FOR THE LOVE OF
ATEN

Published under licence by Brown Dog Books and
The Self-Publishing Partnership Ltd, 10b Greenway Farm, Bath Rd,
Wick, nr. Bath BS30 5RL

www.selfpublishingpartnership.co.uk

ISBN printed book: 978-1-83952-531-5
ISBN e-book: 978-1-83952-532-2

Cover design by Kevin Rylands
Internal design by Andrew Easton

Printed and bound in the UK

This book is printed on FSC® certified paper

FSC
www.fsc.org

MIX
Paper from
responsible sources
FSC® C013604

FOR THE LOVE OF
ATEN

V. ANN CATHERALL-PENTTILÄ

BROWN
DOG
BOOKS

For my grandchildren,
Sophia, Alex, Daniel, and Eva.

With gratitude to Gary Bissmire

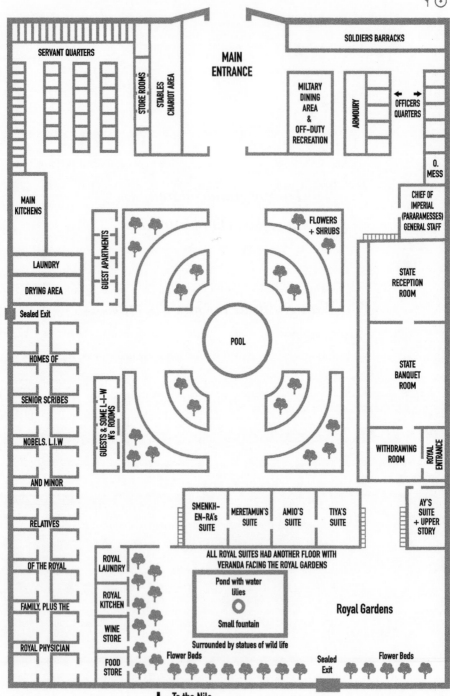

ORDINARY PEOPLE LIVED OUTSIDE THE PALACE COMPLEX

SERVANT QUARTERS

STORE ROOMS

STABLES CHARIOT AREA

MAIN ENTRANCE

SOLDIERS BARRACKS

MILTARY DINING AREA & OFF-DUTY RECREATION

ARMOURY

OFFICERS QUARTERS

O. MESS

CHIEF OF IMPERIAL (PARARAMESSES) GENERAL STAFF

MAIN KITCHENS

GUEST APARTMENTS

FLOWERS + SHRUBS

STATE RECEPTION ROOM

LAUNDRY

DRYING AREA

Sealed Exit

POOL

STATE BANQUET ROOM

HOMES OF

SENIOR SCRIBES

NOBELS. L.I.W

GUESTS & SOME L-I-W N's ROOMS

WITHDRAWING ROOM

ROYAL ENTRANCE

AND MINOR

RELATIVES

SMENKH-EN-RA's SUITE

MERETAMUN'S SUITE

AMIO'S SUITE

TIYA'S SUITE

AY'S SUITE + UPPER STORY

OF THE ROYAL

ROYAL LAUNDRY

ALL ROYAL SUITES HAD ANOTHER FLOOR WITH VERANDA FACING THE ROYAL GARDENS

FAMILY, PLUS THE

ROYAL KITCHEN

Pond with water lilies

Small fountain

Royal Gardens

ROYAL PHYSICIAN

WINE STORE

FOOD STORE

Surrounded by statues of wild life

Flower Beds

Sealed Exit

Flower Beds

To the Nile

PROLOGUE

In order that my reader will more easily understand the background to my story, I will give a brief outline of some of the history of Egypt, with a short description of the peoples of the lands surrounding the Mediterranean Sea at that epoch, prior to the emergence of Atenism.

About 1700 BCE the Greek island of Thera (modern Santorini) had suffered a series of volcanic eruptions over a period of two-hundred years. To the end of this there was an eruption of such magnitude that the ancient island of Caphtor (modern Crete) was destroyed by tidal waves, and of Santorini itself only one-third of the island remained above the waves. Most of the island disappeared beneath the waves within days. The tidal waves and atmospheric disturbances that ensued caused massive floods and widespread destruction in all the lands around the Mediterraneum. More especially, the sophisticated and advanced cultures of Mycenae and Minoa were almost completely extinguished and never afterwards were they to regain their former glory. Even today, the levels of pink volcanic ash on Santorini are up to fifty metres deep in places. All around the coasts of Anatolia and North Africa too there are corresponding levels of this pink ash at levels contemporaneous with the explosion. This cataclysm was very likely the cause of the biblical flood of Genesis. Noah was obviously more far-sighted than many of his countrymen, as was the Babylonian Gilgamesh who also recorded the flood.

Prior to the Theran catastrophe, the civilisation of Egypt was already more than a thousand years old. The ancient shepherd astronomers of old had given way to the highly organised priesthood of Amun. There is a school of thought (me!) who believes that the first pyramid was built to provide a constant, from whose corners the astronomer priests could observe the sky through generation to generation and plot the movements of the heavens.

At that epoch the earth was in the age of Aries the ram, and therefore it is no coincidence that the god Amun was symbolised by statues of a human body with the head of a ram. Other, lesser gods were Anubis the jackal, who represented Sirius the dog star, and Hathor the cow goddess, who represented Taurus the bull. The other symbols of the Egyptian pantheon corresponded with the ancient Babylonian symbols too.

The priests of Amun recognised the temporal sway of the pharaohs, although it is doubtful that even Cheops, the first pharaoh of the first dynasty, could have remained in power without the backing of the powerful priesthood. It may be that Cheops was flattered and cajoled into providing the required investment and manpower to build the first pyramid by the promise of having the most illustrious mausoleum in the world.

Even the scientists of today are compelled to provide pragmatic applications of their research in order to attract the necessary funding for their projects. There is nothing new under the sun.

Prior to the flooding and damage to northern Egypt in the wake of the destruction of Thera, the Egyptian capital was On, close to the later capital called Memphis and situated near modern Cairo.

Throughout the history of Ancient Egypt and the Ancient Greek cultures of Mycenae and Minoa, there appears to have existed close and harmonious social and trading relationships. This may have been because both cultures had diverged from the same original people and culture. It is possible that Ancient Greek and Ancient Egyptian were related languages, although written in different scripts. They may have been as closely related as modern English and Swedish.

At the same epoch, Caphtor's population were known as Keftiu. Extant Egyptian scripts refer extensively to these Keftiu. The tidal waves generated by the explosion of Thera swamped Caphtor, and Knossos, the major city, was destroyed. Refugees from Caphtor and many other of the Greek islands landed on the surrounding coasts of Anatolia, the Near East and North Africa. Sometimes their numbers were large enough for them to re-populate themselves as a distinct people from the indigenous people around them.

The Book of Amos in the Bible tells us that the Philistines (modern Palestinians) were Greek in origin. 'And did I not deliver the Israelites out of Egypt and rescue the Philistines from Caphtor?' To support this evidence, the tale of David and Goliath tells us that the giant wore chain mail. Only the Greeks are known to have had knowledge of iron-working at this stage of history; indeed the Bible tells us that the Hebrews had to take their plough shares down to the Philistines to be sharpened.

The Tuareg of Libya and the Sahara are also thought to be of Greek extract. There is evidence that they were a tribe called Garamantes with a capital at Garama (modern-day

Germa) and had a written script of their own, which even they can no longer decipher. The men cover their faces even today, which could be explained by the evidence that they became brigands in ancient times, attacking the caravans going to West Africa from the East.

Ancient Egyptian was a language like Pitman's shorthand system in that it involved writing down only the consonants. Vowels were only written if they appeared at the beginning of a word or if they were at the end of a word and are pronounced, such as 'lvli' meaning 'lovely', 'agn' meaning 'again' and 'tmrw' meaning 'tomorrow'. Modern Arabic is written like this. From the point of view of later linguistic reconstruction this is not a good thing, because vowel quality tends to change with time and, later in time, the true quality of the vowels is difficult to determine. The word 'Tuareg' shows an opposing consonant sequence to the word 'Garamantes' but this may have been a deliberate attempt to hide their tribal identity to avoid vengeance for the attacks on the caravan routes. 'Tuareg' may therefore be the modern version of this ancient strategic change.

Northern Egypt was seriously weakened by the destruction that occurred in the aftermath of the destruction of Thera. The breakdown in the social organisation of the country that followed left Egypt vulnerable to invasion. Northern Egypt (Lower Egypt) was attacked and occupied by a Semitic horde called the Hyksos. They occupied the north of Egypt for nearly two-hundred years.

During this time a new capital was built in southern (Upper Egypt) at Thebes, which was five-hundred miles south of Memphis. Thebes became the centre of resistance against these hated foreigners who had subjugated their country. They had been able to subjugate Egypt so quickly because they came from the east on horseback. There were no horses in Egypt before this time. Eventually the superior social and administrative organisation of the Egyptians bore fruit and the first pharaoh of the eighteenth dynasty led an army to the north and succeeded in defeating the Hyksos and driving them out of Egypt.

With the re-unification of Upper and Lower Egypt came the realisation that nearly two-hundred years of separation had led to important social changes, especially in the area of religion. In the south, Amun had continued to reign supreme amongst the gods of the Egyptian pantheon, but in the north the position of Re, the sun god, had become immensely strengthened by the large influx of Keftiu refugees who had brought with them their ancient traditions of worshipping the sun god Helios. To the Keftiu, Re was merely the Egyptian name for Ra.

The potential for political strife did not go undetected and in the post re-unification period it was considered prudent to accord Amun and Re equal divine powers and combine the two religious organisations into one dual system of worship. In this way religious unrest was avoided and power could be conveniently retained by the same groups as before. This policy appears to have been successful from the point of view of history, although there might have been some unrest at grassroot levels at the time. It is interesting at this point to note that the Keftiu continued to keep a separate identity in Egypt and, indeed, do so to this day, though their name has undergone linguistic change and they now call themselves Copts. In truth, the Copts are still identified in origin by the Ancient Greek texts of their religious books, although the language is now far removed from modern Greek.

Less than one-hundred years after the expulsion of the Hyksos from Egypt, a pharaoh by the name of Tuthmosis IV came to the throne of Upper and Lower Egypt. Tuthmosis IV had resided at Thebes, which continued to be the capital of the Two Lands, as it was often referred to. Tuthmosis IV is thought to be the pharaoh who promoted the Hebrew patriarch Joseph to the position of grand vizier, the leading advisor to the pharaoh. As a Semite, Joseph must have been looked upon with great mistrust by many of the Egyptian nobles who, no doubt, equated him with the hated Hyksos. The Bible tells us that the Egyptians would not eat at the same table as Semites, so it must have been a sort of cold war situation. In spite of such disastrous beginnings as an imprisoned slave, his intuition and intelligence served him well when he was brought before the pharaoh as an interpreter of dreams.

The Bible (Genesis 41:43) says that Joseph rode in the second chariot after pharaoh, therefore, we know that Joseph could not have been in Egypt before the eighteenth dynasty because there were no horses in Egypt before then. Genesis also tells us that Joseph became 'father unto pharaoh' but this could not be so unless Joseph had a daughter who was married to the pharaoh. Although the Bible gives no direct evidence that Joseph did have a daughter, it does say that he married the daughter of the high priest of On in northern Egypt. His wife was called Asenaath. The Bible also tells us that he had two sons Manasseh and Ephraim. Later on in Genesis we are told that the total number of Israelites who came into Egypt were three score and six (66) and that altogether the number of 'Israelite souls' in Egypt were three score and ten (70). Sixty-six plus Joseph, Manasseh and Ephraim make sixty-nine, so who was the seventieth soul? Being important enough to be considered a soul, but not important enough to be named, indicates that this soul was a female! Simple mathematical deduction implies that Joseph had a daughter and that she married the pharaoh, thus making Joseph 'father unto pharaoh'.

It is obvious that Joseph did not use his own name officially as grand vizier because there is no written evidence of a Joseph, or Yussef, as it was in Arabic and Hebrew, in the Egyptian records. There is, however, a grand vizier called Yuya. He was the only commoner to be buried in the Valley of the Kings, which denotes his closeness to the throne. Yuya was the father of a daughter called Tiya (note the ya- suffix). The Egyptian records tell us that Queen Tiya was the daughter of a slave and that she married Amenophis III, the son of Tuthmosis IV, when he was thirteen and Tiya was nine years old. It is known that Tuthmosis IV died young, and marriage at such an age, young even for that period, could have been used as a method of securing the throne.

It was the custom of the Egyptians to incorporate in their own names the name of their god. This may have been a way of denoting their birth month. In this way Tuthmosis means Moses, whose god was Toth, and Amenophis means Ophis, whose god was Amun. If Joseph also adopted this custom as a way of assimilating into Egyptian society, he may have become Yussef, whose god was Yahweh, i.e. Yuya.

Yahweh is Ancient Hebrew for Jehovah. In this way Joseph would have been able to 'Egyptianise' his name without renouncing his faith, while at the same time no offence could be caused to the priesthood of Amun-Re because they did not know what the Ya stood for. As his father-in-law was the high priest of On, he may have received some judicious advice in this matter.

Added weight is given to the above theory by the fact that the mummy of Yuya in Cairo museum shows that the body was laid out with its arms crossed over its chest, whereas Egyptians were always buried with their arms straight down by their sides. In addition to this, the mummy does not have pierced ears, and yet pierced ears were an integral sign of Egyptian nobility.

It is obvious that Joseph's faith was very important to him; perhaps it was all he had to cling to during the seven years he spent in prison on trumped-up charges. It is probable that Abraham and Sarah, with their small clan, had left Ur in Chaldea (present-day Iraq) because of their strong beliefs on monotheism, in what was a refusal to accept the polytheistic beliefs in the society around them. Babylon and the surrounding states were all societies with a plethora of gods and goddesses. Indeed, both Abram and Sara incorporated the infix 'ah' into their names after leaving Ur, according to the Bible. This syllable obviously had meaning, because it appears in many names in Hebrew, including

Noah. 'Ya' might have been a later form of the idea, which also appears as 'ah' and 'ha'. Unfortunately, I do not have a real knowledge of Ancient Aramaic to research this further! As Joseph's wife also changed her name and assumed the same suffix, Tuya must have converted to her husband's religion and their daughter Tiya also. This conversion was probably kept secret, one would think. It seems that Joseph tried to assimilate as far as he could without compromising his principles. People in love do not accentuate their differences, after all, and Joseph seems to have been a born diplomat.

Amenophis III came to the throne on the death of his father, Tuthmosis IV, when the young prince was only thirteen years old. With Yuya as grand vizier, and effectively regent, he would have had a great influence on the ideas of the young pharaoh and it must be assumed that Joseph would have instructed the young Amenophis in his ideas of religion as he probably also did to Tuthmosis before him. Joseph's ability to interpret the pharaoh's dream as a prediction of the forthcoming famine must have impressed Tuthmosis, the priests of Amun not being able to interpret the dream.

Why did Yuya choose the name 'Aten' for the Egyptian name of Yahweh? According to some texts the word meant 'breath' and also 'ray'. Both these meanings denote abstracts, as in the phrase 'the breath of life', and the meaning 'ray' would have a fortuitous connection with the sun and, therefore, could lull a sun-worshipper into believing that the difference between Atenism and Re-ism was only marginal. I suspect it was crafty manipulation of a very dangerous situation, which allowed him to continue worship of his own god without alienating the priesthood of Amun-Re too much. Genesis describes God as 'a spirit moving over the waters', i.e. their god could not be symbolised with statues like the Babylonian gods or the Egyptian gods. It seems that Joseph tried to stay as close as he could to the Ancient Hebrew word 'ruach', meaning 'spirit'.

For whatever reason, Amenophis III began to elevate a new god called 'Aten' to a position of prominence early on in his reign. The young pharaoh gave Tiya a present of a new royal barge called *The Aten Gleams*. The priesthood of Amun must have looked upon this with displeasure if not downright rancour. It was a definite encroachment upon their power. As Tiya was the mother off Amenophis IV, who later took the name Akhenaten, meaning 'Devoted to the Aten' and instituted monotheism in Egypt, then we can be pretty sure he absorbed monotheism with his mother's milk. The message to the priesthood could not have been clearer.

During the years of famine, so accurately predicted by Joseph, the pharaoh's silos had been full of grain when many Egyptian landowners were suffering hunger. The priests of

Amun had failed to prophesy the famine. Tuthmosis IV must have become convinced that the Aten was at least as powerful as Amun-Re.

The Bible tells us that many people had to sell their land to the pharaoh in order to obtain grain to make bread and fodder to keep their cattle alive. Many old and proud families must have been affected by these events. We are told that when the famine was over they were allowed to continue on their land as tenant farmers who had to pay an annual tax of twenty percent of their income. Such laws as these must have been exceedingly unpopular with the people and the priesthood, as sacrifices too would have become much less generous in a time of hardship. The personal wealth of the royal family was enormously increased, making them much less dependent upon the priests of Amun-Re for their power. No doubt but that Joseph was vilified for his strategic part in all this. In addition, when he brought his sixty-six relatives into Egypt and established them at Goshen in the north-east of the Nile delta, it must have seemed to many that the Hyksos had returned under a different name to usurp the throne of Egypt. Perhaps Joseph changed the name of his family from Hebrew, meaning descendants of Abraham to Israelites, as this was a name unknown to the Egyptians, who were previously cognizant of the Hebrews, whom they called the Hapiru. The poisonous seeds of rancour between the Hebrews and the Egyptians may have been sown during the summer of Joseph's success.

In contrast to the above, the long history of peaceful co-existence between the Egyptians and the Greeks meant that the assimilation of the Keftiu into Egypt was different in degree and quality from that of the Israelites, who were settled into the north-eastern district of Goshen. Perhaps their immigration into this area entailed compulsory land redistribution within the local population. This was an area that had suffered occupation of the Hyksos. Joseph perhaps underestimated the bitterness of the Egyptians' feelings towards the Semites and his own agrarian reforms. We shall never know, but I suspect that the Hebrews were established in Goshen because Joseph may have wanted them at least near to their previous region in case things went badly wrong for him.

My story is not the story of Joseph, however, interesting though he was. It is the story of Nefertiti and Akhenaten, whom history disgraced and time forgot until their statues emerged again from the sands of time, having survived the millennia intact. Nefertiti, with her classical beauty, and Akhenaten, with his body badly deformed by rickets, may have been opposites from the accepted norms of beauty, but history preserved through more than three-thousand three-hundred years clear evidence of the love between them.

It was a love which was intense in its passion and poignant in its manifestations.

The statue of Nefertiti wearing the blue and gold crown of Upper and Lower Egypt shows that she was much lighter in complexion than the Egyptians of southern Egypt. There is a slight rosiness to her skin colour which indicates that she might have been Keftiu in origin. In any case, as a citizen of the north she would have grown up in the more densely populated area of the Nile delta and been influenced by its maritime aspects, a more cosmopolitan environment than the people who surrounded her at the Theban court. Much more important, she would have grown up with the legends of the time the gods were angry and almost destroyed the world with fire and floods. She would have been used to the festivals of Re-Helios to placate his anger. How much closer was Re to her traditions than Amun with his ram's head, whose constellation was far away in the night sky. Re's size and power were apparent every morning and every sunset.

How understandable that her beloved Amio should try to reconcile the differences between their faiths. How normal that the young lovers should be so full of enthusiasm and optimism that they truly believed that they could change, almost overnight, a system which had endured for more than one-thousand five-hundred years. How deep their despair and disappointment when that self-same system finally destroyed all their dreams.

Dear Amio and Neferu. May you rise again from your ashes like the phoenix, to live and love again in another time and space. May this be the will of the Aten.

CHAPTER 1

When Nefertiti was born in Heliopolis, the city was known as On. It was one of the main dwelling places of the Keftiu in Egypt and had preserved its Greek identity even throughout the Hyksos occupation. The town was busy, situated as it was just north of Memphis on the east bank of the Nile. All the river traffic stopped here, and it was an important centre of commerce, though it lacked the large palaces of Memphis and the grand administrative buildings with the comings and goings of its vast military contingent. The second largest division of the Egyptian army was based at Memphis and served to protect the whole of Lower Egypt, though Egyptians did not feel that they were under threat at that epoch.

In the streets of On, the Keftiu language was almost as common as Egyptian, and the dress of the women was also somewhat different from that of the women of Upper Egypt. Here the women wore their hair long and twisted into large chignons at the nape of the neck. Here and there could be seen women who affected the sharp fringes and intricate plaits of the modish ladies of Thebes but, in general, these were the wives of important public officials, and the majority of the wives and daughters of merchants and more minor officials continued to wear the loosely folded dresses and uplifted hairstyles of the classical Minoan period, now long past its glory days.

On was also different in its religious life from Memphis. There were few temples here to the many gods of the Egyptian pantheon so popular elsewhere. The majority of the temples at On, certainly all the important ones, were dedicated to Re, the sun god, known also as Helios to the Keftiu. Helios had always been the most important of the Greek gods. He was thought to drive his chariot across the sky in his daily ritual which brought life and warmth to the earth.

Nefertiti was born in the year that we call 1390 BCE. Her parents were Greek in origin, but her name was Egyptian and meant 'A beautiful one has come'. Nefertiti was born at a happy and prosperous time in her parent's marriage, when her father had recently been made a potiphar of On. Amenophis III was pharaoh of all Egypt at the time, and Tiya was his great queen and chief wife. Egypt was at peace and there had been several years of good harvests. Life seemed secure and unruffled.

Vassiliou, Nefertiti's father, came from a long line of merchants and the family was very close knit, as most Greek families still are today. Their shop in On sold spices, dried fruits, nuts, sugars, pottery, polished mirrors and wines. On the coast at Rashid, the brother of Vassiliou, Nefertiti's Uncle Giorgios, was also a merchant and he stocked and sold silks and other materials of all kinds from all over the Mediterraneum and from the Orient, brought by the caravans led by strange looking men from the east. There were silks from China, beautifully woven cottons from Damascus, lace from Cyprus and light muslin and heavy cottons from Egypt itself. Just as important as the texture of these fabrics was their colour, and in Uncle Giorgios' warehouse it was possible to find every colour that the heart of a little girl could desire.

When Nefertiti was two years old her brother Demetrious was born, but in the second decan after the birth of his son, Vassiliou was widowed and left to bring up his children without his beloved Elena, who died of an infection, an all-too-common occurrence in those days. Neferu and Demi, as Nefertiti and Demetrious were affectionately known, grew up in the day-to-day care of their maternal grandparents and their mother's sister, Aunt Lea. Neferu never later remembered her mother directly and it was mainly from Grandma's stories that she built up a picture of the mother who had died.

Grandma never tired of telling the children stories of her own childhood and of how their ancestors had arrived here in Egypt. Neferu would sit enthralled on Grandma's knee, cushioned by her ample bosom, listening to the frightening tale of earthquakes and explosions. It seemed that those distant ancestors had fled from Mykonos to Crete, but finding that too covered in thick, muddy silt, and death and despair around them, they had continued south until they had landed at Rashid, on the coast of the Nile delta in the west. Other Greeks like them, who had also survived the deluge that the gods had sent on them for their sins, fled to wherever they could find a refuge. Some had gone to Libya, where some of them had become semi-nomadic, travelling by camel at night to attack the rich caravans bringing the silks and spices of the faraway Orient to trade across the wide continent of Africa.

Grandma would purse her lips in disapproval in the telling of this, as their trading boats had also been attacked occasionally by pirates when on the sea at night-time. Still others of the Minoan and Mycenean peoples had been soldiers of the palace guard, and many of these Palastoi had landed on the coast of Byblos and moved south to form a nation of their own called Palestine. Although they had formed an uneasy peace with their Semitic neighbours, they had never again managed to achieve the level of culture that the refugees who came to Egypt had been lucky enough to access. Neferu never tired of hearing Grandma's stories, even though sometimes, when Grandma kissed her goodnight, she would feel afraid in the dark. Occasionally, only if she was very afraid, she would creep into Demi's bed and, if she was very, very afraid, she would poke him until he woke up. Then she would say, 'There is no need to be afraid, Demi. I am here and I won't let the bogeyman get you.' Sometimes Demi would whimper in fright at this, and she would hug him tight to protect him and, in doing so, she would forget her own fright. Retrospectively, when she thought about this as a teenager, Neferu used to feel very guilty, especially as poor Demi was always so grateful for his big sister's protective presence.

Grandfather was a jeweller. He mainly worked in silver, which comprised about two-thirds of his work. Gold was expensive and large pieces were made only on the order of the customer. Grandpa was very proud of his craftsmanship. He made the traditional designs, but he also liked to make up pieces of his own design, and Grandma had many beautiful earrings and bracelets made by Grandpa. When Grandma was in a good mood and her work was done, she would bring out her jewellery box and Neferu would play with the jewels and pretend she was a beautiful princess at the court, and how the pharaoh and all the princes would fall in love with her.

Aunt Lea would smile at her fancies and say 'Maybe', but Grandma had no time for Neferu's fancies and would tell Neferu that her feet were not on the ground properly. She was to marry a nice Keftiu boy from a good family and give her father many grandsons! Neferu would sniff. She didn't know any suitably romantic Keftiu boys. In the mornings she attended school and there were only the neighbour's sons and daughters there. The only other boy she knew was Yussef, her cousin, and he was two whole years older than her and teased her unmercifully. At seven she could already read and write, but she found mathematics difficult. She was good at adding but taking away was a bit of a problem and, if she asked Yussef to help, she had to suffer his arrogant remarks on how girls just were not up to it.

The week in Egypt consisted of ten days and, at the end of every decan, the family would go to the temple to make their sacrifice to Re-Helios. At the age of seven Neferu was allowed to go for the first time, and the occasion was one of great excitement. Grandma brushed her hair until it shone, and then pinned it up on top of her head in grown-up style. Neferu felt very proud. At the entrance to the temple the family divided into two groups, the males on one side and the females on the other. After the intense heat of the sun bearing down on her head and shoulders, the coolness of the shadowed temple was a relief, and Neferu would watch the vestal virgins as they performed the traditional rituals. They looked very glamorous to her, whereas she always found the solemn figure of the high priestess a little frightening. In truth, Neferu found that after the usual rituals had been completed and the chanting of the prayers begun in earnest, her attention would wander. After a while, the smell of the incense and the other pungent smells made her feel sleepy, and only a warning tug on her arm from Grandma or Aunt Lea would bring her back to the present. By the time they left for home, Neferu was always ravenously hungry.

Every summer Grandma would pack all their clothes and they would take the river boat down to the coast to stay at the empty villa by the sea at Rashid. This was the time that Neferu and Demi loved most of all. Yussef would come with them too, and the three children would spend the four hottest decans on the coast. Afterwards, these times always seemed to Neferu to have been halcyon days and she wondered that she had not known at the time to savour them for the future in more detail.

Yussef was an orphan. He was really the second cousin of Neferu and Demi. His grandfather and her grandpa had been brothers, and his father had been Elena's cousin. Like Elena, Yussef's mother had also died in childbirth, and his father had died of a sudden fever four years later. Neferu's uncle, Leandros, had taken the boy into his home and it was planned that he would eventually inherit his father's share of the jewellery business and take his father's place. To this end, Yussef was apprenticed to his uncle and Neferu's grandpa at the age of nine in order to learn all the necessary skills of a goldsmith.

The vast majority of Keftiu in Egypt had done fairly well in their new motherland. Greeks have always had a flair for business, and in the narrow streets of the towns and villages of the Nile delta there were many little whitewashed shops with Keftiu names written over them. Most of these were only three or four metres wide, often consisting of no more than recesses into the long lines of buildings along the street. At the end of the day the little shops would be cleared of their goods and re-stocked the next day, or in the case of the more affluent businesses, thick wooden shutters would be locked into place with large copper keys. There were few Keftiu in positions of real power in government.

Partly this stemmed from the fact that Thebes was located almost five-hundred miles from On and, even though there was a flourishing river traffic on the Nile, it seemed that the Keftiu were not drawn in large numbers to the stultifying climate of southern Egypt. They were a people who liked to feel a proximity to the sea. Those Keftiu who were involved in politics tended to band together and were, in the main, holding middle-ranking administrative positions in Memphis, On and the other important towns of the Nile delta area.

Neferu's father, Vassiliou, who had been devoted to his wife, was a handsome man, and Grandma was constantly trying to marry him off to one of the daughters of her friends. So far, Vassiliou had remained a widower. As a potiphar of On, he was quite well known in the community and the family was respected. Vassiliou had progressed in both his business and official career and was a very busy man, often away from home for long periods. It was Yuya the Israelite who had promoted Vassiliou to the rank of potiphar, during one of his frequent visits to Lower Egypt on the pharaoh's business. Perhaps the old Hapiru felt an empathy with the Keftiu, who were also a minority in this land. As the years passed, Vassiliou was away from home more and more often and Uncle Demetrious, after whom Demi had been named, had to run the business with the help of hired salesmen. Sometimes her father had to travel as far as Thebes and when he returned there would always be presents for Neferu and Demi and exciting descriptions of life in the faraway, exotic capital.

When her father was away Neferu would attach herself closely to Grandpa. Uncle Leandros almost ran the workshop now and Yussef was a very apt pupil. Grandpa often took time off nowadays to sit outside the shop on a plain stool and pass the time of day in conversation with his friends or playing backgammon with them. The old man was very fond of Yussef and treated him just like his own grandson, Demi. When Grandpa was busy there was always Aunt Lea to talk to. She was Mother's older sister and had been widowed many years ago before Neferu was born. Aunt Lea had no children of her own and was somewhat under Grandma's thumb. She reminded Neferu sometimes of a little, bright bird with her sharp, nervous movements and her quiet, self-effacing manner. Lea was as plain as her sister Elena had been pretty, but there was a decided charm about her that stemmed from the goodness of her heart. When she smiled the round twinkling eyes transformed her face, making it suddenly enormously attractive. She was very shy and let Grandma dominate her too much in Neferu's opinion. Still, it was a loving domination, and the mouse-like Lea did not seem to object. Neferu adored Aunt Lea, who could be prevailed upon to support her and Demi if they wanted to resort to strategies contrary to Grandma's will. Aunt Lea was very good at pouring oil on troubled waters. She had taken upon herself the role of surrogate mother to all three children and applied herself willingly to the task.

In the spring of Neferu's seventh birthday her father married again, and for a time a dark and jealous cloud entered Neferu's life. Both she and Demi felt themselves shut out of their father's life. His new wife, Shosen, was Egyptian and therefore they were no longer allowed to speak Keftiu at home. Neferu felt an intense jealousy of the woman who she felt had taken her place in her father's heart. More and more she found herself passing most of her time after lessons with Grandma and Aunt Lea. She and Demi grew much closer, and though Shosen was kind, there was always a distance between them which never entirely disappeared. Neferu loved her father as much as she had ever done, and he remained as warm and affectionate as before, but things were never quite the same. When Shosen's first child was born, Neferu found pleasure in helping to care for it, and the ones which came after, but Demi and Yussef became the most important people in her world.

CHAPTER 2

The summer of Neferu's tenth year was different from all previous ones, yet there was no portent of this in the spring. Grandma and Aunt Lea had packed as usual for the summer move to the coast. Grandpa retired officially that year and Uncle Leandros had to take on extra help so that Yussef could be spared for the summer. He was twelve now and felt himself very grown up. All the men said that he had the talent of an excellent goldsmith, and his designs were much in demand by the customers. Grandpa reckoned that in another year Yussef could be counted a qualified artist.

In previous years Vassiliou had often accompanied them to Rashid for at least part of the holiday, but this summer Shosen was expecting her second baby and she wanted to stay in On so as to be close to her own family, who lived in Memphis. Although Neferu knew she would miss her father very much, nothing could dim the pleasure of anticipation. All the year round she looked forward to the summer holiday in the little whitewashed, mud brick villa a little way along the coast from Rashid. She and Demi talked about it for decans in advance and even the newly sophisticated Yussef was heard to make excited remarks.

Packing was the worst part and Grandma grumbled constantly that she was getting too old for all this upheaval, but while she grumbled, she packed and talked about how she was looking forward to seeing Giorgios and the family again. It was not until their luggage had been put on board the river boat that Neferu felt that the holiday was upon them.

The Nile was constantly busy with traffic. Some of the bigger boats carried crews of fifty or more with the oarsmen counting for about thirty of these. These large boats made very good time and could cover the distance between On and Thebes in just five days. The smaller boats were slower, of course, and their speed depended in part upon the amount of freight and number of passengers they carried. Usually, the journey between On and Rashid took four days, although it was only a distance of two-hundred miles. The cause of this were the many stops to drop passengers off and pick up new ones.

Yussef was two years older than Neferu and therefore it seemed normal to both her and Demi that it should be Yussef who organised their play. That year was no different in its beginning than any of the previous ones and once they arrived at Rashid, they made their usual sorties to the beach to swim, collect shells and generally have a good time. Uncle Giorgios and his family would come and visit them, and they would, in turn, visit them. Every year the grown-ups would remark upon how much taller the children had grown.

When the children left in the mornings to go to the beach, Grandma would make up a basket of bread and fruit and warn them not to swim too far out. They always played in the same cove, which was only five minutes from the villa. This was their secret place and they all made promises to each other that they would never share it with anyone else.

That year Grandma and Aunt Lea decided that the children were growing up past the age of innocence. It was obvious to them that Yussef was maturing fast, and the two women did not wish to accentuate this fact by making Yussef alone wear a loin cloth. To this end all the children were made to wear loin cloths now that they were growing up. That was the first sign that things were about to change, but it was lost on Neferu and Demi, who merely felt pleasure that they were considered in a more mature light. Yussef understood the meaning of the move and was alternatively proud and embarrassed.

As before, the children continued to explore the caves and to collect unusual and beautiful stones and shells, to scratch their names in the rocks and to swim races out to the rock situated about a hundred metres from the shore. Just as before it was always Yussef who won, though occasionally he would throw the race to her or Demi, pretending to be tired. She always knew when he did it that he was just humouring her, but she appreciated the gesture.

In the evenings the family would sit outside with the moonlight and an oil lamp to illuminate their evening. Grandpa would tell stories of Caphtor and the fabulous minotaur who terrorised the island. He would sigh and talk of retiring to the island home of his ancestors, but Grandma would only snort and tell him that he would be going on his own. She understood that it was only his fantasy and that he did not really intend to undertake such a perilous journey. In his heart of hearts Grandpa was amply satisfied by his present circumstances and way of life.

It was a wonderful summer that year and, as usual, the time they all had dreaded began to draw close. Neferu had not even been unduly disturbed by the fact that her father had not even managed to pay them a single visit. Previously his impromptu appearances at the villa had been the cause of great jubilation with the children. This year there had only been greetings sent by one of his business associates who happened to be journeying in their direction. Only one more decan to go before they must commence the return journey to On, Yussef to his final year of apprenticeship and Neferu and Demi to their classes.

On a particularly sultry morning towards the middle of their last decan at Rashid, the children were in the back yard feeding the hens with grain. Grandma and Aunt Lea were in the kitchen preparing the vegetables for lunch. Neferu felt a little overcome by the intense heat and went to sit on the threshold at the back door. She became aware that Grandma and Aunt Lea were talking about them, and she shamelessly began to eavesdrop. Grandma was debating with Aunt Lea the wisdom of allowing the children to continue their unrestricted play together. Aunt Lea observed that Neferu still had the childish figure of a little girl, with the slight pot belly and undifferentiated waistline of that age, but that this time next year things would be entirely different. She begged Grandma not to spoil this last year of childhood innocence by touching upon the subject with Neferu before they returned to On.

Neferu pricked up her ears, her curiosity whetted. What did Aunt Lea mean? Grandma replied to her daughter in a tone of self-congratulation on how well she had instigated the novelty of the loin cloths that were not to be taken off even for swimming. The children had accepted the innovation without question. It was true, Neferu thought. She had noticed, of course, but strangely enough for her, she had not commented upon it or even stopped to analyse the reason for it for more than a fleeting second. Yussef's attitude towards Neferu remained that of a slightly arrogant elder brother, affectionate but with superior camaraderie, and her attitude to Yussef remained that of an adoring younger sister, between their heated exchanges and infrequent quarrels, that is. As Neferu was considering what had been said, Grandma went on to say that it was her intention that Yussef and Neferu would eventually wed. It would cement the family together and be a most advantageous marriage.

In one brief moment Grandma had managed, entirely without her knowledge or intention, to blow away that innocence of childhood forever as far as Neferu was concerned. Fortunately, for Grandma's own peace of mind, she remained unaware of the fact. The noise of footsteps alerted Neferu to the impending approach of Aunt Lea and she jumped up quickly and made as if she had just entered the passageway.

'Aunt Lea, we have fed the hens. Can we go down to the beach now?' she asked with just the faintest hint of a warmth in her cheeks.

'Of course you can, child! The food basket is ready on the side there.' Her aunt replied, pointing at the basket.

Grandma looked up as Neferu entered the kitchen. 'Now mind you don't lie out in the sun too long, Neferu!' she remarked as she always did.

'No grandma,' Neferu dutifully replied.

'And don't go too far out to sea or go swimming alone,' the old lady continued.

'No, Grandma.' Replied Neferu yet again.

'And mind you are back here in time for your rest.'

'Yes, Grandma.'

It was the same conversation they had every day before they went to the beach. It was a sort of ritual which suddenly this morning gained a new importance as Neferu wondered whether next summer she would be allowed to go swimming with the others at all. Grandma looked at her inquiringly. 'Well! What is it child?'

Neferu started. 'Nothing, Grandma,' she said, leaning forward and planting a kiss on the old lady's lips. 'I love you, Grandma,' she said suddenly.

'And I love you too. Now be off with you and mind my words.'

'Yes, Grandma.'

Carrying the basket, Neferu went to the door and called the boys to come. They made their way round the path and opened the gate into the front yard. The smell of the roses was mixed with the jasmine, and it was almost overpowering. Not for the first time she observed to herself that there was something very unpleasant about jasmine when its smell was so concentrated. Once on the little pathway on the cliffs they began to play 'I spy' as they walked, and Demi was annoyed because Neferu guessed 'poppy' right away. They had to give him another turn to appease him. He was only eight, after all.

At a special point on the edge of the cliff the children began to scramble down. Yussef and Neferu took it in turns to carry the basket. It weighed heavy with all the fruit and the pitcher of juice. They made their way to their secret cove. There was almost no breeze and the blue water lapped tentatively the edge of the sand. Even much further out there was very little spume to indicate the presence of those delicious rolls of water which enveloped you when you went further out.

The children made their way to the shallow cave where they usually deposited their food basket to keep it cool. Today they lingered in the cave longer than usual, making shapes and scratches with a sharp piece of rock. Demi was not managing very well and began to insist that Yussef engrave his name for him on the wall of the cave. Yussef did so carefully and with deliberation, taking his time until he was satisfied with the result. Demi was pleased, and after admiring it, he sat down on the damp sand to make a sandcastle with a moat around it.

Yussef continued to carve and Neferu began to be eager to get into the cool water of the sea. Even in the shadow of the cave it was very hot. She wanted to feel the delicious ripple of the tiny waves washing over her shoulders and her sticky face. Just then Yussef called Neferu over to admire his work. Neferu went up close and saw that he had carved his own name and hers in a cartouche. It was not something he had ever done before. Neferu was pleased. Somehow it looked very grown up, and she sensed something of a compliment. Yussef looked at her and smiled before saying lightly,

'When we grow up, we will bring our children here and teach them how to swim.'

'Will we?' Neferu asked, her mind thrown back to the curious conversation between Grandma and Aunt Lea. She looked up at Yussef and was surprised to see him looking at her with a serious expression on his face.

'Of course,' he replied. 'When we grow up, we will get married, and you can help me with the accounts. I will make all the most beautiful jewellery for you.' Neferu happily nodded her head in agreement. She felt pleased at the implied continuity of a world where they would all always be together having fun. An image of herself as a beautiful lady, wearing jewellery of gold inlaid with lapis lazuli, entered her mind. Everyone would be green with envy, of course, she thought dreamily.

'Will you teach me how to make the jewellery too?' she asked suddenly.

'Of course not,' said Yussef flatly. 'That's men's work. Ladies can't do that,' he added, a trifle scornfully.

'Oh,' said Neferu, feeling somewhat put down.

Noticing her crestfallen expression, Yussef added in a kinder tone, 'You will look so beautiful that even the pharaoh will be envious when he sees you.' Neferu's good humour was restored by this gratifying remark, and she smiled again.

'Well, I want to have a beautiful silver necklace so that everyone will notice me when I wear my court dress of silk, which covers my right shoulder and hangs in graceful folds down to my ankles, like the wife of the governor of Memphis. I saw her once when I went with father to visit his friends.' Neferu pivoted daintily around and held out the imaginary folds of her gown.

Yussef laughed, and pulling her arm said, 'Well, you've got a lot more growing up to do yet! Come on, let's go for a swim! Come on, Demi, let's have a race!'

The little boy scrambled up and they all raced down to the shore. Once at the edge they decided which rock was to be their goal and then they gave Demi his usual start. Yussef and Neferu plunged in simultaneously and the race was on. Yussef soon overtook Demi and was well ahead. Neferu was not a fast swimmer, but she soon caught up with her little brother and she hovered just behind him pretending that she just could not quite make it. Demi made valiant efforts, spurred on by her closeness and just managed, he thought, to reach the rock ahead of her.

In his haste to scramble up the rock, Demi caught his shin and an ugly graze appeared on his leg. It bled quite freely, and Demi began to cry when he saw it. Yussef reached down to help him up and looked at the leg closely. 'It isn't dangerous,' he said. 'It's only a scratch.'

Neferu scrambled up the rock after him and took a look. 'Don't worry, Demi,' she said reassuringly. 'I'll wrap a towel round it when we get back to the beach. It will soon stop bleeding.' She put her wet hand over the graze. Whether this was to hide it from Demi's frightened gaze or to stop the bleeding she really didn't know. After a while Demi calmed down. Yussef showed Demi a scar on his arm where he had cut it a few months ago. The scar was about two centimetres long but quite wide. It was fully healed and a white colour. Demi was reassured. They lay back on the rock to get their breath back and enjoyed the warmth of the sun on their wet bodies. Yussef began to prise a limpet off the rock but, in spite of his efforts, it would not budge and after a while he gave up the attempt. He lay back and closed his eyes. After a companionable silence lasting a few minutes he said lazily, 'Tell me when you have got your breath back and we'll race back to the beach.'

'Not yet,' answered Neferu.

When Demi was ready, they gave him a start and watched as his lithe little body dived into the water and, after surfacing, began to swim with strong, sure strokes towards the shore. They gave him a bigger start than usual and allowed him to reach the shore first. He was jubilant. 'I won, I won!' he proclaimed loudly. The graze on his leg had started to bleed again slightly but Neferu patted it with a towel, and it soon stopped. Neferu brought out their basket and they sat down on the sand to eat a leisurely lunch. Swimming always made them hungry. Demi looked up and brought their attention to two people further along the beach about to take a dip. 'I hope they don't decide to come down here and discover our secret cave. This is ours and no one else is allowed in it.'

Neferu laughed but Yussef also looked suddenly annoyed, and he said aggressively,

'You are right, Demi. This is our cave and no one else is allowed to come here. We mustn't tell anyone else about it. Pact?' They each held out their right hand and extended the index finger so that all three index fingers were touching at the tips. It was their own secret sign. Yussef withdrew his hand and said, 'Don't forget, or something dreadful will happen.'

Neferu shivered, in spite of the heat. 'What will happen?' she said with a slight intake of breath.

'Oh, I don't know,' said Yussef, regretting that he had said it. It seemed to give the whole thing a presentiment of fear. 'I only meant that it would be a betrayal of our promise and that is a very, very serious thing.' The other two nodded and felt special, wrapped up in the cocoon of their secrecy.

After eating their fill, the children stood up and began to collect their things together. Looking a little bedraggled, they made their way up the cliff. Somehow Neferu knew that it had been a very special day, though she could not think why. Something important had happened, a day to remember, she knew. She decided, as she sometimes did, that when she went to bed that night she would ponder over the day's events until what it was had crystallised clearly and she could store it in her memory for future reference.

As the little white house came into view, they could see Grandma's plump figure sitting on the porch. Neferu forgot her meditations in the excitement of showing the injury on Demi's leg to her grandmother. Demi basked in the sympathy of Grandma's tut-tuttings and began to enjoy the little drama. Little did they realise that Demi's drama was only just beginning.

CHAPTER 3

The following day, the graze on Demi's leg appeared a little red and inflamed. He declared it tender to the touch and Grandma made Yussef and Neferu take a large bowl down to the shore and bring her back some sea water. Grandma was a keen believer in the beneficial properties of sea water. It was an old Keftiu tradition that the salt in it was very good for healing wounds. Grandma boiled the water and waited until it was slightly warmer than tepid before she began to bathe Demi's leg. Grandma was full of these ancient ideas of folk medicine and Grandpa would often mutter 'mumbo jumbo' or words to that effect. Still, he never interfered, and had cause to be grateful for Grandma's mumbo jumbo in the past.

Demi was a bit tearful and tried to pull his leg away, so Grandpa sat with him and kept telling him about all the accidents he had suffered as a boy. According to him, he had never been known to cry. Demi's eyes met Neferu's, and she smothered a smile. Some of Grandpa's tales were a bit tall even for him. After Grandma had bathed the leg, she bound it up with strips of cotton material left over from an old bed sheet and told Demi to rest. He was not allowed to go swimming that morning with Yussef and Neferu.

Grandpa was unwilling to let the older two go off alone and in the end a compromise was reached whereby Aunt Lea accompanied them. She said that she rather fancied a visit to the beach that day. It was decided that Grandpa would keep Demi company while Grandma prepared lunch. When Yussef and Neferu got up to leave, Demi tried to jump up too, to follow them, but Grandma pushed him down firmly, refusing to heed his objections, and Neferu could hear his angry protestations all the way down the path.

'Poor Demi,' she said, as they turned onto the cliff pathway. 'I hope his leg gets better quickly.'

Aunt Lea smiled reassuringly. 'Of course it will. Mother has always been the careful kind. It was just the same with us when we were small.' Yussef and Neferu exchanged glances and smiled. It was hard to imagine Aunt Lea as a small girl. It was easier to imagine that Helios would come down from the heavens in his golden chariot. Grandma had always been Grandma, that was for sure; no two ways about it.

Once on the beach, Yussef and Neferu showed Aunt Lea their cave, and she was sworn to secrecy. She sat in the shade and watched them as they raced to the shoreline, her hand over her eyes to protect them from the glare. This time it was a race to win, as there was no Demi whose sensibilities had to be protected. In spite of her best efforts, Yussef still beat her to the rock, and she was panting breathlessly when she finally reached out to grab a gnarled outstretch of porous-looking rock whose surface was dented with hundreds of small holes as is typical of old larval eruptions. Carefully Neferu made her way up. It was rather painful trying to find a smooth foothold on the jagged surface of the rock and Yussef watched her with an amused expression on his face. He had found a good position on top of the rock. Finally Neferu sat down, her body glistening as the sun reflected off its wet surface.

For a time, she watched the little drops of water sparkling in the rays of the sun and wondered if that is what diamonds looked like. Grandpa had told her about this very rare, precious stone of which few had passed through his hands in his long career as a jeweller. Grandpa had said that there was no more beautiful stone in the whole world and that the light reflected from such a stone dazzled the eyes. After a moment Neferu lifted her gaze towards Aunt Lea on the beach. She seemed small now in the distance and was sitting up sharply, looking in their direction. Neferu waved to her and said to Yussef, 'Wave to Aunt Lea, Yussef!' He did so and they watched as Aunt Lea relaxed, leaning backwards against the wall of the cave. After a while she seemed to have fallen asleep.

When they had got their breath back, Yussef stood up. 'Look Neferu!' he said, pointing down the beach in the direction away from Rashid.

'What is it?' Neferu asked, scrambling up beside him, the wet loin cloth clinging uncomfortably to her.

'Let's explore down there. We've never been that way before,' he said, looking down at her.

'What about Aunt Lea?' Neferu asked carefully. 'Do you think she would let us?'

'Why not?' replied Yussef. 'If we go right now before lunch she won't mind.'

'We'll have to tell her,' said Neferu doubtfully.

'Of course.' the boy replied with a shrug.

Moments later Yussef dived into the water and Neferu quickly followed. This time she made no effort to race and contented herself by following at a leisurely pace. When she reached a standing depth, he was already waiting for her, standing impatiently at the water's edge. 'Come on, Neferu,' he said and turned away in the direction of Aunt Lea, who was snoozing quietly with a layer of sweat on her forehead, causing it to shine. Yussef bent down and shook her gently. 'Aunt Lea,' he said insistently.

She woke up with a start. 'What's the matter?' she said anxiously, quickly sitting up.

'Nothing! Everything is alright,' Yussef answered reassuringly. 'It's just that Neferu and I want to explore down the beach in that direction a bit,' he said, lifting his arm and pointing to a vague area further down the beach.

Aunt Lea turned her head to look. 'Well all right then. But don't be too long and be careful. My, it is hot today!' she replied, wiping her brow with the back of her hand.

Yussef smiled, having got his way. 'The sun has moved,' he commented amiably. 'Move to the other side and you will be in the shade and able to watch us at the same time.' Aunt Lea looked round again. It was true. Taking hold of Yussef's hand she pulled herself up and went to where he had indicated. She looked longingly for a moment at the sea.

Neferu followed her gaze. 'Why don't you go for a swim, Aunt Lea?' the girl asked.

'Mmm, I'm very tempted,' her aunt replied. 'I might do if you two stay out of the way for a while.'

Yussef grinned. 'We won't peep, will we, Neferu? We are going to explore the caves for treasure left by the pirates.'

This whole coast of the Mediterranean had a bad name for piracy at that time. Stories abounded of wild, barbaric, bearded men in strange longboats from the far western lands, close to where all land ended and a great ocean commenced, which covered the earth. Very few people had seen them, but it was known that they came from countries with strange names like Iberia and Gallia, where the weather was cold, and the people wore the skins of wild animals. 'Pirates?' Aunt Lea shuddered and looked carefully out to sea. Reassured by the apparently empty horizon and the vast expanse of uninhabited white sand stretching in front of her, she smiled. 'I don't think you will find any treasure around here,' she said, in an amused voice.

Yussef shrugged. 'You never know.' he said darkly. With an impatient glance, he turned to Neferu. 'Come on.' With that he turned round and started off down the beach. Neferu followed him. She wasn't quite sure how you recognised a pirate but guessed that they looked pretty awful from the expression of horror which had fleetingly crossed Aunt Lea's face.

'Don't be too long!' Aunt Lea's voice called out one last warning note.

They turned round and waved to her. 'We won't!'

As they carried on down the beach Yussef explained about pirates to Neferu, and she too took a furtive look out to sea. She didn't like the sound of these pirates. As the pair walked, they looked out for interesting shells on the way, bending down occasionally to take a closer look at something interesting. Now and again they would look round to locate Aunt Lea. She looked like a tiny speck in the distance. Suddenly, Yussef tugged at Neferu's arm, and she noticed it too. They had almost missed it at first because of its narrow entrance in an odd L-shape. They went to investigate the cave they had discovered. On closer inspection it wasn't very wide. The opening could not have been more than a metre wide at its widest point and at its narrowest it was little more than half a metre. They took it in turns to peer through into the dimness. It was hard to see much from where they were, and they decided to go in.

Yussef climbed in first and turned to help pull Neferu over the threshold, which was about a metre high. Neferu's heart was thumping inside her chest. What if there were pirates inside? Inside the cave there was a dank, salty smell. The sand underneath was moist, and their feet left deep imprints which cracked at the edges. The cave was much bigger than they had first imagined. What they had seen from the entrance was a kind of vestibule which led into a small grotto with stalactites and stalagmites, hanging like pointed daggers down from the roof, trying to reach down to their counterparts on the ground. Neferu clapped her hands together in wonder. She had never seen anything like this before in her life. She wondered if it was magic. Yussef too was silent. They stared about them. Towards the back of the grotto there was a tiny pool which gave off a fluorescent blue glow. It was magic. Neferu was sure of that.

'Do you think there is treasure here, Yussef?' she asked in an awed voice.

'This is better than treasure.' Yussef's voice held a note of deep satisfaction.

'Is it magic, Yussef?' Neferu asked in a whisper.

'I don't know, but I don't think so,' he replied hesitantly. 'But it is very special all the same, Neferu,' he continued emphatically. Neferu nodded. Yussef was silent for a moment and then he said, 'We must not ever tell anyone else in the whole world about this, Neferu. This is our cave. Not another person in the whole world knows about this. Promise you won't tell?'

'Not even Demi?' Neferu asked.

Yussef considered for a moment and then replied, 'Not even Demi.' He then looked accusingly at Neferu. 'Promise!'

'I promise,' Neferu answered after a slight hesitation.

'Not even if we quarrel and you want to get back at me like you sometimes do?' he said warningly.

'I do not!' Neferu answered indignantly.

'Yes, you do,' Yussef stated baldly, but then added in a softer tone, to mollify her, 'but you must promise that this time you won't.'

'Can't I even tell Demi if he swears to keep it a secret?' she pleaded.

'No!' he said firmly. 'Promise!'

'Alright, I promise,' she said at length. 'But it will be hard to keep such a delicious secret.'

Yussef shot her a warning glance and Neferu shut up. 'Put your finger out,' he said peremptorily, lifting up his arm. Neferu lifted her arm and placed her index finger opposite his. In a solemn tone Yussef began to speak. 'Say "I, Nefertiti Stassopoulos do solemnly swear never to divulge to any other person …"'

'Never to divulge,' here Neferu stumbled over the word which she had never heard before, 'to any other person …'

'"The whereabouts of this magic cave."' Yussef's tone droned on, and she repeated his words.

'"If I break my promise horrid things will happen to me."' Neferu swallowed hard. She wasn't very good at keeping promises.

'What kind of horrid things?' she asked anxiously.

'I don't know, but anyway, very horrid things,' Yussef replied, accentuating the word 'very'.

Neferu swallowed again but saw no way out. 'If I break my promise horrid things will happen to me,' she repeated wide-eyed.

'Good,' said Yussef with satisfaction.

Neferu shivered suddenly, she felt cold. 'Let's go back,' she said, 'Aunt Lea will be getting worried.' Yussef seemed reluctant to move, but Neferu began to retrace her steps.

'Neferu!' Yussef called. Neferu stopped and looked around. Yussef was advancing towards her with a smile on his face.

'What is it, Yussef?' she asked curiously.

'Oh nothing,' he said hesitating. Then, 'You are my best friend in the whole world, Neferu.' He gave her a hug and kissed her cheek. Neferu was surprised.

Yussef was not a very demonstrative boy; in fact, normally he would have called such demonstrations of affection girlish, and girlish was the most insulting adjective Yussef could imagine. Without reflecting further, she sensed that she was very honoured and smiled with pleasure.

'I won't tell anyone about our cave, Yussef,' she said again. Yussef merely nodded.

'We had better go,' he said, 'We can come again tomorrow.' They took a last look round their magic cave and then jumped onto the sand and set off at a brisk pace in the direction of Aunt Lea.

When they arrived back Aunt Lea was very cross and scolded them severely. She said that she had been very worried when they disappeared from view and did not reappear again for such a long time. The children apologised and said that they had been looking for stones and shells and had not noticed the time. Aunt Lea spread out their lunch and they began to eat. She was still a little annoyed and said that she could not imagine what they found so interesting down on the beach every day. She found nothing more boring than sand, personally. The children smiled conspiratorially and made a special effort to be charming to her, to soothe her ruffled feelings. Yussef thanked her for coming with them and told her that she was his favourite aunt of all. Aunt Lea laughed good-naturedly. She realised that he was purposely flattering her, and she peered at him myopically.

'You could charm a song-bird down from a bush, Yussef,' she said with a laugh, pleased, in spite of herself, and no more was said about the cave incident.

After lunch, they gathered the remains together and Neferu put her frock on. Slowly they made their way up the cliff, Aunt Lea going first, puffing and panting. Neferu came behind and Yussef last, carrying the food basket. By the time they got to the top they were all hot and sweaty and Neferu noticed that the sun was past its highest. They were later than usual in getting back. The others were probably taking their afternoon nap already. She hoped that Grandma would not be cross with them.

When they arrived back, Grandma was still up waiting for them. Grandpa and Demi were both asleep. Once assured that there was nothing wrong, she too retired and they all followed her example.

When Grandma woke her Neferu noticed that the sun was already low over the horizon. She rubbed her eyes and sat up. 'How is Demi, Grandma?' she asked.

The old lady pursed her lips and frowned slightly. 'He's got a bit of fever, I think. I'll have to stay behind with him tonight when you all go over to Uncle Giorgios,' she said matter-of-factly. Neferu felt surprised, but she was not particularly worried. She had never known anything that Grandma could not deal with.

'Have you told him yet?' she asked, thinking that Demi was bound to kick up a fuss when he found out that he was not going. He hated to be left out of anything. It was bad enough being the youngest: as if it was his fault, he would say, emphasising the 'his'.

'Not yet,' Grandma replied serenely. She grinned at Neferu. 'Demi has a sweet tooth and I'll bribe him with some bonbons!' she openly admitted. Neferu felt a little shocked at this brazen admission, and also at the thought of missing the bonbons.

'Can I have some bonbons as well?' she wheedled.

'No,' Grandma said firmly. 'I expect there will be quite enough to eat at Uncle Giorgios.' Neferu brightened up at the thought. She and Yussef got on well with their six cousins and Aunt Alessandrina always had a large store of goodies. She decided not to pursue the subject further and got up to go for her wash. Out in the yard Neferu could hear Yussef bringing some water for Grandma.

'Neferu! Come and have your hair washed,' Grandma called. Neferu went out into the back yard. Yussef was winding up some more water from the well. Grandma beckoned Neferu over to her and made her kneel down on a rug. On an old wooden stool was a pottery bowl and Grandma made her bend her head over it. With a jug she poured water over her granddaughter's head until her whole head was thoroughly wet. To wash her hair Grandma used a kind of brown soap which she used to make herself. Liberally, she soaked Neferu's hair and began methodically to rub in the soap. After rinsing the girl's head well, she commenced the whole procedure again and finally finished off with three thorough rinses. As she carried out the job, she tut-tutted over the amount of salt in Neferu's hair. 'You'll have to start acting like a young lady soon,' she grumbled. 'This salt takes all the sheen from your hair,' she continued after briskly rubbing the soap in again. Neferu said nothing, trying to keep her eyes squeezed tightly shut to prevent the soap getting in them. She hated that because it stung so. When it was all over, Grandma wrapped a towel around her head and began to rub roughly. Neferu's face was red from hanging it upside down over the bowl, but it was no use complaining. They had been going through this torture three times a decan ever since Neferu could remember, and there was no arguing with Grandma. She noticed Yussef grinning at her from the well and she stuck her tongue out at him. Grandma noticed and admonished her for behaving like a ragamuffin.

Eventually Grandma was finished and, the towel still over her head, she was sent into the kitchen where Aunt Lea was waiting with a big tub of warm water. In she stepped at Aunt Lea's behest and Aunt Lea watched while she bathed herself all over. When Aunt Lea was satisfied that she was clean, she was allowed to step out and wrap a towel around herself. The ablutions finally over, she went to dress for the visit to their relatives just across the fields. As she left the kitchen, she heard Grandma call Yussef for his turn and, in turn, felt pleasure that now he would have the same torture, as he had laughed at her.

When Neferu had completed her dressing, she went in to see her brother. He was lying quietly on his bed, and she noticed that his cheeks were flushed. He turned his head and smiled when she came close but did not stir himself more than that. Neferu felt a sudden unease. Demi was usually a very lively boy. Although he was shy with outsiders, at home he was noisy and exuberant. Now he was just lying very still, and this alarmed her. She went and sat on the end of his bed. 'Are you alright now, Demi?' she asked him anxiously.

'I've got a bad headache and my leg hurts,' he answered despondently. 'I expect it will be better tomorrow,' he added hopefully.

'Are you coming to Aunt Alessandrina's tonight with us?' she asked, pretending that she didn't know that he was not coming with them.

Demi gave a slight shake of the head. 'No,' he said. 'I'm staying home with Grandma. I don't feel like going.' Neferu reflected that Grandma had had an easier time than she had envisaged in persuading Demi to stay home.

'We'll bring you some bonbons back,' she said, to cheer him up.

'I don't even feel like bonbons,' Demi replied with a wan smile.

'Oh.' This was an unexpected response as it was almost unheard of for Demi to refuse bonbons. It must be serious. Neferu suddenly remembered that her mother had died of a fever. Her heart seemed to contract, and she hoped Demi was not going to die. This frightening thought caused her to stand up suddenly. She paused for a moment and then bent down and kissed him. 'I love you, Demi,' she said gently.

'I love you too, Neferu,' he answered.

'I'll be back later. I have to go and see Grandma about something,' she added. Demi nodded and she went towards the door. At the entrance she gave him a quick smile and then disappeared.

Neferu tiptoed as quickly as she could to the door where Grandma was standing with her hands on her hips overlooking the yard, where Aunt Lea was spreading the towels out to dry over the bushes. She could hear the splash of water in the kitchen, where Yussef was washing himself.

'Grandma,' she whispered urgently.

Grandma turned and frowned. 'What is it, Neferu?' she asked, wondering why Neferu was whispering.

'Grandma, I want to talk to you,' Neferu continued to whisper. Grandma lifted her eyebrows and stepped outside and Neferu went over to her and, putting her mouth close to Grandma's ear she whispered, 'Demi isn't going to die, is he?'

Grandma was thunderstruck, while Aunt Lea looked on curiously. 'Good gracious! No!' said Grandma, putting her hand to her heart. 'Wherever did you get that idea from, Neferu?'

Neferu drew in a deep breath of relief. 'That's all right then,' she said. She looked at Grandma's shocked face. 'It's just that you said that Demi has a fever and I thought ...' Her voice trailed off questioningly and she looked at Grandma waiting for guidance. 'Well. I mean, Mother died of a fever, didn't she?'

'That was quite different,' Grandma said quickly. 'Quite, quite different,' she reiterated.

'Oh, good' said Neferu, simply. Just then Grandpa came to the door. He was eager to be off to play backgammon with Giorgios.

'Aren't you ready yet?' he said impatiently.

Grandma took the towel from Neferu's head. 'Come on, young lady! Let's get this hair sorted out so that you can be off.' Neferu temporarily forgot Demi in the rush to get ready and even when she popped in to kiss him before leaving, she did it with the sure knowledge that he would be better in the morning. Grandma had implied that, hadn't she? Her mind was already following Grandpa and Yussef down the path.

They all spent a very enjoyable evening with Aunt Alessandrina and Uncle Giorgios and their family. Grandpa and Uncle Giorgios discussed business and old acquaintances and friends, while playing backgammon. Aunt Alessandrina and Aunt Lea gossiped all night in an animated way. They always fell silent when Neferu or the others came near and would look warningly at each other. This branch of the Stassopoulos family had six children and they varied in age from the baby of six months to the eldest son, Constantinos, who was the same age as Yussef and was working with his father in the family business. Neferu was reduced to playing hide and seek with the others because Constantinos and Yussef felt too grown up to play with the little ones and made it clear they were not keen on having a girl listen in on their avid conversations. After a while, though, they were attracted by the squeals of fun into joining in the game.

True to form, Aunt Alessandrina had provided a scrumptious spread and Aunt Lea allowed even Neferu to have a goblet of wine, though on the strict understanding that Grandma was not to be informed. Grandpa grinned and crossed his heart that he would not tell. It was very late, and the younger children had been put to bed much earlier, when Grandpa regretfully made the first signs of moving. Yussef said that he was not tired at all, but Neferu could feel her own eyelids drooping more and more.

Together they set off along the little track which led from the lane and made their way home. It was only a distance of five-hundred metres or so, but in the blackness of night it seemed a real adventure to Neferu. When they got back to the villa, Grandma packed the children off to bed at once. She said Demi was sleeping and must not be disturbed. Neferu and Yussef went off to their respective beds unprotestingly. Neferu was so tired that the next day she could not even remember getting into bed. She must have fallen asleep immediately.

CHAPTER 4

Neferu was woken by Yussef the next morning. She sensed the urgency in both his voice and the rather rough shaking of her shoulders, 'Neferu! Wake up!' Neferu was still tired but the very fact that it was Yussef waking her and not Grandma was sufficient for her to register that something was wrong.

'Yussef, what is it?' she asked in alarm, sitting up and pushing the hair out of her eyes.

'Get up quickly, Neferu!' the boy answered by way of reply. 'Aunt Lea says that you are to come and have breakfast right away.' By now Neferu was thoroughly alarmed, and the memories of the previous day came flooding back.

'It's Demi, isn't it?' she gasped. 'He's dead, isn't he?'

Yussef shook his head vehemently. 'He's not that bad,' he said, 'but I have to go to Rashid with Grandpa to bring the doctor.'

'The doctor?' The very word scared Neferu half to death. If Grandma could not sort the matter out, it must be very serious indeed. The doctor hardly ever needed to visit them. In fact, she could not ever remember his having ever visited.

Yussef saw how stricken she looked. 'Don't worry, Neferu, he'll get better.' From the door he smiled at her sympathetically and said, 'See you later.' Neferu felt her lips automatically murmuring the appropriate response.

When Yussef had gone, she started frantically to pull on her clothes and as soon as she was ready, she went to find Grandma. 'Don't bother me today, Neferu. I am very busy.' Was Grandma's short reply to her opening questions. Glumly she went into the kitchen and sat down. She asked Aunt Lea about Demi but only received an evasive reply. She was told that she could not go and see him yet. He had vomited and Grandma was bathing him. She could see him later on.

Disconsolately, Neferu went into the yard after eating her breakfast and she fed the hens. Normally this was a job they did together before going to the beach, but she knew that there would be no outing today. There was a terrible quietness over the place today.

Grandpa and Yussef had gone into Rashid with Uncle Giorgios. They had taken a lift in the chariot and so would be much faster than if they had gone on the donkeys. The usual banging of dishes in the kitchen was missing today. Aunt Lea was going about her business like a mouse, trying to make as little noise as possible. Grandma was with Demi and there were no sounds coming from that room.

Neferu sat down on the old broken stool and let two large tears run luxuriously down her cheeks. She allowed herself to wallow in glorious self-pity. Here she was, alone, almost an orphan. No mother, a father who had forgotten her, and now even her brother was dying. No one cared about her. Even Yussef had gone off with Grandpa. She was all alone in the world. As the tears began to run more freely, she felt her nose begin to run and she wiped it unceremoniously on the back of her hand, sniffing a little. Aunt Lea came out at that moment and saw her. 'What's the matter, Neferu?' she asked in surprise. 'Why are you crying?'

'Because I am an orphan, alone in the world,' blubbered Neferu.

'You are being ridiculous, Neferu!' her aunt replied sharply. 'We've got quite enough on at the moment with Demi being sick without all this sort of silliness!' Neferu glared at her aunt. She might have known that she would get no sympathy. Aunt Lea gazed coolly back at her and suddenly smiled. She knelt down in front of Neferu and, putting her arm around her, said firmly, 'You are not an orphan, Neferu, and no one means to push you away. It's just that Demi is rather ill, and we are all very worried about him. You'll just have to be strong.' Neferu sighed but decided to capitulate. Usually she was told to be sensible, now she had to be strong as well. Grown-ups expected too much of ten-year olds, she reckoned.

'When can I go and see Demi?' she asked Aunt Lea.

'As soon as he has been washed and changed,' answered her aunt. 'But you had better blow your nose and then go and wash your face first,' she added. 'I don't want you to frighten him!' Neferu went to wash her face and then hung around in the kitchen with Aunt Lea until Grandma came in.

'Can I go and see Demi now, grandma?' she pleaded.

'Off you go, but don't excite him,' her Grandma warned.

Neferu rushed off to her brother's room and tiptoed in. When she saw him, she was shocked. Even she recognised that Demi was distinctly ill. He lay curled up in bed, his eyes bright with fever and two flaming cheeks in an otherwise pale face. Under his eyes were deep shadows and his eyes seemed sunken. She felt scared.

'Hello, Demi,' she whispered. His eyes moved to her face, but he did not answer. 'Is it your leg?' she asked in a low voice. An expression of acquiescence flitted across his face and Neferu lifted up the sheet which was covering him. She was horrified to see that the whole of his left leg was swollen and across the front of the lower leg there was an angry red patch. She hurriedly dropped the sheet again, frightened by what she had seen. Now she was truly afraid that Demi was really going to die. Suddenly he seemed so dear to her that she just could not even bear to think of it. A large, heavy lump came to her throat all at once and it stuck there like a stone that she just could not swallow. Neferu knelt on the floor by Demi's bed. 'I'll stay here with you, Demi, and I'll never leave you,' she said fiercely. Demi nodded slightly in appreciation. 'You are the best brother in all the world and when you get better you can play with all my toys. I'll never stop you. I'll give you them all,' she said desperately. A slight flicker of interest animated Demi's face for a moment before that too faded, not, however, before Neferu noticed it. 'Yes. I mean it. You can have all my things if you will only get better. You will get better, won't you, Demi? Promise me you'll get better?'

Demi did not move at all, but his dry lips murmured, 'I promise.'

Neferu felt a huge weight fall from her shoulders. 'Good! Remember it then!'

At that moment Grandma came in and said, 'Come on out now, Neferu. Let Demi rest.'

Neferu leaned over and kissed her brother. 'Remember your promise' she whispered as she stood up.

To pass the time while waiting for Grandpa and Yussef to return with the doctor, Neferu decided to go and pick some of the wildflowers from the field behind the villa. Aunt Lea told her not to go too far. Neferu replied that she would get a nice big bunch for Demi's room. As she picked her flowers, Neferu found herself wondering if Helios knew that Demi was ill. Did he know automatically or were you supposed to pray and tell him? Just in case, she sent up a quick prayer of the 'God, it's me' type. She suddenly realised how much she missed her father. It was already four decans since they had seen him, and she began to wonder if Demi would ever see him again. They had been due to leave for On in five days but what would happen now? Neferu squeezed her eyes tightly shut and concentrated hard. 'If there is a god in the heavens, listen to me now. Let Demi get better quickly and make Father arrive here very soon, please.' With all her might she concentrated on sending her prayer up and up through the ether to Helios in his heaven. Afterwards she felt a little calmer, having done all she could.

After Neferu had collected a nice big bunch of poppies, buttercups and blue speedwell, she started to make her way back to the house. At the edge of the field, she watched a little fieldmouse run across the track to the other side. She wondered if it had a family and if it was happy. A moment later she lifted her eyes to the sound of hooves and watched the chariot as it brought the others back. They were standing in the back with a stranger, who she correctly supposed was the doctor.

As the three men and Yussef stepped down, they greeted her, and she followed them inside the gate. Grandma was already at the front door, ushering them in. Neferu made no attempt to follow them, but went instead to the kitchen, where she took a sharp knife and began to cut the stems of her flowers into the appropriated lengths for the pottery vase she had chosen. She was putting water in the vase when Yussef came up behind her. 'Have you seen Demi?' he asked.

'Yes,' Neferu replied non-committally.

'He seems to be very ill,' Yussef remarked broodingly.

'Yes, but he will get better,' Neferu said firmly.

'I hope so,' Yussef continued in a morose tone. Neferu was too frightened to answer. The strange presence of the doctor in the house only served to crystallise her fears.

She busied herself arranging the flowers in the vase. 'For Demi,' she explained briefly to Yussef.

He nodded abstractedly. 'I don't suppose that we'll be able to visit the cave again this year,' Yussef said after a moment.

Neferu let her gaze flicker over his face. She had forgotten the cave with all the drama of Demi's illness. 'No,' she agreed and felt sorry that she promised not to tell Demi about it. It seemed mean somehow. Still, what did it matter now?

There was a murmuring as the grown-ups came out of Demi's room and went out into the yard. They huddled together, talking in low tones so that she and Yussef could not hear what they were saying. Grandma looked very worried, and it made Neferu feel sick in the pit of her stomach. Grandma was not the kind who worried over nothing and Neferu felt that she and Yussef were being excluded. The doctor left and when Grandma returned from seeing him off, Neferu noticed that her eyes were red-rimmed. Grandma crying? A hollow feeling of despair enveloped Neferu and she could see that even Yussef was frightened now. 'What is it, Grandma? What is wrong with Demi?'

Grandma answered in a tremulous voice. 'The doctor says that Demi has an inflammation of the bone. He might die or have to have his leg off. The doctor is coming back tomorrow to open up the bone and try to get the poison out.' Her words were so stark and unexpected that everyone seemed rooted to the spot, watching as the tower of strength they all relied upon wept openly. Grandpa shuffled uneasily from side to side, refusing to look up. Aunt Lea looked as though she were about to faint, and Yussef looked terrified.

Seeing it all, Neferu suddenly felt very angry. She was not going to give up so easily. 'You are wrong, Grandma!' she said defiantly. 'Demi will get better. He is not going to have his leg off and father will arrive very soon.'

In spite of herself, Grandma smiled. 'You are right, Neferu. We must look on the bright side. It won't do Demi any good if we all start frightening him with our attitudes of doom. But tell me, how do you know your father is coming?'

'I prayed to Helios, the strongest god in the universe, and asked him to send father,' Neferu answered.

'But even if he leaves on the boat today, he still won't arrive for three more days,' Yussef answered logically.

'But if he left On four days ago, he will be here tonight,' Neferu answered blithely. Grandpa shrugged and deigned not to listen. He was not given to the fanciful.

Grandma suddenly pulled herself together and in her usual brisk voice said, 'Well, there is no point in standing here. Lea, can you put the lamb on the spits and sort out the vegetables?'

Without waiting for an answer, Grandma turned to her husband and asked him to bring some more brushwood and dried dung for the fire. Then turning to Yussef and Neferu, she told them to start packing. Whether Vassiliou came or not, they must be ready to leave as soon as it was possible for Demi to travel. She said she was eager to get home as quickly as they could because she knew the local doctor well and there was more help available to them in On. Neferu smiled. Grandma had decided that Demi was going to be fit enough to travel soon, so it must be so! She and Yussef went to begin packing everything they would need during the next couple of days. It was a relief to have something to do.

Demi remained very ill that night and all the following day, but Grandma persuaded the doctor not to touch Demi's leg for a while. The doctor shrugged but he gave Demi some medicine he had made up and it helped to reduce for the first time the high fever that was prostrating the little boy.

Against the total disbelief of all, perhaps with the exception of Neferu, her father arrived the following day. Neferu was credited by everyone as having powers of clairvoyance. Neferu tried to tell them that it was only that Helios had decided to answer her prayer. Grandma declared the truth of that and Grandpa, who didn't really believe in any gods, he said, decided to thank him just in case.

It was Yussef who had seen her father first. The sound of the hooves of the horse and the clatter of the wheels on the sun-baked track had alerted him. Vassiliou stepped down and hugged them all, wondering aloud where Demi was. There was a complete babble as the others rushed out and everyone started talking at once. Her father was very shocked by the news and even more so when he saw Demi tying there. His strong little son seemed to have shrunk. Neferu was so miserable about Demi but so happy to see her father that she simply burst into tears. For once Yussef did not call her a crybaby. His own emotions were just as jangled as hers. He put his arms around her, and they stood locked together, drawing comfort each from the other.

The next day, Demi was no worse and no better and the hope engendered by Father's arrival faded once again. Again, Neferu had a fit of crying. She had gone in to see Demi and was so upset by his lack of response that the tears started to roll down her cheeks and began to plop onto his hand as it lay palm down on the coverlet. Demi looked at her and said, 'Don't cry, Neffie!' using the name he used to call her by when he was a toddler. At that Neferu only cried the harder. She kissed his cheeks and told him that he absolutely must get better, or she didn't know what she would do! Yussef stood awkwardly, in unconscious resemblance of Grandpa. Both of them seemed completely at a loss. It was sad to see Grandpa like this. Normally he was such a confident and articulate man, now he had taken to following Grandma round and muttering despondently at her.

That night when Neferu went to bed, she decided that it was time for another straight talk with Helios. She had long since decided to bypass all the other gods and go straight to the top, as this was such a dangerous crisis. She closed her eyes tightly again and concentrated as before. 'I did tell you that you must make Demi better, but I forgot to tell you that it must be very soon because we are supposed to go back to On very soon.' She let a brief pause ensue before sending off the final part of her message. 'If you could fix it for tomorrow then I will always pray to you, and I won't even consider talking to the other gods. Thank you very much from me, Neferu Stassopoulos.' Soon after she fell asleep.

The next day Demi's fever had fallen. He was still ill but there was a definite improvement in his general condition, and even the leg appeared less swollen. Everyone commented that the doctor's medicine was very effective, but Neferu knew better. She was pleased that Helios had heard and answered her prayer.

Within six days Demi's general condition was vastly better. He was eating and drinking and sitting up in bed. There was still a serious problem in that the leg was still very painful and he could not put his weight on it. Neferu's god had healed Demi, but he had chosen not to do so completely. After a family conference, it was decided to go back to On forthwith, while Demi was able to travel, even if with difficulty. Vassiliou went on ahead to alert the doctor in On about Demi's condition and make arrangements for some provisional nursing help for Grandma so that the home would continue to run smoothly.

After the discovery of the cave there had been no more trips to the beach, and even Rashid was no fun under the present circumstances. For the first time ever Yussef and Neferu were glad that the summer was over. They vowed to come and find their cave again the following summer.

For the journey down to the river, Grandpa had to hire a very posh chariot at an astronomical price so that Demi could be comfortably seated for the journey. Grandma and Aunt Lea travelled in the chariot with him. Grandpa, Yussef and Neferu went by donkey. By the time they arrived at the landing stage the others were safely on board. It was an anxious and uncomfortable trip back, stared at by other passengers and with little privacy. Demi was tired and fractious, and the doctor had not given Grandma enough of the medicine to keep the pain away. By the time the boat docked at On four days later, everyone was tired and irritable. Grandma said for the hundredth time that she was getting too old for all this travelling and vowed that she would not go to Rashid anymore. Father came down to the docks to meet them with two servants and two large chariots. The luggage was loaded onto three donkeys and the two servants accompanied them. The rest of them clambered into the chariots, Father and Grandfather carefully lifting Demi.

It was quickly decided that for the time being, at least, Demi would live permanently with Grandma until he was better. Neferu howled at this and wanted to stay at Grandma's too. Vassiliou looked defeated and hurt at this, but he eventually gave in. From this time hence the children lived with Yussef and their grandparents and visited home on an almost daily basis rather than the other way round. In the end it turned out to be an admirable arrangement and everyone seemed satisfied with it. This time the return to On held none of the usual happy anticipation of meeting old friends and swapping summer experiences. It was a tired, subdued group who had arrived back in their quarter. Grandma's indomitable face was even more lined, but at least it showed the set expression of a partial victory and a determination to wrench more from the situation.

Egyptian doctors were clever, their secrets were passed down in the family from generation to generation, and Grandma trusted their local doctor, whom she had known for many years. Accordingly, he was invited to visit as soon as he could because, although Demi was making a slow recovery, the fate of the leg itself was still uncertain. When the grey-haired, old doctor came to examine Demi, the whole family stood in wait, on tenterhooks. After what seemed an interminably long consultation, the doctor told Grandma that the first doctor had been right. It was necessary to open the bone and let the poison drain out. Grandma wilted visibly at this news, but after a short silence she shrugged her shoulders and told the doctor to go ahead.

The doctor explained to a very frightened Demi what he was going to do and that afterwards Demi would not be allowed to put weight on his damaged leg for six decans. Demi was scared but he was even more scared of his leg never healing so he bravely agreed. The doctor gave Demi a potion to drink and after a while he became very sleepy and soon became deeply unconscious. Grandma brought hot water for the doctor, and afterwards everyone but she was banished from the room.

For Neferu and the others, the procedure seemed to take ages. Vassiliou arrived and was allowed into the room. He did not reappear until much later when all three came out. Grandma looked white. She told Aunt Lea to go in and sit with Demi, who was still asleep. She then went to clean herself and offer the same facilities to the doctor. The fact that they both seemed composed caused the atmosphere to lighten immediately.

Vassiliou told Grandpa that an enormous amount of poison had come away from the leg and the doctor had scraped away the spoiled bone. Afterwards, he had repeatedly washed the wound with hot water into which he had dissolved one of his potions. Following that he had packed the hole in the bone with a cotton soaked in another pungent liquid. He had told Father that it might have to be repeated but that he hoped not. Finally the doctor had splinted Demi's leg to keep it immobile, and he and Grandma had applied many bandages. The doctor had arranged to visit again the following day unless the situation deteriorated.

Demi slept for a long time, and when he woke up, he was very frightened. He looked down at his bandaged leg and was reassured that it was still there. Whatever had been done to it was not visible under all the bandaging. Aunt Lea decided not to wake Grandma up. In her exhaustion she had fallen asleep on the couch, and they were all tiptoeing round her. Strangely, in Neferu's opinion, Demi said that his leg was less painful than before, not more so. In spite of this, Aunt Lea gave Demi some of the medicine which the doctor had left for him. The medicine took away the pain completely but gave him a very strange feeling of floating around which was very odd but not unpleasant, he said.

It appeared that Aunt Lea sat up with Demi for half the night because, in her exhausted state, Grandma did not wake up until nearly dawn. When she entered the room, Demi was sleeping peacefully, and Aunt Lea had fallen asleep in the chair with her head at an uncomfortable angle. Grandma woke her and told her to go to bed. Aunt Lea gave Grandma a pleasing report as to Demi's progress and the two women hugged each other in their relief.

Demi was definitely much improved the next day. Even the slight fever which he had never completely shaken off was now gone. They were not out of the storm yet, but Grandma said that a safe harbour was in sight. Demi began to show a renewed interest in his surroundings and, day by day, he grew stronger. The daily inspection of his leg by the doctor was a procedure truly obnoxious to him, but he never felt any pain because of the extract of poppy juice which he was given to drink, and which effectively took away the pain. Vassiliou was very grateful to his mother-in-law for her competent and loving help. Over the years they had grown very fond of him, replacing his own parents, who were now dead. He, in turn, held them in great esteem and they were no less close now that he had remarried than before.

The doctor had visited daily at first but, as Demi's illness became less acute, he came less often. As his condition improved Demi became bored and fractious and even Grandma grew impatient with his constant calls for attention. In the end Grandpa sent Yussef to the school to bring homework for Demi to do every day. Demi was most annoyed at this but recovered his equilibrium a little when two of his school friends came to do their homework with him.

Over the long months of the cool season, Demi's leg slowly improved, though he was not able to stand up on it until about three months after their return from Rashid. The doctor was not completely satisfied with it either and he told Grandma that he suspected that there was still some poison in the leg which was preventing it from healing properly. He wanted to re-open the leg but both Grandma and Demi were totally against it. Demi said that he could put up with the amount of discomfort he had. He did not want to spend several more months on bedrest and Grandma agreed. In the end, the doctor acquiesced, and Demi learned to get about with the aid of a crutch and it was not until the following spring that he learned to walk fairly well again, in spite of a marked limp. Even then the leg was painful and tended to swell easily. If he over-exercised it, it was prone to turn an alarming reddish-blue colour, and they all gave up hope of his leg ever being normal again.

Gradually Demi changed and became much quieter and more introverted than he had been previously. It was hard to tell whether this was a result of the chronic leg problem or whether he would have developed in this way whatever. Grandma had taken to praying with him, her ankh, the ancient symbol of life, clutched firmly in her hand.

The following summer there was no visit to Rashid. Demi was not fit enough to go, and Grandma had had enough of the long journeying. So it was that Neferu and Yussef never came to visit their magic cave together again. Much later in her life, Neferu came to think of that summer as the last real summer of her childhood.

In the ensuing years the family continued to grow and live together in peace and love. Demi grew stronger and taller, even the damaged leg, though it remained throughout his life shorter than the other so that he always walked with a marked limp. He was a clever boy and flourished at school, perhaps because he was not able to join in the rough and tumble games of his friends. His teacher told Vassiliou that Demi would make an excellent scribe and Vassiliou was very proud because it meant that he had good possibilities of following in his father's footsteps. Demi only occasionally missed the sports and active pursuits of his friends and settled down to the academic work involved in acquiring the necessary skills of a scribe.

As for Vassiliou, his integrity and pleasant personality brought him favour in his career, and on several occasions he had been requested to attend the court at Thebes on business. Once, he had even met Amenophis III, the pharaoh of all Egypt. The family were greatly honoured and very proud of this.

CHAPTER 5

When Neferu was fifteen and Yussef seventeen, he came to make a formal declaration for her hand to Vassiliou. It seemed to Neferu that the whole family had always expected that some time she and Yussef would marry. Many of her friends were married already, but she had not felt ready and Vassiliou had not pressed her. He told her that he had received several offers for her hand in marriage from locally respected families, but he was a tolerant father, and he wanted his daughter to be happy. Yussef was with her father a long time and when they came out of his study they were laughing together. Yussef bowed to her somewhat shyly as he left that day, and it was only later that her father came to tell her the real reason for his strangely formal visit.

Looking back, she should have known that he was no longer her big brother when he had moved out into his own accommodation the previous year. Vassiliou asked his daughter if she had considered the matter seriously of late. Neferu replied that she supposed she would have to marry some time but that she had wanted more. Her father was intrigued and wanted to know what more was it that she wanted. Neferu shrugged her shoulders, not really knowing herself what it was. She replied, for want of a better description of the strange empty place inside her, that she wanted to experience some exciting adventure. Her father laughed and said that she was too much of a tomboy and it was his fault. She had suffered a lack of discipline. Afterwards his tone became serious, and he told her that his beautiful daughter had now become a beautiful woman and must soon settle down and marry. Neferu sighed. She truly did not know herself what she was seeking, so how could she expect her father to understand? She looked so crestfallen that her father said laughingly, 'I can arrange one last adventure for you.'

Now it was Neferu's turn to be intrigued, and she asked her father to tell her more. Vassiliou explained that he had been summoned to the palace at Thebes for a meeting of the regional representatives with the grand vizier, Ay. It would be a very important meeting, but afterwards there would be a grand banquet and ball. The pharaoh himself and the great queen were to be present. As Shosen was now at the beginning of her third pregnancy and had not been feeling well, she had decided not to make the long journey to the capital. If Neferu wished, her father would take her instead. When they returned, he was sure she would settle down and marry Yussef without any further longing for adventure.

Neferu was thrilled. This adventure issued out of the blue immediately lifted her spirits. She could hardly wait to tell Grandma and was already mentally conjuring up a picture of the dream dress she would wear for the occasion. Something light and very elegant, of course, which would set off her hair, which she considered to be her best feature. Her hair was thick and glossy, a rich dark brown with auburn highlights. It had been much admired, and she was rather vain about it. Vassiliou was amused and pleased at her excitement and promised her that she could have a fine new dress to wear for the occasion. She was to choose her own material from the store.

The next day Yussef arrived to have dinner with the family. Although nothing had been said formally, their engagement was now more or less taken for granted. Vassiliou told Yussef that it could take place when they returned from Thebes. Yussef was rather annoyed at what he considered to be a rash offer on the part of Vassiliou in taking Neferu to Thebes. He did not like the idea of Neferu going to Thebes at all, but he could give her no reasonable explanation of why. After all, they would be back in On in less than two decans. Yussef sulked but Neferu was obstinate.

'Why do you insist on going?' Yussef asked petulantly.

'I want to play the fine lady for once,' Neferu told him.

'You are already a fine lady,' Yussef told her quietly. Neferu was silenced and almost capitulated at this; almost, but not quite. 'Those people are dangerous, Neferu. They say that there is a lot of intrigue at court, and they look down on Keftiu like us. We are not pure Egyptian.' Yussef spoke in a brooding tone.

'But we will only be at the court itself for three days, Yussef. Most of the time we will be travelling, and I do so want to see it,' Neferu said in a pleading voice. Yussef's face relented a little and she sought to press her case. 'What on earth can happen to us in three days? Father has no enemies. I am sure you are right, but no one is going to notice a couple of unimportant Keftiu!' Yussef remained unconvinced, but in the face of her pleasurable anticipation and reassurance, he could do no other than give way. Still, a shadow was cast over the evening and he left in a sombre mood. Not, however, before giving her a long and ardent kiss. It was the first time he had ever kissed her in this way, and she felt herself instinctively responding to him. He tweaked her nose and smiled before running down the steps.

More strangely, Demi too was worried about the forthcoming trip and tried to talk Neferu out of going. Grandma and Aunt Lea, on the other hand, were both wholeheartedly for it and were almost as excited as she was. Neferu suspected that Grandma was dying to tell her friends. She kept telling Neferu that it was time she learned how to be a lady. They discussed what she was going to wear and how she would do her hair. There was not much time to arrange anything complicated because the trip was only four days away. In the coming four days Neferu heard her Grandma telling several of her friends, 'When Nefertiti goes to court …' She had the distinct impression that Grandma's friends were already growing a little tired of it.

Aunt Lea accompanied Neferu to the warehouse and they spent a whole morning looking at and discarding materials before finally settling for a beautiful off-white silk material with an interwoven leaf design. The warehouse assistant said it had come from China, on the other side of the world. The very mystery of that thought lent an enchantment to the material, in Neferu's eyes. That afternoon Grandma sent for the dressmaker and all the four women spent about six hours deciding upon a design. Neferu had opted for a design which was very modish amongst the aristocratic Egyptian ladies, that is, one shoulder covered and the other one bare, but Grandma balked at this. It might be all right for stylish Egyptian ladies, but it was not a suitable style for good Keftiu girls of respectable family. Grandma was adamant on this and Neferu was forced to compromise on a style which just screamed 'Keftiu' to her mind. Aunt Lea consoled her, but she was not convinced.

The dress was to be loosely folded from one shoulder to the other and cut to under the bust in the so-called classical Mycenean style. From under the bustline, the dress fell in soft folds to her ankles. Neferu felt sure that everyone would realise that she was a country bumpkin right away. Neferu and Aunt Lea experimented with her hair. Neferu wanted to have it plaited in the tiny braids so popular then in Egypt, but Aunt Lea sensibly told her that she thought Neferu would not be able to manage such a style herself on the day and she thought it was best to stick to a more decorative version of the chignon she normally wore. Neferu recognised the sense of her argument and let her aunt cut some shorter strands around her temples and just in front of her ears. Aunt Lea showed her how to do a large figure-of-eight chignon at the back. Aunt Lea seemed to be full of useful tricks and she wet some strips of cotton rags and twisted Neferu's wet hair around them. When Neferu's hair had dried she removed the rag strips and Aunt Lea carefully arranged the curled hair in graceful ringlets. Neferu was enchanted.

The great dress was not completed until the day before they were due to leave, and Neferu was getting very nervous as she was beginning to think it would not be ready in time. In addition, she was worried about her father's attitude to the coming trip. Now that it was almost upon them, he seemed to be having second thoughts about it. He constantly tried to impress upon her that at court she must not speak unless spoken to first, and then she was only to answer politely what was required. Her father was obviously afraid that her normal exuberance might get her into trouble, and she was scared that he might cancel her trip. She felt that she would never forgive him if he did so at this late stage.

Yussef was quiet, but he made an effort to overcome his displeasure. He told Vassiliou that he hoped that the visit to Thebes would be a kind of last holiday for Neferu before their marriage and all the responsibilities of their future. Oddly, on the day before their departure, it was Neferu who felt a deep sense of loss and she nearly changed her mind about going. Even the new dress seemed to have lost its charm and Thebes seemed a brooding, faraway city full of strangers, while here at On were the only people she loved in the whole world.

That following morning of activity and bustle became a complete blur to Neferu and the only incident which stayed forever afterwards in her memory was that of Yussef coming to Grandma's while she was having a practice run in her new dress. She went out in her new dress into the living room, where he was chatting with Demi. Both of them stared at her in her new finery, as if seeing her for the first time. Yussef said that he had never seen anyone more beautiful in his life. Grandma smiled from behind her and encouraged Yussef to go for a stroll with Neferu in the garden. That morning he told Neferu that he was in love with her and that he would count the days until she came back to him. This was a new Yussef to her, and she suddenly saw him in a different light, as a man she really did not know, rather than the surrogate elder brother with whom she was so familiar. Now, Neferu regretted her decision to go to Thebes. She felt she was being disloyal to him and that she did not deserve such a loyal and loving suitor. She knew that Yussef could have his pick of all the girls he wanted in On. He was tall, good looking, intelligent and well-mannered. In addition to this, he had now taken over his one-third share of the jewellery business with Uncle Leandros, and ably administered Demi's share of the business now that Grandpa was retired. Demi had now started work as a full-time scribe with his father and even in his spare time he was often busy doing extra secretarial duties for father. She abruptly became aware of just how much Yussef's life was interdependent with her own.

Yussef was now completely grown up and independent at seventeen. He was a serious-minded young man, nothing like many of the youths of their quarter who behaved wildly and drank too much. Many of them had found themselves the subjects of Grandma's disapproving gossip when her friends came to visit, as they frequently did. No, Yussef was different, and Grandma was right. He was a man to be proud of. So why was she dithering? She loved him, didn't she? Yes! Neferu knew that she loved Yussef: how could she not do so? And yet the thought of marriage did not completely draw her. She thought of Aunt Lea and Grandma and saw herself through all the long years of the future, organising the household and looking after everybody like they did. Part of her rebelled. Part of her still wanted to run along the beach and find shells. Part of her wished to dress up in fine clothes and have all the young men at court fall in love with her. She, of course, would disdain them all after a brief flirtation and return to her Yussef, who was the only reality she had experienced. Disgruntled, Neferu thought that she would really have liked to have been a man. Men had so much more fun. They could come and go as they pleased, and nobody kept telling them to sit like a lady. She sighed; it was not fair.

A call from Aunt Lea brought Neferu back to the present. Her father had arrived to collect her and her luggage. She would be sleeping at home tonight, at her father's house that is, so that they could have the earliest possible start the following day without disturbing Grandma and the others. Neferu looked around at Grandma's as if seeing it for the first time. She felt a sudden desire to weep but held it in check. How stupid she was! She would be back in two decans. Four days to get there, three days there and four days to get back. Less than two decans. Shaking off her unaccountable depression she went round the family and gave them all frantic kisses and hugs. Yussef left with them to go back to the shop, and they said a poignant farewell in the hallway. He was as upset as she was, and he held her close even in front of Father, who delicately turned away.

Neferu watched him leave with a heavy heart, but she was not allowed to contemplate for long. Her father was eager to get going and Grandma kept calling out last minute instructions. As they left, she turned to wave and her last view of them was as they crowded the doorway to wave, Grandma calling out to her to be careful. It was only a short walk to her father's house, but Neferu could not see properly. Her eyes were misty, and her voice quivered when she responded to some remark of her father's. He looked at her sharply and noticed her lip trembling.

'What on earth is the matter, Neferu?' he said uncomprehendingly.

'I don't know,' she faltered. 'I just have the strongest feeling that nothing will ever be the same.'

Her father gave a small chuckle. 'And you are right. When we return from Thebes you will settle down with Yussef like a good Keftiu girl and provide Grandma with all those great-grandchildren she is always talking about!' Neferu smiled in spite of herself. Her father was right, nothing ever stayed the same. She began to cheer up. She was glad now that her ballgown was in the Keftiu style. It was no good pretending to be something that you were not. They were tradespeople, not aristocratic Egyptians, and she was proud of her origins and knew that Yussef was too. Neferu squeezed her father's hand and he smiled and said, 'That's better!'

That evening when Yussef came to her father's house to see her for the last time before she left, she made a special effort to cheer him up. They talked about the house they would live in, and Yussef became quite animated as they made their plans. They decided that they would stay in the same quarter if they could find a suitable place. Uncle Leandros had told Yussef that very day that there was a nice villa for sale on the edge of the town in the quarter called Neapolis, which bordered their own. Neferu would have liked to have gone and viewed it there and then, but it was dark. Yussef promised to go and see the house the following day and, if he thought it suitable for them, he would try to stall the owner until she got back from Thebes. They did not really want to have to wait for a new villa to be built and they did not want to rent an apartment. That was just a waste of their resources. They would be comfortable but not wealthy, and Yussef said that they must get a place with a reasonably sized plot of land so that they could extend later, if necessary.

Before he left Yussef was much cheered up, but he did admit to Neferu that he was jealous.

'Why?' she asked, surprised.

'You don't know how stunning you look, Neferu,' he said. 'I don't want some prancing Egyptian nobleman falling in love with you and turning your head.'

Neferu laughed at the very thought. 'That is crazy, Yussef,' she said, amazed. 'We will only be there for three days. No one can fall in love with me in such a short time, nor I them.'

'Well. Whatever. If you are not back in fourteen days, I am coming to bring you back. I don't want to lose you.'

Neferu felt pleased and flattered but knew that his concern was totally unwarranted. 'I am not a stupid girl whose head is so easily turned,' she said seriously. 'I love you and I promise you that I am not about to fall in love with some handsome Egyptian nobleman.' She spoke lightly to cheer him up.

'Well, when you see all that splendour and opulence, you might not want to marry a humble Keftiu goldsmith,' he told her, in such an abject tone of self-pity that Neferu just could not stop herself from laughing.

'You, humble, Yussef? Who are you trying to fool? You can't be serious!'

Yussef grinned and then bared his teeth in a mock grimace. 'You had better warn anyone who looks at you twice that he is in danger of losing his life.'

Neferu continued to smile. 'I love you, Yussef. I can't even imagine loving anyone else. The time will go quickly, you'll see!' She leaned forward and boldly kissed him on the lips, something she had never done before, and he took her in his arms and kissed her passionately. Before he left, he made her promise to think of him for five minutes every evening at the time she went to bed so that their thoughts would find each other. She promised to do it.

As she climbed into bed that night, she smiled as she considered Yussef's hidden depths. She felt that she knew him better than anyone. She doubted that any of the others realised the poetic and romantic soul who lurked behind his businesslike and matter of fact facade. With a sigh she closed her eyes, conscious of the fact that she would have to be up at the crack of dawn. She slept soundly that night with no intuition of the destiny that was about to unfold itself before her.

CHAPTER 6

The sun was already up when Neferu was awoken by Shosen's maid. Neferu felt that she could easily have slept for another hour or two. It was already hot even though it was still early spring. It occurred to her that the journey would be very tiring in this heat, and she decided to wear a simple cotton shift. She hoped that the river boat they were travelling on would be comfortable as it would be an awful long journey.

Neferu and her father dined alone as Shosen was still suffering severe nausea in the mornings. This third pregnancy seemed more difficult than the previous two and Vassiliou was worried about her. They went to give her a last hug before they left and Vassiliou told her he would be back as soon as he could. Neferu kissed her stepmother and told her to take care, and with that, they left, accompanied by waving from Shosen and her eldest little boy.

The boat was a large barge-like vessel and was quite the largest boat that she had ever travelled on. It was a special passenger boat, she was informed by her father. This time they would not have to disembark during the evenings to stay overnight at some tavern or other, as they had accommodation on the boat, along with several other passengers. Neferu was pleased. It would be so uncomfortable to sleep sitting up on deck, which they sometimes did when travelling to Rashid. It was faster but also more tiring. On the other hand, to disembark every night and take another boat every morning made one's journey seem interminable. This time they would have the best of both worlds. On deck she looked with a certain pity upon the majority of passengers who would have to sleep sitting up on the benches.

Neferu eyed her fellow passengers with curiosity. She wondered how many of them were going on to Thebes, and how many would disembark at one of the dozens of stops along the way. Leaning over the side she could see the brown muscled arms of the oarsmen as they pulled and pulled in unison, singing a monotonous rhythmic chant to keep their time with. She could not see their faces, which were hidden by the overhead cabins, but she counted the number of arms. There were twenty on this side, so that meant forty altogether. No wonder the boat was able to move so fast!

Neferu wondered whether the oarsmen would row the whole journey, but her father told her that the crew would change further upriver, when the boat docked at dusk. Until then these unknown oarsmen would row continuously. Their only rest being the short stops for passenger disembarkation. It seemed to Neferu that these men had a harsh life. Who were they and where did they come from? What had they done to offend Helios that they had to toil so hard? Today there was no breeze at all so there was no help from the sails even. Today she felt glad that she was a woman and glad also that she was a Keftiu from a comfortable family. She reflected that you did not understand how lucky you were until you were able to compare your life with that of someone less fortunate.

The journey to Thebes was an education in itself for Neferu. Her father relaxed and he enjoyed pointing out to her various places of interest. All his accounts were in order and so he could afford to look upon this trip as a short break from the routine of his duties. Father and daughter felt close again in a way they had not done since Vassiliou's re-marriage. They stood on deck and watched some Semitic nomads grazing their sheep on the opposite bank. They wore colourful knee length tunics and carried crooked shepherd's staffs. Here and there she would notice the irrigation wells with the poor donkeys walking round and round the shaduf in their efforts to raise the water. They too had a hard life, and a boring one too.

The days of the journey passed quickly. Vassiliou took the opportunity to tell Neferu something of the personages she was likely to meet or to see. They were to stay in Thebes at the home of an old friend of her father who was also Keftiu in origin. They had moved to Thebes from On some years ago on his appointment to an administrative position in the archives section of the palace complex called Malkata. It was here that the royal couple lived. Neferu was impressed. It appeared that the family they were visiting had two daughters and a son and, if Vassiliou remembered correctly, the eldest daughter would be about the same age as Neferu. Unfortunately, her father could not remember the names of the children of his friend. Neferu looked forward to meeting them, especially as they were Keftiu also.

Neferu made her father tell her about some of the important personages at court. He had only been to Malkata two or three times previously and he was not well acquainted with the situation, but he shared with her some of the gossip, which he had heard from colleagues. The pharaoh was Amenophis III and he was in his early forties now, her father believed. It was rumoured that in recent years he had begun to live a very decadent lifestyle, and some said that he was addicted to opium. Apparently, he had taken this as a medication for a very painful and chronic gum inflammation from which he suffered. The grand queen, his chief wife, was called Tiya and the pharaoh had had four children with her so far. Although she too was almost forty it was rumoured that she was still a very beautiful woman and Vassiliou had seen her and could confirm this.

'What does she look like?' asked Neferu curiously.

'She is a little shorter than you and still rather slim. She looks very exotic, to my mind. She is not of Egyptian origin that is for sure. They say that her father, the old grand vizier, was a Hebrew who first came to Egypt as a slave many years ago. I don't know about that, and it is very important that you don't repeat it!' he admonished. 'His son, Ay, is the grand vizier now and we wouldn't want to upset anyone would we?' He said this last part with a mischievous grin, but Vassiliou was warning her to be discreet. After a moment, he continued, 'Tiya's mother comes from a very respected Nubian family. Her mother's father used to be the high priest at On and her mother was high priestess at On for some years. Her parents are old now and live at Akhtmin where her mother's family came from. Tiya's cousins and uncles are famous generals in the pharaoh's Nubian guard, and they come from a distinguished military background. I believe that the family was elevated to the aristocracy because of its distinguished service during the Hyksos Wars. Come to think of it, it is strange that her mother should have married a Hebrew, coming from that background. It must have been a love match then.' Vassiliou broke off for a moment to meditate a little on the caprices of life, but Neferu was curious and wanted to know more.

'What about the princes and princesses, Father?'

'Mmm!' Vassiliou answered. 'There are dozens of them. In fact, probably most of the people at Malkata are related to each other in one way or another.'

'How is that?' Neferu asked, somewhat mystified.

'Well, you see, the crown prince usually marries his sister or his eldest daughter as well as having several lesser wives. This means that there are always lots of claimants to the throne if the crown prince dies.' Neferu was shocked. She had never heard anything like it in her life. A daughter marries her father or her brother! It was certainly unheard of in Lower Egypt. She said as much to her father.

'I agree, Neferu. It has only ever been the royal families who have traditionally intermarried within the close family, but in nearly all cases, I am sure, it is a device used to maintain power within the governing family, and most of the pharaohs have had other wives who are chosen for their beauty and wit and for love,' her father said, with an air of disapproval.

After a moments silence, during which Neferu reflected on this, she continued, 'Well, tell me about Tiya's children in that case, as I suppose it will be her son who will become the next pharaoh.'

'He is already pharaoh,' her father replied.

'What do you mean? How can he be if his father is still alive? There can't be two pharaohs, can there?'

'The eldest son, Dhutmose, who was named after his grandfather Tuthmosis the Fourth, died a few years ago. Apparently, he fell sick with a fever whilst on a military expedition in Kush. I believe it was the same year that Demi hurt his leg at Rashid. He was the commander-in-chief. It was a tremendous blow to the pharaoh and the great queen. After that the next eldest son, Amenophis, became heir and he has now been declared co-regent with his father. It is said he is a very strange-looking fellow.'

'In what way?' Neferu was intrigued.

'Apparently, he is quite deformed, with a curvature of the spine and very bowed legs with knock-knees. His face is very long and thin and he has thick lips like the Nubians. He is much lighter skinned than his mother but altogether a very odd-looking person. What is more, his younger sister Meretamun and his younger brother Smenkhenre are also similarly afflicted, though not apparently to quite the same extent. The eldest daughter, Sitamun, is supposed to be exceedingly beautiful. A cross between her father and mother in looks, having the best qualities of both.'

Neferu shivered. 'I hope that my children will be beautiful, or at least not deformed,' she said feelingly.

Vassiliou smiled. 'I'm sure that you and Yussef will have remarkably beautiful children and I will be the proudest grandfather in Egypt.' Neferu smiled as her father squeezed her hand in reassurance.

The leisurely journey came to an end at last. Neferu was almost sorry. It had felt for a time that they were cut off from reality, suspended in time without any worries. Still, ahead lay three exciting days and she intended to enjoy them to the full. She was in the most important city in the whole of the Two Lands and she was eager to explore it.

At the quay Vassiliou and his daughter were met by Athanasios, the Keftiu official whom her father had spoken about. He escorted them to his chariot. He inquired charmingly about Neferu's health and tried to make her feel at ease. Neferu liked him, he seemed so open and friendly. After a while the two men began to discuss business and Neferu was free to watch the street life of Thebes as it passed before her. After a relatively short journey of about ten minutes, the carriage stopped outside a very large, whitewashed villa with extensive, well-kept gardens. It all looked much posher than her own home. Athanasios informed her that his wife, Narida, was Egyptian and neither she nor the children spoke Keftiu. Neferu said it was perfectly all right as she spoke Egyptian equally as well as Keftiu, and from then on they all switched to Egyptian.

The mistress of the house, Narida, seemed rather cool and formal. She was a very fashionably dressed, elegant lady and Neferu felt a little overawed and ill at ease. She clung to the area most proximate to her father and hoped he would not go off with Athanasios and leave her alone with the others. Narida sent the valet to bring her children and shortly after they were joined by a tall, handsome boy of eighteen called Hamid and a girl of Neferu's age called Anula. The youngest daughter was about thirteen and she was called Tagried. Neferu shyly introduced herself and gradually began to feel less strange. She noticed that Anula was a very sophisticated young lady and she saw her eying Neferu's dress with a slight smile. She felt that Anula perceived her as being very naïve and ordinary, but she felt that they were kindly disposed towards her. Tagried told her that she was very pretty, which was rather sweet, and Anula immediately began to chat about the great banquet and the festival which would follow it. Neferu explained that she would not be going to the party and Anula was quite shocked.

'Why not?' she gasped in amazement. 'You have to come to the party. It's the highlight of the event.'

Neferu felt herself blush. 'Unfortunately, I can't dance, except for the Keftiu folk dances, and I don't expect that they will be performing those,' she remarked, with irony. 'And anyway, Father thought it would not be quite the thing as I am to be married when we return to On.' She added this last with an unconscious note of pride in her voice.

'Who are you going to marry?' Anula asked curiously.

'My second cousin, Yussef. He is a jeweller and is very handsome and clever.' She did not know why she felt the need to explain Yussef. She was proud of him, it was just that she felt this girl, who seemed so much older and more worldly than she was, was not easily impressed.

'Oh.' Anula did not seem impressed at all and Neferu wished she had not gushed on. After a short interval, Anula looked at Neferu with compassion and then said, 'I am hoping to be chosen as a lady-in-waiting to the grand queen and to marry one of the princes.'

Neferu felt her eyes widen with awe. 'How splendid!' she gushed, most impressed. At the same time, however, she found herself to be strangely unenvious.

Anula shrugged. 'Hamid is joining the army soon and will be at court very often then, I expect. The grand vizier, Ay, who is a very important man, recommended him to Pararameses, the co-regent's best friend.'

'Oh,' said Neferu, not quite understanding.

Neferu remembered her father telling her about the deformed co-regent but did not remember him saying anything about anyone called Pararameses. She assumed he was important if he was the best friend of the second pharaoh, but she could not quite see how that would affect Hamid. She did not wish to betray her ignorance, however, as to court affairs, so she merely smiled and looked impressed. Anula appeared satisfied with her reaction.

Later on at dinner, Anula asked Vassiliou if Neferu might stay for the ball as well. Vassiliou said that he did not feel it was quite fitting as they knew very few people, almost no one else other than her own family. Neferu would feel lonely and strange if he did not go, and he was too old for dancing now. Neferu was not perturbed but was quite pleased when Anula offered to teach her how to dance the modish Egyptian dances anyway. 'Yes! That will be fun,' agreed Hamid.

After dinner they had a very jolly evening. Even Narida warmed up and hummed the tunes while Anula taught Neferu the correct steps. It turned out to be quite a party and Hamid escorted them all in turn, even little Tagried, who was most bitter about not being allowed to go to the banquet. She had been firmly told by her mother that she was too young. Hamid was very gallant and told Neferu that she was a charming dancer, and he would be most happy to escort her to the ball. Neferu grinned, knowing that she was anything but a charming dancer as she had trodden on his feet at least twice. Hamid continued his gallantry and, turning to Vassiliou, he begged him to reconsider his decision as he would like to make all his friends green with envy by escorting the most beautiful lady he had ever seen. Hamid was a bit of a clown and Neferu giggled. Her father smiled and said he would think about it.

That night Neferu slept on a couch in the same room as Anula and Tagried. They lay awake in the dark, whispering girl talk and discussing the forthcoming festivities.

Anula told her that the city was full of visitors from all over Egypt, as well as a good few foreign dignitaries. It was all very exciting, and it was only at the last moment when she was almost about to fall asleep that she remembered to think of Yussef as she had promised. She closed her eyes tightly and concentrated. When she opened them again, it was morning. The morning of the great day.

There was great commotion in the household that day as everyone was trying to get ready at the same time. Neferu realised that she could not stay to the ball in the evening anyway because the white dress would be worn to the banquet, which was to take up the first part of the day, and she could not wear the same dress to an evening occasion as well. Anula was very disappointed and could not believe that she had only brought one party dress. Narida offered to lend her one of Anula's dresses, but Neferu politely declined, feeling slightly embarrassed.

Neferu was ready before Anula and Narida. She could not understand why it took them so long to get ready until she watched the maid plaiting Anula's hair in what seemed to be hundreds of little plaits. Neferu had herself made special efforts the evening before to wrap the front strands of her hair into the cotton rag strips like Aunt Lea had shown her. She was amazed at the effectiveness of this hitherto unknown trick and was most gratified by the graceful little ringlets which were the end result of a slightly uncomfortable night.

The dressmaker who had made Neferu's dress was a friend of Grandma and she had surpassed herself. The thick crepe silk was cut in a soft cowl shape which stretched from shoulder to shoulder, revealing little more than her neck but completely exposing her arms. Grandma had considered the bare arms as going too far and had been inclined to add long diaphanous sleeves, much against Neferu's will. The dress was very modest by the fashionable standards, which preferred a long, low-cut, v-shaped neckline, exposing the upper curve of the breasts. Still, Neferu felt very daring in it.

Neferu swept her hair up in a loose figure-of-eight chignon and carefully twisted the ringlets around her finger to coax them into the right positions. As an extra at the last minute, she plucked a white flower from the garden and put it in her hair. Vassiliou told Neferu that she looked just like her mother and that he was very proud to escort his daughter to the banquet. Neferu was thrilled and took her father's arm to the chariot. Hamid and Anula travelled in the chariot with them and Athanasios and Narida travelled in their own chariot. Anula kept up a long commentary on whom they were likely to see and when she got to the co-regent, she told Neferu that he always wore a long cloak to hide his deformed body. 'Then at least we will recognise him right away,' laughed Neferu gaily. She was quite intrigued to see this strange personage who attracted so much attention, it seemed.

CHAPTER 7

The two chariots arrived almost together into the palace courtyard, and they had to wait a while for the palace grooms to direct their placement. The courtyards, outer and inner, were thronging with people, although it was still early. There was a holiday atmosphere in the air and Neferu's eyes had never been hit by so much colour. First the multitude of beautiful flowers laid out in the carefully tended gardens of the inner courtyard and then by the women resplendent in their flamboyant gowns. Neferu waited for the others to join them and then they all strolled at a leisurely pace towards the inner courtyard.

Narida and her husband were to be presented to the royal couple, but Neferu knew that her father had not been chosen for this honour, so that they were more or less free to wander around as they pleased, after her father had first presented his statistics to the archives section. Occasionally her father would stop to chat to someone he knew, or someone would hail him and then Neferu would stand shyly until she had been presented. Her father was obviously very proud of her, and it warmed Neferu's heart. Neferu hoped to catch a glimpse of the royal family, but Anula told her that they would not be appearing until lunchtime.

Servants hovered round the courtyard, directing people to long tables where fruit juice was being served to quench their thirst. People were standing round in small groups chatting animatedly, trying to cling to the shade of the roofed corridors rather than in the midst of the brilliant sunshine. Someone came to talk to her father and soon the four grown-ups were deep in conversation. Neferu's attention began to wander a little as Anula too had found an old acquaintance to talk to. She wondered where Hamid was. He had been there a moment ago and now was nowhere to be seen. Feeling very bold, she went over to the drinks table and the smiling waiter offered her a goblet of what she thought was juice. It turned out to be a very sweet, fruity wine. She was very thirsty and drank it quickly, taking another which she took with her back to their group. She was just sipping the second goblet when she felt a tug on her arm. It was Hamid, 'Neferu! Come with me to see the fountains and the lotus pond.'

Neferu quickly finished off her drink and then felt herself a little light-headed. She wondered if she should interrupt Father's conversation, but they had now been joined by another couple and Narida and the lady were making casual pleasantries. As their conversation seemed less serious, she touched Narida's arm and murmured that she would be back in a minute. Narida looked at her briefly and nodded with a smile, before returning to her conversation. Neferu was not quite sure that her hostess had even heard properly but, after standing uncertainly for a moment, she turned and followed Hamid, who was beckoning insistently. The two of them pushed their way through the crowd and went towards the large white block of buildings in front of them. There was an archway to their left, but it was guarded by two soldiers with spears and was obviously not meant for the general public. They turned to the right through a small alleyway, past another block of buildings on their right. They felt the coolness of the shade in the alleyway as they walked. It was only about thirty metres long and soon, on their left, was a gate.

Neferu stopped and said to Hamid, 'Are you sure that it is all right to go in?'

'Yes, yes,' he replied. 'I've looked in and there is no one there anyway so no one will see us. It won't take a moment. I just want you to see the gardens of the palace.'

Neferu's instinct was to leave immediately, and she stood where she was, not daring to go in. Hamid entered without her and after a few seconds she felt conspicuous by herself and, feeling very furtive, she timidly went in. She almost tiptoed past the building on her left but when she reached the edge of it she had a clear view of the gardens beyond. She stopped and looked around in wonder, never having seen before such green lawns, carefully trimmed, surrounded by apple trees and lemon trees and flowers of every kind and colour. In the middle of this enormous park there was a large silvery pond with water lilies on it. In the centre of the pond there were three fountains shooting silvery jets up into the air. She watched the sparkling drops fan outwards. It was like one of Grandma's fairy tales of Caphtor. She glanced round quickly, but there was no one there. To her left there was an open door, but no sound came out of it. She was nervous and so went no further, though she thought it was likely to be the quarters of the most important servants because there were no signs of any guards at all.

Hamid was bolder and went over to the edge of the pool. She beckoned him back agitatedly. She dared not call, in case someone heard her. She understood implicitly that they were trespassing and wanted to be out of there. She decided to retreat without Hamid and, still furiously beckoning to him, she backed away in the direction from which they had come, straight into someone else. Her heart gave a thud of sheer terror as she spun round, almost falling over in her haste. Two arms steadied her, and she found herself looking into the most remarkable face she had ever seen in all her life.

Even before her eyes took in the cloak, she knew instinctively that this was the younger pharaoh. Her gaze dropped before the sardonic look of amusement in the young man's eyes, and she wished that the ground would open up under her feet and swallow her. Why on earth had she allowed Hamid to bring her into this place? They had been trespassing and now they were caught out, horribly. She had let her father down miserably and her mouth felt dry, just wondering what the consequences were going to be. She felt a hand lightly lifting her chin upwards and two steady eyes looking at her. 'Who are you, young lady?'

Poor Neferu blushed crimson. 'I am Nefertiti Stassopoulos, sire,' she said, stammering over her own name. She blushed even more. He probably thought she was lying to him. Quickly she added,

'I know we should not be here, sire. We were just leaving. We only wanted to see the fountains, we are very sorry, sire!' She suddenly remembered that one was supposed to curtsy in front of royalty, and she made a jerky, sudden curtsy. Hurriedly, she wondered if she ought to curtsy to the other man, standing at the side of the pharaoh. Just to be prudent she did so. When she dared to look up again, she saw that there was amusement in the pharaoh's eyes.

'She is certainly well named, don't you think, Rameses?' Pararameses looked at her and nodded before letting his gaze flick over to Hamid, who had beat a hasty retreat from the pond and was now standing before them with a suitably hangdog expression on his face. As well he might, thought Neferu bitterly. 'Is this young man your brother, Nefertiti Stassopoulos?' the pharaoh asked, pronouncing her family name slightly incorrectly.

'No, sire. My father and I are staying with Hamid's family for the festival.'

'You are from Lower Egypt, I take it?' he had noted her northern Egyptian accent.

'Yes, sire.' The pharaoh continued to regard her with his extraordinary eyes, and she became uncomfortable under his gaze. 'I fear that my father may be looking for me, sire,' she said somewhat lamely, her tone decidedly subdued.

'I expect you are right,' the pharaoh replied. His face was quite expressionless. He turned to Hamid. 'Perhaps, young man, you will convey my greetings to this young lady's father and tell him that I will return his daughter to him after I have shown her around my garden.' Neferu looked up quickly. She saw a look of miraculous relief spread over Hamid's features.

'Of course, sire,' he said, bowing low. 'At your command, sire.'

Finding himself unceremoniously dismissed in this way, Hamid hurried off. The pharaoh turned to his companion and asked him to proceed to the meeting and tell the grand vizier that he had returned from the hunt and would be joining him in a while. The man he had called Rameses left and now Neferu was left alone with this extremely self-possessed young man. She felt very nervous and could not bring herself to look at him. Would you like to see my garden properly, Nefertiti Stassopulos?' he asked, again pronouncing her name incorrectly.

'It's STASSOPOULOS, sire. My name, that is.'

He smiled at her. 'I'm sorry if I pronounced it incorrectly. It is a Keftiu name, is it not?'

'Yes, sire,' she said.

'Do you speak Egyptian at home or Keftiu?' He sounded genuinely interested, putting her a little more at ease.

'We speak Keftiu at home, sire, but we all know Egyptian too,' she added hastily.

'I did not doubt it, Nefertiti STASSOPOULOS.' He made an obvious effort to pronounce her name correctly and she laughed. He smiled. 'That's better!' he said. The young pharaoh took her elbow and gently guided her towards the centre of the garden, telling her of its history and pointing out its many specialities. He was charming and intelligent and seemed to know a lot about the exotic plants that surrounded him. The pharaoh's voice was kind, even friendly and gradually she relaxed a little.

In the lily pond there were many different kinds of fish, and it was fascinating to watch them. Some of them she had seen before in the sea at Rashid. She pointed to one of them, recognising it.

'There are lots of those in the sea at Rashid,' she said.

'Rashid?' he echoed the name, looking at her for further explanation.

'We used to go there every summer for a holiday with my grandparents until Demi, my brother that is, became sick,' she offered by way of explanation.

'Has he not recovered then, your brother?' he sounded curious.

'Well, he is a lot better, sire. He was very, very sick then six years ago. We all thought he was going to die but he recovered, although his leg is still crippled.' Neferu sighed unconsciously as she thought of Demi's leg. The young pharaoh raised his eyes in question.

'What happened to his leg?' he asked.

Neferu shrugged. 'I don't know really. We had a swimming race and Demi grazed his leg on the rocks when he was climbing up. The next day the leg began to swell and turn a horrible purple colour. I was really scared.' She shuddered at the memory of it all. 'He was really ill for ages. It was horrible. Grandma was almost out of her mind with the worry of it all. Now he can walk with a stick, but the leg is always painful and that was six years ago,' she spoke confidingly.

'How old is your brother?' the pharaoh asked.

'Nearly fourteen. He is two years younger than I am and I am almost sixteen,' she answered shyly.

'Do you know who I am?' he asked suddenly. For the first time she allowed her gaze to rest fully on his face. It was a strange face but somehow a pleasant face. It pleased her. The eyes were bright and intelligent and an unusual heavy-lidded, elongated almond shape. The nose was long and slightly aquiline, and the mouth was full and sensuous. As a whole, the face reflected both sensitivity and determination. She noticed that he was studying her studying him and she looked away from his half-smiling gaze suddenly, wondering if one was allowed to look at the pharaoh.

She looked up at him again and answered softly, 'You are the pharaoh, sire.'

'Are you afraid of me?' he asked gently.

'No, I am not afraid anymore, sire,' she said finally.

'Good,' he said, smiling. 'I won't eat you, you know, Nefertiti STASSOPOULOS.' Neferu felt a little abashed at his words. Taking her elbow again, he continued to walk forwards. His voice was deep and seemed to suit him very well. She guessed that he would be a good singer, if pharaohs ever sang, that is. She wondered about that too.

After a while, he asked her more questions about her family. She made some humorous observations about Grandma and Grandpa, and he laughed. She looked at him sideways and noticed that he was not very much older than her. Nineteen or twenty perhaps. He was not a god, just a man. A nice man, it seemed. After he had finished showing her around, he called a servant who had appeared at one of the doorways and asked him to bring General Pararameses to him, if he was free. When Pararameses joined them Neferu noticed that it was the man he had called Rameses earlier. The pharaoh requested the general to bring Neferu's father to the garden. She thanked him very much for showing her around and asked him to excuse her effrontery in having strayed from the public enclosure. He promised to forgive her, and she looked down, blushing at the amusement in his voice. His complete self-possession served to make her feel incredibly gauche.

When Vassiliou appeared, looking embarrassed, Neferu was mortified. He looked as though he did not know whether to scold her or not. The pharaoh received him graciously and told him that he had a charming daughter. Vassiliou looked very relieved. The pharaoh told them that he looked forward to seeing them at the festivities in the evening. Vassiliou looked embarrassed again and Neferu was abashed. They were not going and anyway she did not even have a dress to go in. Vassiliou thanked the pharaoh in confusion, on the grounds that one should not be imprudent enough to refuse the invitation of the pharaoh. Neferu was horrified. 'We can't come, sire,' she blurted out.

'Why not?' the pharaoh replied in a cool tone.

Neferu's face was scarlet as she replied. 'We had not planned to come to the evening's festivities and so I only brought one special dress and it is now soiled as you see, sire.' There was a pause and she added. 'We were not invited.'

The pharaoh's face relaxed and he appeared mollified. 'Well! I am now inviting you as my guests. Your dress looks fine to me but if it upsets you, I will arrange for one of the servants to provide you with a dress of your choosing. Would you then be happy to come?'

'Yes, sire. Of course!'

Amenophis IV looked at her keenly and then smiled. 'The problem is solved then. Pararameses here will arrange the matter of your dress and I will expect you both here to dinner and the party this evening.' With these words, he bowed slightly and left them, hurrying off in the direction of the archway.

Pararameses looked at Neferu curiously a moment and then asked them to excuse him for a while. Vassiliou and Neferu were left alone together in the garden. Vassiliou looked around at the splendour on all sides. He seemed troubled at the sudden turn of events whereas Neferu, oddly enough, felt perfectly at ease. She smiled inwardly as she thought of how annoyed Anula would be at having missed such an adventure. Now, in retrospect, it began to appear to her as an adventure, what less than an hour ago she had felt she might have lost her life for.

How grand, she thought, personally invited to dine at the palace. She could not wait to go home and tell Grandma and Aunt Lea. They would never believe this! Grandma would be telling all her cronies, she knew. It would be all over the quarter in two days. On second thoughts, perhaps she would not tell her after all. 'This is a most unexpected event, Neferu,' her father remarked. 'We can't stay at the festivities too late tonight as I have to be up early in the morning for business.'

'I know, Father,' she replied. 'But what an exciting end to our holiday,' she added.

At that moment Pararameses rejoined them and asked them to follow him. They duly followed him up the stone steps to the terrace on the upper floor. Asking Vassiliou to remain where he was, Pararameses asked Neferu to continue alone. She did as she was told, and they entered into a spacious sitting room where a girl of her own age was sitting on a beautiful peacock blue silk sofa. Pararameses bowed low and announced,

'Miss Nefertiti Stassopoulos, Your Royal Highness.' Turning to Neferu, he announced, 'Her Royal Highness, the princess Meretamun.' Neferu promptly curtsied deeply. The girl stood up and Neferu saw that she closely resembled the young pharaoh.

'If you would like to come with me, Nefertiti, you may choose a dress for the party tonight,' The Young woman said graciously. The princess seemed informed and not at all put out by this intrusion. She led Neferu to another room leading off from her sitting room where literally dozens of dresses were hanging in a large alabaster wardrobe. Neferu was almost more impressed by the wardrobe than the dresses in it. They were all beautiful and she felt very shy and did not know how to react.

'Choose any one you like,' the princess said, encouraging her. Then she added, 'I would not take that blue one though, if I were you, because I have worn it several times and someone might recognise it.'

'Oh, no,' said Neferu hastily, still not daring to touch anything.

'What about this one?' the princess said helpfully. 'I only wore this one once and that was ages ago. It didn't suit me. I haven't got a figure as nice as yours,' she said a little wistfully, while lifting the hem of a heavy silk dress of a cream colour. 'This one is similar in colour to the one you are wearing, so it is bound to suit you.' Neferu smiled and nodded, asking if she might try it on. 'Naturally,' replied the princess. 'May I look?' she continued.

'Of course, Your Royal Highness!' Neferu replied in turn.

A maid came out of nowhere to help her off with her dress and then carefully slipped the dress of Princess Meretamun over her own head. It certainly fitted her well. It was a very fashionable dress in the elegant Egyptian mode that she had tried so hard to persuade Grandma to let her wear. Fate was now granting her desire. The dress had a low-cut heart shaped neckline and tiny capped sleeves. It was fastened under the bosom with a ribbon before falling in graceful soft folds to her ankles. She loved it immediately and felt daringly décolleté in it. She also knew that Grandma would have had a fit if she had seen it. 'How do you think it looks?' she asked nervously, wondering how the princess could bear to lend anyone such a beautiful garment.

'You look simply stunning,' the princess said sincerely. 'It never looked like that on me. I think that the dress was meant for you!' The maid added her approbation, and the matter was settled. Neferu was suddenly overcome by doubts. Her face clouded over, and the princess asked her what the matter was.

'My father,' said Neferu guiltily. 'He might have a fit if he sees me in such a low-cut dress. I don't know if I dare wear this.'

The princess laughed gaily. She appeared to be genuinely amused by this. 'Shall I bring him to have a look?' the princess said lightly.

'Oh no!' Neferu responded hastily. 'I'll go out and show him if you could come with me?'

Meretamun seemed happy to lend the required moral support. It was as Neferu had feared.

'It is very beautiful, Neferu, but I am sure that Grandma would not approve of it at all,' said her father.

'Do you think my dress is in bad taste then, Mr Stassopoulos?' Meretamun asked innocently.

Vassiliou realised that he had fallen into a trap, and belatedly tried to undo the disapproval of his words. 'No! No! Your Royal Highness,' he stated with emphasis. 'It's just that the dress is …' Here his voice trailed off for a moment while he tried to collect his thoughts. 'It's so … so Egyptian,' he ended up saying lamely. He paused once more to wipe the perspiration off his brow. 'We Keftiu are not so sophisticated as here at court, Your Royal Highness.'

The princess laughed at his efforts to gloss over his faux pas. 'Well, if you prefer, Nefertiti can cover her arms with a matching stole. Perhaps Grandma would approve then?' she said diplomatically. Vassiliou sighed with relief at having extricated himself from this diplomatic catastrophe.

'I think that would be a very good idea, Your Royal Highness.' He was enormously relieved that the princess had not appeared to take offence at his remarks.

The maid went to bring the stole and the princess arranged it herself around Neferu's shoulders. 'There!' she said, pleased with her handiwork.

Father was now satisfied with the effect and Neferu hurried back inside to change back into her own dress for the lunch. She thanked the princess profusely for her kindness. She still could not believe that all this was happening to her. It was too much like makebelieve. Meretamun informed Neferu that she would have the dress and stole taken to their chariot so that when they returned to where they were staying, they would not be delayed. Vassiliou duly informed the princess of their temporary address and Meretamun bade them both a friendly farewell. Neferu and her father were led quickly downstairs by the aide de camp of the pharaoh and back into the courtyard. The waiters were announcing that the banquet was soon to commence, and people were to take their places at table.

Looking round the courtyard, it took them a little while to find the Charalambides family. When they did so their host and his wife were agog with curiosity. Vassiliou described briefly what had happened while Neferu blushed to the roots of her hair. By now Hamid had regained his composure and was vociferously making himself the hero of the hour. Anula was green with envy that the pharaoh himself should have shown Neferu around the garden. 'Of course, he is not the senior pharaoh, but all the same. Didn't you think he was remarkably ugly?' Anula asked.

'His face is remarkable, it is true, Anula, but I did not find him ugly, and I think that he has splendid eyes.' Neferu tried to be balanced about the man. She had felt it would be very easy to like him.

'What very strange tastes you have, Neferu,' was Anula's only reply.

Once inside of the banquet hall, they found that they were seated far down from the dais so that Neferu could not get a close glimpse of the royal family as they took their places. When the royal family did eventually enter and sit down, everyone else followed suit and a general babble of conversation broke out. Neferu looked and made out the figure of the pharaoh and his chief wife, Grand Queen Tiya, but from that distance of fifty metres or so it was impossible to really tell. She noticed that the young pharaoh was seated next to his mother, and then her neighbour at the table diverted her attention and she settled down to enjoying her meal. She was, in fact, very hungry and tucked in with enthusiasm.

The banquet went on for a couple of hours, but Neferu was replete very quickly and the wine had made her a little sleepy. When the royal family rose to leave, everyone jumped up and remained standing until they had all left by a door at the back of the banquet hall. Afterwards everyone sat down again, and the babble continued. Some of the men drank too much, Hamid amongst them. Narida was angry with him and soon afterwards they made their leave. Neferu was really tired now and looked forward to the afternoon siesta, even in a strange bed. It had been such an unbelievable day. There had been nothing like it before in her routine existence.

When Neferu climbed into the chariot, there it lay upon a seat, wrapped in a soft linen cover so she knew it must be true. It was not a dream. Neferu peered at the dress and the stole and then looked at her father. 'It must have happened, after all!' she stated simply. She picked up a piece of papyrus and showed it to the others. 'The pharaoh, His Majesty Amenophis the Fourth, requests the pleasure of the company of Mr Vassiliou Stassopoulos, potiphar of On, and also his daughter, Miss Nefertiti Stassopoulos, to the grand ball this evening.' The others were speechless. Neferu suddenly smiled at Anula. 'I'm so glad you taught me how to dance, Anula!' Anula stared at her blankly for a minute and then Hamid started to laugh. A moment later they all joined in.

Back at the house they all retired to rest. Anula was still in a talkative mood and Tagried wanted to hear all about their visit. Neferu, however, just could not keep her eyes open and she was the first to fall asleep. The sun was getting low over the horizon when the maid woke them up. Neferu felt that she could easily have slept on for a while but remembered that they had to prepare for the evening's festivities. The maid called the girls to wash their hair. Neferu was curious to see whether Anula's hair would need to be re-plaited, but the maid merely washed it carefully as it was. Neferu found that strange but said nothing. She washed her own hair and had to go through the job of tying in the rags again to make the ringlets again. It was a bit of a bore and this time there was barely enough time for them to dry so she rubbed the shorter hair vigorously with the towel before she inserted the cotton strips.

Afterwards the maid brought a tray of drinks and cakes to their room and Neferu towel-dried the rest of her hair before fanning it out to dry in the sunshine streaming in from the veranda. Tomorrow she would be on her way back to On and so she determined to enjoy this unexpected pleasure. She knew that she would probably never come to Thebes again so she hoped that it would be an evening to remember. She decided that she would try to remember everything so that she could tell the family all about it in detail. She did not think Yussef would be upset. Probably he would laugh when she told him about the affair of the dress. She would have to warn him not to tell Grandma though.

The house began to stir again and Neferu could hear Athanasios and her father laughing. The maid returned to the girls to tell them that the mistress had ordered a light meal which would be served in the sitting room. 'It is a long time until the sun dial shows the start of moon time, and we will be starving if we don't eat something a little more substantial before then,' Narida explained. It was moving fast towards sundown and was becoming comfortably cool now. They all sat down to enjoy the snack.

'The time seems to have passed so quickly since we came,' commented Neferu.

'It always does when happy things are happening,' said Athanasios, smiling.

After their refreshments, the girls went back to their room to prepare themselves once more for the festivities. Neferu felt once again a rising sense of excitement. She brushed her hair thoroughly, enjoying the little cracks of static electricity emitted. Afterwards she sprinkled a drop or two of the perfumed oil which Anula had given to her onto her hair and began to twist it adeptly into a chignon. She tested one of the ringlets, but it was not completely dry, so she re-wrapped it. She would have to leave them to the last minute.

When night fell abruptly, as it always does in Egypt, Narida sent one of her maids to help the girls to dress. The others were already dressed when it was her turn, but she did not feel at all nervous and had waited patiently, knowing that her turn would come. She did a final adjustment of her dress and then put on her sandals. She felt very elegant in her borrowed plumes and felt less exposed when she saw that Anula's dress was similarly low-cut. Father can't say anything now, she thought.

When they left the house, it was pitch black outside, and after the great heat of the day it seemed almost chilly. She wrapped the stole more closely around her. She was glad of it now. In the dark it seemed that the journey took longer, and she feared they would be late. When they arrived at the great reception hall where they had earlier eaten, there were fewer guests and there was more room to move. To the surprise of all of them, they were shown to a table directly beneath the royal platform. Hamid winked at her surreptitiously. 'Of course, you and I have personal contacts, don't we Neferu?' he spoke with a mock superior air. Even Neferu had to laugh. Athanasios warned him not to cause a stir that evening if he had any ambition, and Hamid assumed a penitent expression which fooled no one. Although they were not late in arriving, they were almost last and they had barely settled themselves when they had to rise as the major domo announced loudly, 'Their Royal Highnesses …' He listed all the names from the most senior of the royal retinue to the least of the minor members of the royal family. When the royal family were all seated the major domo announced, 'Please be seated, ladies and gentlemen!'

Neferu looked up to where the young pharaoh was seated and was disconcerted to see that he was looking at her. He gave a slight nod and she blushed immediately and quickly looked down. After a while she looked again and found that he was still looking at her. After a moment's sense of slight shock, she smiled faintly and bowed her head. He turned to talk to an older man on his left and Neferu searched for the princess. Meretamun was talking animatedly to a woman on her right but, as if she sensed Neferu's gaze, she turned and met her stare. Her face broke into a friendly smile which was so spontaneous that Neferu felt herself respond to it immediately by openly smiling back.

An old lady seated to the right of Neferu started to chat to her and Neferu's attention was drawn away from the platform for a while. Later on, she secretly observed them all, one by one. The old pharaoh was quite plump and was eating with gusto. His companion to the right was a beautiful young lady with whom he was obviously on very good terms as they chatted very intimately together, and she held all his attention.

Grand queen Tiya, on the other hand, seemed to confer all her attention on the man to her left. From his looks Neferu guessed he must be the senior pharaoh's younger brother, the grand duke Tuthmosis. He was much slimmer than the pharaoh and she tried to find a word to describe his face in relation to his illustrious elder brother. Eventually she found the word she had sought and realised that it was 'spiritual'. Yes, he was definitely more spiritual looking than his brother, she thought. The great queen looked very regal, and it was true that she was still beautiful. It occurred to Neferu that she must be about the same age as Aunt Lea, but she looked younger than her aunt. When she looked at the young pharaoh again, he was deep in conversation with Pararameses.

The food was served, and it was sumptuous but, once again, she found she could eat only a little, unlike her usual self. Her eyes strayed to the dais once more and she found herself staring into the direct gaze of Amenophis IV. He smiled at her more openly this time and she smiled back shyly before looking away. She felt strangely drawn to him for some inexplicable reason. She knew that she would never see him again after that evening, but she knew also that she would never forget him as long as she lived.

The great queen rose after dinner, and everyone stood up as she left the hall followed by her ladies-in-waiting. The major domo requested that all the ladies follow the queen to the withdrawing room after the royal family had all retired from the hall. The men were requested to remain in the banqueting hall, which would quickly be made ready for the ball that was to follow. Neferu and Anula followed the other ladies to the withdrawing room where the grand queen was seated on a couch, her most senior lady-in-waiting standing behind her. The only men present were Archduke Tuthmosis, the young pharaoh and Pararameses. The older pharaoh had obviously retired with his companion. After a few minutes another man entered the room. Narida whispered to Neferu that this was the grand vizier, Ay, the queen's brother.

The grand vizier chatted quietly to the young pharaoh for a while before beginning to circulate round the room, stopping now and then to exchange pleasantries with one or other of the ladies. Ay stopped in front of their little group and chatted gallantly to Narida, who positively bloomed. Afterwards he said a few words to Anula and then turned to Neferu in an avuncular manner. The grand vizier told her that he was very pleased to make her acquaintance, that he knew her father slightly and thought him a very good sort. Neferu smiled in pleasure, feeling proud that her father was thus appreciated. She found the grand vizier very easy to chat to. Taking her arm, he told her that there was someone he wanted to introduce her to. Ay guided Neferu to a lady who was seated close to the queen. This proximity to the great queen caused a moderate feeling of panic in Neferu. Somehow the queen's bearing did not emit signals of jolly informality.

The lady Maatnofret, it appeared, was also from On. Neferu felt a glow of relief at knowing there was at least one other of her kind here in this awe-inspiring centre of palpable power. The grand vizier introduced the lady Maatnofret and Neferu to each other and then wandered off to continue his pleasant banter with another guest. Maatnofret, it transpired, had been born in On but had actually grown up in Thebes, so that the grand vizier's statement to Neferu was not wholly correct. In spite of this, the two women developed an instant liking for each other, and the older woman was delightfully informal and friendly. Neferu guessed that she was about thirty-five years old, close in age and background to the great queen. Her guess proved to be correct. Maatnofret told her that she and the grand queen had grown up together and that her position at court was as chief lady-in-waiting to the grand queen. Neferu could hardly imagine two more different personalities and yet it seemed that they were great friends. The cool, regal queen and this warm and kindly lady-in-waiting, who seemed so sensible and down to earth.

Maatnofret told Neferu that her husband was valet to the younger pharaoh. She asked Neferu if she would like to be a lady-in-waiting. Neferu was very flattered but told her that she was very clumsy and would be all fingers and thumbs and would soon be sent packing. Maatnofret laughed and did not pursue the matter any further. In the pause that followed this chat, Neferu looked up and found the young pharaoh gazing at her curiously. Maatnofret was so easy to talk to that Neferu quite forgot to be nervous and found herself genuinely amused at Maatnofret's witty descriptions of some of the personages present at court. Ay made his way towards them again, smiling. 'I am pleased you find each other such congenial company, my dears,' he said benignly. Turning to Neferu he added, 'I have some business I must discuss with your father later.' Turning then to the lady Maatnofret, he bowed slightly and said, 'May I leave the young lady safely in your care, Maatnofret, while I spirit her father away for an hour or so?'

Neferu was surprised. Her father had not mentioned any business with the grand vizier directly and certainly not for this evening at all. In fact, he had earlier stated that he had a business meeting the following morning. After a moment's alarm she reassured herself that it must be to do with that. She hoped her father's accounts and statistics were all in order. Maatnofret replied to the grand vizier that she would be happy to chaperone Neferu while her father was busy. This too, Neferu found surprising; after all she was in the company of Narida. That was surely chaperone enough. She decided, however, that it would be wiser to make no comment.

When Ay departed, the young pharaoh took his place. He looked at Neferu's dress with an impish look in his eyes. 'I find your gown very beautiful, Nefertiti Stassopoulos,' he said with a grin.

Neferu had quite forgotten the borrowed plumes and looking down at the dress she burst out laughing.

'I thank you, sire, for your kind intervention.'

The pharaoh merely smiled by way of reply. Maatnofret raised one of her eyebrows quizzically. Neferu opened her mouth to explain but the pharaoh put a finger to his lips and said quickly, 'It is our secret, Maatnofret.' The amiable lady smiled, not seeming to mind being excluded from their complicity.

Neferu's explanation was left unspoken. 'I will have so much to tell them when we return to On!' she said, smiling.

'When will that be?' asked the pharaoh, suddenly serious.

'The day after tomorrow,' answered Neferu. She suddenly felt a little sad that she would never see them again. 'I will never forget our meeting, sire.' She spoke sincerely.

'Neither will I, Nefertiti.' His tone was almost sombre.

As if to lighten the sudden deepening of mood, Maatnofret interjected with a comment on the excellence of the dancers they were soon to witness. She told them that when she was younger, she had loved to dance.

'Do you dance, Nefertiti?' she asked lightly.

Neferu leaned forwards slightly and lowering her voice admitted, 'Well actually, I only learned yesterday.' Maatnofret and Amenophis looked at each other and burst out laughing.

'I don't believe you!' the pharaoh said with amusement.

Neferu raised her eyebrows. 'It's true, sire! Of course! I know all our old Keftiu dances but not this posh stuff they do here.' The pair of them were seized by another fit of laughter. Neferu had not meant it as a joke and felt a little hurt, assuming that they thought her a country bumpkin.

'Oh, Nefertiti!' Maatnofret spluttered. 'You should stay here with us in Thebes. We would have a laugh more often, I think.'

'You are right, Maatnofret,' the pharaoh said. Looking at Neferu, he noticed her crestfallen look.

'Don't worry, Nefertiti,' he continued. 'I can't dance either.' He stood up and his cloak swung about him. 'I hope you will excuse me, ladies. I will see you, anon.' With a slight bow, he left to chat with someone else. Maatnofret looked after his retreating back.

'Well, Neferu. What do you think of our young pharaoh?' she asked with a guileless air.

'I think he is very nice,' observed Neferu. 'I thought pharaohs would be much less pleasant somehow.'

At this Maatnofret really chuckled and Neferu looked up to find the gaze of the grand queen on them curiously.

Presently the major domo came to announce that the great hall was ready for the dancing display and that the gentlemen had requested the pleasure of the company of the ladies. As they filed into the hall, the court musicians were still fine tuning their instruments. Vassiliou was there and came towards her, saying that the grand vizier had requested an audience with him. He looked a bit mystified and Neferu queried, 'Is there anything wrong, Father?' Her father said that he was fairly confident that everything was in order and there seemed to be no reason for concern. He shrugged his shoulders in puzzlement and, suddenly noticing Maatnofret, gave a deep bow.

'I could not but overhear your words, sire!' the good lady commented. 'I will take good care of your daughter. She shall be seated next to me.'

Vassiliou looked even more surprised. 'I would not wish my daughter to be a burden you, Your Ladyship. I am sure our hostess will consent to chaperone Neferu,' he said with dignity.

'Nefertiti is certainly not a burden,' Maatnofret replied. 'I enjoy her company.'

'You are very kind, Your Ladyship,' her father replied with a smile and a quick glance at his daughter, whom he knew could be a bit of a handful. Bowing to Maatnofret, he told Neferu that he probably would not be gone long and gave her a reassuring smile. Neferu nodded and when he left went over to join Maatnofret, who had now seated herself on a low plushly covered stool close to the royal family.

The royal family had seated themselves on ornate chairs of carved wood, the arms of which were plated with inlaid gold filigree. Those members of the royal entourage closest to the royal family were seated on low stools almost at their feet. There was a height difference of about thirty centimetres between the levels of heads. It was a matter of strict protocol that no one should be allowed to sit at a higher level than the ruling family. Thus, it was that Neferu found herself in this illustrious company. Truth to tell, she was almost overcome by a mad desire to giggle when she searched out the figure of her hostess Narida and her family. Narida was gazing at her stupefied, mouth wide open. Her expression implied that there was no justice in the world. Neferu had to look away quickly and clench her teeth to repress the giggle which threatened to come out. As it was, she ended up emitting a tiny snort which almost finished her off. Maatnofret gave her a quick look and Neferu endeavoured to control herself by imagining unpleasant things such as having to help Grandma prepare the vegetables. Fortunately, it worked.

Behind Neferu the royal family were seated at a distance of about one metre. Seated as she was on the outer curve, Neferu could see the Queen Tiya and her companion to her right, the Archduke Tuthmosis. To his left was Teya, the wife of the grand vizier, Ay. She was seated with her daughter, who was called Mutnedjmet, according to Maatnofret. The girl was about the same age as Neferu but quite petite with a dark complexion. She was pretty but looked a little petulant. To the right of the grand queen was seated her husband, the senior pharaoh, and to his right, just behind Neferu and therefore out of her field of vision, sat the younger pharaoh. To the right of Amenophis IV sat his sister, the princess Sitamun, and to her right the youngest princess, Meretamun. Neferu turned her head to the right slightly and caught the glance of the young princess, who smiled at her. Neferu noticed that the smile transformed the face of the girl, suddenly making her look pretty. Maatnofret informed Neferu that only the youngest prince, Smenkhenre, was absent.

Not wishing to appear nosy, Neferu fell silent and let her attention be drawn to the musicians, who had now begun to play in earnest. A group of belly dancers entered the room from the reception hall and commenced their exotic dances. Neferu had never seen anything like this before, though she had overheard her grandma and Aunt Lea talking about such things when they thought she was not listening. Now she understood why Grandma had talked in low tones. Even Neferu was shocked to the core by their scanty dress, if one could call it that. Her eyes almost fell out of her head.

Maatnofret glanced at Neferu and Neferu widened her eyes at her to denote her shock. Once again Maatnofret began to laugh and out of the corner of her eye she noticed that the queen was eying them again. She suddenly felt very conspicuous and resolutely decided not to do anything else to arouse anyone's attention. Gradually she got a prickly feeling on her neck, as though someone was watching her. She tried to ignore it but it would not go away and the sensation of prickliness at the nape of her neck made her want to scratch it. Intuitively she realised it was the younger pharaoh behind her. The knowledge made her feel edgy, and she felt an urge to turn round and look at him. She shifted about restlessly on her stool but remained with her face turned towards the dancers. Perhaps she was just imagining it.

After the dancers left the hall, it was the turn of a group of acrobats. She enjoyed watching their amazing feats and clapped her hands enthusiastically with everyone else to show her appreciation. The act was followed by a woman who contorted her body into such unusual positions that Neferu was afraid that she would never be able to straighten herself out again. Involuntarily, she remarked. 'That is amazing!' Maatnofret responded with a nod. Neferu felt sorry that her father was missing all this. It was truly something special.

When the apparently double-jointed woman finally unwound herself and ran lightly from the hall, a trio of jugglers presented themselves and again there were appreciative 'Ohs' and 'Ahs' from the bemused audience. The jugglers having left the hall, the musicians stopped playing and an interval was announced, during which the dozen or so waiters served out drinks. Neferu thought they were almost jugglers themselves, carrying their huge trays up high on the palm of their right hand.

A voice behind her caused her to turn quickly. 'Did you enjoy the show, Nefertiti?' Amenophis asked.

Neferu looked up and something happened which changed her life, though she did not know it then. Her eyes seemed to become locked into those of Amenophis and she could not draw them away even as she realised it was inappropriate. The gaze was intimate and strange. She felt his eyes search her face, asking unspoken questions, analysing her soul, and she felt her own eyes searching his face and giving involuntary answers to whatever he was asking, but which she did not understand. When she finally managed to pull her eyes away from his magnetic gaze, she felt shaken. It must have lasted only a few seconds, but she knew something momentous had happened between them. Something deep inside her felt that she had known this man a long, long time. She knew it was ridiculous but could not deny the truth of it. She wondered if he had felt it too. She became aware that he was waiting for an answer and tried to draw her wits together. She looked at him again, but this time his eyes were expressionless, and she said in a low voice, 'I thought it was wonderful.' He nodded and turned to talk to his sister, and Neferu began to wonder if she had imagined the incident. The strange exhilarating feeling was still too strong inside her for her to have imagined it. She determined to push it away from her. She did not want her equilibrium to be disturbed in this way.

Just as the second part of the show commenced, the grand vizier and her father returned to the hall. They appeared to be chatting amicably and she relaxed. Ay had his hand on her father's arm in a friendly gesture so she knew that nothing hostile or negative had passed between them. Neferu willed her father to notice where she was sitting, and he did indeed look at her, and there was a turbulent expression on his face. It seemed to her that he deliberately averted his gaze. She rejected the notion, telling herself that she was becoming too fanciful. It must be the sweet but potent wine she was drinking. She felt that once they got back to On it would take her a few days to get her feet back on the ground after this trip. With a guilty pang, she realised that she had not thought of Yussef all day. She determined that when they returned to their host's residence later on, she would spend a good half an hour attempting the telepathic communication he had requested of her.

Vassiliou joined Ay and his family on the opposite side of the group to Maatnofret and Neferu and during the show there was no chance for them to engage in conversation. When the show was over, the royal family rose to leave and everyone else either bowed or curtsied as they made their exit. There was no further conversation between Neferu and Amenophis.

Once the royal family had made their exit, Maatnofret guided Neferu to her father's side and then bade her farewell. 'I have enjoyed meeting you so much, Nefertiti,' she said warmly. 'It is such a pity that you are not staying longer.' The charming lady-in-waiting acknowledged Vassiliou's deep bow with a nod. 'Your daughter, Mr Stassopoulos, safe and sound,' she said with a slight smile. With that she wished them both good night and retreated quickly in the footsteps of the royal family.

Now that the royal family had departed, there was a general movement towards the courtyard. In the hall some people were still standing around chatting and laughing in gossipy groups, but Vassiliou and Neferu went briskly to find their host and hostess, feeling a little rude about having been separated from them.

When they eventually managed to find their friends in the exit to the courtyard, it was obvious that the Charalambides were agog with curiosity. Vassiliou said that the grand vizier was interested in procuring some jewellery of a special design which he had seen on one of his regular, though infrequent, visits to the delta area. Vassiliou had promised to help locate the particular pieces required. The rest of their discussion had been concerning the census which had been ordered amongst general political discussion. The grand vizier had been exceedingly amiable to him. There had not been a census carried out for fifteen years and the pharaoh was interested in knowing the population count and more especially the number of males of fighting age, should Egypt be attacked, though he had conceded himself that this was very unlikely. The others nodded and accepted his explanation, but Neferu sensed that there had been much more to their meeting than that. For one thing her father had looked at her with a troubled expression there in the hall. Out here in the darkness, she could not see his face properly but there was something unusual in his voice, a note of evasion.

Her father was suddenly relieved from the need to continue when Anula said, 'The pharaoh seemed very taken with you, Neferu.'

'Oh, do you think so?' Neferu answered cautiously, although feeling ridiculously pleased at the same time.

'Yes, I do! Didn't you think so, Mother?' Anula threw the question over her shoulder to her mother, who was walking behind with her husband and Vassiliou.

'I certainly did,' Narida replied. She admitted to having been a little put out that the pharaoh had not singled them out too and, curiosity getting the better of her, she asked Neferu what they had discussed.

Neferu smiled in the dark. 'Well, for one thing he told me that I was wearing an absolutely beautiful dress!' There was a mischievous note in her voice. 'In the circumstances he could hardly have said otherwise,' she said rather tartly. They all laughed. 'I think they found me a bit of a country bumpkin too,' Neferu continued 'Because they kept laughing at what I said, and I didn't even think it was funny.'

'Oh, surely not!' Narida replied briskly. Her excess haste making a mockery of her sincerity.

'I didn't mind,' Neferu said good-naturedly. Then, 'What about you, Hamid? Did you have a good time?'

'Hamid is in love!' said Anula laughing.

'Really?' replied Neferu. 'With whom?'

'Yes, I am,' admitted Hamid, not at all abashed. 'And the object of my adoration is Surana, the sister of Pararameses.'

'I don't think you have any chance there, Hamid. There were more court nobles around her than bees around a honey pot.' Neferu smiled at Anula's pessimism. Their bantering reminded her of Demi and herself. Perhaps all brothers and sisters were so hard on each other.

The conversation ceased during the last part of their journey. It was very dark, with just the light of an oil lamp and the moon to light their way. Neferu could not stifle her yawns. She was very tired. Soon she could hear the others yawning too and it was with a feeling of tired relief that they arrived in the small courtyard of the villa. Father had been quiet almost the whole journey, but she was too tired to ponder the cause of it tonight. She knew it could not be anything dangerous causing his preoccupation, and anything else could wait until the morning.

The girls tiptoed into the bedroom whispering. Tagried was asleep and her rhythmic, deep breathing was not disturbed by their entry. The girls whispered tired 'good nights' to each other and very soon the only sound in the room was the deep breathing of all three girls. For Neferu, it had been a day to remember all her life. One more day of this unusual holiday and then she would be leaving this fairytale city to go back to the real world once more, or so she thought.

CHAPTER 8

At breakfast the next morning Neferu became aware of an air of suppressed excitement. She kept noticing furtive exchanged glances between the grown-ups. She guessed that her father had discussed with the other two the conversation he had had the previous evening with Grand Vizier Ay. Several times she noticed Narida glancing at her with a considering look, and Narida would look away each time Neferu caught her glance. Neferu began to feel annoyed. She wished that her father had discussed whatever it was with her first. In an intuitive manner she sensed that whatever the matter was it concerned her and therefore she felt no surprise when her father asked her to be ready to accompany him to the palace soon after their breakfast. He noted her questioning glance but told her he would satisfy her curiosity on the way. Athanasios saw her expression of uncertainty.

'Don't look so fearful, Neferu. It is a question of a great honour.' That remark only mystified her further. She looked at her father and noted the veiled expression in his eyes. He, at least, was not over joyful at this supposed honour. She shrugged her shoulders. There was nothing she could do.

At the appointed time Athanasios and her father called her and she was ready to leave. She was wearing a simple but pretty pale blue cotton shift, more suited to her neighbourhood in On rather than a grand visit to a palace. The previous night she had been too tired to mess around with her hair and this morning the once proud ringlets had become depressingly straight tendrils of hair. She had had to brush them back, and to keep them in place she had pinned them with decorated combs. It was all the style she could manage at such an early hour.

Outside, the sun was already high, but it was not yet as hot as it would become later on in the morning. The three of them waved to the others and climbed into the chariot while the servant steadied the horses. Neferu reflected that the Charalambides must be very wealthy to own such a fine chariot and four horses. Once they were on their way, she became almost afraid to broach the subject she had been so keen to discuss a short time before. Fortunately, she did not need to initiate any questioning. Athanasios was obviously eager to tell her of what he clearly considered was her extreme good fortune. 'Aren't you going to tell the girl, Vassiliou?'

Vassiliou cleared his throat, 'Neferu, it seems that the grand queen has requested you as one of her ladies-in-waiting.' He sounded a little shocked, even to his own ears.

'Well don't make it sound like a death sentence, man,' declared his friend heartily. 'What do you say to that, Neferu?' Athanasios beamed at her. Neferu was totally shocked. This was not what she had imagined at all. She was speechless while conflicting emotions raced through her. Initially there was a feeling of pleasure at the honour, but then came the realisation of all it implied. She would have to stay here in Thebes far from all her beloved family and from Yussef. It did not bear thinking about. It was out of the question, and she said so to her father. He smiled at her wanly. He told her that he fully realised that, but how were they to explain their position to the queen. That was a real problem.

'What?' said Athanasios incredulously.

'You are going to turn it down? Why? Anula would be ecstatic to receive such an offer.'

'Anula doesn't live in On and wants to become engaged,' Vassiliou remarked ruefully.

'What does that matter?' asked Athanasios uncomprehendingly. 'Ladies-in-waiting are often married. Her fiancé can move to Thebes too.'

Neferu tried to explain. 'It isn't that. I am Keftiu, On is my home. I don't even speak Egyptian with the same accent as these people here. I don't belong here.'

Athanasios gave a short laugh. 'With all due respect, my dear, you are in grave danger of offending the grand queen and believe me, it is a very brave person who risks offending the royal family. Brave or reckless, that is.'

Neferu felt alarm course through her. She glanced at her father. He shrugged his shoulders. What would happen to them? Surely it could not be that serious? Would her father lose his position?

Out loud she merely said, 'I'll explain everything. Don't worry, it will be all right.'

'I sincerely hope so,' was Athanasios' ominous reply.

For the rest of the journey they sat in silence, each involved in their own thoughts. She heard her father give a deep sigh, and she felt her soul to be troubled. An idea came to her. If the queen needed a new lady-in-waiting, then why not Anula? She decided to suggest this to the queen. Anula wanted to be a lady-in-waiting and the queen wanted a lady-in-waiting. The answer was clear. Once the chariot arrived within the outer courtyard the three of the quickly stepped out and Athanasios left for his job in the archive office on the upper terrace block above the banquet hall. Before leaving them, he gave Neferu a reassuring smile and patted her shoulder. 'Don't worry, my dear. It will all work out for the best.' Once the genial Keftiu had gone she and her father stood about for a little while, uncertainly eyeing the busy movement of people going in and out of the courtyard. Many of them were soldiers from the army barracks close by. All of them walked briskly, it seemed to her, knowing where they were going and sure of themselves.

Something vague and nebulous seized Neferu. It found expression in a tightening of her stomach muscles, an uncomfortable pounding of her heart and an unpleasant dryness of the mouth. She recognised it as fear, remembering that she had felt the same discomfort when Demi had fallen ill in Rashid, and they had thought that he was going to die. Suddenly she wished that she had never come here. A deep nostalgia possessed her for all those she loved and all the things which had gone before. She had a terrifying feeling that everything was about to change and sought reassurance from her father's face. It was in vain; she saw that he was just as troubled as she was by the turn of these events. He looked at her and shrugged his shoulders slightly. 'We had better get a move on, Neferu,' he said. With a feeling of inner turbulence, she accompanied him to where he had been told to report; the headquarters of the chief of the imperial general staff, Paramameses.

The adjutant who greeted them smiled pleasantly and asked them to wait for a moment. He showed them into a pleasant sitting room, which was cool and in the shadow of the morning sun. Vassiliou and Neferu sat quietly. The man seemed to be gone no more than a minute when Paramameses appeared with him in the doorway. Both Vassiliou and Neferu stood up quickly. The two men bowed slightly to each other and then Paramameses asked them to follow him. Neferu wondered where the meeting was to be held. They passed the stone steps at the side of the state reception room and followed a partly covered corridor running the length of the reception room, the state banquet hall and the state withdrawing room. The flowers in the carefully laid out flower beds were a mass of brilliant colour, and their perfume filled the air in the heat of the morning sun.

At the end of the courtyard to the left was the arched opening she and Hamid had ignored the previous day because of the presence of the two guards. Today, the grand vizier came forward to meet them from an entrance on the left, just inside the archway. The grand vizier was obviously in a jovial frame of mind, and he welcomed the visitors informally, signalling Pararameses to leave them. The young general gave a low bow and walked quickly away in the direction from which they had just arrived. 'Come, my dear!' Ay said kindly, leading them forward into the garden into which Neferu had trespassed the previous day, but from the opposite entrance. Vassiliou and Neferu exchanged glances. Following the grand vizier, they turned right at the corner of the building and began to go up the stairs on the outside of the building. At the top they stepped onto a terrace which ran the length of the whole block. That part of the terrace closest to the suite of rooms was covered by a roof. It was facing east and so at this time of the morning it was flooded by sunlight, there being no shady spot to be seen. From the number of tables and chairs out on the terrace, it seemed that it was a popular place of relaxation in the afternoons when it offered welcome shade from the burning sun.

The grand vizier led them through to a spacious sitting room. Although it was quite large it was nevertheless a very cosy room. Neferu looked at the costly rugs on the floor and the walls and the beautifully made furniture and ornaments. She had never seen such an elegant room. In spite of its opulence, it was tastefully furnished, and her eyes found pleasure in contemplating it. The grand vizier asked them to sit down for a while and a servant silently entered, bearing a tray of drinks which he set on a very large, round brass table covered with intricate ngravengs and motifs of birds and animals. Everything in the room spoke of vast wealth and it only served to make Neferu feel more nervous than ever. She was seated on the edge of a couch, knees pressed tightly together, as if to spring up if necessary, when the great queen entered.

Hurriedly both father and daughter rose and made prolonged obeisance as the rest of the royal family to be involved in the discussions followed the queen. Also present were the young pharaoh and Princess Meretamun, Teya, the wife of the grand vizier, and to Neferu's intense relief, Maatnofret, the queen's chief lady-in-waiting.

Once the royal family were seated, the queen bade them both to sit. This was just as well for, by now, Neferu felt that her legs had turned to jelly. She noticed that the muscles in her calf were trembling slightly. The queen briefly welcomed them in peace and then went straight to the point.

'Sir, I am assured that my brother, the grand vizier, has already informed you of what I wish to discuss,' she said composedly.

Vassiliou swallowed slightly, and after a pause he answered in a voice that faltered a little. 'That is so, Your Majesty. If Your Majesty will permit me to say so, I am quite stunned.'

The queen raised her eyebrows slightly. 'Stunned?' she said coolly. Vassiliou hurriedly tried to explain that it was, of course, a great honour for them both, and a very unexpected one, but that he did not think his daughter would make a very suitable lady-in-waiting for Her Majesty. Again, the queen lifted her eyebrows ever so slightly. It made Neferu afraid. 'On the contrary,' the queen continued, 'I find your daughter perfectly charming and my chief lady-in-waiting,' here she indicated Maatnofret, 'tells me that she is both intelligent and witty.'

In spite of himself, Vassiliou looked gratified for a moment. 'It is not that, Your Majesty,' he said hesitatingly, as if searching for the right words. 'It is just that we Keftiu are simple tradespeople and have been for generations. Neferu has not led a sophisticated life and has no experience of the manners of the court. Not only that, she is soon to be married.' He stopped short for a as if to get his breath. Neferu wished that he had not used her pet name in front of these people. It made her feel vulnerable. She felt that she needed the dignity of her full name rather than the familiarity of Neferu in this situation.

'So, your daughter is formally engaged to be married, Mr Stassopoulos?' the queen stated slowly.

'Well, not yet formally, Your Majesty. We plan to announce it formally as soon as we return to On. You see, Your Majesty, Neferu and my great nephew Yussef have grown up together and the family has always understood that one day they would marry. It has always been perfectly clear to everyone that they are very well suited, so you see, Your Majesty, that it is not really possible for Neferu to stay.' After this long speech, Vassiliou mopped his brow.

'Anything is possible, Mr Stassopoulos,' the queen replied drily. She turned to Neferu. 'And what do you have to say for yourself, young lady?' The queen asked with a veiled expression.

Neferu hesitated, not knowing how to express what was in her heart. 'What my father says is true, Your Majesty,' she said slowly. 'I am very deeply honoured but I would be very homesick if I had to live away from all those I love. In any case, I wouldn't know what to do,' she added lamely.

The queen answered rather tartly. 'The duties are not very onerous; I do assure you. It is mainly a matter of laying out my clothes and dressing my hair.'

'But I don't know how to dress anyone's hair,' Neferu said miserably.

'Who has dressed your own hair?' the queen asked slyly.

'Well, I did it myself, but it is very easy, look, Your Majesty.' With that she grabbed her chignon and pulled out the pins and shook her hair down. Then, to illustrate her point, she took the unruly locks and re-pinned her hair back into a chignon. The whole group stared as if mesmerised and Neferu noticed a gleam of amusement in Maatnofret's eyes. 'I would not know how to braid someone's hair as intricately as yours is, Your Majesty,' she said as she stuck the remaining pins in her hair.

'I am sure, Nefertiti, that you are capable of learning anything you put your mind to,' the queen said firmly, as if brooking no argument. She was silent for a while and glanced at her son. He seemed discomfited and the queen looked at him reflectively before turning back to Neferu. 'This young man, Yussef, have you never been separated from him before?' she asked quietly.

'No, Your Majesty, I can never remember a time when Yussef was not there,' Neferu also answered quietly.

'And what does this young man do for a living?' the queen asked.

'He is a jewellery maker,' Neferu answered proudly. 'The best in the whole of On, Your Majesty.'

'Is he indeed? Then he is the very person to do some work for us. We have a great appreciation of excellent craftsmen and artists, young lady.' The queen observed Neferu.

'I am sure that Yussef would be very honoured to make whatever you wish, Your Majesty,' Neferu answered in a pleased tone. She knew that Yussef would be thrilled to receive a commission from the royal family.

There was a moment's pause, then, 'In the circumstances, Nefertiti, I do not think it would harm your relationship with this young man to be separated from him for a little while. It would give you both an opportunity to test your feelings and to see how deep your love really is. In the meantime, I would like you to stay here with me as a trainee lady-in-waiting for a period of three decans. During that period, I wish this Yussef to carry out a commission for me. I am desirous of having a set of earrings, necklace and bracelet made in an unusual and elegant design. I will supply the gold and lapis lazuli. Your father may convey them with him to this young man and the young man will return with your father in three decans with the completed pieces. If I am satisfied, I will give him a further commission and there will be others from other members of the court probably,' Neferu digested the queen's words. So, she was only to stay here for a period of three decans. But that did not make sense. On the other hand, it was a fantastic opportunity for Yussef. She could not afford to throw it away unthinkingly.

'And at the end of three decans I will be allowed to go home?' she asked tentatively.

The queen smiled slightly. 'If at the end of that period you feel unhappy and do not wish to stay any longer then, of course, I would not wish to keep you here any longer.'

Neferu's brow cleared. That was all right then, they did not intend to force her to stay. 'Is that a promise, Your Majesty?' she asked in a tiny voice. She was afraid and knew she was being grossly impertinent, but she wanted to be sure. Her father looked shocked at her temerity.

The queen looked at her coolly for a moment and Neferu cringed. 'It is my word, Nefertiti Stassopoulos,' she said emphatically. Neferu smiled and exchanged glances of relief with her father.

Three decans were only thirty days, much less than the time they used to spend at Rashid, and that always seemed to fly by. She nodded slightly to her father. He too, was also obviously immensely relieved that the situation had been resolved so understandingly. He knew that Yussef would be furious and disappointed that it meant a delay in their marriage, but no doubt the fortuitous opportunity to gain fame and fortune as a royal jeweller would do much to lessen his amertume. On reflection, it was perhaps a good thing for the two young people to test the depths of their feelings by a short separation. What was the old saying? 'Distance is like the wind, it extinguishes the small flames, but only fans the big ones.' There was no doubt that this period at court would certainly raise Neferu's status in On society, he thought. Perhaps there were more advantages in this turn of events than he had originally perceived. On one further point though, he wished to be clarified.

'Your Majesty,' he said slowly.

The queen turned her cool gaze upon him. 'What is it, Mr Stassopoulos?'

'It is only a theoretical question, ma'am. If one of the family became dangerously ill, or conversely, if Neferu should suffer some tragic fate, I trust that she would be released from our agreement forthwith?'

The queen conceded the point. 'Naturally. It is quite understood, Mr Stassopoulos.'

Vassiliou smiled in relief. 'I thank you, Your Majesty.'

During this whole conversation none of the others had spoken. The young pharaoh's expression was hard to define, and the others had shown only curiosity. Now that a successful conclusion had been reached the queen told Maatnofret to order the servants to bring refreshments. One servant served the fruit juice and another one brought fruit and sweetmeats. Maatnofret smiled at Neferu in a friendly fashion and the grand vizier welcomed Neferu to the household. They were both invited to stay overnight at the palace in the guest block room across the courtyard and Ay undertook to send one of the servants to bring their belongings from the Charalambides' residence. Princess Meretamun told Neferu that she hoped they would become friends. Neferu nodded shyly, not knowing quite what to say.

The queen told Neferu that she would be under the personal charge of Maatnofret, who would look after her and guide her on matters of court protocol. Neferu felt overwhelmed. Her life seemed to be taking one unexpected turn after another. She had a sense of being swept along by the tide rather than steering her own course. In spite of the honour of the queen's invitation, there was a sense of helplessness which she did not find pleasant. She wished to hold the hand of destiny in check and decide her own fate.

Amenophis told her he was pleased that she was staying and looked forward to seeing her at the evening social occasions with Maatnofret. Maatnofret saw that Neferu did not understand and explained that the closest members of the royal entourage were invited to spend the evenings after dinner in the queen's private withdrawing room downstairs, where they chatted, played backgammon, sewed, played music and sang. She said they were very enjoyable occasions. Neferu nodded and smiled, replying that she would be honoured to attend. Shortly afterward, the pharaoh left and Ay said he would accompany them to where they were to stay. He suggested that they rest before lunch after all the excitement of the morning. Neferu nodded gratefully. It was true that she was tired, at least. After the tension of the morning, she now felt like a wet rag.

The grand vizier seemed remarkably informal. Neferu did not anticipate any problem in relating to him. She felt very wary of the queen, however, and she could not imagine ever coming to feel at ease in her company. When she was ill at ease, she was invariably clumsy, and she hoped that she would not do anything dreadful while she was here in Thebes. As they walked across the courtyard, the grand vizier told Neferu that he was sure that she would enjoy herself at court. Neferu was silent. She nodded her head for want of finding the right words and she felt a sense of relief as he turned towards her father and began to discuss affairs relating to the administration of On. At the entrance to the guest block a servant hurried to receive them and the grand vizier wished them a good day and left them in the capable hands to the valet.

The servant led them to the apartments they were to occupy for the next twenty-four hours. The followed him silently and remained silent while he showed them round. After he had departed, Vassiliou seated himself upon a couch and said, 'Well! I really don't know what to make of all this, Neferu. The queen seems to have really taken to you.' He smiled, in spite of his disquiet. 'Of course, you are the most beautiful girl in the whole of the Two Lands, so I suppose I shouldn't be surprised!'

Neferu laughed for a moment. 'I think you are biased, Father,' she said, and then became serious as the greater implications of the situation became uppermost in her mind again. 'What on earth will the family think?' She frowned at the thought. 'Yussef will be really upset.' She felt stricken at the thought of Yussef and their last conversation before she had left On. She sighed. 'It would have been very difficult to have totally rejected the queen's offer without causing an offence which could possibly have had repercussions on the family,' she pondered, half to herself.

Her father nodded. 'I think now that it would have been better if I had never brought you with me in the first place,' he stated seriously. 'Your adventure has taken a most unexpected turn, I'm afraid.'

'Well, it isn't for very long after all, Father,' she interjected quickly. 'The queen did promise that at the end of the month I will be free to go home if I am not happy here, and it is unthinkable that I should stay longer.'

Her father nodded. 'But it is not only a question of that, Neferu, and I do appreciate that this is a great opportunity for Yussef's advancement, it is just that I don't want you to have your head turned by any of these court noblemen. I intend to have a word with the grand vizier to ensure that you are properly chaperoned. The manners of the court seem very free and easy compared to our way of life,' he said somewhat critically.

Neferu allowed her surprise to register. 'I'm certain that there is no need to worry on that score, Father.'

'That's as may be, Neferu, but I feel sure that knowing you are protected from unwanted attentions will be a prime source of reassurance to Yussef, as well as myself.' Neferu nodded hurriedly. She had not thought of that point. Again, she assured her father that she couldn't possibly imagine becoming attached to any of the young noblemen they had met, and in any case, he must surely be aware that she would never do anything to bring disgrace upon their family name. Her father patted her arm and said that he understood all that and he had implicit faith in her. He suspected that she would become very homesick and voiced this opinion. A lump did indeed come to her throat as she envisaged not seeing the family for another thirty days. In order not to upset her already anxious father, however, she made grand efforts to overcome her sadness and tried to say airily.

'I will miss you all so much, but I expect that the time will pass quickly with all my duties, and it is a great honour. I think that the lady Maatnofret seems to be exceedingly pleasant, don't you, Father? She was born in On apparently.'

Her father was momentarily diverted. 'Is that so? What is her family name?'

'I didn't think to ask. Do you think that you might know the family?' she asked curiously.

'Well, On is not such a big place as Thebes and we know most of the more important families,' he said, speculatively. 'When you get to know her a little better, perhaps you could ask her. I guess she is my age or thereabouts, although I don't recognise the face at all,' he continued.

'I believe that their branch of the family moved to Thebes when Lady Maatnofret was six years old, Father,' Neferu answered.

'Ah! That explains it then,' her father replied. 'Well, young lady. I think we had better go and rest ourselves before lunch, don't you?' Neferu nodded and they both rose and went to their respective rooms.

Neferu lay down on the strange bed and began to go over the events of the last few days. She wondered whether she would be returning to the Charalambides' home ever again or whether their acquaintanceship would be allowed to continue at the court. She would have to wait and see. In fact, she thought, there was no way of knowing anything at the moment and she would just have to wait and see about everything. Almost against her will, her eyes began to droop, and she fell asleep.

It seemed to Neferu that she was awoken almost at once. The young maid, who had slid so silently into the room, told her that lunch was ready, and she was to prepare herself to share it with the grand vizier and his wife and family in their apartment suite, close to the state withdrawing room and just behind it. Neferu rose quickly and washed her face in the brown pottery bowl in the bathroom, just off the chamber. Taking up a large mirror made of highly polished silver, she checked her hair and smoothed it into place before quickly slipping on her dress again and going to find her father. The servant escorted them across the courtyard and into the cool confines of the foyer of the grand vizier's apartment. The butler ushered them forward into a large reception room where the affable Ay was waiting to greet them.

The lunch turned out to be a cheerful affair. Teya, called 'the royal nurse' by her official title, seemed very aptly named. She was a small, rather plump lady with a pleasant face, and she greeted Neferu in a very motherly manner. Neferu thought that she would like this lady and warmed to her immediately. Mutnedjmet was, it appeared, the couple's only child. It seemed a pity to Neferu because Teya seemed to be made to have a large and close brood of children. Mutnedjmet was very similar to her mother in looks but appeared to be totally different from either of her parents in personality. She was a quiet, rather sullen girl and Neferu suspected that she could be a little difficult. Her introversion was surprising in face of the affability of both her parents.

Once the lunch was over, Teya arranged to take Mutnedjmet and Neferu to spend some time with Princess Meretamun. Her father remained with the grand vizier to discuss any final matters of protocol or to answer any questions that had remained unresolved. Neferu knew that her father would bring up the subject of being chaperoned. The Keftiu were much stricter as regards the care of their womenfolk than the Egyptians.

Princess Meretamun greeted her charmingly and said that when they were alone like this there was no need to curtsy. She told Neferu that the family called her 'Mereta'. She said she would be pleased if Neferu would call her that too. Neferu told Mereta that her own family always called her Neferu. The princess kissed her lightly on the cheek and commented that she had never seen such a beautiful girl in all her life. Neferu flushed with pleasure at the compliment. Once their initial reserve had subsided and the three girls were chatting easily together, the royal nurse left them.

After a little while the three girls were joined by a fourth, slightly older girl of nineteen or twenty, who curtsied deeply to them as she entered. Mereta introduced Neferu to Asenaath, her chief lady-in-waiting. Neferu was disconcerted to find that her spontaneous smile was answered by a cool stare and a polite nod. Obviously, the newcomer resented her presence as an intruder. Neferu sensed it keenly. Mereta's glance intercepted this little incident and she squeezed Neferu's arm gently, saying, 'Neferu is going to be mother's new lady-in-waiting, Asenaath. Both mother and Maatnofret are very taken with her.'

'Indeed! How nice!' The voice was soft but there was no warmth in the eyes. Neferu almost felt the girl's antipathy reach out and touch her. She felt cold inside but reminded herself that she would not be acquainted with Asenaath very long, so there was no sense in letting the girl's coldness upset her. Later she discovered that the girl's father was a half-brother of the older pharaoh. His mother had been one of the lesser wives of Tuthmosis IV. It made Mereta and Asenaath some kind of half-cousins. Still later Neferu discovered that the great majority of the court entourage were more or less interrelated and that this was the cause of much envy and intrigue and arranging of marriages with an eye to procuring status nearer to the throne. In time Neferu learned how to disengage herself from taking any part in their quarrels and squabblings, but at the present she was mercifully unaware of the situation and the mean-spiritedness which it sometimes caused.

'Asenaath's brother, Sinefrew, is one of the best hunters and sportsmen in the court,' Mereta said to Neferu with a smile. 'It is usually a very keen competition between Amio, Rameses and Sinefrew to see who will take the most game,' said Mereta, smiling.

'Amio?' Neferu asked.

'My brother, the pharaoh,' answered Mereta by way of explanation.

'Oh!' said Neferu, thinking that Amio suited him very well.

A servant entered the room and bowed deeply. 'The great royal nurse requests that her daughter the lady Mutnedjmet and the lady Nefertiti accompany me.'

Mutnedjmet told Neferu that it was siesta time, and it was always very strictly observed here at court.

'In the evenings, after dinner we congregate in the withdrawing room, and we have fun. You will enjoy it, Neferu.' The girl's rather sombre face smiled, showing white, even teeth.

'See you later, Neferu!' Mereta said as Neferu curtsied, following the protocol demanded of her position, in spite of the princess' earlier words to the contrary. She did not wish to appear forward, especially in front of the critical eyes of Asenaath. As she descended the steps, Neferu thought to herself that she would have much preferred to be Mereta's lady-in-waiting than the queen's.

That evening Neferu and her father were invited to dine at the home of the grand vizier and his family. She was suddenly seized by the sadness of the imminent parting and found it difficult to respond to the atmosphere of joviality which pervaded the room. In spite of the splendid cuisine, which included many kinds of foods alien to Neferu's palate, she could not eat much and the royal nurse, Teya, appeared concerned. 'Come, come, my dear! You must eat more than that if you are to conserve your strength,' she said. Neferu made an effort to comply but found it difficult to swallow because of the ominous lump which had settled from out of nowhere in a region between her throat and her stomach.

'I am sorry, ma'am,' she answered. 'The food is delicious, but I am not hungry.'

'I expect you are feeling a little homesick now that your father is leaving,' Teya observed with sympathy. The sympathy in her voice caused a sudden prick of hot tears at the back of her eyes and she had to stare hard at the plate in front of her to prevent the tears from falling. She hoped that no one else would say anything or it would be her downfall. When she regained control of her feelings she looked up. The grand vizier was peering at her closely. The royal nurse patted her hand and then turned away from her as if she understood what was happening. Neferu perceived that the tiny lady was incredibly kind. Her initial perception was to be reinforced again and again throughout the many years of her contact with this woman, whom she later learned had suffered much from the constant philandering of her husband. The grand vizier never publicly showed other than constant devotion to his wife, however.

The dinner over, the whole group made their way to the state withdrawing room where a group of nobles and their ladies were already seated and engaging in social conversation. Neferu felt several curious stares as she and Father entered the room. The room looked much larger than it had the previous day when it had been full. Now that there was only a dozen or so people present, it was rather imposing. Gradually, other people trickled in, in twos and threes and found themselves places. One of the men had a lyre and he began to strum the instrument and sing. Other people began to play backgammon and the group started to take on the atmosphere of a familiar club.

The royal family arrived; the older pharaoh with the lady who had accompanied him the previous day, the grand queen with Archduke Tuthmosis ever close by. Neferu was puzzled by the bizarre nature of this set-up and could not quite bring herself to believe the nature of the true relationships that it implied, although her inner woman knew and was somewhat shocked by it all. Both the pharaoh and the grand queen seemed genuinely fond of each other, smiling and chatting with each other and also with their (dare she think it?) respective lovers. None of them made overt gestures of intimacy that would have confirmed her suspicions or betrayed the true nature of their liaisons. On the contrary, their behaviour was very correct and what could be more natural than that the queen should be on good terms with the archduke, who was, after all, her brother-in-law? And yet, and yet. Here Neferu decided to abandon her speculation which was, she realised, potentially dangerous. Best not to be curious about the lives of any of these people, she thought.

When the princesses and the younger pharaoh came in with their younger brother, the delicate looking Smenkhenre, the group was complete. Again, everyone rose to bow or curtsy and after the rest of the royal group had been seated, everyone sat down again. Neferu reflected humorously to her father that it was going to be a month of bobbing up and down. To her embarrassment the grand vizier overheard her remark and emitted a loud guffaw which caused everyone to look at them for a moment. A look of chagrin crossed her father's face and poor Neferu realised that she had better learn to curb her tongue. From the royal circle Neferu saw Maatnofret smiling at her, and she smiled back warmly. She felt that she had at least one friend in this imposing company.

Ay was very attentive to Neferu and after a while she began to relax. The grand vizier told her that he spoke Hebrew, Egyptian and Akkadian, but that he did not know a single word of Keftiu. He asked her to say something for him and he tried to copy what she said. She had to smile at his odd accent but when he inadvertently said something very rude, she and father laughed uncontrollably. She laughed so much that tears came to her eyes, and she refused to tell the grand vizier what he had said. She felt many eyes on her and tried to control the giggles. The grand vizier insisted upon knowing what he had said and eventually Vassiliou gave in and, leaning forward whispered the offending crudity into the ear of the grand vizier. The grand vizier raised his eyebrows in pretended shock upon learning what the word meant and then he too began to laugh.

Eventually the grand vizier rose and, excusing himself, he began to circulate round the room chatting to the guests. Princess Meretamun came to sit with them. She told Vassiliou that she would take good care of Neferu, and he appeared grateful for her promise. 'I wish I was to be your lady-in-waiting instead of …' Neferu stopped hurriedly.

Mereta laughed and looked amusedly at Neferu. 'Mother is not as frightening as you think!' she said softly.

'I didn't mean …' Neferu broke off in mid-sentence, lamely.

'Of course not! Don't worry, Neferu!' The princess spoke understandingly. Vassiliou shot his daughter a warning glance. A moment later Pararameses tapped on his shoulder and told him that the queen desired a private word with him. He stood up and followed the general over to the queen.

'Sir,' she said to him. 'My brother has informed me as to your anxiety regarding Nefertiti's welfare and I am very happy to give you my personal assurance that I certainly would not allow any of the noblemen or courtiers to take advantage of your daughter, upon pain of death!'

Vassiliou's face cleared, and he smiled involuntarily, fears completely allayed. 'Thank you, Your Majesty, I am immensely relieved,' he replied, bowing.

The queen continued. 'I have had some gifts sent over to your quarters for your family and tomorrow the grand vizier will deposit with you the gold for the jewellery which I have commissioned this young nephew of yours to make.'

'I thank you once again, Your Majesty,' Vassiliou replied.

'I think I will not see you in the morning, sir, so I will wish you a safe and speedy journey this evening. May the Aten be with you.'

'Peace be with you, Your Majesty,' replied Vassiliou, who had not the faintest idea who or what the Aten was. The queen inclined her head and Vassiliou perceived that the interview was over. He bowed once more and returned to sit on the couch where he was presently joined by Maatnofret.

Pararameses came over to Neferu and told her that the younger pharaoh would like to speak to her. She looked over to where he was seated and thought that he made an enigmatic and even mysterious figure, wrapped as always in the dark cloak. His deformities must be repulsive, she thought, for him to feel the need to keep his body shrouded thus all the time. Amenophis made room for her to sit beside him as she curtsied. 'I have heard that you are feeling homesick already, Nefertiti,' he said quietly.

'It is nothing, sire,' she said, looking into the strange eyes again.

'We will try to make sure that you are happy with us, Nefertiti,' he said in a tone of sincerity.

'You may call me Neferu, sire,' she said impulsively. 'All my friends call me Neferu. That is, I do not presume to say that we are friends, sire,' she said hurriedly, aware that she had broken protocol by speaking so openly.

Amenophis smiled. 'I know what you mean, Neferu. You don't need to be so defensive all the time. My family call me Amio, and you may call me Amio too when we are in private.' Neferu blushed. She could not imagine calling him anything other than 'sire'. 'If you have any serious problems, will you come and tell me?' he asked, raising his eyebrow questioningly.

'Yes, sire,' she answered. He smiled again but said nothing. From across the room someone called.

'Are you going to sing for us tonight, sire?' Neferu suddenly noticed a lyre by his side.

'Tomorrow we are leaving early for the hunt so tonight there will be only one song,' he said leisurely, picking up the lyre. He smiled at Neferu and saw that she looked surprised. 'It is a song you all know. An old Egyptian love song.' This last was said to Neferu.

The pharaoh began to sing the lovely old song and Neferu listened in astonishment. This strange looking man had an incredibly good singing voice. The room was silent.

Everyone listened as he sang the song with great feeling in his voice. The words were sad and Neferu felt an echo within her own heart as the last sounds of the melody were swallowed in the silence. She found herself clapping spontaneously with the others. 'Did you like it?' he asked with a smile.

'It was beautiful, sire,' she replied, and it was true.

He inclined his head slightly. 'Now I will take my leave of you, Neferu,' he said and wished her a good night. He stood up to leave and, as if by some prearranged signal, the rest of the royal family also rose to leave. Everyone stood up to bow or curtsy again but when the royal family had gone, they sat down again, and the conversation continued as before.

Ay, who had not left with the rest, came over to Neferu and suggested that she have an early night as her father was leaving soon after dawn. Vassiliou approached and explained that he would have to leave early as he wished to call and thank his friends the Charalambides. Neferu nodded her head in agreement. After reminding Vassiliou that he must come to collect the gold for the jewellery commission next morning, Ay bade them farewell and left.

Father and daughter bade the other guests a shy goodnight and made their way across the courtyard. The great, round, silver moon was clear in the sky and its light cast shadows in the courtyard, making everything strange and unreal. After the tremendous heat of the day, it felt chilly, and she shivered a little. A great sadness came over her as she was reminded that she would not see her father for a whole month.

In their apartment a surprise awaited them – the presents sent by the queen. Each one appeared to have been chosen with each particular recipient in mind. There was something for everyone. Layer upon layer of dress lengths of the most beautiful materials for Grandma, Aunt Lea and Shosen. For Grandpa there was a ceremonial dagger on a waistlength ornate chain, and for Demi an ebony walking stick with a solid silver head, and a sheaf of precious papyrus with the works of the royal poets artistically written and beautifully decorated with delicate drawings. For Yussef there was a box of gold coins and a piece of papyrus with instructions for him to make for Grand Queen Tiya, Queen of Upper and Lower Egypt, a set of matching jewellery, comprising earrings, necklace and bracelet, in a design of the artist's own choosing. It was signed with the seal of Amenophis III, the senior pharaoh, and stamped with the royal seal of the exchequer. They gazed at it all silently. 'Such a royal favour is going to make Yussef very sought after. He will be the most important jeweller in the whole of Lower Egypt,' her father said, slightly in awe. Neferu nodded. 'It should make Yussef feel better about the delay in your marriage,' he added.

Neferu felt the brink of their separation upon them, and she blurted out. 'Oh, Father! I shall miss you all so much.' She threw her arms around her father's neck.

'I will miss you too, my darling daughter, and I don't know how I am going to explain it all to you grandparents. I have to leave though, my darling. I am worried about Shosen. This pregnancy has been much harder on her than the others and I don't want to lose a second wife in childbirth,' Vassiliou said anxiously.

Neferu felt guilt at her recent obsession with her own affairs. 'I understand, Father. Remember to give them all my love and tell them that I will pray for them every day.' A deep sense of her love for them invaded her being, and with it an overwhelming desire to be with them. They hugged each other tightly until Neferu's father reminded her that it was going to be a very early start. They said goodnight to each other and retired.

At the first light of dawn, Neferu woke up and, opening her eyes, looked around the room for a moment in puzzlement before remembering where she was. The rays of the sun were already filtering through the high narrow window, and she watched them streaming in and illuminating some small dust particles in their rays. She remembered that her father was to leave early today, and she jumped up without further ado. After washing and doing her hair, she hurried into the sitting room. The same maid who had been present the previous day was laying out drinks and food upon a low table. She straightened up as Neferu entered. 'I was just coming to call you, my lady,' she said.

It felt very odd to Neferu to be called 'my lady', more especially as the maid was some years older than she was. She felt somehow an imposter. She smiled at the maid. 'Is my father already up?' she asked, after wishing the woman a good morning. The maid informed her that her father had risen some time ago already and would be along shortly.

Vassiliou did indeed appear very soon after and wished his daughter an affectionate good morning. The two of them sat down to eat. When they had eaten their fill, Vassiliou left to go to Ay's office to collect the gold bullion for Yussef to work on. A tall well-built man appeared and removed the luggage to the chariot waiting in the outer courtyard. A second man appeared to help the first one but, even so, it took them two journeys each to remove the presents and other luggage. Neferu looked around the room and felt it empty, as though its soul had gone. It looked desolate and impersonal without her father's belongings, and she decided to go out and wait for him in the courtyard.

Neferu sat down on the edge of a flower bed and waited for her father to reappear. In the meantime, she could see in the far courtyard the hunters preparing the chariots for the hunt. She could see plainly the cloak of the young pharaoh as he issued orders to the grooms. There were perhaps a dozen young noblemen altogether and the hunt always took place early in the morning before the heat became unbearable.

Vassiliou and Ay left the latter's office above the level of the great banquet hall and walked toward the direction of the steps near the suite of Pararameses. Neferu hurried in that direction along the ground floor and waited for her father to descend. They all strolled toward the outer courtyard and were shown the chariot, which had been loaded. Some of the hunters were checking their bows and arrows. Neferu saw no sign of the pharaoh. Her father put his arms around her and embraced her. She felt the tears rolling down her cheeks, in spite of her resolve to be calm. 'Now, now, Neferu,' her father said, patting her back. 'The time will go quickly.' His voice was gruff with emotion too and she felt her heart would break with the love she felt for all of them.

'I know,' she said, trying to smile through her tears. 'It's just that I will feel so terribly alone when you go. On is so far away.'

The grand vizier said nothing but only observed them. Vassiliou gave her one last emotional hug and kissed her on both cheeks in the time-honoured Keftiu fashion before finally releasing her and climbing into the carriage. Neferu waved her father away through a mist of tears. The avuncular Ay seemed not in the least put out by this show of emotion. He took Neferu's hand and led her toward the inner courtyard. Neferu did not notice the young man with the sombre expression who watched her wipe her tears away and walk hand in hand with his uncle back to the royal suite.

CHAPTER 9

As Ay walked towards the living complex of suites, the grand vizier told Neferu about some of the court's coming programmes, in which she would automatically be included. She felt that this charming man was her ally and impulsively she squeezed his hand. 'I'm so glad you are here,' she said ' At least I'll have one friend.'

Ay smiled, perhaps at her slightly mournful tone. 'One friend, my dear? You'll have dozens of friends, you'll see.' The grand vizier informed Neferu that her work schedule had been changed a little. For the moment, she was to act as lady-in-waiting to Mereta, along with Asenaath, until she became accustomed to the duties involved. The queen herself had suggested this. Neferu felt relieved on hearing this; she really did not want to be too close to that cool and regal woman. She smiled her pleasure to her companion. 'Thank you,' she said gratefully.

Ay looked at her keenly and then said conspiratorially. 'Come with me and I will show you where my office is. If you feel really desperate about anything, you can come there to see me.' They climbed the stairs to the first-floor offices and followed the terrace along until they were almost at the end. The grand vizier stood aside to let Neferu pass into his office, which contained two large, beautifully carved desks, one of which was full of papyri. There were two comfortable hide couches and two chairs, one behind each of the desks. 'This is where I am when I am not supervising state functions,' he said. 'So now you know where to find me if you need me.' There was a pause. 'You must be discreet though, Nefertiti. Normally I never allow anyone to come here without an invitation.' Neferu nodded, feeling very flattered by all this attention. 'I know that I can trust you,' he added. Neferu told him that she would only come if she felt absolutely desperate. Ay patted her hand reassuringly. 'Come now, let me arrange for you to visit Mereta again.' This time they left the office and came down the steps that were nearest to the grand vizier's living suite. Having crossed to the other side of the archway, they were forced to walk up the steps of that side. Ay left Neferu with Asenaath and Meretamun before he left to resume his state duties.

Princess Mereta beamed at Neferu and told her how pleased she was that her mother had arranged the swap. Asenaath did not seem much impressed, but she began to outline Neferu's new duties with cold politeness on Mereta's request. Whenever she needed to refer to Neferu by name, she insisted on calling her Nefertiti. It was obvious that she had no intention of encouraging any intimacy between herself and the Keftiu girl.

In truth, the duties which Neferu was expected to carry out were anything but difficult. For the next few days, she was to accompany Asenaath until she learned the routine, which began at seven in the morning. She was to wake the princess and check that the maid who was responsible for heating the water had laid out the bathing room. The princess would have decided what it was that she wished to wear the evening of the previous day, and the lady-in-waiting would ensure that the laundry staff had them in impeccable condition, ready to don. After helping the princess to wash and dress, she would then do her hair. From then onward the lady-in-waiting acted as companion to the princess throughout the day until lunch time. After lunch the princess was helped to undress for siesta. At three-thirty it was the duty of the lady-in-waiting to wake the princess, make sure that there was warm water for bathing, help her to dress and then accompany her for refreshments, which usually the royal family ate together.

If the evening was to be spent informally then there was really nothing for her to do except keep the princess company until it was time to settle down. On state occasions there were fresh clothes to be prepared and put on and the princess' hair to be stylishly adorned. In practice, it appeared that more often than not Mereta performed many of these functions for herself, apart from doing her hair, and so the job of lady-in-waiting was even easier than Neferu had been led to believe.

Acting as companion to Mereta meant that Neferu had to take part in sewing, embroidery, singing to the accompaniment of the lyre and joining in various games such as backgammon, charades or puzzles. It seemed that Mereta was very keen on lace making and so Neferu tried to learn. It was an art that nature had not meant for her. Her results were untidy and uneven, and in the end she admitted defeat and elected to tell stories instead. Some of the stories she made up herself and some were old Keftiu legends. Mereta enjoyed listening to these adventures, so much so that she would sometimes put her lace down for many minutes at the exciting parts. In addition, Neferu made up poems and recited them, though only rarely in the company of Asenaath, who made her feel gauche and clumsy. Neferu was used to helping Grandma with chores and did not even acquaint her new tasks with work proper. It was more like playing, and she began to understand why there were so many applicants for any vacancies which cropped up.

In the evenings, the royal family dined together with the royal entourage and afterwards they would all retire to the withdrawing room where a general buzz of conversation and jolliment could be heard most evenings. No one was ever allowed to leave the room before the pharaoh or the queen retired, unless with special permission or on some errand of state. The old pharaoh rarely joined these evening occasions at all, and in principle, the queen usually left early at about nine o'clock, along with the older members of the royal family. After this, the younger noblemen would sometimes get a little drunk or become a little wild, but Amenophis could be brutally sharp if he felt someone was stepping out of line and so nothing unpleasant ever happened. Little flirtations were common, occasionally stimulated by an excess of wine, but the evenings rarely lasted beyond midnight unless it was some special holiday or state banquet occasion.

In the beginning Neferu felt very much an intruder at these events. Asenaath and many others remained very cool towards her and even suspicious of her. The friendliness of Mereta, however, more than made up for the barriers of the others. The princess turned out to be a genuinely nice girl and she and Neferu quickly became firm friends. Neferu decided that she would have liked a sister like Mereta with whom she could have shared girl talk and things. Demi and Yussef had never been interested in talking about beautiful gowns and hairstyles, or about falling in love. Suddenly a whole unexplored conversational area was opened up to her and the two girls spent hours chatting about these delicious things.

On this first afternoon of her first day, however, all this was still in the future and Neferu sat on the couch opposite to the other two, feeling like a black sheep amongst all the white ones. When Asenaath had finished her job description, the princess thanked her and said, 'I would like to talk to Neferu alone for a while, Asenaath, and afterwards I will see to myself, so you are free until three-thirty.' She smiled sweetly at the other girl, who rose and lightly curtsied. She seemed a trifle put out by the dismissal, although more often than not she was usually dismissed at this hour. Neferu guessed that the girl was annoyed by the friendliness of the princess towards her. She hoped it would not sour the girl further. She needed all the help she could get in treading the minefield of court protocol. When Asenaath had disappeared, the princess smiled at Neferu and then patted the seat beside her and said easily, 'Come and sit here, Neferu.'

Neferu rose obediently and went to sit down next to the princess. The two girls looked at each other in a friendly, questioning way for a few moments and then Mereta said, 'I hope that we can be real friends, Neferu. Do you think you will like me?' Neferu felt that the question was rather touching and humble. She knew in that moment that she would like the other girl.

'I would like us to be friends, your Royal Highness,' she spoke shyly.

Mereta shook her head slightly. 'You should not say "Princess" or "Your Royal Highness" when we are alone, that is just protocol for the court. Mother is very strict about it in public though, she even tells Amio off on occasions if she thinks he is too familiar with his friends.'

'I understand, Mereta,' Neferu said with a nod. She thought again that the name 'Amio' suited the pharaoh very well. For the first time it showed a different facet to her picture of him. He was not only the pharaoh, even more importantly he was a man, someone with feelings and needs as all men do. Nothing like the demi-god picture she had conjured up before her visit to Thebes.

'I look very much like my brother, don't I?' Mereta asked abruptly. It was undeniably true.

'Yes, you do, Your … Mereta,' replied Neferu, stumbling over what to call the princess. Mereta smiled ruefully at Neferu.

'I wish I were beautiful like you, Neferu,' she said wistfully. Neferu felt a pang. This girl managed to touch her heart. She forgot their differences of rank and leaning forward, gently touched her arm.

'You are beautiful in your own way, Mereta. I like you anyway. People who are beautiful on the inside are the nicest of all, I think, don't you?' she said gently. 'Anyway!' she continued. 'You have beautiful eyes and skin,' she was able to say sincerely.

Mereta's lips curved in the slightest of smiles. 'I know that we will be good friends, Neferu. I felt it the first time we met.' This latter remark reminded Neferu of the dress she had borrowed on that occasion and Neferu thanked her for the loan of it. Mereta laughed. 'You may keep it if you wish,' she said ruefully. 'It looks much better on you than on me anyhow.'

'I couldn't possibly,' Neferu replied quickly.

'Why not?' asked Mereta.

'It is such a costly gown!' Neferu was shocked. Mereta laughed.

'Nonsense, it is yours and there is an end to it. In fact,' she said, with a frown, 'I will have to speak to mother about getting you some more as you cannot possibly have brought many with you.'

'Oh no!' said Neferu in consternation. 'I really won't need them. I can manage with what I have. After all, I will only be here a short while.'

Mereta gave Neferu a strange look as if she were about to say something, but whatever it was she changed her mind. After a slight pause, she said gently, 'You will still need several gowns, Neferu. There are several state occasions during the next three decans, and you can't possibly wear the same two gowns all the time.'

Neferu was mortified. She felt like a poor relation. 'I have many pretty dresses at home,' she said, looking down, her face scarlet.

'I know that, Neferu, but if we send for them, it will take a whole decan, five days there and five days back. Believe me, it is much easier this way,' said Mereta, noting Neferu's chagrin.

'It's just that I don't want to be beholden to anyone,' Neferu said slowly. She looked up quickly, hoping that she had not offended the princess.

'You will not be beholden, Neferu. You do not need to be afraid of that. The clothes of all the ladies-in-waiting are paid for out of the treasury coffers.' The princess looked at her gravely. 'We are friends, Neferu! You need not be afraid of speaking your mind with me. Whatever we discuss will go no further if that is what you wish.'

Neferu hesitated a moment. 'Well, if the others receive their gowns, then I suppose it is all right for me to too,' she said doubtfully.

Mereta smiled. 'Good! I will tell mother this evening so that she can arrange for the dressmaker to come and measure you. In the meantime, I have a few dresses which I have not yet worn so you are saved from a social disaster,' she said melodramatically, putting her hand to her heart and rolling her eyes. Neferu giggled and the uncomfortable moment was over. 'Right! Now that has been settled, I suppose that we had better go to rest,' said Mereta, standing up. 'By the way, Neferu. I almost forgot. One of the valets will be moving your things into a suite of rooms downstairs, directly below mine. He will bring your belongings over this evening. You won't be lonely there because Maatnofret and her husband also have a suite there, just opposite yours.'

Neferu smiled with relief. She had envisaged a lonely time over there in the guest house without her father's company. 'Thank you, Mereta. I am pleased because I was a bit afraid of being lonely over there by myself.'

Mereta laughed. 'You are very unflattering in your expectations of our hospitality.

But I will forgive you. See you later, Neferu!' Neferu started to curtsy but the wave of Mereta's arm reminded her that she did not need to do so. She grinned and turned to go as Mereta disappeared in the direction of her bed chamber. She walked off alone along the terrace, down the steps and across the courtyard to the guest block. 'I am finding my way around already,' she thought with a burst of confidence as she walked.

At half-past three o'clock, Neferu duly presented herself again at Mereta's apartment. She found that Asenaath was already there and waiting for her. 'I have already woken the princess,' she said coldly. Neferu felt a little abashed, though she was quite aware that the other girl was trying to break her confidence. Because she realised it, she felt anger stir in her. Knowing that to vent it would be useless, she did her best to quell the negative feeling. She was sure that she was on time because she had asked the maid to wake her at three and she had checked the sun dial in the courtyard as she came over. She decided to give the other girl the benefit of the doubt and put her hostility down to jealousy of a newcomer taking her place. Perhaps she would have been just as jealous in a similar situation, she thought, knowing jolly well that she would have been. She bit back the sharp retort she had intended. Better not to antagonise these people; she had to think of her family's position. A moment later Mereta joined them.

'Oh, Neferu! You are here already!' she said with a smile. 'Normally, we have refreshments with the rest of the family in mother's sitting room, but today she and Uncle Ay have to sort out some affairs of state, so we are eating here. Amio and Smenkh are joining us too, Asenaath tells me.'

Neferu had not yet met the youngest prince, although she had seen him during the festivities. He had seemed very shy.

'Smenkh usually has his meals with his friends in the Kap,' the princess explained.

'The Kap,' reiterated Neferu, completely in the dark.

'You don't know what the Kap is?' Mereta sounded astonished.

'No.' Neferu confessed, wondering if she was always going to be caught out by her ignorance.

Asenaath smiled with an unrestrained air of superiority, which completely flattened Neferu's previous good intentions.

'The Kap is a secret military society,' said Mereta in mock hush tones. 'We women aren't supposed to know anything about it, of course. Only noblemen whose loyalty to the throne is above question are allowed to join. Its headquarters are at a huge fortress camp in Nubia and its leaders here in Thebes are the Nubian generals. All the pharaohs and the princes of the blood have to learn the rules of the Kap and pass its initiation ceremonies. The pharaoh is the leader of the Kap,' explained Mereta.

'Oh!' replied Neferu, doubtfully, not quite understanding the formidable political and military might that the Kap represented. It sounded more like a friendly men's club to Neferu. Certainly, she did not equate it with war at that time.

The pharaoh arrived shortly with his younger brother, and they all stood up to curtsy.

'Sit down, sit down,' Amenophis said informally, and they re-seated themselves. Today he was wearing a purple cloak down to his calves. As he sat down his legs became partially exposed and Neferu noticed that his legs were extremely thin. She looked away quickly. She noticed that the younger prince stayed very close to his elder brother and Amenophis said to him affectionately, 'Come on, Smenkh. We aren't afraid because we are outnumbered, are we?' The boy smiled and looked at Neferu sideways. She noted the glance and smiled at him. He was still only a little boy. She remembered how shy Demi had been at that age.

'Hello, Your Highness,' she said simply. Amenophis looked at his brother to see his reaction. The boy blushed and smiled at her shyly before quickly looking away.

'This is Nefertiti, Smenkh. She is going to be Mereta's lady-in-waiting for a while,' the pharaoh said with a grin. 'She doesn't know yet what an ogre Mereta is!' The boy smiled again but remained silent. Mereta slapped her brothers' knee lightly and told him not to frighten poor Neferu. 'Ah, Yes!' he said with a grin. 'Neferu is what you like to be called.'

Neferu flushed slightly, wishing it didn't sound so babyish. Nefertiti suddenly sounded far more grown-up and sophisticated. 'It's what my family and friends call me, sire,' she said.

'Well, in a way we are your family and friends now so we will call you Neferu too, won't we Smenkh?' The boy nodded, looking openly at Neferu for the first time. She smiled at him again, hoping to put him at ease. He was remarkably shy, she thought. Even Demi had not been this shy. 'Remember that when we are alone with the family like this, you may call me Amio,' said Amenophis easily.

'Thank you, sire,' she replied, not quite able to bring herself to call him by his name.

In spite of his affable manner, she felt he was not an easy person to know, and she felt their relationship was too uncertain for her to feel comfortable using his first name in such an intimate manner. He looked at her with a glint in his eye, as if assessing her manner. She saw Asenaath looking at her with what seemed to be a smirk and realised that she had made another faux pas. She felt a spiteful desire to box Asenaath's ears.

Within forty-eight hours her life had swung upside down and she didn't know whether she was on her head or her heels. She felt as though she was drowning in all these changes. It was only that same morning that her father had left, but already it felt like ages. Neferu fell silent and Amenophis turned his attention to Asenaath, teasing her familiarly about her brother's prowess at hunting. Asenaath laughed, completely at home in the company of Amenophis, and there followed a detailed discussion of the hunting programme for the summer season. Asenaath's brother was obviously a very popular and skilled member of the hunt.

Now and again, Mereta directed a friendly remark towards Neferu to try to draw her into the conversation and Neferu would answer gratefully, feeling totally out of her depth amongst these people who knew everything about each other and about whom she knew absolutely nothing. Her sense of alienation was profound, and an overpowering feeling of homesickness flowed over her. She knew nothing whatsoever about hunting and was repelled to hear them discussing how many animals had been killed and by whom. She kept her opinions to herself, however.

For Neferu the meal was quite an ordeal. She was ever conscious of being an intruder on their lives. Asenaath did not direct a single spontaneous remark to her during the whole meal and Neferu came to understand that she would always be an outsider. She was different, in accent, customs, manners and background. No matter how nice they were to her, she would never fit in here. To her surprise she gained an ally in the young prince. He seemed to divine her mood and responded to it as if to a kindred spirit. 'I hope you will like it here with us, Neferu,' he suddenly said diffidently. Neferu could have kissed him for his sensitivity. There was a moments silence as Amenophis broke off his conversation with Asenaath to glance at his brother in surprise. He soon turned his attention back to the lady-in-waiting and they resumed their animated conversation. Smenkh and Neferu were left to chat together.

'I've got a younger brother too,' Neferu told him.

Smenkh responded with interest. 'What's his name?' he asked.

'His name is Demetrious really, but we call him Demi,' she replied.

'Demetrious! That's a strange name,' he said in surprise and then added quickly. 'But I like it!' She realised that he thought he might have offended her.

'It's a Keftiu name,' she explained. 'My ancestors came to Egypt when Caphtor was destroyed. It was hundreds of years ago when the great flood almost destroyed the world.'

'Yes, my history teacher has told me about it,' he replied.

'Really?' She was surprised.

'Of course,' he answered, realising that he had captured her interest. 'I love learning about history, don't you?' he said eagerly.

'Well, sometimes,' she said dubiously. 'But I didn't like learning about the destruction of my people.'

'No,' The boy agreed. 'But all the northern coastline regions of Egypt were destroyed too,' he said in a scholarly tone. She saw that it was an attempt to share her discomfort and thought it was sweet of him to make the effort when he would so obviously been happier elsewhere other than sharing this situation with them. Now that he was on a subject that really interested him, he seemed to come alive and lose his shyness.

'I didn't know that.' Neferu did not mind admitting her ignorance to him.

'Yes. It was completely flooded and there was massive destruction. Almost everyone died in the coastal areas. The sand absorbed it very quickly here, of course, and the multiple tributaries of the Nile took it back out to sea so in many ways we were lucky compared to our neighbouring countries.' He spoke with animation. Smenkh discussed the matter with confidence and obviously knew a lot about it. They were talking as equals now and both had forgotten the others. 'It was after the destruction by the flood that Egypt, seriously weakened, was invaded for the first time in its history. The Hyksos came on horseback and Thebes became the capital after the fall of Memphis.' Neferu listened, enthralled. It was just as exciting as anything that Grandma had told her about Caphtor. Seeing that he had all her attention, Smenkh continued. Leaning forward confidentially he said, 'Of course, that is why some people here don't like us. They say we are the same as the Hyksos.'

'We?' Neferu answered, mystified.

'Smenkh!' Amenophis sharp retort brought their attention to the fact that the others were listening to them in silence. Smenkh promptly blushed and Neferu glanced from one brother to the other, wondering what the boy had been about to tell her. She was consumed with curiosity.

In order to break the rather pregnant silence which followed, Neferu said, 'You are so clever, Smenkh, to know all that. It was really interesting. I will tell you all about Caphtor sometime. If you want to hear, that is!'

'Oh, I do, Neferu! I want to know about the whole world,' he said enthusiastically.

'Me too!' Neferu grinned. The two looked at each other conspiratorially, and both realised they had found a firm ally. The shy Smenkh was never afterwards shy in the company of Neferu. Amenophis was looking at them curiously. He had noticed their look of complicity. Almost immediately afterwards he said that he had to go over some letters of state with his uncle and rose to go. He indicated for his brother to follow him and gave them a slight bow.

At the doorway he suddenly turned, his long cloak swishing round him and he spoke, 'Don't worry, Neferu. You will soon feel at home here. Asenaath will look after you closely. Won't you, Asenaath?'

It was a statement rather than a question, and Asenaath responded with an airy tone. 'Of course, Amio. You know that I will.'

For some reason Neferu did not bother to define, Asenaath's response did not make her feel any happier. Still, she nodded at the pharaoh and smiled her thanks to him. She knew that he had just tried to manoeuvre Asenaath into being a little more friendly. He had shrewdly correctly assessed the ambience between them. He looked at her across the room. 'If you are very tired, Neferu, I am sure that Mereta will excuse you from dinner tonight if you wish, won't you, Mereta?'

Meretamun leaned forward and gave Neferu a concerned look. 'Of course, Neferu. You must be really tired. Amio is right. Perhaps it is best to have an early night tonight. I will check whether your belongings are downstairs or not yet. Let's arrange for you to have a tray in your room this evening.'

Neferu looked gratefully at them.

'You are all so kind.' She was touched by their concern. 'Perhaps it might be wise to have an early night. It has been such a long day,' she answered. The pharaoh nodded kindly and bade her goodnight drily.

Asenaath reminded Meretamun that she was to be away for the following three days to visit her sister, who was expecting a baby any day, and she was anxious to be there for the event. She said reluctantly that she could cancel it if Mereta wished, or she could arrange for the lady-in-waiting, who was to have taken over her duties, to instruct Neferu too. 'No. It won't be necessary,' Mereta said slowly. 'In fact, you may cancel Shenade's transfer from mother's rota. I think Neferu and I can manage alone, can't we?' she looked inquiringly at Neferu, who didn't know what to say.

Asenaath looked at Neferu and said, 'It is only a matter of checking that the housemaid has put the hot water on. Mereta manages everything by herself anyway.'

Neferu nodded. 'I'll try,' she said uncertainly, not even knowing where the bathroom was.

Meretamun smiled. 'Don't worry, Neferu. Everything will be fine.'

After refreshments Mereta instructed Asenaath to show Neferu where the various chambers were and then to take her to rest. She wished her an early goodnight and said she looked forward to seeing her in the morning. Neferu was glad to be back in her room and reflected that it was really a very good thing that destiny had arranged for Asenaath to be absent for a few days. It would give her time to find her feet without that rather supercilious expression following her around everywhere. Just because she spoke with a Lower Egypt accent did not mean she was a country bumpkin. Neferu pulled back the curtains to the adjoining bathroom and was pleasantly surprised to find out that someone had been to heat the water and the room was brightly lit. After a while a maid came to help her bathe, but she sent the girl away, saying that she had always attended to these things herself and would prefer to continue to do so. The maid clearly thought her very eccentric but said nothing.

One of the valets arrived immediately afterwards and supervised the transfer of her luggage from the guest room to the royal block. Neferu strolled over to the royal block again, thanking fate that she had not let the maid begin to bath her. She followed the valet round into the royal garden and continued along the ground floor until they reached the second entrance. Once inside, the major domo greeted her and accompanied her to her suite. She had three large rooms to herself and felt very posh. Both her bedroom and her sitting room looked out onto the royal gardens. The third room looked out onto the inner courtyard. She had her own bathroom and a changing room. 'Yes,' she thought, she could definitely get used to living in a palace.

Neferu set about arranging her few personal objects and then went to investigate the luxurious tub. She dipped her fingers into the water and found it pleasurably warm. Everything around here seemed to be organised with the utmost silence and efficiency. Neferu undressed slowly and let herself sink into the tub. Emptying a small vial of perfumed oil, she let its delicate scent pervade her nostrils. When she got out, she felt that she glowed. She began to wash her hair and rinsed it until the water ran clear. Carefully, she wrapped her head into a big towel, turban style. Soon afterwards, the maid returned with a small tray. Neferu was almost too tired to eat. She took a few bites of an apple, drank a glass of fruit juice and then went to bed. She fell asleep almost as soon as her head touched the pillow.

The following morning Neferu was awoken early by a young maid, and she quickly washed and dressed herself before eating some fruit and having a drink. She left her apartment at the same time as Maatnofret was leaving hers and they met in the corridor. 'Good morning, Neferu. Did you sleep well?' the older woman asked. Neferu answered in the affirmative and they made their way together, exchanging pleasantries, to the stairs leading to the upper storey. On the terrace they separated, Maatnofret turning into the grand queen's suite, while Neferu continued down to Mereta's suite.

On entering she checked that the maid had prepared the bathroom with sufficient hot water before going in to wake Mereta. She shook the girl's thin shoulder gently. 'Good morning, Neferu,' said Mereta sleepily.

'Good morning, Mereta, your bath is ready for you,' she said softly. The princess opened her eyes again and sat up. After a moment she swung her legs over the bed and stood up. Yawning widely, she went through to the bathroom and Neferu followed uncertainly, not quite sure what she was expected to do next. Remembering Asenaath's instructions, she helped the princess to lift off the cotton shift she had as a nightgown.

'It's all right, Neferu. I do everything myself. I prefer it that way.' She saw that Neferu was looking at her pathetically thin body and she grimaced. 'Not pretty, am I?' Neferu averted her gaze quickly. The princess had a slight curvature of the spine. The lower, inner curve was accentuated, forcing her abdomen outwards and her thighs bent inward, making her markedly knock-kneed. Although Neferu did not know it, the princess was showing all the signs of rickets. Neferu did not reply to the princesses' remark. There seemed to be nothing she could say which would not sound either insincere or patronising. The princess looked down at her body, ruefully. 'We are a great disappointment to mother,' she said. Neferu looked puzzled. 'Amio and I,' Mereta explained. 'Amio's condition is worse than mine. That's why he always wears his cloak. He hated people staring at him when he was small.' Neferu nodded. She could well understand why he wore the cloak. She would hate anyone to stare at her if her body was deformed. 'So you see, Neferu, we are not a beautiful family.' There was a note of sadness in Mereta's voice. 'Sometimes I wonder if I will ever find a husband who will love me for myself. I know there are plenty who would marry me for my position.'

Neferu thought that was just dreadfully sad. 'I think that true love conquers everything,' she remarked eventually. 'I hope that is true anyway.'

Not without a little bitterness Mereta replied, 'I think that is easy for you to say, Neferu.' She began to wash herself down vigorously. Neferu was at a loss and so remained silent.

'Well, you do have a very tiny waist and well-shaped breasts,' she said finally, a trifle self-consciously. She was glad that her own limbs were straight and strong.

'What about you, Neferu?' Mereta asked. 'Could you ever fall in love with anyone as misshapen as Amio, for example?' Neferu tried to think honestly. She thought of Demi and his leg, short and badly scarred. She loved him, didn't she? The kind of love one felt for a brother and the kind of love one felt for a husband were different, of course. After careful consideration she came to the conclusion that the difference was merely another aspect of a universal single emotion.

'I could not love even the most handsome man in the whole world if I did not love him as a person. I think that physical attraction alone would soon pall and yes, I do believe that if I loved a man as a person then I could also love him if the physical aspect of him became misshapen. If I met such a person and did not know him at first, I think the personality of him would have to be strong enough for me to see that more than his physical defects. Once I could see past those then they would no longer have any importance.'

'Mmm, I wonder,' said Mereta doubtfully. She seemed satisfied by Neferu's reply and jumped out of the bath. 'I shall have to search out a man who is your male counterpart, Neferu,' she said with irony. ''Have you ever been passionately in love?' Mereta asked her after a pause.

'Well, I have Yussef. I love him,' Neferu answered.

'But are you in love with him passionately?' Mereta asked insistently, drying herself with a soft towel.

'Yes, I think I am,' Neferu replied, slightly confused.

'You only think you are!' said Mereta mockingly.

'Well, I guess I am,' Neferu responded uncertainly, conscious that in her fatigue she had forgotten the five minutes concentrated telepathic communication with Yussef the previous evening. Immediately, she felt guilty.

'What does he look like, this Yussef? Is he handsome?'

Neferu replied with pride. 'Oh, Yes! Everyone says that Yussef is very, very handsome. And he is clever and strong too. He can swim much faster than I can.'

'I would like to meet him sometime,' Mereta said. She eyed Neferu curiously for a moment but did not pursue the matter further. 'Perhaps we'd better get a move on, or we'll be late for breakfast and mother hates that,' she said abruptly, moving towards her dressing table after putting on her clothes.

Neferu hurriedly picked up the hairbrush and began to brush Mereta's hair. It just would not do to be late on her first day. Mereta showed her how to braid her hair but when Neferu tried it did not go well at all. They both looked in the polished mirror in dismay and Neferu begged Mereta to let her do her hair in another style that she knew how to do. 'What style?' Mereta said doubtfully. Neferu told her that it was a style very much in vogue with the important Keftiu women. She told Mereta that she felt sure it would suit her. In the end Mereta agreed.

Neferu brushed Mereta's hair thoroughly again and then backcombed the front and sides. She then pinned this hair up temporarily. She divided the remaining hair into three sections and made a large elaborate figure-of-eight chignon. Taking the brush again she carefully smoothed over the front hair and blended it into the chignon, gently lifting it off the face. She stepped back to admire her handiwork and was very pleased to see that she had given Mereta a completely new look. The new style made her thin face look fuller and was far more flattering than the hard outlines of the braided style she normally wore. Mereta saw her pleased expression and took the mirror. She stared intently at herself and then looked up at Neferu, well satisfied. 'You have managed to make me look almost pretty, Neferu.'

Neferu clapped her hands with pleasure. 'It really suits you,' she said. 'It balances your face much better.'

'It's true,' agreed Mereta, in a pleased tone. 'I think destiny meant you to come here, Neferu.'

'Destiny is in the hands of Helios,' said Neferu.

'Is Helios the Keftiu name for Amun-Re?' asked the princess.

'Yes,' replied Neferu.

'Here in Thebes we think that the Aten is the most powerful god of all,' Mereta informed her.

'The Aten.'

'Yes! The Aten is the breath of all life, and he is the sole creator of the universe.'

'Is the Aten the god of the sun?' Neferu asked.

'Yes. He is the god of the sun and of the moon and of everything else. Grandfather says he is the only god. There is no other god but Aten. In grandfather's language he is called Yahweh.' Mereta spoke with conviction.

'I have never heard of Yahweh-Aten before. It is a strange name,' Neferu found this odd.

'Well, Grandfather is a foreigner. He came to Egypt when he was a young boy and that is the name of the Aten in his language.'

'Oh!' replied Neferu. She wanted to ask where Mereta's grandpa came from. He could not be Keftiu anyway, she knew that. Mereta, however, did not enlighten her further.

'If we are ready, we had better go,' The princess stated. As they left the apartment, they noticed Maatnofret coming in their direction. As soon as she saw them, she turned round, and the two girls exchanged glances. They were late! They began to hurry their steps and Mereta said playfully. 'You had better pray to your god that mother won't eat us!'

The grand queen was seated at the table when they entered. All the rest of the family was there, plus three other ladies and a gentleman. The other ladies were all ladies-in-waiting, Neferu found out on a rather hurried introduction, and the gentleman was the tutor of the young Prince Smenkhenre. The queen raised her eyebrows at the two girls. 'We almost started without you,' she said in a tone of reproof, her eyes taking in Mereta's new hairstyle. Neferu curtsied deeply then almost fell over as Mereta tugged at her arm, pulling her down onto the couch. She blushed crimson and met the glance of Amenophis, who tried to suppress an amused smile as she caught his eye. Did she always have to be such a clumsy clown? she thought with irritation. All that was left now was for her to spill her drink and the introduction would be complete. 'Sorry,' mouthed Mereta silently and Neferu sighed. Fortunately attention was focused on Mereta's new hairstyle, and the incident was quickly forgotten. After due admiration had been expressed, in which Neferu basked in the afterglow, the queen asked, 'Why were you so late? Surely the hairstyle did not take that long?'

'No, Mother,' Mereta answered serenely. 'I am afraid that Neferu and I became so involved in our conversation that we completely forgot the time.'

'Gossiping, I suppose,' said Amenophis teasingly.

'Certainly not!' said Mereta indignantly. 'Intelligent conversation, no less!'

Amenophis smirked slightly, knowing this would irritate his sister.

'I suggest that we get on with eating,' the queen said matter-of-factly.

The meal passed off pleasantly and the young prince asked Neferu if she was interested in seeing his collection of beetles and butterflies. She realised that she was very honoured when Sitamun told her that Smenkh had never offered to show her his collection. The boy flushed slightly and Neferu said quickly that she would love to see them. The boy smiled and his tutor said that the best time would be in the afternoon as they had a lot of work to do that morning. It transpired that Smenkh's knowledge of Akkadian left a lot to be desired. Well, one cannot be good at everything, Neferu told him with an expressive shrug, as if to say 'never mind'. The boy grinned.

At the end of breakfast Ay appeared on the terrace. Smenkh and his tutor were just leaving and Sitamun also excused herself, saying that she was going to visit a friend. Ay looked at the girls and asked them what they had planned for the day. 'We haven't thought yet,' replied Mereta, airily. Amenophis said that he was hunting. They were welcome to come and watch if they wanted. Mereta said she could not imagine a more wonderful way to get covered in dust, but that she would come if Neferu wanted to go.

'I have never seen a hunt before,' answered Neferu carefully.

'What are you going to hunt?' she asked warily.

'Lions,' replied the pharaoh. Neferu's eyes widened. She did not like the sound of that.

'I thought they were very dangerous,' she said cautiously. 'They eat people, don't they?'

Amenophis laughed out loud. 'I won't let them eat you, my dear! I did promise your father I would look after you and I shall. You will be completely safe in a chariot,' Neferu felt sure that this was not going to be her kind of entertainment, but she felt that he expected her to go, and she knew that he was very proud of his hunting ability so, after a quick glance at Mereta, she nodded. Amenophis seemed pleased. He told the girls that he expected them to be ready and in the courtyard in half an hour. 'I must go and prepare my arrows and choose the horses for the chase. Do excuse me, ladies,' he said and inclined his head slightly.

Mereta looked at Neferu merrily. 'I think you might come to regret this experience, Neferu,' she said. 'Don't say that I didn't warn you.' The queen and Ay exchanged glances, smiling slightly, and the group broke up.

The girls strolled back to Mereta's apartment and Mereta said wryly. 'I don't think my new hair style is going to last long unless I take steps to protect it.' The girls looked through the vast wardrobe of clothes and Mereta chose a long scarf of blue silk, which she wrapped around her head and neck. She told Neferu to choose a scarf for herself.

'My hair is firmly in place,' remonstrated Neferu.

'It won't be for long at that speed,' Mereta warned her. With a shrug Neferu chose a long white silk scarf and wrapped it around her head. A trifle vainly she picked up the mirror and admired the effect.

'It's too loose,' said Mereta sensibly. 'It will blow out of those folds in no time.'

Obstinately, Neferu refused to pull it any tighter. She did not want to look absurd after all the other contretemps she had managed to accomplish thus far. Mereta gave a shrug. 'It's up to you,' she said, with a 'wait and see' look. The two girls crossed the inner courtyard a short time later and saw the hunters assembling in the outer courtyard.

'Why did you say I would live to regret this?' Neferu asked curiously.

'Because we are going to end up with half the desert in our mouths and noses,' replied Mereta sarcastically. 'I hope you aren't afraid of horses,' the princess continued.

'No, I don't think so,' answered the Keftiu girl.

When the two of them reached the hunting party, its members seemed to have completed their preparatory tasks. Neferu counted seven chariots and twelve men. Six of these were carrying lethal looking bows and arrows over their shoulders. The other six were the drivers, she thought, and a few minutes later her assumption proved correct. Neferu noticed that the chariot she and Mereta were to use was the only one with seats. When their driver appeared, he was a little old man whom Neferu could not envisage as a hunter. Mereta greeted him affectionately and there was an intimacy between them. She told Neferu that when he was younger, he had been her father's hunt driver. Now his reactions were too slow, but he loved to accompany the hunt with visitors whenever he could. The old retainer greeted Neferu with a warm smile and he assisted the girls into the chariot. Finally, the entourage left through the palace gates with the pharaoh's chariot leading at a smart trot. In their chariot Neferu noticed a number of hide water bottles and a basket of fruit. Mereta explained that the hunt was very hot and thirsty work in the morning sun and the men were always dry at the end of it.

Behind the pharaoh's chariot and in front of their own was the chariot of Pararameses and his driver. Behind the girls, the other four chariots kept at a safe distance from each other and went in single file through the narrow streets of the city. Neferu noticed that one of the hunt members was Sinefrew, the brother of Asenaath. The others were unknown to her. The princess told her that they were all members of the Kap.

'Where do the lions come from?' Neferu asked curiously.

'From deep in the hinterland where the people have black skin. The Nubians bring them in cages,' Mereta told her. Neferu digested this information and then asked where the animals were kept. The princess did not know but told her that they had to be fed with red meat every day to stay healthy and that Amio had told her that the animals were starved the day before the hunt to make them aggressive. Neferu felt disgust. Privately she thought this both cruel and dangerous, but did not voice her opinion.

Neferu looked about her with interest, watching the citizens of Thebes going about their business. Soon they reached the outskirts of the city, and the hovels of the very poorest people came into view. Here the women were dressed in black from head to foot and there were small children all around. Presently they had passed these outer limits too and were on the edge of the desert proper. The scrub and the sandy ground underneath them was hard and rocky. Ahead of them a large cage came into view. It was on four wheels and pulled by four horses. As they approached, the driver freed the horses and mounted one. His companion mounted another, and they rode away, each holding the reins of the other two horses.

The hunters rode up close to view the lions, but the girl's chariot stayed well back. After some animated discussion the other chariots also pulled back and set themselves into line to await the release of the lions. A man whom Neferu had not previously noticed stepped from behind the cage and with agility climbed to the top of it. From the top he pulled up a side of the cage. Almost immediately one of the lions jumped out snarling. Neferu felt her heart beat faster. The creature made off into the desert at a loping pace. Soon it was followed by the other three beasts. The huntsmen made no haste to follow them, to Neferu's surprise.

Amenophis came over to the girls and explained that Neferu could join his chariot if she wished, and that way she would have the best view. He then tried to persuade Mereta to join Pararameses. At first she declined, saying that she hated the speed at which they travelled, but when Pararameses came over too, she eventually allowed herself to be persuaded. Now that she had seen the lions, Neferu was not at all keen to join the hunting chariot. She did not want to dampen the atmosphere, however, so even though she felt scared she put on a brave face and followed Amenophis. He explained that it was possible that with the weight of an extra person in the chariot, they would be slowed down enough that they might not be able to get a kill today. Neferu swallowed. She sincerely hoped that would be the case, but she merely smiled sympathetically at him. The young pharaoh helped her into the chariot and showed her the bar in front onto which she must hold tightly with both hands. She was so close to him now that she could smell his skin. It was a clean, slightly fragrant, masculine smell. She felt aware of him as a man. She looked away embarrassed as he noticed her looking at him. He did not seem put out and merely smiled slightly. It was very hot now and she could feel the perspiration above her lip. The glare of the sun was so strong that she had to screw up her eyes to see anything.

The hunt got underway, and they were off. Gradually the speed of the chariots built up and it was difficult for Neferu to see the lions, who were almost the same colour as the sand. They seemed to have disappeared. Her headscarf flew open, but she could do nothing about it at that speed. She dared not let go of the rail in front of her. She could hear the constant flap of the silk behind her.

'What will you do if the lions escape into the desert?' she had to shout to make herself heard in the thunder of all the chariot wheels. 'The horses won't be able to follow them into the desert proper,' she shouted.

'They won't go that far,' yelled Amenophis back to her. 'They are thirsty, they will try to keep within close distance to the river.' She saw that made sense and noticed his exhilaration. He was enjoying himself. The wind was blowing his straight black hair everywhere and his normally pale cheeks were tinged pink with the excitement of the speed of the chase. He smiled at her, and she responded before being temporarily blinded by the collapse of her chignon and her hair blowing everywhere. She shook her head backwards as best she could, to try to flick the hair out of her face. For a moment she was tempted to take one hand off the rail but had second thoughts.

Neferu noticed that Amenophis seemed adept at staying upright without holding onto the rail. He had had plenty of practice, of course. All the chariots seemed to be neck and neck now and it was a bumpy ride over the small rocks on this semi-desert. Amenophis shouted to her that the aim was to kill the lion with one blow if possible so that the animal would not suffer. Neferu began to feel a bit queasy. She was not sure whether it was from the jolting ride or the thought of the coming kill. He shouted something to her, but she caught only a part of it as he turned to the left and back as the chariot swerved, trying to get the first lion into the best line of shot. Neferu felt her teeth rattling in her head from the jerky movements of the vehicle and suddenly she was at an angle where she could see the lion panting as it ran for its life. The chariot suddenly swerved abruptly again and Amenophis stumbled against her, losing his aim. She put out an arm to steady him as he fell against her, and their eyes met for what seemed a long moment before he quickly regained his equilibrium and retrained his aim. This time he was too late, and it was one of the others who shot first. The arrow went deep into the lion's skull between those wild staring eyes, and it fell over. Amenophis clicked his tongue in annoyance and shouted to the driver to go after the other lion which was about a hundred and fifty metres away. Neferu noticed that a second lion far away to their left had fallen prey to an arrow from one of the other chariots. The chariot swerved again as they set off in pursuit of the one nearest to them and she lost sight of the others, who were now behind them.

Seemingly from out of nowhere, the chariot of Pararameses came up on their right and a furious race began. Neferu noticed that Mereta's scarf was still in position, though she looked anything but comfortable, in spite of that. She was gripping the rail and her face was screwed up against the glare. Mereta had known what she was talking about, Neferu thought. Next time she would heed her.

Suddenly it was all over. Pararameses bagged the lion with a direct hit, and it made a half somersault before falling heavily to the ground. A stain of red blood began to ooze from around the arrow in its chest. It was still alive. Neferu looked away quickly, shivering in spite of the heat. When she looked again, the animal was dead. The general had finished it off with an arrow between the eyes. Amenophis shrugged his shoulders ruefully. 'It seems that the gods are not with me today,' he said.

'I'm glad!' said Neferu vehemently.

'Why?' he asked in surprise.

'I think it is very cruel to kill anything for the pleasure of it.' She felt herself almost on the verge of tears.

Amenophis was noticeably taken aback. 'Do you think I am cruel?' he asked, looking at her obliquely.

She shook her head. 'No. I think you have not considered the matter, that's all.' He looked at her silently then abruptly stretched out his arm and smoothed the hair out of her eyes. She put up her hand and felt the hair straggling all over the place. She noticed that she was still gripping the rail tightly with her right hand and she became aware that she must look a complete mess. He said nothing, just watching her as she removed those pins which had not already fallen out.

'Do you like my sister?' he asked suddenly.

Neferu was startled by the sudden change of subject. 'Mereta?' she inquired, somewhat superfluously. 'Yes. I do like her. She seems to be a very kind person,' she replied.

'She likes you too,' he admitted. He hesitated. 'It is very difficult to find sincere and trusty friends if you belong to the royal family. There are so many people who are willing to abuse our friendship. I am pleased that you get on so well.' Neferu nodded, recognising that his words must be true.

'Do you like me, or do you find me repulsive to look at?' he asked coolly. Neferu was totally shocked by his words. She wished he would stop doing this to her. She looked down, away from his piercing gaze while she tried to collect her thoughts.

Looking up again she answered carefully, looking him straight in the eyes, 'No, I don't find you repulsive to look at and yes, I do like you as far as I know you.'

He smiled. 'Good,' he said briskly. Because I would like us to be good friends too. Will you be my friend?'

She smiled. 'I would like to be your friend, sire,' she replied.

'My name is Amio,' he said looking intently into her eyes. 'Say it!'

'Amio,' she said obediently. The name sounded strange on her lips.

'Good,' he said once again. They could speak no more then as the others joined them.

There was much laughing and explaining amongst the men as they drank the water and ate the fruit, standing and leaning against the chariots. 'I did tell you, didn't I?' Mereta groaned.

Neferu laughed and admitted that she had been right. 'Yes! I don't think I will be coming on any more of these expeditions, but it was an experience, I suppose!'

'Didn't you enjoy it?' Mereta asked.

'Not really,' Neferu replied with a shake of her head. 'The worst bit was the killing of the poor lion. I thought that was horrible.'

'My sentiments entirely,' Mereta said with a grimace. 'I expect Amio is furious at not getting a hit,' she continued, glancing at her brother.

'Annoyed, I think, but not furious,' Neferu commented. Mereta merely smiled by way of reply. Back at Malkata, the dusty group settled down to a hearty lunch still in their soiled garb. Amio commented to Neferu that he always felt that the meal tasted much better after the strenuous activity of the hunt.

'I rather thought it was the poor lions who had the strenuous activity,' she said ironically.

He burst out laughing. 'Witty as well as beautiful, are we?'

Neferu blushed. He had an answer for everything this man.

After dining, Neferu accompanied Mereta back to her apartment. The housemaid had prepared the bathroom and the princess bathed and washed her hair. Afterwards Mereta insisted that Neferu should use her bathroom too. The maid returned and refilled the tub and the pitchers. Neferu stripped and climbed in. As she washed herself the two girls chatted. 'I wish I was as beautiful as you, Neferu,' Mereta said, almost re-echoing their conversation of the morning.

'Grandma says that beauty is in the eye of the beholder,' Neferu replied. Mereta nodded. She could see the sense in that, but it was not exactly what she had had in mind.

'What should I do if I meet a handsome man and fall in love with him? How could I get him to fall in love with me?' she asked insistently. Neferu considered the matter with all the accumulated wisdom of an almost-sixteen-year-old.

'Well, first of all, if I were you, I would arrange to be in regular casual contact at first until he began to see you as a friend and got used to seeing you around. Then you would always have to be charming to him and let him see how interesting and intelligent you are. Just to be on the safe side you should pray to the god who created everything, your Aten. He will make the young man fall in love with you if all else fails.'

Mereta laughed with genuine amusement. 'I will try it when I meet the man of my dreams,' she said.

The princess yawned. Neferu got out of the tub and washed her hair. She wrapped a towel round her head and then suddenly thought.

'I'll have to borrow something to go downstairs in,' she said.

'Take your pick!' said Mereta, waving her hand toward the wardrobe from which Neferu took a comfortable cotton shift.

'I will miss you when I go home, Mereta,' she said fondly.

Mereta looked startled. 'Go home?' she echoed.

'I meant at the end of the month,' Neferu said reassuringly.

Mereta lowered her eyes with an enigmatic look. 'Oh, yes!' she said neutrally. She yawned again. 'I'm going for my snooze, Neferu, and I suggest that you do too.' Neferu nodded. The yawn was infectious, and she too felt very tired. She removed the wet towel from her head.

'See you later, Mereta,' she said as the princess climbed into bed.

'See you later, Neferu,' the other girl replied.

Neferu walked across the terrace and down to her apartment. The sun was at its highest now and there was a shimmering haze over the garden. She could feel her hair drying already in its heat. When Neferu climbed into bed she lay on her side with her hand under her cheek. She thought she would analyse the events of the day for a while but, within seconds, she was asleep.

CHAPTER 10

By Neferu's standards, the queen's chief lady-in-waiting was a middle-aged lady. Maatnofret was, in fact, slightly over thirty-six and was a cousin of Tiya. Maatnofret's father had been the brother of Tuya, the wife of Yuya, the previous grand vizier to Ay. Maatnofret was, in turn, married to one of her distant cousins, Paranefer. Her family originated from On in the north of Egypt where her paternal grandfather had held the position of high priest at the temple.

The family had been surprised when the Hebrew Yussef had made an offer for the hand of her aunt Asenaath, who was the daughter of the high priest of Amun-Re. Although he was a foreigner and a believer in a god they had never heard of before, he held the most important office in the land after pharaoh, that of grand vizier. He was handsome and sincere to boot and therefore they considered him a good catch for their daughter. Of course, it was unfortunate about the religious aspect, but Asenaath's father thought that a little judicious massaging of the facts would suitably blur the differences from any nosy outsider. It could not be doubted that the young pair were in love. The young vizier was stickler for matters of conscience but knew that it would be frowned upon for him to bring a wife from his own tribe so close to the throne. The old high priest had congratulated himself on the success of their compromises. Asenaath had taken her husband's religion privately and changed her name accordingly to denote her following of her husband's god, but had not made a public noise about it. No one could doubt her Egyptian origin or the high status of her family.

The marriage had been a happy one, blessed with two sons: Manasseh, who had died in early adulthood, leaving a daughter but no son; a second son, Ephraim, known publicly as Ay, had married and produced a daughter, Mutnedjmet, but no son. Yussef's only daughter, Tiya, had been his crowning success and had married the pharaoh Amenophis III. Maatnofret was therefore the product of a mixed heritage that had survived and flourished in the relatively peaceful culture of Egypt.

In northern Egypt where the Hyksos had reigned for nearly two-hundred years there had naturally been a fair amount of interaction between them and the Egyptians they had subjugated. In time a more positive situation had arisen with some intermarriage and a general lessening of hostilities. Because of this the very area that had been under occupation was also the area that, in time, developed the most tolerance to these Semites. Southern Egypt, on the other hand, had been the military centre of the struggle to drive them out of Egypt and here a fanatical hatred of the Hyksos had been constantly fuelled by the feeling of exile from their former home territories. Consequently, the Semites were still regarded as potential enemies even then, nearly two-hundred years after their expulsion from Egypt. There were many mixed families in northern Egypt but almost none in the south. To be Hebrew here was to be akin to the hated Hyksos, illogical though this was. As Smenkhenre had already intimated to Neferu, even the royal family was not immune to suspicion on this score and Ay, for one, had to do a lot of diplomatic work to alleviate the situation. He was, for instance, extremely strict about their flaunting of their belief in the Aten and was constantly warning his sister Tiya on this score. Like his father he never used his Hebrew name but had assumed Ay as a compromise because it contained the element of Ya, but had no connotations of heresy to the usual Egyptians they came into contact with. If the capital had been in Memphis as in the old days, life would have been much easier as there were many old, aristocratic families who were in a similar position. Ay personally would have preferred to live in Memphis with its more tolerant maritime and cosmopolitan atmosphere. To have transferred the court there would, however, have caused a political upheaval whose consequences might have been dramatic in view of the percentage of high-ranking Nubians in the army, for whom Thebes was their home ground. He knew that the prosperity of life in the Nile delta far outranked that of the arid Thebes region, which was being artificially fed from the more fertile north, and he knew that sometime in the future the north would have to gain ascendancy once again. Already, for some decades there had been grumbles about the draining of resources to the arid south.

Now that the enemy had been expelled from Egypt there was no real reason for the southerners to be constant receivers of northern largesse anymore. It was a delicate political balance for Ay and his personal inclinations were with the north, but he also knew that he could make no move without the backing of the army and that would not be forthcoming. He had occasionally mentioned a halfway compromise with them and with his nephew. That of the building of a new city halfway between Memphis and

Thebes. It would function as a major army base and store depot and be far enough away from the delta area in time of war for there to be no danger of it being invaded. The plan had aroused little sympathy, however, as at four-hundred kilometres from Memphis and the fertile areas, it would still suffer all the problems of self-sufficiency as Thebes. The project had been abandoned some years previously, but the problems remained, and Ay knew that eventually they would have to be dealt with. He hoped the crisis would not occur during his lifetime.

Amun had been the god central to Egyptian culture for thousands of years. He was always depicted with the head of a ram, which represented his star position in the sky as Aries. The earth was in the constellation of Aries at that time. Re was the god of the sun, and during the separation of Upper from Lower Egypt, his position had become increasingly important in the north, where a large influx of Greek refugees from Caphtor and many other of the Greek islands had brought with them their history of worship of their sun god Helios. Their beliefs were so close that Helios and Re had become synonymous and the worship of Amun had declined. This was not good news for the priesthood of Amun in the south as it represented a dangerous loss of power. To combat this a loose duo system had been set up to conveniently absorb all opinions under the one priesthood power grouping and it functioned quite well as it necessarily implied a loosening of rules and attempts to accommodate differences. Yussef the Hebrew had been able to take advantage of this politically expedient situation. The danger was that times of tolerance are often followed by periods of repression and intolerance, and never more so than in times of political or economic instability. All the religious sects were, however, under obligation to recognise the roles of Horus, Isis and Seti, which were central to the theme of being Egyptian.

In this legend, Horus the good king-god of creation was killed by his brother Seti, who wanted both the power of Horus and Isis, the sister-wife of Horus. In order that Horus could have no afterlife, Seti dismembered his body and scattered all the parts over the Two Lands. The grief-stricken Isis refused Seti and set about collecting all the parts of Horus together so that they could be united in an afterlife. She managed to find them all except one, his phallus. Because of this Horus was able to live in the afterlife but Seti retained part of the power of Horus, which included the power over death. Until the final part of Horus is found, all human beings must die and be laid to rest. The afterlife they saw as a pale but similar condition to earthly life. Immortality would only return to them when Horus was restored to his full strength. To Maatnofret, all these things

were part of her heritage and thus second nature to her. If she thought to question any
of the precepts which ordered her life, she did not do so out loud. She was a kind and
tolerant woman who had never been able to have a child herself and who sublimated her
maternal instincts in the care of others. For all these reasons she was an exceptionally
popular person at court and was able to interact harmoniously with everyone seemingly.
At that time, the future of her friendship with Neferu was still an unknown chapter, and
their acquaintanceship was only just beginning. Thus it was that just after three o'clock
Maatnofret slipped into Neferu's chamber to wake the girl. 'Are you awake, Neferu? I
couldn't hear any sounds, so I thought I had better check.'

Neferu forced her eyes open and squinted through them at the lady-in-waiting. 'Oh,
am I late?' she said, sitting up suddenly.

'No, no! There is plenty of time, don't worry,' the other woman replied serenely. 'I just
came to see how you are getting on, as we haven't had much time to chat.'

Neferu swung her legs over the side of the bed before replying. 'I'm not quite sure. All
right, I suppose, but I think everyone is of the opinion that I'm a total country bumpkin,'
she said ruefully.

Maatnofret chuckled. 'Oh, I don't think so, Neferu,' she replied. 'How are you getting
on with Asenaath? She can be a bit difficult, that one,' she continued.

To Maatnofret's amusement, Neferu rolled her eyes. 'I sense that she resents me very
much, but so far it hasn't been too much of a problem because she is away and won't be
returning until tomorrow night.'

Maatnofret meditated for a moment over this information. 'Well, it shouldn't prove
too difficult because you will rotate your shifts so that you will never really meet apart
from mealtimes, and not always even then.'

This was welcome news and cheered Neferu up no end. She didn't want to show her
relief too openly, however, so she merely asked, 'How is that, Maatnofret?'

Maatnofret gave her a quick look, not at all fooled by Neferu's apparent meekness.
'Well, at the moment Asenaath lives with her family in one of the villas just within the
walls of the palace complex, so that when she is off duty she usually spends her time
with them. Secondly, I happen to know, and this is confidential, Neferu,' here she shot a
warning look at Neferu, who nodded vigorously to show that she would remain silent,
'that one of the pharaoh's distant cousins has requested her hand in marriage.'

'Oh,' was all that Neferu could think to say to this undeniably interesting news.

'The man in question is one of the army commanders, and he is based in Kush, and

I think Kush is just the right place for Asenaath,' Maatnofret said cynically, with a smile.

Neferu burst out laughing. She adored this woman already. 'I never would have thought that you had such a nasty streak, Maatnofret,' she commented lightly.

'Oh, I can do much better than that when I really try,' the lady-in-waiting said with emphasis on the word 'try'. 'But, Neferu, in the meantime you had better watch your step. She has got a very poisonous tongue and she may be very jealous if she feels that Mereta likes you more than her.'

Neferu nodded. She had felt the same herself and she knew that the warning was kindly meant, and it served to reinforce her own intuition.

'Thank you for the warning, Maatnofret. I will be careful.'

'Good,' replied the other. 'I think I'd better get a move on or well both be late.' She stood up to go but stopped when Neferu called her name. 'What is it, Neferu?' she said, turning again to look at the Keftiu girl.

'Thank you for being my friend, and will you come again to talk to me?' Neferu asked shyly.

Maatnofret smiled. 'Of course! I'd love to,' she said and then continued, 'You must come and spend an evening with us when you are free. You'll like my husband, Paranefer. He is very down to earth and good at sussing out what people are really like.'

'He is Amio's personal valet, isn't he?' asked Neferu with a slight hesitation. She did not wish to be thought impertinent.

'Yes,' responded Maatnofret. 'And he is chief scribe and architect to the queen.'

'He must be very clever then,' said Neferu on considering this information.

'Yes, he is, and he is a good man,' Maatnofret said with a proud smile. Then, with a mischievous laugh, she added, 'But how could he not be with such a good wife as me?' Neferu burst into a peel of laughter which resounded round the room. 'Bye, Neferu. See you later,' Maatnofret said, and with that was gone. Neferu jumped up cheerily to complete her tasks, knowing that she had a friend.

When Neferu and Mereta were ready, they made their way down to the gardens where Ay's wife had arranged refreshments for them. Even the older pharaoh was present and affably chatting to his wife. It was the first time that Neferu had occasion to speak to him, and she noticed that the pupils of his eyes were tiny and that his eyes had a very glassy look. He ate very little and appeared sleepy. Teya appeared very concerned about him and when he excused himself, she accompanied him to the suite of rooms directly below theirs on the ground floor. Neferu was consumed with curiosity. So, the elder pharaoh was her neighbour. Did he and the queen not live together then? It seemed a very strange set-up to the Keftiu girl. There was no one whom she dared to ask though, so her curiosity remained unwhetted. When the royal couple had departed, they all sat down again and Mereta said privately to Neferu, in a low tone. 'Father is ill.'

'I hope it isn't anything serious,' Neferu replied.

Mereta shrugged enigmatically and said, 'One never knows!' With that she turned aside and began to chat to Teya, her aunt, who had just re-seated herself.

Ay caught her eye and indicated that she should go and sit beside him. She did so and he asked her charmingly, 'How did you enjoy the hunt today, little one?' Neferu looked at Amio, not wanting to hurt his feelings, but he was chatting familiarly with Shenade, the middle-aged lady-in-waiting who shared her duties to Tiya with Maatnofret. He did not appear to be listening. Ay noticed her sideways glance.

'I don't think I really care for hunting,' she said truthfully, in a low voice.

Ay laughed a deep-throated laugh. 'I don't care for these hunting games myself,' he declared. 'You get hot, bothered and covered in sand.' Neferu smiled. He was an understanding audience. After passing a few more pleasantries with her he rose to depart, telling her that he had work to attend to but hoped he would see her again that evening after dinner. Neferu looked after the small, thin, but authoritarian figure as he walked away. 'Uncle Ay', as Mereta called him, had a certain charm, although he was not a handsome man. Perhaps he had been when he was younger, but now, in his mid-thirties, his face was rather thin and sallow. He was without doubt, much more approachable and easier to talk to than his regal, rather cold sister who was every inch the grand queen. Neferu found that she could respond more normally to him than to all the others except Mereta. From the things he said, Neferu knew that the grand vizier prided himself on his knowledge and intuition concerning people, considering himself an expert on human nature.

Refreshments over, Neferu and Mereta made their way across the lawns of the gardens to the lotus pool. The sun was not so hot now and it was very pleasant. Neferu felt vaguely disappointed, though she did not know why unless it was that Amio had not spoken to her during refreshments at all, other than to give her a nonchalant smile. For some reason she felt herself slighted. She then felt irritated with herself. She would be going home soon. There was no point in letting these people get under her skin. With the thought of home came the realisation of how quickly time was passing at court. This was her third day here, and so far she had not had time to think about the family for more than a few minutes. Already she felt as though she had lived here for ages. In front of the pool Neferu stopped and looked longingly at the water.

'What are you thinking of, Neferu?' Mereta asked quietly.

'I was just thinking how lovely it would be to jump in and just swim up and down, up and down,' Neferu answered.

'Oh!' said Mereta. 'I can't swim. I would be afraid.'

Neferu looked at the princess in genuine surprise. 'You can't swim? I will have to teach you. It is very easy once you get the hang of it, and it is so much fun.'

'Is it really?' she sounded interested.

'Oh, yes! We go swimming every year in the summer,' Neferu spoke enthusiastically.

'Where do you go to?' asked the princess.

'Grandpa has an old family villa on the coast near Rashid,' she explained. 'His parents used to live in it when they were first married, and he was born there. Nowadays it is mostly empty except when Uncle Giorgios puts up guests there or we go to spend the hottest summer months. Uncle Giorgios has a big shop in Rashid, and they live there nowadays, but they have an old villa on the cliff tops too and when we were small, we all used to spend the summers together. It was such fun.' She became aware that her voice sounded wistful and stopped abruptly. She didn't want to bore the princess with the minutiae of her own life. The princess looked interested, however, and asked her to tell her more.

'We used to go swimming every morning,' she continued, more briskly. 'The beach nearest to us has a little sheltered cove so there is always some shade to be had. Grandma would pack a lunch basket for us with fruit and juice and we always put the basket in the shallow cave in the cliff to keep it cool. We used to have swimming races out to the rock. Yussef would win mostly but I did win one now and again. I think he might have let me,' she said laughing. She looked down at the clear water of the lily pool again and a great pool of homesickness welled up in her. Suddenly tears began to course down her cheeks, although she made no sound.

'Neferu, I didn't mean to upset you,' she heard Mereta say anxiously.

Neferu wiped her eyes roughly with the back of her hand and laughed at herself. 'I am a silly prune,' she said. 'At the end of the month they will all be coming to get me. It was just that I had a strange feeling that I would never go back there and never feel that tangy salt taste of the sea on my lips again. I just got carried away,' she apologised, smiling at Mereta. 'Grandma says I have too vivid an imagination. She says it is the

Keftiu in me. The Keftiu always have been a sea-going people and it is true that I love the sea,' confided Neferu.

'Say something in Keftiu for me,' Mereta requested with a smile.

Neferu frowned. 'What shall I say?' she asked, at a loss.

'Say "Mereta is my friend, and I will teach her how to swim."'

Neferu obliged and Mereta listened intently, with her head to one side slightly. 'It sounds a pleasant language,' she conceded, after giving it a little thought.

Neferu felt pleased. 'If I were staying longer, I would teach you how to speak Keftiu,' she stated magnanimously.

'If you stay longer, I promise to try and learn,' Mereta said slyly.

Neferu laughed at the other girl's guile and leaned forward and hugged her. 'I've never had a sister,' she said simply. 'I always wanted one. We can be like sisters. When I go home you can come and visit me.' Mereta nodded but made no reply. Instead, she pointed to the big red ball which was almost filling the sky over the horizon.

'It will be dark very soon. Shall we go in?'

They strolled back towards the main building and the stairs. Inside the living quarters they could see the servants already starting to light the oil lamps. Once inside Mereta said, 'Choose a dress for this evening, Neferu. I have spoken to mother, and she has arranged for the dressmaker to come to measure you tomorrow. It might be a few days yet though before she is able to complete the order.' Neferu picked out a simple shift in a crepe material in pale rose. It was a colour she had never worn before, but she liked it.

'This is pretty,' she said. 'I would like to wear this.' She held the dress up against herself.

Mereta looked and then said, 'It really does suit you. The only thing is that I have worn that dress several times and some of the ladies of the court don't have very nice manners. I don't want any of them sniggering at you because they have seen me in it before. Some of them are bitches!' she said candidly. Neferu was touched by the kind thought behind these straightforward words. It showed that the girl had a nature sensitive to the feelings of others. Mereta checked through the wardrobe impatiently. 'This, this and this. These are all unworn,' she said in a businesslike fashion. Neferu chose a pale blue damask cotton dress with a lace-covered bodice. It was very closely fitting to show off the bust line and it gently curved outwards in a soft A-line.

'I would like to wear this one if it fits me,' she said.

'Yes. It is pretty, that one!' Mereta said approvingly. 'Try it on!' Neferu tried on the dress. It was a tiny bit tight across the bosom, but Mereta felt it was acceptable. 'It only defines your bosom better,' she said. 'I think it looks very good.' The matter was decided and Neferu took the dress off again and laid it carefully across the couch ready for after her bath.

'You don't think it's too daring, off one shoulder like that?' Thinking of Grandma, she glanced down at the dress again and then doubtfully at Mereta. 'Grandma would have forty fits if she saw it,' she admitted.

Mereta's laugh rang out loudly. 'You are very safe with me, Neferu. I am a good chaperone, and I won't tell her!'

Neferu smiled. 'What will you wear tonight, Mereta?' she asked.

'I don't know. What do you suggest?' Eventually they chose a creamy dress of heavy silk which flattered Mereta's olive complexion well. These important decisions made, Mereta told Neferu that she was free until just before dinner, when she would like her to come and do her hair for her. Neferu promised to come in good time and left with the three dresses that Mereta had given her. On the terrace it was already very dark, and the temperature was much cooler. She was a little afraid of the dark, so as she walked she sang an old Keftiu song to keep herself company.

Neferu did not see him, but Amio was standing on the terrace further down, just outside his own suite. He watched her as she walked along quickly, singing to herself. Intuitively, he guessed that she was scared of the dark. He vaguely remembered doing something similar as a child and he smiled at the thought. A moment later he entered his sister's apartment.

At about half-past six, Neferu twirled before Maatnofret for a final word of approval and then left her apartment to go upstairs. She skilfully arranged Mereta's hair, and they set off for dinner, which was to be held in the state banquet hall that night to honour the arrival of several foreign emissaries. In the large hall she wondered where she would be seated. She knew that as a non-royal she could not expect to be seated close to Mereta and she was afraid of being put between absolute strangers. Mereta noticed her nervousness. 'Don't be afraid, Neferu. You will be sitting next to me.'

Neferu was very surprised but glad that she would not be with anyone strange. She wondered, however, if it would cause a stir, because she had already noticed some hard looks from some of the still unfamiliar courtiers and their wives. She felt very much an upstart.

At the table she was placed next to Ay and Mereta. Next to the grand vizier on her right was his wife, the royal nurse, Teya. Opposite to Neferu was seated General

Pararameses and his fiancé, whom she had not yet met. An informal introduction over the table was made and Neferu smiled at the girl shyly. On the other side of Pararameses was Mutnedjmet. Seated at a higher table were the two pharaohs and the grand queen, with their guests the royal emissaries from Byblos and Mitanni.

During the meal Neferu noticed that she was the subject of several half-veiled glances, but Ay kept her so well entertained in his witty and amusing manner that she was not able to dwell on them. What she had feared as a difficult social test became an enjoyable meal in a friendly atmosphere. It was a lively and amusing little group and she thoroughly enjoyed it. She felt grateful for the generous admiration of Ay, which she was sure was a purposeful strategy on his part so that others would perceive that she was in favour. This instinctive guess was confirmed when Mereta whispered to her.

'Now no one will dare be rude to you, Neferu. They are all afraid of Uncle Ay.' Neferu could not imagine why.

When the queen and her lady-in-waiting rose, all the ladies followed her through to the withdrawing room while the men were served their after-dinner drinks. Neferu was introduced to several more of the court ladies, some of whom seemed very pleasant and some whom she felt were decidedly less so. She was graciously received by everyone, however, thanks to the grand vizier.

Later the gentlemen rejoined them and again Ay made a point of singling her out and paying her a great deal of attention. There was a hubbub of conversation in the room and Neferu guessed that perhaps more than a hundred people were present. When Amio came over to her little group he said playfully, 'It seems, Nefertiti, that you have become my uncle's favourite.' His remark came clearly just as a lull occurred in the conversation. Several eyes turned upon her and Neferu felt herself blush. Ay turned an amused glance at her and said, 'Have you no finesse, sire? Could you not spare the blushes of the subject of my admiration?'

Amenophis smiled good-naturedly at Neferu. 'I did not mean to embarrass you, Nefertiti. I hope that I am forgiven?'

Poor Neferu blushed even more. 'I forgive you, sire,' she said quietly. She gazed from Ay to Amio. Did she detect some kind of subterfuge or was it her imagination? They both smiled at her just a fraction longer than the adjective 'innocently' could fairly be used to describe. She was left to grope around in the recesses of her mind at some grey, obscure question mark which had begun to form.

Amio turned his attention to someone else and Ay excused himself, leaving Neferu to address herself to the remarks of Pararameses, who was politely inquiring how she had enjoyed the hunt. She responded animatedly in her desire to prove that she was not so easily put out. She wished she could get rid of this revolting habit of blushing whenever she was caught off guard.

Later Neferu and Mereta were called to pay their compliments to the queen, and she began to realise that the queen was also in on 'this', whatever it was. She definitely had a twinkle in her eyes. Neferu looked twice to make sure. The queen's eyes did not normally twinkle, at least not at her.

'What a superb dress you are wearing, my dear. It is very becoming,' the queen remarked admiringly.

Neferu felt her eyes almost pop out of her head. She wondered how to react. Finally, she decided that she too would play a supporting role in this strange act. She curtsied again and replied nonchalantly, 'I'm so glad you like it, Your Majesty. I must say I love it myself. It is one of the nicest gowns I have ever worn. You don't think it is perhaps a little tight across the chest?' She stopped, wondering if she had overdone the little charade. No one else appeared to have noticed anything. The queen's mouth had twitched upwards in an involuntary ghost of a smile.

'Not at all, my dear. It seems just right.' She gave Neferu a piercing look, as if to say 'perhaps she is not a complete goose, after all.'

Several inquisitive ladies came over to her and she answered them coolly, determined not to give away anything about herself. Shortly she was joined by Ay again, this time with his wife. Maybe it was a ploy, but she did feel that he was genuinely fond of her as well. When the grand vizier retreated once again, they were joined by Amio, who apologised again for teasing her. He told her gallantly that she looked beautiful in her gown, though he did not like it quite as much as the one she had worn on her first day at the palace. He had said it sincerely. Neferu smiled with pleasure. Grandma and Aunt Lea would be thrilled when she told them. It was a great compliment to them. She looked again to make sure he was not teasing her. He was smiling at her with a real warmth in his eyes. After that he too rose and began to circulate once more and Pararameses took his place.

Some might have thought Pararameses too straightforward and down to earth with his military bearing and his intelligent eyes, which missed nothing. He was a serious man by nature, and he did not put on airs and graces. He seemed to be genuinely what he was, and she liked that about him. He was not a person to turn on the charm, but she felt he was the kind of person you could trust. He in turn seemed to sense her approbation and treated her with a gentle respect, which was quite independent of her position but which he would have accorded her anyway.

Pararameses informed her that he had been put in command of an army battalion operating across the border in Palestine to the east, to quell some unruly tribes amongst the Hebrews and the Palestinians who kept challenging Egypt's authority by not paying their taxes. He was to leave the following decan. Neferu did not really understand what was going on, but she told him she liked him and would miss his presence. She told him that she would probably be gone by the time he got back but she hoped that they would meet again some time. He smiled and said that he was sure that they would. Bowing low, he took his leave of them and returned to join his fiancé and some others unknown to her.

Next in succession came Mereta, who had been waylaid by friends earlier. Mereta told her that the queen was very pleased with her and that she had heard many admiring remarks from the others. The princess attempted to roll her elongated almond eyes dramatically and hissed, 'They are all green with envy because you are so beautiful.'

'Mereta, please be quiet,' Neferu whispered, but the princess only laughed. Neferu looked across at Amenophis, who was seated on a couch and chatting with a pretty, rather elegant girl. 'Who is that girl with your brother?' she asked casually.

'Oh, she is the girl Amio used to be in love with before his affair with Asenaath. She used to lead him a real dance, so he ended the relationship,' Mereta replied, having glanced over her shoulder to see whom Neferu was referring to. Neferu was shocked. Asenaath had been Amio's lover? She suddenly remembered the easy familiarity between them. This girl too. For some reason she felt jealous. Why she should, she could not imagine. She was not in love with him herself. The sensation jarred her nerves. Mereta seemed unaware of her discomfort and continued. 'I think Asenaath would have liked to have become queen, but I don't think she really loved Amio, and he knew it. It cooled down ages ago.' It seemed to Neferu that Amio was quite a fickle person; she felt disappointed in him. Why did it annoy her so much?

'Has Amio had many lovers?' she bit her lip at having voiced such an impertinent question. It was none of her business. Still, she had made her voice as neutral as possible, so it sounded more like a point of minor interest rather than a deep question.

'Quite a few, but no one lately,' Mereta conceded. Now Neferu was really annoyed with herself for her cheap curiosity. What an idiotic question, she thought, of course women would be flocking to sleep with the pharaoh. Probably most of the women in this room had designs on the crown and he, no doubt, could not be blamed for accepting the privileges of his position. All the same some of the shine went off him for her. She knew she would hate to be used like that. 'I'll go and ask Amio to sing for us,' Mereta informed her. She walked over to her brother and, bending low, spoke quietly into his ear. His companion rose and went to bring a lyre that was one of several in a corner of the room. Mereta came back to Neferu and asked her to move closer as there was so much noise in the room. Neferu did as Mereta bade her, and they were joined by a few more ladies and friends of Amio.

'What shall I sing?' he asked. Someone told him a song and he began to sing it. Once again Neferu was surprised by the sweetness of his voice. He caught sight of Neferu and smiled at her, but she was feeling distinctly nettled and did not return the smile. Someone mentioned what was obviously a popular army song next and he began to sing obligingly. Some of the others began to join in and the rest of the room fell silent as the singing took over. Neferu had never heard the song before, but she listened. It sounded so different from the intense songs of the Keftiu, sung to the music of the bouzouki. Suddenly she felt sad and out of place again, but set her face so that no one would know it.

Enthusiastic applause greeted the last strains and there were cries of 'More, more.' Amio started to sing again. This time it was a haunting love song. Its mood was more in tune with her own and she listened appreciatively.

'Did you like it?' Mereta asked.

'Yes! I could have listened to that one forever. Your brother has a lovely voice, and the words of the song were very touching too,' Neferu replied.

'Glad you enjoyed it!' the princess said with a smile.

Soon afterwards the queen rose and was escorted out by the archduke and her brother. Many others of the older generation left soon after that. This seemed to be the signal for a sudden upsurge of conversation and Neferu found herself suddenly surrounded by a group of admiring young noblemen giving her extravagant compliments and asking the princess to put in a good word for them. One of them spoke with the accent of Lower Egypt and with him she chatted longer, pleased to make the acquaintance of a fellow countryman. Their conversation became more animated as they realised they had mutual friends and some of the others drifted away. The young man, whose name was Snofru, was from Memphis, but his mother's sister was married to a Keftiu from On.

A smooth voice to the left of Neferu interrupted their conversation. 'I am afraid that I must break up this little entourage. I promised the lady Nefertiti's father that I would rescue her at the first sign of an attack by you smooth-talking fellows.' Amenophis put his arm out to Neferu, indicating that she should rise. She did so and he took her firmly by the elbow, and looking at Mereta he said, 'I think it is time that you two ladies retired.' Mereta started to protest, but a steely glint in her brother's eyes warned her to comply.

'Oh, all right,' she said, somewhat ungraciously to him as he, with every show of gallantry, escorted them from the room.

'Sometimes things get out of hand later on when some have a little too much to drink, Neferu,' he gave as explanation. 'I don't think either mother or my uncle would care for you to be present.'

Neferu nodded. She felt tired anyway. Another long day of change. At Mereta's apartment he kissed his sister lightly on the cheek and pushed her inside, saying that she could manage by herself for once, he was sure. Mereta laughed.

'I can see that I am going to have to,' she said, but there was humour in her voice. Mereta wished Neferu goodnight and humming under her breath she went into her suite.

Amio escorted Neferu down the terrace towards the stairs, saying, 'I hope you are settling down with us, Neferu.'

'I think so,' she replied. 'It has all been so strange and new, but everyone has been very kind.'

'Good,' he said pleasantly. At the bottom of the stairs, they turned left, and he led her to her door. It dimly registered with her that he knew where her room was. 'It has been a long day. Goodnight, my little friend, sleep well.' With that he leaned forward and kissed her cheek before turning round and retracing their path back to the withdrawing room.

She watched him go and when he stopped and turned before passing round a bend she waved and called, 'Good night, Amio.'

She felt very tired but tonight she just could not sleep. She tossed and turned, first to the right and then to the left, then back again. She felt troubled, in a situation in which she had lost all control. Her mind was a jumble of conflicting emotions and when she did finally fall asleep, she dreamed weird and confused dreams, which in the morning she could not remember

CHAPTER 11

The following morning Neferu had a slightly pensive air about her as she laid out Mereta's clothes for the day. This did not go unnoticed by the princess, and when she was styling her hair Mereta asked, 'Is anything wrong, Neferu? You look a bit downcast.'

Neferu sighed but gave a smile to offset the impact of it. 'Oh, it's nothing. I was just thinking that tomorrow Asenaath will be back,' she replied.

'Does that upset you?' asked Mereta, looking troubled.

'No,' said Neferu hesitantly, knowing that it was a lie but not wanting to cause any trouble.

Mereta, being quite astute, realised the lie immediately. 'Don't you like Asenaath?'

'It isn't important,' Neferu answered her. The princess noted the slight depression in her voice.

She glanced at the Keftiu girl sharply. 'Asenaath is all right when you get to know her,' she answered. 'She isn't as sharp as her words would suggest.'

Neferu shrugged. 'It isn't important,' she repeated. They breakfasted together on the veranda in the sunshine. The rest of the royal family was tied up with the important visiting dignitaries. There was a lot of business to sort out evidently. Neither Ay, Tiya nor Amio were to be seen and Neferu and Mereta spent the day almost entirely cut off from the others.

Later in the morning, the two girls sauntered down to the young Prince Smenkhenre's apartment. Smenkh was busy at work with several other pupils, copying out a text on their papyri. The tutor did not seem very pleased at their interruption, but the boys, on the other hand, were delighted at the unexpected break when the princess asked if Smenkh could be freed for a moment to show his butterfly collection to Neferu. Smenkh took them to his room and removed the cases carefully, one by one, from the shelves. They contained dozens of butterflies of all colours and sizes and Neferu admired their beauty, but she felt sad that they were dead. Smenkh showed her how the markings varied, and he seemed to know a lot about them. 'Don't you think it is sad, Smenkh, that they were cut off at the height of their beauty?' she asked a little sadly.

The boy looked at her gravely. 'They have such a short life anyway, Neferu.'

She nodded. 'I hope there is no one outside in the wide universe who thinks along those lines about us though, Smenkh!' she said feelingly.

Smenkh looked up at her, startled. 'Sometimes I think that I am like one of my butterflies. I am in a sort of case too. I can't go where I want to or do what I would like to,' he said sadly.

'What would you like to do, Smenkh?' she asked. He seemed very intelligent for such a young boy, she thought.

'I would like to go and visit other countries and see other peoples, animals and the insects in their countries,' he said stoutly. 'Do you know that far, far away in the north of the world, the climate is very cold, and rain comes frozen from the sky and stays on the ground like a soft white rug covering half the earth? In those countries the people are white skinned and yellow haired, and they have to wear thick furs just to keep warm,' he continued.

Neferu stared at him. 'How do you know all this?' she asked, amazed.

'My tutor met such a man once, a long time ago when he was young. A ship of the Northmen landed on our coast in the delta, and they left one of their dying crew behind when they left. But he did not die. Our people looked after him and he lived. After a time he learnt how to speak our language, and he told us about his land and his family. He was very homesick, but he could not go back to his loved ones, so he settled down here and stayed many years until eventually he died. He was an old man when my tutor knew him, and he had four children from his Egyptian wife. One of them had red hair, one of them yellow hair and two of them were dark haired, though not as dark as we are.'

Neferu was enthralled with this story. 'What was his name?' She wanted to know for some unaccountable reason.

'It was Hans. Strange, isn't it?' Smenkh commented.

'It certainly is. I would be afraid to travel to such places though. I would hate to lose the people I love.' In spite of the heat, she shivered at the thought.

'I would be afraid too!' admitted Smenkh, with a smile.

The two girls left the boys to their schoolwork and took a walk around the gardens. They took some figs from a tree and ate them as they walked. When the heat became oppressive, they returned to Mereta's apartment and chatted until lunchtime. In the afternoon, just after the refreshments had been served, one of the valets came with a message that there would be no family dinner that night. The two girls would be eating alone, but afterwards they would meet with the others in the withdrawing room, as usual.

Neferu was still under the blight of the vague unease she had been feeling the whole day. Mereta wanted to hear more about Neferu's life in On and about the other members of her family. It all seemed so different from her own upbringing. They discussed life, their hopes of love and what they each perceived as the ideal characteristics of a lover. A bit later they had got around to fashion and beauty, whence it was only a short but daring step to Mereta allowing Neferu to cut her hair shorter at the front to make the Keftiu-style ringlets so favoured by her people. Neferu dampened the tendrils and twisted them into the now familiar rag strips. Mereta squeaked at times as Neferu inadvertently pulled too hard on the roots. Neferu merely assured her that the results would be worth it. When Mereta looked in the mirror she said she looked like a monster with two little horns sticking out. They both giggled at the sight and then Neferu did her own hair too.

In the evening the girls dressed and Neferu styled Mereta's hair upward, but now with the addition of the two tiny ringlets falling from her temples. Finally Mereta admitted that the pain was worth the results, and she watched as Neferu did her own hair. She brushed it into a loose ponytail high on her head. Taking a small handful of hair, she wrapped it round and round the base of the ponytail, which was held in place with a strip of silk tied tightly. It was a style she often wore during the summers at Rashid when she went swimming every day. Tonight, the long hair lay in loose waves down her back from the effects of the chignon it had earlier been wound into.

It was quite late when the girls entered the withdrawing room, and it was already half full. There were several faces new to Neferu. The two girls curtsied deeply to the senior royals and Teya indicated that the girls should sit down close by her this evening. Teya always seemed to give an impression of great height, but in reality she was no taller than Neferu herself. It was solely the effect of the slightly raised platform on which the royal chairs were placed which gave rise to this illusion of height. Neferu knew that from such a vantage point they could easily observe anyone in the room, even when it was full. In any case, sitting there below the platform, Neferu always felt those above to be enormously tall.

There was a lively conversation going on when they entered. It concerned what constituted the definition of beauty. At first the subject was general and included artistry, scenery and so on, but eventually the subject narrowed to that of specifying female beauty. As there was a majority of men present, it was inevitable that some of the comments came as near to the bounds of good taste as was possible without risking offending the queen. Ay was taking an active part in this animated conversation and he suddenly alluded to Neferu in a bantering tone. The others turned to look at her and the Keftiu girl was forced to avert her eyes from this concerted gaze. She could feel the tell-tale signs of a blush suffusing her face again. It seemed that Ay was deliberately trying to give the court the impression that he had amorous designs on Neferu, though Neferu sensed instinctively that this was nothing more than subterfuge. She was puzzled. The charade of the previous day seemed set to continue. She was fast beginning to realise that here at court things were rarely what they seemed to be on the surface.

'Neferu, what do you think constitutes beauty?' the grand vizier asked with a warm smile. Neferu was embarrassed but answered as best she could, trying to emphasise the spiritual facet of beauty which she felt to be more important than the mere physical aspects. In the midst of her modest monologue, she was suddenly interrupted by Amio.

'Well, Nefertiti,' he said, in a faintly supercilious tone, 'now that you have defined beauty for us, please carry on and define ugliness. Am I ugly, for instance?'

Neferu sensed without looking the shock of the people all around her. There was an audible sigh of people sucking in their breath. She lowered her eyes quickly from their curious gazes and felt panic, lost as she was in a chaotic limbo of silent expectation. Taking her courage in her hands and knowing that there was no way she could win this moment, she looked up again at her tormentor. Amenophis was smiling down at her sardonically and she immediately lowered her eyes again from their searching gaze. She felt he was publicly reading her soul again and it made her feel angry. She sought to tell the truth as honestly as she could but without hurting him in front of all these people. She swallowed, knowing that she could not lie without despising herself but scared to accept the consequences of her reply. The room was absolutely silent now as they all awaited her answer with bated breath.

She lifted her gaze to his face once again, said squarely, 'I think you are not handsome, sire,' and lowered her gaze again. She could hear the audible gasps all around her but miserably wondered what else she could have said. She could not have lied and told him he was handsome. On the other hand, she did not find him ugly, and anyway, even if she had, it was just not the sort of thing you said to the pharaoh. Defiantly, she lifted up her head again and looked straight into his eyes and fixed them on him. She wondered what his reaction was going to be. Would he be furious? Mereta had told her that he had a very hot temper when aroused. Gradually she became aware that he was smiling at her and that more importantly, the smile reached his eyes.

'So! You think I am not handsome!' he said smoothly.

'No, sire,' she said, lowering her eyes from his intent gaze again. There was still no sound in the room. Neferu felt a desire to cry, and she wished the floor would open up and swallow her. It just remained solid and tangible beneath her feet, however, and she knew there would be nobody to save her.

Amenophis spoke softly, 'It is true, Nefertiti, I am not handsome.' She looked up quickly at the kindness in his voice and she saw that she had nothing to fear. He was not angry with her. He was smiling warmly at her. After the briefest of hesitations, he turned to Pararameses and said with humour, 'Honesty in one's subjects is always to be commended, don't you think, Rameses?' Pararameses laughed in genuine amusement and after a second the rest of the room joined in.

The rest of the evening passed in superficial chitchat for everyone else except Neferu, whose nerves had been badly jarred and was in turmoil, which she had difficulty hiding, try as she did. After the queen had retired, Mereta asked permission from her brother for herself and Neferu to be excused also. This was given good-naturedly, and the girls made their way through the chilly night air up the steps and down the terrace to Mereta's apartment.

'Do you think Amio is ugly, Neferu?' Mereta asked casually. 'You can tell me; I won't tell him.'

Neferu had had time to think of the matter since the incident and had formulated her thoughts more clearly on the subject. 'No! I don't think he is ugly. He has an unusual face, but it is not ugly. He looks intelligent and sensitive like you,' replied Neferu honestly. Feeling that it really was not possible for her to put her foot in it any worse than she already had, she added, 'It was very unkind of Amio to make such a public spectacle of me, Mereta. He is obviously not as sensitive as his face would suggest.'

'Amio doesn't mean to bait you, Neferu. He is very kind underneath,' Mereta said, defending her brother. Neferu sighed but said nothing. At the entrance to her apartment, Mereta turned and kissed her cheek. 'You go straight to bed, Neferu. I can see to myself tonight.'

Neferu hesitated. She didn't want to get into any more trouble. 'What would Asenaath say?' she asked.

'Don't worry about Asenaath, I often put myself to bed. Anyway, I had a chat with mother earlier this evening and I asked her to let you stay with me and let Asenaath join her team. She said she would think about it and let me know in the morning,' Mereta replied cheerfully. Neferu felt her spirits lift immediately. She really did not wish to be under the eagle eye of the grand queen all day, even though Maatnofret was such a dear. For her to be rid of the company of Asenaath as well was a gift out of the blue. Something good had happened to her today, at least.

'Oh, I do hope she will agree, Mereta!' she said fervently.

'Let's see in the morning, Neferu,' the princess replied. 'Good night, Neferu. Peace be with you!'

'Good night, Mereta. Peace be with you too.' That night Neferu prayed that she could spend her remaining time at Malkata with Mereta.

The next morning Neferu found that the god had answered her prayer. At breakfast the grand queen informed her that she was to continue as lady-in-waiting to Mereta and that Asenaath would be transferred to the service of Tiya herself. Although the arrangement was perfect for her, Neferu was nervous that Asenaath would be upset and take it out on her later. She told Mereta of this, but Mereta told her not to worry. The queen would word the information in such a way that it would be seen as a promotion for which the queen had specially selected her.

Neferu felt taken aback that the royal family were prepared to make such strenuous efforts to accommodate her and could not decide whether they were being particularly kind to her, or whether they treated all guests like this, or, in view of Ay's odd behaviour, if there was some ulterior motive in which she was merely a pawn. Eventually she dismissed this latter assumption because they had nothing to gain from someone with origins as humble as hers. She realised that Mereta was very fond of her and that she had quite a lonely life within the confines of the court. She probably had brought a different dimension to her life and the queen appreciated it. She was too lowly for there to be any other reason.

For the next few days Neferu caught no glimpse of Amio. She surprised herself by catching herself looking out for him. No one mentioned the reason for his absence and although Neferu wanted to ask, she felt that she would appear impertinent and therefore kept quiet. Gradually she became aware that she was not so homesick now. People were nice to her, and it was all very grand and exciting. Still, in her heart of hearts, she felt that life here ran at a very superficial level. The socialising in the withdrawing room, for instance, was fun, but you could not get to know anyone well. She was also becoming aware that in the seeming cohesion of the large social gatherings, separate groups of influence existed side by side, but separated by barriers other than those caused by the constant awareness of protocol. She was an intuitive girl and sometimes the invisible barriers were almost tangible to her. It was not something she was used to, and she found it very tiring, always having to be on her guard.

When Amio finally did reappear, it seemed that he had been on an official visit to a garrison of troops stationed in one of the cities north of Thebes. He looked rather tired and drawn but was very cheerful. Neferu felt glad to see him again but did not bother to complicate her life further by analysing the reason why.

The problem regarding Asenaath turned out to have been just as easily resolved as Mereta had envisaged. This self-assured young lady had arrived back from her short visit rested and aglow with confidence as if she were hugging some secret good fortune to herself. Neferu guessed that her good temper was the result of her recent engagement, which was not yet official news at court. As Maatnofret had already divulged the news to Neferu and Neferu to Mereta, the two girls were hard put to raise the necessary expressions of pleased astonishment when Asenaath grandly informed them of the forthcoming event.

When the news had been proffered and received with due pleasurable exclamations of congratulations, Asenaath was in an even better mood. She unwound sufficiently to give even Neferu a warm smile and seated herself on the couch. With only the very faintest of patronising tones in her voice, she looked directly at Neferu and said, 'Neferu, I have some news for you. I know that Mereta is aware of what the grand queen and I discussed this morning, but I feel it is only fair that we should inform you too as soon as possible, don't you think so, Mereta?' Neferu affected a puzzled look of incomprehension. Asenaath's geniality knew no bounds today. With just a trace of superciliousness, she turned to Mereta and said, 'Perhaps it would be better coming from you, Mereta!' Neferu felt a little startled at this, wondering if what was about to come was indeed what she had been led to believe or whether it was another matter entirely.

'Yes, I suppose so, Asenaath!' the princess stated. Mereta turned to look at Neferu from such a position that it was difficult for Asenaath to see her eyes. Neferu noticed that her eyes contained an irrepressible glint of amusement and that she was having difficulty in controlling a tendency for them to crinkle at the edges. Mereta assumed a serious tone, somewhat at odds with the merest ghost of a smile on her face. 'Neferu! Mother has had a chat with me about her lady-in-waiting roster,' she said sweetly. Neferu nodded and looked from one to the other expectantly. 'You know, of course, that one of her ladies-in-waiting has married and moved from Thebes. She had originally considered you as her replacement, but she now wonders if perhaps you need more time to get used to palace ways, and indeed you have the option of returning to On very soon anyway. She has considered the matter and thinks it would be better in the circumstances to take someone who has more experience. For those reasons she has decided to offer the position to Asenaath. I know you will be very disappointed, but I hope you won't begrudge her the favour.' Neferu gave a quick glance at Asenaath, who in all fairness tried to wipe a look of triumph off her face as fast as she could. Neferu did her very best to appear both very annoyed and magnanimous simultaneously. She wasn't quite sure whether she managed to pull it off perfectly and so assumed a downcast expression instead. She even managed a suitably thwarted tone to her voice as she replied.

'The queen may, of course, choose whomsoever she pleases as her lady-in-waiting, Mereta, though I would have thought that if Asenaath is getting married and moving to Kush, as she has just informed us, it will mean yet another replacement will have to be sought shortly.' Here she directed her glance innocently across to Asenaath who quickly replied.

'It will not be for some months yet.'

'I see!' said Neferu, as if she were more than a little put out at this news, as indeed she was.

Mereta smiled with bonhomie. 'I'm so happy that you have taken the news so well, Neferu. Never mind. I'm sure that the two of us will get along just fine.' Neferu nodded as if conquering her disappointment. In truth she was amazed at this newfound ability to be so duplicitous. She played her assigned role superbly, she thought, and was rewarded by Asenaath's interjection, in a tone of friendly compassion.

'I'm very sorry, Neferu! I really am. I have been at court for a long time now, however, and I am much more senior than you are. I suppose that the queen needs someone who she knows can deal with whatever situation may arise. As you yourself have said, the queen may choose whom she pleases.'

'I understand, Asenaath,' Neferu continued her slightly hurt tone. 'Of course, it is only right that you take up the post, in the circumstances. In any case, it is a position very much in the public eye and I really do feel that I am not ready for it yet.' Asenaath nodded, brimming with affability, and throughout breakfast she made a special effort to be nice to Neferu, emphasising that if Neferu had the slightest difficulty she only had to ask herself and the required assistance would be forthcoming. Neferu murmured effusive words of gratitude and the meal ended in an atmosphere of warmth and friendliness.

After breakfast Mereta gave Asenaath the rest of the day free, saying that with all these new plans she knew that Asenaath must have a million things she had to do. Asenaath thanked her prettily and acknowledged that it was true. She had to have her trousseau made up and she had to help her mother plan the menu for her engagement party.

Once Asenaath had disappeared and was safely out of earshot, Mereta laughed. 'I didn't know you could be so devious, Neferu. You almost had me believing that you were overcome by chagrin which you could barely disguise.'

'I am much deeper than you think, Mereta,' she said.

Mereta leaned forwards slightly and said seriously, 'Oh, it's not your profundity that I doubt, Neferu. It is your acting ability which amazes me.'

Neferu considered the other girl's statement and then replied just as seriously. 'Since I have been in Thebes, Mereta, not a day has passed when I have not sensed in the conversations of those around me deeper undercurrents. Several times I have observed people saying with smiling faces what their eyes are completely denying. Perhaps I too am developing the habit, though it is not what I want.'

Mereta nodded sagely. 'It is true, Neferu,' she said frankly. 'There is much intrigue and insincerity at court. Now that you are aware of it, you will be better able to protect yourself. You don't need that ability with me, however. I hope you will believe that.'

Neferu smiled her acquiescence. ' I believe you, Mereta.'

The two girls decided to go for their morning stroll around the garden, which was cut off from the noise of the busy courtyard. It occurred to Neferu that Mereta had led a very sheltered life here within the confines of the palace environment.

'Don't you ever go anywhere, Mereta?' the Keftiu girl asked idly.

'What do you mean?' Mereta looked surprised.

'Well, I mean, like I go to Rashid. Don't you ever leave Thebes?'

'Well, not in the summer anyway, it would be far too hot to travel. It would be much too far to travel to the coast from here, except for the coast across the desert in the east, and no one wants to cross the desert for a holiday.' Mereta laughed merrily. 'I would like to see the coast of Lower Egypt though, if it is as beautiful as you say it is.'

'Oh, it is, Mereta, it is!' was Neferu's enthusiastic response.

'We are going somewhere soon, I think,' Mereta said grandly.

'Where?' Neferu was unashamedly curious.

'In three decans I shall be going with mother, Amio and Smenkh to Goshen to visit mother's relatives. My grandparents, who live at Akhtmin, are coming with us. My grandfather has several brothers who are still alive, and they all live in the district of Goshen.'

'But that is not a great journey from us,' declared Neferu delightedly. 'As I shall be home then, will you come and visit me?'

Mereta was silent for a moment. 'Wouldn't you like to stay here with us, Neferu?' she asked almost pleadingly.

'I would like to take you with me,' Neferu said with a sigh. 'I will really miss you, Amio and Maatnofret when I go home.'

Mereta shrugged her shoulders. 'If you go home, I will really miss you too.' After a pause she continued, 'I don't know if I will be allowed to visit you, but I would like to'

'I understand,' Neferu said comfortingly.

Neferu sat down on the side of the lily pond and rippled the water with her fingers. They both turned as they heard high-spirited voices talking and laughing. It was Amio with Pararameses and another young man, whom she later discovered was a military scribe called Horemheb. They had obviously just returned from the hunt. Amio called out a cheery greeting to the girls and came over. The other two stayed where they were, but both bowed low to the girls.

'You are back early today, Amio,' Mereta remarked.

'Yes! It is getting too warm now that the hot season is in full swing. Even the animals are too lethargic to run. You will be pleased at that, Neferu, I think.' He studied the Keftiu girl carefully. She returned his gaze steadily.

'Yes, I am, Amio. I don't like hunting. I would prefer to go swimming. It is much more pleasant,' she answered with a smile.

'Are you fond of swimming?' he asked.

'Very fond. I am going to teach Mereta sometime. She can't swim, you know?' Her surprise at this lack was apparent in her voice. The young man continued to gaze at her with his inscrutable eyes.

'Well, perhaps when we go to visit my relatives soon, she will be able to learn,' he replied. 'Would you like to learn how to ride a horse, Neferu?' he asked in an abrupt change of subject.

Neferu felt herself brighten up immediately.

'Can I?' she asked eagerly.

'Why not? Mereta can,' he replied, shrugging.

Neferu looked at Mereta impressed. 'You didn't tell me that,' she said accusingly.

'Never thought of it,' the other girl said, amused. 'It is fun though, when once you get over the initial fright. Mother doesn't really approve, though,' she said to her brother.

'Mother doesn't mind so long as we are discreet and look after Neferu carefully. I have already discussed it with her,' Amio said with a grin.

'Oh, Amio, that was very nice of you,' Neferu jumped up, suddenly all excited. 'Can we go today?'

'This afternoon if you like.' He looked pleased at her enthusiasm.

'I would love it! It will be so much fun!' Her eyes sparkled.

'It isn't as easy as you might think at first,' warned Mereta. 'Getting on and off is a problem in itself at first.'

'I'm not afraid,' Neferu declared. 'I think horses are such beautiful creatures.'

'They are,' Amio assured her. 'I will choose a suitable one for you, Neferu. There is no cause to be afraid.'

'Thank you so much, Amio,' she said. He nodded his head, gave them a small bow and returned to his friends, saying over his shoulder that he would come for them after their siesta.

Neferu was so pleased that she clapped her hands and Mereta was relieved. Neferu had been getting very restless of late. Perhaps it was just the lack of physical exercise.

'What shall we wear, Mereta?' Neferu asked, wanting to get organised as soon as she could.

'The most practical dress for riding, I feel, are the long, baggy trousers that the women of Mitanni wear,' answered Mereta. 'You may borrow some of mine.' Neferu did not have a clue what they were but knew they must be suitable for her if the queen considered them suitable for Mereta. She had no idea how the women of such a faraway country as Mitanni were given to dressing. It sounded very exotic though.

That afternoon siesta seemed to go on for ever and she just could not sleep to save her life. She tried to lie still and not make a noise to avoid disturbing any of the others, though she thought it was probably impossible for sound to penetrate the thick walls. After tossing and turning for what seemed an age, she got up and began to prepare herself. Remembering what had happened to her on the hunting trip, she combed her hair and wound it into a ponytail, which she wound round again and again into a large bun at the back of her head and pinned it securely with combs. She put on the black satin harem trousers and a white, loose cotton tunic, with sleeves down to her forearms. She felt very strange and foreign in such attire, but it was modest, and she reflected that Grandma would undoubtedly have approved. To complete the outfit, she wound the creamy silk scarf donated by Mereta around her head and neck securely.

'It makes me look foreign,' she remarked to Mereta who was similarly attired.

'I think it is very becoming,' the princess assured her. Amio and Pararameses joined them for refreshments and looked them over approvingly.

'Better not eat too much,' he warned Neferu. 'The jogging of the horse may make you feel a little nauseated at first.'

'I never feel sick,' Neferu assured him with total confidence. It was true. Once in the courtyard Neferu was dismayed to see that a chariot had been harnessed. 'I thought ...' Her voice trailed off in disappointment.

'I know what you thought, Neferu,' Amio said with amusement. 'But I think your pride might be severely damaged if you fell off here in the courtyard, don't you?'

'Is that likely then?' she asked carefully.

'Not necessarily,' he replied cheerfully. 'But it sometimes happens and that is why we always find a secluded spot to learn.'

'Yes. I should hate it if everyone laughed at me,' she admitted, grateful for his forethought on the matter.

'That's what I thought,' he said, handing her into the chariot after his sister. The groom led out the horses of Amio and Pararameses and Neferu watched them as they mounted. It did not look all that difficult. She thought she would be able to manage it.

With no more ceremony than that, they left the complex of Malkata and entered into the city itself. The driver of their chariot had been given instructions to avoid the main thoroughfares and he took a winding and lonely route around the town, in a north-easterly direction. The Nile lay on their right and the river shimmered in the afternoon sunshine. They drove on until they left the town well behind. The only people they could see were the tiny figures far away on the riverboats, sailing up and down. Amio reined in and dismounted.

'All right girls, you can get out now!' he ordered. He came to help them down. Pararameses also dismounted. The driver dismantled the two horses from the chariot and began to put the leather saddles upon them ready. 'Come here, Neferu,' commanded Amio, and she obediently followed him. Now that she was standing beside the horse it suddenly seemed taller than she remembered it. She looked at it again a bit doubtfully.

He laughed a little, noting her expression. 'It will be fine, Neferu. I'll help you,' he said confidently. 'First, though, you must make friends with the horse. Here, give it these!' He took a little pocket from his knife belt and opened it. 'Open your hand!' he ordered. She did as she was told and he poured a handful of dried fruit, chopped into small pieces, into her hand. Then he poured some into his own palm and said, 'Just do what I do.' With his right hand he patted the horse's flank and spoke soothingly to it. Then he went to stand in front of it and offered his open palm to the horse's mouth. The horse sniffed the contents and then began to eat the dried fruit. 'Right, Neferu! Now it's your turn,' he said, when his palm was empty. 'Talk to him softly and tell him what a fine fellow he is,' Amio advised. Somewhat nervously, Neferu complied. She jumped a little as she felt the warm moist mouth against her palm, but she relaxed when she noticed that the horse did not attempt to bite her. She began to talk to the horse, telling him who she was and how beautiful she thought he was. She continued to talk after the fruit was gone and she patted him. The horse gently nuzzled her and seemed to be listening. 'I think you have made a friend, Neferu,' Amio stated matter-of-factly. 'Now that he knows you, I'll show you how to mount.'

Neferu moved to the side of the horse and Amio explained the procedure. She listened carefully. He explained all the parts of the saddle to her and then helped her to mount. The first time she did not succeed, and she fell heavily against him. He caught her in his arms and steadied her. Their faces touched for a moment and for the second tim she felt aware of him only as a man rather than as Amio, the pharaoh. Neither of them said anything and he released her. 'Let's try again,' he said casually. The second attempt was successful and all at once she was aloft. It seemed terrifyingly high, and she drew in her breath quickly. 'Steady, boy!' Amio patted the horse soothingly. 'Are you all right?' he asked.

'I think so,' said Neferu.

'I'll mount my horse then and we'll go slowly, side by side,' Amio spoke reassuringly. He mounted and came up close, then, carefully giving her instructions, they started off slowly. It was exhilarating and with each short distance passed, Neferu grew a little more confident. The others were already mounted, and they set off ahead at a smart trot. Amio and Neferu followed at their own slow pace.

'This is lovely, Amio.' She smiled her pleasure.

'You will enjoy it even more when you grow more confident,' he told her. When he felt sure that she could handle her horse, he told her how to indicate to the horse that it should go a little faster and he increased his pace to match hers. She soon lost her fear and they trotted along together. She had full confidence in Amio's equestrian abilities. After a while the others came back towards them at a canter.

'The sun is getting low now, Amio,' Pararameses reminded him.

'Oh, no! Do we have to go back already?' wailed Neferu. 'I've only just got the hang of it.'

Amio grinned. 'We can come again early in the morning if you want to,' he promised.

'Oh, yes please!' said Neferu pleadingly. 'If Mereta wants to, of course,' she added quickly. She looked at the princess, who was nodding good-humouredly.

At a gentle trot, the four of them returned to where the chariot was waiting. Neferu waited for the others to dismount first. She was not quite confident about tackling it. Amio came to help her. She came down a little clumsily and he took her by the waist to steady her. Once on the ground she turned to thank him, their faces only a few centimetres apart. 'It was such fun!' she told him, 'I hope we can come every day. Thank you for being so kind.'

'I am glad you enjoyed it so much, Neferu. We won't be able to come every day but as often as I can manage it,' he promised. She leaned forward and reached up to plant a kiss on his cheek. He stood quite still afterwards. She wondered whether he was shocked. She should not have acted so impulsively, she realised. She became aware of the other two watching and blushed.

'I'm sorry, Amio. I didn't mean to be so familiar,' she said shyly.

'I am not offended, Neferu. I am honoured,' he said gently. He smiled at her, and she smiled back. For that moment there were just the two of them and then the memory of Yussef came flooding back and she backed away, looking down.

The driver harnessed the two horses back to the chariot and they drove back to Malkata at a sedate pace. In the courtyard, Pararameses took his leave of them and the other three strolled leisurely back to the royal apartments. The sun was beginning to set and there was a deep pink glow filling the horizon. 'What a nice day it has been today,' declared Neferu. The other two exchanged glances and smiled.

As they neared the apartments Mereta told Neferu to go straight to her own suite and get ready and she would look after herself. At the inner corner of the block, Neferu took her leave saying she would see them later. She went along to her chambers, humming a familiar Keftiu melody as she walked. Maatnofret called her for permission to enter as she was dressing for dinner.

'I have had such a delicious day, Maatnofret,' Neferu exclaimed. Maatnofret requested a further explanation and Neferu regaled her with the story of her adventure. 'Wasn't that kind of Amio, don't you think, Maatnofret?' she declared warmly.

'Yes! Amio is a very nice person, I agree,' replied the older woman with a smile. 'I am glad that you have taken to him. I think he is quite lonely,' she added.

'Lonely?' asked Neferu in real surprise. 'I don't think he is lonely. He is always the centre of attention and surrounded by friends.'

'You can be lonely in a crowd, Neferu,' Maatnofret said enigmatically.

'Why do you think he is lonely?' Neferu countered.

'Well, for a start I think it is time he settled down and married. In another three decans he will be twenty and he still has no wife. It is very late for a pharaoh to be unmarried,' Maatnofret retorted.

'But why has he not married? I am sure there are hundreds of girls just dying to marry the pharaoh!' She sounded curious.

'That's exactly where the problem is, Neferu. You see, Neferu, Amio has always said that he will never marry until he gives his heart and the woman he loves loves him too.'

'That is the way it should be,' agreed Neferu.

'Well unfortunately, he has now given his heart to someone, but she does not love him,' answered Maatnofret cryptically.

'Oh!' replied Neferu. 'What is to be done?'

Maatnofret sighed. 'I really don't know what to suggest. It appears that the lady in question seems fond of him but no more than that. What do you think he should do? He could order her to marry him, but he is afraid that he will never win her love if he does that,' said the lady-in-waiting.

'Yes. I see what you mean. Poor Amio,' Neferu said sympathetically. 'I think he should continue to court her. He is so nice I don't see how she could resist him in the end. If all else fails I think he should pray to his god, the Aten.' Neferu felt her advice was very practical.

'Yes! I think that would probably be a very good idea,' said Maatnofret.

'Have I met her?' Neferu asked curiously.

'Yes. She is one of the ladies-in-waiting at court, but I'm afraid that she is soon to marry someone else.'

'Asenaath!' exclaimed Neferu. Maatnofret did not reply and Neferu understood that she did not want to betray a trust by saying it outright.

'Poor Amio,' she said heatedly. 'I think he deserves someone much nicer than her. Even if he were not the pharaoh, he would be worth a hundred Asenaaths.'

'I agree with you entirely, Neferu,' said Maatnofret.

That evening, they congregated as usual in the withdrawing room. There were less people than normal. Some of the military noblemen had left that day on an exercise and would not be back for several days. The queen and the older royals left early, and there were just a dozen or so of them left. Neferu kept looking at Asenaath and Amio. Somehow, she just could not imagine them together.

One of the court ladies asked Neferu about a Keftiu love song she had once heard. The woman hummed the melody for her unselfconsciously and Neferu recognised it. The others asked her to sing it for them. She was loath to do it because she did not have a good singing voice, but she did the best she could. Fortunately it was a song she knew well and had sung frequently, so she gave it her best. Afterwards, at their request, she translated it for them. It did not sound so poetic in Egyptian, she explained, because it lost the rhyming in translation. It was a sad song about two lovers who became separated from each other, through no fault of their own, and their lives were torn apart by circumstance. The man vows to find his love again in his next life, even if he has to search the world over until he finds her. He does find her again, but it is too late, and she has just died. The song tells of how her spirit listens to his words and vows too to keep to his promise and wait for him.

'What a sad song.' Mereta was quite aghast.

'Yes,' said Neferu. 'Now I think about it, we Keftiu almost always sing sad songs. About love, death, pain or about the sea usually. Not always in that order though,' she said laughing. 'Perhaps our history has left us this legacy, who knows.' She shrugged her shoulders.

'Interesting!' said Amio. 'You must teach me some of your songs, Neferu.' She looked at him in surprise. It was the first time he had called her 'Neferu' in public. He did not seem to be aware of the slip in protocol.

'I would be happy to, sire,' she replied. 'If your ears can stand the pain of my flat voice.' There was a general laugh at this and soon afterwards the party broke up.

CHAPTER 12

A new easy intimacy grew between Neferu and Amio while she was learning to ride. They were good friends, she thought. She thought of her family often and of Yussef, but there was no sense of guilt in her thoughts. She was well into her second decan at Thebes, almost at the end of it, in fact, and so in another ten days or so her family would be arriving to convey her back to On.

In this sense of well-being, she threw herself energetically into that part of court life which was open to her and she was able to observe objectively some of its less pleasant aspects, such as the eternal bickering between rival factions of the large and complexly interrelated families. It was, after all, nothing to do with her. If she felt sad at all, it was because she knew that she would miss Mereta, Amio and Smenkh when she left. She doubted that she would ever see them again afterwards and that thought gave her quite a pang.

Gradually she had come to know the names of many of the other people, mainly young, who formed the royal entourage. On several occasions at the evening social events, she found herself slipping into easy familiarity with those who had caught her fancy. If anyone had asked her, she would have told them that Thebes was hotter and not so pretty as the fertile delta region from which she had come, and which throughout her life she continued to feel as her real home country. She found Thebes dry and dusty, without the pleasant breezes which blew from the sea across Lower Egypt.

There were objects of architectural awe here in Thebes, though nothing to compete with the ancient pyramids of her part of the world, whose history was a closed book to Neferu. All she knew was they had been built in an ancient time, long before her forebears had ever come to this land. The colossi of Thebes had, on the other hand, been built on the orders of Amio's father, Amenophis III, to line the route to the great temple of Amun-Re on the east bank of the Nile. They were only now nearing completion and the whole family was enormously proud of them. To Neferu, they were the most imposing things anyone could imagine. She had already been once down this grand way, travelling with the royal family in a splendid chariot when they had all gone to offer sacrifices and to pray.

Amio had admitted playfully that he was not a great believer but that the priests of Amun had to be appeased. He had put his finger on his lip as a signal that she was not to repeat what he had said. She had been quite shocked but had promised that she would not say anything. He had given her a conspiratorial smile. She was nowadays often the recipient of some enigmatic remark or other that he would make and never quite finish. It was disconcerting to be half pulled into intimacy in this way and then just as suddenly pushed away, almost as if she was his enemy. He seemed afraid to say too much.

During the last decan of her visit, Neferu began to feel a sense of conflict. She wanted to go back to On and things to be as they had always been, but she was already aware that that could never be. Something in her had irrevocably changed. She was not certain what it was but sensed that it was something momentous and even frightening. She thought often now about the carefree days of her childhood and the love and security which her grandparent, Lea and her father had given to the three children so unstintingly. She wondered now how difficult it would be to fit into her old life again.

She had missed Yussef, and yet her heart was not torn by the separation and that troubled her. She was half afraid of what she would feel in that moment when they met again. She knew that the ones who remain behind often grieve more than the ones who leave, simply because they carry on in the sameness of their routine whereas the leaver has his or her existence filled with new experiences, to which they are constantly being forced to adapt. They therefore change more within than the ones who stay behind. Neferu clung to the truth of the old Keftiu saying, 'Distance is like the wind, it extinguishes the small flames but only fans the large ones.'

Sometimes when Neferu was out in the garden with Mereta and Amio, she would glance up casually to find that Tiya was quietly observing them from the terrace. Her intuition told her immediately that she was being assessed and tested. Neferu always felt the presence of an invisible barrier between herself and the grand queen. They both ignored it but they both knew it was there, nevertheless. Just before her family were due to arrive there occurred an incident which was entirely Neferu's own fault.

The summer heat had arrived in force, inflicting a deep lethargy over the citizens of Thebes. No one wanted to be outside unless it was absolutely necessary. Even the river traffic was reduced to a minimum. Inside the palace complex the only sound to be heard in the afternoons was the buzzing of the crickets. Inside her chambers, Neferu felt hot and sticky. She could not sleep well, and this left her irritable and restless. There was no sound in the rest of the house and so she went to the door. There was no sound to be heard anywhere.

From the doorway, Neferu looked out at the lily pool. Wavy rays of heat moved above it and she remembered with nostalgia the feel of the sea as it washed over her body in the lazy, hazy days of summer at Rashid. A sudden thought came to her, and she stepped out into the garden. Immediately the full force of the heat struck her, and she felt as though she were in a baking oven. She walked over to the pool and spread her fingers around in the water. It felt deliciously cool. She had an unbearable urge to jump in. Carefully she looked round. There was no one visible. The pool was only in the line of vision of those in the palace block and the place was deserted. It was mid-siesta time. No one would emerge for ages yet. Carefully she let her eyes scan the upper floor again but there was no sign of life. Without further ado, Neferu took off her shift and slid as quietly as she could into the pool. It was bliss. She swam up and down, occasionally checking with a quick scan the living area. There was no one. She promised herself just a couple more lengths and then she would scurry back to her apartment. Lazily she swam and it was only on the downward length that she heard her name being called. Horror of horrors, it was the grand queen herself who had come onto the terrace and was watching her. Her heart somersaulted.

'Nefertiti! Nefertiti!' The queen's voice was deliberately kept low and subdued, to avoid alerting anyone else to the spectacle before her. The queen looked extremely shocked. Neferu swam to the edge of the pool and climbed out, scratching her thigh on the side as she hauled herself up. Once out of the pool she gave a quick examination of the graze and then picked up her shift and put it quickly over her head. Her haste was such that she made no attempt to dry herself and felt the shift clinging to her uncomfortably and becoming increasingly wet as her hair dripped down her back. She remained unaware of the figure of Amio, whose attention had obviously been caught by his mother's voice. He watched the scene from a recess on the terrace. Tiya hurried down to the pool.

'You must not swim here, Nefertiti!' she scolded. 'You might be seen.' Here she turned round to look if anyone had noticed them, but Amio had withdrawn into the shadowed part of the terrace and was not visible to either of the women. Satisfied that they were not observed, she turned back to Neferu, who was now feeling abjectly miserable and dripping all over the place. The queen's face softened a little. 'For another thing, this water is very dirty. It does not replenish itself like the sea. You must promise me that you will never swim here again!' she said emphatically. Neferu nodded vigorously, thanking her lucky stars that she was not being reprimanded more severely. The queen gazed at her and then said, almost graciously, 'I suppose there has been no harm done this time, but this must not be repeated. We need not discuss it further. Go back to bed.'

Neferu nodded again and said in an apologetic voice, 'I am sorry, Your Majesty. I thought everyone was asleep.'

'Obviously!' declared the queen, drily. She accompanied Neferu to her door, as if to make sure the girl would definitely go inside.

'Sleep well, Neferu,' she said as she walked away.

'Thank you, Your Majesty. You too,' she replied.

Neferu ran into her room and dried herself before climbing onto her bed. She had taken an absurd risk and been caught, but what was the most amazing thing about the affair had been the exceedingly lenient attitude of the queen towards her. She felt very relieved. At dinner that night she felt very nervous. The queen, however, made no reference to the escapade of the afternoon. It was as if it had never happened, and her anxiety subsided. She did wonder if the queen would mention the matter to her father, but she realised on further reflection that it was far too an embarrassing subject for the queen to discuss with her father.

It was late that evening when Ay made his entrance, and when he came over to chat to her he had some news. Her father, Yussef and Demi would be arriving in Thebes the following day. He said that the messenger had also informed them that the family had had a good journey. Neferu was so happy. She realised how much she had missed them. The queen chatted to her and, for the first time, Neferu detected some trace of warmth in her manner. Perhaps it was the cheering thought of her imminent departure, Neferu thought. Whether it was that or whether the arrival of her family loosened her own tongue, for the first time Neferu was able to relax and chat gaily to this formidable woman.

When morning came, Neferu could hardly contain her excitement. Sitting with Mereta in her sitting room, she must have asked the other girl at least a dozen times when she estimated her family would arrive. Finally Ay sent one of his valets to escort her to the state withdrawing room. It appeared that Vassiliou, Demi and Yussef had already paid their respects to the royal family, and they were waiting for her to appear. On seeing them, she broke into a run and flung her arms around her father, almost smothering him in her hug. She then turned to Demi, repeating her exuberance and finally to Yussef she turned, taking his outstretched hands, and giving him a glorious smile she kissed his cheeks. Too late she became aware of spectators. At the back of the hall, behind and to her right her father indicated the royal family seated on the dais. She had thought themselves alone together and had therefore not even considered protocol. Hurriedly she turned to do obeisance and apologised fervently for her rudeness. The queen said she understood that Neferu was overjoyed at seeing her family again and gave her full leave to speak privately to them, before the discussion of business began. Neferu hugged them all again and was so overcome that tears began to course down her cheeks. 'Surely, Neferu, you have not been so unhappy with us?' Ay asked in a hurt tone.

'No, No!' she replied quickly. 'I haven't been unhappy at all. How could I have been when you have all treated me so well? It's just that I am so happy to see my people again.' She spoke quickly so as not to hurt their feelings. Yussef took her hand and did not let go of it. A gesture which did not go unnoticed by the royals. Demi moved around a little restlessly and Neferu noticed that he was looking very pale and that he seemed to have lost weight. She looked at him anxiously. 'Is your leg worse again?' she asked.

Demi shook his head reassuringly. 'Just the same old thing. The doctor says he will have to open it again when we get back. It has got a little worse on the journey, but it isn't bad,' he replied stoically.

Neferu's face clouded over. She guessed that it was worse than he was telling. Her brother noticed her expression and said gently, 'I must learn to live with it, Neferu. It will not help for you to worry!'

Amio had been listening to their conversation and now he requested them to be seated. He studied Demi carefully as he limped painfully to the couch, using his new ebony walking stick. He turned aside and quietly mentioned something to his uncle. The older man nodded meditatively. The royal family were remarkably informal and made no attempt to impose their presence on the little group in any way. Amio told Demi that he would arrange for the court physician to see him and examine his leg. If he could do anything to help, he would be pleased to do it. Demi thanked the pharaoh tiredly. Neferu bit her lip. She could clearly see that he was unwell. It was more than the tiredness due to a long journey, though that had not helped, she thought guiltily. Vassiliou proffered his thanks to the pharaoh and said he would be very grateful for their assistance as his son's condition had deteriorated over the past two days. Her father was anxious too. Neferu felt a little scared now. Her father did not easily become worried.

Ay suggested that the travellers be escorted to their quarters in the guest block to rest and have refreshments. They would all meet up again in the evening when they were refreshed. With that the queen rose to leave and Neferu and the others, including poor Demi, who struggled to his feet, rose and paid obeisance. The pharaoh put out his arm to indicate to Demi to stay seated, and with that the royal family left. A servant conducted the little group across the courtyard to the guest block and Neferu, accompanying them, asked continual questions, which they endeavoured to answer all talking at once. 'Yes!' her father replied. Shosen was now well, the nausea had stopped, and she sent her love.

'Did you remember to tell grandma and Aunt Lea how much my dress was admired?' she persisted.

'Yes, I did. They were very pleased, of course.'

Neferu had felt strangely shy on seeing Yussef once again, and not a little guilty because she had largely forgotten to put into practice their pact to concentrate on each other every evening. She had let her new life distract her. She realised it was no excuse. Yussef, however, seemed just happy to see her again and did not attempt to question her on this score just yet at least. He cast her frequent passionate glances which she shyly noted, and which caused her to look down, blushing.

Neferu told them about her position as the lady-in-waiting to Princess Meretamun and how nice a person the princess was. She told them that she would really miss her when she returned to On because she and Mereta were like sisters. Vassiliou was very pleased to hear this. He told her that he had been very afraid that she would be miserable in such different surroundings and away from all her family and friends.

Seeing that Demi was exhausted, Neferu said she would leave them to rest and come back later. Yussef pulled her to him closely and kissed her passionately on the mouth, saying that he was looking forward to seeing her alone. A servant came in with a tray of drinks and they pulled apart. Neferu took her leave, saying she would return later.

As she walked back across the courtyard, she felt her heart pounding. For some reason she could not decipher, she had not been wholly compliant in Yussef's embrace. She had had the feeling that the gesture, in front of her father and without waiting for her to respond, had been a movement of possession rather than an indication of love. It had made her feel like a prisoner. It had spoiled the idea of what she felt should have been a romantic moment. She had never felt like that in the past. He was rushing her, and she was not ready for it. Slightly troubled, she returned to her duties. Mereta looked up questioningly when she entered. 'Are they all well?' she asked with a smile.

Neferu frowned as she thought of Demi. 'I think Demi is ill again. I am afraid that he might have a fever. I am really worried about him,' she stated anxiously. 'He says it is just the usual pain, but I think he is hiding it for my sake.'

'It was probably the long, arduous journey in this heat,' Mereta answered reasonably. 'Probably he will feel better tomorrow, after a good night's sleep.'

'You are possibly right, Mereta. I certainly hope so,' Neferu sighed.

'What about the handsome Yussef? Are you completely bowled over?' Mereta teased. Neferu was discomfited by this question because she realised that she did not know the answer. Mereta noted her hesitation and her eyes narrowed.

Neferu replied uncertainly, 'Of course, I am enormously pleased to see Yussef again. We are soon to be married, as you know.'

'But?' inquired Mereta with her eyebrows raised.

'Nothing,' said Neferu feeling distinctly disloyal to Yussef. 'Naturally, I am very happy to see him,' she said hurriedly. She averted her eyes from Mereta's direct gaze. The other girl was silent, and when she did finally speak, it was on another matter entirely.

'Tomorrow you are to have the day free, Neferu. My uncle has arranged for a carriage to take you all to see the sights of the city and to visit the temple of Amun-Re to admire the new road which my father has had built. He does like all visitors to see it,' she said with some amusement. 'You must praise it extravagantly afterwards, naturally!'

Neferu grinned. 'I understand,' she answered. 'It was very good of your uncle to think of it.'

'It was Amio, actually. He thought it would give you a better opportunity to be alone with Yussef.'

Mereta's tone was studiedly casual.

'That was very kind of Amio,' Neferu said, touched. 'I shall miss him so much when I go back.' Tears pricked her eyes and she felt them water.

'Will you really miss us so much?' the princess asked curiously. Noting the moist-eyed look.

'Only you, Amio, Maatnofret and Smenkh,' Neferu said stoutly. 'Not the others, really. Oh, they have been kind, but it is only you and the others that I have grown to love.'

Mereta seemed touched by this outburst. 'I do wish you could stay, Neferu. I too shall miss you so much.' The girls hugged each other at the thought of the imminent parting.

A housemaid entered with lunch for them. Today they were having it in the apartment because a delegation of dignitaries from the kingdom of Hatti had arrived. In the evening there was to be a state banquet for them.

'Uncle Ay wants your family to attend too,' stated Mereta.

'I had better go and inform them then,' Neferu spoke anxiously.

'Don't worry! Uncle will arrange everything. Just have lunch then go for your rest. You can see them again after they have rested and are more refreshed.' Mereta was showing her very practical side, thought Neferu. She felt very unsettled. The excitement plus the heat were just too much for her, she reckoned.

Neferu returned to Mereta's apartment after siesta to find that the princess had arranged for the company of Asenaath so that Neferu could be free to spend the afternoon with her family. Neferu kissed her and left her to go to the guest block. The sun was still very hot even now when it was much lower in the sky. The smell of the jasmine was overpowering and made her feel a little sick. She crossed the courtyard and entered the doorway of the guest block with relief. The shade appeared almost gloomy after the brilliance of the glare in the courtyard. Her eyes took a moment to adjust.

A major domo came forward to greet her. He recognised her with a smile.

'Have my family rested well?' she asked him casually.

'Your father and one of the young men are over with the grand vizier, my lady,' he informed her. 'They left a few minutes ago.,'

'Oh!' she said in surprise. Then, 'You do not need to escort me. I know that you are very busy with the houseguests. I know where my brother's room is and if he is still resting, I will come back later.'

'As you wish, ma'am,' he answered and bowed slightly before withdrawing.

Demi was awake and lying on his bed. He looked white and strained but he told her that he was feeling better. At her insistence he showed her his leg and she saw it was swollen. She felt inner unease but made no comment. 'You needn't come to dinner this evening, Demi, if you don't feel up to it. I can easily arrange a tray for you,' she said with concern.

'I wouldn't dream of missing such a grand occasion,' he said smiling. 'It isn't far to walk, anyway, so don't worry about me.' He spoke matter-of-factly.

'When will the others be back, I wonder?' she asked, more to herself than him.

'Not for some time, I suspect. They have only just left. I believe the queen wished to see the jewellery that Yussef made for her,' he stated.

'I would have liked to have seen them first,' she said, pulling a face.

Her brother laughed. 'Yussef is so proud of them that he is quite unbearable to be with at the moment. He can talk of nothing else. I can tell you, what with him, Grandma and Aunt Lea boasting round the neighbourhood I'm quite ashamed to walk out.' Neferu laughed. Grandma was not exactly subtle.

'Was Yussef very angry when I didn't come home with Father?' Her tone was careful.

'Angry? He was furious. He immediately developed this theory that one or other of the pharaohs wished to seduce you and put you in his harem.' He laughed outright.

Neferu was not amused. 'I don't think that is at all funny, Demi,' she said. 'Where on earth did he get such a crazy idea from?'

'Just jealousy. I expect,' said Demi. 'Anyway, there was obviously nothing to worry about,' he said placidly. 'I expect he feels a complete ass now!'

Neferu was not appeased. 'I should think he does. Does he think I am so cheap that I would let myself be treated like a toy?' she asked indignantly.

'I rather thought he was afraid you might be given no option,' Demi replied seriously.

'That is ridiculous. I have hardly seen the older pharaoh and Amio would never do anything so low.' Neferu was offended on behalf of her friend.

'Amio?' Demi asked curiously.

'Amenophis, the younger pharaoh whom you met earlier. He is very kind and honourable. Why, he has even arranged for us to be shown the sights of Thebes tomorrow by chariot so that we can be together.'

'That is kind, I must say,' commented Demi. 'You must forgive Yussef, Neferu. He loves you, that is why he is so jealous.'

Neferu smiled, not wanting to upset him. 'I will let you rest a while, Demi. I will come back later. You still look tired.' She kissed her brother and then left him to try and get some more rest. His condition left her distinctly uneasy.

Neferu dressed at a leisurely pace. There was no rush this evening as she was free until dinner. When she was ready, she decided to see if her father and Yussef had returned from their meeting with the queen and the grand vizier. They had indeed finished their meeting; both were in high good humour, Vassiliou, because he and his daughter had received so much praise, and Yussef because the queen had expressed deep satisfaction with the articles she had commissioned. Yussef was, therefore, looking forward to receiving more work from the court, Demi groaned to her that he would be impossible to live with now. The only thing which had marred their pleasure was that both the queen and Ay had expressed a proposal that Neferu's stay should be extended. Neferu was surprised and told them that she guessed that Mereta had requested her mother to say this as she had already asked Neferu herself many times.

'Why do they want you, Neferu? They could have anyone,' he said suspiciously.

Neferu couldn't help but be slightly annoyed at this. 'Well, perhaps it just so happens that she is as fond of me as I am of her, strange as that might seem to you, Yussef,' she said sarcastically.

Demi laughed. 'Just like old times, eh?' he said.

Yussef was not at all convinced. 'I don't like this set-up at all,' he said bitterly. 'I think this pharaoh has designs on you.'

Demi and Neferu exchanged glances. 'It isn't true, Yussef. You are letting your imagination run away with you. In any case the pharaoh would never be allowed to look at a commoner Keftiu girl of all things. You aren't even being sensible.'

'Why not?' he said jealously. 'He is only the grandson of a slave himself!'

Neferu was shocked and Vassiliou was angry. 'Be quiet, Yussef! You don't know what you are talking about. That kind of talk is treason! Guard your tongue. This grandson of a slave can have your head if he wishes it!'

'Yussef, you are being ridiculous,' Neferu said placatingly. 'The pharaoh is as kind to me as he seems to be with everyone else. He certainly has not gone out of his way to pay me any attention. I surely would have noticed it if he had. In fact, I happen to know that he has lost his heart to a certain lady at court, though you must never, never say anything to anyone. I see very little of him actually, and never alone. It is always in the company of people who are far more important to him than I am. As for me, you surely can't imagine that I am going to throw myself at him because he is the pharaoh, can you?'

'No, of course not,' Yussef replied more calmly. 'It isn't you I doubt, it's him! I don't think for a moment that you could be attracted to him, or any woman could for that matter!' Yussef's tone was spiteful and Neferu was mortified, both for herself and for Amio. She had never heard Yussef ever speak in such a malicious way about anyone before and she suddenly saw him in a new and more objective light. When he had criticised Amio in such an ugly fashion she had felt real pain and she became aware of just how much he meant to her. She felt an angry desire to defend him but was afraid that to do so would only fuel Yussef's fury. In the end she thought it more prudent to leave the matter at that. Yussef clearly felt her displeasure because his tone changed, and he said softly, 'Perhaps I am being jealous, Neferu, but I have missed you so much. I won't be happy until I get you away from here!' Neferu inclined her head. She felt confused and miserable. She did not know anymore what was going on or what she felt.

'Let's not talk just now, Yussef. It is time for dinner, and we must not be late.' She saw a look of anger cross his face, but her father agreed.

'I think you are right, Neferu. All these things can be discussed tomorrow.' Demi winced as he put his foot to the floor and Neferu saw that his limp was far worse than it normally was.

'What is it, Demi?' she cried. 'Can you manage it?'

Demi nodded and, with difficulty, raised a smile. 'I'll be fine tomorrow,' he replied reassuringly.

Neferu hovered by her brother's side as they crossed to the banquet hall. It was very dark, but the lights of the hundreds of oil lamps reflected out through the high narrow windows gave them a glow to find their way by, even if those lamps that lit the courtyard had not been there. Inside the hallway the family were directed to a table lower down than she had become accustomed to. It felt strange but she was not offended. She looked up to see Mereta, who gave her a warm smile and an unobtrusive wave. She smiled back. They were a little late. All the royal family had seated themselves. They all did obeisance prior to seating themselves. Neferu held onto Demi's arm as he leaned heavily against her. She noticed a film of perspiration above his lip. Against her will she felt a slight feeling of panic. She knew that he was far sicker than he was prepared to show.

During the meal Demi ate very little. She gave her father a telling look, but he gave her a non-plussed look, as if to say 'What can I do?' The after-dinner show began and for her sake Demi made an effort to seem appreciative. Neferu found it almost impossible to keep her attention on anything except her brother. She felt herself again the frightened little girl she once had been, when she had been sure that he was going to die. The same tight knot was in her stomach again and there was no Grandma to turn to this time.

When the queen retired to the withdrawing room and the ladies were requested to follow, Demi said that he felt tired and would go back to his room. Vassiliou refused to let Neferu accompany them when he and Yussef helped Demi back to the guest quarters. Neferu knew that once in the queen's company, she would not be able to leave until the royal family retired. She followed the others through to the withdrawing room where the royal family was surrounded by the usual crowd, and she found herself a place alone on the outskirts of the group from where she could slip away with the minimum of fuss. She was too worried about her brother to be in the mood for chattering.

'What is the matter, Neferu?' It was Maatnofret, who had come to sit with her.

'You are looking very sad for someone who is about to go home,' she said with the hint of a smile.

'My brother is very ill I fear, Maatnofret,' Neferu blurted out. 'I feel that I really should not be here at all but over there with him. My father and Yussef are just taking him over to the guest block.' She looked beseechingly at Maatnofret. 'Do you think you could possibly beg the queen for me to have permission to leave,' she said almost in tears. Maatnofret looked sympathetic and went back over to the royal group. She returned shortly afterwards.

'You have permission to leave, Neferu, and the grand vizier has sent for the court physician,' she said kindly.

'Thank you so very much, Maatnofret,' she said miserably. 'I am so sorry to cause such a fuss.'

'It is not a fuss, Neferu. Call me if you need my help later,' the older woman proffered. Neferu thanked her once again and jumped up, bidding her adieu. She saw that the royal family was surrounded by attentive courtesans so she curtsied hurriedly to everyone in general and slipped out as unobtrusively as she could.

Once outside, Neferu picked up her skirts and ran as fast as she could. The air felt chill now after the drop in temperature from the great heat of the day. She felt goosepimples on her arms when she reached the other side. Yussef was pacing up and down in the sitting room when she arrived. He told her that her father and a servant were helping Demi to undress. He looked worried.

'It's the same thing he had in Rashid, isn't it Yussef?' It was more a statement than a question.

Yussef bit his lip and tried to sound cheerful. 'It might not be, Neferu. It could be just a fever after the long boat journey.'

But Neferu knew that he could not even convince himself, let alone her. 'I want to go and see him as soon as he is in bed,' she said. Just then her father came out of Demi's room looking dispirited.

'He has a lot of pain,' he said to them. 'We'll have to get a physician. I wish Grandma was here.'

At least on that score she was able to reassure him that a court physician was probably on his way even now. Her father's brow cleared a little in relief. She knew that he always felt out of his depth in illness. He sat down glumly, watching Yussef pace up and down.

Neferu went through to her brother's room. Now that the leg was at rest, he looked a little bit more relaxed. She felt his forehead and looked at his flushed face closely. 'You have a high fever, Demi,' she noted.

'Yes. I can feel it,' he answered tiredly.

'The court physician is coming to see you soon,' she told him. Demi nodded listlessly.

The court physician arrived and with him the grand vizier. Neferu left the room while her brother was being examined. Afterwards, when her father was called in, she too entered, in spite of their protests. The court physician was a tall, thin, saturnine man in his mid-thirties, she guessed. He looked very grave, and he began to explain to Vassiliou that his son needed urgent treatment. Indicating with his forefinger the area in question, he declared, 'The infected bone needs to be scraped out from here. It is poisoning your son's vital systems. It was allowed to heal over from the surface last time and part of the poison has remained inside. Now, for some reason I am unable to ascertain, it has become active again. He may die if I don't do it. The treatment will take a long time. Six to eight decans, maybe more.'

Neferu's legs felt weak, and she could feel her lips quivering, but she composed herself with a struggle. This was much worse than she had thought. Surely Helios would not let Demi die now, when he had lived with it for so long? Demi himself seemed resigned to his fate, she thought, when she looked at him. He seemed exhausted. The physician explained to Demi exactly what he would do and then he gave him a draught of medicine to drink. Demi began to become very drowsy. The physician left to bring the equipment he would require, and they were left alone in the room with the grand vizier. The grand vizier addressed himself to Vassiliou.

'Your son will need to stay a long time, you realize? There is no way he could stand the journey home in this condition.'

Vassiliou nodded. There was no arguing with that. 'We have been through all this before, years ago,' he replied, running his fingers through his hair distractedly. 'I can't stay here for that long and Yussef must be back at the workshop soon. His uncle can't manage alone anymore!' The two men looked at Neferu, just as Yussef came in. He went over to Demi.

'How are you feeling, old man?' he asked fondly.

Demi smiled. The potion he had been given was beginning to take effect and his eyelids felt heavy. 'I feel a bit drunk,' he said sleepily.

'I will stay with you, Demi,' Neferu said, moving closer to the bed. She sat down carefully on the bed away from his damaged leg and took her brother's hand in hers. There was silence in the room. As they watched, Demi fell into a deep sleep. He did not even stir when the physician returned. The man looked doubtfully at Neferu and then lifted his eyebrows at her father and the grand vizier. 'I am staying here,' she said defiantly.

'Neferu, I think it would be better if you left us now,' said her father firmly. Knowing better than to argue with him when he was in that mood, she stood up.

'I will wait outside,' she said stubbornly.

Her father sighed. 'No, Neferu. I think it is best if you go to bed.'

'I won't be able to sleep!' she retorted.

'Your father is right, Neferu,' remarked the grand vizier, whose bright eyes had darted from one to another of them. 'Have no fear, we shall call you if your brother's condition worsens,' he added.

'Is that a promise, Father?' Neferu pleaded.

'Yes, it is.'

'All right, I'll go then,' she conceded, admitting defeat. She bent to kiss her brother's cheek and whispered against his ear. 'I love you, Demi. God be with you!' Wishing them goodnight, she left the room. Yussef followed her and said he would accompany her back.

In the sitting room she pressed her fingers to her eyes to stop the tears from coming. 'I'm so scared for Demi, Yussef,' she cried softly.

'Don't be, Neferu,' he said, putting his arms around her. 'He got better last time, didn't he? This royal physician must be the best in the land, or he wouldn't be physician to the pharaoh, would he?' he argued reasonably. 'He can probably do a lot more for Demi than our physician in On.'

'I hope so!' Neferu wept bitterly.

Ay came out of the room. He looked slightly disapproving. 'Are you still here, Neferu?' He said, somewhat superfluously as he could see very well that she was.

'I am taking her back now,' Yussef said smoothly.

'Good!' Ay replied. He looked at Neferu's bare arms and took off his cloak. 'Here, put this on, my dear!' he said solicitously, throwing it around her shoulders.

'Thank you, sire,' she said and wished him good night before stepping out of the room.

Yussef and Neferu walked across the courtyard and round the side of the block. He accompanied her along the pathway to her door. She wondered whether she should go straight in or whether it was all right to talk outside for a little. In the moonlight the surface of the water on the pool was shimmering.

'We can sit over there and talk for a while,' she said.

Yussef followed her gaze. 'Yes. I would like that,' he said. They walked over, hand in hand. The noise of the revelry from the state banquet hall was cut off here by the block of living apartments and the air was still.

'Life is so complicated, Yussef,' she said with a sigh as they sat down on the edge of the pool.

'The only important thing is that I love you and you love me,' he said. 'You do love me, don't you?'

'Of course I love you,' she said softly.

He leaned forwards and kissed her on the mouth and then put his arms around her. 'We must get married soon,' he said urgently. 'When we get back, we must arrange it right away,' he added.

'But what about Demi?' she asked, alarmed. 'We can't leave him here alone. He might die!' she cried. 'I couldn't bear it!'

'Of course not,' he said quickly. 'We will stay a few more days until he is out of danger then we will go back, and Aunt Lea will come to look after him!'

'Yussef, you know very well that that is not a practical solution. I am the one who must stay to look after him. I now the way of the place and some of its people. Poor Aunt Lea would be absolutely lost here. Anyway, it would be another decan at least before she arrived, even if she left immediately after she got the news.'

Yussef's chagrin was enormous. He was absolutely furious at this quirk of fate, which was about to snatch his prize, it seemed, just when it was in his grasp. Neferu felt disappointed. Was that all she was, a prize? Didn't she have a soul because she was a woman? Was that all that being a woman was? Was she really worth less than a man? She felt deep inside her that she was the equal of any one of them. Perhaps she wasn't as strong, but she was sure she was just as intelligent. She had been told many times that she was beautiful, and she was happy beyond measure for that gift, but now for the first time she began to perceive that she was in the same boat as Amio. He wanted someone to see past his deformities and she needed someone who could look past her face. How could she be sure that she was loved for herself? It was easy to have one's head turned, but if someone only lusted after the outer shell then she could end up a very bitter old woman when her lover found a younger version. She suddenly came to doubt Yussef's real feelings. She couldn't push the thought away.

They both looked up as the sound of voices carried to them. She recognised Amio as he escorted his mother and his sister to their apartments. There was the tinkling sound of Mereta's laugh as she responded to something amusing in their conversation. Their voices carried well in the still night air, although the words were indecipherable. She could make out the sounds of their goodnights and then watched Amio continue to his own apartment. He seemed to look towards the pool but did not say anything. Neferu's heart stopped for a moment. Had he seen them or not? For some reason she felt guilty again. She guessed that he probably had not noticed them or he would have wished them goodnight, wouldn't he?

'I think I had better go in, Yussef,' she whispered.

'Not yet,' he said petulantly.

'Yes,' she insisted. 'Father may be needing you.'

The handsome youth stood up reluctantly. 'I will be glad when all this is over,' he said with irritation.

'Demi hasn't done this on purpose!' she spoke indignantly.

'No,' he replied with a sigh. 'But if he had, he could not have timed it better to spoil all our plans.'

'Oh, Yussef. Remember what Grandma always says. Distance is like the wind!'

'It's all right for Grandma,' he said morosely. 'She is old, and her life is almost over.' Neferu nearly cried at the thought of losing Grandma. He was no comfort at all.

'Yussef. Don't say things like that! We have quite enough problems as it is.' The thought of Grandma's demise as well was too much.

They had reached the entrance to the building now and Yussef took her in his arms. He kissed her with all the ardour of his passionate wait and therefore did not see the approaching arrival of Maatnofret and her husband until the pair were almost upon them. The young lovers drew apart with embarrassment, Neferu said a hasty goodnight and ran in. Yussef stood looking after her for a moment, wished a goodnight to the couple in response to their greeting and then left towards the guest block.

Neferu lay awake for a long time. She said her evening prayers and made a massive plea for her brother's life and health and that the creator god should also sort out the life of one Neferu Stassopoulos, if he could possibly spare a little time from his more pressing duties, as she didn't have a clue what to do about any of the emotional storms she sensed brewing around her.

CHAPTER 13

Next morning Neferu was awoken by one of the house servants who informed her that Yussef and her father were to have breakfast with the grand vizier, and it had been arranged that she would have breakfast with her brother. Neferu asked how her brother was, but the housemaid had no information other than that which she had already given.

The Keftiu girl jumped up quickly and as soon as she was dressed, she left the building to go to her brother's block. As she neared the stairs on the corner, she noticed Amio and stopped for a moment to wish him good morning. She curtsied lightly.

'How is your brother, Neferu?' he asked. He seemed a little remote.

'I don't know, Amio. I am just going over to see him. Would you like to come with me?' There was a slight pause. 'Of course, I know that you are probably too busy,' she said hurriedly.

Amio looked at her seriously. 'I would like to come a little later if I may,' he said courteously.

'Of course. Whenever you wish,' she replied. She felt decidedly nervous with him this morning.

They parted company almost immediately and he entered into his uncle's household while she went out into the inner courtyard and across to the guest block. Her heart was thumping with an unpleasant intensity by the time she entered its portal. She was afraid of what she would find. Her father and Yussef greeted her with a kiss, and her father was able to allay her greatest fear. Demi was seriously ill, but the operation was over and though he would need careful treatment, the doctor thought a full recovery was possible.

Poor Demi. He still had a high fever, and his eyes were over-bright. He lay passively and to her eyes he looked worse than he had in the evening.

'How are you, Demi?' she asked quietly as she bent down to kiss him. He turned his feverish eyes upon her.

'Hello, Neferu,' he said, trying to smile. 'Not too good I'm afraid.'

'Don't worry, I am going to come and sit with you,' she said and pulled up a heavy wooden stool.

'The physician will be here soon,' her father informed her. 'His assistant sat with Demi all night and left at dawn. His master will be here after breakfast.'

Neferu nodded. 'Perhaps you had better go and eat, Father. It would not do to be late,' she said evenly.

'You are right, Neferu! There is a lot to discuss,' her father replied resignedly.

Demi had closed his eyes and Neferu could not tell whether he was asleep or not. It was obvious he had not the energy to talk, so after the other two had left she just sat by him quietly with her hand resting on his arm as if she could transfer some of her strength to him by touch. She turned as she heard a sound, thinking that the physician had arrived. It was Amio standing in the doorway. He looked a little like a giant bird of prey with the voluminous folds of his cloak around him, thrown into shadow with the slant of light rays behind him. He gave a slight cough as if to signal his presence. Neferu rose from her seat and curtsied, but Amio shook his head, and she was left standing awkwardly by the bed, wondering what to say. Demi opened his eyes and Amio advanced into the room.

'I hope you are feeling better,' Amio said solicitously.

'I am sorry I have caused you so much trouble, sire,' Demi said by way of reply.

'The doctor tells me you will need to stay with us for a while. It is no problem. It means we can keep your charming sister with us a little longer,' he said, smiling. After a moment he asked, 'Do you have any pain?'

'Not for the moment. The medication the physician has given me is very strong, sire,' Demi answered.

'Good,' replied Amio, pleased. 'I have arranged for you to be transferred to the royal apartments as soon as the physicians say it is feasible to move you. You will be in the same block as my younger brother. He is quite a bit younger than you, but I hope you will find him good company when you are feeling better.'

'I'm sure I shall,' replied Demi, before closing his eyes again. Neferu was touched by Amio's kindness, and this coupled with her worry over her brother caused the tears to come to her eyes.

'You are very kind, Amio,' she said, moved.

He saw her tears and said softly, 'Don't cry, Neferu. He will recover, I'm sure. We will do everything we can for him, I promise.' Neferu's tears only fell the faster at his tone of sympathy and she clasped his hand and squeezed it tightly.

'I am grateful for your help and your friendship, Amio.' She smiled at him through her tears. Amio seemed thrown by her emotional reaction.

'Well, that is settled then,' he stated uncertainly. 'If you will excuse me, Neferu, I must go. There is much to be done today before the Hittites leave.'

'I understand, Amio,' she said, softly aware that he found her mood difficult to cope with. With a slight incline of the head, he took his leave and Neferu was left alone again with her brother.

A maid brought in a breakfast tray, and she ate what she could. When Demi opened his eyes, she made him drink a little, but he refused to eat anything. Soon after the physician arrived with his assistant, and she insisted on staying to watch as they dressed his leg. What she saw almost made her faint. The bone of his left shin was almost broken in two, there was such a big hole in it. The assistant made her hold up a sheet so that Demi could not see his leg if he sat up, though she felt this was not much likely.

While the physician poured a cleansing solution into the wound, the assistant gave Demi some more of the potion for pain. When the physician had cleaned out the mixture of solution and exudate from the wound, he packed it with strips of cotton, soaked through with lotion from another vial.

'What is it?' she asked him, curious, in spite of her horror at the sight of the wound.

'It is a secret.' The physician grinned. 'It has been handed down from generation to generation in my family,' he said with pride.

'Oh!' she exclaimed, wondering what on earth it could possibly be. It had no particular smell as far as she could discern.

By the time her father and Yussef arrived, the leg was bound and splinted up and Demi was out cold again. His breathing was deep and stertorous. The doctor told her that that was as it should be, but when her brother woke up, he was to drink as much fluid as she could get him to take, in order to ensure that the fluids he had sweated out by fever were replaced as soon as possible. She nodded in acknowledgement. It appeared that Vassiliou and Yussef had been invited to offer a sacrifice for Demi's recovery at the temple of Amun-Re and that they were to go almost immediately.

'It seems a good idea, Father, as there is nothing to do here except wait. I am happy to sit with Demi. You two go. It is a very impressive sight!' she told them earnestly.

'I wish you could come with us, Neferu,' said Yussef disconsolately.

'One of us has to stay,' she said sensibly. 'We'll go together another time,' she added, to comfort him. As an afterthought she asked, 'Have you been given any further commissions?'

The handsome face brightened momentarily. 'Yes. several,' he replied proudly. 'We shall be the most famous jewellers in the whole of Lower Egypt.' Neferu smiled. It was good that there was some consolation for Yussef in all this history of delay and accident.

'Go and make your sacrifices. I am sure it will help. Pray to our own god. I will pray too, here,' she promised. Yussef nodded, came over and embraced her and then they left, knowing that they could do nothing for Demi at the present moment.

It was some hours before Demi woke up and so Neferu had plenty of time to think. So much had happened in the last month and especially in the last forty-eight hours. Tomorrow she should have been leaving for home and now she and Demi were to remain for an indefinite period. Not only that, she was confused over her feelings. She had grown close to Amio and Mereta, but she missed Yussef and her family. She decided to have a talk with Maatnofret when she could. She needed to air her views with someone she could trust to give her an honest opinion.

When Demi did finally wake up, he seemed refreshed. He still had very dark shadows under his eyes, but the fever seemed less, and a faint flicker of hope began to stir in her. She knew that he was not out of danger yet, they had been through this once before, but maybe the prayers had borne fruit.

'How are you, Demi?' she asked with concern.

'Better, I think. I don't feel any pain anyway,' he said as if slightly surprised.

'That's good,' she stated. 'Father and Yussef should be here soon.'

'I feel thirsty.' Her brother tried to lick his parched lips, so she poured some juice for him and supporting his head and shoulders lifted the cup to his lips. He drank it with enjoyment, she was pleased to see. It was a good sign. 'What time is it?' he asked. He was showing an interest in his surroundings again, she noted. It all pointed to an amelioration in his condition.

'Almost lunch time, I should think,' she responded with a small shrug. Neferu tried to help him to sit up a little. He winced a little as his leg pulled up the bed, but the pain settled as soon as his leg was immobile again.

'What will I do for a whole month in bed?' he said, depressed already at the very thought. Neferu refrained from saying that it might be much longer than that. No point in upsetting him at this stage, she thought.

'I'm sure they will find good use for a qualified scribe,' she said practically. 'You don't need your leg for that.'

Vassiliou and Yussef arrived back. Yussef had not been in the mood for admiring monuments, and he was feeling rather fractious. Neferu sighed. It was going to be a difficult day, she could tell. Demi was the least of her problems. The return of the two men must have been observed by the grand vizier because a messenger came over presently to invite them all to lunch with the royal family. The housemaid was called upon to sit with Demi for the duration. As was usual, the elder pharaoh was not present, neither his companion. Archduke Tuthmosis was seated on the queen's left and Amio on her right. Neferu found herself placed between her father and Mereta.

Mereta went out of her way to be charming to the visitors, it seemed to Neferu, and Yussef responded well to her vivacity. She was witty and amusing and made him laugh openly on several occasions. Amio was rather quiet and chatted mainly with her father. He told Vassiliou that the doctor had given permission for Demi to be moved from the guest block to the palace apartments the same afternoon and after lunch six servants would be coming to transfer him on a stretcher to his new room. From here it would be much more practical to care for him and he would be able to sit in the gardens when he was better. His young brother was looking forward to having a guest apparently. Neferu noticed that the queen appeared pensive but observant and once again, Neferu noted that nothing missed her attention.

After the queen and the archduke departed, Neferu was despatched to rest and she accompanied Maatnofret down to their mutual entrance, leaving the others on the terrace, chatting together.

'How are you, Neferu?' Maatnofret asked.

Neferu sighed. 'I don't really know, Maatnofret. I had really hoped to have a word privately with you.'

'What about?' Maatnofret said, raising her eyebrows.

'I feel I am being pulled in so many different ways, Maatnofret, that I may break, and I don't know what to do for the best.' Neferu felt annoyed at the self-pity in her voice, which sounded whingy even to her.

'You can always pray to Yahweh,' Maatnofret told her.

'I don't think he will listen to me, Maatnofret. He isn't my god,' Neferu replied.

'Aten-Yahweh is everyone's god,' Maatnofret assured her. 'He is the only one who can help you.'

'Where is his temple then?' Neferu asked, mystified.

'Come into my home, Neferu and I will tell you,' Neferu followed Maatnofret into her suite and looked around. She noted with surprise that it was very plainly furnished.

In view of the senior lady-in-waiting's position at court, this simplicity was obviously a matter of personal taste. There was none of the opulence of the other apartments. 'Sit down, Neferu,' Maatnofret said, smiling. Neferu sat down. She wanted to hear more about the god whom Maatnofret believed in so fervently. She liked and respected Maatnofret a lot.

'Aten-Yahweh is the great god who saved mankind from the great flood long ago,' she told Neferu. 'His name is from the Hebrew language, and it is not really a name like Neferu or Maatnofret. It means in that language "The Great I Am". In Egyptian we call him Aten to signify the "Breath of Life". The spirit which animates us all and which makes us a part of Him. Neferu was fascinated. She could see that Maatnofret was totally sincere and that her belief was profound and steadfast.

'Isn't Aten the same as Re then?' she asked, a bit perplexed. Maatnofret hesitated a little before answering.

'Amun and Re and Hathor and Toth are all parts of Aten, if you like, Neferu. He is the whole who comprises many parts. He is greater than any of the parts.' Neferu could understand that. Like the segments of an orange in a way. Each segment was orange, but it was only a part of the whole orange. Maatnofret smiled at the analogy. 'Well, sort of, Neferu. But there is a better description,' she said. She could see that Neferu was interested and so she continued. 'Think of yourself, Neferu. The whole person. That part of you which thinks and feels is a part of you, and it is the part that tells your hands what to do when you sew. Your hand is precious, but if it withers, you still live, and although life will be more difficult for you, you can manage. If the spirit which moves you is cut off, then nothing can work, and you are dead. The life force in you is part of the Aten and your hands and useful parts are like the lesser gods. Aten is like the crystals of lapis lazuli; he has many facets. When you die the Aten stores only this essence of you in his memory until he chooses a suitable time and place for you to come again. Your essence, the spirit of you, will never die.'

Neferu felt nervous. She knew that this was heresy, and one could be severely punished for heresy if the priests of Amun found out. At the same time, she loved the sound of this religion. She had never been able to believe those stories that the bodies of the dead come to life again. She had sometimes seen the bodies of dead animals and knew that they decomposed and smelled horrid. She would never want for her dead body to come back to life again rotted. The very thought made her feel sick. On the other hand, it seemed a much more practical solution for only the most important part, the spirit of her, to be saved. She would much rather have a whole new body starting from a baby again. Yes, this was much more comforting to her. She liked this and she could believe it too. She said as much to Maatnofret, who smiled at her.

'There is much more to it than that, Neferu,' she said. 'But that will do for today. I will tell you more later on, when the time is ripe. Just make sure that you pray to the Aten, if you really need help.' She paused before continuing. 'The Aten doesn't need a temple, Neferu, He is all around you. You can contact him from within you, not with the aid of symbols.' Neferu nodded. Maatnofret looked at her sharply. 'Do not discuss this with anyone outside the family, Neferu. It could be very dangerous for me if the priests of Amun find out.'

Neferu nodded. 'I understand that, Maatnofret. It was brave of you to tell me. I would have to stand with you, if you ever get into trouble for it, because I too believe in your Aten and from this day onward, I will pray to him every day. He shall be my god too. If he wants me, that is.'

'He wants you, Neferu,' she said, giving the girl a hug. 'Now. Go and get some rest. It is getting late.' Neferu got up to go. At the door she stopped.

'One more question, Maatnofret.' The older lady inclined her head in acquiescence. 'When we die, is it necessary for our body to be embalmed for our soul to be preserved.'

'Not at all,' was Maatnofret's swift and emphatic reply.

'That's good,' said Neferu simply and was gone.

Neferu meditated over the things Maatnofret had told her and she thought of new questions that she also needed to know the answers to. She had heard long ago that in the faraway east where the silk caravans came from, the people burnt the bodies of their dead loved ones and scattered their ashes to the winds. Afterwards they listened in the wind for the voices of their loved ones. It had seemed a frighteningly barbaric custom to her at the time but if Maatnofret was correct then there was nothing to be lost with the death of the body anyway. In that case, she found it infinitely preferable to have her ashes thrown cleanly to the wind than to rot in a casket. Much more preferable. Her sense of romance was drawn to the thought of whispering to her loved ones in the wind.

Maatnofret came to wake her at the end of siesta and Neferu broached the subject again.

'I have prayed to your god, Maatnofret. I have chosen him above the other gods.'

Maatnofret laughed. 'No, Neferu. You don't understand at all. Aten has chosen you, not the other way round,' she declared.

'How do you know he has chosen me?' she asked in puzzlement.

'I have seen the signs,' Maatnofret said cryptically, but refused to be drawn further. Neferu shrugged. She didn't understand what Maatnofret could possibly mean. All the portents of her present situation were at best very difficult and at worst potentially catastrophic. She had decided to leave the matter alone when Maatnofret suddenly said, 'Aten is a jealous god, Neferu. If you forget him later and pray to other gods, he will punish you. But if you are faithful to him as your only god, he will show you the secrets of your heart and of life. Once you learn to know him, he will give you the strength to overcome your fear of danger, death and disease.' Maatnofret spoke with such intensity that Neferu stood transfixed. Maatnofret was sharing with her the secrets of her soul, and it was a precious gift because she understood that people rarely give of themselves to strangers in this way. She recognised the generosity of the moment and felt a little humbled by the other woman's courage in putting herself at risk in this way.

'I want to know the Aten, Maatnofret. He will be my only god from this time onward,' she promised.

There was an air of expectancy in the room and Maatnofret sank to her knees and assumed a position of prayer. Neferu felt herself compelled by something within her to do the same. Maatnofret asked the Aten in a simple prayer for his blessing to be on Neferu from this day forth to the end of her life, and to the eternal life beyond the tomb. Neferu echoed the amen of Maatnofret. Thus it was that Nefertiti Stassopoulos abandoned the sun worship of her forefathers and became a devotee of the Aten, the one almighty god of the universe. She felt herself a small inconsequential speck in his universe and could never have imagined that for a brief span of time, her conversion would lead to momentous events in the history of her beloved Egypt.

After the brief prayer session, Neferu left Maatnofret and, having dressed and prepared herself, decided to go and see Mereta. Although she was still officially off duty, their friendship had grown to the stage that they considered each other best friends and it was this social instinct which was uppermost in her mind. Mereta was sitting at her dressing table, having her hair attended to by Asenaath. Mereta had pressed Asenaath to do her hair in the new style instigated by Neferu, but she did not appear to mind.

'It takes much less time than the braiding,' she conceded to Neferu with a smile. There was a hair pin between her teeth, which rather obscured her words. Neferu was amused to notice that it looked like a little ivory horn growing out of each side of her mouth.

'I can see that your Yussef is very handsome, Neferu. I can see why you love him,' Mereta said, trying not to turn her head and looking out of the corner of her eyes at Neferu.

'I have known Yussef since I was born; we grew up together. He is my friend, and he is a good person. Yes, he is handsome, but that is not why I love him, Mereta,' Neferu said gravely. 'I cannot imagine my life without Yussef in it. He has always been there.'

Mereta nodded understandingly. 'I know, Neferu. I think you are lucky to have such an admirer, but I also think he is lucky to have such a nice person as you!' She abruptly changed the subject. 'I expect you are going over to see your brother now, aren't you?' Neferu affirmed this and Mereta said, 'Give him my best wishes then. I'll see you and the others later at dinner then.' She gave Neferu a playful push to indicate that she was not summarily dismissing her. Neferu smiled and took her leave.

Demi was awake when she made her entrance. The doctor was just leaving and pronounced himself satisfied with Demi's progress so far. The fever was abating gradually and had ceased the previous spiking which had exhausted her brother so much. He told Neferu that his assistant would sit a night watch with Demi again the coming night. All in all, Neferu found herself cheered by the news. Things seemed to be taking a turn for the better in general, she thought.

Neferu observed that Yussef was also in a much happier frame of mind. He seemed to have been totally charmed by Mereta and said he could see why Neferu liked her so much. He was further flattered when Neferu repeated Mereta's comments on his handsome looks. It appeared that the queen had extended, via Amio, an invitation for the whole family to visit Thebes to see Demi whenever they wanted. It was to be hoped that he would make a prompt and excellent recovery. but they could be assured, in the meantime, that he would receive the very best of care. To Neferu's relief, Yussef appeared to have lost his paranoid mistrust of the royal family. Things were going to be less traumatic than she had feared.

Further conversation between them was interrupted by the arrival of the servants, who had been sent to undertake the transfer of Demi to the royal block. Moving Demi was a slow and painful process, even with him still under the effects of the pain potion he had swallowed earlier. He was terrified of them jarring his leg. In the end it took Yussef and her father, as well as the four men, to lift him onto a stretcher. Once on the stretcher they all relaxed for a moment before lifting it and bearing him out of the room to the other block. When it was accomplished, Neferu felt herself breathe out and realised that she had been holding her breath in sheer nervousness. The three of them gathered Demi's belongings together and followed the four stretcher bearers.

When Demi had been settled into his new room, he leaned back on his pillows with relief.

'It wasn't as bad as I thought it was going to be,' he confessed. He was echoing the thoughts of all of them and there was a general relaxation of tension in the room and some relieved grins.

'May I come in?' asked an unknown voice from the doorway. They turned round and saw Smenkh with his tutor, General Nakhtmin. Vassiliou and Yussef bowed deeply, and the two newcomers inclined their heads slightly. Neferu introduced them without formality. Not noticing the slightly raised eyebrow of the general.

'Father this is Prince Smenkhenre and General Nakhtmin, his military tutor.' The general remained very much in the background while the two youths became acquainted. Although Smenkh was much younger, he was very intelligent and had already received a good education, so that he was already able to converse well on varied subjects. The two youths appeared to have a natural affinity for friendship and Neferu thought this would make her brother's enforced immobility much easier to bear. Smenkh was very open with Demi, not showing his usual shyness.

'It will be nice to have a new friend living so close by,' he said. 'Your sister is my friend. She is quite clever for a girl,' he said politely.

Demi laughed. 'Yes. She isn't bad, for a girl,' he admitted. Neferu let the remark pass, though she would normally have retorted something rude if her brother had said it. She knew it was meant as a compliment.

Vassiliou and Yussef left once they were sure that Demi was completely comfortable, as they had business with the grand vizier still to sort out. They would be taking refreshments with Ay and there were messages and documents to be collected for despatch to On with them. Both men appeared remarkably cheered up from their attitude of dismay the previous day, which had gloomily pervaded the room and everyone in it.

When they had gone Smenkh became much more voluble, and the two boys began a game of backgammon. This more than anything denoted to Neferu how much better Demi was feeling. Neferu told Nakhtmin that Demi was a qualified scribe and that when his condition was improved a little, he would probably benefit from having something to challenge him, to prevent him becoming bored. The dark Nubian general turned out to be quite fatherly and offered to supply Demi with papyrus and drawing apparatus in the meantime, to while away the hours.

Seeing that Demi was rapidly becoming exhausted, the general neatly manoeuvred his charge out with the promise that they would return later, when Demi was more able to enjoy company. A servant brought in some refreshments and Neferu forced her brother to take something. He refused to eat anything solid but did take some juice. Neferu fussed about it until he told her in a slightly irritated tone, 'You are getting just like Grandma.' It brought her up with a bump. She contented herself by eating more than she normally did and when she looked up, he had fallen asleep. She sat watching him for a while, but he seemed perfectly comfortable, so she rose and departed to her own suite to prepare for dinner. While dressing she pondered Maatnofret's words again.

Neferu found herself seated between her father and Mereta at dinner. To the right of Mereta was Yussef and Neferu noted that the princess engaged him in lively conversation. There were frequent discreet laughs from the pair of them and Yussef seemed at his most charming, with no hint of the animosity he had earlier expressed towards the royal family. She felt relieved and smiled slightly at her father, who was also observing their geniality.

Dinner over, the ladies followed the queen to the withdrawing room as usual and Mereta told Neferu that she found Yussef intelligent and charming. Neferu was pleased. She realised that Mereta posed no threat to Yussef's serenity because she was female. He had therefore, been able to be his usual self with her.

Later, the men joined their company and Neferu noticed that her father and the grand vizier spent a long time in conversation. Yussef came over to join her and Mereta and seemed quite his old self. He told Mereta funny stories about Neferu when she was little, some of which Neferu felt would have been better left unsaid. They made her appear an idiot and she felt quite irritated with him. He, however, only ignored her warning looks and continued, which only amused Mereta all the more. At one stage Mereta laughed until tears actually came to her eyes, as Yussef told her about the time they had climbed over a hedge to take a shortcut to the beach in Rashid and found themselves being chased by a bull. They had run so fast that in their efforts to climb over the gate quickly, Neferu had slipped in a large patch of dung and gone crying all the way home, the long way round, to Grandma.

'You can imagine how she stank!' he told Mereta. Neferu could have really strangled him at this point. He was deliberately trying to humiliate her. Mereta laughed uncontrollably while Neferu was hard put not to thump him. Her chagrin was multiplied a hundredfold when an amused voice at her elbow asked, 'And what is the cause of all this mirth and merriment?' It was Amio, and the sight of his questioning face only sent Mereta into more paroxysms of laughter. She was laughing so much that her words ended up coming out as a sort of snort and she was, mercifully, forced to stop her attempts to speak. Neferu felt her cheeks burning and her discomfort was obvious to them all.

'I'll tell you later, brother dear,' Mereta gasped. 'It's impossible to talk now.'

Amio raised his eyebrows. 'I shall look forward to hearing the tale,' he said lightly, looking at Neferu and taking in her mortified expression and flaming cheeks. He glanced towards Yussef, who was exuding charm and good humour, then back to Mereta, who was still laughing so much that she could not sit still. To Neferu he remarked that the queen had charged him to tell her that if she wished to be excused to go and sit with her brother, she already had permission. Neferu was more than glad to flee the scene of her embarrassment and got up to leave.

Yussef jumped up. 'I didn't mean to tease you, Neferu. Don't be angry with me.' Amio looked at them curiously.

'It's all right, Yussef,' she said trying to control her irritation as they were to leave so soon. 'I suppose it was very funny for you. Maybe for me too, in about twenty years,' she said cynically.

'I'll come and see Demi too, later,' Yussef replied.

As she was leaving, she heard Mereta say to Yussef, 'Tell me more. It is fascinating!' Neferu shuddered to think what he would tell them next. Nothing too awful, she hoped.

Demi was awake and alert, when Neferu arrived at Smenkh's suite. He was sitting up in bed trying to read by the light of two oil lamps. As his head was partially in their shade he was squinting markedly, trying to make out the script in the inadequate light. Neferu moved the lamp closer.

'That's better!' he said, with a smile of welcome.

'What are you reading?' she asked, trying to look over his shoulder.

'These are some of the stories and legends that Smenkh brought me, to help pass the time,' he replied.

'Are they interesting?' she asked.

'Very!' he responded. 'I might write some of our stories down for him to read,' her brother added, glancing up at her. 'What's the matter, Neffie? You look a bit glum.'

'I was just thinking how fast these past few days have gone and how eventful they have been. I haven't really had a chance to speak to Father alone at all. I wish that I had some presents to send to Grandpa and Grandma and Aunt Lea, at least. Something to remind them of me.'

'Don't be a chump, Neferu. How could they possibly forget you?' he spoke in a tone of brotherly disrespect. She gave him a playful dig.

'Don't push your luck, Demi Stassopoulos, just because you are sick.' He grinned at her but did not say anything. 'My life has been thrown completely out of focus by this visit to Thebes,' she said, half musingly. 'I'm beginning to think that destiny has arranged some obscure fate for me and I'll never see home again.'

'What a lot of twaddle, Neferu!' her brother retorted. 'You are getting as fanciful as Aunt Lea. In six decans at the most, we'll be home, and you will be married. I couldn't help my leg now, could I?'

From his tone, she realised that he was blaming himself for the outcome of events, or he thought she was blaming him.

'I am not blaming you, Demi,' she stressed. 'It's just that I am beginning to think that fate brought me here for a purpose,' she said darkly.

'Yes, it did!' Demi said with a grin.

'What then?' Neferu queried, non-plussed.

'To make Yussef the richest jeweller in On, and you the most envied wife, of course.'

Neferu was genuinely amused. 'Well, that definitely isn't it,' she laughed. 'I'll just have to leave it in the hands of the Aten,' she said good-humouredly.

'The Aten?' Demi queried. 'What the heck is the Aten?'

Neferu reflected guiltily that she was not to mention this subject in wider circles, so she promptly made Demi swear to secrecy. Curious, he did so. Neferu told him about the existence of the god of the universe who was well known outside of Egypt but less known here. She told him that she was meant to keep quiet about the subject because she did not want to get her friend or herself into trouble with the priests of Amun. Demi was shocked. His cautious nature saw problems here that Neferu had not even envisaged, he could tell.

'You can certainly count on me to remain silent, Neferu,' he said. 'You could get yourself into a lot of hot water over this. Does it mean that much to you?'

'Demi, I believe in the Aten. It would be much more convenient for me not to, probably but I can't deny what I believe to be true. It would be like denying you or Grandma. You may be sure that I will be very careful not to expose myself,' she said, privately alerted by her brother's reaction to a more realistic sense of the danger she trod.

'We won't talk about it anymore,' she said.

'Good,' he said, with evident relief. 'Better not mention it to Yussef, Neferu.'

'No,' she agreed. It was the first time in her life that she had calculatingly left Yussef in the dark about something fundamentally important to her. He was the one person she should have been able to discuss anything with, she realised, but she knew he would be her enemy in this. Intuitively she shivered. Yussef her enemy? She was being fanciful.

Demi looked past her all of a sudden and she caught a warning look to her before she turned around. Her father was standing in the doorway. 'Father!' Neferu cried and went to put her arms around his neck. He hugged her and patted her back.

'I shall miss you so much, and Grandma and the others,' she cried brokenly.

'It isn't the end of the world, Neferu. Sometimes life changes and we have to adjust as best we can,' he said reassuringly. 'The time will pass, and Demi will have you to keep him company. We have to believe that this is for the best. He is having the best care in the whole of the Two Lands. We are very lucky. If any physician can heal Demi, it must be this man.' Her father spoke sensibly, and a degree of calmness came back to Neferu.

'I would like to send Grandma a present, but I don't have anything to give,' she said sadly.

'What about a lock of your hair? Nothing could be more personal than that?' He seemed pleased with himself for having thought of this.

'My hair?' she repeated. After a pause she said, 'If Grandma would like that then I am happy to send it. It doesn't seem very much though.'

Her father smiled. 'She keeps a lock of your mother's hair, doesn't she?' It was true. Grandma treasured the lock of hair which she had cut from her dead daughter's head. Neferu had seen it many times when Grandma would unwrap it to show her the glossy black curls. Neferu decided that she did not wish to donate quite so much, and her father agreed that it wasn't necessary in the circumstances. Just a few centimetres from the ends would be quite sufficient.

It was getting very late, and Neferu was on the verge of leaving when Yussef arrived. He was genuinely sad to be leaving Demi behind. He had always thought of Demi as his younger brother.

'We will come and visit you and Neferu again soon,' he assured Demi. 'I'll come with Grandpa if your father is busy. Maybe you will be well enough to travel by boat then, if we lift you carefully.'

Demi nodded. 'I am feeling a lot better already,' he assured Yussef.

They continued to chat for a little while longer and they left when the doctor's assistant arrived to sit by Demi during the night. They were all very thankful for the care and attention he had received. It was the sort of care Grandma had always provided for them in the past. Vassiliou walked on slowly after kissing Neferu good night, diplomatically leaving Yussef a little time to say goodnight to her alone. 'I have hardly seen you, Neferu!' he complained bitterly. 'But I'll be back, you'll see. Remember you are mine.' She only had time to nod briefly before he took her in his arms, and she felt his lips on hers. She found herself responding automatically and when he released her abruptly and walked away, she went in slowly. She got ready for bed and then lay awake, going over the events of the crowded day. She felt overcome by their coming departure and tears of self-pity welled up in her. She cried long and hard in the dark, giving vent to a host of mixed emotions, which the night received kindly, without betraying her. When at last she fell asleep she felt completely empty.

The next morning, Neferu woke with swollen eyes and a heavy head. She looked into the burnished mirror and got a shock. 'I look a fright' she thought with a shock. She knew that everyone would notice that she had been crying so she hurriedly soaked a piece of white cotton in the cold water in her pitcher, squeezed it out and lay back on her bed with the cloth pressed over her eyes. She continued to do this for some time, wetting the cloth occasionally to cool it. She pressed her eyelids so hard that she saw a series of colours in front of the closed lids. A pretty green with white speckles in it which turned to pink when she pressed harder, finally the pink turned into a reddish brown which she did not find so attractive. She released her fingers from her eyes and opened them. Yes. It definitely felt better. She looked in the silver mirror again. Her eyelids were still a bit swollen, but it would have to do. She jumped up to start getting ready for breakfast.

While Neferu dressed, she thought about how quickly she had fallen into the way of life here at Malkata. It was like having a foot in two different worlds, she reflected. Worlds which had no possibility of ever meeting, she realised. She knew that when she did finally go home there would be no coming back. The thought of leaving Amio and Mereta was very painful to her. She felt that they belonged to her just as much as Grandma and the others. She wondered how this could have happened in such a short space of time. It seemed strange to her. Even the redoubtable grand vizier had become a part of her daily life as if he had always been there. They had assumed a familiarity which was as natural as it was peculiar. She had the sensation that she had known them a very long time, even before she was born. She cut herself short here. Demi was right, she was getting too fanciful.

That morning she dressed with care. She applied kohl around her eyes more carefully than usual to disguise the puffiness. She dressed her hair carefully too. What was it that the Aten intended with her, she wondered as she put the finishing touches to her hair. 'Don't examine everything for hidden meanings!' she told herself silently in the mirror. She looked around for something to cut a lock of her hair with, but not finding anything suitable she decided to go and ask Maatnofret if she could borrow her husband's shaving knife.

The lady-in-waiting seemed surprised at Neferu's unusual request, and the girl quickly explained to her why she wanted it. Maatnofret looked intrigued and stared at Neferu's beautifully coiffured hair.

'You should have done it before you styled your hair, Neferu,' she said with a frown.

'Oh, that's no problem,' Neferu assured her. 'I shall just pull some out from the side.' Maatnofret looked doubtful but went to bring the required object. 'May I borrow your mirror, Maatnofret?' Neferu felt she was being a nuisance. Maatnofret dutifully went to get it and held it up helpfully while Neferu removed one of the ivory pins from her chignon and teased down some of her hair in the region of her temple. When she was satisfied that she had enough, she repeated the procedure on the other side of her head and then cut them both to the length required. Neatly, she placed the cuttings on the table and, using the pin as a comb, she deftly blended the shortened hair into the top of her chignon. Maatnofret was impressed.

'You did that well, Neferu,' she granted.

Neferu smiled. 'It will soon grow again,' she stated optimistically.

'It's true!' observed the older woman.

Breakfast was shared with the grand vizier and his family that morning. An easy familiarity seemed to have grown up between her father and Ay, and even Yussef appeared to get on well with the older man. There was no doubt that Ay could be extremely charming when he wanted to be.

There was an inevitable feeling of sadness in the air and Neferu was hard pressed to make pleasant small talk in the circumstances. Ay was quick to tease her, saying that she was behaving as though they were going forever, whereas it would not be long before they would be coming again.

Once the meal was over, the dreaded period of leave-taking was upon them, and she was very sad. Ay hurried the moment along as much as he could, with the obvious approval of her father and the just as obvious chagrin of Yussef, then he conducted her father and Yussef to convey their last words with the queen prior to their leaving. While this was going on Neferu hung about in the garden hoping to get a last moment of conversation with them before they left.

The morning was still young, but the air was oven hot. It would be an uncomfortable journey for them, she knew. The movement of the boat would create a little breeze, at least. In spite of that, she knew that the next four to five days would be very boring for them. Eventually she heard their footsteps and went out ahead into the inner courtyard, where she waited until they caught her up.

'Where is your luggage?' she demanded of her father.

It was Ay who responded. 'All these matters have been attended to, Neferu. The luggage is already loaded onto the chariot.' His tone rebuked her a little and she accompanied them across the courtyard in silence.

In the outer courtyard there was a hubbub of noise and people scurrying backwards and forwards through the main gates of the complex. She noticed that Ay seemed to be known by everyone. She became aware of an attitude of reverent respect accorded to this man whose presence provoked a general stir of interest and a glut of deferential bows, which the grand vizier invariably acknowledged with the very slightest inclination of his head while continuing to walk on. At the chariot standing ready to take the two Keftiu to the harbour, Neferu threw her arms around her father's head and hugged him tightly, murmuring message after message to Grandpa, Grandma and Aunt Lea. Eventually her father managed to untangle himself from her hug and said that it was time to leave. The grand vizier stood by, watching but silent.

Neferu turned to Yussef with an unaccustomed shyness in her manner. The young man swept her to himself and kissed her boldly. He told her to remember what they had discussed two evenings ago. She nodded and he climbed into the chariot. Neferu stood watching through a blur of tears as the chariot left the palace confines. Her arm remained high in a wave until they disappeared from sight. She felt a touch on her arm and turned to look at Ay. 'We should return, my dear!' he said kindly. He seemed a little disapproving and she suspected that it was the boldness of Yussef's embrace which had upset him. The grand vizier did not make any comment, however, and they returned to the royal block in silence. As they reached the entrance to the royal gardens the grand vizier informed her that the queen would like to have a word with her. Neferu's cheeks were still a little flushed at what she considered as Ay's unspoken criticism of her conduct in the public courtyard. Her anger grew inside. These people were not her family, and they had no right to criticise her. She felt like a naughty child. Sustained by this sudden spurt of anger, her tears receded, and she was able to greet the grand queen with bright eyed composure. She curtsied deeply. After all that, it appeared that the queen only wanted to tell her that if she wished to have the day free for her brother then she would be welcome to do so, but that the great royal nurse had taken it upon herself to care for the young man.

Neferu was so surprised that she could have been knocked over by a feather. This was the biggest surprise possible and a great honour. No one could have had a more exalted nurse. The wife of the grand vizier! Neferu guessed that Demi would like the plump little woman. In a very aristocratic way, she had a great deal of the quality of Grandma about her. Neferu digested the information, nodding slightly.

'In that case, Your Majesty, I would prefer to continue my duties as lady-in-waiting to the princess from today, if I may visit my brother first,' she spoke quietly, her anger having dissipated by the kindness of the grand vizier's wife. The queen smiled and agreed with her decision. She had looked questioningly at the girl, with her head on one side, before dismissing her. Amio merely smiled at her and hoped that she would not be too sad.

As she walked to her duties, Neferu reflected on Yussef's suspicions and hoped that he was now at his ease. Unfortunately, since he had voiced them, she had not been able to forget them herself. Was it possible that she had been installed here as a plaything for the pharaoh? It seemed totally absurd, but then again, it seemed absurd that the queen should have suddenly offered the position to her out of the blue. Why her, a nobody from On? She remembered Ay's flirtatious manner with her in front of the court and her vague suspicion that something intriguing was going on.

When Neferu entered Demi's room, she put her speculations aside and concentrated her attention on him. He had no fever this morning and had actually eaten some breakfast, he said. The doctor seemed pleased with him. His leg had been freshly dressed and he looked comfortable.

'I have some news for you,' he said importantly. Neferu raised her eyebrow questioningly.

'Oh, what is that?'

'The pharaoh has invited me to join the Kap and I am to follow the same timetable as the others, as far as I can, anyway,' he said with a flourish.

'What exactly is this Kap?' she demanded.

'Well, I can't tell you very much because I am sworn to secrecy,' he volunteered. 'I think it is going to be very interesting though, and I am going to be carried into the main room for lessons with the others,' Demi assured her.

'I am very pleased for you, Demi. I was afraid that you would be bored, even with the great royal nurse to look after you,' she said with an outer smile, but wondering again at all these things.

Neferu sat down beside his bed. 'I shall continue to work as lady-in-waiting to the princess Mereta, but I can come and see you often, so you won't be lonely, Demi.' Demi suddenly looked down for a moment before he started to speak to her again.

'Neferu, I think Yussef was wrong about the pharaoh. He seems very nice to me. I don't think he is planning to use you as a plaything at all.'

'I think it very unlikely, Demi,' she spoke coolly. 'Why on earth would he go to such complicated lengths when he could have anyone he wanted just by a single command? I am not important enough to warrant such an elaborate subterfuge.' Demi nodded and Neferu stood up and abruptly changed the subject. 'I think it is time for you to rest, Demi. I will come again after lunch. I will return to Mereta now if you are quite comfortable.'

'See you later, Neferu,' he said amiably.

'See you later, Demi,' she replied.

When Neferu arrived at the apartment of the princess, she and Asenaath were sitting in the shade of the sitting room, chatting in a friendly fashion. Mereta told Asenaath that she was free to return to her duties with the queen if she wished so that Maatnofret could be free for a little while, or, if she wished, she could take the rest of the day off to continue her preparations. Asenaath was delighted and left almost immediately.

When she had gone, Mereta looked at Neferu keenly and asked her what was wrong. Neferu replied, 'Nothing at all.' And gave a forced smile.

'I don't believe you, Neferu. What is it?' the other girl replied. Neferu saw there was no point in lying and explained about the incident in the courtyard and Ay's silent disapproval, which had stung Neferu.

'Your family do not own me, Mereta. I am sorry if I have embarrassed you all and I am very grateful for all your many kindnesses, but I am beginning to wonder why I am here at all,' she said, her lower lip trembling violently.

'Why you are really here?' Mereta reiterated slowly.

'Yes! Why me, Mereta? Why was I singled out to be offered the post of lady-in-waiting? I was not even suitable. Yussef is right. It is most unusual, isn't it?' Neferu spoke with some heat.

'Did Yussef say that?' Mereta inquired. Neferu now felt uncomfortable having brought Yussef's name into the conversation. She realised that she had made a bad mistake.

She shrugged slightly. 'If he hadn't said it, I would have wondered myself sometime,' she replied a little defiantly. 'Why did they want me to stay, Mereta?'

Mereta looked at Neferu with a hurt expression. 'My family does not feel that it owns you and none of us would want you to feel like that either, Neferu,' she said quietly. 'If you really dislike us and want to leave, I am sure that mother will arrange it right away. We all truly like you and want you to be happy here with us. If my uncle was cold then I expect it was because we are all so continuously aware of how everything we say and do is subjected to public scrutiny and, believe me, there are many, many people who would only be too happy to criticise or misrepresent us. Where there is power there is always loneliness. It is very difficult for people like us to give anything of our real selves away. To know whether someone likes us for ourselves or merely for our positions. You have never had to live with that, Neferu. You know when someone says they like you that it is not for some ulterior motive. I have never had the pleasure of knowing that except with my family and a very, very few others. I have felt it with you, and I am very sad if you feel that you are in subjection.' Mereta's voice had broken and Neferu noticed that her eyes were bright with tears. Neferu felt very ashamed of hurting her friend in this way. She had never considered things from this point of view.

'I am so sorry, Mereta,' she said regretfully. 'It must be awful to feel like that and I didn't mean to bring criticism on your family by my behaviour.' She felt really miserable. 'I really do like you. You are my best friend and just like a sister to me. I never want to hurt you,' she said contritely, watching as tears fell down Mereta's cheeks. The other girl shook her head and wiped her eyes. The two girls hugged each other for a moment before drawing apart and looking at each other.

'What about Yussef, Neferu? I felt he didn't really like us,' Mereta said.

Neferu looked away evasively. 'It wasn't that, Mereta. He certainly likes you very much anyway. It's just that …' Her voice trailed off here uncomfortably. She felt she could not quite look Mereta in the eyes. It was a horrid feeling.

'It's just what, Neferu?' prompted Mereta softly.

'Oh, it's nothing,' Neferu said too quickly.

'Tell me what it is, Neferu!' questioned the princess.

'I just can't, Mereta,' Neferu said miserably, sorry now that she had ever opened her big mouth in the first place.

'Tell me, Neferu. I promise that no harm will come to Yussef whatever it was that he said to you. I promise you that on my life. I don't want any suspicions between us.'

'I still can't tell you, Mereta,' Neferu said desperately. 'Please forgive me.'

Mereta was silent. 'It must be very terrible if you are so afraid to tell me,' she said finally. Neferu was silent and Mereta did not press the subject further. She began to talk about Demi and how Amio had thought of a good idea to keep his mind occupied while he was on bed rest. Neferu felt even worse at what she had harboured and almost burst into tears on the spot, she was so upset. When she regained control of herself, she told Mereta that Demi had already told her about it, and he was pleased and honoured to be a member of the Kap.

The housemaid brought in lunch a little earlier than usual and the girls began to eat. Mereta had a very small appetite and she finished first. As Neferu was also about to sit back, the princess brought up the subject of Yussef again and Neferu sighed deeply. She began to feel that Mereta would never let the subject rest until she knew everything. She regretted with all her heart ever having started their earlier conversation. After more probing by the insistent Mereta, Neferu eventually replied emphatically. 'I will only tell you if you promise never ever to tell anyone.' Mereta promised that she would not tell her mother or Ay as long as she lived. 'That is not enough!' pressed Neferu. 'You must not tell your brother either, or anyone else.' A strange look passed over Mereta's face, but she promised not to tell her brother or anyone else either.

'Is it about Amio?' she asked slowly.

Neferu nodded shamefacedly. 'Yussef believes that your brother intends to take me as one of his mistresses and that is why you are all being so nice to me.' She looked down, blushing furiously. 'I told him that he is completely mistaken, but he wouldn't believe me.'

Neferu looked up and saw that Mereta was sitting like stone, her face gradually becoming flushed with two angry dots in the centre of her cheeks.

'I can promise you with all my heart that Amio has no intention of making you his mistress, Neferu. He likes you so much more than that. He would never do anything to cheapen your reputation, I can assure you of that. If he had wanted to use you in such a way, he would have made his intentions clear a long time ago. He respects you far too much to ever put you in that position.' Mereta had spoken angrily and Neferu was now completely demoralised. On the one hand, she was relieved to know that she was not to be used as a plaything, but on the other hand she was annoyed that the pharaoh wasn't even interested in her. How mortifying. Mereta saw Neferu's horrified face and said, more kindly, 'Why do you think Amio is not married, Neferu? He is almost twenty years old and there are many women who would be eager to become queen. Why, my father was thirteen when he married, and my grandfather was sixteen.'

Neferu shook her head miserably as her only reply.

Mereta continued, 'I will tell you! He once told me he would never marry until he loved with all his heart and was loved for himself in return. You see, he still hopes that he will find someone who can look past his physical defects and his position and love him as a husband and lover should be loved.'

Neferu had never felt so small in all her life. She realised how Yussef and herself had misjudged the young pharaoh. She felt so awful that she just sat there knowing that she could never take back what she had said. How Grandma would be ashamed of her if she knew how she had let them all down.

Mereta sighed. 'Amio would never force you into any kind of relationship with him, Neferu! Do you believe me?'

'Yes,' answered Neferu. 'Mereta, I do wish that we could both forget that this conversation ever happened.' Mereta stood up and rubbed her eyes as if she were tired.

She looked at Neferu silently for a moment. 'Yes. We'll pretend that it never happened.'

On the terrace a young man drew back and returned to his own apartment. Mereta grieved for her brother, knowing how much their conversation must have hurt him, but she never gave any sign to Neferu that she had been aware of his presence. In this way she had ensured that her brother knew without her having to break her promise to Neferu.

'I hope this will not cause a barrier between us. Yussef was goaded by jealousy, Mereta, and I was foolish enough to allow myself to believe it.' Neferu's voice was very penitent.

'Let's forget the whole conversation, Neferu, and please don't let it spoil your friendship with Amio. I know that he truly likes you as a person and he would never hurt you.' Her eyes filled with tears again and Neferu hugged her fiercely.

'I won't let it spoil our friendship. I really, really like him as a person, and I value his friendship for its own sake,' she said passionately. Mereta nodded, her equilibrium recovered.

'Go and rest, Neferu. We shall be having dinner on mother's veranda this evening.

Just the close family. Be at ease with us.'

Neferu thought how very kind this girl was. 'I will be,' she assured Mereta. As she went down to her apartment to rest, she felt that she had been through a terrible storm and was not yet sure, even now, that she was safely into harbour.

A little while later Amio entered his sister's apartment. His face had a sombre look and Mereta went to hug him. 'Don't be sad, Amio,' she said.

CHAPTER 14

Neferu felt jumpy that evening as she left to dinner. She had confided in Demi earlier and he had rounded his lips and given a low whistle to signify that he felt she had made a terrible mistake. Still, what was done was done now. If they were soon to be sent packing, then at least they would know why. Demi was worried that Mereta would not honour her promise not to tell her brother. Neferu became distraught at hearing this, and Demi had to practically push her to dinner. Even her joy at seeing Demi so much better was dimmed by the thought of a possible oncoming tempest.

At the entrance to the grand queen's suite, Neferu was met by a butler and escorted to a sitting room where Asenaath and the queen were already seated. Neferu made her entrance and was cordially invited to sit. She looked surreptitiously at Tiya but there was no indication that she was at all put out.

Meretamun, Teya and Ay soon made their respective entrances. Mereta, it was true, gave her an enigmatic look, but her manner was calm and in no way out of the ordinary. Finally, the moment that Neferu had been dreading, the arrival of Amio. She hardly dared look at him and after curtsying deeply, she kept her eyes averted for as long as she could without causing comment. Amio, however, seemed to be in good spirits and when he did speak to Neferu, it was merely to comment on Demi's improved condition, which the doctor had reported to him. Then Neferu was compelled to look at him. To her relief there was no expression in his face which that faintly indicated that Mereta had spoken to him.

Inwardly, Neferu began to breathe freely again, and she shot a quick glance of gratitude to Mereta. Presently her attention was drawn by Ay and whenever she glanced at Amio, he appeared to be enjoying an intimate conversation with Asenaath. There certainly was no doubt of the easy flirtatious manner between them. Neferu was a little shocked, considering the girl's forthcoming marriage.

Asenaath basked in the attention she was receiving from both Amio and the queen.

Neferu chatted shyly with the archduke, who seemed to be a very dignified man. For some reason she felt that her nose had been put ever so slightly out of joint. For this reason, when the wily Ay began to pay her some attention, she was constrained to be as charming as she could possibly be, even to the point of the mildest of mild flirtations.

Ay seemed to be enjoying her attentions and the meal continued in what appeared on the surface to be a relaxed and vivacious manner. Neferu could not forget the awful lunch. She felt cheap and nasty and whenever she looked at Amio, she felt guilty too. When Ay offered to accompany her to her quarters, she accepted thankfully. He regaled her with interesting stories about Thebes and its inhabitants. At her room, he kissed her hand and wished her a good night. Once inside her room, Neferu let her mask fall. She felt like crying. It had been a most unsatisfactory day in every respect, and she hoped never to have another one like it.

During the next few days, Neferu fell back into the routine of being a lady-in-waiting proper. She found that, in spite of her words to the contrary, a little barrier had grown up between herself and Mereta. Neither of them commented on this in any way, nor referred to the conversation which had disturbed their friendship.

Demi continued to mend and whenever she had a spare moment, Neferu was frequently to be seen sitting by him. Soon he was able to be carried out into the garden to enjoy the evening sunshine. The damaged leg was well splinted to keep it immobile and, according to the daily reports of the doctor, it appeared to be healing well. During this period, Neferu did not see much of Amio, but, whenever they did have occasion to exchange a few words, he was invariably kind and friendly and slowly she began to relax with him again. Amio had visited Demi on several occasions and seemed interested in her brother's progress. There were no more private dinners with the royal family and all in all a period of slight retreat set in, it seemed to Neferu. On the one hand she felt it was probably wise but on the other she had the feeling that something important had been bruised.

Gradually Neferu and Mereta began to regain the mutual trust which had been temporarily shattered between them. Neferu remembered that the royal family had planned to visit their relatives, yet since then nothing more had been said.

'Is it not that you are soon going to pay your respects to your grandparents, Mereta?' she asked one day.

'The visit has been postponed for a while because of state business,' the princess answered her. The girl did not give any further information except that she did not think it would be too long before they went.

During the coming days, Neferu also received a spontaneous explanation as to why she had been chosen as lady-in-waiting. Perhaps Mereta had said something to her uncle, but perhaps not, as, in a way, it was Neferu herself who brought the subject up. She had been feeling a little restless one day and instead of going to rest after lunch, she decided to go for a walk round the walled inner complex of Malkata. She had told Demi about it and although he had tried to dissuade her, she had replied that there would be no one about and she was perfectly safe in the complex itself. She promised not to go through the outer gates.

Neferu put a cotton scarf over her head to protect it from the sun and to help maintain her anonymity. She left the palace gardens by the lower south gate and passed the royal laundry, turning right into the thoroughfare behind the guest house block. To her left were villas, which she knew to be inhabited by lesser royals and court noblemen, including some of the senior officers of the Kap. She walked at a comfortable pace and looked about her with curiosity. After a while, she came to a large laundry and drying area, obviously meant for general use.

Everywhere was quiet and, up till now, she had not seen a single soul. It seemed that the whole of Egypt was asleep except for her. A homely smell of roasting meat wafted to her nostrils as she passed the large general kitchens where the food for large banquets was prepared. She heard a man's voice shouting to someone and knew that here, at least, someone else was also awake.

In front of Neferu were the long lines of smaller interconnected villas where the servants lived. From one of these whitewashed mud brick houses she could hear a child crying. She listened to it for a while, wondering about these people, whose lives revolved around the whims and desires of the pharaohs and their entourages. It seemed unfair to her that some people lived all their lives in subjection to the will of other more powerful men. What was the purpose of all this, or was there even a purpose in it at all? Was it all some chaotic accident of nature which the Aten only interfered with now and then? And did he interfere only on the behalf of a chosen few? She didn't like the thought of that. Her god had to be fair. To be partial meant not to be perfect and her god had to be perfect. If he liked some more than others, how could she be sure that one day he wouldn't like her less than someone else?

Neferu's meditations were disturbed by the pungent smell of the stables. She was very hot now and beginning to feel tired. Also, there were more people about in the outer courtyard now and she did not want to arouse undue attention to herself. She turned into the inner courtyard and along the more familiar open corridor adjacent to the state reception room and the banquet hall. Purposefully, she crept past the open door of the grand vizier's residence and turned right onto the pathway to her own apartment. As she entered the doorway, she was dismayed to see the grand vizier leaving the suite of Maatnofret and her husband. He looked at her in surprise, noting her covered head and her dusty feet in her sandals.

'Where have you been, Neferu?' he asked with a slight frown.

'I have been for a walk around the palace complex. I spoke to no one,' she said, feeling like a naughty child once again.

'I see,' said Ay, with a calculating look.

'I just wanted to be on my own for a short time,' she said rebelliously. 'I have the feeling that I am being observed and assessed the whole time, here.'

Unexpectedly, the grand vizier laughed, and when he spoke it was in a kinder tone. 'You are being observed and assessed, Nefertiti,' he said candidly. 'We must be sure of the people who move around us. Appearances can be very deceptive, and the royal family are very vulnerable in that respect. Our friendship can be and sometimes has been abused. When something like that happens, it makes us very suspicious. You must be able to see that.' Neferu nodded; she had heard the gist of this before, from Mereta. The grand vizier continued, 'At your first visit we saw you and thought you a very beautiful and pleasant girl. Sometimes the best ladies-in-waiting are those who come from out of Thebes, from a more simple and unspoiled background, far from the intrigue of the political life of the court. It is your naturalness we like in you, Neferu. We don't want you to be unhappy here, just the opposite, but our positions force us to live our lives in the role which destiny has arranged for us.' He inclined his head in her direction slightly. 'Perhaps it was destiny which sent you to us, Neferu. Perhaps it means you to stay with us. Have you thought of that, my dear?'

Neferu looked and felt a little bemused as she was surprised to hear Ay speaking of destiny. He was to all intents and purposes a practical and political man. She did not know what destiny required of her, but she was sure that it did not mean her to stay here in Thebes all her life. This city could never be home to her, she reckoned. Outwardly she only nodded and remained silent. At least she now had the sure knowledge of Ay's words that there was no ulterior motive for their invitation for her to stay. 'I think it would be better, Neferu, if you would give me your undertaking that you will not leave here alone anymore. I must be able to honour my promise to your father that you will be chaperoned at all times.' His tone was serious.

'I promise that I will not do it again,' she reassured him. She thought longingly of her visits to the market with Grandma and Aunt Lea. It seemed a life of total freedom, compared with the palace.

The rest of the day passed peaceably and at the evening social get-together in the state withdrawing room the same little cliques sat together. She enjoyed the evening, but she was conscious of a certain aimlessness in herself. She wondered if it was the heat getting her down. Here, so far inland, there was not even the hint of a breeze and, in spite of the fan wafting servants, the air was heavy and still. The soil of the flower beds outside was thick and baked with endless cracks in it, though the irrigation system supplied them regularly with a supply of water. It was never this hot in Lower Egypt and there was always a slight breeze. Somehow it affected her spirits badly. Both she and the heat seemed to be waiting for something to happen. She did not know what.

The next day something did happen. It completely changed her attitude to Amio and paved the way for a completely different relationship with him. Neferu had been feeling more and more a prisoner. Her prison was beautiful, and her warders were kind, nevertheless she was a prisoner. Demi was much better now, and it seemed more likely that he would make a full recovery. Neferu decided that it would be possible for them to go home very soon. The next time that her father and Yussef came she would leave with them and get back to her real life, instead of living in this suspended animation.

After breakfast with Mereta, she went down to sit with her brother for a while and shortly afterwards Amio entered the suite. She stood up abruptly, interrupting their game of 'I spy'. Amio told Neferu to sit down and then he seated himself informally on the end of Demi's bed and began to chat comfortably with him. Neferu noticed that Demi was now quite at ease with Amio and called him Amio quite naturally. They seemed to like each other, she thought. When Amio got up to leave, he looked directly at Neferu and asked if he might discuss something privately with her. Neferu nodded and followed him outside, intrigued. Amio looked around and then said with a smile. 'Let's sit by the pool to talk.' She nodded again, and they walked across the garden to the lily pond and sat down next to each other. Neferu could see the queen seated on the terrace with several other people, but they were too far away to be heard. Amio turned his face to her, and it was so close that she could see where he had missed a few hairs of his beard on shaving. There was a softness in his face also that he had not shown her for a long time.

'I have noticed, Neferu, that you are not happy here with us anymore. Can't you tell me what is troubling you?'

'It is not anything of importance, Amio,' she answered hurriedly.

'On the contrary, it is of considerable importance. I like you very much and I want my friends to be happy, not miserable, Neferu,' he said sincerely.

'I am not miserable, Amio, it's just that … I don't know myself what is wrong,' she admitted with a rueful smile.

Amio looked at her intently and then spoke quietly. 'Don't worry about Demi, Neferu. We will keep him here until he is quite well enough to travel, and I give you my solemn promise that he will receive the very best care and attention. That being understood, I want you to know that if you feel that you really want to go home now, you are free to do so and I will make the appropriate arrangements for you to travel so that your journey can commence as soon as you wish, and it will be safe and speedy.' There was a pause and Amio looked away toward Demi's suite. 'I think Demi will miss you very much and I too will miss you very much too, but I will understand.'

Neferu felt her heart thud and then stand still. She did not have to stay here. Amio had given her the lifeline she had needed. She thought it over for a moment, but she knew that his generosity had decided for her. She waited for him to turn to look at her again, to receive an answer.

'I really am more grateful than you could ever possibly know, Amio, for your kind offer, but I would prefer to stay until Demi is completely well. If I left now, I would miss him and worry about him.' She stopped for a moment to savour the truth of it before adding. 'I would miss you very much too,' she replied shyly.

Amio smiled at her and the atmosphere suddenly relaxed. 'I am pleased, Neferu,' he said simply.

'Amio,' Neferu began. 'I don't really feel that I belong here. I am too different and have little in common with many of the people at court, but I am very, very fond of you and Mereta. I want you to know that.' Amio looked at her for a long time with that frank, direct gaze, which she sometimes found so disconcerting. He put his hand over hers as it rested on her knee.

'Thank you, Neferu.' He lifted his hand away. Neferu jumped a little. She had the strangest feeling of shock through her arm. She glanced at him quickly. Had he felt that peculiar feeling too? It was impossible to say, he was already geting up to leave.

With a change of atmosphere already, he spoke a few pleasantries and then crossed towards the building. Neferu stood for a moment and pondered that feeling of momentary shock as his hand had touched hers. She had never felt anything like it in her life before. She sighed, she definitely was becoming too fanciful these days, there was no doubt about it. He had not reacted at all, so she was probably imagining something which did not exist. Unconsciously, she gave a slight shrug of her shoulders before she too began to cross the lawn toward the steps which Amio had so recently ascended. She crossed the veranda to Mereta's apartment. The princess greeted her with an exuberant hug.

'Amio has just told me that you have decided to stay with us for a while yet, Neferu. I am so happy.'

'I am sorry I have been so grumpy, Mereta,' replied Neferu.

'Oh, let's forget it! What shall we do this morning? I am so bored!'

'It's too hot to go out. We could sew or make up poetry?' suggested Neferu, helpfully.

'No! Let's do something quite different,' Mereta said enthusiastically.

'What then?' Neferu asked, at a loss.

'I know! Teach me Keftiu!' said Mereta.

Neferu laughed. 'It isn't that easy,' she declared. 'And anyway, what use would it be to you? You said Akkadian is difficult, but at least it is of more use to you,' she replied logically.

'That's true,' Mereta acknowledged reasonably. 'The difference is that I am compelled to learn Akkadian whereas Keftiu is the language of my friend and therefore I want to know it.' After a pause she continued with a shrewd look, 'Besides, Keftiu could be our secret language. There are very few Keftiu here at court, and none, except you and Demi, close to us personally. I have heard you and Demi talking together and it sounded very mysterious to me!' she said with a secretive smile.

Neferu laughed with real amusement. 'We were probably only discussing what we had for lunch!' she chuckled. 'Still. If you really want to learn I will teach you. It won't be easy though, I warn you.'

'What won't be easy?' It was Amio speaking. He had just entered the room.

'Neferu is going to teach me Keftiu,' Mereta said coyly. 'It's going to be our secret language.'

Amio looked interested. 'You can teach me too. I like secrets as well,' he said to Neferu with a smile.

'Are you serious?' asked Neferu, surprised.

'Yes! It sounds a melodious language. Not like Akkadian with all those guttural sounds,' he said.

'Oh, no!' Neferu said, loyally. 'Keftiu is a beautiful language. Grandma said it is a language made for love.' It came out impulsively and then she felt embarrassed and looked down.

Amio laughed. 'In that case there is no doubt but that I should learn it. Perhaps,' he continued drolly, with his hand over his heart, 'it may be just the magic I need to woo the woman of my dreams.'

'It won't work unless she understands what you are saying.' Neferu smiled.

'You never know,' he answered in a light, bantering tone. 'Maybe the magic is in the very sound of the words. Let's start now. How do you say "I love you" in Keftiu.'

'Sagapoa,' Neferu pronounced clearly.

Mereta repeated the words softly.

'Not quite right, Mereta,' Neferu said, repeating the expression more slowly this time.

'Sagapoa,' Mereta mimicked correctly this time.

'Now you,' said Mereta to her brother, chivvying him a little. Amio looked at Neferu and repeated the phrase carefully and expectantly. Neferu caught her breath. The words suddenly assumed an unfamiliar nuance for her. She blushed slightly and averted her eyes involuntarily. Then immediately felt she was giving herself away and she looked up again lightly saying.

'That was almost correct. Only a very slight accent.'

He seemed pleased and said, 'Say it again so that I can remember it properly.'

'Sagapoa,' she repeated the words slowly and emphasising them, forcing herself to look at him with a non-committal look on her face. He grinned and she blushed again. He repeated the phrase to her once more and then switched subject abruptly by saying that he was hungry and where was lunch?

Both Mereta and Amio stated that they were really serious about learning Keftiu and Neferu planned to spend about half an hour a day teaching them. Times would vary according to Amio's state duties, naturally. She was happy to do this, gratified that they should be interested in her beloved language. As far as she knew, they were no other Keftiu speakers at court so she would have to formulate her own teaching methods. Amio told her he would practise any new vocabulary on Demi and if her brother understood then he would know his pronunciation was correct. Neferu smilingly encouraged this plan as it seemed to give good feedback. They decided to keep the lessons a secret from the others. Neferu enjoyed hugging their little secret to herself. It was her little bit of individuality.

This small beginning was the start of a new period of closeness between the three of them, which healed the rift caused by the conflicting emotions Yussef had aroused. Neferu knew now that her life was moving towards something momentous, and she lacked the will to fight it. At the same time, she wanted the Aten to choose her path for her. She was basically quite a passive person who hated discord and conflict and went out of her way to avoid them. Her passivity was thus sometimes a cowardly way of not taking responsibility for making decisive moves. She always felt keenly her position as a woman with no chance of succeeding against these powerful men if she did run into problems. Unless she was cornered, therefore, she preferred to avoid any unpleasantness. If she was cornered, she would come out fighting for her rights.

Neferu knew that although nothing had been said in words, her relationship with Amio was changing into something more than platonic friendship, but was it love? For that matter, was what she had with Yussef the right kind of love for a marriage? It seemed to her that she had drifted into her forthcoming marriage because Grandma and Grandpa and everyone else wanted it, and he was safe and known. She really did not know what she wanted for sure. That was the only thing she was sure of: her uncertainty. There was no way she could reconcile two such different worlds, so she preferred someone else to decide for her. Let it be the Aten, if he was the most powerful of the gods. At present she had a respite from the tug of loyalties.

After siesta that day, Maatnofret came to find Neferu with some news for her. The queen requested her presence in the royal suite the following morning for a visit by the dressmaker. She was to have a new wardrobe. Neferu, like all women faced with such a prospect, felt pleased and eager. She wondered whether she would have any choice in the matter of material or style, but she did not like to ask. As her father would not be paying for them, she did not rightly feel that she could make too many suggestions.

The withdrawing room was full that evening. There were many strange faces present. Mereta informed Neferu that a large contingent of troops had just arrived back from a mission in one of the eastern countries. The room resounded with chatter, noisy and cheerful. The pleasure of the officers and their wives was self-evident. It is always good to be home, and home for them was Thebes. With the troops came news of Pararameses, who was due back in two decans.

Neferu found these officers and their wives a different kind of people from the intrinsic court noblemen. She felt that she had more in common with them. They were more open and spontaneous than the group comprising the inner court circle of mainly minor royal relatives, some of whom were very distant. With this latter group, things were never as they appeared. Even she could see that they were scheming and devious – many of them, that is. Neferu had noticed that when they smiled it never quite reached their eyes. She felt very ill at ease with them, and they obviously felt a great deal of curiosity about her.

Amio seemed very happy to receive these military personnel, many of whom appeared to be on very close terms with him. She assumed they were his friends from the Kap. He was surrounded by a laughing group of officers as she observed him and occasionally peels of bawdy laughter would ring out at some ribald remark or other. Once she caught his eyes and he gave her a warm smile before someone caught his attention again. Neferu turned her gaze to Mereta, who was chatting with a handsome young officer. Neferu thought she detected a flicker of romantic interest in Mereta's eyes and hoped that the young man would reciprocate. She would like her friend to find love.

Sporadically people would move on from one group to another and Neferu was content to sit alone on a couch and watch these animated groups with interest. Ay and Teya came over to chat to her for a while before moving on and then she was joined by Asenaath, her fiancé and her brother, Sinefrew. Neferu was a little surprised. Asenaath did not normally seek out her company and she assumed that Asenaath wished to show off her fiancé, who was one of the returning senior officers. Neferu did not really care for Sinefrew, although she knew that he was apparently one of Amio's close hunting friends. She found him supercilious and arrogant, though their conversation was always amiable enough on the surface. Asenaath's fiancé seemed to be a nice young man. He was, it turned out, another cousin of Amio, the son of Amenophis III's youngest sister. Neferu found all these things very complicated. She found the young man a rather strange choice for Asenaath, who had always seemed a rather haughty person. There was a little verbal prodding on their part, as if they did not quite know what to make of her. She was sufficiently on her guard that she felt she had not given away anything of herself. The incident did ruffle her feathers though; she realised that she would never be able to be herself here. When she tried to analyse why she felt so defensive, she isolated a seeming remark of no consequence thrown airily into the ether by Sinefrew in a tone just a shade too casual for the sharp glance which had accompanied it. Sinefrew had said to his future brother-in-law what a favourite Neferu had become at court. While she was still wondering what to say to that, if anything, he had asked her, 'Do you find it difficult to adjust to life at court after leading such a quiet life hitherto?'

On the surface it was a very innocent question, but she sensed an undercurrent. He managed to make her feel a complete country bumpkin. To add insult to injury he had followed this with extravagant compliments to her beauty which were quite over the top and which only succeeded in making her feel like a plate of meat on display. She responded with what she hoped was a bright confident smile. Inwardly she breathed a sigh of relief when they moved on. What on earth was it that irritated her about them so much? Her intuition told her that she had made enemies but for the life of her she could not think how she had accomplished it.

Neferu stood alone for a while, feeling a bit lost. She had met quite a few people this evening, but she did not have the confidence to move around from group to group, it would have been considered very bold in Keftiu company and she was at heart a Keftiu. She wanted to leave. She glanced over at Tiya, but she was involved in a deep conversation and obviously was not contemplating retiring for a while. A cool hand touched her elbow and she turned to see Amenophis.

'Would you like to leave, Neferu?' he asked.

She smiled gratefully and nodded. 'Yes, please, Amio,' she replied.

'I'll take you back,' he said easily and began to guide her through the crowded room.

Once outside in the darkness she turned to him and said, 'I don't want to drag you away from your friends, Amio. I will be fine if you want to go back.' He shook his head in the darkness and they continued on toward her doorway.

'Are people being nice to you?' he asked suddenly.

'Yes, very! Everything is fine, Amio. You know me; I would complain bitterly to the pharaoh if they were not.'

There was a smile in her voice, and she saw a corresponding curve of his lips in the darkness. 'I expect the pharaoh's shoulders would be broad enough to take it,' he ventured lightly. At the entrance to her chamber, he stood still in front of her then kissed her on her cheek before wishing her goodnight and leaving her. Neferu entered her chamber. The housemaid had left the oil lamps burning and it looked welcoming. Already she thought of it as her very own room. As she undressed, she pondered how her perceptions had changed. She now found Amio's reputation for ugliness incredible.

She had never found him ugly, but now his face had become very dear to her. Almost without noticing it she brightened up when she saw it coming toward her. She felt that his features portrayed a certain sensual attraction. The unusual very elongated eyes and the full mouth gave his face a hint of passion and sensitivity. She had grown accustomed to his face, and she knew that she would miss him terribly if she went home. She knew that her very use of the word 'if' instead of 'when' meant that her emotions were in a state of flux. On top of all that she felt that the display of favour which the royal family had always accorded her was making her powerful enemies. Where would it all lead to? In the end she became tired of worrying about what other people thought of her and put herself to bed. She said her prayers to the Aten and decided that from now on she would live only one day at a time. Let the future take care of itself.

CHAPTER 15

Summer continued in full cycle and the heat remained stifling. People became irritable easily and tempers were short. Neferu found it impossible to sleep during the afternoon siestas. Her old ploy of pretending that she was shiveringly cold no longer worked. Her imagination was just not up to this. She and Demi spent their time together talking of Rashid and the delicious, cool sensation of the sea on their skin. Demi's condition improved daily and both he and Neferu began to entertain real hopes of the leg finally healing once and for all. They both felt a profound debt of gratitude to the court physician and his assistant for the constant and skilled care they had shown to Demi. He knew that it would still be some time before he would be allowed to put any weight on his leg and his enforced immobilisation was becoming very chafing. People did come to visit him, especially Amio and the grand vizier, and as well as Smenkh he had come to know the other pupils in the Kap. Notwithstanding this, he began to suffer real pangs of homesickness and spoke constantly of the family and life in On.

Following the visit of the court dressmaker, the queen had stunned Neferu by ordering an extensive wardrobe of clothes for her. Whatever Neferu may have felt about the queen, and she was not at all sure that she liked her, it was undeniably true that she dressed with the most exquisite taste. Neferu had felt herself overawed by the scale of this gesture but her attempt at thanks were somewhat imperiously waved away. She was given to understand that it would be unwise to mention the matter further. With Mereta she felt free to show her delight in the beautiful gowns and to discuss in delicious indecisiveness, which dress she would wear on which occasion.

The only real times when Neferu felt thrillingly alive during this period was on those days when Amio took herself and Mereta riding. Now that Pararameses was away they went with only the two of the old grooms for company. Although Neferu was not yet an accomplished horsewoman, she was confident and improving all the time. She adored riding and the sense of freedom it gave her. She loved the wind blowing through her hair that the speed of the horse gave her in the otherwise sultry air. Eventually the queen prohibited the lessons until Pararameses came back. She was cross with Amio for taking them on his own. The pharaoh was not at all put out by his mother's remonstrations and assured that as soon as Pararameses returned they would commence their riding again.

Throughout all this time messages were sent to her family in On via the riverboat system and she and Demi received frequent loving messages from Yussef and the family, delivered to them by the grand vizier. The family were much heartened by the good news of Demi's continuing recovery and Demi himself began to harbour hopes of returning home before the complete healing process had pursued its course. The matter was brought up with the physicians, but it received a cool reception. The physicians were proud of their accomplishments so far and said that it was in Demi's best interests to stay until he was able to weight bear on the damaged leg. They estimated another two or three decans. A whole month. Demi was disappointed and Neferu resolutely refused to let herself think about the matter further. She would not get back into that maelstrom of emotion again.

One morning at breakfast, the queen began to speak of visiting her family, first her parents who lived at Akhtmin, as she had received news that her mother was ill. Both her parents were very old. 'I think that I will be ready to leave by tomorrow morning,' she told Amio. 'Your father is reasonably well at the moment and Tuthmosis is here.' She was referring to his uncle, the archduke. Amio nodded in agreement. 'I have to inspect the military base at Darmish in four days, but it is only three hours ride from here and I will be returning the following day.'

The queen nodded, as there was no reason to expect anything untoward in any case. 'Ay need not stay as long as I intend to,' she said. 'Fortunately, your grandfather is still fit and well for his age. He sent a message saying that they have everything that they need, but that mother wants to see me as soon as possible. She has been ill for a long time now and we have been through all this before, but I would hate anything to happen and me not to be there.'

Neferu listened to this conversation silently, apart from their family problem. It did show her a facet of Tiya she had not imagined before, that of the dutiful daughter. It made her seem slightly more of a human being and less of the regal queen. Even Mereta did not interfere with the plans and merely looked sympathetically at her mother. Neferu realised that it was almost impossible for this family to demonstrate emotion of any kind publicly. She wondered if they ever let themselves go in spontaneity and what they were really like. The queen and her son quickly formulated their plans.

'After I return, I wonder whether we should make a trip to see the rest of the family in Goshen. I haven't seen my pleasure gardens there for a long time. Let's see how state business permits it.' The queen meditated silently for a while before continuing. 'It is so very hot here now that a short visit to the coast might do us all good. The sea breeze would be very refreshing.' She paused here, looking at Neferu. 'Haven't I heard you say, Neferu, that you usually spend your summers by the sea?'

Neferu inclined her head. 'Grandpa has a villa by the sea in Rashid,' she answered. 'It is very old though, Your Majesty. Not at all grand enough for you and your family, ma'am. I don't think you would care for it at all,' she said apologetically.

The queen smiled slightly at her. 'I wouldn't dream of imposing on your family in such a way, my dear,' she answered regally. 'But perhaps it would be a good idea to hire a villa on the coast for a while after visiting my family in Goshen. Perhaps the potiphar of Rashid could be prevailed upon to find us a suitable place.' Here she looked at her son. 'Don't you think it might make a pleasant change, Amio?'

The pharaoh nodded his approval and added lightly. 'It would be fun to go swimming in the sea.' He looked slyly at Neferu. 'Though I have heard that it is not necessary to go as far as the coast!'

Neferu stiffened in horror and looked at the queen, who was smiling with amusement.

Amio began to laugh. 'Sorry, Neferu. I could not help teasing you after hearing what a good swimmer you are!' Neferu blushed and the talk turned to other things, the incident being quickly passed over.

The preparations took longer than expected and it was not until two mornings later that the queen and her brother left with a military escort and a full retinue for the journey to Akhtmin. Two days later Amio left with a troop of officers of the Kap for the visit to Darmish. This was a very unusual situation according to Mereta, but life at court was very quiet at that point. The senior pharaoh and the archduke were left in command and Tiya also left Maatnofret in charge of the ladies-in-waiting. Teya, the royal nurse, was to host the social life of the court until they returned. Ay had planned to stay only two days with his parents and he would return therefore about the same time as Amio.

At the last moment Amio decided to shorten his visit to Darmish. Before he left, he told the girls that he would be back by sundown the following day. He told them that Sinefrew would sort out any practical problems that might crop up, though he could not envisage anything. When he and the other officers left, the palace seemed almost deserted. A hush settled over the place. The elder pharaoh ate with his favourite in private and so Mereta, Neferu and Maatnofret ate with Teya and Mutnedjmet in the sitting room of the princess' apartment.

After siesta the ladies decided they would make lace and chat. Neferu told them a Keftiu legend about a monster called a minotaur and then they sang songs while their nimble fingers worked the threads. Not being very proficient at lace making, Neferu asked permission to go and sit with Demi for a while. Permission was granted and Neferu left the relative coolness of the sitting room for the brilliant sunshine of the hot terrace. As she stepped down the stairs, she became particularly aware of the stillness of the place. She could not remember it ever having been this silent. Demi was wide awake. He said it was impossible to sleep in this heat and that he was longing to be ambulant again. 'The royal family will be travelling to Goshen soon,' she told him. 'They will pass On on the way so I suppose that is when we will be taken home,' she added. Demi received the news with enthusiasm. He anticipated being back on his feet very soon. He was totally fed up with being in bed and said his back and bottom were very sore. The news of a return home in the now foreseeable future cheered him up enormously.

Later, Neferu returned to the upper apartment to find the others about to disperse for siesta. Neferu had imagined that the dinner that evening would be a very quiet affair, but Teya said she felt honour-bound to continue the evening tradition in the withdrawing room and she expected them to attend. When she had gone, Mereta said with a grimace, 'It will be deadly boring with the others gone!' Neferu nodded. She could well believe it. It would be a congregation of the lesser royal relatives mainly, and she had already perceived what a lot of intriguers they were. Forever working out their lineage, planning suitable marriages which would bring them nearer to the succession and effecting ways of one-upmanship on their nearest rivals. What a thrilling evening was in store, she thought sarcastically. Not only that, but this was also the group who most looked upon her with jealous disfavour as an upstart outsider with not even an ounce of royal blood to recommend her.

Most of the middle-ranking army officers were also commoners like herself, and their lesser proximity to the centre of the royal family enabled them to make jokes about the seriousness with which the others viewed themselves. Not only that, Amio was a popular commander, she had noticed, because he did not put on airs and graces with them. Now, with most of them away, she was in for a very dull evening. 'Perhaps I could be excused after dinner, Mereta?' she requested hopefully.

'No way!' Mereta replied firmly. 'If I have to put up with them, so do you!'

Neferu sighed, before adding with a malicious smile. 'They are your relatives. I thought you might like them better!'

'Wrong!' replied Mereta drily. 'They are my relatives, so I have to put up with them.' Neferu laughed at the other girl's sour expression.

That evening was just as Neferu had imagined. Neither the elder pharaoh nor the archduke put in an appearance, and Teya was left to host the evening alone. She carried it off superbly, however, and was obviously very popular with everyone. People seemed genuinely fond of her. Sinefrew, left in charge as the senior officer was rather loud and pompous, in Neferu's opinion. He loved being the centre of attention now that Amio and Pararameses were away.

Neferu did not court the company of anyone and contented herself by sitting with Maatnofret and Mereta. Mereta went over to chat to a group of ladies and several people came over to chat with Maatnofret. Neferu was regarded with curiosity, but by and large she was mercifully ignored. She knew that they considered her to be far beneath them, but she did not think much of them anyway so there was no ill feeling about this.

It was a relief when Teya decided to retire, giving them the opportunity to make their escape too. As they walked across the terrace, Mereta remarked that tomorrow would be just as quiet. The girls bade each other a goodnight and went each to her own suite. Neferu called out goodnight to Maatnofret as she heard her passing, knowing that she was also alone, her husband Paranefer having accompanied Amio to Darmish. Maatnofret called out a cheerful goodnight to her and Neferu smiled to herself at her good fortune in finding such a kind friend. She climbed into bed and fell asleep quickly, with nothing to disturb her serenity nor the expectation of anything about to do so.

Neferu woke early the next morning. It was just after dawn, and she watched as the gloom in the chamber receded before the strength of the sun's rays. Her mind homed in on the thought of the forthcoming journey home. Demi had progressed incredibly well, and the physician had said that he thought that recovery would be complete this time. The leg would never look normal because of the scarring, and he would always walk with a slight limp because the leg was a little bit shorter, but he did not expect any pain or further infection. Demi said he could accept everything else just to be pain free. Neferu was overjoyed for him. As for her own life, she intended to wait passively for destiny took its course. She did not wish to jar the threads the Great Weaver was weaving of her life in a pattern she could not see. Some would say that Neferu was a dreamer, but if she was, then she only acted out her part in a dream that others stage managed and in which she could not influence events without hurting someone or other. There was only limited action left open to her after the scene had been set by others. Although she hated that feeling, and some part of her deep inner being rebelled against the injustice of it, she remained a woman and therefore in the eyes of the world only someone of minor importance.

Neferu drifted off again into that strange half-sleep state which sometimes occurs, where dreams and reality become mixed. She was eventually awoken by Maatnofret shaking her and calling her 'lazy bones'. She stretched herself out before sitting up. That morning the two girls breakfasted with Teya, Mutnedjmet and Maatnofret in the home of the grand vizier. There was an air of languor over the place already. Everyone agreed that the day was going to be another abnormally quiet one. Teya made them laugh with her comment that she never realised how noisy her husband was until he went away.

After breakfast, Neferu was excused to go and visit Demi. The others promised to visit him a little later on. Demi had just washed and had had his leg re-dressed when she entered, and he was about to start on his breakfast. Neferu watched with satisfaction as he began to tuck in hungrily. Just as she was about to make some comment on this, she heard an agonised scream from outside. This was repeated after a very short interval and then again. The sound of it made her blood curdle and she and Demi looked at each other in horror.

Neferu stood up. 'What do you think it is?' she asked in horror.

'I don't know,' Demi answered in almost a whisper.

'I'm going to find out,' Neferu said impulsively and made for the door. The screams were coming from the right, just outside the garden gate and, as she hesitated, another scream firmed up her resolve and she ran towards the gate. The latch was heavy, and it took her a moment to lift it, but once she had done so it swung outward easily, and she went out into the courtyard. She followed the painful sounds to just in front of the guest house block where she had taken her earlier surreptitious walk. A horrible sight confronted her eyes. A young man was stripped down to his loincloth and was being whipped over and over again. There were long, bloody weals across his back, thighs and arms and the man wielding the whip was Sinefrew. On his face was such an expression of cruel bestiality that Neferu felt a fury such as she had never ever known rise up within her.

Neferu ran as fast as she could to Sinefrew and tried to wrench the whip from his hand. Obsessed with the enjoyment of what he was doing, he barely noticed her and pushed her away, almost knocking her over and without even looking at her. The people standing around gasped in horror and called her to step back but Neferu was like someone possessed. She managed to grasp the whip and tugged it with all her might to try to wrench it from his grasp. This time he pushed her so hard that she did fall backward into the dust. She jumped up again unhurt, enraged only the more by the crack of the whip on the victim's back again. She screamed at him hysterically to stop and this time he looked at her properly. He drew up his hand and with a stinging blow across the cheek, allowed the whip to fall to the ground.

Sinefrew now turned his anger on her. The crowd fell strangely silent and began to back away. The victim of the outrage lay on the ground, almost unconscious and whimpering with pain. The stinging slap had caused the tears to come to Neferu's eyes and she felt an immediate and overwhelming urge to retaliate. She curled up her fingers and with all her force she brought her nails down Sinefrew's right cheek. She watched as if from afar as the four bright red scratch marks lit up his face. 'And how do you like it, animal?' she hissed at him. By way of answer Sinefrew lunged at her and, pressing her down by the shoulders, forced her onto her knees.

'You will pay for this, bitch!' he hissed malevolently. 'I am in charge, and you will not get away with this, you little upstart! In insulting me you have insulted the royal family.' He almost snarled at her, 'You too will be whipped!' With that he pushed her insolently to the ground and marched off. No one came to help her up. She scrambled up as fast as she could and went over to the victim. Her own heart was thumping madly even before she pulled his arm and half dragged him up. She felt as frightened as he looked, but he was with it enough to look straight in her eyes, as if wondering who she was. She had an impression of intelligence and gentility. Even in her distress she wondered how such a soul had landed in this position. A woman came to help her, she wondered if it was his wife, and suddenly relieved in this way she whispered to the woman to hide the man as fast as she could. The woman agreed and Neferu was suddenly free to look to her own position.

'Neferu! Neferu!' she looked up at Maatnofret's distressed face.

'Wait a moment, Maatnofret,' she managed to say. Turning to the crowd, who still stood silently by, she appealed for someone to come forward to help the woman with the man who had been whipped. Most turned away with their eyes downward. After a short hesitation, a man came forward and took the man's arm, helping the woman to lead him away.

Neferu found that she was trembling violently. Maatnofret took her arm and led her off hurriedly back in the direction from which she had come. Just before they turned into the gardens, they came face to face with the cold set face of Asenaath. Her look of cold enmity was chilling, and her tone was full of hatred as she said to Neferu. 'There is no one to protect you now, Neferu! The pharaoh will surely sentence you to be whipped for such a crime.'

Neferu felt fear crawl up her spine, but her pride was sufficient to help her pull herself together enough to say coldly, 'We will see!' before allowing Maatnofret to take her to her suite.

Maatnofret guided her into her room and now that they were alone, the tears began to run down her cheeks, and she began to sob uncontrollably. She was hot, dusty, frightened and in dire disgrace. She wondered that Maatnofret dared even to be in her company. The older woman put her arms around her and held her tightly until her sobs quietened. When she had become calmer, Maatnofret asked her what had happened. Neferu tried to explain but kept breaking down again. Eventually she managed to get her story out. 'I must go and tell Mereta,' Maatnofret said. 'She must be told first.' Neferu tried to persuade Maatnofret not to tell Mereta. She did not want to get the princess into trouble too, by appearing to support her now that she was more or less finished. Maatnofret was insistent, so Neferu begged her to go and tell Demi that she was all right. She did not want him to know what was happening. Maatnofret promised to reassure Demi and then left her.

Once Maatnofret had gone, Neferu threw herself down on the bed and began to cry again. She allowed the tears to well up and run down her cheeks in little rivulets as the self-pity took over. She knew that she was almost certainly going to be whipped and sent packing in disgrace. She had disgraced her family, and no one would look at her even in On after this. She heard the sound of running footsteps and looked up to see Mereta in the doorway with Maatnofret just behind her. She started wailing again. Mereta sat down on the end of the bed and waited for Neferu to calm herself.

'What happened, Neferu?' she asked finally. Once more Neferu related her sad tale and started to tremble again. When she had finished, Mereta said, 'I must go and see my father.' Her voice was sombre. 'Sinefrew dare do nothing without my father's authorisation, but he is a relative and a man. I don't know how much sway I hold with

Father. It may be that he will not listen to me.'

'I beg you not to do anything which would bring distress on you as well,' Neferu replied miserably.

'I must go right away,' was Mereta's only reply, and she got up and left immediately.

Maatnofret put her arms round the weeping girl. 'If they order you to be whipped, I will obtain a special ointment from the physician to cover your skin with first, so that it will not hurt as much. I already have a potion which you can take by mouth, which I have taken from Demi. He no longer needs it. It is said to be very effective,' she said reassuringly, trying to console the Keftiu girl. Neferu began to weep even more and Maatnofret decided to be silent. She was very fearful of what the outcome of all this was going to be for the young Keftiu girl.

Mereta was gone a long time and when she returned, her face was white. 'There is nothing I can do, Neferu. Father had already been approached by Sinefrew and has signed a warrant for you to receive nine strokes of the whip at sundown. The most I could get him to do was to change the venue from the public courtyard to the state reception room.' The princess began to cry softly, and terror struck anew in Neferu's heart at the thought of the public humiliation she would receive. 'Even Amio has not the authority to rescind an order signed by father,' the princess wailed. 'What can we do?' Her voice was despairing.

'We can pray,' said Maatnofret, releasing Neferu and falling to her knees on the floor. 'Oh, Yahweh, the one true god of all creation I humbly ask you to save your servant, Neferu, from this cruel fate. I, your humble servant, Maatnofret, ask this of you.' Maatnofret prayed aloud and after this outburst she stayed on her knees for a while in silent meditation with her eyes closed. Mereta and Neferu looked on mesmerised for a moment before they too fell on their knees and started to pray. After some minutes Maatnofret looked up and said, 'I am going to find the archduke and ask him to send a message to Amio and Pararameses to bring them back before nightfall. Sinefrew goes too far!' She sounded firmer and calmer now. 'Neferu, go upstairs and have some lunch with Mereta, just as you usually do. I will go and tell your brother that you are upset about the incident you saw earlier.' She was silent for a moment, as if planning some strategy. 'I think it would be best to carry on as if nothing has happened. Stay with the princess and do not leave her suite. The journey to Darmish takes about three hours on horseback for the troops. By a special envoy at express speed, it will be less than that. If the pharaoh can be located immediately then he can be here before sundown,' Maatnofret declared to them.

'But Amio can do nothing to save me!' Neferu cried in despair.

'Amio is resourceful. He will think of something,' the good lady replied. 'I must go now. There is a lot to be done and not a lot of time.' With that she left and Mereta looked at Neferu.

'You had better wash and change, Neferu. You are covered in dust,' she said with the ghost of a smile. Neferu rose and went to the bathroom. When she came out, she put on a clean dress and brushed her hair. Mereta nodded. 'We must do exactly as Maatnofret said and behave as though nothing has happened,' the princess said. It was easy for her to do, thought Neferu. A brief thought for the poor young man who had received the whipping crossed Neferu's mind. She hoped he would recover and avoid further trouble. If she ever got out of this scrape, she must find out how he fared somehow. She said a quick prayer for them both.

Together, they left the ground floor and ascended the stairs to the veranda. Neferu noted dismally that the gardens still looked beautiful, and the air was as silent as ever, as if she half expected the world to have changed too. With a big effort she could begin to think it had all been a nightmare she would presently wake up from. She knew it wasn't, though. With a tremendous effort, she tried to push everything away from her. At lunch she could not eat anything and Mereta also appeared to have no appetite.

Maatnofret reappeared after lunch to tell them that Pararameses' most senior adjutant, who had been on leave, had been despatched in all haste to bring the pharaoh back. She reported that she still had a lot to do but would be back fairly soon. Mereta told her that the two of them would remain there together. Maatnofret nodded. 'I think it is wise,' she replied and left in a hurry.

Soon after that there was an uncomfortable moment when Asenaath arrived. She seemed amazed to see Neferu with Mereta and, after a devastating look at Neferu, she turned pointedly to Mereta and said, 'Do you think it is wise, Your Ladyship, to be in the company of a person so disgraced?'

Mereta stiffened. 'Don't be insolent, Asenaath! This incident is not yet over, I do assure you. Your brother will live to regret what he has done,' she replied coldly. Asenaath's eyes blazed momentarily and Neferu was frightened for Mereta's having so openly shown her hand.

'The pharaoh has given his judgement and there is nothing that can change that!' Asenaath was unable to keep a note of triumph out of her voice. And then she added further, 'I always knew this girl would cause trouble. She is spoiled by her good looks and is undisciplined and too headstrong. She does not have the breeding a man like Amio needs.'

Mereta's voice was icy. 'Asenaath, you have lost my goodwill. I demand that you leave my apartment now and never set foot in it again. Do you understand?' The other girl was very taken aback by Mereta's unexpectedly strong reaction, as was the terrified Nefertiti. Asenaath hesitated for a moment, looked uncertain, then curtsied and left. Neferu felt grateful for her loyalty, but afraid for her too.

'I think that was very unwise of you, Mereta. You have made an important enemy now.' Mereta smiled wanly.

'She was never my true friend, Neferu, and sometimes a person has to stand up for the people and things she believes in,' she said sombrely. Neferu was silent. She felt very sad that her adventure should have come to such an ignoble end. She wondered if there were some ill omen hanging over her. She felt the tears prickle her eyes again and did not object when Mereta insisted that they rest until dinner time. As dinner was after sundown, Neferu found the thought comforting.

The princess lay down on the couch and instructed Neferu to spread herself out on the other one. It was almost as if the princess wished to prepare herself for any eventuality. Neferu was glad not to be left alone and did as she had been bidden. She became possessed now of a strange tranquillity, as if, once again, she had no part to play in the events that were to take place other than to be there physically. She had not thought it possible that she could fall asleep but, amazingly, she did so. She awoke with a start when Maatnofret entered the room.

The older woman was obviously anxious and told them that as yet there was no sign of either her husband or the pharaoh. She put a large pot on the table and said she would come back well before sundown and smear the ointment all over Neferu. Both girls were thoroughly frightened now at the implications of Maatnofret's words. Maatnofret put her hand into a pocket in her gown and withdrew a small phial which she had obtained from the physician, she said. If the worse came to the worst, Neferu was to drink it quickly before being taken down to the hall by the guard sent to bring her. It was extract of poppy seed and it was known to be a powerful painkiller. Maatnofret left once again and shortly a maid came in with some refreshments. She looked curiously at Neferu but otherwise proceeded as deferentially as she normally would have.

In spite of herself, Neferu now felt hungry. She had eaten nothing since breakfast, neither had Mereta. Neferu ate carefully, as if it were her last meal. She carefully analysed

the texture and taste of the food as if in reference to some future period when she would
be expected to remember it. Mereta watched her for a while and then she too began to
eat slowly. She ate very little, playing with her food, seeming to take Neferu's fate more
cruelly than Neferu herself. Neferu had, by now, steeled herself to be resigned to enduring
what her fate had thrown at her.

Maatnofret returned after the meal and made Neferu drink a small amount of the
potion from the phial she held. It made Neferu very sleepy, and her eyes started to move
out of focus. She slept again. Not long before sundown Maatnofret woke her again. She
felt very strange but understood that there was still no sign of Amio or Paranefer. She told
her that Horemheb, who had left to bring back the pharaoh, had had the foresight to send
messengers back from each stage of his journey, so that they knew he had arrived safely
in Darmish. Tuthmosis had also sent word to Ay in Akhtmin. Through her drugged
haze, Neferu could still sense the air of foreboding in the room.

Maatnofret asked Neferu to undress and with the help of the other two, she managed
to do so, although her movements were very uncoordinated. She lay down naked on the
couch as she had been bidden and Maatnofret smeared her carefully and methodically
with the ointment she had brought in the afternoon. It made her skin tingle a little
and Maatnofret told her this was to be expected. Afterwards, Neferu re-robed and
Maatnofret poured the contents of the phial into a goblet of fruit juice, telling Neferu to
drink it. Mereta sat silently watching. Neferu hesitated a moment then, with a shrug of
her shoulders, she swallowed it. Maatnofret told her to sit down and wait. She was going
down to the courtyard so that she could intercept Amio and her husband as they arrived.
She would bring them straight to the state reception hall. Mereta came to sit by Neferu
and held her hand. Neferu was grateful for the comfort of it, although she had begun to
feel very dizzy.

A housemaid entered with Yonel-Re, the adjutant of Sinefrew. Yonel-Re was very
apologetic. He bowed deeply before Mereta and Neferu. 'I am very, very sorry, Your
Ladyship,' he said to Neferu with plain reluctance for his unpleasant duty. 'This is totally
against my personal wishes, but I am bound by my duty to carry out the order of the
pharaoh.' Through the ever-increasing haze around her, she felt extremely sorry for him.
He had always seemed one of the nicer young men at court. It was not his fault. She tried
to say so, but her words came out so thickly that her speech was unclear even to herself.

Mereta answered for her. 'I understand your position, Yonel-Re and I appreciate your
feelings on behalf of the lady Nefertiti.' The young man put out his arm and very gently

steadied Neferu to her feet. From a great distance, she heard Mereta say, 'I am coming with you.' She shook her head, but Mereta insisted upon taking her arm and assisting her to walk with her legs, which now appeared to have great difficulty in bearing her. She tried to pull herself together as she wanted to face this with dignity for her family's sake, as well as her own. As they crossed the darkness of the courtyard something of her predicament began to force itself through the fog of unreality and she became more alert.

Once inside the state hall, she made an effort to see who was there. There were about twenty people, all of them familiar as minor palace royals and most of them either close friends of Sinefrew and Asenaath or close relatives. She was surprised there were not more. She had expected a crowd to observe her downfall. In spite of her situation, both physical and physiological, she could not contain her acid wit. 'I am surprised that you could not manage a bigger audience than this, Sinefrew! Do your friends not share your partiality for whipping people?' she managed to say.

She managed to focus her gaze on Sinefrew but found that he could not meet her look and lowered his face. So, he had lost some of his bravado. She felt a moment's triumph, but this was quickly dispelled by the realisation that her vision was doing very strange things. It took all her control now, to focus on Asenaath. 'Enjoy this, Asenaath. I think you have been looking forward to this since I came.'

Her cutting manner appeared to goad Sinefrew into brutality. Pointing to one of the female servants, he ordered, 'Strip her!' The woman came forward and Neferu stood motionless as she lifted her shift from over her head.

'That too,' said Sinefrew, pointing to her loincloth.

'Is that necessary, sire?' the woman protested quietly.

'Do it, woman!' the man repeated. The woman untied the knots on either side of Neferu's hips and the cloth fell to the ground. 'Well, my fine lady! You are not so proud now, are you?' Sinefrew said sneeringly.

'Every dog must have its day, even a jackal like you,' Neferu replied quietly, her words slurring a little. Her insult hit the nerves of the man, who had now moved in front of her. He raised his hand to hit her.

'Do not dare, or I will have you thrashed to death!' an icy voice spoke menacingly from the entrance to the hall. Everyone turned to look, including Neferu. Striding across the room towards them was Amio. His face was contorted with anger. Close at his heels were Horemheb and Paranefer, with Maatnofret hurrying behind. Sinefrew began to bluster that he was carrying out the orders of the pharaoh.

'I am pharaoh!' said Amio with contempt. 'I cannot rescind my father's orders, but I can issue my own order that you will be sentenced to death if you dare to lift that whip, and what is more, I will have you and all your family driven from Egypt on the death of my father. Take your choice!' Turning round, he barked. 'Get out of here, every one of you!' They did not wait to be asked a second time. Amio went up to Neferu and looked closely into her face, lifting her chin with his forefinger. 'Are you all right, little one?' he asked tenderly. Neferu heard his words from very far away and nodded. He opened the clasp of his cloak and took it off. With great care, he wrapped it around her shoulders and carefully fastened the clasp. With a sudden terrifying change of attitude, he turned to the now terrified looking man and said, 'Down on your knees, dog, and apologise!' The cowardly Sinefrew fell to his knees and abjectly apologised. Neferu, however, appeared totally unaware of him. Her eyes stared unseeing ahead. 'Now get up and do not ever appear in my court again,' Amio said savagely.

The man rose and left without further ceremony. Neferu stood like a statue, lifeless. Maatnofret, Mereta and Amio all started towards her as she suddenly crumpled to the floor.

When Neferu came round it was pitch black almost and she was lying on the couch in Mereta's sitting room. The room was lit by a single oil lamp, and she saw it as a blur. She could hear voices talking and distinguished them as Mereta and Maatnofret. She turned her head in their direction and they stopped abruptly as they noticed she was awake.

'At last!' Mereta said in a tone of relief. 'You have been sleeping for hours, Neferu. We have not been able to wake you at all. It is past the hour of midnight! Are you alright?'

Neferu tried to sit up. Her head felt very heavy. 'Have I really been asleep so long?' she asked wonderingly.

'I think I put too much of the potion in your drink,' Maatnofret explained apologetically.

Neferu began to recall the events of the afternoon. She looked down and noticed she was still wrapped in Amio's cloak. 'Where is Amio?' she asked. 'I must thank him for saving me.'

'I will fetch his majesty,' Maatnofret answered gravely. 'He is sitting with your brother. I was told to inform him the moment you came round.' Maatnofret rose to go and bring the pharaoh and Mereta came to sit by her, taking her hand.

'A lot has happened since you fell asleep, Neferu,' she said carefully.

'What Amio did was very serious. My father could banish him from Egypt for it. I hope you will take this into account when Amio talks to you.' Neferu was horrified and nodded her head emphatically. She had not realised that Amio had put himself at such grave risk by saving her. She had foolishly thought of the pharaoh as being above the laws that governed his citizens.

When Amio entered, Mereta went up to him, kissed him and then left. Neferu was left alone with him in the room. Her head was clearing rapidly now, and she sat up, conscious as she did so that she was still naked under the cloak. Amio looked at her very gravely and asked her if he might sit down.

'Of course!' She patted the sofa beside her, and he sat down next to her. He was wearing another cloak now, identical in style but of a darker blue than the one she was wearing. She looked down at the floor for a moment as the gravity of the situation enveloped her. After a moment she lifted her gaze to him. 'I would like to thank you with all my heart for saving me from ...' Her words trailed off. Amio said nothing, waiting for her to continue. After a moment, she did so. 'I suppose you are going to send me home in disgrace now,' she said miserably.

'No. I had planned another, quite different fate for you,' he said coolly.

'What is it?' she asked quickly.

'I plan to marry you,' he said.

'Marry me?' she repeated stupidly.

'Marry you,' he repeated.

'But why? Haven't I brought enough disgrace on you all?'

A glimmer of a smile appeared on Amio's set face. 'Well, not quite. I told my father that I did not think it wise that the future queen should suffer a public flogging. He understood my position immediately and said he hadn't realised that we planned to marry when he had signed the order, or he would not have done so. Now he is very angry with Sinefrew for the whole situation.'

Neferu was speechless. 'But we are not in love with each other,' she said finally. Remembering that there was someone else he was in love with.

'But we are very good friends are we not? And we are very fond of each other, isn't it so?' he said laconically.

'Yes,' she agreed.

'Good. We are agreed on that. I hope that love will grow between us, Neferu. You never need to be afraid of me. I promise you I will never touch your body unless you want me to, in love,' he said gravely. 'And, after all, I think it is time I married and there is no one else I can think of.' This latter was said lightly, with a dash of humour. He looked at her sideways as she remained silent. 'Don't tell me that you are refusing me.' He sighed drily.

Neferu's thoughts were chaotic. She thought of him being banished for defending her. She thought of her family being disgraced, of the royal family being disgraced. Finally, she thought of Yussef. She felt she had betrayed him, but what option did she have? It was either Yussef, who had much less to lose, or Amio, who had put his own life at risk for her. She realised he was looking at her intently.

'No! I will not refuse you, Amio,' she said quietly.

'Good,' he said simply. 'I will try never to ask of you more than you can give, Neferu. If love grows between us, I will be very happy. I hope that one day soon, you will want to make love with me. I am a normal man and I find you a beautiful woman, but I will never rush you. When you are ready for that, you must show me clearly. Until then I will never touch you. Do you understand?'

Neferu nodded. She felt shy discussing such things so openly. 'I feel that I have betrayed Yussef,' she said honestly.

He looked at her sharply and nodded. 'Tell me truthfully. Are you in love with him?' he asked quietly.

'In love with him?' she repeated. 'I don't know. I love him. Is it the same? I don't know.' She felt like a parrot, repeating everything, but she wanted to give an honest answer.

'It is not the same thing,' he replied emphatically. He did not pursue the subject further and appeared satisfied with her reply. 'In the circumstances I think it is best that we marry quickly and quietly. I will send a message to my mother in the morning. Do you agree?'

She nodded. 'Yes,' she said.

'I think it is best if you go to bed now,' he said. 'I will take you down to your room and then I will go to tell Demi that you are fine and will see him in the morning.' Neferu nodded shyly. Amio held out his hand and she took it. He pulled her to her feet and, still clasping her hand, led her across the veranda. He went down the stairs ahead of her, still holding her hand in his. At the bottom he waited for her foot to touch the bottom and then led her to her suite. At the door to her chamber, he leaned forward and gently kissed her full on her lips. Involuntarily, she felt herself respond to the sweetness of it.

'Goodnight, Neferu. Sleep well.'

'Goodnight, Amio.' She lifted her hand to his cheek and touched it lightly. 'I am sorry for all the trouble I have brought to you,' she said softly. He touched her hand with his own and brought her fingers to his lips, kissing them.

'Forget the past, Neferu,' he said in a low voice. 'Only the future is important now. We will try to build a good future together.' With those words, his lips brushed her forehead and he turned and was gone.

Neferu entered her chamber and she sat on her bed for a while in the dark, before lifting her fingers to unclasp the cloak. In the darkness she could not find her nightgown and after a futile effort, she climbed naked between the sheets, shivering a little at their coldness next to her skin. She felt strangely calm. The thought came to her that Yahweh, Maatnofret's god, had saved her from the whipping. He had answered their prayers. He was obviously a very powerful god. He had saved her so now she belonged to him. Neferu closed her eyes. She still felt a little dizzy from the effects of the potion. Within a few minutes the only sound in the room was that of deep, regular, rhythmic breathing.

CHAPTER 16

Next morning Maatnofret came as usual to wake her. She shook Neferu awake and bent over her, smiling. Neferu opened her eyes, and the events of the previous day came back to her in a rush.

'Oh, Maatnofret,' she exclaimed, putting her arms round the motherly neck. 'How can I ever thank you for what you did yesterday?'

Maatnofret beamed. 'It wasn't me Neferu. It was Yahweh. I told you he could do anything!'

Neferu planted a kiss on the plump cheek. 'Well, from now on I shall pray only to him, my god who controls the sun, moon, stars, and all creation.'

Maatnofret laughed and told Neferu she should get a move on. 'I think it is well that we are soon leaving Thebes for a while,' Maatnofret said. Neferu felt a sudden rush to tell Maatnofret her other news but, after considering the matter she thought better of it. It would be best to wait until everything was official. She did not want to get into any more hot water.

After washing her hair and bathing, Neferu felt like her usual practical self. Every now and again, she would stop to consider the events of the evening, but such confusion would fill her that she would immediately push the thoughts away. As she climbed the steps up to Mereta's suite, she wondered how she would broach the subject. As it happened, she need not have worried on that score. Neferu gently shook Mereta awake, the princess yawned. She opened her eyes and said sleepily, 'Good morning, sister!'

Neferu was taken aback. 'You know already?' she cried.

'Of course!' Mereta said smugly. 'Amio came to tell me last night.'

'What is your opinion of the matter?' Neferu asked gravely.

'I am thrilled about it, Neferu. I know that you and Amio will get along splendidly together. You are exactly the right person for him.' Mereta beamed with pleasure.

Neferu looked at her doubtfully. 'Do you think so?' she said uncertainly. 'It seems to me that I am hardly the stuff that queens are made of.'

Mereta laughed. 'It is true that you are a little impulsive,' she agreed. 'But I think you will be fun as a sister-in-law, and I am sure that you will grow to love each other. I love you both anyway, so I am very happy about the situation.' Neferu had to smile at the other girl's enthusiasm. She appeared to have forgotten already the uncomfortable position her recklessness had put them all in. Her smile disappeared suddenly as she remembered something.

'What's the matter?' asked Mereta quickly.

'I am just wondering what your mother and the grand vizier will say when they hear about yesterday,' Neferu answered anxiously.

'I have no doubt that they will have been informed about it already,' replied Mereta calmly. 'We will just take what is coming. There is no point in worrying!'

Neferu looked at her seriously. 'You really have been a good friend to me, Mereta. It was so stupid of me to lose control yesterday. I just couldn't stand by and let another human being be treated like that. It was so cruel,' Neferu burst out.

Mereta was silent for a moment before choosing her words carefully. 'I understand how you feel, Neferu, nevertheless, I feel that your intervention did more harm than good. Uncle Ay will investigate the matter to the very last detail, I am sure. In putting yourself at risk like that, a much larger tragedy could have occurred. You must see that yourself, Neferu.' Neferu nodded by way of reply. There did not seem to be anything to say which could adequately explain the matter, and she did not want to make the situation worse. 'I think that our trip to Rashid was planned for a very judicious time. With any luck the matter will have blown over by the time we return.' The princess added matter-of-factly.

'Well!' she said. 'I think I had better get up and ready for breakfast. It wouldn't do to be late on top of everything else, would it?' This last was a rhetorical question, not demanding any reply, and Mereta jumped out of bed with an unaccustomed spurt of energy.

As the two girls neared the breakfast table, Neferu noticed the great royal nurse, Teya, looking closely at her. She observed their due curtsies and merely wished them both a good morning, however, saying that they would wait for Amio before starting. Mutnedjmet looked at Neferu curiously but did not mention the previous day at all. It was as if it had never existed. For the umpteenth time Neferu reflected upon the strange family set-up which comprised the royal family. She had only ever once seen the queen and her husband breakfast together, although their relationship at formal state lunches and dinners seemed to be extremely cordial, even warm. Neferu felt that they behaved more like brother and sister than man and wife. It was not the kind of subject that she was free to discuss and her conjecture concerning them remained private. She wondered if that would be the kind of relationship she would live out with Amio. She hoped not.

Amio joined them at table, his cloak brushing her arm as he passed, and she forgot the enigma of the old pharaoh in contemplating that of her own position. Amio seemed to be in good spirits. He gave his aunt a kiss on the cheek and then turned to give Neferu a brilliant smile. Neferu felt overcome by shyness as she noticed everyone staring at her. She blushed as she smiled back at him. Mereta intercepted the look and smiled her satisfaction at both of them. Without further ado, they all began to eat. Several times Amio caught Neferu's eye and smiled at her warmly and reassuringly.

When breakfast was over, Teya looked around the table and said, 'What happened yesterday was most regrettable. It is done now, however, and something good has come out of it. I am expecting my husband back quite soon. He will know best how to deal with the practicalities of the situation and salvage what he can from all the bad feeling which has been engendered with Sinefrew and his family.' Teya's words made Neferu feel extremely uncomfortable, and she sighed audibly.

Teya looked at Neferu directly and with the very slightest of a twinkle in her eye, said, 'Amio tells me he wishes to marry you, Neferu. For your sake I would have preferred more romantic circumstances for his proposal but perhaps what it lacked in romance it made up for in drama.' At this point, Neferu blushed furiously again and looked down at her feet.

'Never mind, Neferu!' Amio laughed gently. 'We will have all the time in the world for romance later.' There was tenderness in his voice, and she looked up again. His eyes seemed to embrace her.

'I think it would be best to arrange the marriage as soon as possible. That way everything will be settled before our visit to Goshen to visit your grandfather's family.' She spoke practically and directed her speech to Amio.

'I agree, Aunt. The visit to Goshen would give time for the atmosphere at court to settle down and would also be a suitable occasion for our relatives to meet Neferu.' Amio spoke airily. He seemed content to leave the organisation to his aunt.

Teya seemed pleased. 'I hope that my husband will be back this morning. There is much to arrange. Possibly your mother will come back with him, unless your grandmother's condition is very serious.'

Amio nodded to her and glanced over at Neferu and the others. All were listening with avid interest. Neferu was privately thinking how complicated it all sounded. She wondered what steps would be required of her in all this planning.

It came almost as a relief when Amio asked her directly. 'Do you trust me to make all the arrangements I see fit, Neferu?'

The Keftiu girl nodded after a slight hesitation. 'Yes. I trust you, Amio. I ask only that if it is possible, I would like my father to be present. I know that it is impossible now here in Thebes, but if we could have a simple ceremony in On where my people could be present, I would be grateful.' She looked to him for support in the matter and he responded immediately.

'Of course, my darling.' It was the first time he had ever used such an endearment to her, and she wondered if it was for the benefit of his family. 'It seems wrong that they can't be here now. I would like to have your father's blessing on our marriage, and I don't see why a ceremony of blessing cannot be performed in the temple of Re at On.'

His tone was very understanding, and Teya was also nodding her approval to the plan. 'I will discuss it with my husband today, Neferu,' she interjected.

Amio said after a pause, 'My great-grandfather used to be high priest of Re at On. Uncle Manasseh also held that position until he died, so I think it is very appropriate that your family celebrate our marriage in a ceremony at On.' He smiled at her again. She wondered once again at how quickly those long almond-shaped eyes could change expression.

'Now that it is all settled, I will request my husband to see to it as soon as he returns,' Teya said crisply. 'No doubt your mother will also have her own ideas for the ceremony too, Amio,' she added.

'Yes. No doubt,' he remarked with a touch of cynicism.

Neferu began to feel that she was vaguely out of touch with reality. She was pleased to have been unburdened of the responsibility of making the decisions of a practical nature, but on the other hand, this was not how she had ever imagined her wedding would be, and she was not even going to marry the man she had always imagined she would marry. Once again, she was like a boat with no oars, carried by an unpredictable tide.

'I feel I ought to go and tell Demi what is going on,' Neferu said suddenly.

Amio looked at her thoughtfully. 'I spoke to Demi already this morning, Neferu.

He was worried because he had not seen you since yesterday and Smenkh came to tell me very early before you had awoken. You have no need to worry about shocking him, therefore, but I do appreciate that there is much that you may wish to discuss together.' His voice sounded concerned. 'After you have spoken to Demi, perhaps you would come to my apartment. I think that we too have much to discuss,' he said quietly.

Neferu inclined her head in the affirmative. 'What time shall I come, Amio?'

Amio glanced at Mereta. 'If Mereta does not mind I will come to collect you after you have spoken to Demi, and we can have lunch together in my sitting room.'

'That is fine,' she said quickly. Neferu requested Teya's permission to leave and she and Amio stood up. He lifted back her chair for her and the two of them began to walk along the path towards the end block where Smenkh and Demi were resident. Amio made no attempt to touch her at all but merely chatted in his usual manner. Neferu was very much aware of the eyes of the others following them as they left. Everything was changed and yet it was still the same on the surface.

When Amio guided her into Demi's chamber and told her brother that he would be back to collect her in an hour or so. Demi's first reaction was one of relief at the sight of his sister.

'What on earth happened?' he asked anxiously.

Amio bowed slightly. 'I will leave you and your sister alone, Demi. I am sure there are lots of things you want to talk about.'

Amio took his leave and Demi looked to his sister. 'I almost thought that I wasn't going to see you again,' he said with relief. 'Is it true that you are going to marry Amio?' The questions came thick and fast and Neferu sat down on his bed, bemused. 'I can't imagine what Father will say, let alone Yussef!' As coherently as she could, Neferu began to relate the turn of events which had commenced when she left his chamber the previous morning. The telling turned out to be easier than she had foreseen because she was still so dazed by events that it was almost like telling a story that had happened to someone else.

Demi was full of disquiet. Naturally he would come to her wedding, he told her, though he knew that the folks at home would be heartbroken not to be present. Neferu felt upset too but she told him it was not really important because she and Amio were not in love and theirs would be a marriage of convenience. She told him of the risk Amio had taken to save her. Demi was silent. At last he spoke sadly. 'It is not what I would have wanted for you, Neffie!'

Neferu shrugged. 'It is what destiny has arranged for me.'

'Do you really believe that?' her brother asked.

'I believe it is what Yahweh wants for me,' she said sincerely.

Demi looked perplexed. 'Yahweh? Who is Yahweh?' he queried.

'I mean Aten in Egyptian,' Neferu answered. 'I prayed to him yesterday to save me from the flagellation, and he did so.'

'And I thought it was Amio!' her brother said cynically.

Neferu looked at him sharply. 'There is no need to be sarcastic, Demi,' she retorted.

'Do you love Amio?' her brother asked, looking at her intently.

'I am very, very fond of him,' she replied.

'Is that enough?' he sighed.

'If the Aten has planned it, it will be enough. I like him very much. Yes, I do love him as a person,' she stated firmly.

'But Neferu! He will expect you to sleep with him,' Demi said impatiently. 'You can't have a brother and sister relationship with him for long! Are you physically attracted to him?'

Neferu considered the matter. 'I don't know,' she said simply. 'I find it sweet and pleasant when he kisses me.' She spoke frankly. Demi told her that he felt he was much older than her, not two years the other way round. He said he thought it was a situation fraught with problems. After that he was silent, and she understood that he did not want to say more because he was afraid of disturbing the delicate balance between his sister and the pharaoh. In any case he was precluded from speaking further by the sound of conversation outside the room and the consequent appearance of Amio in the doorway. Demi wondered if Amio had heard any of their conversation but, if he had, he gave no indication of it.

'I have come to escort Neferu to my suite to discuss all our new plans,' he said, smiling. 'How do you feel about our forthcoming marriage, now that you have had time to consider the matter a little more?' he asked Demi in a seemingly casual fashion.

Demi looked from one to the other of them and then said slowly, 'I hope very much that it will work out happily for you both,' he answered. 'I will not pretend that I am not upset. Yussef is my best friend, more like my brother, and I know how much he loves Neferu. His world is going to be shattered by this. I know what he is like, and I know that he will never be able to forgive either of you.'

Amio looked upset to be reminded of the existence of Yussef. 'I know that what you say is true, Demi, and I know that I cannot make up to him for the loss of Neferu, but I will do my best to make sure that his life will be successful along other lines. I will make him the wealthiest jeweller in the whole of Egypt, and I will grant him a high position in the administrative palace at Memphis.'

'I know that you mean well, Amio,' her brother replied with a sigh, 'but it won't help his feelings. Not only that but Yussef is a very deep person. I am afraid that his bitterness will be such that to offer him such a high position may backfire on you.'

Amio seemed slightly annoyed by Demi's continuing pessimism. He brushed the argument aside and said a little curtly, 'I will do what I can to assuage his grief. Perhaps mother will be able to find a beautiful girl for him to marry instead of Neferu. I will ask her to find some suitable women of good family. We can deal with it when she returns.'

Demi realised that further comment from him would be unwelcome, so he merely added. 'I truly wish you both all the very best happiness that it is possible for a man and woman to feel, from the bottom of my heart.'

The look of annoyance passed from Amio's face and was replaced by a broad smile. He thanked Demi generously and then turned to Neferu. 'Are you ready, Neferu?' Neferu rose and came toward him. He put his arm lightly around her shoulders and bade Demi a friendly adieu. The Keftiu boy waved his arm at them in response.

At the foot of the stone washed steps, Amio removed his arm and gave Neferu a gentle push to signify that she should climb in front of him. With a slight shock, she realised that he was ceding rank to her as his forthcoming wife. At the top of the stairs, she waited for him for a moment until he was abreast of her. He took her fingers lightly in his. His hand was cool in spite of the heat. She felt a little awkward but made no attempt to take her hand away. It felt pleasant and she felt it was a demonstration of his affection for her.

Neferu had never entered Amio's suite before and she felt a little strange and shy when they reached the entrance. On the veranda she half turned toward him, hesitating, waiting for him to go first. He went forward to the doorway and then turned to ask, smiling, 'Won't you come in?' Neferu crossed into the room and looked about her. It was not the kind of room she had supposed the pharaoh to have. Like Maatnofret's room it was comfortably but plainly furnished. There was no sign of opulence. Amio sensed that she was a little surprised and he observed her face as she looked around her.

'Well! Do you like it?' he asked curiously.

She spoke softly. 'It is not what I imagined the pharaoh's room to be like. It is much plainer and simpler. Somehow I had expected that the pharaoh would have a very grand apartment.'

Amio was amused and laughed a little. 'It is a plain room for a plain pharaoh,' he said without rancour. His remark seemed to indicate no answer, so she said nothing. Amio indicated a long couch made of hide, scattered with plump, soft-looking cushions. 'Sit down please, Neferu,' he said.

Neferu did as she was asked and he seated himself beside her, studying her face for a long moment. Oddly, she no longer felt ill at ease in the slightest and steadily returned his gaze. His eyes seemed to be probing hers, moving slightly and yet holding her gaze all the time. It was a very long moment and yet when he spoke it was in a casual voice. He referred to their forthcoming wedding preparations.

'I regret very much that everything will be so rushed. I would very much have liked to have your family here for you. I never imagined that when I married, it would be quite like this!' he said ruefully. He paused for a moment as if to find the right words before continuing. 'I sense that you are a very deep and private person, Neferu. I look forward to getting to know you as closely as it is possible for one soul to know another. To be pharaoh means to have power, but it also means to be lonely, even in a crowded room sometimes. To be lonely and yet never to be alone. A paradox, don't you think?' Neferu nodded but said nothing as she did not wish to interrupt his train of thought. 'I would like us to be alone together as much as possible from now on so that we can get to know each other properly, but I know that it is going to be almost impossible. It will make our relationship difficult, Neferu. There will always be eyes on us, watching us all the time. Will you be able to accept that and still not lose sight of your friend Amio, underneath it all?'

Neferu looked at him as if seeing him for the first time. They had never spoken so intimately before. She understood that he was making a special effort to show her that he understood her feelings. She was touched by his concern. He took both her hands gently in his. 'I want you to be happy, Neferu. I want it with all my heart. Do you believe me?'

Neferu felt a lump come to her throat. She was unable to speak for a moment. 'I like you so much Amio. I want to love you as a wife, but at the moment there are too many other feelings which are in the way.'

His dark eyes were expressionless as he nodded. 'I understand that it will take time for your feelings for Yussef to fade, Neferu. I promised that I will not take you to wife until you are ready for it. Will you promise to tell me when you are? I desire you,

Neferu. It will be very hard for me to keep my promise. Do not make me wait longer than I have to.'

'If Yahweh has arranged for us to be man and wife, Amio, then he will also arrange for love to grow and unite us,' Neferu replied.

'Yahweh? Where did you get that idea?' Amio asked with a slight frown. 'You sound like grandfather!'

'From Maatnofret. She says that Yahweh is the Aten and is the most powerful of all the gods, and I believe it. I think it is his will that I have come here, and he will make everything right.' She spoke with more confidence than she felt.

Amio laughed, in spite of himself. 'I didn't realise that Maatnofret had been so wily as to convert you too, Neferu! When I was small, my grandfather used to talk about the god of his forefathers. Now he is old, he talks about nothing else.'

'Don't you believe in the Aten, Amio?' Neferu sounded surprised.

Amio replied in succinct fashion. 'Yahweh is a Hebrew name, Neferu. As you know, the Hebrews are not a popular people in this country. They are still hated by many, who erroneously confuse them with the Hyksos who once invaded our country. I am a quarter Hebrew, but I don't speak the language as well as mother or Uncle Ay. We prefer to refer to our god in Egyptian terms to avoid the unfortunate connotation of the Hyksos. It is one of the reasons that my mother is always very careful to respect the old traditions of Egypt. Personally, I don't think about the gods very often, Neferu. When I was small, I used to pray to them to make me strong and handsome instead of ugly and deformed, but nothing happened, as you see,' he said wryly.

'I do not find you ugly, Amio,' Neferu said firmly.

His mouth tightened a little and he answered curtly. 'You do not need to flatter me in any way, Neferu. What I have always liked about you is your honesty. I want you to promise me that you will always be honest with me.'

'I am being honest with you, Amio. I have never found you ugly.' She paused to find the right words herself now. 'Your face is very unusual, it is true, but it is an intelligent face and a sensitive face, and you do have remarkably beautiful eyes. Eyes are the first thing that I notice in someone. I don't know what it is, I know it is not colour or shape, but some people have the kind of eyes that warm your soul, and you know that they are your kind of people. You have eyes like that, Amio. You must be one of my kind of people. I assure you that it is true,' she said earnestly.

Amio sat very still and looked at her directly. Finally, he said in a neutral tone. 'I find it hard to believe but I thank your kind heart.' He leaned forward and kissed her softly on her lips. It felt sweet to her, and she thought that it would not be difficult to respond to this man in other circumstances. Simultaneously as he drew back, he began to discuss their plans. 'I hope that afterwards you will not regret the hurriedness of our marriage ceremony, or let the circumstances leading up to it dwell in your memory,' he commented anxiously.

Neferu shook her head. 'No. I shall be happy if the ceremony could be as simple as possible. I am not used to pomp or ceremony,' she assured him.

Amio sighed. 'I feel the same, myself. We will be forced to endure a protracted ritualistic tradition though, Neferu. It is going to be very wearing,' he warned her. He brightened as another thought occurred to him. 'When we have visited my relatives in Goshen, we will take a holiday in Rashid so you will feel at home with your past and know that it can be united with our future. We will take as few people along as protocol will allow and try to make it as simple as we can. Would you like that?' he asked softly. Neferu's eyes prickled, and two large tears fell down her cheeks. She nodded emphatically. He looked distressed and with both hands he gently wiped away the tears. 'There is nothing to be afraid of, Neferu. I will help you; I promise.' In an attempt to lighten her mood, he said, 'I promise not to be a domineering husband!' Neferu smiled in response to the effort he was making. She took his hand and lifted it to her lips.

'I promise to try and be a good wife,' she replied. Amio put his arms around her and pulled her to him. She rested her head on his shoulder and there was a sweet intimacy between them. It was not passionate or full of sweet romantic words and yet for the rest of her life, the memory of those few moments stayed with her as a treasure even through her darkest periods. There was something so special about them that she knew she would take the memory of them through to her afterlife with her.

A man coughed discretely, and they drew apart. It was Paranefer, Amio's valet. He bowed slightly, surprised to see Neferu there.

'The grand vizier will arrive sometime after noon, Your Majesty,' he declared formally.

'Thank you, Paranefer.' Amio spoke easily. 'Will my mother be with him?'

'Yes, sire. That is the message we have received, sire.' The valet bowed and made as if to retire.

'There is no need to be formal in front of Neferu, Paranefer. We are going to be married soon and I would like you to be friends.' Paranefer smiled and offered them his congratulations. He told Neferu that he was sure that they would always be friends.

Their time together had passed quickly and yet Paranefer informed them that lunch would soon be served. Amio informed him that they would eat with the others and, still lightly holding hands, they went across the terrace. Mereta also left her apartment at the same time and noticed the entwined hands. A small smile caught her eyes, but she said nothing about it and instead said lightly, 'Here comes one very thirsty princess! Where are the refreshments?'

Ever afterwards, all the trivial details of that day seemed to stand out in Neferu's memory, sharp and clear. Lunch was always a delicious meal at Malkata, but Teya had ordered an especially nice menu for them that day, and Neferu felt hungry. It might have been just a recovery of their appetites following the sheer drama of the previous day, which had shocked them all so. Today they all ate hungrily, even Mereta, who normally ate only tiny amounts. There were cubes of beef and lamb, roasted on skewers and served with plenty of fresh warm pitta, to accompany a salad of onions, carrots, lettuce, cucumber and beans dressed in a vinaigrette of vinegar and oil of bak. They washed it down with fresh date juice and the very sweet wine produced from their own grapes. The servants regularly replenished the little finger bowls so that they could rinse their fingers between courses. For dessert there were sweet cakes and bowls of fresh fruit comprising pomegranates, figs, dates, apples and slices of melon. It was an excellent meal and when they were replete, Teya suggested they go and rest. Amio escorted Neferu to her chamber but made no move to enter. He kissed her gently on the lips again before leaving her.

It was Maatnofret and not the housemaid who woke Neferu up just before three o'clock.

'The queen and the grand vizier have arrived, Neferu,' the lady-in-waiting whispered. 'I have just been summoned. I am telling you so that you can prepare yourself.' Neferu had been dreading it but there was nothing to do except to face up to it. She wondered whether Amio would be present when she was summoned. She sincerely hoped so. She felt that she could not face the formidable pair without him. Neferu dressed as quickly as she could. She took special care over her appearance, as she felt she needed the moral support of knowing that she looked at her best. She decided that she would pop in and see her brother before going upstairs. She told him nervously. 'I can't stay long, Demi. They are back!'

'Good luck, Neffie,' he said sympathetically to her as she left him.

The terrace was deserted, for which she was thankful. She did not want to bump into the queen just yet. Mereta was up and dressed and making lace when she entered.

Neferu raised her eyebrows inquiringly and Mereta responded, 'It's all right, Neferu. I told mother everything.'

Neferu was dismayed. 'Already?' she gasped. She felt it boded badly that the queen had started to interrogate them immediately on her arrival. It denoted her anxiety about the events.

'Amio is still with her,' Mereta added. She smiled. 'He is so happy that I don't see how mother can be angry. She has been nagging him to get married for two years, at least! Ever since he became co-regent with my father. Her goal is now in sight!'

Neferu grimaced. 'I don't think she had anyone like me quite in mind.'

Mereta laughed merrily. 'Amio could not possibly have a more beautiful wife, Neferu.'

'But I am a commoner, and Keftiu at that. She will surely not approve of that even without the contretemps which I have caused,' Neferu stated.

'But we are also partly of foreign blood,' Mereta admitted honestly.

Neferu shrugged. 'Perhaps that is all the more reason for her to wish to have a full-blooded Egyptian as queen. I think that the court will not accept it,' she replied.

Mereta considered for a moment and then said with emphasis. 'I know that nothing will turn Amio from his decision, Neferu. And if destiny has decided that you will be queen of Egypt, you will be queen.'

Neferu was shaking with nervousness when Maatnofret came to escort her to Tiya. The senior lady-in-waiting spoke reassuringly. 'Your future is in the hands of the Aten, Neferu. You have nothing to fear.' Neferu wished that she could be convinced. Tiya looked at Neferu closely as she entered. The Keftiu girl curtsied low. When she rose, she was pleased to see that Amio was also present, as was the grand vizier and his wife, Teya.

'Well, Neferu!' the queen said with her usual cool regality. 'It seems you are the harbinger of great changes.' Neferu did not reply. She was very conscious of the queen's piercing gaze on her. The queen's voice was grave when she resumed her speech. 'It seems that the future of Egypt will lie in your hands, Nefertiti. It will be a great responsibility. Do you think it is one you will be able to discharge?' Neferu felt so scared that she was forced to look to Amio for reassurance. Her eyes implored him, and he gave her a warm look and a slight nod in support.

She turned to face the queen again. 'I have never thought about this until this moment, Your Majesty,' she said honestly. 'But as I now do consider your question, I find it is not what I assume my future life to be.' Here she noticed the queen raise her eyebrows and so she continued hurriedly. 'I feel that my future duty lies to my husband. I will try to be a good wife to him, and I leave Egypt to him and to the Aten.' Neferu spoke the words from her heart. Tiya looked startled at her reply, but she noticed that Ay, at least, was on her side as he was smiling at her warmly.

The queen remained silent and Ay said to her reassuringly, 'You are right, Neferu. That is all anyone can reasonably expect of you, and it is the most important role you could have in ensuring the future of Egypt. A pharaoh who is well supported at home is in the best position to lead his country wisely.' He spoke in a kind tone and Neferu relaxed a little.

The queen looked sideways at her brother. 'It seems that you have made a staunch ally in my brother, Nefertiti,' she observed drily. 'My son's happiness is of prime importance to me. If you succeed in making him happy then you will find a staunch ally in me too, Nefertiti! In the meantime, there are many preparations to be made. The dressmaker will be coming this evening to start on your wedding dress. The ceremony is to be held the day after tomorrow. The priests of Amun will come tomorrow to teach you the correct responses. We have very little time to prepare.'

It had begun, just as Amio had said it would. From now until the wedding was over there would be no time for her to think about anything. Her life was no longer her own at all now. Her only relevance was to be as an appendage to the glory of the pharaoh. She pushed away the vague amorphous sense of disquiet. Neferu looked into the eyes of the great queen and knew herself to be merely a pawn. She looked across at her future husband. Would he be strong enough to protect her from the domination of this woman, or was she to be merely his plaything, after all? Suddenly she felt very alone. As if recognising her inner conflict, Amio came over to her and lifted her hand to his lips in front of them all. It was a gesture of solidarity with her, and a faint hope flared in her heart. If he respected her as a person, it would be all right.

Neferu was anxious that her family be informed as soon as possible about the momentous events taking place in Thebes and she pleaded with Amio to make sure that they knew as soon as possible. On this score her fears were settled by Ay, who informed her that he had sent a messenger to On. From this time on, Neferu gave herself over to the machinery of state and the next twenty-four hours were spent in a whirlwind of activity and organisation, controlled and co-ordinated by the grand vizier and the queen.

Amio and Neferu were brought before the elder pharaoh. The plump, rather paunchy man seemed affability itself and appeared to have lost all recollection of the unfortunate events which had almost culminated in her public flagellation. His span of concentration seemed short and once again Neferu noticed that the small pinpoint pupils gave his eyes a glassy look. This time she suddenly realised where she had seen that look before. It had been on Demi while he was under the influence of the potion the court physician had given him to take away the pain in his leg. Was it possible that the elder pharaoh was a user of opium? It would certainly explain his lack of interest in the affairs of state. Neferu decided that sometime in the future she would discuss the matter with Amio.

That moment came much sooner than she had thought. It was the morning following the arrival back at Thebes of the queen and Neferu and Amio had a free moment, following their audience with the elder pharaoh. They stepped out onto the dry grass of the gardens. In spite of the awful heat, Amio still wore his cloak. 'My father is sick, Neferu,' Amio said to her as he guided her toward the lily pond with gentle pressure on her elbow.

'Yes. I have heard that, Amio. But what is the matter with him?' asked Neferu, trying not to appear over-curious. They sat down on the side of the pond and Amio was very frank with her. He told her that over the past few years his father had changed out of all recognition. It had started with bouts of terrible toothache, which he still suffered from occasionally. Several of his teeth had had to be taken out, but the physicians had not been able to cure the inflammation inside his gums and he had been prescribed extract of poppy seed. This medication had proved to be very effective at relieving the mouth pain, but gradually his father had become addicted to the medication and became very unstable and tempestuous without it. With continued use, his personality had deteriorated, and he had come to depend more and more on his brother-in-law and his wife to run the country. Now he spent his time indulging himself with whatever lady of his considerable harem took his fancy and swallowing ever more of the opium.

Neferu shuddered. 'I hope that will not happen to Demi!' she cried anxiously, remembering her brother's eyes when he had received the stuff.

'No!' Amio reassured her quickly. 'I am sure that it will not. The physician is very careful, and it is something I have, in fact, already checked with him myself. I also have a horror of it after seeing poor father become a slave to it. In any case, Demi only receives it for the dressing on his leg and the physician says he has no pain now and so is no longer given it.'

Neferu was surprised. 'Have you been following Demi's treatment up?' she questioned him. When he nodded, she asked him why.

Amio smiled. 'He is your brother and our guest. It is only natural, don't you think?' he replied with a quizzical look.

'I think that you are remarkably kind, Amio,' she declared. He shrugged, slightly embarrassed. After a pause Neferu said bluntly. 'Your mother does not like me.'

'It is not that, Neferu,' Amio said quickly. 'My mother has not had as easy a time as you might think. My grandfather was a Hebrew slave who was imprisoned in the military fortress at Zoan for many years when he was a very young man, for a crime he did not commit! He was saved from that fate by my grandfather, the Pharaoh Tuthmosis IV. There are still many Egyptians who still hate the Semites without differentiation for the crimes of the Hyksos. It was very difficult for both my grandfather and my mother when she was young, especially when she married my father, even with the blessing of the pharaoh. Many of my close Egyptian relatives saw their ties to the throne irretrievably sundered and many sought to deny the legality of my elder brother's claim to the throne. When he died in Kush, the succession passed to me and they see that as a further weakening of our rights, as I do not have my grandfather's forename.'

Neferu was totally mystified by this latter remark, until Amio explained the tradition of the eighteenth-dynasty pharaohs that Tuthmosis and Amenophis were ancient family names, and it was the custom that each elder son should carry the name of his paternal grandfather and he in turn should name his firstborn son after his father. This tradition had been broken by the death of his elder brother, so that now one Amenophis had been followed by another. Amio went on to inform him that the young Tiya had suffered very much as a young queen from the jibes of the royal family around her, from which she had little protection. She had grown a protective shell around her to act as a barrier against this, still always aware that she would always be considered an outsider, only half Egyptian.

'They tolerate us, you see, the high priests, but they do not like us. It is time for you to know these things,' he said in a prosaic manner.

Neferu was alarmed. 'Then it would have been very much better for you to have married an Egyptian woman, one of your cousins, perhaps, Amio.'

'Yes, it was my mother's wish, but fate has ordained otherwise!' He said with a grin.

'No wonder that she is not pleased, then,' breathed the Keftiu girl.

Amio shrugged again. 'I think that you are a very suitable wife for me, Neferu. It is true that you are of Keftiu origin, but your family have lived in Egypt for several generations. I am a quarter Hebrew but born in Egypt, you see! We have much in common.'

Neferu looked at him intently. 'I have no idea how to be a queen, Amio. The most I can promise you is to give you my loyalty as a good wife.'

'It is all I will ever ask of you, Neferu,' he said with some passion. The large, brown, almond-shaped eyes seemed to bathe her in their warmth. He leaned forward and kissed her. Her lips began to respond as his kiss became more insistent. They were disturbed by the call of the great royal nurse. Amio clicked his tongue in annoyance as Teya approached.

'Neferu! The dressmaker is here for a fitting for your wedding dress, and the priests are here, Amio, to carry out a practice ceremony. Neferu will join you as soon as the dress fitting is over.' Amio sighed and then lifted his eyebrow to Neferu, as if to say, 'I told you it would be like this!'

Teya, at least, seemed to be enjoying all this activity and she led Neferu up the steps to Tiya's apartment, where rolls of heavy white silk were lying about. The material was, without doubt, the most beautiful that Neferu had ever seen. It was patterned with the faintest of lotus designs, which were barely visible from afar. It offset the simplicity of the style of dress which the others had decided upon.

Neferu stood dutifully while the queen, Teya, Maatnofret and the court dressmaker made folds, draped material round her and generally decided the details. Neferu was quiet and compliant, and the others barely seemed to notice her, so caught up were they in all the preparations. The dressmaker and her assistants had worked hard since starting the dress the previous evening only. Neferu was amazed at the speed of the work. The dress so far was a good fit and the dressmaker seemed pleased with her efforts. She deftly swathed the material into the desired ruches and skilfully manipulated them to produce the effect she wanted.

Teya seemed very pleased with the results and Neferu looked down. It was indeed a dress fit for a queen. It draped gracefully over her left shoulder and left the right one exposed. The bodice was made of a simple double swathe of silk around her bosom and then down and around in loosely drapes ruches over a simple loose skirt. The swathe was lifted at the back to cover the left shoulder and ended in the top part of the left bodice. It was simple and easy to wear, and the result was elegance and formality.

When they were all satisfied, the queen brought out the blue and gold crown of Upper and Lower Egypt with the golden serpent around it. The queen asked Neferu to seat herself while she placed the leather crown on her head. The Keftiu girl was overawed. She did as she was told and practised walking up and down with her head held slightly backwards to balance the weight of it in the way that Tiya indicated. When Tiya was finally satisfied that they had done all they could for the present, Neferu was allowed to step out of the dress and to quickly put her own clothes on again, to be taken down to the state withdrawing room where the high priest and priestess were waiting with Ay, Amio and several others. The procedure of the ceremony was explained to her and the responses she would be required to make. Neferu began to feel very jittery. This was supposed to be her wedding and yet she felt she was almost superfluous. After what she supposed to be an hour or so, the priests left, and she was told to go and rest until the evening when there was to be a visit to the temple of Amun for a full-dress rehearsal for the following day.

Maatnofret accompanied Neferu back to her suite. Although she was irritable and tired, she could not help but be pleased by Maatnofret's news that after the wedding, Maatnofret was to become Neferu's own lady-in-waiting. Neferu's relief was great at having her trusted friend in close proximity.

'Oh, I am so pleased, Maatnofret!' she exclaimed, genuinely touched. 'I must say that I don't need a lady-in-waiting to do things for me. I can look after myself! But I do need a good friend.'

The older woman laughed. 'You will find that once the babies start to arrive, you will need a lady-in-waiting too.'

'Children?' Neferu was startled. She had not given a thought to such matters so far. She could not even imagine herself as a mother. Babies meant sleeping with Amio and she had not even really given any thought to that as yet. He still felt a stranger to her in many ways. She had just felt it during the ceremonial practice they had just worked through together.

Maatnofret glanced at her. 'Yes, Neferu, children! I hope that you will be blessed with many. They will be like my own grandchildren. Don't you want children?' Maatnofret asked, a little taken aback by Neferu's lack of enthusiasm.

'Yes. Of course! It's just that I hadn't thought about them yet. I don't want any just yet,' she stated firmly.

'They will come when the Aten wills,' Maatnofret remarked. 'When the Aten wills,' she reiterated pensively.

After the afternoon rest period, Neferu was awoken by the housemaid as usual. She dressed quickly and went to visit her brother. Demi also had news of a kind. The physician had told him that he was gradually to become ambulant again. Just a few minutes at a time at first and then, if that went well, for longer and longer periods. He was thrilled and scared at the same time. Demi also told his sister that he had been visited by Amio just prior to siesta and that they had had a long talk.

'What about?' Neferu was curious.

'Oh, about love, marriage, you, Yussef!' There was a brief pause. 'I think he is in love with you, Neferu,' he stated, looking at her closely.

Neferu shook her head. 'I know he is very fond of me, as I am of him, but I don't think he is in love with me,' she said. 'He has never said so and I expect that he would have done if it were so.'

Demi shrugged. 'If it were not for Yussef, I would be really happy for you. I think he is a really nice fellow, in spite of being the pharaoh!' Neferu smiled at this. Demi continued, 'He does feel really bad about Yussef, but I don't think he realises that doing all these things for him won't make Yussef feel better. You and I both know that Yussef will feel bought and that will make him even more angry. Yussef can be very spiteful when he is thwarted too. I am afraid for all three of you.' He looked worried. Poor Demi, she could see how deeply divided were his loyalties. Her cautious and methodical brother was just not able to cut himself off from the everyday realities in the same way she was able to. He would not even have wanted to. He was a born worrier, she sometimes thought. Still, she reflected, he could be right. It was possible that Yussef would feel he was being bought off rather than how Amio envisaged the process as a making up for what he could not alter. She gave her brother a kiss and left his suite.

Mereta looked up at her with surprise. 'I thought you had deserted me,' she said, smiling.

'Not at all,' Neferu replied casually. 'It was just that I was commandeered for fitting and practising responses. I don't think I like weddings, at least not my own. The others are having a good time, I think, except for Amio, of course, who I can see is not having much fun either.'

Mereta wrinkled her nose in a frown. 'Neferu, Neferu! Just a little more time and then it will be over. Try to be patient.'

Neferu sighed. 'I'm sorry, Mereta,' she said disconsolately.

In the end the preparations were not completed in time for a full-dress rehearsal that evening, and they ended up going to the temple in their day dress for the rehearsal. Just before sundown the chariots arrived to pick them up at the riverbank and take them to the temple. It was quite late when they returned, and she noticed that Amio was just as tense and tired looking as she was. In the chariot he took her hand and squeezed it. She leaned against his shoulder and slept for a few minutes until they reached the bank again. The boat only took a couple of minutes to ferry them back to the west bank, where the palace chariots waited to receive them. Everyone seemed subdued when they arrived back at Malkata. There in that gigantic and solemn temple, the first real understanding of the enormity of what this all meant had begun to filter through to her consciousness, as the voices of the priests and the chanting had rung out around the vast stone walls of that place. Today was the last day of Nefertiti Stassopoulos, and tomorrow would be the first day of who?

Maatnofret and Shenade, Tiya's other senior lady-in-waiting, came to settle her down that evening. They told her that they would come to wake her and prepare her for her wedding the following morning. Maatnofret gave Neferu a potion that she said would relax her. The physician had said it would ensure a good night's sleep for her. It reminded Neferu of the unpleasant incident just a few days earlier and she was reluctant to take it. In the end, she allowed Maatnofret to persuade her, and she swallowed the liquid. The taste was bitter and made her shudder, but it was effective, and she slept dreamlessly that night.

The next morning Maatnofret and Shenade appeared early and took her through to the bathroom where she was washed with a thoroughness she had never known. A special cleansing paste was used on her first, then it was washed off with water, to which salts of natron had been added. It made her skin tingle. Shenade washed her hair next and then wrapped a large towel round her head. Her body was wrapped in another large towel, and she was requested to return to her chamber and lie down on her bed while Maatnofret massaged her with perfumed oils. This completed, Maatnofret took her hands and began to manicure her nails while Shenade began to do the same to her toenails. She sat up, unprotesting until the two ladies were satisfied that she passed their inspection. Worse was yet to come, she discovered. Maatnofret left to bring her wooden toilet case, and Shenade took the linen towel from her hair and began to comb it carefully. Neferu winced as various knots were teased out and Shenade began slowly and skilfully to braid her hair. It took hours, it seemed to Neferu, as Shenade over and over again divided the hair into sections and began the job of plaiting. The lady-in-waiting cut the ends evenly when she had finished. She had wanted to cut a fringe for Neferu and plait that, but here Neferu rebelled. A fringe she would not have. In the end Shenade made her compromise by having a false hairpiece, which she attached with an unobtrusive silver comb. By that time Neferu just could not have coped with anymore. Once the hairdressing was completed all of them sat down to breakfast. Neferu felt most peculiar. Her hair felt as though it was sticking out from her head in all directions. Maatnofret gave her a mirror to have a look. She stared at the unfamiliar reflection in the mirror as though it was someone else. She wondered what else was to come.

After breakfast, Maatnofret brought out the little wooden box again. She made Neferu sit down on a stool so that her face was at the right level for her to work and then she began to prepare Neferu's face. Shenade took some silver tweezers and plucked a few stray hairs from Neferu's eyebrows. Apparently, she found them to be offensively out of line. Maatnofret then took a small brush and pressed it into a little casket of kohl. Carefully she drew a soft line around Neferu's eyes in the elongated style of the court noblewomen, which Neferu could imagine Grandma would never accept. It just was not Keftiu. Not at all. Maatnofret even applied the kohl to her upper eyelashes to make them look thicker. When Maatnofret was satisfied with her handiwork, she put down the kohl brush and picked up another one. This she pressed into a casket of powdered red ochre and then carefully brushed some onto Neferu's cheeks and then some onto her lips. Shenade tinted her nails with henna and Neferu heaved a sigh of relief. The process of beautification was complete.

When Neferu looked in the mirror this time, she scarcely recognised herself. Maatnofret brought her a long linen shift, which she put on carefully, her hair protected by a veil of thin muslin. With Shenade leading the way, the three of them went up the stairs to the first floor. Maatnofret told Neferu to stay with Mereta while she would go to find out how things elsewhere were proceeding. Mereta was full of admiration for Neferu's new look. 'Sit down, Neferu, while I bring Amio to have a look,' she said. Neferu sat down gingerly on the edge of the couch. She felt a little afraid to move her head. The hair pulled at all angles. Mereta returned in a couple of minutes with Amio in tow.

'Don't you think she looks beautiful, Amio?' Mereta enthused.

Amio came over and peered at her closely. 'I like you better as you are normally, Neferu,' he said at length.

'I think you could call this the triumph of artistry over nature,' Neferu said ruefully. Brother and sister looked at each other and began to laugh. 'Will you be wearing something special this afternoon, Amio?' asked his bride to be.

He smiled. 'I shall be wearing full ceremonial dress, Neferu. But remember it is only me underneath all that, won't you?' His voice was gentle. Neferu nodded. She lifted her head, and pulling him down she kissed his cheek. He jumped as if burnt and blushed a little. It was the first time she had made an obvious move in such a way.

'Neferu, this will be the fastest coronation in Egyptian history, no doubt, but I believe that you will be the most beautiful queen that Egypt has ever had and so, for your coronation name, I have chosen for you "Nefer-Neferu-Aten – the Beloved of the Aten". I hope you like the title I have chosen to honour you with and to honour the Aten, the god you have chosen for yourself. Do you like it?' Amio seemed anxious that she should like her new title.

The beloved of the Aten, she repeated in Keftiu. 'Yes. I am very honoured to be given such a coronation title. What will your title be, Amio?' she asked.

'Nefer-Khephrure.' He sounded almost shy, she thought.

'I like Amio better,' she said softly. 'It suits you very well, I think.'

The mood was broken, as it always seemed to be just when they were on the verge of getting to know each other, by the intrusion of someone, in this case by Maatnofret. Mereta gave a discreet cough and the young couple turned. 'Excuse me, sire,' the good lady apologised. 'But it is lunchtime, and the dressmaker would like to complete the final fitting of the wedding gown yet.'

Amio inclined his head. 'I understand, Maatnofret.' He turned back to Neferu and took her hand to his lips. 'I will see you later, my queen.' He bowed to them all and left the room.

Mereta came and hugged her. 'I hope so much that you will both be supremely happy,' she exclaimed passionately.

'I hope so too,' Neferu said fervently.

Maatnofret led the young bride into Teya's sitting room, where the queen was waiting for her impatiently. The gown in question was lying over a couch, carefully spread out. Neferu removed her shift and Maatnofret took it away. The dressmaker lifted the wedding gown and placed it over Neferu's head. Neferu stood very still while the last alterations were made to it. Tiya stood back attentively and surveyed the overall effect. 'Hmmm! It needs something in the way of jewellery to balance the crown,' she said, half to herself. The queen opened a large rosewood casket and took a pair of long, dangly filigree earrings. Maatnofret removed the small gold loops which Neferu normally wore and inserted the long drop earrings instead. The queen next took out a heavy gold collar necklace and some bracelets. Maatnofret placed them onto Neferu's arms and neck and then stood back to observe the effect. The queen appeared satisfied and clicked her tongue to show her appreciation. Tiya herself had also had her hair coiffured that morning and was wearing her state make-up, but was not yet gowned. Neferu looked at the housecoat and stifled the urge to smile. It looked strangely incongruous in the midst of all this splendour, and even lent to the normally formidable woman an air of homeliness, although homely was not an adjective Neferu would ever normally have used to describe Tiya.

Finally it was all over, and Neferu retired exhausted to Mereta's apartment for lunch.

'Will there be many people there this afternoon, Mereta?' she asked casually.

'Hundreds, I expect,' Mereta answered nonchalantly.

'Hundreds?' Neferu was aghast.

'Everyone from the court and all the senior officers, at least.' Mereta shrugged. 'It would have been thousands if there had been time, Neferu, so just think yourself lucky! There would have been representatives from all the vassal states and all the principal towns and cities of Upper and Lower Egypt. I can't think why you are so upset about it. If I had a face like yours, I would want everyone to see it,' Mereta said carelessly. 'By the way,' she added as an afterthought, 'will you teach my new lady-in-waiting how to do my hair. She is very young, a niece of Shenade's.'

'Of course! But I can continue to do it for you. Why not?' Neferu stated. 'In any case, I will certainly do it for you myself today.'

'You might as well rest here for siesta,' the princess spoke practically.

'I can't sleep with my hair like this!' Neferu commented.

'Well, lie down anyway,' Mereta advised. Mereta went off to bed and Neferu lay down on the couch. She was a little perturbed that she had not yet heard anything from her family. She wondered what they were thinking about at this time. She moved her head around on the cushion. It felt very uncomfortable with all the plaits. In the end she lay with her hands by her side and her neck straight and closed her eyes. In spite of herself she slept.

At the appointed hour Maatnofret woke them and Mereta went to bathe while Maatnofret carefully washed Neferu's face with a damp cloth and repaired her makeup. When Mereta returned Neferu went to bathe. Afterwards it was time for more scented oil and a last examination of her makeup and hair. Neferu quickly dressed Mereta's hair for her and then followed Maatnofret to the apartment of the queen. Tiya was already dressed. She was resplendent in a gown of blue pleated silk and was wearing the blue crown of Upper and Lower Egypt. When Neferu was finally ready, Tiya placed on her head a gold circlet with pearls in small nutcase-shaped gold cups hanging from it. It had the bonus effect of improving Neferu's deportment no end – this was because she was so afraid of it falling off that she simply did not dare to look down.

Pararameses came finally to tell them that all the entourage had already left and that their chariots were waiting if they were all ready. Amio's aide de camp led the group downstairs and across to the royal withdrawing room where they took the positions ascribed to them by the high priest. Amenophis III and Tiya led the way, followed by Amio and Neferu. The others followed. Slowly the elder pharaoh and the great queen followed the high priest through the great banquet hall, which was lined by servants, and out into the courtyard through the state reception room. Neferu stole a look at her husband to be. Amio's robe was of the finest white linen with long sleeves. It was tied at the waist with a wide belt of purple braid, knotted in such a way that its tassels formed four tails. Around his neck was an enormous gold collar necklet formed of small links. It was so large that it came to the edge of his shoulders. Neferu guessed that it must be very heavy, because even hers felt uncomfortable and it was much smaller. On his head Amio wore the blue crown. It matched the smaller one worn by Tiya. The cobra encircling it and the disc of the sun with the ankh at the front represented the indissoluble union of the pharaoh and his two kingdoms. Amio looked resplendent, awesome and thoroughly a pharaoh. He also looked like someone she did not know. As instructed, she had placed herself on his left and they walked with his left arm and her right arm outstretched, her right hand on his left hand. Neferu felt as though she were in a dream. She was no longer nervous. It was one of those moments which seem to be suspended in time, totally cut off from reality. Vaguely she wondered what she was doing here.

The footman helped Amio into their chariot first and then her. For a moment she allowed herself to turn slightly towards him. He was looking at her. He clasped her right hand in his by his side. 'It's only me, Neferu. Don't be afraid of all this pomp.'

In response she squeezed his hand and he smiled. She said in a low voice, 'I am afraid to move my head in case my coronet falls off.'

A low chuckle escaped him. 'I hardly recognised you,' he said. So, he too had had a shock, she thought, and it gave a sense of kinship with him.

The chariots took them the short distance to the riverbank, where the royal barges were awaiting them. In spite of the hurriedness of the planning, there were thousands of the citizens of Thebes lining their route. Neferu wondered how they had known about it. Later she found out just how effective the town crier system really was. On the royal barge, *The Aten Gleams*, Neferu and Amio were seated just below Amenophis and Tiya. People lined the banks on both sides. Once everyone had embarked, the barge pulled away from the bank into mid-river. It took only a few minutes to reach the other side and they waited until the gangway was safely in place.

Once on the east bank, they were assisted into other chariots for the journey to the temple, along the avenue which Amio's father had had built in the early years of his reign and which had only fairly recently been completed. The avenue was about thirty metres wide and was flanked on both sides by sphinxes in the shape of the heads of rams, as befitted the constellation which dominated their night sky. As they neared the end of the avenue, the first of the ten colossi loomed up. They passed this and three more before the chariots fame to a final stop in front of the southern door of the temple itself. Here at last they stepped down and into the temple of Amun-Re itself. To the Egyptians, Amun-Re combined the power of Aries with that of the sun, and the temple itself stood on the east-west axis, the worshipper standing with his face to the east symbolising the rising of the sun. Purple robed priests came forward to meet them from the confines of the gloom of the solemnly lit temple. The chanting ceased temporarily, and the sound of trumpets blasted the air as a signal of the pharaoh's arrival. Slowly the procession moved forwards and the chanting began again.

Amio and Neferu were led to kneel in front of the altar, which was piled high with sacrificial offerings. The high priest performed the rites of fertility and the vestal virgins danced around them. The chanting was hypnotic and Neferu lost all sense of time. Only when the moment came in which she had to make the required vows did she regain a sense of the reality of the occasion. Once the high priest pronounced them man and wife the coronation ceremony began. The high priest removed the circlet of gold from Neferu's head and Tiya came to kneel by her side. Carefully the high priest removed the crown from Tiya's head and placed it onto the head of Neferu, calling her now by her coronation title of Nefer-Neferu-Aten, chief wife of Nefer-Khephrure, new queen of Upper and Lower Egypt.

Afterwards Tiya solemnly kissed her on both cheeks and Neferu did homage to her husband in the traditional way by kneeling at his feet and kissing his hands. Then came the music of the trumpets again and the new royal couple passed down the central aisle to the waiting chariots outside. It was already dark outside, but the sky was lit by thousands of stars and a large full moon. It felt chilly and Neferu shivered a little as she climbed into the chariot with the man who was now her husband. Later Neferu found it very difficult to conjure up precise details of the service that made her a queen. There lingered a memory of the smell of incense and other rare and costly perfumes, but what she did remember most clearly was the moment when their chariot descended the long avenue towards the river when, in the cover of the night, Amio clasped her to him and whispered, 'I wish us a long and happy life together, my queen,' before kissing her with a restrained passion.

Neferu also remembered afterwards the brightly lit barges and the sudden joyous upsurge of the conversation and laughter which accompanied their return journey across the river. It was in stark contrast to the quiet, solemn outward journey. Perhaps everyone had been nervous, she thought. The realisation that she was now a married woman came to her. It was a strange thought. She did not feel married, she pondered. She considered that less than three months ago she had not ever set foot in Thebes, and Amenophis was just the name of a stranger who happened to be the pharaoh of the country in which she had been born. Now he had called her 'my queen'.

Back at the court there were refreshments laid out in the banquet hall for those who wished. It was now very late, and the hurried circumstances of the wedding were such that long jovial celebrations were out of place. Toasts were drunk to them, and Ay informed everyone that there would be great celebrations when the royal family returned from their holiday. By now Neferu was deathly tired, and she noticed that Amio too was also pale and drawn. She felt only relief when the redoubtable Shenade and Maatnofret led her away. To her surprise, somewhat foolishly, she thought afterwards, they led her to the pharaoh's apartment. Here they undressed her, bathed her and unplaited her hair. Maatnofret brushed her hair and suddenly she saw her own familiar face in the mirror again.

Maatnofret took her to Amio's bed chamber and helped her into the large double bed, which was placed next to the wall. The two ladies then left discreetly. In spite of her tiredness, Neferu lay awake wondering when Amio would come into the room. She heard him enter the suite with his valet and then the noise of the valet's footsteps as he retreated across the veranda. Quietly she lay and waited. Amio entered the room silently. He said nothing as he came over to the bed. Leaning over her he kissed her, then he looked at her for a long moment with an enigmatic look before saying quietly, 'Goodnight, Neferu. The peace of the Aten be with you.'

'Goodnight, Amio,' she whispered into the darkness as he left.

He had kept his promise. He was the pharaoh, and he could take any woman he pleased, yet he had respected his promise to her. A warm feeling grew inside of her. She was not yet in love with him, but now she felt for the first time that she wanted to be. Unbidden a picture of Yussef came into her mind and a feeling of guilt enveloped her. She felt she had betrayed him and everything that had gone before. 'But there was no alternative,' she whispered out loud to herself in the dark. She would explain everything to Yussef when they met again. He would understand. He must understand.

CHAPTER 17

The next morning Neferu woke and looked around her. She sat up, suddenly nervous as she waited expectantly for Maatnofret to appear. What would her friend say when she discovered her alone in bed? She wondered what she should do. She jumped up quickly and put her wrap on, just in time as she heard Maatnofret and Paranefer enter the apartment. Maatnofret looked surprised to find Neferu alone and her eyes strayed round the room and then looked back at Neferu accusingly. Neferu interpreted her look correctly and bit her lip.

'Please don't tell anyone, Maatnofret,' she begged the lady-in-waiting.

'My discretion is assured, Neferu. You know that. I must confess though that I am disturbed and curious,' the older woman replied. 'It does not bode well,' she added sombrely.

'Do I have your promise that you will not tell the others?' Neferu's voice rose nervously.

'You have my promise, Neferu,' Maatnofret replied.

'I can manage my toilette myself, Maatnofret,' Neferu stated.

'Then I will go to breakfast, Neferu,' Maatnofret replied. 'There is a lot of packing to do if we are to leave for Goshen tomorrow.'

After Maatnofret had left, Neferu washed and dressed quickly. She was brushing her hair when there was a slight cough behind her. She turned to see Amio standing in the doorway. He wished her a good morning rather coolly and she returned his response. Already she felt the barrier between them. She was afraid to speak but felt that one of them must broach the subject.

'Maatnofret was surprised and upset that we were not together,' she said shyly, looking down under his unwavering gaze.

'What did she say?' His tone was now a little cold.

'Not very much. I made her promise not to tell a soul.'

Amio nodded gravely. 'What will you tell the others?' he asked, narrowing his eyes.

'I will not tell them anything,' Neferu replied in surprise. 'As far as they are concerned, we are man and wife, unless you choose to tell them otherwise.'

'I will not pretend, Neferu, that I am happy with this arrangement. You know that I desire you and I want our marriage to be a true marriage as soon as possible.' Amio's expression was set and his tone a little bitter. Neferu was unhappily aware that he had used the word desire and not the word love. Her heart sank.

'I will sleep with you any time you wish to, Amio,' she said proudly, lifting up her head. 'You may take me now if you wish.' There was an electrifying moment of silence between them. When she looked up at him again, she could read nothing from his face.

'I do not wish to take you, Neferu. I want you to give yourself to me in love. I have given myself six months to win your love, If I cannot do it by then I shall set you free. I do not want you to be unhappy.'

Neferu remained silent as she digested his words. 'I suggest you take my arm,' he said. 'And at breakfast we try to appear happily in love.'

As they walked across the terrace, they both made a conscious effort to appear bright and smiling. The queen observed them closely at breakfast and Ay made a few innuendoes, which caused Neferu to blush deeply. This caused Ay to chuckle, thinking he had scored a bull's eye. Fortunately, breakfast was a hurried affair with all parties anxious to plan for the trip. The queen was much preoccupied with the expected arrival of her parents, who were to accompany the group to Goshen. Her mother was still very fragile, and the queen was very worried about her. Perhaps for this reason she was not her usual perceptive self. Neferu was much relieved as she did not think her acting ability was up to an acute cross questioning.

Neferu was seriously aware that her relationship with Amio had deteriorated since the previous day. His words to her before their marriage had largely been a bluff, she realised. He had thought her so empty that her head could be turned like a baby's and that she could be manipulated at his will to do anything he wanted her to. She knew that they could not continue like this without a storm. Contrary to what he had said previously, he now resented her deeply.

Against her will, Neferu remembered the words of Yussef. She understood that no one could have foreseen the incident with Sinefrew and Amio's rescuing her from a very public disgrace, but that aside, she was now really suspicious that her original detention in Thebes had not been entirely innocent. Amio had admitted that he desired her, but had he originally meant to toy with her? Neferu tried to suppress these thoughts. She realised they were extremely destructive in her present circumstances.

There was much to be done to prepare for the forthcoming journey. The court physician declared at the last moment that he would be ready to sanction Demi's travelling, if he could be carried on and off the boat, and at no time was he to bear weight on the damaged leg. Initial tests had confirmed that the bone was not strong enough yet to take the strain of walking. The deputy court physician was to accompany the group to Goshen so that the five-day journey would not handicap Demi in any case, as he could be called upon for assistance if necessary. Demi was overjoyed to be on his way home at last. Not least because he had had enough of the stifling heat and the enervating stillness of Thebes.

That day was different in many respects from all her previous time in Thebes, in that Neferu seemed to be on the verge of stepping halfway again at least into her former life in the north. She had now come to hate Thebes and all the complications it had caused in her life. She was once again between one life and another, except that she was now a prisoner of her new husband. She had at least the prospect of a respite from the obsessively overbearing atmosphere of the court. She knew that she would never ever belong there, whatever the outcome between her and Amio.

That part of her wardrobe which was not being taken on board the royal barge was being transferred to Amio's apartment that day so, after her morning visit to see her brother after breakfast, she found herself shyly returning to the suite of her new husband. After his attitude of the morning, she expected the situation to be strained and she wondered fearfully how he would react. He seemed to have reverted to his usual friendly self, however. They played backgammon and chatted about her family and his. It was almost as if the barrier of the morning had disappeared. She could not quite forget it though, and it made her a little jumpy with him. By and by, she began to relax again, except for the thought of the siesta period in the afternoon, which bothered her in advance. She fully expected him to either approach her again or to begin to sulk again and she steeled herself for whatever mood he might assume.

After lunch, however, Amio advised her to go and rest and he retired to his own room. Maatnofret came in as usual but made no comment. On the other side of the corridor, Neferu heard Amio chatting with Paranefer, and at one stage she heard the sound of laughter, so she deduced that he was not sullenly thinking of her.

Shortly before sundown, Yuya, the former grand vizier, and his wife, Tuya, arrived.

To Neferu, they both looked immensely old. Amio told her that his grandfather was sixty-seven years old. Neferu had never known personally anyone that age and she could not help being impressed. The old couple were so wrinkled and bent, however, that she felt there was no way that she would ever like to live that long.

The old grand vizier had a very prepossessing appearance and Neferu could see that in his youth he must have been a very handsome man. He had a strong square jaw and full lips. His eyes were large and heavy lidded, and he had a long face and elongated skull. Neferu could see from whom Amio had inherited his elongated almond eyes, though the noses of the two men were completely different. The old Hebrew had a markedly aquiline nose whereas Amio's nose was long and straight with a slight uptilt at the end, similar to his father's nose. Tiya had inherited her mother's round face and full lips and her Nubian dark skin. Her eyes and her square jaw were from her father. Amio's skin was much lighter, almost an olive colour, though not as light as her own, which was much more typical of the Keftiu and other mixed peoples of northern Egypt. Neferu felt a little in awe of the couple, they were so old. Tuya especially was so fragile that she seemed like a little dried-up puppet doll, so tiny and wizened and thin, with a dowager's hump. Neferu was afraid that she might break in two like a dried twig. Neferu also noticed that Yuya still spoke Egyptian with the slightest of foreign accents. Although it was only detectable in certain words, she noticed it because of her own bilingual background.

Amio's grandparents welcomed Neferu into the family and apologised that they had not been able to arrive in time for the wedding. She was happy to note that they did not appear to know the reason for its rapid execution. The old couple smiled affably at her, but in the main, they were obviously more preoccupied with talking about the past and the prospect of seeing the old man's relatives. Most of his brothers had passed away, it seemed, with the exception of his youngest brother. They reminded Neferu of her own grandparents and she thought about the times when she and Demi had poked fun at Grandma behind her back because she also spoke Egyptian with the occasional mistake, even though she had been born and brought up in Egypt. The Keftiu were such a close-knit community that they still spoke their own language as a mother tongue at home and amongst fellow Keftiu. Grandma's mistakes had sometimes been a source of embarrassment to them when her father brought his business colleagues around. Neferu wondered if Mereta and Amio had ever felt the same.

Tiya was very anxious to settle her parents in. Her mother especially was exhausted after the long journey in the heat of the summer. Privately Neferu thought that the old lady was in no fit state to travel to Goshen, though they seemed insistent upon making the journey. Neferu had never met anyone who had so many relatives as Amio had.

After the family dinner was over and the old couple had been settled in their quarters, Neferu and Amio received the message that the old couple wanted to talk with her and Amio privately. When they entered the apartment of the former grand vizier, Tuya said to her husband, 'Yussef, our new granddaughter is here.' The name brought a flush to her cheeks, and she wondered if Amio had noticed. It must increase his present chagrin, she thought. He appeared not to have taken anything amiss, however, and she relaxed again.

The former grand vizier had charming manners. He told her she was beautiful and understood why his grandson had fallen in love with her. He told her that being part Keftiu was not a bad thing, as it led to a greater understanding of other peoples and their customs. He ended their brief meeting with a prayer and a blessing on them from his own god and reminded Amio that his sons should be circumcised, like all his forefathers had been. She and Amio had been rather embarrassed, as neither of them had considered the question of babies yet, at least, as far as she was concerned. Not really knowing anything about the ritual of circumcision, she had nevertheless agreed to it, because it had seemed of fundamental importance to the old man.

Later that evening, Teya, the great royal nurse, agreed with Neferu that she did not think the old lady fit to make such a long journey and it was agreed that she and her husband would stay behind to look after them. She felt the relatives in Goshen were better placed to visit her father-in-law than the other way around. Neferu was happy that the family affairs and talk had obviated any need for Amio and herself to act out any charade of being passionate young lovers. Everyone was taken up with the journey ahead. The queen suggested that they must have a lot to talk about and rather coyly hinted that they have an early night. The two of them rose and Amio put his arm around her waist in the attitude of a young lover. The others watched them depart with knowing smiles.

As they walked to their suite, Amio said, 'I have talked with my mother and told her that I am extremely anxious to spend some time together with you away from the court. It is important for us to get to know each other better, don't you think?'

Neferu stopped for a moment to look at him and formulate her words with care. 'Of course. I want to get to know you, Amio.' She hesitated before continuing as gently as she could. 'I want to be in love with you, Amio. I cannot force myself to be, but I do love you as a person. Do you believe me?' Her voice was quiet and intense.

'I am trying to understand your feelings, Neferu,' he said slowly. 'I pray that love and passion will grow between us.'

'I hope so too, Amio,' she said earnestly.

He continued with the veiled expression he so often used with her, so that she did not know what he was really thinking. 'With that end in view, I have arranged that when mother and the others sail east to Goshen, after our visit to On, we will continue north, northwest to Rashid with just a few of the palace personnel. That way we will have some privacy to develop our relationship. Pararameses, Maatnofret and Paranefer, plus a few of the servants only, will accompany us. After mother and the others finish their visit, they will sail to Rashid and spend a few days with us before we return to Thebes. On the return journey, we will make a private visit to your family and to pick up Uncle Ay, who will remain there on business after our re-affirmal of our marriage in the temple of Re at On. I do think that you should be aware, Neferu, that on the outward journey there will be little time for a long reunion with your family, because of all the ceremonial duties. It will be different on our return journey!'

Amio looked at his bride for her comments.

'Won't we need two boats then, when we leave here?' she asked puzzled.

He smiled at her ability to jump to the pragmatics of the situation when she was otherwise such a dreamer. 'No. We will all travel outwards on *The Aten Gleams* as far as On. The others will continue on board to Goshen. We and the rest of our little group will continue our journey north on the army's battle cruiser from On to Rashid,' he explained. He looked at her speculatively. 'We will arrange for Demi to be put ashore and accompanied home to your grandparents, then, in the evening, we will attend a formal banquet where we will meet many of the personnel who will be present at our vow ceremony on our return. Your family will naturally be our guests of honour and you will have a short time for private greetings between you to take place. The following day we will continue our journey north. I would like our marriage to be stabilised before we meet your family in a more personal unit, Neferu. I don't want us to be uncomfortable with each other then,' he admitted in a thoughtful tone.

Neferu perceived that he was expecting this brief holiday to be the catalyst for a ripening of their relationship into married love. He seemed to have planned everything down to the last detail. She began to understand that Amio was capable of devious strategy and was not at all the uncomplicated character she had perceived him to be. She wondered what he really was capable of, this all-powerful young man whom she had married, and about whom she knew almost nothing.

In their apartment Amio kissed her goodnight on the cheek. In spite of his seemingly artless words, she felt a controlled aggression in him. It disturbed her. It was almost a battle of wills. She sensed that he really did not understand her at all. It left her with only two alternatives, as far as she could see. She could go to him tonight and submit to him. He would be appeased, she knew, and he would feel that he had won her over, but she knew herself well enough that she would come to hate him for using this menace of dominance over her to obtain what he wanted. She had to decide now, if she loved him enough to challenge him, and possibly cause him to destroy her, or if she cared little enough for him that she could allow him to physically dominate her and for her not to give a damn for him. The second alternative would make her life a lot easier, and she could keep the innermost part of herself separate from him so that he would never know. She supposed that lots of women did do that, especially at court, where most marriages were made for financial or power considerations. But there was something about Amio that did touch her heart, if only he could learn to really love her and not just to possess her. She wanted more from her husband than to be just his chattel. She wanted to really love him as a husband and a lover, and that would only be possible if he recognised her as his equal in every way. Anything less would be subjection and degrading to both of them. She knew that for her it was imperative that she respect the man who would be father of her children, not because he was the pharaoh, but because he was a superior human being. Neferu sighed. She wondered why she had to be so complicated. Were other women like her? There must be some, she thought.

The next morning it was Amio who woke Neferu up. 'Neferu, wake up!' he spoke insistently.

Neferu sat up quickly. 'Amio, what is wrong? Where is Maatnofret?' she asked anxiously.

'Nothing is wrong,' he declared, shaking his head. 'I sent Maatnofret and Paranefer to oversee the loading of your luggage. You must get up. We have a lot to do before breakfast and we leave immediately afterwards.' His voice was brisk. Neferu wondered how long he had been there. She had not heard him come in. She swung her legs over the side of the bed.

'What about Demi?' she asked, remembering that she had not visited him the evening before.

'Demi is already ready. The physician has given him something to calm him prior to the journey. He is having breakfast now and he will be transferred to the boat first. Paranefer is dealing with that,' he said slightly impatiently.

'Oh, good!' Neferu said, jumping up.

'Good morning, wife,' he said sardonically. Neferu was conscious that he was looking at her expectantly.

'Good morning, Amio,' she said and reached up to kiss him on the cheek. He accepted her embrace without moving and she drew back, a little self-consciously. Again, she felt that parrying of wills in his cool gaze on her. Was he stalking her like one of the lions in the hunt? But this was not a hunter versus hunted relationship. Was it? What a complex man he really was beneath that charming courtier mask he wore. Her sense of his hostility was so palpable that she asked, uncertainly.

'Amio. We are friends, aren't we?'

He smiled at her so charmingly that she began to wonder if she had imagined that earlier covert tension. 'Of course we are friends, Neferu,' he said with a deliberately comic bow. 'What a strange question!'

Neferu's brow cleared. She was just being over-sensitive again. 'Sorry!' she said with a smile. 'I don't know what made me say that. Stupid of me, forgive me.'

'Of course,' he replied smoothly. 'When you are ready, come down to mother's suite immediately. I must go. There are some decrees I should sign and seal before we leave.' With those words he turned to leave.

At breakfast everyone had something to say, and the atmosphere was unusually chaotic. Mereta told Neferu that when she was little, the family had travelled frequently to Goshen and Akhtmin to see their relatives, although these visits had been cut down since her father had become ill. After all the eating was over and the final affairs settled, they set off.

In the courtyard Ay, Teya, the senior pharaoh, Archduke Tuthmosis, Tuya and Yuya all came to wave them goodbye. Tiya and her ladies-in-waiting travelled in the first chariot and Amio and Neferu in the second. Pararameses and three soldiers were in the third chariot and the rest of the entourage were almost evenly divided between the remaining six chariots. The journey down to the river was short and there was a holiday atmosphere about it. Neferu immediately felt a lightening of her mood.

'I am so happy to be leaving, Amio,' she whispered to him excitedly.

He raised an eyebrow inquiringly. 'Is it so bad here?' he asked with cool reserve.

'No. Of course not. It's just that … This is not my home.' Poor Neferu realised that she had said the wrong thing yet again. She took his hand. 'Oh, Amio! I always seem to say the wrong thing. I didn't mean it the way it sounded,' she said miserably.

'I understood what you meant, Neferu,' he answered, more kindly. He squeezed her hand and she kept it in his. It seemed like a gesture of peace between them.

Neferu embarked on *The Aten Gleams* for the third time in her life and for the longest river journey she would ever make. In order to speed up the journey time, it had been decided that the fifty oarsmen would take it in turns and would row through the night on those nights when the moon was full or large in the sky, which was now the case. It would be more tiring for the passengers but there would be frequent stops at the cities along the way, to take on supplies and to change tired crews for fresh ones. At these stops they could find their land legs if they wished.

The first morning was full of interest. There was a large canopy on deck under which they could sit, shaded from the omnipresent glare of the sun. Demi and Smenkh played jacks and when they grew tired of that there was a general game of 'I spy'. When they grew tired of this there was a general knowledge quiz organised by Amio and Pararameses, and the time passed quickly until lunch. Everyone ate a hearty lunch; no one seeming upset by the movement of the boat or the rhythmic chanting of the oarsmen.

There were two cabins on the boat and after lunch the queen and her lady-in-waiting, Shenade, retired to sleep. Amio declined to go below when Neferu asked him. There was an immense couch for the pharaoh and the queen under the canopy area, but Amio told her that he was not tired. Demi and Smenkh, therefore, were taken down below to rest and Neferu was left undecided what to do. Amio and Pararameses were engaged on army talk, which was of no interest to Neferu. She went to sit next to her husband, but he said, as if slightly surprised at her being so close to him, 'Sleep if you want to, Neferu!'

'Not if you are not,' she said somewhat shyly, in front of her husband's aide de camp. Amio smiled and then turned back to Pararameses. While she chatted, she let her thoughts wander to the family. How had they taken the news of her marriage? More important, how had Yussef taken it? She would soon find out. Strange that Amio's grandfather should also have the same name.

After a while, Neferu got up and went to look over the rail, remembering her journey to Thebes some three months previously. So much had happened since then. She had come as the daughter of a minor river security representative, and she was returning as the second queen of Egypt. Amio had informed her that the fact her father was to be elevated to the pharaoh's chief security guard of the Nile had not meant any manipulation of the present incumbent, who had been coming up to retirement anyway. She was glad about that, though it did not rule out the possible bitterness of the person who had assumed that the title would fall to him, she realised. She hoped her father would not incur any enmity.

Gazing into the waters of the Nile, as if searching for her own future, she continued to digest all these events. She rolled the word 'queen' around her tongue, but it still had a hollow meaningless ring to her. It certainly did not seem applicable to her. Her eyes slid downwards to the oars as they glided in and out of the water with monotonous regularity. After a while she rejoined her husband's side. Amio was still talking animatedly, and she slid silently into place beside him. He acknowledged her presence with a smile. Most of the others were asleep now and Neferu too began to feel her eyes closing. She felt hot even under the canopy. The heat was very oppressive now. Although the sun was slightly lower on the horizon now, it was entering the canopy at such an angle that its glare was impossible to evade. Even the movement of the boat brought only the very slightest of breezes and it was not detectable unless you were standing at the sides. Neferu wondered how Amio could bear to wear his cloak all the time. It must have been very irksome. Amio noticed her lolling against him as she became increasingly drowsy. Only a few of the servants were awake. 'Come along, Neferu. We will rest,' he said. She was too tired to do her analysis of his mood by now and allowed herself to be adjusted unprotestingly on the couch. Pararameses rose and retired to his own sumptuous, curtained couch.

The two almost-but-not-quite lovers were left alone to take their rest under the covered canopy and were then curtained off from the sight of the others except from certain angles. They lay back on the soft cushions. Neferu suggested that he take off his cloak, but he shook his head with a smile and refused to remove it. He told her to turn towards him and sleep so that they would appear to be in close contact. She did so and he half turned towards her so that from the vantage point of the servants it must have seemed like the whisperings of lovers. Neferu could smell the closeness of him and the perspiration on his upper lip. She felt, in spite of her intentions, an awakening of her body in response to his closeness. She thought it would be impossible for her to sleep but she closed her eyes and drifted away almost immediately.

When she awoke, it was almost sundown and was much cooler. Amio was still asleep, his chin resting on her forehead. She hesitated to move, not wanting to disturb him. She could not see his face, but she could hear the sound of his rhythmic breathing. She smiled to herself, there was something vulnerable about him like this. She felt him stir. Although she had not seemed to move at all, he suddenly woke up and lifted his head, looking down at her. She smiled up at him.

'I did not mean to wake you,' she said softly.

'How long have you been awake?' he asked by way of reply.

'Only a few moments,' she told him. For some reason, he appeared reassured. She shivered a little as the sun sank and the temperature dropped.

'Are you cold?' he asked.

'Just a little chilly. The sun is going down fast,' she answered.

He lifted slightly and spread out his cloak to cover them both. 'Do you feel comfortable with me as close as this?' he suddenly asked, with an odd look.

'Yes,' she answered, nodding.

'I am glad,' he said, putting his right arm across her waist and saying. 'Come closer, it will be warmer.' She drew closer to him and leaned her head on his shoulder. She felt warm and protected. They lay in silence, but it was a friendly silence that neither of them felt constrained to break. He leaned his cheek against her head and was still for a long time. She thought he had fallen asleep again, but when she moved her face to look up at him, his dark eyes gazed down at hers.

'What is it?' he asked.

'Nothing,' she replied. 'I was just wondering if you were sleeping.'

'No. Just thinking,' he said quietly.

Some of the servants began to light the oil lamps and soon the boat was shimmering with the light shining from dozens of different directions. They could hear the others chatting and laughing. It seemed to Neferu that there was something special about this evening. It was one of those moments, cut off from all time, when the soul seems to crystallise a moment of truth and beauty so that it remains forever imprinted, to feed off in an uncertain future. She felt that she wanted to preserve it exactly as it was, with all its essence of tenderness and poignancy. Did Amio feel it too? At any rate, he remained silent, and except for the movement of his chest, he did not move for a long time. The mood was finally broken by the approach of Paranefer, to tell them that dinner was served, and the others requested the pleasure of their company. Amio looked annoyed for a moment, but then shrugged his shoulders. 'We had better rise, Neferu.'

The queen observed their approach with satisfaction. They had smoothed their crumpled dress and came hand in hand. The queen informed them that the boat would soon dock at Al-Amra, where the crew would change over. After that they would travel on overnight, if this was acceptable to them, and they should then arrive at Panopolis at sunrise. If they wished to stay overnight at Al-Amra they should state it now. Amio shook his head. There was not much traffic on the river at night and in the cool night air the oarsmen were able to pull faster and more strongly. There was no need to institute all the boring requirements of security that protocol demanded, not to accept the lengthy habits of obeisance from the local citizens that custom demanded but that he was in no mood for. The moon was almost full and there was plenty of light to steer by; in addition, he was eager to reach their destination as soon as possible.

Privately, Neferu was a little put out by the toilet arrangements on board the boat. She realised the difficulties with so many people on board, but she felt repugnance at using the special chamber pots to the rear of the boat, in the small cabin-like structure built for that purpose. The servants were meticulous about keeping it clean, but she could not help wrinkling her nose in disgust at the pervading smell of urine there. When she mentioned it to Amio, he laughed and told her that she would never be able to cope in the army then, when they were out on manoeuvres or patrolling the border area. She told him she did not doubt it and noted his genuine amusement. It occurred to her afterwards that she was able to discuss with him most things that she would have been able to discuss with Demi or Yussef, without embarrassment. There was something very down to earth about Amio and she felt at ease with that. If only this question of their emotional relationship would fall into place and they could start to live as lovers, she began to feel certain that they could be happy. It seemed that the veiled pattern of dominance was now receding and for that she was grateful. Mereta, at least, shared her desire to bathe and clean herself up more satisfactorily than their present arrangements permitted. Both the girls would have dearly liked to dock at Al-Amra for home comforts, but they understood Amio's enthusiasm to reach their destination. They cheered themselves up by private jokes about nasty smells and living rough. Although their conversations were conducted in whispers, Mereta's tinkling laugh caused the others to look at them with querying expressions, which they deigned to ignore. Neferu noticed that Amio and Pararameses were smiling broadly, having overheard their remarks.

Night sleeping arrangements were forced to be simple by the sheer necessity of numbers. All the ladies were billeted downstairs in one or other of the two cabins. Amio and the other royal entourage, including Demi, were to sleep under the canopied areas on deck. There was a plentiful supply of soft rugs to keep out the cold night air and they would be ever present to deal with any emerging situation which might arise. The remaining personnel, including the minor servants, slept on the deck on small roll-up rugs. They too had rugs to cover themselves with to keep out the night chill.

At Al-Amra, the boat pulled into dock and an emissary of local dignitaries came on board to welcome the royal family. They seemed a touch put out on hearing that the royal visit was to be an exceedingly curtailed one. By now even Tiya was having second thoughts about whether or not they should stay overnight. She was hot and sticky too, it appeared. In the end a compromise was reached, and the ladies were escorted to the home of the chief potiphar, where they were graciously received. Here they were able to bathe and change. The men were taken to the local military headquarters and accomplished the same tasks under less opulent conditions. When the men rejoined the ladies, Amio convinced Tiya to continue onwards, in spite of their fatigue. Neferu felt certain that the queen would have made a good military commander. She had a tireless discipline that Neferu knew she would never be able to acquire.

Back on board, Amio accompanied the ladies to the door of their cabin and, in front of all the others, he took Neferu in his arms and gave her a long kiss. Neferu assumed that this was at least partly for the benefit of his mother and Maatnofret and so she played her part too, though in truth, it came naturally to her to respond. She put her arms around his neck as he held her and responded to his kiss spontaneously. Abruptly, he released her and wished them all goodnight somewhat grumpily. When he had gone, the queen smiled at Neferu sympathetically.

'Poor Amio! I think he is finding this journey most frustrating,' she remarked. She seemed completely unaware of the true state of their relationship and Neferu felt some misgivings at the deception. She remained silent, not wanting to alert the queen's suspicions.

Notwithstanding the cramped conditions in the cabin, Neferu slept soundly and only woke as the craft pulled in at Panopolis at dawn. Word had already reached Panopolis by equestrian messengers that the royal barge was due to dock there earlier than originally planned. Such communication posts were situated regularly along the Nile from the southernmost point of Upper Egypt to the northernmost point of Lower Egypt and throughout the tributary areas of the Nile delta. It was faster even than the river traffic and was a method much favoured by Ay.

The welcoming party at Panopolis escorted the royal party to the pharaoh's official residence, normally occupied by the mayor in the absence of the pharaoh, as was the custom in all the major towns and cities of the Two Lands. Here the party were able to freshen up and bathe prior to a sumptuous breakfast on dry land. Afterwards, a much more comfortable party departed back to their boat, which now had a fresh crew and fresh supplies.

The rather cramped conditions on board the ship were conducive to an increased familiarity which had sprung up between the various parties, and there was much good-natured bantering. The lady Maatnofret turned out to be a superb storyteller and she and Neferu sat together, Neferu listening intently while the lady-in-waiting regaled her with stories of Amio's family. It was fascinating and gave her an insight into her husband's secretive and complicated character that she had hitherto lacked. In particular, she found the story of the old grand vizier's life almost like a fairy story, though Maatnofret assured her it was true. Neferu wondered at the lack of rancour in the old man. She had detected no bitterness in him.

'Nothing in our lives can happen to us without the will of Aten, Neferu,' Maatnofret explained with great firmness. 'Yahweh can use even the bad things that happen to us to our advantage if we believe in him. It was all a long time ago and Yahweh caused Amio's grandfather to prosper in Egypt and to save his tribe from being wiped out by starvation during the great famine. There is a reason for everything, even if we don't understand it at the time. So, you see, Neferu, it was the will of Aten that you marry Amio!' Neferu nodded, it was clear that if Yahweh could have effected such monumental changes in the life of Amio's grandfather, he could surely do it in her life. Neferu found her new grandfather an immensely interesting man.

They had lunch on deck and the heat began to feel oppressive again. Amio went to rest with the other men and, instead of going downstairs with Tiya and the others, Neferu went to be on the couch with him. The charade of lovers which they were acting out was proving to be less false to her than it had previously appeared. There was a growing familiarity between them, in spite of the constant enforced companionship of the others present, plus the cramped surroundings. Life on board ship seemed to suit Amio and he appeared to be in good spirits. He was always friendly towards her, though she still detected a momentary ambivalence in him in his attitude towards her occasionally. It was as though an invisible barrier would suddenly be erected between them when she least expected it and she would find herself retreating ever so slightly until there was almost a coolness between them. The unpredictability of it all made her constantly on her guard, even jumpy at times. She found it strange, this never quite knowing whether he would ever let her know what he was really like or whether the expressionless eyes would one day open up permanently and show her the real man inside. Although they lay closely together, he never made any attempt to touch her body other than in a friendly way. She felt they had reached an impasse and wondered at her use of such a military term.

The following two days passed in this mould and a pall began to descend upon them. There was an instinctive desire for them to feel their feet on terra firma again. It was with widespread relief that when the boat docked at Memphis on the evening of IV day. Here they were to stay overnight after delivering Demi into the hands of her family.

In Memphis there was a large reception committee to meet them. Tiya had strictly primed her on how she should act but she could not damp down her excitement at the thought of seeing her family again. They were so dear to her heart and her support system. She could hardly suppress her disappointment when she failed to locate any of her family amongst the crowd as she carefully scanned it from the deck. She turned to Amio with bitter disappointment.

'Where are they, I wonder?' she asked him.

'I expect they will be waiting for us at the state palace in the city,' he observed. He did not seem to share her enthusiasm for her relatives and there was an air of cool reserve about him which she found much worse than his occasional bursts of irritability. After all, she had to put up with his relatives all the time, didn't she?

Firmly sandwiched between Tiya and Amio, Neferu found herself acknowledging over and over again, smiling, the salutes of the dignitaries. She felt rather bemused by it all, feeling a total fraud, knowing that just a few short months ago none of these people would have considered her worth a second look. When they reached the palace, they were all shown to their apartments to prepare for a state banquet to celebrate their arrival. Neferu found that she and Amio had been given the pharaoh's suite, which was an enormous, opulent room, flanked on either side by two smaller bedrooms. It was not the sort of cosy room that their relationship would have needed at that period perhaps. Maatnofret brought in their gowns and toilette articles and Paranefer began to attend to Amio's clothes. There was no time to rest before the banquet was due to begin. Tiya entered to give Neferu a runthrough of how she was to act and to check the final details of her dress. The crown of Upper and Lower Egypt was placed on her head and Neferu felt strange wearing the blue and gold piece. She wondered out loud if she could remove it while she was with her family.

'They will have very little opportunity to see you alone this time, Neferu,' the queen warned her. 'You are the queen first and their loved one second. You must control your impulse to bestow too much attention upon them. The high priests of Re will be present and will be criticising your every speech and movement. You must be every inch a queen!' she admonished the Keftiu girl.

'But when can I see them alone, then?' Neferu asked with dismay.

'When we return, we will spend some time privately with them,' Amio interjected. With that Neferu had to be content.

The banquet occasion went well. Neferu was allowed to speak to her family all together after the official presentation of the grand queen, Amio, Mereta and the young Smenkhenre. Most of those few precious minutes went in hugging and kissing them. Yussef took the back of her fingers after first bowing formally. She saw that his eyes were bright with fury and that his face had a pinched look. Amio's presence clearly had a restraining influence on him and Neferu felt Amio's eyes on them constantly. For the first time Neferu's courage failed her and she felt tears come to her eyes. While she and Yussef spoke only pleasantries out loud, she felt his thousand and one questions and her own unspoken answers tearing at them both. He saw the tears in her eyes and misconstrued them, whispering between clenched teeth, 'He will pay for this, have no fear, Neferu!'

'No, Yussef!' she whispered back, fearful of being overheard.

'Where are you going to, my lady?' Yussef signalled with his eyes.

'We are going for a short holiday to Rashid.' She tried to reply in her normal voice, but even to her it sounded strangled. She tried hard to regain her composure but found it well-nigh impossible, feeling as she did that the eyes of everyone were upon her, examining her every reaction.

When Tiya entered the room, all private talk came to an end and, unexpectedly, she found relief in this. The queen took command of the situation and told them it was time for goodbyes to be made. Grandma hugged her and Neferu thought her heart would break. Grandpa was gruff as usual when his emotions were ruffled, and Aunt Lea was in tears. Vassiliou and Shosen were most in control of the situation and whispered their best wishes to her. Neferu whispered to her father that he should take good care of Yussef and try to make things easier for him. He nodded understandingly but it was impossible to talk further. She kissed them all goodbye, feeling the heat of Yussef's cheeks as she kissed him. Then they were gone with last waves and loving glances, and she was left alone with Tiya and Amio. The tears spilled down her cheeks in an unstoppable fashion, and she turned her back on them so that they should not see.

'You will see them again,' Tiya said calmly. Neferu felt a sudden and enormous anger towards this woman, who seemed to be incapable of considering the depth of pain of others, but only what was best for preserving the public status of the throne. Nothing else really meant anything to this cold woman, she felt.

'But I will never know them again in the same way, will I?' Her question was only a rhetorical one. She tried to steady her voice as she spoke.

'Things change, Neferu! You will see that it is for the best.' The queen spoke more kindly this time.

Neferu had no handkerchief to wipe her eyes and she wanted to erase all trace of tears from her face before she turned to face the two of them. Carefully, she wiped her face with her hands, still with her back towards them. She knew now that in order to meet these people on their own terms, she must make herself invulnerable. They could manipulate her at will otherwise. She knew that it was Tiya she had most to fear from. Amio would do whatever his mother wished. He did not love her, Neferu, he merely wanted her. Her love was just another goal he had set himself to winning. If she had ever been foolish enough to have given him her heart, he would have used it however Tiya had wished. She had no intention of being Tiya's pawn via her son. She could at least do something about that. Soon she would have to acquiesce in their physical relationship, but she decided that that was all he ever would have. She would show him only that part of herself she wished to. He would never own her heart. What a fool she had been.

Neferu turned round reluctantly. She guessed that her face was smeared by the kohl on her eyes and probably looked ludicrous, but she held her head high. Amio stepped forward with a look of distress on his face, as if he would comfort her, but Tiya laid her hand on his arm as if to restrain him. The gesture was not lost on Neferu, who smiled bitterly.

'I shall go and clean my face,' she said coldly.

'Neferu.' It was Amio who spoke.

'Yes?'

'I am sorry you are so upset,' he answered. But not enough to desert your mother's side to comfort me, she thought.

'Thank you, Amio,' she said coolly. 'I will return in a short while.'

'Don't be long, Neferu,' Tiya said smoothly. 'It is unwise to keep people waiting.'

Those people. Who did they think they were? Neferu asked herself. She felt explosively angry, so much so that the feeling buoyed her up the whole evening. She smiled brilliantly at everyone they met and outwardly devoted her full attention to each visitor and guest, conveying just the right degree of attention and formal cordiality.

Later that evening, Maatnofret congratulated her on her handling of the situation. 'You were every inch a queen, Neferu.' She smiled, unaware of the emotions that were really powering Neferu. 'You were superb, anyone would have thought you were born to court life,' she added.

'It was easy, Maatnofret. All I had to do was to hide the real me away and play Queen Nefertiti,' she replied sombrely.

'Is there anything wrong?' Maatnofret asked anxiously.

'No! On the contrary,' replied Neferu slowly, looking at her worried face, 'tonight, I have learned exactly what my role is to be.'

When Maatnofret had gone, Neferu put her jewellery by the side of the royal bed and climbed into the huge bed. As carefully as she could, she moved herself into a comfortable position right at the edge of the bed, and when Amio came in she pretended to be asleep. She felt him come over to look down at her, his body blocking out the light of the lamp and casting a dark shadow over her closed eyelids. He did not say anything and after a moment he climbed in on the other side. She lay with her back towards him, wondering if he would approach her, but he lay still for a long time and finally she felt him moving around and then settle down again. Eventually she heard the rhythm of his breathing change, and become more regular and deeper, and she knew that he was asleep.

Gradually she began to relax. She lay awake for a long time. She felt sad, angry, cheated and defeated. She had only ever wanted to be in love with someone who was in love with her, preferably her husband. Her soul had wanted a great love, which would ask everything from her she was capable of giving and which, in turn, would be reciprocated in kind. Now she was trapped in a marriage whose terms would be forever dictated by the grand queen or the grand vizier. Amio may still be an unknown quantity, but he had clearly shown where his primary loyalties lay already, and they were not with her. Tiya would never relinquish her domination over him. Neferu knew that she would grow to lose all respect for him. It was many hours later before she finally fell asleep.

Maatnofret woke Neferu early the next morning. Neferu felt that she could sleep for many hours but Amio's stirring in the bed reminded her of the previous evening and she jumped up quickly, not wishing to be involved in a difficult sparring conversation of the usual thrusts and parries. She needed friends around her this morning. When she had bathed and dressed, she turned to wish him good morning. He returned her greeting coldly. If Maatnofret noticed an additional coolness between them, she did not comment on it. During breakfast Neferu was subdued, but perhaps it passed unnoticed in the lethargy of the morning. The main thing that had been accomplished as far as Tiya was concerned was the successful finalising of their second coronation service on their return visit to Memphis. To Neferu it was an unwelcome omen, but she pushed it to the back of her mind. People were reluctant to return to the ship. What had been an enjoyable change in the beginning had now lost its air of adventure and become a succession of hot, sweaty days with limited possibilities of recreation and reduced comforts of living. Still, Mereta reminded her, the longest part of their journey was over, and the group was to part company that day.

The grand queen, Mereta and most of the others were to continue on *The Aten Gleams* from Memphis, past On, turning north-east down river to Pithin and Goshen proper. Amio, Pararameses, Neferu, Maatnofret, Paranefer and the other half of the palace guard would continue north, north-west in a riverboat from the Memphis military detachment. Neferu was heartily glad to be rid of the company of the great queen's constant scrutiny. Bitterly she asked herself if Amio was concerned at this cutting of the umbilical cord, even if only temporary. The marriage was doomed to failure, she thought miserably. The closeness between them that had earlier developed had now completely dissipated.

Later that morning Neferu stood with the others and waved off the queen's flagship. She felt sure that there was no one happier to see it go. She had lived in terror the whole morning that at the last moment the plans would be changed, and she would be forced to accompany them to Goshen. Soon afterwards they boarded the *Glory of the Two Lands* and made set to sail. The boat was a military craft and was built, therefore, with much less elegance than the royal barge. Nevertheless, it was comfortable and actually boasted four cabins instead of the two of the royal boat. A canopy had been specially erected for them and Neferu and Amio took their places as protocol required.

As the boat travelled downriver, they could see the royal boat ahead of them and could actually communicate with the others by shouting, for some time. When the craft passed On, Neferu felt a terrible lump in her throat that would go neither up nor down. She got up to watch the city more clearly as it slid by. Everything that was dear and familiar to her was there and she sensed that she had no business here on this ship, watching it all recede into the distance. She felt she was watching her happiness slip away and wondered if she would ever be happy again.

During the morning Amio made great efforts to liven up the staff. The heat was getting them all down now. He spent much of the morning in animated conversation with some of the guard and there was a good deal of laughter. Occasionally he made the effort to speak to Neferu and showed her all the public respect that he felt her position required. There was no warmth in his manner, however. Though Neferu thought it was for the best, she was nevertheless upset by his coldness. Did he expect her to forget Yussef and all her former existence as if it had never been? Was it always she who would have to make all the adaptations? She knew that if he had come to comfort her the previous evening, ignoring his mother's gesture, she could have forgiven him this turning of her life upside down. When she saw him stayed by the movement of Tiya's arm, something inside her had grown cold towards him. Well, it was his decision. As a woman she was only a passive respondent in their lives anyway. Now he, in turn, had coolly withdrawn and he seemed to be avoiding her. For the first time, Neferu began to contemplate the possibility of divorce. She felt stricken. Such a thing was a terrible disgrace, but it was far preferable to losing her head, which he had the power to do.

Neferu did not notice the approach of Maatnofret until the lady-in-waiting was almost in front of her. 'What is wrong, Neferu?' she asked worriedly. She had noticed the icy politeness between Amio and Neferu and wanted to help to repair the rift if she could.

'Oh, Maatnofret! This is all a terrible mistake,' Neferu said in a panic-stricken voice. 'I should never have come to Thebes. I should have stayed in On where I belonged.'

'Nonsense!' responded Maatnofret firmly. 'We have been through all this before. I don't know what has triggered this present situation, but it will be put right when we reach Rashid. The rigours of this journey are getting too much for all of us. You must give things time, Neferu. The Aten has brought you this far, he will sort things out between you and Amio.' Privately, Neferu wondered if the Aten had bitten off more than he could chew. Still, Maatnofret's sympathetic manner and down to earth attitude raised her spirits a little. It was true that they were all tired from this long, hot journey. It was very arduous at this time of the year, but soon they would be approaching the coast and the wind would blow in from the sea.

At lunch Neferu ate almost nothing but drank thirstily of the fruit juice. Maatnofret clicked her tongue worriedly and Neferu promised to eat something later. Afterwards, the moment she had been dreading arrived, and Amio asked her coolly, 'Well, my dear! Shall we retire to rest?' She rose and followed him down to the cabin, where he helped her onto the couch and then sat down beside her.

'Are you ill, Neferu?' he asked, in a mock solicitous tone.

She looked at him warily. 'I am afraid, Amio. Not ill,' she said cautiously.

'Afraid?' he asked coldly. 'Of me?'

'Not of you,' she answered. 'Of what we have done. What do we have in common? It would have been much better for you to have married someone from your own circle who would have fitted into your way of life much more naturally than I do.' She could not help sounding dispirited. She was tired and miserable.

'It is done now,' he continued in his cold tone. 'If your unhappiness continues, we can divorce, but it cannot be accomplished immediately. I do not wish to be humiliated in front of all my subjects. We must wait at least three months,' he said bitterly. 'If our marriage is not consummated by then and you continue to find me so repulsive, you may go back to your Yussef.' His harsh words caused Neferu's cheeks to flame with shame and her eyes felt hot with the unshed tears. She knew it would be useless telling him that she did not find him repulsive, but that she wanted to be loved, not merely lusted after, and she wanted to feel that he put her before all others, including his mother. She wanted him to tell her he loved her. In the end she did not have the courage to say any of this and just closed her eyes. He lay down beside her but not touching her. They were both silent and awake for a long time but, in the end, she knew from his breathing that he had fallen asleep. Carefully, Neferu turned her head to look at him. In sleep he looked sensitive and vulnerable. It was hard to believe how cruel and cold his voice could be. He stirred and turned on his side towards her. She closed her eyes quickly, in case he woke up, but he merely drew up his knees a little and continued to breathe deeply and regularly. She could feel the heat of his breath on her face.

Neferu opened her eyes again and saw that his face was very close to hers, too close for her to observe him properly. Carefully, carefully, she inched herself up onto her elbow so that she could see him better. It was a truly remarkable face. Unlike many Egyptian noblemen, Amio almost never wore a wig. He wore his thick, black, glossy hair relatively long, rather than sporting the close-cropped style of the wig users. In sleep his lips were parted slightly, and it gave him a defenceless appearance which she found endearing. In a sudden rush of tenderness for him she carefully leaned over and lightly kissed him. Satisfied that she had not disturbed him she lay back down and closed her eyes.

When Neferu woke up, the couch at her side was empty. She remembered Amio's bitter words and felt desolate. Would it ever be possible to repair this great divide between them? She did not think she knew how. When Neferu went up on deck, Amio was talking with Pararameses. He acknowledged her presence by standing up and bowing slightly.

'I hope I do not disturb you,' she said quietly.

'Of course not, my dear!' he replied with a sardonic look. Pararameses had also jumped up and he seemed entirely unaware of the tension between them. The two men began to play backgammon and she sat quietly. As unobtrusively as possibly she stared at her husband. Once he looked up suddenly and caught her looking at him. The first time, she looked away quickly, but the second time she returned his gaze coolly. A questioning look came into his eyes. The moment was interrupted by Pararameses completing his move and glancing up at them. Neferu looked away. After a minute or so she got up and went to the front of the ship. She saw that *The Aten Gleams* was no longer visible. With a subconscious sigh she realised that the oppressive presence of Tiya was no longer with them.

Neferu returned to where the two men were seated. It suddenly occurred to her that Maatnofret was not on deck and had not visited her.

'I wonder if Maatnofret is all right,' she muttered, more to herself than to the others.

Amio lifted his head. 'Maatnofret was feeling a little nauseated, so she has gone down below with Paranefer,' he explained.

'I hope it isn't anything serious,' Neferu said worriedly. 'She was fine at lunchtime.'

Amio shrugged. 'Perhaps you had better check up on her,' he agreed.

'Yes. I think so,' answered Neferu, standing up. She crossed the deck and went down the steps. She knocked at the door of Maatnofret's cabin and the voice of Paranefer answered. 'Come in.'

The royal lady-in-waiting was lying down on the couch with very flushed cheeks and was shivering violently. She was obviously ill. Neferu was immediately worried. The assistant court physician was now on his way to Goshen with Tiya's group.

'It must be something I have eaten,' Maatnofret said miserably, by way of explanation.

Paranefer was looking decidedly out of his depth, Neferu noticed.

'I'll look after Maatnofret, Paranefer,' Neferu said to him. 'You go upstairs with Amio and Pararameses.'

Paranefer hesitated a moment, then he bent over and kissed his wife and said, 'All right, but call me if you need me, Neferu.'

'I will,' she assured him. Paranefer left the cabin, and the sound of his footsteps penetrated the thin cabin walls.

'I would have come earlier if I had known,' she said chidingly.

'I told Amio not to disturb you. You were still sleeping,' Maatnofret replied.

'I hope it isn't the tertiary fever,' Neferu exclaimed. 'We have no herbs on board and there are no large towns now before we reach the coastal area. The nearest doctor may be a long way from here,' Neferu fretted.

'Don't worry, Neferu! I don't think it is the tertiary fever and the captain's assistant on all the military vessels is a military physician.' Maatnofret was quite in command of herself, in spite of the fever. 'I think the fish I ate at lunchtime might have been bad. You did not eat any, fortunately.'

Neferu shook her head, and then an alarming thought struck her. 'I think most of the others tasted it though,' she said worriedly.

Their fears were confirmed sometime later, as five more people came down with vomiting and stomach cramps. Fortunately, neither Paranefer nor Amio had eaten the fish. It was decided that all the sick should be billeted downstairs, away from the chill night air. All the cabins were now full, and the servants were instructed to look after the sick and the healthy would fend for themselves on deck. The ship's physician appeared with a potion that all the victims of food poisoning were given to drink. He assured Neferu that it would be effective. It certainly worked quickly, for Maatnofret who had settled down and slept after Neferu had washed her. Paranefer was much relieved.

'What a way to spend our last night on board,' groaned Amio. 'Is it possible for anything else to go wrong?'

'Hopefully it will not be serious,' Neferu answered, surprised. 'We can cope with this, I think,' she added serenely.

Amio looked at her and gave a slight smile. 'How very strange you are, Neferu!' he said softly. 'We'll have to sleep up on deck now, you realise!'

Neferu shrugged. 'There are plenty of cushions and the couch is comfortable enough,' she declared uncomprehendingly. He laughed softly. She wondered what he found amusing in the situation, but he did not enlighten her.

Dinner was a hollow affair with everyone left viewing their plates with suspicion. To be on the safe side, they made do with pitta and cheese with fruit and wine to follow. Maatnofret had been the first to become sick and she was the first to show signs of recovery. When the moon was high, Neferu went downstairs to see her friend again. She was awake and feeling much better, and the others were sleeping. The physician's potion was working. Neferu went back up on deck.

Up on deck, the night was chilly now and most of the servants were now asleep on their sleeping mats, warmly wrapped up in their rugs. There was quite a strong breeze now and Neferu could smell that delicious salty smell that always heralds the proximity of the sea. It brought back memories of the freedom of her childhood for a moment before the chill began to get to her and she began to shiver. Amio had already retired to the couch but had left one of the curtains up so that he could see the direction in which they were travelling. Neferu realised that this was the first time she had ever followed him to bed.

As she climbed in beside him, he said curtly, 'I wondered whether you would come or whether you would find some excuse to stay below.'

Neferu sighed. It was beginning again. 'Amio, it is not at all how you think. I do not find you repulsive at all, it's just that I want there to be love between us and not just lust.'

He reached out and pulled her towards him. Her breasts were crushed against his chest, and she felt the hardness of his arousal. He pushed her face backwards with his head and pressed his lips on hers. Just as suddenly, he pushed her away again abruptly. 'I have not forgotten my promise, Neferu, but try not to make me wait too long. If we were not now in a public place, I would not be strong enough not to take you.' In the moonlight she could see his outline, but his face was in shadow under the canopy. She could tell from his voice that it was hard for him to control himself. Although she had had no sexual experience, she had felt him hard against her body and had felt her own body respond to him automatically.

'If we were not now in a public place, I would not be able to stop myself from surrendering to you,' she whispered. With a groan, he suddenly pushed her down onto the pillows and clutched convulsively at her right breast. She put out her arms and dragged the rug over him to maintain a semblance of decorum, should any of the crew be watching. Between her legs she could feel the strength of his arousal through her gown and his loin cloth. The sound of his panting as he tried to overcome his frustration. She felt a warmth in her lower abdomen and wanted to touch him. She put her arms around him and began to stroke his head, unaware that she was whispering to him in her own language. She repeated the words over and over again as she kissed his face.

'Everything will be all right, my darling. Everything will be all right.' Finally, she felt the tenseness leave him and Amio lifted his head, repeating the Keftiu words he had heard.

'What does it mean?' he asked dully.

Neferu smiled at him as she realised what she had been saying. 'It means in Egyptian, "Everything will be all right, my darling".' she answered softly.

'And will it be all right, Neferu?'

'It will be all right, Amio,' she whispered in reply. She kissed his forehead, and he rested his head on her breast again with a faint sigh. Neferu felt a deep tenderness towards him rise up in her and she continued to stroke his head. 'It feels good,' he murmured. She lifted her head from the pillow and kissed the top of his head. She dared not speak for fear of breaking this moment of peaceful surrender between them.

Gradually Neferu felt Amio become limp and heavy, and she noticed that his breathing had become deep and regular. He had fallen asleep. She felt herself smile and wondered if what she was feeling was what people called 'being in love'. She was tired and he was heavy, but she knew that she wanted him to be always this close to her. He was a complicated man, and she knew almost nothing about him, but he was now her husband and she had promised him that she would try to be a good wife to him. She let her hand fall down over his arm. Her heavy eyes began to droop and soon she too was asleep.

Neferu woke to find Amio tracing the outline of her eyebrow with his finger. It travelled lightly down her cheek and around her lips. Neferu opened her eyes. She was lying on her right side, and he was facing her on his left.

'Everything will be all right, my darling,' he whispered in Keftiu. She smiled at the words. He had recalled them perfectly. He continued in Egyptian, 'I have never seen such a beautiful woman in my life.' Neferu opened her mouth to say something, but he quickly put two fingers over her mouth and shook his head, indicating to her not to speak. 'Don't say anything,' he said quietly. 'I want to remember you as you are now,' Neferu felt moved by his words and she lay still, watching him as he watched her, examining her as if to store the memory on his mind for ever. She had the distinct feeling of being in a world of their own, bordered by the confines of the canopy. All around them was silence, apart from the strange rhythmic chanting of the oarsmen. 'Our last day at sea begins,' Amio said, still gazing at her. 'Tonight, we will dock in the harbour at Rashid. I am waiting for that moment, Neferu, as I have never waited for anything in my life before.' He spoke ardently.

Neferu nodded. She put out her left hand to brush away a lock of his hair, fallen over his forehead. He leaned forward and kissed her passionately on her mouth and she lifted her mouth to his in passionate response. Only the sudden sound of voices and movement on deck around them caused them to draw back reluctantly. Paranefer came to inform them that everyone had recovered from the indisposition of the previous evening and, if Neferu would like to go down to the cabin below, a pitcher of water had been placed for her to wash and freshen up. Neferu gave her husband a quick kiss and jumped up.

Down below, Maatnofret was pale but insisted that she was completely recovered. Neferu washed and changed, happy that this was the last day afloat. Maatnofret smiled at her obvious high spirits.

'My! You are much more cheerful today,' she exclaimed.

'Yes, Maatnofret. You were right and I was wrong. I'm sorry I have been such a sourpuss,' Neferu murmured apologetically.

Maatnofret smiled thoughtfully. 'I think we are going to have a wonderful holiday,' she announced.

'Oh, I do hope so, Maatnofret,' was Neferu's cheerful comment.

At breakfast Neferu thought that the whole world must surely notice how much closer she and Amio had become to each other. After breakfast he clasped her fingers and brought them to his lips in front of everyone, causing her to blush and him to tease her about it. The others smiled indulgently.

The last day on board seemed to pass so slowly. Amio was by turn cheerful and impatient. For the first time on the trip, he took his lyre and began to sing. It was a cheerful little ditty that the palace guards took up with enthusiasm. It told the tale of a soldier and the wives he had in every garrison. This song led to others and the atmosphere on board lightened considerably, attaining almost the holiday excitement it had carried seven days previously when they had left Thebes.

Lunch came and went, appetites still blunted by the effects of the food poisoning of the previous day. After lunch Amio and Neferu left hand in hand to go to their cabin. This time there was no restraint between them and once inside they embraced passionately. Strangely, now that she was ready for him, Amio made no attempt to take her. She looked at him, mystified.

'I can wait now until we are completely alone,' he said tenderly. 'I want our marriage to begin tonight in beautiful surroundings, where there is no danger of anyone overhearing or interrupting.'

'You are such a strange and complex man,' she replied, at a loss.

'That's good,' Amio assured her. 'You won't easily become bored with me.'

'I can't ever imagine becoming bored with you, Amio,' she laughed. They lay down on the couch together in companiable mood. She urged him to remove his cloak, but he refused.

'Why do you keep it on all the time, even with me?' she asked curiously.

'It is not the time to remove it yet,' he replied mysteriously. 'Besides, it helps to keep me safe from you,' he said enigmatically.

'Safe from me?' Neferu echoed, amazed. 'Am I dangerous, then?'

'Extremely so!' he assured her light-heartedly.

Neferu shrugged and lay back, at a loss. Amio made no attempt to approach her physically and she closed her eyes. After a few moments she opened them again quickly. He was looking at her and he grinned.

'Go to sleep!' he said amiably.

When Neferu woke up Amio was still asleep. He was lying on his left side, his body against hers. This time she felt no shyness in waking him up.

'Amio, wake up!' she said. He opened his eyes, still sleepy. She leaned forward and kissed him.

'Grrrrr! he said, imitating the roar of a lion as he grabbed her. She squealed.

'Are you going to eat me?' she asked playfully.

'Worse!' he said melodramatically. There was a sound in the cabin next door, and they suddenly remembered the others.

Neferu put her fingers over his lips to shush him and she whispered, 'I think we had better go up on deck.'

He groaned. 'I think I am fated never to be alone with you.'

On deck they shared refreshments with Paranefer, Maatnofret and Pararameses. There was a pleasant sea breeze now and the tang of the sea in the air. The sea was very close now, Neferu could smell it. When the familiar piece of coastline, so dear to her heart, finally came into view, Neferu felt a real thud of joy.

'It's Rashid! It's Rashid!' she yelled, jumping up and down like a little girl. There was a spontaneous cheer from the others at the thought of disembarking soon. Neferu grabbed Amio's hand and excitedly began to point out various landmarks to him. He looked down at her face, flushed with pleasure and excitement. His eyes had lost their veiled look and he was infected with her enthusiasm.

'I hope we'll be able to get rid of the reception committee quickly,' he grimaced.

Neferu nodded her head vigorously. 'I'll take you to see my villa tomorrow,' she said eagerly.

'I look forward to seeing your villa,' he said sardonically, emphasising the word 'your'. Neferu looked at him quickly, but he was smiling warmly at her. She felt happier than she had done for a long time. Only the thought of Yussef's anguished face sprang up occasionally to remind her of unresolved conflict. As always, she dealt with it by pushing it out of her mind. There was no point dwelling on it. She was in love with Amio now and there was no reason to doubt that their relationship would grow and ripen.

Unfortunately for the little group, the good citizens of Rashid had made great preparations for this unexpected pharaonic visit. They had congregated in great numbers to greet them. Neferu had never imagined that so many people inhabited the seemingly sleepy little coastal town. When they landed, there was a great display of cheering, dancing and seemingly never-ending speeches. Amio received it all with the customary dignity of his lifelong education, although he too was having trouble containing his irritability in his desire to be gone. They left as soon as it was diplomatically possible for them to do so but the sun was already getting low in the sky, and they were anxious to reach their destination before dark. They refused the offer of a military escort, in order not to delay themselves further. As the chariots pulled away from the small harbour in the direction of the eastern coastline, the sound of loyal cheers followed them.

'We could be monsters and yet they cheer us,' Neferu commented, as they stood in the chariot, giving their final wave.

'It is not us they are cheering, Neferu. It is the pharaoh and the queen,' was Amio's discerning reply.

The villa, in front of which the chariot finally pulled up, was a little further along the coast than that belonging to Grandpa and Grandma. It was much larger and altogether finer too. In spite of its size, however, it had a picturesque appearance in the rosy glow of the setting sun, which gave its white stuccoed walls a faint pink hue. Neferu vaguely remembered the villa from her youth. She and the boys had walked in that direction a couple of times when they had been exploring the area. She did not remember ever having seen anyone there. She guessed that it was only about a couple of kilometres from their old place at most. The villa was set in very beautiful gardens, she noticed.

As their chariot drew up, she noticed a staff of about fifteen people waiting to greet them. She felt a moment's disappointment. It was hardly going to be the holiday alone she had been expecting. She realised that her idea of a small group and Amio's idea of what constituted a small group had nothing in common. The house servants began to unload their luggage immediately, after a short welcoming that Amio rapidly cut short, though in a friendly manner. The last pieces had to be brought in in darkness, as the sun slid so quickly over the horizon that only the light of the oil lamps remained for them to see by.

After Amio and Neferu had been situated in their suite and Maatnofret and

Paranefer in theirs, Pararameses set about allocating the remaining rooms to the rest
of the staff. The large house reverberated to the sound of all the comings and goings as
they all began to settle themselves. It felt wonderful to be billeted again in proper rooms
with the appropriate bathing facilities that Neferu had missed so much. It felt like sheer
heaven to Neferu, after the smelly chamber pots and limited water supplies on board the
boat. The Theban servants were relieved to be able to hand over their responsibilities to
the household staff. Delicious savoury smells had been apparent on their arrival and as
soon as they had washed and changed, they all hurried to the banquet that was laid out
for them.

Neferu had bathed luxuriously, enjoying to the full the solid feeling of the floor
beneath her feet and looking forward to the possibility of swimming the following day.
She washed her hair and then massaged herself with the perfumed oil. Maatnofret had
brought her dress in, clicking her tongue at a crease in the skirt. She hung it in the steamy
atmosphere of the bathroom for a while to get rid of the offending crease. Neferu had
chosen a simple cream shift of fine cotton lawn, cut in a straight simple style across
the neck. She brushed her hair herself and wound it into a large chignon. She wore no
jewellery except her wedding ring, but she put a lotus flower in her hair. When she was
ready, she entered the small private sitting room she was to share with her husband.
The first thing she noticed was that Amio's hair had been cut. He stood up as she came
into the room. He was wearing a new blue cloak of heavy silk. Once again, she wished
he would not always wear a cloak. It gave him a secretive air and it seemed to create a
distance between them. Amio stood expectantly as she came over to him and kissed him
passionately on the mouth.

'Is this your way of telling me that you are really ready for me?' he asked in a
controlled tone.

Neferu looked at him directly and nodded. 'Yes, it is my way.'

'You know that once we have made love, I will never let you go, don't you?' he
continued in the same tone. Neferu nodded once again and this time she threw her arms
around his neck and pulled his head down to hers. He put his arms around her and pulled
her feverishly towards him. Paranefer coughed discreetly in the doorway. Amio sighed.
'I think I am fated with you, Neferu. I begin to wonder if we will ever consummate this
marriage,' he whispered as Paranefer retreated.

'We will tonight!' she whispered in reply.

Dinner was a happy affair. Now that the journey was over, they were all looking forward to a decan of relaxation, swimming and exploration of the milieu around them. Maatnofret told Neferu that the garden was beautiful in the moonlight and smiled knowingly at Neferu. The older woman said she had slipped out before dinner and it had seemed eerie and romantic, with all its statues and foliage laid out in strange shapes. When Neferu was replete and the men were chatting light-heartedly about hunting possibilities, Neferu told Maatnofret that she was going to explore the gardens. Maatnofret replied that she would accompany her. Neferu leaned forward and whispered to Amio that she was going to walk in the garden and asked him to come too. He nodded and said he would join her in a few minutes. Neferu and Maatnofret strolled onto the terrace and down the three wide steps.

Maatnofret shivered. 'I will go and get our shawls, Neferu. Wait here for me!' she said. Neferu nodded and stood looking about her. Even in the moonlight she could see that the garden had been laid out magnificently. The perfume of the flowers was almost overpowering. She looked up at the deep dark blue of the night sky above and admired the millions of stars visible in its clarity.

The smell of jasmine mixed with the glorious smell of the large velvety roses was a little too strong and she stepped down onto the lawn and strolled casually towards the statue of a naked female figure prominent in the centre of the garden. She looked at it carefully, realising from its style that it was Keftiu in origin rather than Egyptian. She wondered about the people who had built the villa. She felt the pride of her people's glorious past, now long since extinguished. She turned away and bent to smell a large, fragrant rose in front of her. Someone called her name urgently in a hoarse whisper. Neferu straightened up and spun round incredulously. There in the shadows in front of her stood Yussef. For a long moment she stood there paralysed with shock.

'Yussef!' she whispered. 'How did you get here?'

He laughed bitterly. 'I will not bore you with the details. I left as soon as I found you were coming here.' He spoke in a hoarse, low voice.

'Does my father know that you are here?' Her voice was frantic with worry.

'I expect he has guessed by now,' was his answer. Yussef stepped forward and took Neferu's arm in a firm grip. Neferu tried to free herself.

'Let me go, Yussef. This is no good. You can't change anything now! I am married.'

He gripped her arm tighter. 'Have you lain with him? Are you lovers? Demi says it is a marriage of convenience. Have you made love?' he demanded insistently. Neferu was anguished. Torn between two loyalties. She could not answer. 'Have you?' he asked again.

'No! But we will tonight,' she cried in a whisper. 'This won't help, Yussef! You must go now!' She was terrified that Amio would discover them. She expected his furious presence to appear at any moment. She feared for Yussef's life. She realised he was half mad with jealousy.

'He has stolen you from me! I will never give you up. Never! Never!' He crushed her to him.

'Please, please go, Yussef. Amio will be here any moment and I don't want to be the cause of you getting into trouble. Please go!' Neferu felt she was beyond terror now as she listened to the frightened sound of her own voice.

Reluctantly he let go of her arm. 'I am staying at our villa tonight. Tell me, Neferu! Do you love me?' His voice was wild and Neferu was petrified. For a split second she hesitated, torn between her divided loyalties. It would not have been the truth to deny it.

'I love you, Yussef, but I love Amio too,' she cried in a low voice.

'It isn't love you feel for him, it's pity,' he hissed as he slipped through a break in the hedge. Neferu stood for a moment, trembling with the shock, looking at the hedge where Yussef had disappeared. She whirled round with a sick feeling in her stomach when a cold voice said icily, 'How charming! We have scarcely been married a decan, and my wife is having a tryst with another man.'

'Amio!' she said shocked.

'Don't you think you had better come in, my dear. You look as though you have seen a ghost.'

'Amio, it wasn't what you are thinking,' she cried sharply. He took her arm in exactly the same grip as Yussef had a few moments before and he firmly guided her back towards the villa without speaking. In truth, Neferu could not have felt worse if she had seen a ghost. Amio avoided the terrace, which lay in full view of the dining room and led her round to the patio outside their bedroom. Still holding her arm in a grip, he took her into the bedroom and pushed her roughly onto the bed.

'So!' he said icily. 'Yussef followed you here. Well, my dear! I don't intend to give you up so easily!'

Neferu was thoroughly frightened. She hoped that Amio would not order Yussef to be severely punished.

'Please, Amio,' she cried miserably. 'Please don't punish him. It isn't really his fault. He is half crazed with jealousy. He doesn't know what he is doing!' Tears blurred her eyes.

'You plead for him so eloquently, my dear, that even if I had not heard you tell him you loved him, I would have guessed it anyway,' he said savagely.

'Then you also heard me tell him that I love you too,' she wept.

'Yes. I did hear you say that,' he admitted, less harshly. Neferu bit her lip.

'Tell me! Is it pity you feel for me?' he continued.

She looked up startled and shook her head. 'No. It is not pity I feel for you,' she replied truthfully.

Amio was not the kind of person one could feel pity for, she reflected. He came over to the bed and leaning forward, he lifted her chin with his hand. She saw that his face was white with fury.

'I don't want your pity ever! You had better understand that!' His voice was ferocious. 'I want your love and I intend to have it. The time will come, Neferu, when you will beg me to touch you.' She looked up at him, but she no longer felt any fear. She preferred Amio in a fury to Amio cold and icy.

'I told you that I love you, Amio, and I do. I love Yussef too. It is not something I can cut out of my heart at a moment's notice, and it has nothing to do with what I feel for you. You cannot ask me to forget the whole of my life before I met you. Can't you understand that?' She spoke more calmly than she felt. He was looking at her intently and gradually she saw the anger leave his face.

'I am a jealous man, Neferu, and I want the love of my wife for myself alone. I won't punish Yussef this time, but I will not tolerate his presence here in Rashid, undermining my marriage, which still stands on such shaky legs. He is to leave for On tomorrow morning. Do you understand?'

Neferu nodded, relieved, and Amio continued. 'I will send Rameses to the villa first thing in the morning.' Neferu felt herself calm down. In spite of Amio's undoubted temper, she had already discovered that he was basically fair and just.

'I thank you for that, Amio. It is fair and just,' she granted.

'He is staying at your grandfather's villa,' he said with narrowed eyes. It was a statement, not a question. 'You must describe the route to me!' he commanded.

Neferu described as best she could the route, using the edge of the cliffs as the bearing point. She hated the thought of Pararameses being informed of the incident and asked if she and Amio could not go together. He categorically refused.

'You promised me that you wouldn't punish him,' she reminded him.

'I don't break my word,' Amio said haughtily.

'No. Of course not,' Neferu replied, feeling small.

'Goodnight, Neferu,' he said. 'When Yussef has gone from your heart and you want only me, come to me!' With that he stood up haughtily and left the room.

Neferu was stricken. She could not understand how an evening which had started out so promisingly could have ended so disastrously. Why had he not taken her? He knew that she was attracted to him and that she loved him. He had on the other hand never even told her that he loved her! He wanted her to initiate their physical relationship. It was just a matter of pride with him. What more could she do? He was reacting unfairly in her opinion. He wanted her to beg for him. How dare he. Poor Neferu. She felt so sorry for herself that night. She supposed that she must have offended the Aten or done something terrible in a previous life, to be punished like this. She got up and took off her gown, tears running down her face. After washing her face, she climbed into bed. Maatnofret came in. She looked at the sobbing girl and came to sit next to her on the bed.

'I couldn't stop Amio from coming, Neferu,' she said sadly. 'He was on my heels, and I couldn't think of anything to detain him quickly enough.'

'I don't want there to be any secrets between us anyway, Maatnofret,' Neferu sobbed. 'I didn't know that Yussef would come here. You do believe me, don't you?'

'Yes. I believe you, and so does Amio. I have known him for a very long time, Neferu and I love him, but he is a very strange mix of pride and humility, and this has really hurt his pride,' Maatnofret said with an air of resignation.

'I know,' replied Neferu. 'What can I do?'

Maatnofret sighed again. 'I don't know, Neferu. Let us just pray that from now on there will be no more problems between you!'

'I don't think the Aten is listening to my prayers,' Neferu began sobbing anew.

'Yes, he is!' the older woman reassured her. 'We just have to wait for him to act. 'She bent over and kissed Neferu. 'Goodnight, Neferu! May the Aten bless you!' Neferu was left alone again to consider her plight. It was a terrible start to what had promised to be a new beginning. When she finally fell asleep, it was in dread of what the following day would bring.

CHAPTER 18

When Maatnofret came to open the shutters the next morning, she noticed that Neferu's eyes were swollen, and she made her lie back while she applied hot compresses and cold compresses in turn to the offending eyelids. It proved impossible to reduce the swelling completely in the time available before breakfast, but a massive improvement was obtained. Neferu wanted to plead a headache and miss the meal completely, but Maatnofret would not have it, and in the end she took a seat in the sitting room to wait for Amio so that they could enter together. It appeared that he had risen very early to advise Pararameses on the errand discussed the previous evening. Pararameses had not yet returned.

When Amio reappeared his manner towards Neferu was polite and slightly formal. He kissed her coolly on the cheek and wished her a good morning, noting the swollen eyes. He offered her his arm and she took it nervously. They breakfasted on the terrace, just the four of them. Neferu was heartily glad that Tiya was not present. She had the feeling that if that had been the case then possibly Yussef's and her own head might have rolled. She was dreading the moment when the queen would return. Maatnofret and Paranefer made much more sympathetic companions.

In the morning light the garden was a different place. It exuded none of the mystery of the shadows of night. The atmosphere at breakfast was subdued and Neferu did not dare to bring up the subject of swimming. It was Amio who brought up the subject of the programme for the day. He asked Maatnofret and Paranefer if they felt up to a walk to the shore. Maatnofret hesitated, wondering how far it was. 'It isn't very far, Maatnofret,' Neferu assured her, eager to see her beloved shoreline. In the end the older couple agreed to go on the donkeys. Amio and Neferu elected to walk. They all wrapped themselves in light cloaks to shield themselves from the sun before setting off.

As Neferu knew the terrain, she acted as guide and led the way down the track towards the cliff top. Four-hundred metres or so along their journey they turned right at a fork in the track and carried on to where they could see a villa. 'The villa there belongs to my Uncle Giorgios,' Neferu said, pointing self-consciously. 'We could go and see them, if you like,' she added, looking at her husband.

Amio shook his head. 'We will visit your relatives when they are prepared to receive us,' he responded. They walked past the villa and Neferu strained her neck to see whether she could see her aunt or any of her cousins, but there was no one visible. At a turning fifty metres or so on, they went left and began to walk in the direction of the Stassopoulos villa. Just before they reached the coast road itself, they met the chariot of Pararameses coming towards them.

Pararameses reined the horse and stepped down and Amio halted, waiting for him to approach. He waved Neferu and the others on and he stood talking quietly with the general for a while. Neferu noticed the quick glance that Pararameses gave her. She felt embarrassed and she turned away in humiliation. Maatnofret saw her look. 'Amio is just jealous, Neferu!' she said quickly but quietly. Neferu shrugged. There was nothing she could do. They had stopped to wait for Amio a discreet distance from where the two figures were standing. Eventually Pararameses turned to their direction and bowed deeply then climbed into the chariot.

Amio rejoined the group. 'Would you like to show us the villa of your grandparents, Neferu?' His tone was outwardly serene. 'It appears that your cousin has already left Rashid, but he did leave a message for you.' Neferu felt her cheeks flame as he handed a piece of papyrus to her. Neferu put out her hand to receive the papyrus and saw that Yussef had written. 'Never forget that I love you, Neferu. Our day will come!' She was thankful that he had written it in Keftiu. She read the message and then gave it back to Amio. He did not ask her what it said but did look at her with a questioning look, wondering whether she would tell him. She did not wish to discuss it in front of the others and so she answered. 'We can discuss it later if you wish.'

Amio inclined his head in affirmation and put the papyrus carefully into the pocket on the inside of his cloak. He was obviously curious. 'I would like to visit your home, Neferu, but perhaps you would prefer to go another day?' he said. Neferu remembered promising to take him, but everything was changed between them now. She hesitated, not knowing what to do, but then she shrugged slightly. What did it matter? If they were to go someday, they might as well go today.

'It isn't far,' she answered in reply, turning into the coast road left, towards the old villa.

Five minutes later they were at the old gate and Neferu unlatched it to step into the yard. She led the other three through the gate and into the small garden, now sadly overgrown. The old villa was beginning to look a little derelict. They had not visited it for several years now and it had clearly missed Grandpa's loving annual repairs. The whitewash had peeled from the walls in some places, exposing the brown colour of the sun-baked brick underneath. She realised that the old place was not a very prepossessing sight, but it embodied all the happiest times of her childhood and she stood on the pathway as if transfixed. She remembered the way Grandma had stood and waved to them as they went off to the beach.

The Keftiu girl became aware that Amio was watching her closely and she quickly brought herself back to the present. She walked to the front door and tested it. It was locked, as she had expected, of course. To the right of the door was a large boulder and she stepped on it and lifted up her right arm to the stone framework above the door and groped around with her fingers, until she located what it was she was looking for. Neferu grasped the key and stepped down from the stone. She blew the dust away from her hand and then meticulously inserted the key into the lock and twisted it. The old cedarwood door slowly creaked open and Neferu stepped inside. Once inside, she stepped aside to let the others enter. It was cool in the gloom. All the shutters were closed.

Going from room to room, Neferu flung all the shutters open and checked to see if everything was as it should be. This was her domain. Amio was only a guest here, she thought to herself. As she went, she looked about her surreptitiously for any signs of Yussef's presence. The only signs which she discerned were in the small kitchen, where some of the cooking utensils had been left upside down on the stone level where Grandma and Aunt Lea washed the dishes. Neferu went over and carefully lifted them up onto the shelves where they belonged. Amio looked but made no comment. Everything was covered in a thick layer of dust and Neferu sighed. The others said nothing and just followed her around.

From the kitchen, Neferu went to the back door and opened it. She stood on the threshold for a moment, looking at the empty chicken run and remembering the many happy hours they had sat outside and enjoyed their meals here. Full of nostalgia she went into the yard to where the once neat vegetable garden had been overtaken by weeds. The small mint patch had trebled in size since she had last seen it and she idly bent down and plucked some, absent-mindedly putting it into her mouth. It tasted fresh and tangy, and she offered some to Amio. He did not refuse it as she had half expected.

'Would you like me to arrange someone to come and maintain the house and garden on a regular basis, Neferu?' he asked her quietly. Neferu looked up at him sharply. Was he being pleasant or was it a trap in case Yussef came back? She weighed the matter up and judged the balance to be in favour of the former motive. After a brief consideration, she nodded.

'I would like that, Amio, if you would,' she replied.

'You really love the place, don't you?' he asked softly.

'Yes.' She nodded. 'I spent all the happiest times of my life here. Someday it will belong to Demi, but some part of it will always be mine.' She stopped, not wanting to give too much of herself away to this man who had shown her both kindness but also icy superciliousness. She did not want to sound over-emotional.

Amio only nodded and replied, 'I will arrange for a man to come once a decan to maintain it. It would be a shame to let it become derelict after it has been in your family so long.' It was kind of him, and she thanked him.

'Unless you would like to see some more, I am ready to leave,' she said. Amio nodded and they went indoors again. They began to help her to close all the shutters once again prior to their departure. After locking the front door, Neferu carefully placed the key back on the stone ledge above it and they set off down the path. At the gate she took one long, last, lingering look before beginning to retrace steps in the direction from which they had come.

By the time they arrived back at the holiday villa they were hot and sticky. No one had spoken much on the journey. All of them had seemed locked in their own thoughts. The villa was quiet, and they went to wash before having lunch. When Neferu was ready, she went to the sitting room where Amio was already seated. 'Do you want to tell me about the message?' he said, taking it from the couch beside him. Neferu sighed. She did not want to discuss it, but she was beginning to get to know her husband better and she knew that he would be unbearable if she did not translate the message. In a voice as expressionless as she could make it, she stated what was written on the papyrus. His lips tightened a little, but he did not reply at all, merely folding the papyrus into two and handing it to her. She took it from him with trepidation. She guessed that he probably wanted her to destroy it, but she could not bring herself to do it and, as she did not have a pocket, she put it on the table. She could have put it into the bosom of her dress, but she felt sure that, had she done so, he would have misconstrued her action as an indication that the message and, by implication, its sender were close to her heart in a way that was not fitting in her present circumstances.

A little later they were joined by Maatnofret and Paranefer and, shortly after, by Pararameses. Over an enjoyable lunch they purposely discussed trivial subjects of a non-emotional value until Maatnofret said artlessly. 'Well, Neferu, are you going to take us to the secret cave you told me about?'

Neferu's heart turned a flip. 'I'm sorry, Maatnofret, it is a secret which we promised not to divulge to anyone.'

Maatnofret smiled. 'Of course. I understand, Neferu. It was quite rude of me to ask.'

'We can explore other parts of the beach though, Maatnofret,' Neferu replied quickly, not wanting to hurt the other woman's feelings.

'Yes, that would be nice,' the lady-in-waiting agreed, and the conversation turned to other things.

Later on, when the others left, Amio asked. 'What is this about a secret cave?'

Neferu shrugged. 'Oh, it is just a cave we found as children and made a secret pact never to show to anyone else,' she explained.

'By "we", you mean Yussef and Demi, I take it?' he asked carefully.

Neferu looked down, she did not want to tell him that it only belonged to herself and Yussef. 'Yes,' She Said. They rose to go and rest and Neferu lifted the papyrus message from the table. Amio's eyes narrowed a little, but he made no comment. Neferu was tired after the morning's walk and was also suffering a kind of emotional exhaustion. She slept heavily, but when she woke up, she felt little refreshed and not at all in the mood for the planned dinner that evening to honour the local dignitaries who had arranged the practical details of their visit to Rashid. Maatnofret was chatty but not probing as she helped Neferu to dress. She told Neferu that she felt very tired and Neferu advised her to go to bed early and not to attend the dinner if she did not feel up to it. Maatnofret was indecisive, wondering if Neferu would need her moral support, but Neferu was confident she could handle the situation alone. It was only to be a small gathering. Before Maatnofret left, Neferu asked her, 'Is Amio up yet?' She had not yet entered Amio's room.

'Yes, I believe so,' Maatnofret replied. As there was no further comment Maatnofret retired.

Neferu went to Amio's room and stood in the doorway. He was fastening the clasp of his cloak and was standing sideways to her.

'May I come in?' she asked uncertainly. Amio turned towards he and gave a slight bow. He looked surprised.

'What can I do for you?' he asked, raising his eyebrows.

'Amio, may we go swimming tomorrow?' she pleaded. 'I haven't been swimming for such a very long time and I would just love to go.'

He considered the matter for a long time and then asked, 'The four of us do you mean, or just the two of us?'

'Just the two of us if we can,' she replied.

'No. I don't think so,' he said slowly.

'Why ever not?' she protested petulantly.

'You will find my body repulsive,' he said, after a pause.

'No. I won't!' she said indignantly. 'What a poor opinion you have of me.' She was stung.

He was silent for a while and then he said, 'All right then. Just the two of us.' He paused. 'If you promise to show me your secret cave.'

Neferu looked at him in dismay. 'But I can't do that, Amio. I made Yussef a solemn promise. Terrible things will happen to me if I break it,' she said anxiously. 'I will show you our other cave,' she said, after a moment.

'So, there are two caves, then?' he asked slyly.

Neferu was silent for a moment. 'Yes.'

'All right. You can show me whichever one you wish,' he conceded finally.

Neferu smiled. 'All right,' she responded with relief.

'We can leave as soon as breakfast is over' Amio stated.

'I will ask Maatnofret to arrange for a picnic basket to be made up,' she said with another smile.

Thus, in a reasonably companiable mood, they went to have refreshments on the terrace, and it was then that Amio told Neferu that he had received a message that he expected his mother and sister to arrive in two days, along with her entourage. The news of the queen's imminent arrival filled Neferu with dread. Her outward reaction was minimal but inwardly her fragile peace was shattered. Only the thought of the outing on the following day could cheer her up.

That night Neferu threw herself into the social evening with gusto and pretended an outward serenity that was entirely absent from her real self. Amio noticed and commented appreciatively upon her efforts, and she was pleased to have won his approbation. The party disbanded late and in good spirits and Amio congratulated Pararameses on the amount of patriotic good will which the evening appeared to have engendered. When they reached their bedroom Amio kissed Neferu lightly on the cheek and said, 'Goodnight, Neferu.'

'Goodnight, Amio,' she replied.

Neferu was in a state of flux, and she wondered how long their relationship was doomed to remain on this level. Should she go to Amio? If only he would tell her that he loved her, then she knew that she would be happy to spend her whole life with him, but Amio was more pharaoh than man and he was determined that it would always be her who would be submissive. Perhaps it was Yussef who really loved her and Amio who only lusted after her.

As she lay there alone in the darkness, she knew she only had two days before her hand was forced. She knew now that she was in love with him, but he was spoiled and used to getting his own way in everything. Once Tiya returned she would strengthen that selfish and commanding part of him and the man behind the crown might be lost to her forever. It was this Amio she wanted to reach and yet there was no way she knew how to. Neferu said a quiet prayer to the Aten and asked him to put her relationship with Amio right.

When she awoke the next morning, it was with a sense of time running out. Only one more day left after today before Tiya's omnipresent domination returned. At breakfast they encountered an unexpected problem. Pararameses was adamant in his objection to their going to the beach alone. In the end Amio and he came as close to quarrelling as Neferu ever saw them. Pararameses was obviously worried about what the queen or grand vizier would think if there was an accident. In the end Amio would brook no arguments and they set off on the two donkeys available.

Neferu was glad of Amio's decision to have his way. She was so totally tired of strangers in her life. There was a light-hearted sense of truancy between them during the journey. When they arrived at the top of the cliffs, leading down to her part of the beach, they tethered the donkeys to two fig trees to give them some shade. There was some good grazing for them round about.

Climbing down the cliff Amio found it difficult. Whether it was due to his deformities or the unknown terrain, she did not know. Neferu took the basket from him and led the way down, waiting anxiously for him. Once at the bottom, she led him over to the cave where they used to hang their clothes on a rock as children.

'Look, Amio!' Neferu said excitedly going to one of the rock faces and pointing with her finger to where her name was carved. He came over to look. The earliest one said

'Yussef eight years, Neffie six years, Demi four years', and the last one was 'Yussef twelve years, Neferu ten years, Demi eight years'. He smiled and outlined 'Neffie' with his finger.

'Why were you called Neffie?' he said with a grin.

'Demi couldn't say Neferu when he was small,' Neferu explained. Amio nodded comprehendingly and he moved to another part of the rock face, where clearly etched was written 'Yussef loves Neferu'. She realised that she had taught both Amio and Mereta the verb to love in Keftiu, so he understood what it meant. He looked at her with an inscrutable look.

'It was a long time ago, Amio,' she said quietly.

'But it is still true, Neferu,' he replied.

She stood silently for a moment and then turned with a slight shrug. 'Let's go to swim,' she said matter-of-factly, and began to undress. She lay her clothes neatly on a high jutting section and then turned round naked. To her surprise Amio had removed none of his clothing. He watched her as she stood naked. Neferu went to confront him with a bit of a frown on her face. She knew that he was self-conscious about his body, and she had to convince him that it would not alter her feelings towards him. But how?

'Come on, Amio. Let's go!' she said eventually, looking up at him questioningly.

He replied through set teeth. 'I am ashamed of my body, and I do not want you to see it.'

Neferu was cut for a moment by this honesty, but she could not let him see that. He would misconstrue it as pity. At the same time, she was afraid of not finding just the right words to explain to him that his deformities were not a factor which could influence her feelings towards him one way or another. She knew from past experience that she had the perfect knack of offending him. She was just too blunt.

After a moment's hesitation, she put her fingers to the clasp of his cloak. He gave no reaction and when she opened it and pulled the cloak from his shoulders, he made no move to prevent her. She folded the cloak carefully and put it with her own clothes and then went back to where he was standing in his tunic. He lifted it over his shoulders himself and she reached out to take it from him. He was now standing only in his loin cloth. She could see that his body was quite misshapen. He was very thin, and he had a pronounced curvature of his spine. Amio's eyes bored into Neferu, noting her every reaction as she looked at him. 'Stop it, Amio.' Her voice was emphatic. 'I truly promise that I find nothing disgusting about your body. Please believe me. It is the truth, I swear it.' Amio did not reply but began to take off his loin cloth. She put his tunic with his cloak, and he came behind her and put his loin cloth on the top of the pile. Neferu looked at him involuntarily and noticed that he did not seem at all shy about exposing that part of himself. She turned her face away blushing. He noticed it and smiled, seemingly having fully regained his composure now.

'We will have a swimming race to this famous rock you have been telling me about,' he remarked cheerfully.

Together they walked across the hot sand to the edge of the water. It felt so deliciously cool that Neferu squealed a little in sheer delight. She drew in a deep breath. 'Don't you think it smells lovely, Amio?' she asked. He bent down and flicked some water at her. She ran forwards into the waves and scooped some up to spray him. He quickly moved forwards too and soon they were both thigh high.

There were several rocks jutting out of the sea, and he said competitively, 'Which one?'

Neferu grinned and pointed to the one she meant. 'Not just yet though!' she said playfully. 'Only on the signal.'

'What signal?' he replied.

'Ready, steady, go!' she answered. 'And I say "go"!'

'Fair enough,' he replied. 'Let's get set!'

Neferu bent down and quickly douched herself with the sea water and then stood up again. She put her arms forward and Amio followed suit. 'Ready … Steady … Go!' she said loudly and they both launched themselves into the water.

Both of them made an all-out effort in the breaststroke towards the rock. He beat her easily and stood on the rock with a look of elation on his face. Neferu was surprised. He had given her to understand that he did not swim very often. Amio made no effort to hide his satisfaction at beating her so easily. Panting a little, they clambered up the rock and lay back to regain their breath. Neferu told Amio about Demi hurting his leg. Lying down, she noticed that his deformities were much less apparent. She herself felt no shyness in exposing herself to his gaze. She had always felt comfortable in her skin. 'Tell me when you are ready to go back!' he said, frankly looking at her. She nodded.

'Don't you think it looks beautiful, Amio, when the sun makes the drops of water on us sparkle so?' she said artlessly. He smiled a little and nodded but remained silent. After a while he closed his eyes and she looked at his chest. She was glad it wasn't hairy like Grandpa's. She did not like very hairy chests. After a while she sat up.

Amio opened his eyes. 'Ready to go?' he queried, squinting at her in the glare of the sun.

'Yes, let's go!' she responded.

Carefully they made their way down the rock, holding hands for mutual support. When they had both managed to find a secure foothold in the water, they repeated their warm-up procedure and launched off again. She tried her very hardest, but he repeated his previous success and he waited on the sand as she waded the last few metres. They walked a little up to the dry sand and Neferu threw herself down. He came to sit by her on her right and leaned towards her on his left elbow. There was an easy atmosphere between them. When they were no longer breathless, he said 'I am very curious as to where this secret cave might be. I feel inclined to go and explore!'

'Not this time, Amio,' she said quickly.

'So, you want to come again?' he said, looking at her sideways.

'Yes,' she replied. 'Don't you?'

'Yes. I have enjoyed it.' His eyes gazed down at her body and a hungry look came into them.

'This is the first time we have been truly alone together,' he said. Neferu wondered whether he would kiss her. If he kisses me now, she thought, I will do as he wishes and embrace him sexually. She waited expectantly but he did not kiss her. Instead, he withdrew slightly and asked her testily, 'Well. Do you not think that you have acquired a strange husband?'

Neferu looked up sharply, wondering at the sudden change of mood yet again. This was what threw her most about him. Just as they were approaching a moment of truth, he would do an about-face and spoil everything. She was clear that he was exceedingly anxious about his body image and Neferu sought to reassure him. Aware that his eyes were following her own, she allowed herself to gaze upon him and observe him carefully. When her eyes wandered down, she saw that he was very aroused.

She looked at him directly. 'You are not strange in any way, Amio. I find you very manly,' she said feeling very shy.

'And yet you hold back from me, knowing that I want you,' he said angrily. He jumped up furiously and walked back towards the cave.

Neferu sat quite still for a moment, shocked by the abruptness of the change in him again. She felt that she could not take much more of this; it was jangling her nerves. She wondered if there was something wrong with her that she always managed to irritate him in this way when she was trying her hardest to get closer to him. Sadly, she stood up and walked slowly towards the cave. They had not even eaten their picnic, she thought. In the cave, Amio was brusquely knocking sand from his legs and bottom. Angrily he put on his tunic. Neferu stood there unhappily.

'What did I say, Amio?' she asked in a distressed voice.

'Nothing,' he snapped.

'Aren't we going to eat our picnic?' she said, on the verge of tears.

'I'm not hungry,' was his reply.

Suddenly Neferu felt deathly tired of all this. She turned away and began to flick the sand from herself before beginning to dress in silence. She just wanted to go home to On and never leave there again. Just when she had learned to love this man, she knew that they could never be happy together. He was far too complicated and sensitive for her. Every moment she had to be watching her tongue, and even then she was always disappointed or displeased him. He waited in silence for her, then when she was ready, he took the picnic basket and started towards the cliff. Tiredly she followed him, dragging her feet up the cliff face. Irritated, she wondered at his ability to get to the top so quickly, when he had appeared to have so many problems getting down it. When Neferu reached the top, Amio was already seated on his donkey and waiting impatiently for her. She swallowed her frustration and untethered her donkey. Talking softly to it, she perched herself sideways on it and then patted it. Amio was already several metres in front of her. He did not even want to ride by her side, it seemed.

During the journey back they exchanged not a single word and when they finally arrived back at the villa, Neferu was devastated to find that Tiya and her entourage had arrived already. It could not have been at a worse time. Neferu curtsied deeply to her mother-in-law and replied to the queen's pleasantries as best she could, but she knew that Tiya's perceptiveness had already detected that something was amiss. When Neferu begged to be excused, she did not demur.

Mereta followed her to her sitting room. 'What is wrong, Neferu?'

Neferu shook her shoulders, unable to reply at first. In a strangled voice, she eventually managed to say, 'Everything!' before bursting into tears. Neferu looked around quickly to see where Amio was. He was not in the vicinity, however, so she was able to give vent to her true feelings. Mereta came to sit with her, extremely distressed.

When Neferu's sobs quietened down a bit, Mereta asked, 'What exactly is wrong, Neferu?'

'I don't know, Mereta,' Neferu wailed. 'I just can't be in his company for more than half an hour without him becoming totally enraged with me.' Mereta was silent. Neferu continued, 'I don't think we can ever be happy together. I suppose it would be better for him to divorce me.' She broke down into a fresh burst of sobbing.

'Divorce you!' Mereta said in a horrified voice. 'Amio loves you, Neferu.'

'No. He does not love me,' Neferu said, more quietly now. 'He wants me, but he does not love me. That is quite different.'

'You could not be more wrong, Neferu. Amio is in love with you. He loved you from the first day you met. He told me so,' Mereta's voice was quite certain.

Neferu was dumbfounded. 'Are you absolutely sure, Mereta?' she asked slowly. 'Why has he never told me. Is he ashamed to love me because I am a humble Keftiu, and he is the pharaoh? Is it beneath him to tell me that he loves me, if he does?'

Mereta glanced at her sharply. 'I know that he does love you with all his heart, Neferu, and I know that he is not ashamed of it. Does what I have told you make a difference to your feelings?' Mereta's voice was sad.

'Yes. It makes all the difference, Mereta,' answered Neferu.

'Neferu?' Mereta hesitated a little. 'Are you in love with Amio?' she said uncertainly.

Neferu looked at her directly and wiped her eyes. 'Yes. I am in love with him,' she said, tremulously smiling. 'I am going to find him. It is time we had a long talk,' she said.

Mereta smiled. 'Be gentle with him, Neferu,' she said softly.

'I will,' Neferu said, just as softly.

Neferu rose from the couch. She wondered where Amio was. He was not in his room, and he was not in the reception room with Tiya, when she peeped in. She went quietly out onto the terrace but there was no one there. She was about to cross the terrace into the garden when she heard footsteps behind her.

'Ah, Neferu!' Amio said, taking in her red eyes and streaky face. He came out onto the terrace proper. 'There is something I wish to discuss with you in private. Will you come with me to where we will not be disturbed?' he asked tonelessly. A feeling of dread came over Neferu. She followed him through into their suite and he opened the shutters onto their private veranda. It was cool and shaded and entirely private.

'What is it, Amio?' Neferu asked fearfully.

He turned away from her so that she would not see his face and after a moment, he said in a controlled tone, 'I understand now that love can never be forced and that our marriage was a serious mistake. What Yussef said was true. I did steal you from him and that was wrong. I did it because I love you.' His voice broke slightly. 'I never meant to hurt you and I can't bear to see you unhappy, so you are free to go whenever you wish. I will arrange to divorce you as soon as possible.' Neferu stood staring at his cloaked back and his black hair. He had said it out loud finally. He loved her. Slowly she moved forward and round to the front of him. She saw tears in his eyes and her heart contracted at that moment.

Slowly she unclasped his cloak and let it slide to the floor. Underneath he had only his loin cloth. He must have been about to take his rest when he felt he must speak with her. Amio stood like a statue, not moving a muscle but tense as if ready to explode. Neferu went round to his back and put her hand on his shoulder. She kissed the nape of his neck, standing on her tiptoes. Swiftly moving downwards, she kissed his back, his waist, his buttocks, thighs and calves, bending as she went. Still crouching, she moved round to the front of him, and she kissed each shin in turn, each knee and thigh until she gently took his manhood in her hands and kissed it too. He emitted a great shudder and suddenly they were on the cold mosaic floor together. Amio lifted her gown feverishly and pulled at her loin cloth. She helped him to remove it and then lay back to receive him. There was a wildness about him as she felt him thrust into her body, and she gasped momentarily, and then pulled him convulsively towards her. She wanted him as she had never wanted anyone or anything in her life before. She lost herself in the wildness of their passion, totally out of control until suddenly he uttered a cry, and she felt a sweet warmth radiate through her.

'I love you, Amio, I love you, I love you, I love you.'

He sighed heavily and murmured, 'I love you too, Neferu.'

Afterwards they lay together on the stone floor, he still inside her. She kissed his forehead.

'My darling, my husband,' she murmured. After a while he lifted his head, and she felt his body move.

'Don't go yet,' she whispered.

'You will get cold,' he said caressingly. She could feel him still inside her body. He lay his head on her breast again and caressed the other breast through her gown. In her haste it had not been properly removed. 'I will never give you up now, Neferu. Nothing can ever separate us now,' he said with a deep sigh.

'I will never leave you now,' she promised.

They separated finally and he helped her up from the floor, kissing her. Hand in hand, they went through to the washroom and performed for the first time what was to become a kind of ritual of love throughout their marriage, a mutual washing, him of her and she of him. There was something supremely sensual in the feel of his hand washing her most sensitive areas. Afterwards they dried themselves, and this time, Amio led her through to his bedroom. He got into bed first and she climbed in beside him, lying on his left. He drew her towards him, and they caressed each other over and over again until, out of sheer replete exhaustion, they slept.

Neferu awoke to the touch of Amio's hand on her face. She opened her eyes and he leaned forward to kiss her. 'I love you, my dearest wife,' he murmured softly.

'I love you too, my darling,' she murmured back to him. He put his hand on her breast and began to caress it with his fingers. Aroused, she moved her hand down to his groin and began to caress him lightly and rhythmically. Again, the great tumult started and ran its course, leaving them limp and quiet. He looked at her wonderingly.

'When did you begin to love me?' he asked, lightly stroking her cheek with his index finger.

'I don't know,' she answered. 'Perhaps it was happening all the time, but I didn't notice it. But when we lay together on the boat that first time, I realised that I did love you,' she continued in a husky voice.

'Why did you not show me?' he asked brokenly. 'We could have saved ourselves a lot of heartache.'

'I did try, Amio,' she said. 'But each time, something would go terribly wrong. I knew that you wanted me, but I didn't know if you really loved and respected me.' Her voice was serious and her tone low.

'How could you doubt it?' he sounded amazed.

Neferu shrugged. 'You didn't say it!' There was a note of accusation in her voice.

'I couldn't say it because I knew that you loved Yussef. I couldn't compete with him in looks and I didn't want you to feel sorry for me,' he explained touchingly. She pulled him down upon her and put her arms around him tightly. She felt a sudden fiercely protective desire to shield him from all hurt. He lay quietly in her arms until they became hot and sticky, a consequence of both their passion and the summer heat. Reluctantly, Amio rolled away from her.

'Shall we go to bathe again?' he asked. Neferu smiled and nodded. He got up and went to the bathroom and she followed him after a moment, with a sheet wrapped around her. First, he washed her carefully, exploring every part of her body gently and without shyness, then he rinsed her, kissing her breasts afterwards. Then it was her turn, and she did the same for him. When it was over, they each went to their respective rooms to dress.

Neferu was doing her hair when Amio entered. He sat down on the bed to watch her. When she was ready, she turned and noticed that, for the first time, he was not wearing his cloak over his tunic.

'Aren't you going to put your cloak on?' she asked. surprised.

He stood up and leaned against the wall near the doorway. 'I don't need it anymore now I know that you really love me,' he said simply. Neferu was once again forced to breathe in sharply. This way he had of suddenly exposing his vulnerability caused her heart to somersault. Although he did not know it, it was his most potent weapon against her will. She felt that her heart would burst inside her and she wished that she could take away all the hurts which had existed between them. She moved to him and brought his fingers to her lips. She wished with all her heart that they would never need weapons against each other ever again. Amio put his arm around Neferu's shoulders and murmured.

'We had better go for refreshments. The others will be wondering where we are.' Neferu was suddenly struck by the absence of Maatnofret and Paranefer. She smiled a little to herself. Perhaps they had entered and gone unnoticed, she thought.

At refreshments Neferu noticed that Tiya and her chief lady-in-waiting, Shenade were absent.

'Where is your mother, Amio,' she asked in surprise. The others exchanged glances and Amio's face suddenly assumed a worried expression.

'She has left to meet my uncle and will be returning with him. He is on his way from On,' he said slowly.

Neferu did not understand. 'But why couldn't he have found his way here on his own?' she asked, perplexed.

'They had some business to discuss,' he said. His brow suddenly cleared. 'It was a mistake for her to go, but everything will be sorted out when they return,' he added with a reassuring smile.

'Oh!' she replied, not quite understanding and she left it at that for the moment.

In front of the others, Amio took her hand and brought it to his lips. 'Don't worry, my darling wife, there is nothing wrong.' Once again, the others exchanged glances and the atmosphere suddenly lifted. 'Neferu and I are going swimming again tomorrow morning,' he announced cheerfully. 'We are going to have a picnic on the beach.'

Pararameses cleared his throat. 'The queen is totally against you both going out alone like that,' he said. 'At least take one of the guards with you.'

Amio dismissed his reservations. 'I have little enough opportunity to be alone with my wife and I dare say that once we return to Thebes, there will be hardly any opportunity. We wish to spend some time absolutely for ourselves, don't we, my love?' he asked tenderly. Neferu pulled his hand to her lip and kissed it. She nodded. The others appeared to be entranced by the openness of their endearments.

'There is no reason to be worried.' Neferu assured them all in general. 'We are both strong swimmers and we are not so foolish as to go too far out. We stay very close to each other, don't we, darling?' She looked at her husband as she said this, and he nodded vigorously in support.

Maatnofret, who had quietly entered the room, caused them to turn and look at her as she said, 'All life is in the hands of the Aten and I, for one, would not stand in the way of your happiness together,' she said with a broad smile. Neferu knew that the older woman was genuinely happy for her. She herself felt bursting with such love and happiness that she felt her face must be plastered with an idiotic smile.

Pararameses indicated that he wished to discuss some business with Amio, and the latter agreed good-naturedly. The two of them rose to go and, unexpectedly, Amio bent to kiss her cheek.

'See you later, darling,' he said lightly, before crossing the terrace to where Pararameses stood waiting. Mereta smiled at Neferu with a knowing look, and when Paranefer had also excused himself and the three women were alone Neferu threw her arms exuberantly into the air and said joyously.

'I am the happiest woman in the whole world.'

Maatnofret and Mereta exchanged smiling looks. 'It came right for you at last, Neferu,' Maatnofret said.

'Gloriously right,' the Keftiu girl said happily.

Mereta sighed. 'I do envy you both, Neferu. I wonder when I will fall passionately in love and someone with me?'

'Oh, you will, Mereta. You will,' Neferu said confidently.

Mereta smiled. 'I was beginning to think that things would never settle between you both,' she admitted.

'I love Amio with all my heart, Mereta. You need have no fear for him,' Neferu replied shyly.

'I know that now,' her sister-in-law answered.

Amio returned and Neferu got up to meet him. Maatnofret rose, saying with her usual practicality, 'Well, there are things to be organised before dinner now that the queen has left. I suppose I had better do it.'

Neferu looked across at her guiltily. 'Do you mind if I leave everything to you and Mereta, Maatnofret? I don't want to do anything today except to be with my husband.' She turned to him as she spoke, putting her arms round his waist and leaning her face against his cheek. Amio kissed her forehead.

'I don't mind at all in the circumstances,' Maatnofret replied good-humouredly. 'Why don't you go for a walk, but don't be too late back now!' she added in a maternal tone.

The two promised not to be late and wandered off, arm and arm, across the garden towards the gate, relishing the easy, relaxed mood that existed between them.

'It feels very strange to go from the depths of despair to the heights of ecstasy all in one day,' Amio mused. 'It makes it seem a very long day,' he laughed.

'I don't want there to be any more depths,' Neferu responded. He squeezed her shoulders for a moment in reassurance.

'You are a foolish girl,' he said teasingly. 'How could you possibly not have known that I loved you. My eyes followed you everywhere and when you were out of my sight, I was always looking out for you!'

Neferu stopped in her tracks. 'But sometimes you were so cold and cutting,' she reminded him.

'I couldn't help it,' he told her. 'I was so miserable because you didn't feel the same.'

'Perhaps I did but I just didn't know it,' she said slowly. 'I looked out for you too and I always felt that there was something familiar and special about you.' Amio too had stopped, and he took her in his arms. They just clung together as if they were afraid of losing each other again. It was exhilarating and seemed so miraculous to them both that they should have found each other.

Neferu found it hard to believe that anyone could have felt quite the way she did, even though she had frequently heard talk of being in love. In the way of all lovers, she felt that what she and Amio had was quite unique, and the coming dinner party that evening could only be an irritating intrusion into their special and magical world. She did not want to share it with anyone. They broke apart and walked on for a while until they came to the edge of the cliff. Here they sat down in the evening sunshine and watched the seagulls and the far horizon. The sun had dropped, and she knew that they should be getting back before Maatnofret began to worry. It was so hard to pull themselves away and she leaned back against him as they watched that gigantic red ball in the sky as it began to sink over the horizon.

'It is beautiful, isn't it?' she remarked softly, marvelling at the quickly changing variety of hues which formed the sky.

'It is,' he agreed softly, as profoundly touched as she was by the vision of beauty mutating before their eyes. They watched in silence until only a small arc remained above the horizon, giving a blue twilight merging into a pinky orange horizon.

'We had better return, Amio,' she sighed regretfully.

'We'll come back tomorrow,' was his reply. They stood up and began to walk back towards the villa, and it was dark by the time they arrived.

Maatnofret was waiting for her and scolded her for their lateness. 'I was getting very worried,' she said sharply. Neferu apologised and quickly went to bathe and change for dinner. Happily, there were to be guests from outside that evening. Still, with those of Tiya's entourage, it would not be a small intimate group anymore, she reflected.

The dinner group was animated and there was plenty of lively and amusing conversation. Neferu found it pleasurable torture to mix with the others, purposely parting herself from her beloved for longish periods, just to experience the pleasure of returning to his side. Their eyes would meet at frequent intervals and glow with their secret signals across the room. They stayed up late with the group until their hunger for each other became impossible to suppress and they bade the others a goodnight.

This time their lovemaking was slow and sensual, without the hurried explosiveness of the afternoon. Now they were secure in their love for each other, exploring each other tenderly and arousing their passion gently. Afterwards she snuggled up against him in the chill of the night and they fell asleep like small children, wrapped around each other. Throughout their marriage Amio and Neferu always retained the ability to gain strength and nourish their inner reserves from the ecstasy of their physical passion for each other.

CHAPTER 19

The next morning Neferu woke up to find Amio pressed up against her. She could feel the hardness of him and see that expression he always had in his eyes when he desired her. 'Mmmmm! You make me crazy, Neferu,' he said nibbling her ear.

She smiled pleasurably at the sense of her power over him. 'Good,' she said with satisfaction.

'Minx!' he said, correctly interpreting her expression.

'Should we bathe first?' she asked teasingly.

'No point! Afterwards will do,' he said practically. His right hand came to her right breast, and she felt that now familiar sensation again. She pulled him closer to her and gently he began to suckle her. He knew exactly how to arouse her, she thought. Afterwards Amio lay back. 'You were right, Neferu,' he said suddenly.

She turned her face towards him, puzzled, wondering to what he was referring. 'About what, my darling?' she asked with a frown.

'About the Aten.' His voice was serious. 'I prayed to them all, but it was only the Aten who was strong enough to make you love me.'

Neferu was silent for a while and then she replied, 'I think you had a great deal to do with it, Amio. Sometimes you are so unexpectedly frank and open your heart to me, like now. I just can't resist you.'

She saw a smile cross his face. 'I must remember that,' he said laughing. 'It is a good strategy. I want to be irresistible to you.' He nuzzled his face into her hair. 'Mmm! I love the smell of you, Neferu. You have your very own smell, did you know?' He murmured romantically.

'I think it is really only the perfumed oils I apply, Amio,' she answered prosaically, and they both burst out laughing. As well as passion, their new relationship had uncovered a deep vein of humour between them that had not been apparent before and was exciting too in its own way.

'Remember we are going swimming this morning!' Neferu reminded him.

'Yes, if you show me your secret cave,' he said teasingly, but with a glint in his eye.

Neferu sighed a little. 'Amio, you have absolutely no cause to be jealous, my darling,' she replied, slightly exasperated at his determination to prise the secret from her.

'I know, I know,' he answered soothingly. 'It's just that I want to know everything about you. I want to be a part of all your life and everything that has ever happened to you. I am greedy for you, my love.'

Neferu kissed him. 'You are unreasonable, my darling. No one can have everything. You are already part of Rashid for me. Here with you I have experienced the happiest day of my life so far. You are my future. The past is already gone,' she told him earnestly.

'I can't help it, Neferu darling. I have not yet learned to be secure in our love,' he said quietly.

She pulled his lips to hers and kissed him again. 'I pray that the Aten will give us many years in which we can come to feel secure in our love and have faith in the tomorrows of our life together,' she said. Amio drew in his breath sharply. 'You are my inspiration, Amio, and you have the music to give melody to my life. Sing to me often.'

'I will,' he promised.

There was a discreet cough in the doorway and the two lovers drew apart. Maatnofret and Paranefer stood there. 'Is it time to get up already?' Amio said laughing.

Paranefer answered with an apologetic smile. 'I'm afraid so, Your Majesty.'

'Don't forget that you are going swimming this morning,' Maatnofret reminded them. 'It is best to go early before the sun becomes too high in the sky.'

'You are right, as usual, Maatnofret,' Amio said nonchalantly. 'We can get ourselves ready, can't we, Neferu?' He turned to his wife, eyes signalling furiously.

'Of course. We help each other, don't we?' Neferu responded with a smile. Maatnofret laughed and she and her husband exchanged amused glances and withdrew.

Amio jumped up and put out his arm to pull her up. 'Come on, lazy bones!' he said and went off to bathe. Neferu followed and they washed each other sensually.

'Being married is much more fun than I thought it would be,' observed Neferu.

'And this is just the beginning,' Amio answered gleefully, nipping her bottom playfully. Their ablutions completed, they dressed quickly and went to breakfast.

After breakfast the housemaid brought a basket of food and juice for them, and they left the confines of the villa on the two faithful donkeys. Once they were a safe distance from the villa, Amio began to sing funny songs about various people at court. He had obviously composed them himself and some of them were very funny and most were at least a tiny bit ribald. Neferu laughed. He really was very witty, and he had a pleasant singing voice.

At the top of the cliff, they tethered the donkeys and Neferu took the basket. She went first and held on to his left hand with her right as they went down. At the bottom of the cliff she paused until he was down and then they made their way over to the cave. This time Amio showed no reserve, and he was undressed and out before she was. They waded out into the water up to their thighs and launched themselves off towards the rock. Amio got their first and waited for her to help her up the rock. They lay back happily, letting the sun dry their wet, glistening bodies.

'How come you managed to scale that damn cliff so quickly yesterday, Amio?' Neferu asked suddenly.

'What do you mean?' He said innocently.

'I mean that you had problems getting down it but going up you went as if lifted by air,' she said indignantly.

Amio laughed. 'I was so furious with you,' he explained.

'And that helped?' she retorted.

'Of course!' he replied, laughing again.

When they had rested and were hot again, they climbed down the rock and into the water and began to swim around the rock, playing in the water, kissing and touching each other. The water was gloriously cool and gave an added eroticism to their play. When they were tired, they swam back to the beach and flung themselves down on the sand. Amio idly picked up a shell. It was lined with mother of pearl on the inside, and he peered at it. 'Pretty, isn't it?' he observed.

'Mmm!' she replied. 'Let's find some nice ones and take them back for a memento.'

They hunted around, up and down the beach like children, looking for shells, and when they had found the desired amount, they put them in the cave with their clothes. They took the picnic basket outside into the sun with them and sat down again to munch some fruit.

After a while Amio said, 'I want to see the secret cave.'

Neferu glared at him, but he just stared obstinately back. 'I can't show you, Amio,' she pleaded. 'I made a promise.'

'You can tell me which direction it is in, at least,' he said huffily. 'I'll find it myself.'

'You are an impossible man,' she uttered, exasperated, pointing to the left of them.

Amio grinned. 'I'll find it, you'll see,' he said. He got up and walked off up the beach. His head seemed glued to the left as he examined the cliffs. Neferu watched him until he had gone quite a way and then got up to follow him. She could not remember, herself, exactly where the cave was located but she remembered that it was quite a distance from their little spot of the beach.

Amio turned round to look back and saw her following him in the distance. She stopped. She was not going to help him in any way. He understood her gesture and turned round again. She realised that his obstinacy was such that she had now probably only increased his determination to locate the cave. He carried on walking, and she followed behind at a distance of fifty metres or so. Suddenly ahead of them she saw the oddly shaped rock in the sea which she recognised as the landmark she and Yussef had used to mark the vicinity of the cave. She wondered whether Amio would miss it. After all, the opening was very narrow.

Every time that Amio turned round she stopped dead in her tracks and made no reaction. Indeed, he did go on past the cave and she followed him with a slight smile. They walked on still for quite a distance until he turned again, and she stopped too. She knew that he must be very tired. It was hard for him to walk long distances even on smooth ground and on the uneven sand it must be twice as difficult. This time he started back towards her. He looked cross. 'Well, I can see you aren't going to give me any help,' he said irrritably.

'No,' she said serenely. 'You said you would find it yourself.' She reminded him.

'Hmm!' He sounded niggled. 'Don't think I am giving up. I'll come again tomorrow.'

'Just as you wish.' She smiled. Neferu took his hand. She did not want him to be upset but she was not going to let him intimidate her into showing him the whereabouts of the cave. 'I love you and you are a dreadful, stubborn fellow,' she said.

He was only slightly mollified. 'Don't think you are going to distract me,' he said, suspicious, his head now turned to the right in a continuous reappraisal of the cliff face.

'I wouldn't dream of it,' she said blithely.

Hand in hand they continued down the beach and suddenly he saw it. He gave a cry of triumph and let go of her hand as he hurried towards it. Neferu felt her heart lurch. As if in explanation or private apology, she whispered out loud. 'I didn't show him, Yussef.' Amio was already at the narrow, slit-like entrance to the cave. He climbed up and went in sideways and there it lay before him. She heard him whoop with excitement before he reappeared at the entrance. 'Neferu, come on!' he exclaimed impatiently. With a real sense of betrayal, Neferu went over to the aperture and Amio put out his arm to help her up. Inside it was just as she remembered it from six years ago. There was the pool with the little fish in it. Idly she wondered how many generations of fish had passed since she was last there. It was very cool inside the cave, but not cool enough to dampen Amio's passion to put his own indelible stamp on the place. He put his arms around Neferu possessively and pulled her body close to his. Almost methodically he began to rub himself against her until he was aroused to such a pitch that it demanded a union. Carefully but forcefully, he pulled her down with him onto the wet sand and then he took her quickly. Neferu recognised that it was the stamp of his ownership.

Only now could he be satisfied that she was truly his. 'This is our cave now, as well, and you will always remember that I was here with you,' he said, replete. Neferu said nothing but merely stroked his face. She wondered at the intensity of his desire to establish his dominance over her past. She hoped that one day he would come to realise that there was no need for his insecurity.

The wet sand was cold and Neferu began to shiver. Amio pulled her up and they submerged themselves in the pool to clean themselves. It was a pleasure to return outside into the warmth of the sun again and they wandered back, hand in hand along the hot sand until they reached their part of the beach. Amio lay down to rest while Neferu went to get the fruit basket and the hide water bottle.

'Perhaps we should be going back soon, Amio,' she remarked.

'Not yet,' he said, spitting out a date stone. 'Let's have one more swim first when we have had a rest!' he said contentedly. She lay back on the sand, but the sun was very high now and it was far too hot for sunbathing.

'We can't lie here, Amio, we will get burnt,' Neferu protested, standing up.

'All right!' he said. 'One last swim.'

The sand was so hot now that they almost had to run to the water's edge, and they ploughed through the water until they were thigh high again before plunging into the waves. This time they swam leisurely towards the rock and did not bother to climb up it but stayed, resting on its underwater edge, before swimming slowly back to the shore. For both of them, the morning's outing had changed something fundamental. It had given Amio a new quality of control over her life he felt he needed and for Neferu came the final realisation that her life in On was permanently over. A new book was beginning.

The pair of them clambered clumsily up the cliff. It was so hot now that they almost felt that they had not been for a swim at all. They were tired by the time they got to the top and untethered the donkey. For the second consecutive day they pursued their journey back to the villa in silence, but this time it was a relaxed, easy silence, born of fatigue and not of despair.

Mereta came out to greet them. 'You two were gone a long time,' she said, thankful that they were back. 'Pararameses was just thinking of sending out a search party for you,' she informed them.

'We were exploring,' Amio explained briefly.

'Oh, well, never mind! You are just in time for lunch,' the princess observed.

'Will I have time to wash my hair?' Neferu asked. Neferu hurried off to wash her hair and bathe before lunch. She felt much better afterwards. She looked up inquiringly as Amio came into the sitting room. 'Where were you?' she asked.

'Just discussing a hunt with Rameses,' he said. 'We have been invited to a hunt over in Rashid itself, the day after tomorrow.'

'Ugh!' Neferu said, wrinkling her nose. 'Well can we go swimming again tomorrow, in that case?' she asked.

'You bet!' he answered. 'I'll only beat you again, though.' He grinned at her, and she suddenly remembered something she had wanted to ask him previously.

'You gave me to understand in Thebes that you were not a very good swimmer,' she remarked pointedly.

'It was true,' he said, with a shrug. 'In fact, it was only a few decans ago that I learned how to swim!'

'When?' asked Neferu in surprise.

'When I found out that you could swim,' he confessed. 'I took secret swimming lessons. I did not want you to do anything I could not share with you,' he continued. Neferu was flabbergasted at the amount of competitiveness he perceived between them, and of which she had been completely unaware.

'But I would not have liked you less if you could not swim,' she explained, mystified.

'No, but I would have liked myself less,' he retorted.

Neferu felt a sense of anxiety. 'Amio, you do know that I love you for yourself, don't you? I would have loved you whatever you were or whatever you looked like. It is not because you are pharaoh that I love you. You don't have to be the best at everything for me to love you. I love you because you are you. Can you accept that?' She wanted to have the matter straight.

Amio nodded. 'I suppose that I am not an easy person to know, Neferu. Ever since my elder brother Tuthmosis died, I suppose that I have been trying to prove that I am worthy of the crown. Tuthmosis was handsome and his body was normal. He was all the things that I am not, but he died of a fever in Kush and instead Egypt got me, second best. Even in your life I came second to Yussef.' He spoke without self-pity, but with a kind of defiance.

'You only came second in time, Amio,' Neferu tried to explain. 'You are second to no one in my heart.'

'I know it, Neferu,' he replied quietly. 'But never stop telling it to me.'

'I won't,' she promised. They kissed and then he left to bathe before lunch. Neferu sat down on the couch to wait for him. Only now was she beginning to understand the complexities of the character of the man she had married. She was beginning to realise that he had suffered a lot in spite of his wealth and position, and she knew that it might be a long time before he really came to trust her.

When Amio was ready, they went out onto the terrace for lunch. The others were already present. Neferu was not very hungry after the morning's picnic, and she ate little. When they later went to rest, they were both tired and after snuggling up together they fell asleep quickly and slept until Maatnofret came to wake them. 'Come and join us for refreshments,' she invited them. Neferu yawned. Amio wanted to sleep for a while still, so she told Maatnofret that she would forego the occasion and have a glass of juice later. She turned over onto her right side and put her left arm around her husband's waist. He had already gone back to sleep. Neferu smiled. He was funny, she thought. He always insisted on sleeping on her right for some reason, even though his side of the bed was against the wall, and he hated that and having to climb over her to get out. Still, he had refused to get one of the servants to move the heavy bed because he did not want to appear to be complaining about the arrangements. He was finickity but endearing and she loved him very much.

Eventually Amio woke up and turned round to face her. 'I was really tired,' he observed, yawning.

'I'm not surprised after all the efforts of the last two days,' she said.

He laughed, squinting at her. 'I am not too tired,' he said amused.

'We need to recuperate ready for tonight. I do anyway,' she said drily.

'All right, until tonight,' he conceded.

She kissed him. 'I love you,' she said.

'I love you too.' Was his reply.

They got up and went out onto the terrace. Mereta was sitting with her lace-making bobbins and Maatnofret was embroidering a square cloth. 'Are you hungry, Neferu?' the older woman asked.

Neferu shook her head. 'Not at all. I'll just have a drink,' she replied, pouring one for herself and one for her husband. She gave the goblet to Amio, and he went to join Pararameses and one of the other officers, sitting on the top step of the terrace.

Neferu looked at Mereta. 'I wonder when your mother and uncle will arrive?' she remarked curiously.

Mereta looked a little uncomfortable, which Neferu misconstrued as worry concerning her mother's safety. 'I wish she had never left here,' she said firmly.

'It must have been something important,' Neferu observed. Mereta bit her lip but said nothing.

'I expect that they will be here tomorrow sometime,' Maatnofret said matter-of-factly.

'So soon! From Memphis?' Neferu asked.

'No. Not from Memphis. From Hamidin,' Maatnofret said.

'That is where my uncle was heading for from Memphis, to lead a court hearing between two quarrelling officials from that province. It has been causing some unrest,' Mereta informed her.

'I find the whole expedition perplexing,' Neferu said slowly. 'It seems to me that there is something of a mystery about it.'

'Perhaps Amio knows something about it, Neferu. Ask him about it,' Mereta suggested.

Neferu had the definite feeling that both Mereta and Maatnofret were withholding information from her. She did not worry unnecessarily about it, however, as she felt that Amio would have told her if it were something important.

Later that evening as she and Amio prepared for bed, she brought up the subject of the queen. 'Your mother is due back tomorrow, isn't she, Amio?'

He frowned momentarily. 'Yes, but do not worry about the matter, Neferu. The problem which caused her to go no longer exists. I am afraid she has had a fruitless journey. Let's forget about it,' he said soothingly. A minute later he changed the subject.' Would you like to go and visit your aunt and uncle?' He asked with a smile. Something of a shadow had flown across Neferu's mind, a sudden intuition that the queen's journey concerned her, but Amio's words diverted her.

'Why, yes! Of course!' she was pleased.

'I will see to the matter tomorrow,' he responded. They climbed into bed, leaving only one of the oil lamps to glow. It gave off large shadows with soft outlines in the dark and it seemed a cosy and romantic setting for their love. She turned towards him, her face in shadow. His face was partially reflected in the glowing haze of the lamp, and his large almond-shaped eyes looked at her softly.

'Do you love me?' he asked her. She nodded. 'Say it!' he insisted.

'I love you,' she said quietly. 'I always will.'

'Through life, past death and into the afterlife?' he asked.

'Forever,' she answered.

'Forever is a very long time,' he murmured as he traced the outlines of her face with his finger.

'Forever,' she repeated. He leaned forward and kissed her lips slowly.

When he drew back, he said, 'You are my life and happiness, Neferu. Only death can separate us now.'

Neferu accepted that completely. 'I know it,' she said. Amio began to caress her breasts and soon their naked bodies were united again. It was as if after all the barren decans of waiting, they could not get enough of each other. Later they slept.

The air had the damp chill of pre-dawn when Neferu was woken by the sound of a man's voice calling in a low tone. 'Amio! Wake up, Amio!' The voice seemed to come from just within the doorway. At first Neferu thought she was dreaming and tried to close her ears to it. Gradually she woke up properly as she felt Amio climbing over her to get out of bed. She sat up suddenly, anxiously jerked into wakefulness by his departure into the blackness.

'Amio,' she cried softly, reaching out for him. 'Is there something wrong, darling?'

Amio stopped in mid-movement and kissed her. 'Go back to sleep, darling. I'll be back soon. It's only Uncle Ay!' he urged. Neferu struggled to make out the figure of the grand vizier in the darkness of the doorway. Ay spoke to her.

'There is nothing to be afraid of, Neferu. I only want to talk to Amio.' His voice was calm. Neferu sank back onto her pillow. Why could it not wait until the morning? she wondered uneasily.

'Don't be long, my darling!' she whispered. When Amio had gone, Neferu could not get back to sleep. All her instincts screamed at her that there was something wrong, but she could only lie back and wait. She shivered slightly and pulled the rugs around her more closely.

It was past dawn by the time Amio returned and by this time she was extremely perturbed.

'What is wrong, Amio? Please tell me,' she said, clinging to him when he was once more beside her.

'There is absolutely nothing wrong now, my dearest love,' he said soothingly. Amio explained that on the fateful day that they had returned estranged from their first visit to the beach, his mother had immediately noticed how distressed they both were, and she had questioned him closely. He had been so upset that in the end he had broken down and told her that their marriage was still unconsummated and that he despaired of ever winning her love. His mother had been horrified and had decided to bring her brother to discuss the situation and sort out a solution before the return to Thebes. They had decided that the marriage must be annulled at once and that Amio must take another wife immediately.

It appeared that Ay had thought his sister was grossly overreacting to the situation and his feelings had been reinforced by finding them in bed together. Neferu became very distressed at hearing all this and wondered how she could respond to them later in the morning. Amio told his mother that he would never divorce Neferu. He had been quite furious with her. He told her that the crisis was over, in any case, and they had been lovers since that very same afternoon. Neferu felt very exposed and vulnerable and asked Amio why he had not told her the true nature of the queen's errand earlier. He told her that he had not wanted to upset her and, especially after they had become lovers, he felt there was no longer any reason to mention it.

'How will I face your mother now?' Neferu wailed.

'Mother won't say anything,' Amio assured her. She saw that for him the matter was over, but Neferu was sure that from now on she would be under the eagle eye of the queen at all times. It was not that she disliked the queen, it was that everything inside her told her she could not trust this woman.

The royal family sat down to breakfast altogether that morning. Tiya greeted Neferu rather stiffly and Neferu also responded without any warmth in her manner other than that due to the queen's position. Several times she noticed Tiya looking at her and her heart sank as she realised the woman was checking up on her in everything as if to catch her out. It was rather unpleasant but, in spite of this, Neferu was so happy in her newfound love that she was unable to worry about the queen's distrust of her for long.

When Amio and Ay began to discuss swimming, her husband told his uncle about their swimming sessions and how enjoyable it was. Ay decided that he would organise a trip to the beach with some of the others, stating that he had not had the pleasure of swimming for fifteen years, at least. Tiya somewhat acidly remarked that he had better not go too far out or he might end up as the rather undigestible lunch for some large fish. The grand vizier seemed slightly put out at this and gave Neferu a conspiratorial wink from behind his sister's back. Neferu was unable to suppress a smile, which fortunately the queen took to be a consequence of her own wit. In spite of Neferu's expectations to the contrary, the queen made no reference to the night incident and seemed at a loss as to what to make of the new developments between Amio and herself. Tiya watched as Amio nuzzled her cheek before sitting down next to her at breakfast, and she followed the many half-secret glances between them.

Some inner instinct warned Neferu not to mention the proposed swimming session she and Amio intended to make, and she left the table without saying anything to the others. She perceived that if Ay and the others intended to go swimming that morning, then she and Amio would have to move their session to the afternoon. The number of personnel around the villa and in their immediate vicinity had just about doubled with the arrival of the queen and Ay and their entourages. To Neferu it seemed that the place was fast becoming a miniature replica of Thebes and that her possibilities of spending time alone with Amio were fast being eroded. Her holiday feeling was quickly disappearing.

When Neferu got a moment alone with Amio after breakfast, she quickly steered him down the terrace steps and into the garden.

'What about our swimming? We can't go this morning!' she said urgently.

'I've thought of that,' he said with a frown. 'We'll go this afternoon.'

'What will your mother say?' Neferu demanded.

'She will probably insist that we take a guard or Maatnofret and Paranefer to accompany us,' he admitted.

'That's what I was afraid of,' Neferu said, with a resigned air.

Amio smiled. 'So that's why we won't tell her,' he murmured. 'We'll have to enlist Maatnofret's silence and Mereta's too.'

'Do you think they will agree to cover for us?' she asked anxiously.

'They don't need to lie,' he said. 'We'll say that we are going for a walk together and want to be alone and that is what they will repeat if asked. We need not say that our walk will end in a swim, need we?'

Neferu frowned. 'It seems a bit dishonest,' she said doubtfully.

'I'll tell my uncle and he will keep her occupied so that she doesn't miss us,' he explained innocently.

'Do you think he will agree?' she asked.

'Of course! I have covered for him several times,' Amio admitted with a grin.

'Oh.' Neferu was quite shocked.

Amio laughed. 'I'll go and see him about it before he goes off himself,' he declared, much amused at her reaction.

Amio spent most of the morning with Pararameses organising the hunt for the following day and a private visit to the home of her aunt and Uncle Giorgios and their family. Afterwards he spent some time with his mother and when they emerged just before lunch, he looked satisfied with the results of their meeting.

Over lunch, the grand vizier caught her eye several times with amusement and once even gave her an almost imperceptible nod. After lunch was over Neferu yawned ostentatiously and professed to a tiredness from which she was not really suffering.

'Are you coming to rest, Amio?' she asked him shyly.

He narrowed his long eyes and looked at her with a glint of amusement. 'Yes. I think it's a good idea,' he said guilelessly. The queen's eyes followed them as they left the room, but any speculation in her eyes was to do with quite other aspects of their relationship than their afternoon schedule.

The two truants lay down, and in the heat they were soon overcome by drowsiness. They slept fitfully for a while, but when the sun had sunk a little and the whole house was in silence, they got up and stealthily made their way to the yard. They led the two donkeys quietly past the two guards on the gate. These latter did not display any surprise or alarm at their departure and merely bowed low as they passed. There was a delicious feeling of breaking the. It was not long before they had got as far as the coastal road and were out of sight of the villa. They chatted in a relaxed fashion. In the still of the heat, the only sound that was audible was that of the crickets chirping and the only movement they could see was the flitting, erratic flights of insects as they flew from flower to wildflower on the verge at the side of the track. It was so quiet that Amio was moved to say, 'It is easy to imagine that we are the only people alive in this stillness, isn't it?'

Neferu nodded. 'The whole world is ours,' she said, throwing out her right arm expansively and then leaning backwards slightly to maintain her equilibrium on the donkey.

At the edge of the cliff, they tethered the two donkeys to the tree at their usual spot, where they were in the shade and watched as the donkeys began to munch contentedly at the scrub grass around them. This time it was easier to get down the cliff as they had no basket to carry. Amio had brought two hide water bottles and grabbed a couple of apples as they left. Gingerly they made their way down the side of the cliff, surer of their footing now that they were familiar with the terrain.

At the bottom, they went forward to the cave hand in hand, hot and sticky. When they were naked and they had neatly stacked their clothes on the rock, Amio took from the pocket of his discarded tunic a knife. Neferu looked at him, puzzled, and he smiled. He went over to the rock where Yussef had carved their names so many years previously and began laboriously an outline. She knew immediately what he was going to do. 'Amio, leave it until later. Let's swim first,' she said, anxious to feel the coolness of the water on her skin. Her stubborn husband refused to budge, however, until there was a legible outline engraved on the rock: 'Amio and Neferu'.

Afterwards, he threw down the knife on the sand and said, 'All right, let's go swimming now!'

They made off towards the water's edge. It was lapping softly on the shore and Neferu stood with her hand over her brow, looking out over the sea to the horizon. The sea was almost still. Here and there were small flecks of white as the foam of tiny waves came towards the shore. 'Come on!' Amio said impatiently, pulling her by the hand, and she followed him out. They swam around leisurely for a while, relishing the coolness and watching the little fishes that swam by in their myriads, on their way to who knows where. In the water they kissed and touched each other playfully. He tried to take her in the water, but her wet skin was so slippery that he could not keep her close enough to him and eventually they had to give up the attempt, laughing. He began to swim strongly towards the rock, and she followed after him at a slower pace.

On the rock they lay together, bodies glistening until the sun dried them off. Today it was so hot that they moved back into the water again and swam around until they were tired. When they reached the shallows, they found that the sun had moved sufficiently to give them a little shadow at the rock cave and they lay down there at the entrance, side by side. Neferu closed her eyes, but Amio cupped his hand over his brow and lay back quietly, observing the birds flying overhead.

In an effort to cut out the glare, he frowned to try and get a better look and it was then that he noticed a figure high up above them on the cliff. It was Pararameses. He guessed that either his mother or his uncle had sent the general, his best friend, to make sure they were safe. At first, he felt annoyed, but then a thought occurred to him. He looked quickly at Neferu to see whether she had noticed but her eyes were still shut. A small smile came to his face.

'Neferu!' he said in a lazy tone.

'Mmm?' she answered, not bothering to open her eyes.

'Neferu, I want you to make mad, passionate love to me,' he said urgently.

Neferu lifted her head to squint at him. 'But we just made love this morning,' she said.

'No,' he replied, unreasonably. 'I made love to you. Now I want you to make love to me.'

'Amio!' she protested mildly. 'We are both going to be exhausted soon.'

'Don't you want to?' he asked sulkily.

'Yes,' she conceded. 'But I don't know if I am up to it right at this moment, or if you are either.'

'Try!' Amio insisted. 'Take it as a challenge. If you do it well, I will be able to. See how good you are,' he said craftily. Unable to resist this challenge to her erotic talents, Neferu obligingly rolled over onto her right side and passed her fingers lightly over his abdomen to his groin. Amio lay back passively, and she began to massage him faster and faster until she had attained the desired effect and he was thoroughly aroused. Sometime during this experimental procedure Neferu began to forget its scientific nature and she became completely aroused herself, caressing him with her mouth again and again, until in a frenzy of abandon he suddenly threw himself onto her and took her quickly. When, finally, they rolled apart, Neferu said triumphantly. 'Well! I was pretty good, wasn't I?'

Amio laughed exultantly. 'Yes. I think we can say that you were pretty good!'

Amio lay back down on the sand and squinted through narrowed eyes at the figure on the ledge. He closed his eyes, satisfied that Pararameses had witnessed everything. It was only much later when Neferu was pregnant with their first child that Amio told her of this incident. He told her that he only half-understood at the time what made him act in this way. He told her it was some kind of defence that he hoped would curb any rumours that their marriage was not a love match, or that it had remained unconsummated. At the time it was a compulsion that his instincts told him he must do. He swore to her that he had not done it out of exhibitionism. He just wanted the whole world to know that she loved him truly. Although his thoughts and motives were chaotic, the outcome made him feel infinitely more secure. She had to forgive him because she understood the depth of his insecurity.

After a few moments Amio sat up. 'Race you to the rock!' he said. They stood up and ran clumsily across the burning sand down to the water. When they had finished their swim and they had carried out their highly personal cleansing ritual, they headed back for the shore. There was no sign of anyone and Amio deduced, correctly, that Pararameses was already on his way back to report that they were safe.

Getting dressed, Neferu began to worry about the time. She was afraid that their absence might come to the attention of the queen, in spite of their elaborate subterfuge. Amio seemed quite nonchalant about it. They were both feeling thirsty and hungry by now and they drank the contents of the hide water bottles and then they made for the cliff face. They climbed to the top, tired, hungry but happy. At the top they untethered the donkeys and set off back. Neferu knew that this memory of love would remain with her forever.

On the way back, Neferu pointed out the sign to Asruti, the name of the village where her uncle and aunt lived. Amio pulled the rein in. 'Shall we go and visit them now?' he asked impulsively.

Neferu shook her head. 'I think it is getting late already, and anyway the villagers would recognise you because of your distinctive looks,' she said gravely.

'Are you trying to tell me nicely that I am ugly?' He laughed good-naturedly.

'No,' she said with a smile. 'Your looks are very special! However, no one could mistake you for anyone else.'

His eyes twinkled and he leaned over to kiss her. 'You are very sweet,' he said. 'All right, let's go home.'

Refreshments had already been eaten when they arrived, hot, sweaty and slightly crumpled. Mereta rolled her eyes to them, which only made Amio laugh. Ay asked innocently of Neferu, 'Did you enjoy your swim, my dear?' Neferu blushed and replied that they had had a wonderful time. 'I believe you, my dear!' Ay chuckled.

The queen was rather cross with them. 'Going off alone like that! What if you had drowned or been attacked?'

Amio shrugged his shoulders and answered somewhat curtly. 'I wanted to be alone with my wife, Mother, and it doesn't seem to be possible here.' The queen appeared hurt at his tone and Neferu was silent. She hoped that they would not quarrel, because she felt sure that the queen would blame her for it if they did. The queen remarked, finally, that in her opinion the pharaoh must think of his position and in future he should take two guards at least with him! Amio thought about it and responded to the signalling from Neferu. 'Very well! On condition that they stay on top of the cliff out of sight.' The queen had to be content with this. It was obvious that she was loathe to argue with her son in front of the others and she let the matter rest there. Neferu wondered how soon their departure had been noticed and determined to ask Mereta. Mereta informed her, however, that it was only at refreshment time that her mother had been informed of their absence as Tiya had specifically asked her if she knew where they were. Neferu was relieved. Mereta also informed her that Pararameses had been despatched earlier to check that they were all right. Neferu assumed that he must have seen them and left immediately as she had not noticed anyone and Amio had said nothing. It did not occur to her that Pararameses might have witnessed their lovemaking.

For the rest of their holiday, whenever they went to the beach, they were accompanied by two guards at a discreet distance. As promised, they did remain out of sight, but it was not quite the same and Neferu always felt slightly restrained during their erotic play, wondering if the guards were secretly observing them. For her, Amio was first and foremost her man, to most other people he was the pharaoh. There were many times in her life when she would come to wonder if her life and marriage would have been happier if they had been able to escape the confines of the court and all its restrictions of protocol. To her dying day she bitterly blamed the court and his position for the loss of her happiness.

The following day, Ay and his entourage left for Thebes. According to him, someone had to hold the fort. At Neferu's earnest request the second wedding ceremony planned for On was cancelled. She told her husband that in the eyes of the Aten she was already his wife in every way. Amio was unconcerned but Tiya told her that it was a foolish move politically as it would have brought the people of Lower Egypt closer to the pharaoh, especially as he had married one of their own. She felt it was a lost opportunity, and in the end, she only agreed to scale down the occasion to make it a rapid blessing by the high priests of Amun-Re to appease them. The public banquets were to continue, albeit without the continuous presence of the young couple. Once again Neferu felt she had crossed swords with her mother-in-law, and she felt an unhappy dread that it might come back to haunt her in the future. Tiya was a little cool and distant with her son for a while afterwards, but Amio told her that it would pass, and she was not to worry. He appeared to be more concerned about her family who might be upset. She told him that when her family saw how happy she was, they would forgive her.

On his way back to Thebes, Ay was to call at On and make a private visit to her family to organise arrangements for their visit, which Neferu and Amio intended to spend at Grandma and Grandpa's. They only had another five days to spend at Rashid now. They were carefree days for Neferu and Amio, which she came to treasure in her memory. The two of them made a visit to Uncle Giorgios and his family, and although at first the elderly couple were a bit shy and tongue-tied, Amio proved adept at putting them at ease with his humorous manner and unaffected ways. It was not long before the two men were swapping tales over a goblet of wine and a game of backgammon. 'He seems very nice, dear!' her aunt whispered to her. 'Not at all what I expected a pharaoh to be like.' Neferu realised it was a great compliment. Her aunt had been particularly impressed by Amio's attempts to converse with them in Keftiu. She was totally won over when he told her he fully intended to become fluent in the language. When they left Alessandrina had hugged them both totally unselfconsciously and begged them to come again, just as she would have for any other member of the family. Amio was very satisfied with his conquest of them and Neferu felt it was important for him to know how ordinary people lived and thought. He was delighted and said he definitely wanted to come again.

The day before they were due to leave Rashid, Neferu asked Amio to come with her to visit the old villa for the last time. Somehow, she felt that she had neglected it in some way, and in doing so that she was somehow hurting her grandparents and the role they had played in her life. She wanted to say goodbye to it. To her surprise, Tiya asked if she could come along with them to see it. Neferu agreed, of course. Mereta decided to make up a fourth member of the party, for which Neferu was privately grateful. They set out at a sedate walk to the old villa.

Neferu smoothed her hands lovingly over the old walls of the living room, while Amio and the others continued their exploration. She stood alone with her eyes closed and could almost bring those other summers back to life in her imagination.

'Seeing ghosts from the past?' Amio said softly in her ear. She turned sharply, not having heard him enter.

She smiled at him and nodded her affirmation. 'They are here, all of them,' she said sadly.

He showed once again his immense sensitivity to her mood. 'We will come to stay every summer if we can, and we'll bring our children.' Neferu nodded and took his hand. She was glad that he had shared in her past in this way.

That evening was the last before their departure and Neferu became increasingly nostalgic. Amio seemed to echo her mood. So much had happened here and she wanted this time never to end and yet, in just a few short hours they would be gone. After dinner she and Amio went for a walk in the garden and they talked about each happy highlight of their holiday and the unhappy moments too, for now they only served to make the happy ones all the sweeter. She tried to impress each moment enduringly on her memory, together with its perfumes and ambience.

She remembered that first evening there when Yussef had stepped out of the bushes. Yes, she would always love him and keep a special place for him in her heart, but she was in love with her husband now and willingly committed to spending her life with him. She stopped pensively at the spot and Amio knew what she was thinking. Her face was in shadow, and he could not read it.

'Are you still angry with me?' he asked.

Neferu shook her head. 'I am just so sad for Yussef. He is a good man, and I will always keep a place for him in my heart. I just pray to the Aten that he will soon find someone he will love with all his heart and who will love him. You are my love and my life now.' Her voice was subdued. Amio pulled her close to him. It was not a passionate embrace, but one of solace.

'If it makes you feel any better,' he said softly. 'I believe that my need of you is greater than Yussef's.' Neferu was silent and he continued. 'Yussef is handsome, healthy, intelligent, charming and he has a good career too. He has never had cause to wonder whether he is liked for himself or his position. I loved you from the first moment I saw you. Your love for me was slow in growing but it has made my life sweet. My life would be empty without you. Being pharaoh would mean nothing to me.'

'Oh, Amio!' Neferu wept softly. 'I wish that you were not the pharaoh. We will always be surrounded by vast numbers of people, living out our most important moments almost in full view of them all the time. I want you to myself.'

Amio kissed her and said reassuringly, 'It won't be as bad as you think, Neferu, once you get used to it.' She nodded to please him but in her heart of hearts she did not really believe it. They continued their circuit of the garden, savouring for later memory the dusky romantic perfumes of the flowers and shrubs. When they went in, she went straight to her room, took Yussef's note and gave it to Amio. She knew he had been very upset because she had kept it. He gave it back to her without speaking. Slowly and symbolically, she tore up the papyrus. 'You did not have to do that, Neferu, but I feel happy that you have done it,' he stated quietly.

'I do not want any barriers to remain between us,' she told him.

'I understand that, my love,' he replied.

In spite of her sadness at leaving Rashid, the journey back upriver proved to be a very enjoyable one. Neferu and Amio were very relaxed as there was no longer any kind of strain between them. Their happiness glowed, giving off an aura of contentment around them which was almost palpable. Loving with this kind of intensity changed one's perspective of the world, Neferu realised. It was as if they were isolated from the rest of mankind, only seeing each other. She also noticed a heightened sensitivity to all matters pertaining to the senses in general. Colours seemed brighter than before, and the singing of the birds seemed sweeter to her ear. The touch of skin against skin and the quiver of his body when aroused made her feel that she must have been only half alive before. Now she felt vibrant and truly alive, as if for the first time.

As the boat approached On, Neferu began to feel apprehensive, wondering how the family would really react to Amio when they met him privately. She wanted them to like him, in spite of their hurt for Yussef. She wanted the opportunity for them both to spend some time at her former home without the accompaniment of any of the royal entourage and she was afraid that Tiya would not allow this to take place. Amio supported Neferu wholeheartedly in this desire to spend some time alone with his wife's family and Tiya was forced to give way on the issue. So it was that when *The Aten Gleams* finally docked at On, the grand queen and the entire royal entourage, with the exception of Amio and Neferu, went to take up their residence at the old royal palace in the centre, while the young couple travelled in a private, unmarked chariot to the home of Grandma and Grandpa. Such transport was not unusual and caused little stir. It would have caused much more stir if she had stayed at the home of her father and Shosen in the main thoroughfare on the busy port.

At first Grandma and Grandpa were a little stiff, just as Uncle Giorgios and Aunt Alessandrina had been. When Grandma curtsied, Amio lifted her hand to his lips and told her to treat him as one of them. He wanted no special care or attention. Switching to Keftiu, he said, 'I hope you will accept me into your family.'

Grandma was won over in one swift coup. She turned to Grandpa and said in Keftiu, 'There. You see, Nikis! He is a good boy. He speaks Keftiu.' Neferu laughed and told Amio what Grandma had said. Grandma looked at him carefully and said in her quaint Egyptian, 'If Neferu loves you, then we love you too!'

Tears came to Neferu's eyes, and she said to her grandmother in Keftiu, 'He is a good man, Grandma. He loves me and I love him. I want you to love him too.' Grandma was much smaller than Amio, but she stood on her tiptoes and kissed him on the cheek.

Grandpa was gruffer and not so easily won over, but he took his cue from Grandma. If she was prepared to accept him, then he would too. Neither Grandma nor Grandpa knew anything of court manners, but they were good, friendly people and Grandpa spoke excellent Egyptian. He patted Amio's arm and said gruffly, 'Look after our little girl, won't you?' Amio promised him firmly that he would. Aunt Lea who had been hovering nervously in the background, like a puppet on a string was ushered forward. Amio enveloped her in a bear hug and kissed her cheek and even Aunt Lea relaxed then. She commented to Grandma on how brown Neferu had become.

Grandma told Neferu that Demi was staying at his father's, so that she and Amio would be having his old room as it was bigger than Neferu's old room. She told Neferu that his leg had improved tremendously, and he was now walking quite well and was pain free. He still had a limp because of the leg being a little shorter and was using his stick still, until he was sure that it was completely safe to give it up. She would be able to see for herself when Demi arrived for dinner that evening. Neferu's grandparents were sensible, down to earth people, and it was difficult for them to associate their granddaughter's new husband with the faraway senior pharaoh. He was just a nice young man to them, perhaps not the son-in-law they had been expecting, but well-mannered and acceptable nonetheless. They were all soon chatting away without reserve. Grandma tried her best with her Egyptian, but managed to give Neferu a bit of embarrassment from time to time. Although she and Demi had often mimicked Grandma's mistakes in the past, behind her back, of course, Neferu did want Grandma to perform well in front of her new husband. Amio did not seem to mind Grandma's mistakes, though she noticed that his eyes twinkled now and again.

Aunt Lea was worse. In her efforts to be refined and not let the family down, she went a bit too far and Neferu just wished she would be her normal self. Fortunately, it was only Amio. If Tiya and the others had been there she would have been mortified. One of Amio's nicest characteristics was that there was no snobbery about him at all.

When Demi arrived later with her father and Shosen and their two eldest children, pandemonium broke out with everybody talking at once. Demi was keen to show off how well he could walk and to show them how well the scar had healed. The scar was still wide and purple, but Neferu was thrilled to see him mobile and pain free at last.

After dinner, Amio tactfully left Neferu alone with her father and they walked out to the garden.

'How are things with you, Neferu?' he asked hesitantly. 'You can tell me everything,' he added.

'I am very, very happy now, Father,' she said with a wry smile. 'All kinds of things have happened, about which it is probably best not to speak, but it has all turned out for the best. I love Amio and he loves me.' There was a pause before she asked carefully. 'What about Yussef? How is he?'

Her father was silent for a while. In the gloom she saw his expression of resignation and heard him sigh. 'He has taken it very badly,' he said at last. 'At first, I thought he would go crazy with fury and grief, but he is quieter now. He has become very cold and bitter. I am afraid for him,' he admitted, glancing at her. Neferu's heart plunged to her sandals. It was not what she had wanted to hear. She felt very badly about it and yet she knew that there was nothing she could possibly do about the situation. Anything she said or did would only make matters worse. Why had all this had to happen, she wondered.

She sighed a deep sigh. 'I will never ever forget Yussef, Father, or stop loving him. He will always have a special corner of my heart, but Amio is my husband now and I truly love him. He is a good man and when you come to know him better, you will appreciate that.' Her voice was sad.

Her father kissed her lightly. 'All is well then, Neferu. It grieves me to see Yussef suffering like this. He is like a son to me. I will do all I can to help him, you can be assured of that.'

Neferu was grateful. She knew she could depend on her father. 'Thank you, Father,' she said quietly.

Taking her arm, her father led her back to the house. 'Everyone will be wondering where we have got to,' he remarked.

Later on, when Neferu noticed her father talking quietly together with Amio in the corner, she guessed that they were discussing Yussef. The family made much of Neferu that night and she too hugged and kissed everyone constantly, aware that it might be a long time before an opportunity arose to be with them together privately in her old home again.

That night Amio and Neferu slept together under her grandparent's roof for the first time as man and wife. Amio told her that he had arranged via her father for Yussef to receive large commissions for jewellery from Thebes and from elsewhere to ensure that he would prosper in business on a grand scale, on condition that Yussef was never to know that he was behind this. In addition, Yussef was to be given an appointment as an administrator at the civil headquarters in Memphis. Neferu knew that this was Amio's way of trying to make up a little for the other man's unhappiness. She knew by intuition that it would not work but she loved him the more for trying, at least.

Amio did not initiate any lovemaking that night and she knew that in some obscure way that it was in penance for Yussef's pain. She was gradually coming to understand better her complicated husband. Neferu did not want him to feel guilty for loving her. It was not a crime. She tried to explain to him how she felt. He lay quite still. She sighed at her clumsy words, not knowing if he had understood what she was trying to say to him. Finally, she understood that the only way she could make it clear to him was by loving him in the way he understood best. She turned towards him and began to kiss his body all over. She took him in her mouth and caressed him with her tongue until he was aroused and then she moved up on him and took him. In the aftermath of their lovemaking, she felt his face wet with tears. 'What is it, my darling?' she said, suddenly distressed. 'Did I hurt you?'

He shook his head, and she felt her forehead wet where he pressed her face to his. 'No. You didn't hurt me, my dearest Neferu,' he whispered. 'I am crying because I feel so happy. It was so beautiful.'

Neferu lifted her face and kissed his eyes, tasting the saltiness of his tears. They clung together for a while and then slept.

Half an hour later or so, they woke up and Neferu decided that she would like to wash.

Facilities at Grandma's were nowhere near as fine as at the palace or the splendid villa in Rashid where they had been staying, nor were there any personal servants to supply all wants at a moment's notice. Fearful of waking the others, they crept to the washroom and began to wash as quickly as they could because the water was cold. The sudden shock of it damped down any possibilities of eroticism and they completed their ablutions at top speed. On the way back to bed, the sound of Grandpa's loud snores sent them off into a fit of the giggles, which they tried in vain to suppress, in case Grandma thought there were burglars in the house.

Once they were back in bed, Neferu murmured apologetically, 'The next time we come, darling, I will arrange for some hot water to be available.'

Amio answered magnanimously, 'If you promise to arrange a similar programme beforehand, then I promise to put up with the cold water.'

She began to laugh. 'Oh. I should think it could be arranged,' she said impishly.

He laughed in turn and pulled her to him. 'I love you,' he said drowsily. A few minutes later only the sound of their deep and regular breathing could be heard in the room.

Neferu and Amio spent the following morning quietly with the family and, after lunch, they set off for the old palace to rejoin the others. This was the worst time for Neferu, and she wept openly to leave behind these people whom she loved so much. 'I wish that the court could be at Memphis, like in the days of the ancient pharaohs,' she said bitterly to Amio. He tried to comfort her, but he knew how deeply she loved this part of Egypt. Neferu never lost her deep yearning to go 'home' to Lower Egypt. Like his uncle, by whom he had been well-taught, he knew that in some future time, the north would once again re-assert its importance as the centre of life in the country of the Two Lands. Like his uncle, he also knew that it was a politically explosive issue while the Kap was predominantly led by generals who were primarily Nubian in origin. He told her that he and his uncle had a dream of building a new city sometime, which would be situated halfway between Thebes and Memphis. It would have been built already if they had been able to resolve the problems of logistics. Neferu listened with interest. It caught her imagination. It would not give her what she wanted but it was a compromise and the fact that it would give her an escape from the hot-house atmosphere of Thebes ensured that any such plan would receive her rapturous support. Thus, it was that the seeds of the new city 'Horizon of the Aten' were sown.

At the old palace, they met up with the rest of the royal family and retired to rest before attending the official banquet that night for the dignitaries of Memphis. That night it was a different Neferu who carried out her duties from the unhappy Neferu who had presided over the banquet on their outgoing journey to Rashid. Now the restraints of protocol were no longer fearful for her. Her newfound confidence was obvious to everyone. Maatnofret was delighted and Neferu felt that Tiya felt her nose ever so slightly put out of joint. She sensed that this could lead to trouble that she did not want, but she decided that she could not let herself be put out by such factors anymore. She had not asked or planned for this position. She had been thrown into it. Maatnofret was right. Let it all go as the Aten willed. Neferu was powered by the strength of her love for Amio and saw it all in a different light now. She was no longer a girl, but a woman, and she had to follow her man back to his home. Home is where the heart is, they say, and her heart was there wherever Amio was.

CHAPTER 20

Thebes became Neferu's place of permanent residence now, but although it was a bustling and affluent city, Neferu never became attached to it or came to feel it was her home. Thebes was the domain of Tiya and Neferu always felt she was a guest there.

The first two decans after their return to Thebes from Rashid were a kind of honeymoon period for Neferu and Amio. Ay and Tiya kept a tight grip on the reins of power and Amio seemed happy to relinquish his duties to them. In truth, Neferu was grateful to them for this. No demands of an onerous nature were made upon her, so that she felt that there was no real cause for complaint. She was able to spend as much time with Amio as their passion demanded. In return, their presence was demanded at certain formal functions. One of these was the celebration of Nefertiti as official queen to Amenophis IV. Ay and Tiya organised the whole ceremony and Neferu and Amio performed their roles as previsaged. For the first time she wore the blue and gold crown of Upper and Lower Egypt in public, before a large audience of foreign guests and of her own people. It seemed to crystallise the situation for her. She was no longer a private person; she had become the property of Egypt. It was a high price to pay for the man she loved, but in the end, she considered he was worth it.

At court, Neferu became aware from the very beginning that she was a constant source of gossip. The circumstances preceding their marriage were common knowledge now and continued to be whispered around the court. She became aware that she was frequently the target of surreptitious glances and sudden turnings of heads. It came to her knowledge that certain of the court believed that she was an opportunist who had taken advantage of the young pharaoh's affection for her. On hearing this gossip Neferu was torn between fury and self-pity. She told herself that she did not care what people thought of her, but this particular item cut her deeply, and she knew there was no way she could defend herself from it all.

As soon as a suitable moment occurred Neferu told Amio, but he calmly brushed aside her anger, telling her not to worry about it. 'I know what is going on,' he told her. 'I hear all the rumours that go around this place, and I happen to know for sure that this one is not true and so if it does not worry me nor should it worry you.' He drew her to him and, as usual in his embrace, she forgot the irritations of the court and its superficialities.

At the beginning of the fourth decan after their return to Thebes, Neferu was violently unwell and Amio, very concerned, insisted upon the court physician attending her. The doctor told her that he suspected pregnancy was the cause of her sickness, but it was still too early to tell for sure. Tiya was very happy with this news, but Neferu was not quite so pleased, as she did not want to share her new husband with a child just yet.

Later in the morning Neferu's condition improved and she joined her husband and Pararameses on the terrace where they were taking light refreshments together. They both rose as she came towards them and Amio, pleased to note that she looked much better, ushered her towards the table and pulled forward a chair for her beside him. He turned to Pararameses and said, 'Poor Neferu was indisposed this morning, but she is feeling much better now.' Pararameses looked at her curiously. He and Amio were discussing a forthcoming chariot race that was the talk of the whole of Thebes. It was a bi-annual event and competitors came long distances to take part in it. The race itself was part of a wider sporting event. Amio had earlier told Neferu that he had invited her family and included Yussef in the invitation. Neferu had been wholly uncertain whether or not this was a good thing in the circumstances, but Amio was keen to normalise his relationship with Yussef and he wanted the Keftiu man to accept the situation once and for all. He seemed to believe that Yussef would acquiesce, and that detente between them was a possibility.

It appeared from the information passed to Ay from his information gatherers that Yussef believed Neferu did not love Amio, and that their marriage was unconsummated. Indeed, Yussef had also publicly made a statement doubting Amio's ability to exercise his conjugal rights. Amio had discussed these things with Pararameses, and he wanted his friend to have a private discussion with Yussef to impress upon him that his beliefs were unrealistic. 'Yes,' Amio had told him. 'It is time to disenchant him on that score. My marriage is a true marriage. My deformities have never hindered me on that score,' he had declared with a laugh before continuing. 'I suppose that the rumours will continue until Neferu becomes pregnant and is delivered of our child.' Pararameses had been silent for a moment, wondering at Amio's frankness on the subject.

He cleared his throat before asking delicately. 'Is the queen pregnant, do you think?'

Amio had shrugged his shoulders. 'I don't know, but I almost hope not. I don't want to share Neferu with anyone, even my own child, for the moment. I want to have her undivided attention. My marriage is supremely happy, Rameses,' he had said with a smile. Pararameses had nodded sagely. Now, as Neferu approached them, Pararameses observed her closely, wondering if her indisposition was the consequence of an early pregnancy. For Amio's sake he hoped so, it would squash many rumours.

Neferu ate a hearty lunch, showing no signs of her earlier nausea. Whatever had been the cause of her malady, it now seemed to have disappeared. The three of them enjoyed a light-hearted conversation over lunch until Pararameses left to brief some of his senior officers about major military manoeuvres soon to take place. By now Neferu was aware of the extent of the trust between her husband and the general. They had grown up together and they had learned how to ride together as Pararameses' father was captain of the horse guard and one of Tuthmosis' most trusted officers of the Kap. Neferu herself felt a natural liking for Amio's best friend, which was fortunate. She in return sensed a natural respect and liking towards herself from the young general, although he was not a naturally social personality like her husband. She sensed that both men were keenly looking forward to the competition to take place in a few decans. Indeed, it seemed to be becoming the only subject of conversation at court these days, which she found a little tedious. Even many of the ladies appeared to be in a state of excitement about the forthcoming event. Neferu supposed that she would find out what the attraction was on the day.

By the time that the great competition was upon them, Neferu knew for certain that she was pregnant. The morning sickness was an unfortunate daily reality that the doctor had informed her would soon pass. She could not wait for the day. In spite of his words to the contrary, Amio was delighted by the knowledge of the coming child.

Within the royal family itself, Neferu noticed that her position had become pivotally different, and she became the recipient of constant care, advice and attention. Tiya began to take a much closer interest in her welfare than before and Neferu knew beyond doubt that this interest was not so much for her benefit but for the child within her, which Tiya was hoping would be the son to continue the dynasty of power. To Tiya she was the producer of the future pharaoh.

Neferu felt a little irked by all this excess of attention her pregnancy had stimulated. The grand queen invariably referred to her unborn child as 'he', and names were discussed with great interest. Mereta held a gold medallion over her abdomen and attempted to determine the sex of the unborn child. The outcome of this dubious experiment was said to be positive. The baby was definitely going to be a boy. Amio professed not to be unduly interested in whether the child was male or female, as he intended to have many more. Neferu herself worried that her child, male or female, would be healthy. She was afraid that it could inherit Amio's pathological bone condition, especially when Tiya told her that Amio's limbs had been perfectly straight until the age of three or four. She prayed nightly to the Aten that her child would be perfectly normal.

When the day of the chariot race came there was much excitement and they all left early for the sports arena, which had been set up outside the city on the edge of the desert where the ground was rock hard. For the nobles and their wives, seating had been arranged in tiers along the length of a wide strip of hard track. Across the track, which was about seventy metres wide, there were the peddlers and the purveyors of refreshments and the sports equipment to be used in the archery contests. The cooler season had begun but it was still very hot, and the spectators were protected from the glare by an overhead cotton awning fastened down with poles. It afforded them some shade at least. When the royal family arrived, the place was already crowded. They were led away to their special seats in the centre of the seating system. The atmosphere was one of excitement and noisy conversation.

Amio and Pararameses were both entered in the archery contests and for the chariot race. His physical condition precluded him from taking part in the speed and strength sports such as running and wrestling so that his ambition for those events he did enter was all the greater. He had been practising for decans and his determination to win was intense. Neferu could not help feeling an unease at this competitive streak in him. She pointed out to him that it was his physical restrictions that had enabled him to develop his sensitivity to others, which was one of the characteristics about him which had first attracted her to him. He had such a naturally aggressive nature that if he had had no weaknesses, his impulsiveness and temper might have resulted in a far less sympathetic character. Amio smiled at her fancifulness, as he called it, and went on practising. Neferu pondered on the workings of the Aten. It was true that Amio had a natural sense of justice and he had learned to curb some of his impulses to act precipitously and Neferu felt sure that it was as a result of his deformities that he had developed some of the finer points of his nature. What Amio had always seen as a curse may have worked to round out his personality in a positive way.

His enthusiasm for the games was matched by that of the other participants and there had been much placing of wagers on the outcome of each event. The whole of Thebes seemed to be present. People had come by chariot, horseback, donkey or on foot and they lined both sides of the track. Many of them were young men using the public holiday to follow their interest in sport. For the lucky few, these games were an opportunity to gain fame and fortune. The poor of the city were just as interested as their more illustrious fellow citizens and, in truth, on foot it was not a long distance from the town to the games' arena.

As soon as Neferu and Amio were seated, she began to look around for her father and Yussef, whom, she knew, had accepted the invitations sent to them by Ay. Much to her disappointment, they had elected to lodge with Athanasios and Narida Charalambides, rather than at Malkata. She guessed it was her father's way of trying to dilute what might have been a very emotionally fraught situation between Yussef and Amio. She had tried to explain this to Amio, but she knew he had felt slighted by her father's decision to some extent. Now as she looked around, she could not see them and supposed that they had not yet arrived.

Neferu and Amio were seated about four rows back from the front with Mutnedjmet, Mereta, Pararameses and his fiancée and Horemheb, Pararameses senior adjutant, whom Neferu sensed was more than slightly interested in the daughter of the grand vizier. Neferu noticed secretive glances passing between the two and smiled. Behind them sat Tiya and the senior pharaoh, Ay and Teya and Archduke Tuthmosis and his family. Amio's events were not until the later afternoon, but he was keen to watch all the morning's events too and they had an excellent view of the programme from their vantage position. They settled down to watch the opening dancing and juggling programme.

Halfway through the dancing her father and Yussef arrived with the Charalambides. Neferu waved to them, and the group bowed before being escorted to their seats just across the aisle from Amio and herself and slightly behind them. Neferu realised that Yussef must have a clear and direct view of herself and her husband, but after the initial greetings she could not turn round to look at them. She was under the eagle eye of the queen, pharaoh, her father, and the rest of the court, and she knew they were alert to her every reaction. Neferu felt very nervous. She knew that Amio wanted everything smoothed over. Because he was happy, he wanted everyone else to be happy, and she felt that for once his sensitivity left a lot to be desired. His desire to openly display his conquest of her heart had overcome his good sense. She knew Yussef better than he did, and she knew that much too little time had elapsed for such experiments in diplomacy as this.

Throughout the morning programme, Neferu could feel Yussef's eyes boring into her and willing her to turn around. It made her stiff and uncomfortable, but she made great efforts to appear casual and relaxed as she chatted to other members of the entourage around her. Amio was in high spirits, his adrenaline flowing for the afternoon's events. He made no attempt to disguise his affection for her, putting his arm round her shoulders and even kissing her. His mother openly rebuked him in a low voice, shocked by his public display of affection. Amio laughed good-naturedly, making no attempt to restrain himself. The queen seemed irritated but said nothing further. Neferu was quiet. She felt that the queen was blaming her in some way for Amio's exuberance.

The finale for the morning, after the wrestling, was a daring juggling duo on horseback. Neferu had never seen anything like it before and was thrilled by their daring leaps and turns as they stood on the backs of the horses. The spectators rose and watched as the royal family departed down to the front of the arena, where their chariots and carriages were waiting. Amio and Neferu travelled back in a carriage with Tiya and the grand vizier. Amio took Neferu's hand and kissed her fingers. Ay smiled indulgently but the queen looked studiously away. Unabashed, Amio cried, 'Mother! Before heaven, I cannot hide my happiness. Do not begrudge it to me.'

Tiya turned towards him and her look softened. 'I do not begrudge you your happiness, my son. I merely ask that you don't display it so openly.'

Amio smiled at Neferu before replying, 'I suppose that you are right. It seems mean to flaunt my treasure when so few others can have experienced anything so profound.'

To which remark the cynical Ay replied, 'Why do the young always think that they have invented love for the very first time?' The queen smiled at this and nothing more was said on the subject.

The games were the major subject of conversation during lunch in the state banquet hall, with lively arguments going on all around regarding the various skills displayed and who really was likely to win the various afternoon events. Vasilios, Yussef and the Charalambides were seated at the second table and Narida, at least, appeared to be in great good humour. Neferu noticed that Yussef was making expansive conversation with Anula and the girl was laughing, genuinely charmed. She noticed that Anula's eyes strayed often to the handsome face of Yussef when he was in conversation with her father or Athanasios. At one stage he looked across and for a moment their eyes met. His were unsmiling. He nodded slightly and turned away to Anula, who was trying to hold his attention. Anula was definitely more than interested in Yussef, Neferu thought.

When lunch was over and Tiya withdrew to the withdrawing room and Neferu with her, Anula and Narida were amongst the lady guests invited to attend the short reception. Narida plainly did not quite know how to treat Neferu. The sudden change in status had left her confused. Tiya, however, left her in no doubt and standing at Neferu's side, she commented to Narida, 'I hear that you are well acquainted with Queen Nefertiti.'

In front of the formidable grand queen, Narida was shocked into formality. 'Yes,' she replied quickly. 'Her Majesty and I are acquainted previously.' Neferu felt a mad desire to giggle but bit the insides of her cheeks painfully to suppress the tendency. She really could not blame Narida, she thought. From country bumpkin to queen in half a year, it was all too much for herself, never mind Narida.

When the men entered, Neferu was given no chance to speak alone with either her father or Yussef. The subject of conversation in the group was limited to who was or was not the most talented wrestler or acrobat. In the privacy of their bedroom Neferu told Amio of her uncomfortable feelings about Yussef and asked him not to be too open in his affectionate displays, as she did not want to hurt her childhood friend unnecessarily. Amio nodded thoughtfully and admitted that he had been partially motivated by jealousy and a desire to show Yussef that Neferu was his and completely his. Neferu nodded. She could understand this, though again she reminded him that his jealousy was without foundation. He drew her towards him and said, 'Prove it!' She responded to his touch as she always did and so it was rather later before they fell asleep.

Siesta was short that day and Maatnofret woke them earlier than usual so that Amio could practise his archery in the garden. Neferu got up more slowly and when she was barely ready, Amio entered to give her a quick kiss before leaving for the games' arena with Pararameses. She wished him luck and promised not to take her eyes off him.

Later, as she sat in the carriage with the queen and Ay and Teya, she felt more relaxed than she had in the morning. She had not had time to talk to her father alone and she thought it best not to even try to talk to Yussef alone, but she wished an opportunity would arise whereby perhaps all four of them, herself, Amio, her father and Yussef, could sit and chat amicably together. To make a superficial peace at least. She knew that this was what her father was hoping for, and it was also what she wanted. Destiny was to lift the matter out of her hands, once more.

They were a little late arriving back at the arena and they made their way to their seats immediately. Neferu waved to her father and Yussef. She surmised that there would be little chance of speaking with them before the evening's entertainments. Neferu sat down next to Mereta and looked out for her husband. She recognised his distinctive cloak in the crowd, although his back was turned towards her.

There were two archery contests and Amio was in both. The first contest involved piercing a small article thrown into the air and it was won by a northern nobleman from Memphis. Amio came second. She knew that he would be very annoyed with himself over that. In the bull's eye contest, there were ten contestants and in the first stage all of them did well and passed on to the second stage. After the second stage there were four contestants left; Amio, Pararameses, a nobleman from Kush and a military officer, recently arrived back in Thebes after serving a tour of duty over the eastern border.

All the four contestants passed to the third stage of the contest and the pace started to heat up. This was the most difficult part and involved aiming from a chariot moving at speed towards a painted board. Amio had told her that it was very easy to release the arrow just too late and if the chariot had passed the line, the bowman was automatically disqualified. Pararameses shot first and just missed the bullseye by a fraction. It was an excellent shot and there was a great 'Ooh!' from the crowd. The nobleman from Kush was next and he hit the board but with a wider aim than that of Pararameses. Next was Amio and Neferu was on tenterhooks. He took off his cloak and the chariot started. Involuntarily, Neferu said, 'Please let him win!' inside her head. As the chariot neared at speed, she could hardly bear to look but finally the arrow flew and there was tumultuous applause from the family behind her as the arrow was definitely inside the bullseye area. She watched as his chariot came to a stop and he jumped out, impatient to see his result. The fourth contestant's chariot set off and began to near the line. His arrow flew and it too entered the bullseye. It was a very close contest. Amio won it by a matter of millimetres, his arrow being more centrally placed in the bullseye than those of the others. He looked towards her place in the stand, and she smiled her pleasure at his victory. She could see that he was jubilant.

There was to be a display of acrobatics before the day's main event, which was a gruelling chariot race, and Amio came to sit with her for a while in the stand. All the family were congratulating him on the recent victory, but already his mind had turned to the forthcoming race. He explained to Neferu that the most important thing was to get into the lead right away at the start because it would be extremely difficult to overtake later in that narrow field. After a while, he and Pararameses got up to go over to where the grooms were doing last minute checks on both the horses and the chariots.

To Neferu, the number of chariots taking part seemed excessive for the width of the track. She began to feel a certain unease about it. When the chariots were lined up, side by side, she could not help noticing that only about one metre of space existed between the wheels of the chariots. She thought it was dangerously little and mentioned so to Mereta. Ay overheard her and told her.

'Don't worry! This race is always popular and once they start, the fast ones get away quickly. There is much more space for the others then, you'll see!'

At one point, before the race began, she turned to look at her father and Yussef. They were both looking at her. She smiled at them and noted with relief that Yussef also returned her smile. The crowd began to quieten as if in anticipation and she turned back to look at the track where all the chariots were now lined up. Amio was on the far side of the track, second in line. Pararameses was on the near side of the track fourth in line and closer to Neferu. The starting point was about fifty metres down the track to her right and Neferu could see everyone clearly. The course was an oval shape and the chariots had to complete three circuits.

The blast of a trumpet signalled the start of the race and Neferu watched Amio closely as he pulled away. He obtained a good start as he had hoped for, and the chariots flashed by. By the end of the first circuit three of the chariots came round together; one of them was Amio's, easily distinguishable by its purple drapes. People were standing now, excitedly shouting encouragement to the various participants, and the atmosphere was charged. The second circuit was completed and Amio was now clearly in the lead. Neferu rose to her feet to watch as he went by and after that everything happened as if in slow motion. The horse up front stumbled slightly, kicking up a stone which caught Amio on the left temple, knocking him out. She saw him fall sideways over the side of the chariot and land on the ground. He lay motionless. Afterwards they told her that she screamed 'No' loudly and then shouting 'Amio, Amio!' she leapt forwards down to the barrier and out onto the track towards him. She had a vague recollection of chariots going by but her only thought was to reach him. She was afraid that he was dead. There were people round him now and when she got to him, she pushed them away. They had straightened his body out and she knelt down in the dust, the tears streaming down her face. At that moment he opened his eyes and saw her.

'I'm all right, Neferu!' he said.

'I thought you were dead.' She was sobbing hysterically now. He sat up, rubbing his head, which now had an enormous bump on it. He took her face in his hands and began to wipe the tears away, saying soothingly, 'It's all right, my darling, it's all right.' There was quite a crowd around them by then, but it silently parted to allow Tiya access to them. She appeared very pale and shaken, and after ascertaining that the situation was not the disaster she had feared, she called for her carriage immediately. Amio rose to his feet with no seeming ill effects and Neferu visibly calmed down now that he was so obviously in command of his senses.

In the carriage she clung to her husband. Amio could not remember exactly what had happened but seemed no more than shaken by his accident, apart from the deep blue lump on his temple. Neferu felt enormous relief. Tiya was still ashen in colour but seemed to have recovered her composure. She was obviously shocked by what had happened.

During their journey, Tiya told Neferu that she too had almost been killed when she had run out onto the track. An oncoming chariot had had to swerve violently in order to avoid her and, in doing so, it had narrowly missed crashing into another chariot to its left. The grand queen said she had never been so frightened in her life, watching all the chariots coming up the track, unable to pull up in time. In Tiya's opinion it was nothing short of a miracle that Neferu was still alive. Neferu had noticed none of it. Tiya said she thought she had lost her son, her daughter-in-law and her grandchild all at the same time. No wonder she had been so ashen, Neferu thought, for once feeling almost sorry for the queen.

Once they had arrived at Malkata, Tiya insisted upon sending for the court physician and packed them both off to bed. The doctor came and pronounced both of them fit but ordered that Neferu should stay in bed for the rest of the day. Neferu protested that she felt fine and wished to be present for the dinner in the evening, or to have her father brought to her at least. Tiya agreed that her father should be brought to visit. Amio was also told to rest and to take it easy for a couple of days. He was more worried about Neferu than himself. 'I don't want you to lose the baby,' he told her.

Neferu shook her head. 'I don't feel ill at all,' she said. 'I don't know what I would have done if you had died.' She shuddered, remembering again the scene as it had passed before her eyes.

'I could never die as long as you love me,' he said tenderly. 'You could have been killed yourself. That was a very foolish thing to do.'

She was quiet now as the shock began to recede. She began to feel sleepy. She looked at him. 'What are you thinking of?' she inquired.

'I would have won,' he said. 'I was first!'

'Amio,' she said crossly. 'Just be glad that you are in one piece.'

He turned onto his side, looking down at her. 'I am, I am,' he replied. 'I was only joking!' He kissed her and then lay quietly beside her. When the queen and the doctor looked in on them sometime later, they were both fast asleep, apparently none the worse for wear.

By the evening the pair of them appeared to be completely recovered from the events of the afternoon and Neferu's father was brought to their apartment. He hugged her tightly. 'You gave me such a fright today, Neferu,' he told her. 'I didn't know until afterwards that you are expecting a baby. The queen told me,' he continued in answer to her questioning look.

'Where is Yussef?' she asked.

Her father looked at Amio before replying. 'He waited until he knew you were both safe and then he returned with Athanasios. He felt it best that you never see each other again. I told him that you are with child.'

Neferu sighed. 'I suppose it is for the best,' she said sadly. 'Oh, Father. You do understand, don't you, that I never wanted to hurt Yussef in any way?' Vassiliou nodded sympathetically. 'I still love Yussef in my own way, Father. I won't ever forget all that he has meant to me, and I know that none of this could have happened without the will of the Aten. I think he meant me to marry Amio and I have come to love him so much that if he had died today, then there would have been nothing left for me either.' Neferu paused and he saw there were tears in her eyes. 'I wish that Amio was not pharaoh and that we were an ordinary family. I hate having to live my life in front of a continual audience, most of whom do not care one iota for me nor I for them. It is now the price I must pay to be with the man I love. I loved my life with you all in On so much. I wish I could have everything, but I cannot.' Her impassioned speech ended on a note of desperation. Her father sighed heavily. Amio stood apart, listening closely but not interrupting in any way.

Vassiliou looked at him before replying. 'Amio loves you and will be a good husband, I know,' he stated quietly. 'What has happened is not anyone's fault. Love comes without our expecting it and it cannot be measured. My grandchild needs a serene mother so do not let yourself become upset like this. Perhaps you and Amio will come to On now and again to visit me and the rest of the family, eh?'

He hugged her as he said this and tried to speak lightly.

Amio came forward. 'We will come and see you as often as we can at On,' he said to Vassiliou. He pulled his wife closely to him and put an arm around Vassiliou's shoulders. 'When we come to see you all, we will come quietly as private people with just a few servants so that we can be together as a family,' he promised.

Neferu's father nodded. 'I would appreciate that, Amio. You are my son-in-law now and the father of my grandchild and that is how I will think of you. The court life is not for me, I'm afraid.'

Amio smiled. 'I understand,' he said simply.

'I must go now,' Vassiliou said. 'Yussef is alone now, and he is very upset. It is not good for him to be left alone now too much.'

Neferu nodded and hugged her father again before he left. When he had gone, she leaned against her husband and said sombrely. 'Life is so complicated isn't it, Amio?'

'Yes,' he replied.

She looked up at him. 'We have a duty to love each other steadfastly to the end of our lives now, in order to make all the hurt we have caused to others worthwhile,' she said this firmly.

'What strange things you say, Neferu!' he answered, brushing her forehead with his lips. 'Come on, let's go to meet the others and show them that we are still alive and well.'

The following day when Pararameses came to give his report of the morning, Amio asked him about the previous day. 'Did I make an awful fool of myself?' he asked with slight embarrassment.

'Well, I think the eyes of the crowd were all focused on Nefertiti. She almost got herself killed. I myself had to swerve violently in order to avoid running over her. If anyone doubted her love for you before, there can be no doubts now,' he said drily.

'Perhaps the events of yesterday did accomplish something then, after all,' replied Amio thoughtfully.

'I think the same results could have been obtained in a little less dramatic fashion,' Rameses said again in the same dry tone.

Amio laughed. 'Yes. Perhaps it was all rather overdone.'

Soon after the day of the games, Tiya found out that she was pregnant too. The father of the baby was, without doubt, Archduke Tuthmosis. In spite of her age, the grand queen remained well and seemed to take her pregnancy into little account when planning the state functions. Only later in the pregnancy, when her figure was already thickened and cumbersome, did she retire from public. Tiya gave birth early at thirty-six weeks to a little girl whom she called Baketaten. In spite of her small size, Baketaten thrived and was a strong baby.

CHAPTER 21

The months that followed were a time of great personal happiness for Neferu and Amio. To a great extent Neferu was able to forget the court and the constant flow of people in and out of it. She realised that she would never belong there. To Ay and Tiya, she was a mere doll who made the younger pharaoh happy. She performed a function, and as such she was useful, even important, but none of them cared who she really was, what she really thought. At this stage of her life Neferu had not yet come to resent this. She was even grateful to Tiya and Ay, who so assiduously kept the reins of power firmly in hand and the practical details of court life turning over smoothly.

Neferu wanted to concentrate on her new husband and the child they were going to have. Amio was a constant source of delight to her. She wanted to know everything about him and bombarded him with questions. He too was eager to explore her mind. As her abdomen swelled, they spent many happy hours in contemplation of this product of their union. Amio would put his ear to her abdomen and listen to the swishing sound of the baby's movements or feel them with his hand. She felt they were locked away in a magic time where only they really existed. Her only real worry was that she had begun to understand that her husband was subject to periodic fevers and strange limb pains. He always tried to shrug them off, but they worried her. Sometimes his knees would become swollen, or his elbow would feel hot to the touch. When this happened, the court physician would prescribe one of his herbal potions and very often they did seem to help. Neferu worried, nevertheless, about these sporadic inflammations. They brought home to her the fragility of life and of their happiness. She took comfort from the fact that Amio had told her that these attacks were far less frequent than in previous years. Every night she prayed to the Aten for his life.

The time came for Neferu to give birth and she was delivered of a normal, healthy baby daughter who was perfect in every respect. They named her after Mereta but gave her the name of Neferu's god, the Aten. Neferu and Amio were overjoyed with Meretaten.

She was the crown to their first year of marriage. If the family were disappointed by the birth of a girl, contrary to the boy they had been hoping for, they held it in check. After all, there was always next time. As was the tradition, the pharaoh had been present to witness the birth of his child, and was witness to its right to inherit.

Meretaten was universally pronounced to be a beautiful baby. According to Tiya she showed the elongated skull of her father's family and the pale skin of her mother. Her eyes were large and almond shaped, and her tiny pink lips had the definite full, slightly turned down shape of her grandmother, Tiya herself. Neferu felt proudly that she was the perfect blend of both their best characteristics. Neferu fed the baby herself and the little girl thrived. She was the happy centre of a large circle of admiring family, not the least of whom was the young Prince Smenkhenre.

Tiya glossed over her disappointment at the sex of her grandchild easily. She was genuinely thrilled by her first grandchild, who was only a few weeks younger than her own Baketaten. After the birth of her daughter, relations between the grand queen and Neferu warmed considerably. From the time of the events of the fateful games' day, the grand queen had become convinced of the authenticity of Neferu's love for her son and she had made more of an effort to win the friendship of the Keftiu girl.

Previously Neferu would occasionally become very annoyed by what she perceived as an undervaluation of her intelligence by Tiya and sometimes she wondered whether Tiya felt threatened by the depths of Amio's love for his wife. Now and again, she had discerned a little jealousy on the older woman's attitude. Perhaps she had been afraid that Neferu sought to assert political power at her expense. If so, she must have gradually come to realise that Neferu had no interest in the affairs of state. Neferu's family life was all important to her and as much as possible she tried to maintain a semblance of private life for her husband and child. As the months passed Tiya came to realise that Neferu was not a threat to her control of state affairs. Later on still, she would come to castigate Neferu for her lack of political enthusiasm and to blame her for Amio's increasing indifference to Theban politics. For the present, Tiya and Ay effectively continued to administer Egypt and Neferu's own existence was more than adequately filled by her beloved husband and child.

The functioning of family relationships at the Malkata palace never ceased to amaze Neferu. They were quite unlike anything she had been used to before. First of all, there was the role of the elder pharaoh, Amenophis III. He took less and less of a part in the administration of his realm and seemed more than happy that this should be so. It was very rare during the years that Neferu was acquainted with him for him to instigate actively any policy protocol at all. He seemed to have implicit faith in both Ay and Tiya, and they in turn did all they could to smooth all obstacles from his path and assure him a comfortable existence. His obvious and frequent amorous adventures seemed to be completely accepted by Tiya and she showed no jealousy. The two were more like brother and sister than husband and wife.

In spite of Amenophis III's physical decline, his sexual prowess was not in doubt, and it was widely known that he had a predilection for women with very ample breasts but otherwise slender proportions and Tiya must have witnessed many such rivals as her husband's harem contained ninety or more concubines of several races.

Although Neferu's initial acquaintanceship with the elder pharaoh had not been as fortuitous as it might have been, he appeared to have completely forgotten the incident and forever afterwards displayed great friendliness and politeness. In spite of this, Neferu remained a little aloof from him. He could be very temperamental and irritable, and she was unable to decide whether this was due to the opium to which he was addicted or whether it was a natural aspect of his personality.

Twenty months after the birth of Meretaten, Neferu gave birth to her second child, also a daughter, whom she called Meketaten. This time, murmurs of disappointment mingled with the congratulations which accompanied the birth. Neferu felt she had failed Amio in not producing a son for him. She knew that he was disappointed, and she was distressed, but he was more concerned over her distress than his own and therefore he was careful not to show it.

The marriage continued to blossom, and their happiness was supreme, in spite of the fact that Neferu had never really settled down in Thebes and always felt herself a guest in what was essentially Tiya's domain. While Neferu was still breast-feeding Meketaten, she became pregnant for the third time. It was a difficult pregnancy, possibly because she had not fully recovered from the birth of her second child, and she suffered greatly from nausea throughout the first trimester. She lost a lot of weight and also became very tired and lethargic. Psychologically she became obsessed with the need to produce the son for whom the whole court was waiting. She was afraid of failing yet again.

By now, Amio had developed enthusiastic, though not fully formulated plans for the building of a new city, which would be situated halfway between Thebes and Memphis. It was important to his concept of the new city that it be built on virgin soil and be dedicated to the one, sole god of creation, the Aten. For support in this enterprise, he had

Ay and his grandfather, Yuya. Yuya had moved back to Malkata on the death of his wife Tuya, a few weeks after the birth of Meketaten. In spite of his advanced age, he was very fit and was a frequent visitor to the apartments and Amio and Neferu. The new city had long been a dream of his and Ay's too. With both her father and her brother, as well as her son, behind the idea, it had not been difficult to enlist the support of Tiya. Ay's interest in the project was primarily a political one. He was not a religious man and showed no enthusiasm for the religious base of the building projects. In reality, he worried about this aspect as he was afraid of irritating the priests of Amun-Re. He was hoping that the new city, to be called Akhetaten, Horizon of the Aten, would act as a kind of halfway house so that gradually the centre of power could be shifted imperceptibly away from the hot south with its lack of resources back eventually to the historical northern capital based at Memphis.

The plan was to replace some of the retiring Nubian generals with younger northern officers such as the young Horemheb, whose antipathy to such a return was minimal. He pressured Amio to ensure that all such moves were to be taken with the utmost discretion and diplomacy. They were part Nubian through Tuya, whose brothers were retired generals of the Kap, and he hoped that these blood ties would serve to strengthen their hand. Although he hoped it could be accomplished faster, the three men discussed a possible time period of twenty-five years to accomplish such a transfer of power. It was envisaged that the transition would be painless.

Amio was as much swayed by Neferu's ideas in this as in his uncle's and his grandfather's concepts. The old Hebrew felt he had an ally in Neferu and was a source of instruction in the tenets of his beliefs. He did his best to strengthen her faith and support her when she was depressed and tired during her pregnancy. In this she also had the unfailing support of Maatnofret, whom she considered her very best friend and confidante.

Support generally for the building of the new city was poor amongst the establishment. Partly this was because there was a fear of offending the powerful priests and partly because the problems of logistics were enormous. It was not only the ferrying of building materials and supplies to the site, it was also the problems of accommodation for the workmen and the employing of sufficient numbers of workmen to ensure the rapid construction rate necessary to make it a viable proposition. Young skilled artisans were loath to leave the centres of wealth where most of their employment was to be obtained. In the end they came up with a novel plan that would uphold the principles of

Atenism and hopefully provide a practical solution to the logistics problems.

After surveying several areas, the project committee, which consisted of Amio, Pararameses, Ay, Yuya, Horemheb and Archduke Tuthmosis, with secondary support and advice from Tiya, Neferu, Maatnofret and Paranefer, decided on a site on the east bank of the Nile opposite Hermopolis. It was first of all almost on the halfway mark between the two ancient capitals and secondly, Hermopolis, although a small town, was a central communications post for the messenger link between north and south, had a good harbour for the riverboats and was well policed due to the military garrison stationed there.

Belief in Atenism precluded the use of slaves and therefore new methods of acquiring workers had to be thought of. In the end it was decided to use the extensive messenger communication system from north to south to advertise for the poor to pioneer a new system of freedom from serfdom in exchange for populating and helping to build the new city. Struggling scribes, architects, painters, and artisans of all kinds were offered the chance to make their fame and fortune, or at least a better life, in a new city, under new laws of freedom and equality. In the new city all men were to be of equal rank, but everyone had to vow allegiance to the Aten. Merit only was to determine the acquisition of honour.

Amio became very impatient with the initial slow response to any of the ideas and Neferu had to constantly encourage him. Support came from surprising quarters, including many of the Hebrews of Goshen. They had only ever worshipped one god anyway, so the idea was not alien to them. Young nomads and misfits came from the eastern desert areas and urban poor from the northern seaports. Amio sometimes rolled his eyes after one of his periodic visits to the site to tell her about the hotchpotch of people who were turning up to take up the challenge. Most of them had nothing to lose and possibility only to gain. Most were poor and many starving. He said that it was costing them a fortune just to get them fit enough to work. In spite of everything he was fired with enthusiasm for the project.

During her third pregnancy, Neferu was jealous of all the time and energy that Amio put into his plans for Akhetaten, and she began to oppose the idea. She was tired, dispirited and had no energy. It was not long, however, before she began to see the possibilities of the new city, which was to be administered by herself and Amio. Tiya and Ay were to continue in Thebes as they were, and she and Amio were to build the city up and create a strong social fabric and culture to attract the young and ambitious. This alone appealed to her strongly but there was also the added attraction of commencing a whole new life far from the intrigue and protocol of Malkata and its hundreds of scheming relatives and hangers-on.

When Neferu was delivered of yet another daughter, her disappointment was intense, and she burst into tears. She had put all her psychic energy into willing her child to be a boy. After the birth of Ankhsenpaaten, Neferu remained depressed for many weeks. Her milk dried up and the baby had to be fed by a wet nurse. It was a low ebb in Neferu's hitherto charmed life. Around the court it was being whispered that the queen was unable to produce male heirs. For the first time Tiya began to talk of Amio taking another wife and Neferu was desolate. She could not bear the thought of sharing her husband's love with another woman.

Throughout this difficult period, Maatnofret was a great source of strength and comfort to her and there were many times when Neferu cried on her shoulder. The older woman was like a mother to her, in a way that the formidable Tiya could never be. Amio was very distressed by Neferu's condition, and he assured her that the very idea of taking another wife was repugnant to him. He had no desire to lie with a woman other than his own wife, he said. Neferu took strength from his support.

Gradually Neferu began to recover and take an interest in the life around her again. Although her inability to produce a son caused her acute distress, her three daughters were all healthy and she felt she had a lot to be grateful for. Maatnofret reminded her of this daily. Perhaps the Aten was testing her and would give her a son when she lived in a city dedicated wholly to him. It was a belief that gradually took root in her mind and changed her whole attitude towards the building of Akhetaten. From this time onwards she became just as enthusiastic as he was in the ambitious building project. Surely there the Aten would grant her the son and heir her husband so earnestly desired, to complete their otherwise perfect happiness. Comforted by this thought, Neferu recovered her equilibrium and went about her tasks with composure.

The months following the birth of Ankhsenpaaten were difficult for Amio, who felt the necessity of balancing the future of the throne with that of his wife's happiness. Unknown to Neferu, there was an increasingly concerted campaign from both of his parents and the grand vizier for him to reconsider and take a second wife. Amio shielded Neferu as far as he could from the knowledge of these arguments. He knew very well that she had never felt herself at home in Malkata and he was aware of the seemingly impenetrable barrier between his wife and his mother. He loved them both but was unable to help the situation and sometimes he felt he was being torn between them. It may have been made worse by the close affection which had grown up between his grandfather and Neferu. Yuya was fond of her and showed her an affection which Tiya sometimes appeared to be jealous of. Neferu's conversion to Atenism was profound and his grandfather constantly encouraged it and sought to deepen her comprehension of his own ideas. Now Amio prayed to the Aten for guidance as to what to do in the present emotionally difficult circumstances.

The problem was considered to be so severe that to provide an alternative solution, the appropriate arrangements were made, and a ceremony of marriage was performed uniting Amenophis III with his eldest daughter Sitamun. In this way it was hoped that an alternative male heir would be produced who would be officially directly in line to the throne if all else failed. This arrangement was received well by the priesthood of Amun, as any offspring of this union would have a reduced amount of the hated Hyksos blood in its veins than that which circulated in the veins of Amio and Smenkhenre.

Soon after this marriage had taken place, Yuya, the old grand vizier, died. He was seventy-two years old and on his death bed he took the hand of his grandson and of Neferu and made them swear to remain faithful to Aten-Yahweh, the living god, until the end of their days. Both of them promised what he asked, as did Tiya, his daughter. Tiya was prostrate with grief and a pall descended upon the whole court. The family were compelled to go into mourning for the traditional seventy days it took for the embalmers to complete their work at the necropolis. A tomb had been prepared for Yuya in the Valley of the Kings, where the body of his wife already lay. Yuya became the only commoner and only foreigner of male sex ever to be accorded the honour of being buried there.

During the period of mourning for Yuya, many guests came to the court to offer their condolences. For the first time, Neferu was introduced to many of Amio's relatives, the Israelites of Goshen, the Nubians of Akhtmin and distant second cousins from here and there everywhere, it seemed. All other state functions were reduced to an absolute minimum during the period of mourning. Although Amio had been close to his grandfather, he was not a close family man in many ways, and he did not relish long drawn-out conversations with older relatives reminiscing about the past. He had the vision of the new city, one which he had shared with his grandfather, still in front of him.

In order to appease the demands of Ay and Tiya, Amio agreed to marry Tadhukipa, known as Kia. She was a Mitannian princess who had been sent to his father's harem. After much heart-searching, Neferu was eventually placated by the knowledge that Amio did not intend to consummate the marriage. It was to be his elaborate smokescreen to satisfy his parents and the priests of Amun and to bring the ties between Egypt and Mitanni closer. The marriage was arranged to take place after the funeral of Yuya was over. Neferu knew that she was very unpopular with the priests of Amun for her espousal of her faith in the Aten, which she had publicly acknowledged in the names of her children, as had Tiya herself with the birth of Baketaten. Ay had been very displeased with both of them over this but Neferu had found it impossible to compromise on her beliefs in something so important to her.

In the meantime, Amio continued with the work on Akhetaten. The two main architects of the new city were Paranefer and Pararameses' adjutant, who was also Tiya's official scribe and architect, the young northern officer Horemheb. In honour of the new city and its religion, Horemheb changed his name to Pa-atenemheb. Both of these men undertook their task with talent and zeal, seeing in the project an opportunity to imprint their own vision of Egypt on reality. Pa-atenemheb was a handsome, young commoner, only a year younger than Amio. He was intelligent and had a charming, easy manner. Amio was so impressed with his ambition and talent that later on he was prompted to make him officer-in-charge of the pharaoh's recruits. This was a powerful position with much direct influence over the rank and file of the army units.

During the two-year building of the first stage of Akhetaten, Horemheb began to be a regular visitor to the inner circles of Malkata. Neferu always found him charming and attentive, and it was not long before the handsome young officer caught the eye of Mutnedjmet, the daughter of Ay. In the hot climate of Egypt love blossoms quickly and it was not long after the wedding of Sitamun and her father, the senior pharaoh, that the wedding of Mutnedjmet and Horemheb took place.

By the end of the fourth year of their marriage, Akhetaten was ready for settlement by those of the palace retinue who had thrown in their lot with Amio and Neferu. Neferu had become her husband's most ardent supporter in the project of building a whole new city from scrub, virgin land. His project was giving her the chance to have a new beginning, living out their lives as they wished to do, away from Malkata with its interminable intrigue and never-ending family squabbles.

The more opposition the priests of Amun laid before his plans, the more obstinate Amio became in his intentions. He was never the kind to be put off by difficulties. He intended to change the face of Egypt forever for the better. He truly thought that the experiment in changing the structure of society along more humane concepts of equality that Akhetaten stood for would eventually be adopted throughout the whole of the Two Lands. His further project was to make Egypt truly one land once again. Neferu gave her husband her complete support in every way she could. When he quarrelled openly with the chief priest of Amun, though, she became afraid. Ay did his best to smooth the situation over. The people were afraid of the priests and were superstitious too. This superstition was against everything that Amio stood for. Tiya became increasingly cautious and muted in her public support of the project, although in private she continued to do everything she could. In the end, Amio became just as sick of Thebes as Neferu. He made many dangerous enemies during this time. When they left Thebes, they left behind the senior pharaoh, Tiya, Ay and Tuya, the Archduke Tuthmosis, Horemheb and Mutnedjmet to appease the priests of Amun as best they could.

CHAPTER 22

Life at Akhetaten was a totally new chapter in the marriage of Amio and Neferu, and they lived it to the full. Amio was constantly full of plans for enlarging and beautifying the town and there never seemed to be enough hours in the day to do what he wanted to do. He maintained constant contact with Paranefer, Tuthmosis the sculptor and with Maya, the head of security for all the work, sometimes going with them to take an active part in it. This would have been considered scandalous behaviour for the pharaoh in Thebes but here, at Akhetaten, there was a warm and friendly familiarity between the royal family and their friends. Here there was very little standing on ceremony with these close allies and Amio and Neferu enjoyed a happy social life.

Amongst their dearest friends were Penhasi and his wife. Penhasi was the chief servitor of the temple to the Aten and had been chosen for the position by Amio because of his deep faith in the power of the one god. Penhasi was from Goshen in the north-east of Egypt and was a distant relative of Amio through his mother. He was older than many of the newcomers to Akhetaten, being in his forties and having both grown-up children and young ones.

In that first year at Akhetaten, Neferu became pregnant with their fourth child. This time she tried not to dwell on the thought of the child, in order to avoid the disappointment, she had suffered after the birth of Ankhsenpaaten. Amio's hopes, however, knew no bounds, and he was certain that this time the child would be a boy. He made plans to go hunting with him and talked all the time of 'him'. Neferu suppressed her disquiet and prayed to the Aten that the child might be the son that Amio longed for. As always, she prefaced her prayer with the words 'If the Aten is willing'. When her fourth and most beautiful daughter was born, she realised that the Aten did not mean her to have a son. Amio's disappointment was bitter. He could not understand why the Aten should deny him this favour when he had built this city specially to honour him and when he had even helped to build it with his very own hands, engaging in manual work as no pharaoh had done before him. They called their daughter Nefer-Neferu-Aten after her mother, because this child more than any of the others had the look of Nefertiti about her from her birth. Although the blow was a heavy one, Amio took comfort in holding his little daughter and helping to care for her. He was a loving father and though temperamental by nature, he was basically an optimist.

All still seemed not lost when they learned that Tiya was pregnant again. The grand queen was now forty and the birth was expected to be a difficult one because of her age. Amio and Neferu were worried but regular news arrived by the river transport, and so far, things in Thebes were going well. Eventually the grand queen gave birth, and the child was a boy who was duly named Tutankhaten. Because the child's father was Archduke Tuthmosis, the circumstances of the queen's pregnancy had been kept as hushed as possible. The birth had left Tiya very weak, they heard, and she would not be able to visit them for some time. There was talk of gossip around the court as Amenophis III was in poor condition now and it was common knowledge that he could not have fathered the child. Neferu knew that it was all ammunition for the weapons of the priesthood of Amun and felt the occasional tremors of fear. In the long run, however, Akhetaten was far enough away from Thebes that the intrigues of the court were more or less a dark dream which did not unduly impinge itself upon her life. Amio was very happy about the birth of his half-brother but, at the same time, it only served to underscore Neferu's inability to produce a son. Perhaps it was his occasional depression on the matter which helped to bring about the next drama which unfolded in their lives.

Barely had Neferu recovered from the birth of her fourth child when Amio was struck down by a fever. The day it started, he appeared hot and flushed and complained of abdominal cramps and pain in his limbs. Neferu was worried, but not greatly so as Amio had always been susceptible to attacks similar to this and they had always responded to the medication of his personal physician. Neferu made him lie down and she tried to make him drink, but he was reluctant to do so, complaining of a very severe headache. Worried, Neferu sent for the physician, who prescribed something for the abdominal pain and told her that he must drink plenty of fluids.

Outside the room, the physician looked worried and told her that during the past two days he had seen twelve similar cases in the city. There seemed to be a danger of an epidemic of dysentery. He was not yet sure if this was what the pharaoh was suffering from, but he thought that it might be.

'Where is it coming from?' Neferu asked.

The doctor shrugged. 'I don't know, Your Majesty. Perhaps it is being brought into Akhetaten by the people coming up the river.'

'We must isolate them then,' Neferu said anxiously.

The physician agreed to quarantine the newcomers until the situation was under control. 'I think it would be best to keep the children away from his majesty until his condition stabilises,' was the physician's parting comment. Neferu agreed and told him that she would nurse her husband herself and arrange for the baby to be wet nursed in the meantime. Little did she realise that she would have almost no contact with her children for nearly four decans.

By the following day Amio had become much worse, and his fever was so high that he became delirious and shouted and rolled restlessly around the bed, not seeming to recognise her at all. Then he began to suffer from severe diarrhoea and Maatnofret had to enlist the aid of two other older ladies-in-waiting to help Neferu to nurse her husband. Between the four of them, they had to ensure that he was never left alone for a moment, and they seemed to spend most of their time constantly changing his bed. Neferu became extremely frightened for her husband's life and sent word to Thebes to Ay and the grand queen that Amio was desperately ill. The physician's worst fears were confirmed by now and Neferu was further alarmed by the news of the deaths of many of the quarantined newcomers from the same disease. There was little that the physician seemed able to do and Neferu felt herself verging on panic. She refused to leave her husband's side, in spite of the efforts of Maatnofret and the others to persuade her. As with Demi so many years before she felt that if she let go of her husband's hand he would slip away. Somehow, she hoped and willed some of her strength to flow through to him and save him.

It was almost impossible to get Amio to swallow the medicine left for him by the physician except in the increasingly rare lucid moments between the outbursts of delirium that left him completely exhausted. When he did manage to take the medicine, he would soon vomit it back. By the fourth day the vomiting and diarrhoea were constant, and he was losing large clots of blood. In his semi-consciousness he would cry out in pain, holding his abdomen. Neferu could see her husband's face shrinking before her. His eyes were sunken and hollow, and his lips cracked and sore. She would hold his head to let the water trickle in but was all the time aware of how pitifully little he was taking in and that she was losing this fight.

He was comatose most of the time now and unaware of his situation. She never left him at all now, even to make her twice daily visits to the temple to pray for him. She slept on a couch which the servants had brought in for her and no longer even noticed the stench in the room, which in spite of all their efforts they had been unable to eradicate. To make things worse she had initially been bothered by the pain of her engorged breasts as she had not had the time or foresight to bind them when the baby had been given over to the wet nurse for feeding. Gradually though, her discomfort had subsided as she had had no time for eating and drinking properly and the milk had dried up of its own accord. Maatnofret was a tower of strength, and she too was now on her feet for eighteen hours a day. It was the darkest and most frightening time of her life, but she refused to look ahead and thought only of that day and the needs of the moment.

Day and night, they washed and cleaned Amio, lifting his skeletal body onto the clean bed to change his own with as little movement as they could. Neferu slept in fits and starts on the couch, which was pushed up close to his bed. Maatnofret would sit on the other side and would promise to wake Neferu if there should be any change. On the fifth day Amio seemed to be barely alive, his coma was so deep. After the physician had visited him that morning, he took Neferu outside the door and told her that the pharaoh was dying and that there was nothing more they could do for him. He anticipated that the end would come sometime during that day and certainly before the following dawn unless a miracle would happen. Stricken, Neferu sent the message on to Thebes, not having yet received a reply to her earlier messages yet. Neferu was at her wit's end now and felt that she was only half alive herself. She did not know what more she could do and had begun to resign herself to the fact that she would soon be a widow. The thought was so painful that she cried out and clung to Maatnofret, who tried in vain to comfort her. A thought came to her befuddled, exhausted brain and she asked Maatnofret to send for Penhasi. Penhasi arrived at all speed, thinking that the pharaoh had died. She was at least able to reassure him on that score for the moment.

Neferu asked Penhasi to call all the citizens who were able to do so to come to a special prayer meeting in the temple that evening before sundown. She asked him for special permission to speak to them herself in the temple. She knew that it was almost sacrilegious for a woman to do such a thing, but Penhasi was surprisingly accommodating and agreed to let her speak within the temple.

That afternoon Ay and Tiya at last arrived on the royal boat from Thebes. On seeing Amio they were both in a state of shock and Tiya sank into a stupor of grief and hopelessness. They were both assured of Amio's imminent death. Neferu told them that she had called a special prayer meeting in the late afternoon and asked them both to attend. Tiya scarcely seemed to hear her.

The temple was packed when Neferu and the royal group arrived. There was an air of pent-up feelings and an atmosphere of gloom overall. Penhasi opened his religious ceremony as usual and then asked all those present to listen carefully to the queen. Neferu stood up in front of them all and told them that the pharaoh was dying. As she spoke, the tears began to run down her face. She asked them all to get down upon their knees with her and pray for the pharaoh to live. Facing them, she knelt down on her knees and started the prayers. 'Dear father above, Aten, creator of the world, I, your humble servant Nefertiti, ask you to spare the life of my husband, the man that I love more than my life, my Amio, the pharaoh. If you will do this, my god, I promise I will dedicate my life to doing your will, how and where you wish it.'

When Neferu finished her prayer, she stood up. She noticed that many of the congregation were crying too. One old, grey-haired man came forward to her and knelt down in front of her.

In a deep and sincere voice, he said, 'I am old, Your Majesty. I will pray that the Aten will take me instead of the pharaoh.' Neferu was so moved that the tears fell faster for a while, until a sudden tranquillity came over her.

She touched the old man on the head. 'I would not wish you to forfeit your life, my old friend. It is I, who have so little faith, who should be ashamed. The Aten can save the pharaoh and I have asked him in faith. The pharaoh will be spared.' She smiled down on the honest, open face and said, 'I thank you for your kind offer. May the Aten be with you always.' With that, she turned and curtsied low before the altar and the chief servitor before turning to curtsy before her mother-in-law and slowly leaving the temple. Outside in the fresh air, she breathed in deeply and began to walk back to the palace, not waiting for her chariot.

The distance to the palace was not far and in the darkness of the evening the lamps of the houses shone out with a kind of haze around them. This was the first time she had walked out alone since her other life in On. Part of her knew that Tiya would be scandalised, but she needed this time to herself, and she continued briskly until she reached the palace courtyard. The walk had done her good and she felt more refreshed than she had done for days. Having had a full ritual cleansing before going to the temple, she felt it would be safe to go to the nursery to see the children. Teya and Mutnedjmet were there, playing with the two older girls, and the baby was fast asleep in her cradle.

Mereta, the eldest, was being prepared for her bath by the nurse. After a quick chat and loving hugs and kisses, Neferu left and made her way to Amio's sick room. Maatnofret was already there, and for the first time, she noticed how exhausted Maatnofret was. 'You should go to bed, Maatnofret,' she said as she bent over her husband's still body. His breathing was very shallow, and his pulse felt rapid and irregular. 'Has he drunk anything?' she asked tiredly.

Maatnofret shook her head despondently. 'I tried but I don't think anything went down,' she replied.

'I feel better now,' said Neferu. 'I will sit by him. Go to your suite and rest tonight. We will know one way or another soon.'

She spoke calmly and Maatnofret, seeing that she was in control of herself, nodded and said, 'I do feel particularly tired tonight, Neferu. I will go to bed. Call me if you need me.'

Neferu looked at her sharply. 'You aren't ill, are you, Maatnofret?'

The other woman shook her head. 'No. Only tired. Goodnight, Neferu. May the Aten protect you both and all of us.'

'Goodnight, Maatnofret. May the Aten bless you too. Keep well.'

When Maatnofret had gone, Neferu checked that her husband was clean, and she massaged some perfumed oil onto his body where the skin was dry and taut. Afterwards she sat by his side, holding his fingers in her hand. Tiya entered the room quietly. 'I will stay with my son tonight,' she said softly. Neferu nodded and asked if she had eaten. The grand queen nodded. She looked well, Neferu thought. She was slightly plumper now than she had been when Neferu had last seen her, but it suited her. It softened the imperious face a little. Tonight, she looked sad.

'You must rest, Neferu, otherwise you will become sick too,' she said, looking at the dark circles under Neferu's eyes. Neferu shook her head.

'I will rest afterwards, when this is all over, one way or another,' she replied. The grand queen said nothing but put her hand on her son's forehead and gently stroked the hair from his face. He was quite still. The two women spoke little but the silence between them was comfortable. Both of them were at their best in a crisis and now they were both fighting on the same side. After an hour or so Tiya fell asleep, her head at rather an uncomfortable angle. Neferu got a cushion and a rug and arranged them for her. Tiya opened her eyes. 'Thank you, Neferu. I didn't mean to sleep.'

'No. No. Sleep on. I will wake you if there is any change,' Neferu answered quietly.

Throughout the night Neferu sat, dozing off now and again and awaking with a guilty start. When the morning came Amio was still alive. He was no better, but he was no worse. She wiped his face and tried to get him to sip a little water, but it was useless. Ay left back to Thebes that day; it would have been dangerous to stay longer. The priests of Amun seemed to be restless. Perhaps they sensed that their moment was near. The death of Amio would be a major crisis for them all, she knew. 'Amio will not die!' Neferu told him firmly. Ay looked at her directly but did not reply. He plainly thought she was being totally unrealistic. Sympathetically, he squeezed her hand in his, for once seemingly at a loss for words.

'Your loyalty is a credit to you, Neferu,' he said finally.

'I love him,' she said simply. He nodded.

Teya and Mutnedjmet were to stay on and travel back with Tiya when the time was appropriate. Left unspoken but hanging in the air was the implied suggestion that Neferu and the children would also be returning with them. Ay embraced her before leaving to give some final orders for his wife and daughter's return to Thebes.

Neferu went back to her husband's side. She bent down to kiss him, and he seemed to stir a little. She looked at him closely, but he seemed just as deeply asleep as before. When she touched his forehead, it seemed that it was not quite so hot as before, but she could not be sure of it. She had felt like that so many times and it had just been wishful thinking. She touched it again, wondering whether it really was cooler.

Maatnofret entered and after their greetings, they set about washing Amio and transferring him to the other bed while they changed his own bed. Tiya watched, shaking her head gently.

'Go and lie down properly, Mother,' Neferu said, noting her distress. She realised that it was the first time she had ever called Tiya 'mother'. Tiya replied that she would go and bathe before having something to eat and visiting the children. 'Yes,' replied Neferu. 'I am afraid that I have sorely neglected them for many days now.' The queen mother left and once Amio had been made as comfortable as possible, Neferu too left and went to eat. Maatnofret took over the watch.

When Neferu returned, the servant had just finished cleaning the room and there were fresh flowers in the urn. She sat down on the couch and held out her arm, taking Amio's hand in her own. She felt completely exhausted and after a while she fell asleep. When she woke up the first thing, she noticed was that her hand was inside Amio's. Had he woken? She leaned forwards and said softly, 'Amio? Amio?' His eyelids flickered but he did not open his eyes. Still, it was a response. The first for several days. She felt a sudden upsurge of hope within her. Again, she spoke quietly into his ear.

'Amio, darling! I love you so much. Please don't die!' There was no response and she leaned back disappointed. After a while she dozed again.

Maatnofret shook her shoulder. 'Lie down and sleep properly, Neferu. I promise I will wake you to any change,' Neferu nodded. She went to the bathing room and undressed tiredly. Maatnofret came to see if she should send for the lady-in-waiting, but Neferu shook her head. 'I prefer to look after myself, you know that, Maatnofret,' she replied.

Slowly she washed her hair and bathed. Afterwards she massaged in her favourite perfumed oil and put on a clean shift. She felt good. She entered her husband's sick room again and pushed her couch next to his again and lay down. Almost before she knew it, she was in a deep sleep.

When Neferu awoke, the grand queen was sitting by her quietly, 'Neferu, your family have arrived to see you,' she said. 'Would you like to go and prepare yourself.' This latter was more a statement than a question. Neferu nodded and asked if there had been any change in Amio's condition. The grand queen shrugged. 'He has stirred and made some noises, but it was indecipherable,' Tiya replied.

'But that is excellent!' said Neferu, who was now ready to cling to straws. She bent over her husband to look closely at him. The skin was stretched so tight over his high cheekbones that it was almost possible to imagine him as a skeleton. She touched his face lovingly. The black, well-defined eyebrows had not changed at least. Her index finger traced the outline of them and then skimmed over the black lashes. He stirred a little. 'Amio, darling. I am here. Hold on. Don't give way to this. I need you so. I know you can hear me, my darling,' Neferu continued. 'Try not to be distressed. Your mother is here. We are all praying for you. You are going to get well. We all love you so much.'

As if with a tremendous effort, Amio opened his eyes. He looked at Neferu and she knew that he knew her. There was a look of love in his eyes. His parched, cracked lips tried to speak but nothing came out. The lips mouthed her name 'Neferu'. Neferu was overjoyed. The tears ran freely down her cheeks again. 'Amio, darling. Everything is going to be all right. You are going to get well. You must drink though, my love. Will you take a little water for me?' He nodded and she lifted the cup to his lips. Tiya cradled his head in her arms, and he took a little of the water. 'More, darling, more!' Neferu begged and tried again and again. Even Tiya's face now showed an expression of hope. Neferu looked at him closely after he closed his eyes again wearily. 'I think he is now sleeping normally,' she commented to her mother-in-law. 'He feels cooler.' She looked up at Tiya.

The older woman nodded and said, 'He is not out of danger yet, but I begin to feel that there is a chance.'

Maatnofret entered the room, and the two women recounted their good news. Maatnofret promised to watch carefully while the grand queen went to rest and Neferu went to receive her family. Vassiliou came forward grimly. He could see at a glance how thin Neferu had become, and the strained expression on her face. Neferu was so glad to see him that she clung to him like the little girl she once had been and he held her tightly, saying nothing. After a long moment he said gruffly, 'We came as soon as we got your news, Neferu. Demi and Yussef have come with me. Can you come through to see them?' Indicating the reception room across the corridor.

'Of course, Father. Don't worry! Amio is going to be all right, whatever everyone thinks!' Her father said nothing but, taking her hand in his own, he led her through to the reception room. Demi and Yussef rose to greet her. Demi came forward first. He looked so strong and handsome.

He clasped her to him and whispered. 'Are you all right, Neferu?'

She replied quietly, 'Tired, that is all.' Then she turned to greet Yussef. 'And Yussef came too! Thank you for coming, Yussef.'

Yussef stepped forward. He was twenty-five now and she had not seen him for many years. He looked at her gravely. 'Hello again, Neferu,' he said at last and came forward with his arms open. He hugged her to him, all the bitterness gone. He was her friend again. She felt the tears sting her eyes again. They came so easily nowadays.

'It is good to see you again, Yussef,' she replied, drawing away from him gently.

'It is good to see you again too, Neferu,' he said softly. 'It has been a long time.'

Everyone turned and bowed as Tiya entered the room. The queen invited them to eat, and they followed her to a small cosy room overlooking the veranda. Tiya was so used to being the chief hostess that she assumed the role automatically. At any other time perhaps Neferu would have been annoyed, but now she was merely grateful to be able to relax.

After eating, Neferu asked the servant to bring the children to them. Meretaten was not at all shy. She wanted to know if her grandfather had brought her presents. She seemed disappointed when he told her that he had not had time this time.

'Did you come because daddy is so ill?' she asked him.

Her grandfather was rather put out by the directness of her question. 'Well, yes, my dear,' he said.

'I have been very good and quiet too, Grandfather,' Mereta continued importantly. 'I have been helping to look after the baby.'

Her grandfather could not help smiling. 'I'm sure you have been a great help to your mother, Meretaten,' Vassiliou answered chivalrously.

'Yes. A great help,' Meretaten assured him. 'Meketaten is always crying for Mummy and Daddy and Ankhsenpaaten is still almost a baby, so mummy depends on me to help to look after Neferu-tashery.' Everyone laughed, even Yussef, who examined all the children with an intent gaze.

'Yes. I depend on you, darling, to look after Neferu junior,' Neferu replied to her somewhat precocious elder daughter. The nanny returned with Neferu junior and handed the child to Neferu, who cuddled her baby greedily for a few minutes.

Her father came to look at the baby. 'Why! She looks exactly like you did as a baby, Neferu!'

Neferu laughed. 'Yes. Everyone says so. That is why we named her Neferu-tashery.' Yussef came to look at the baby but said nothing.

Demi looked and said, 'All babies look the same to me.'

Tiya tut-tutted. 'How can you say that! They certainly don't look the same to me!' She smiled.

Neferu began to feel a little restless. 'I must go and see how Amio is,' she said to no one in particular.

'May we come and see him?' her father asked.

Neferu hesitated but Tiya nodded at her and told him. 'He is dangerously ill. We don't know if he will survive. Perhaps it is best you see him now.'

Awkwardly they got up and followed her through to the sickroom. Maatnofret rose quickly when they entered the room, but Neferu told her to sit down again. The three men looked at Amio. They were plainly all shocked. After a minute or so, Neferu told Maatnofret that she would take her family back and then return. She bent down and kissed her husband's lips before turning away to return them to the sitting room. She was glad that the children were still there, as she did not want to go into any details or explanations right now. Tiya told her she would look after the guests and Neferu bent down to kiss her cheek. She was glad that Tiya had come. She was being a tower of strength.

Maatnofret told Neferu that Amio had woken again, and she had managed to get a little more water down him before he had drifted off to sleep once more. Neferu was pleased, encouraged by this apparent progress. Sitting down by Amio's side, she told Maatnofret to go and take a rest. The pair of them washed him carefully and massaged oil onto his limbs before her friend departed. Afterwards, Neferu combed his hair and put some salve onto his lips to help heal the fissures caused by his dehydration. While Neferu was applying the balm, Amio opened his eyes again and allowed her to give him some water. Neferu was very hopeful now. This day he had not passed any more blood and he was now obviously cooler to the touch. Neferu was sure that the Aten had answered her prayers. This time Amio was awake a little longer. He said nothing but his eyes followed her all the time and when she lifted his hand to her mouth and kissed it, a slight smile came to his mouth. After a little while, he fell asleep again, sighing softly. Neferu felt quite serene now, her faith in the Aten total. She knew without doubt that Amio would live.

Later that evening Maatnofret returned and Neferu took time off from her charge to spend with her now extended family. The presence of the children livened up the atmosphere, and conversation was even more animated. Meretaten had taken an interest in Yussef and the beautiful jewellery that he was wearing and was trying to make him promise to make some for her. Neferu watched her. There was much of her father about her. She had the same kind of lips as her father and grandmother and the long face of her father, but she had the eyes of Neferu herself. Somehow Neferu felt that Meretaten was a fifty-fifty blend of both of them with her looks.

Neferu felt that all her daughters were beautiful, and she was naturally pleased about it. All of them, except the youngest baby, had the unusual skull shape of their father's family. Tiya had once told her that it came from her paternal grandmother, as did the long neck and pale skin. Tiya herself resembled her Nubian mother in skin colour and shape of face, although she too had the unusual skull shape of her father's family.

When the children had been put to bed, Neferu went to say their evening prayers with them and then went back to her husband. Maatnofret said she was satisfied that the fever was definitely subsiding and that he was sleeping properly now. Together they washed and changed him again and he woke up during this. He winced a little as they moved him, and they both apologised for the pain they were causing him. Amio shook his head, as if to say that it was nothing. After, when he had recovered a little from their efforts, he said quite distinctly, 'I love you both.' The two women looked at each other and Neferu saw tears in Maatnofret's eyes. The older woman bent and kissed Amio and Neferu smiled on them both.

'I love you more than anyone in the whole world,' she told him. 'You must get better. Promise me!'

He nodded. 'I promise,' he replied.

'Sleep now, darling, and conserve your strength,' she said, taking his hand. Neferu sat down beside him again and motioned Maatnofret to go to bed. One of the other nurses would be arriving soon. The girl in question came and with her came Aunt Teya. Teya was quiet and motherly, unlike her extrovert husband. She insisted upon sitting with Amio throughout the night and told Neferu to take a proper night's rest. For the first time in eight nights, Neferu slept in her own bed. It seemed strange without Amio. She slept until after dawn when her lady-in-waiting came to tell her that her bath was ready. Neferu relaxed and enjoyed the luxury of a slow and soothing bath. She allowed Esmeni to towel her dry and then she sat before her dressing table and arranged her hair with no hurry. As she dressed herself, she noticed that her figure had completely reverted to its former non-pregnant state and even her breasts were now totally dry of milk.

Before going to the sickroom, she ate a quiet breakfast by herself. Teya looked exhausted when she arrived and was pleased to see her. She had refused to leave Amio until Neferu arrived to relieve her. Now she stood up tiredly and gave Neferu a hug before going for a much-needed rest. After checking that Amio was clean and comfortable, Neferu sent the nurse away. Maatnofret appeared but saw that all was quiet and went to help to get the children ready. Esmeni was requested to help Tiya with the visitors. Neferu was sitting quietly by Amio's side when she looked up to see Yussef in the doorway. She was a little startled but smiled up at him. He was alone and unsmiling as he came toward the bed. He looked down at Amio's prostrate figure.

'He is dying, Neferu,' he said slowly.

'No!' Neferu said sharply and then, 'Shhhhh!' wondering whether Amio could hear. She got up quickly, indicating to Yussef to come out of the room. 'You mustn't talk like that,' she said. 'Amio could hear it even if he can't react.'

'He is dying, Neferu! Just look at him!' Yussef said with emphasis. He continued in a low tone. 'Don't you understand, Neferu. This is our chance to be together. He tore us apart, but when he dies we can be together.'

Neferu was shocked. 'No, Yussef! You don't understand. I love Amio. I won't let him die. He is my husband and the father of my children. I love him and I will never give him up. I am sorry, Yussef, but I cannot listen to you talk like this,' she said hotly.

'You never loved me!' Yussef said bitterly.

'You are wrong, Yussef. I did love you and part of me still does, but it is no longer the same kind of love. Too many things have changed between us, and time does not go backwards.' Yussef turned away angrily and Neferu watched him go, distressed by his reaction.

She returned to her husband's side, touching his forehead and then kissing him. He opened his eyes. Troubled, she asked him, 'Did you hear?' For a moment the old, veiled look came into his eyes but then he nodded.

'I am sorry you had to hear it, my darling. Forgive Yussef.'

Amio nodded and squeezed her hand. 'I was afraid,' he whispered.

'Afraid that I would leave you?' she asked softly. He nodded. She bent over him. 'I will never leave you, my dearest love.' She kissed him tenderly. He smiled.

'I know it now,' he said.

As the days passed, Amio began to grow stronger and it became obvious that unless he were to suffer a relapse, he would live through this disease after all. Day after day, Neferu sat by him. Sometimes she would fall asleep, and when she awoke, he would be looking at her. The loss of blood had ceased, and the diarrhoea was much less. Amio still complained of pains in his abdomen, but the physician's medication helped that and seemed to improve the diarrhoea too. After three more days he was able to sit up and to take some soup. At this point, the party from Thebes felt secure enough to consider going home. Her family had taken their departure the day following the quarrel she had had with Yussef.

The day that they left, Amio smiled at her cynically and said, 'I suppose that their leaving means I am going to survive!'

'Of course!' Neferu said. 'Did you doubt it?'

'I can't remember too much about it,' Amio said. 'How long have I been like this?'

'One and a half decans,' said Neferu quietly.

Amio was shocked. He could remember something from the beginning of his illness but very little in between. 'I remember once waking up and seeing you sitting asleep in the chair. You looked exhausted and your head was at an awkward angle. I was afraid that your neck would ache, and I wanted to wake you, but you looked so tired that I could not.'

Amio's illness brought him and Neferu even closer than before. The knowledge that they had been so close to the separation of death made them appreciate anew all the qualities which they had first loved in each other. Amio's convalescence was long, and it took almost four more decans before he regained his strength and could make his daily visit to the temple to give praise to the Aten. For Neferu it was a draining time but, well before her husband, she went alone to the temple to give thanks to the Aten for the life of her husband.

The people rejoiced and filled the temple with flowers on that day. Neferu was deeply touched by the warmth and sincerity of the people of Akhetaten. The crisis was over, and the great black cloud of uncertainty was lifted from the minds of the citizens of the city. Their faith was safe from the persecution of the priests of Amun as long as Akhetaten lived.

Everyone came to give thanks for the life of the pharaoh, the Keftiu from On and Memphis, the Israelites from Goshen and the many artisans, scribes, artists and workmen from the ordinary Egyptian population of the poor who had migrated here in search of a better life. There were very few old faces to be seen in the congregation. Most of the population was young to middle aged. The elite classes were on the whole unrepresented. They had had no interest in moving to Akhetaten, not being motivated to eschew their comfortable homes and lives in Thebes and to other large towns for a pioneering new town in central Egypt.

Life in Akhetaten slowly returned to normality and as soon as he was physically able to, Amio began to be seen at state and public functions again. His close encounter with death and the seemingly miraculous safe delivery from its clutches made a deep impression upon him. It reinforced his decision never to leave the city and he decreed that when he did die, he was to be buried at a tomb in the eastern mountains. He chose a site about six kilometres into the mountains by the side of a dried upriver bed called a wadi. The superintendent of the necropolis made the arrangements and work commenced on excavation of the chambers and tunnels. Amio also decreed that if Neferu or the children were to die elsewhere, their bodies were to be brought back to Akhetaten for burial.

Akhetaten was built in the shape of a rough D and the wadi was situated about halfway around the curve of the D. In gratitude for sparing him his life, Amio wrote his 'Hymn to the Aten'. He regained his enthusiasm and lively wit, but he gained also a new determination to carry through his will to make the Aten the only god to be worshipped in the whole of the Two Lands.

Things came to a head when word reached Akhetaten that during Amio's illness,

the priests of Amun had made overt overtures of a treacherous nature to several of
the senior army officers. It appeared that a false report of the death of Akhenaten had
arrived at Thebes and there had been open rejoicing amongst some of the priesthood.
They had been spreading hostile and insulting remarks about the pharaoh, ridiculing
his appearance and background and stating that he was mentally unbalanced. Both
Pararameses and Pa-aten-em-heb had been approached and offered backing if they
would instigate a coup by the army. Both had refused and remained loyal to Ay and to
Amenophis III, although the latter was now incapable of taking any direct action and
was virtually isolated in his drug addiction, preferring the delights of his harem to the
realities of political life.

Amio was stung into a furious response by these reports and sent word back to
Ay that the priests of Amun were to be deprived of their powers at all costs. The name
of Amun was to be removed from every place it appeared and was to be denigrated
as hocus-pocus. Citizens were no longer to pay tribute to the priests, nor to make
sacrifices to Amun. The only god to be spared was Re, who was merely another facet
of the god Aten. All other gods and rituals were to be abolished forthwith. Neferu was
uneasy, although she fully approved the thoughts behind his actions. 'It is violence,
Amio,' she told him. 'You cannot change the hearts of men with violence.' It was to no
avail. Once Amio's temper was aroused, it was like a raging tempest. One could only
wait for its force to be spent. Neferu was never afraid of her hot-tempered husband,
and she never wasted time nor energy by attempting to reason with him when he
was in a fury. She knew from experience that after the storm had passed peace would
come, and then he would sit and discuss with sweet reason whatever it was that had
to be discussed. To argue with him when he was raging was only to incite him further,
sometimes causing him to do things he would later regret. Whenever the pair of
them quarrelled, she would state coldly, 'I do not wish to discuss this with you in your
present mood.'

She would then leave the room. Once he had reminded her that he was the pharaoh
and ordered her to stay. To punish him for this childish behaviour, she had behaved as
an underling and called him 'sire' for twenty-four hours until he was so heartily sick of it
that he had called a truce.

This time Amio was not placated until he had taken action to reverse the loss of
prestige he felt he had suffered by the actions and statements of the priesthood of Amun.
Tiya and Ay tried as best they could to affect some kind of compromise by removing the

high priest from his office, but Amio would not be satisfied until his decree had been carried out to the letter.

If the elder pharaoh had been in a fit state, some kind of compromise could have been reached, but only six months after Amio's illness, the elder pharaoh suffered a severe stroke which left him paralysed and unable to speak properly and he remained in this pitiable condition for another year before his eventual death. Tiya now reigned supreme in Thebes with her son's full backing, ably supported by her brother, Grand Vizier Ay, and her lover, Archduke Tuthmosis.

Eventually, Amio's basic good humour won through, and his anger subsided. Neferu remained calm, dealing with the situation in the only way she knew how to; by loving and supporting him. She told him that the opinions of the priests were of no consequence to them. Their reputations were safe in the hands of the Aten. His was the only opinion who mattered. Amio conceded the truth of this and became once more immersed in the affairs of Akhetaten, which was growing fast and had already developed a pronounced beauty and culture of its own.

Perhaps Neferu did not properly understand what Amio had always known, that the power of the priests had always been a threat to the pharaoh, even from the earliest dynasties. They held great sway with the people, threatening them with all kinds of evil consequences if they did not do as the priests wished. There was the political angle as well as the theological one. Many of the higher priests were minor royal relatives or the descendants of former pharaohs, bearing grudges for former wrongs, real or imagined. Amio knew that they would seize power if they got the chance. He did not intend to allow that to happen.

It was towards the end of their second year at Akhetaten that the senior pharaoh died in Thebes and Neferu found that she was pregnant yet again. This was her fifth pregnancy and once more high hopes were placed on the birth of a son. Neferu understood the enormous pressure that Amio now felt, his father now dead and a hotbed of intrigue and resentment existing in Thebes. Even for the death of his father, however, Amio refused to break his vow to leave the confines of the new city. This was unheard of and caused great heart-searching even in their own household. Amio conceded that his vow had been ill-thought out but could not in all honour break it. For a pharaoh to break his promise was an even greater dishonour than non-attendance of his own father's funeral. They were caught in a quandary of their own making. They considered having the body brought to Akhetaten for the seventy-day embalming process and burial, but the practical considerations forced them to abandon that plan. Decomposition of the body would have been profound by the time it arrived and Amenophis was after all not a great believer in Atenism. He had looked upon his wife's family background with tolerance and accepted it fully as part of his marriage to her, but he had remained an irreverent follower of Amun-Re, if anything. In truth, he had really been a hedonistic atheist. The priesthood would not have tolerated the Atenist funeral of the very man who had instigated the building of the great avenue of pillars leading to the temple of Amun at Luxor. On top of that, Amio had to take into account that his father would have been outraged at the very thought of being buried anywhere else but in the chamber specially prepared for him in the Valley of the Kings, close to the funeral place of his own father, Tuthmosis IV.

Trapped by his predicament, Amio sought to minimise the effects of his absence from the funeral by sending Neferu to represent him. He wanted her to take the opportunity to talk to as many people as she could and to bring back as much information as possible concerning the true state of affairs. Neferu was reluctant to leave her husband and children behind to embark on the three-to-four-day journey to Thebes in her pregnant state, but there was nothing for it except to go. At least she was now four months pregnant and over the first three difficult months of nausea. This was her fifth pregnancy in nine years though, and she felt very tired of childbearing and its attendant discomforts. She prayed daily that the child would be a son and that he would be healthy. Finally, she prayed that it would be her last child.

Neferu left for Thebes with a sense of her own inadequacy for this important diplomatic task, very much aware that she was, and always would be, a rank outsider to these people, coming as she did from the north and being a Keftiu in origin. On arrival in Thebes, Neferu was received with tremendous acclaim and outward approval, but she remained aware that on the fringe of the court itself there existed the same group who had always considered her the black horse in their hand. She realised that her Keftiu background only served to accentuate the foreign Hebrew quality in Amio and his family, and she knew, or rather felt, that many of them blamed her for the pharaoh's persecution of the priests of Amun. It was not true that she had instigated Amio's furious plans, but it was true that she had supported him one hundred percent in his ultimate aim to spread Atenism throughout the Two Lands. Neither of them had really anticipated the ensuing bad feeling.

Now, for the first time, Neferu came face to face with the results of the upheaval that Amio's decree was causing. In Akhetaten there was no ripple to disturb the calmness of their days but here in Thebes there was still profound turbulence, albeit suppressed, following the desecration of the temple by the removal of Amun's name. For the first time also, Neferu came to realise the extent of the diplomatic roles being played out by Tiya and Ay in order to maintain control over a difficult situation.

Tiya looked very tired. She had had a difficult time with the birth of Tutankhaten and since then with all the problems of Amio's illness, her husband's death and the political unrest, all coming closely upon the death of her father, she appeared exhausted. Tutankhaten was a delightful little boy of two now, and in many ways he was Tiya's antidote to all the problems. Neferu found him adorable. He was loving and good-tempered and handsome and was obviously the apple of the eye of his parents. Tiya and the archduke were now living openly together as man and wife. Privately, Neferu wondered how Orelia, Tuthmosis' chief wife, felt about the matter, but she did not dare to raise such a delicate matter. She herself could never have tolerated Amio living in such a situation, and she felt that here was another weapon against them which could be turned to the priest's advantage in a weak moment. Tiredly, she brushed the matter from her mind. There was too much to think about as it was.

Tiya was overjoyed about Neferu's pregnancy. It was the symbol she needed that a son was still possible who would secure the throne once and for all. She voiced openly now her anxieties about the succession and during this visit a genuine friendship began to blossom between the two women for the first time. Tiya had lost some of what Neferu had always felt to be her hardness and desire to manipulate any situation to her own advantage. The grand queen was clearly very secure in her love for the archduke and his for her. She confided that she would like to formalise her relationship with him by marrying him, but she was afraid to do so in case Neferu failed to produce the much-needed son. If she married Tuthmosis she would lose her position as chief wife of the former pharaoh and, in doing so, she would weaken the rights of Tutankhaten to the throne. As Neferu had refused to allow her husband to marry another wife, Tutankhaten was their insurance for the future. Officially he was the son of Amenophis III, and as such he had an incontestably close link to the throne.

'I am sorry, Mother. I can never give Amio up,' Neferu told Tiya.

Tiya smiled. 'I never realised what kind of woman my son had married, Neferu,' the grand queen replied. There was a short silence while she appeared to meditate before continuing. 'Do you remember the sports day when Amio was knocked unconscious by the stone?' she asked. Neferu nodded her head vigorously. How could she ever forget such a day?' It was only then,' the grand queen continued, 'that I began to understand the depths of your feelings for Amio. It has been a truly remarkable marriage, Neferu, and I am happy that my son has found such contentment in his marriage.'

Neferu was touched by Tiya's words and this late blossoming of their relationship. 'I pray once again that this child will be a son,' she said, patting her rounded abdomen. 'But if it is not, I still cannot give him up or share him with someone else.'

Tiya was magnanimous in her defeat and nodded in understanding. 'We will just have to work something out,' she replied with a shrug, pulling her youngest child onto her knee. 'We have Tut,' she said, hugging him to her and kissing him. Neferu smiled at the little boy. What a handsome little fellow he was, she thought. If the worst came to the worst, he would make a splendid pharaoh.

Ay seemed much more confident than his sister that the damage to the throne caused by Amio's decree could be contained. 'The treachery was always there!' he stated laconically. 'The only difference is that now we know from which quarters it would come, should it be given the chance. As long as I am grand vizier, it will not be given the chance!'

Neferu felt very relieved. She had a lot of confidence in Ay. 'I have the greatest confidence in you, Uncle Ay,' she openly acknowledged. 'Without your interest in administering state affairs, it seems clear that Amio and myself could not continue our good life in Akhetaten with impunity.'

Ay smiled and bowed his head slightly at the implied compliment. 'I enjoy doing my job, Neferu. Amio is not interested in the routine details of state affairs, but someone has to attend to them. Amio is a painter of vast vistas. I am a man for the smaller details myself,' he said with a grin. They all laughed at his metaphor and Neferu reflected that what he had said was true in many respects.

'Perhaps it is just as well that we complement each other's talents so well,' she remarked.

The day following the final laying to resting of her father-in-law, who had remained an unknown quantity to her right up to his death, Neferu embarked on *The Aten Gleams* for the long journey back to Akhetaten. This time she left behind a new friend, her mother-in-law, Grand Queen Tiya. This Tiya was new to her. A woman softened by the depth of her relationship with Archduke Tuthmosis and the birth of their son Tutankhaten. For the first time Tiya was showing clear signs of wanting to relinquish her grip on the affairs of the Two Lands of Upper and Lower Egypt. Pleased though Neferu was for the formidable woman, she felt the slight uneasiness of one who senses that the mantle of responsibilities might ultimately fall on her unwilling shoulders. She made a sudden prayer that Tiya would live to be a very healthy old woman, and that if this coming child would be the girl she felt it to be, then Tutankhaten would make an excellent and upstanding pharaoh should anything untoward befall the sweet but shy and introspective Smenkhenre when she and Amio were gone.

CHAPTER 23

Neferu's last pregnancy was the most difficult one of all. She was still young at twenty-five, but this time she became easily fatigued and suffered from swollen limbs. Maatnofret was worried and the court physician insisted that she rest much more than usual, coupled with the swelling was a constant backache, which made her grumpy and impatient with the children. When her time for delivery came, she went into a normal labour, but it became prolonged and there was still no crowning of the baby's head. Amio became worried as Neferu laboured two days with no baby. The court physician began to talk of an operation to remove the baby, but Amio would not allow it. He said that too many such operations ended in the death of the mother.

In the end, after almost seventy-two hours, an exhausted Neferu gave birth to her fifth daughter. It was a breech delivery, and this had made everything complicated. The baby remained blue and unbreathing for a while and a distraught Maatnofret hung it upside down to dislodge mucus from its lungs. It worked and the baby gave a weak cry, gradually becoming a more normal pink tone instead of the abnormal bluish colour it had been. Neferu was too tired and disappointed to care much either way. She sank gratefully into a deep sleep. When she awoke it was to find a deeply worried Amio sitting by her side. She tried to sit up but a painful thumping inside her head caused her to lie down again. She realised that she had a fever and she felt very weak. 'Lie still, my darling,' her husband whispered worriedly as Maatnofret came to wipe her forehead and give her water to drink.

'You have lost a lot of blood, Neferu,' her friend said. 'You must rest until this fever goes.'

'How is my baby?' Neferu asked.

'Better now. She will thrive, I think,' the lady-in-waiting spoke with satisfaction.

'Did you get a wet nurse?' asked Neferu

'Of course,' Maatnofret replied sedately before leaving the two of them alone.

Neferu looked at Amio and her eyes filled with tears. 'No son, my husband. I cannot give you a son.' She turned her head away in bitterness.

Gently he turned her face towards him again. 'The most important thing is that you get better,' he said softly. 'I love you, Neferu. I thought that you were going to die. I was so frightened.'

Neferu shook her head. 'The Aten is not ready for me yet. My children are all too small.' She paused before continuing. 'Why won't he grant me a son?'

Amio shook his head almost angrily. 'I have lost faith in the Aten! I cannot accept that he allows all these negative things to happen to us. We! His most ardent followers!' Amio's tone was bitter and demonstrated the depth of his disappointment. It had been a very trying time for them all and at such times it was somehow like that with Amio. When things were going well, he was the most fervent believer, but when things began to go badly, he became the deepest doubter. He was not different from other men in these things.

They called their youngest daughter Satenpare. It was an indication of Amio's deep despair at this time that she was their only child who carried the name of another god as well as that of the Aten within her name. It was his express wish and Neferu gave way in this matter, though with deep misgivings. The name had been suggested by Ay, who thought this would act as a sop to the prestige of the priests of Amun-Re. Between them, Amio and Ay were developing a strategy to strengthen the priests of Re in the north, especially around Memphis and On, to balance the power and antagonism of the priests of Amun in the south. It was now year nine of Amio's reign and they were into their fourth year at Akhetaten.

Neferu recovered fully from the puerperal fever and by the time that Satenpare was six months old she was taking a prominent part in the social life of Akhetaten once more. Neferu felt now that she was stronger both physically and mentally than she had been ever before in her life. The trials and tribulations she had come through had strengthened her and she was no longer the shy and naïve girl she once had been, but a strong, determined and self-confident woman with well-developed ideas of her own. For this she felt in large part a gratitude to Amio because it was her security in his love which allowed her to feel she could cope with anything. Their marriage continued to be strong and happy and though Amio was a forceful character and could be stubborn and unyielding, he was basically cheerful and optimistic, and he had a keen sense of justice. Generally, their relationship was serene and harmonious. Occasionally they would disagree and Amio would explode in temper while Neferu would respond with icy and biting politeness, and the atmosphere around the palace would be turbulent for a time until a truce was made, and everything went back to normal. These occasional quarrels never lasted long, and the sweetness of reconciliation was always greater than the resentment engendered by the rupture between them. Both of them cherished the love they shared and were aware of how rare and precious the quality of their relationship was.

Over the next three years, the process of building and expansion in Akhetaten continued. None of the children had ever left the city since their arrival to take up residence and knew nothing of the atmosphere of life at court in Thebes. Ay and his family were fairly frequent visitors, as were Tiya with her youngest children, Baketaten and Tutankhaten, but they had almost no contact with the rest of the royal relatives. Meretamun, Amio's younger sister, was now married to a nobleman from Kush and they had only seen her twice since then. It came as a very heavy blow to him in year eleven of his reign to receive news that she had died in childbirth. Neferu was very upset. She regretted that she had been so involved in her own affairs that she had had very little contact with Mereta in the years since moving to Akhetaten. She had lost a dearly loved friend who felt like a real sister to her. Amio ordered special prayers to be said for the spirit of his beloved sister and was once again placed in the unenviable position of having to stay in Akhetaten while her funeral took place in Thebes. The seventy-day embalming process was carried out in Kush and the body then transported by military escort to Thebes, as once before for the funeral of his eldest brother, Tuthmosis. Amio now deeply regretted the vow he had made to stay within the confines of a city built to the honour and praise of a god he was no longer sure he even believed in. It seemed ironic. He could not, however, repeal a vow he had made as the pharaoh to suit the needs of Amio, the private man. He raged against himself and Neferu was powerless to help. Again, Neferu travelled to Thebes for a funeral, this time taking Meretaten with her.

After such a long time, it felt very strange to be returning to Thebes again. The royal barge was met by a large group of dignitaries in ceremonial dress, many of whom were obviously very curious to see her. Ay and Tiya came to greet her. She was very conscious that she was representing Amio and the authority of the crown, and she had dressed regally with this in mind. On her head she wore the blue crown of war, as it was called. It was the blue and gold crown that symbolised the union of Upper and Lower Egypt. The grand queen curtsied very deeply in this strange reversal of their public roles, as did

Ay. Somehow, none of it mattered to her anymore. It was more like a game they were all playing for some reason that had escaped her. It was a very serious game, but a game nevertheless.

Neferu went to visit the body of Meretamun as it lay in state and paid her public respects. Hot tears pricked behind her eyes but in her persona of Nefertiti the grand queen she could not allow them to fall. Fortunately for her, she was aided in this by her difficulty in connecting the pale, lifeless, statue-like body with that of the lively and warm personality of her sweet friend. She knew instinctively that wherever the spirit of Mereta was, it had nothing to do with the body she was now looking at. With a sigh she turned away. She did not wish to think of death. She had so much to live for.

After the funereal ceremonies were all completed, Neferu stayed on in Thebes to attend some of the social gathering for which Ay had specially requested her presence. She was surprised to see Yussef at some of them. She knew, of course, that he now had considerable wealth and position and was an army officer of some importance in an administrative capacity at Memphis. She noticed that he appeared to be on very good terms with Pa-aten-em-heb, the former adjutant to Pararameses who had taken an important role in the planning of Akhetaten and later married Mutnedjmet, her cousin by marriage. Neferu was privately disturbed to learn that he had now reverted to his original name of Horemheb, and her unease was further heightened by the icy response to her friendly greeting from Yussef. Although her returned her greeting deferentially, in the manner appropriate by a subject to the pharaoh's queen, there was a steeliness in his eyes which made her quake inside. She knew she was looking at an enemy. There was no trace of her childhood friend in this hard and cold man. He was a stranger to her.

As if to offset this disturbing turn of events, Neferu found herself received with real warmth and affection by Pararameses and his family. The field marshal had spent some years on active service in Palestine with Horemheb, though with frequent trips back to the home country so that he had not lost touch with what was going on. Neferu knew that he was now third in command of the Kap after Amio and Ay. She wondered if this was perhaps also salt in the wounds of some of the older Nubian generals. What Neferu liked most about Pararameses was his genuine niceness. He remained unchanged by the years, quiet, cautious, meditative and undemanding. He promised to come and spend a prolonged holiday with his family at Akhetaten in the near future. He said he was curious to see how it had changed since his last visit. Neferu shamelessly boasted about her beloved home and its delights. For the first time she now met Pararameses' two sons and his baby daughter. It brought to mind her own lack of a son, but she could not envy this sincere friend of her husband. She could not then know just how good a friend this man would prove to be to her later on. She did know that the prospect of a visit from Pararameses would greatly cheer Amio up.

When the time came to return to Akhetaten, Neferu was happy to leave. She had thoroughly enjoyed her visit, in spite of its sad beginning, but she realised how much she and Amio had achieved in Akhetaten. Neferu was more than happy to leave behind in Thebes the many little cliques of squabbling nobles and relatives with all their intrigues. Although her new position as grand queen allowed her to remain apart and above these things, even so, she was constantly aware that it was there in the background.

Meretaten had enjoyed herself enormously and was loth to leave. The lively nine-year old had made many new friends and had been thoroughly spoiled by her relatives. In addition, she had developed a crush on one of her second cousins and declared to her mother that her heart would break to leave him. Neferu's rather hard-hearted reply to this was, 'I've noticed that your heart breaks rather easily. Any time you can't get what you want, in fact.' Meretaten had scowled at her and sulked for a couple of hours and Neferu lost her patience, threatening never to bring her again. Mereta junior could be as stubborn as her father, but Neferu found it hard to resist her. She was so like Amio in many ways. All her children were healthy, none of them had contracted the bone and joint condition from which Amio suffered, and through them Neferu could see what Amio would have been like if he had been healthy. Neferu was content to perceive that all her daughters were beautiful in an exotic way, but Amio revelled in the beauty of 'his women' as he called them. He had always felt himself ugly and had suffered sometimes as a child from the spiteful remarks of other children. Beauty was important to him, and he sought it in everything around him. It was one of the reasons he had so frequently exalted artists to high positions in their social hierarchy in Akhetaten. He admired people around him who were able to make the world a more beautiful place to live in.

When the royal barge docked at Akhetaten, Neferu felt her spirits soar. It was so good to come home. Amio had come to meet her with the rest of the children and came forward to take her in his arms. Here in Akhetaten she could be herself. There was no pompous formality here in front of these people. After giving her a joyous hug, Amio released her, and her trusty friends and fellow citizens came forward to greet her. Openly Neferu told her husband how good it was to be home. Although she had been away only a little over a decan, it now seemed to her to have been an age. These were her people, and this was the only place of importance to her. She put her arm around Amio's waist as he put his arm around her shoulder, and they walked to their chariot. Such a display of affection would have been impossible in Thebes, but here it went without question or comment. How she loved them so, these people, this place, this man and these children. This must be what heaven was like, she thought.

Thebes had calmed down a lot in Neferu's opinion, in the intervening years since the decree to abolish the worship of Amun had been issued. Neferu was pleased to be able to report to Amio that there were no longer any outward signs of resentment at least. Some of the younger priests had been incorporated into the temples of Re, whose worship was still allowed, along with Maat, the goddess of truth, who was still worshipped by many.

Amio had been content to leave these deities alone, one because they used no bestial symbols to represent the gods, and secondly for a very important political reason, which was that these gods were more favoured in the north of Egypt, and it was of paramount importance to keep the fertile delta region loyal to the pharaoh. This was aided by the strong Hebrew population in Goshen, monotheists themselves and totally loyal to Amio. Loyalty to Amio in the north was also reinforced by the presence of the large Keftiu minority in Memphis and On and in many of the coastal cities, who felt a strong tie with their Keftiu queen.

Ay and Amio hoped that the strength of their following in the north would be sufficient to suppress any opposition from the traditional conservatives in Thebes and the predominantly Nubian cities of the south. A recent census had revealed that the population of the fertile northern region was more than twice that of the arid southern region, whose only fertile land lay on either side of the Nile itself. This land comprised no more than narrow strips in some places. In short, both Amio and Ay considered the Lower Land to be of paramount importance in retaining control of Egypt proper and curbing the power of the intriguing priests of Amun, who resented Amio's foreign origins and the rise of the wealthy Israelites in the north. Gradually they developed a plan, with the aid of Tutu, the foreign minister who was resident at Akhetaten, to re-establish Memphis as the capital of the Two Lands. This represented a compromise on Amio's part as he had hoped to make Akhetaten the new capital but now, still without an heir, he listened to Ay and conceded that it might be possible to convert those who were not sympathetic to Akhetaten into accepting Memphis as the new capital. After all, it had been the ancient capital of Egypt from the first dynasty onwards for more than one-thousand years. With this end in view, Amio conceived the plan of sending Pararameses as governor-general of the delta region to be resident at the old palace in Memphis. In order to enlist the support of Orelia, Pararameses' wife, the title of Duchess of Memphis was to be bestowed on her at the time of Pararameses taking up his appointment. Amio empowered Ay to carry out the necessary administrative procedures.

Life at Akhetaten went on in a lively fashion and more and more the court became the centre of diplomacy and culture. Guests and ambassadors arrived from Byblos, Kush, Mitanni and even the kingdom of Hatti away to the far north in Anatolia. Increasingly, people were attracted to Akhetaten, and the city continued to grow, sometimes to the disadvantage of the architectural design that had originally been planned. Being a new city, it drew many young families and the vast majority of its personages of importance were men whom the pharaoh had raised from the ordinary people. Mostly these were people who had had little chance to show their talents and mettle under the Theban regime, which was in the stranglehold of nepotism. Here at Akhetaten, the people were, in the main, young, talented, ambitious and optimistic. It was a city in which there was an ambience of things happening and a sense of the avant-garde. Young men arrived, attracted by the possibilities of making their name and fortune by their own talent and hard work.

There was more of a mixture of races in Akhetaten than in any other Egyptian city, with the possible exception of the northern ports. It was a melting pot of Upper and Lower Egyptians, Nubians, Semites, Keftiu, Philistines, Hittites and other races. Here they lived and worked side by side and each contributed new and different ideas to the art and culture of the new city. To be part foreigner here was almost the norm rather than the exception, and in many households languages other than Egyptian were spoken alongside the vernacular Egyptian. Amio enjoyed this aspect of his new city in particular. By now he was fairly fluent in the Keftiu language, which was related to Egyptian itself, though distantly, and in addition he knew Akkadian and Hebrew, both Semitic languages. He was able to get along in Hebrew well enough with his mother's relatives, though his mistakes caused them some mirth at times.

This diversity of heritage at Akhetaten was significant in giving momentum to a new form of art, of which Amio was inordinately proud. The concept of truth was a quintessential part of Atenism, and he extended this principle to the representations of the various art forms. He insisted that he be portrayed as he really was, rather than in the stylised forms of the past. His deformities were not caricatured but neither were they minimised when he had a colossal statue of himself carved by the artist Tuthmosis.

When the statue was displayed publicly for the first time, it caused quite a stir amongst the population. There were those who considered that Amio had gone too far and that a pharaoh's physical deformities were best left covered from the curious eyes of posterity. Others applauded the act of a pharaoh who was not afraid to be himself, a man. Neferu adored this statue and it symbolised for her Amio's determination to accept himself as he was and to rise above his defects. She felt that the Aten had created him as he was and loved him as he was. Neferu admired Amio's courage and spirit in overcoming things that would have destroyed a lesser man.

There were several first-class artists and sculptors at Akhetaten, but undoubtedly first amongst these was the sculptor Tuthmosis. He was a man of humble origin, whose father had been an artisan in Thebes. He had first come to the notice of Maya, the superintendent of the necropolis, at an early age because of his consummate skill in drawing and painting and he had obtained a position at the court as one of Tiya's junior artists. He was a strong, sturdy man of ambition, but not excessively so, and Amio was drawn to him because of his outgoing personality and wit, which had a decidedly sarcastic flavour to it. His lesser characteristics were his pride and his slight touchiness about his origins. In modern parlance, he could be rather class conscious at times and sometimes saw slights where none were intended. Both Amio and Neferu were particularly fond of him. He was straightforward and honest and without a doubt he was not only outstandingly gifted as an artist, he was also outstandingly intelligent and articulate.

In coming to Akhetaten right at the very beginning, Tuthmosis had seen his opportunity of moulding his life into what he wanted it to be, just as he carved his statues until they were how he wished them to be. It was a unique chance to advance his position and become his own man. In addition to this, he was genuinely attracted by the concept of one living intangible god who had created all men equal. It coincided with his ideas of justice and what society should be like. Although the word had not been coined at that period in time, Tuthmosis was in spirit what a later world would call a true democrat. He felt that he was just as good as anybody else, and he wanted a chance to prove it. His chance came at Akhetaten. Amio would often go to the studio where the great artist worked. Although he would listen carefully to what it was that the pharaoh wanted, he felt himself free to suggest improvements or modifications and he knew that Amio respected his opinions. An easy, informal friendship grew up between them and Tuthmosis would show Amio his own private work, which was in an entirely different style to the official pieces which he usually executed. Amio was entranced with the natural, realistic style of the work which Tuthmosis was producing for his own customers and for himself. He commissioned many statues of birds and animals for the decoration of the palace and the temple. One day he asked Tuthmosis to draw him in the natural style. Tuthmosis did so and Amio was very impressed with the result. It was an excellent likeness. He took the drawing for Neferu to see, and she too was impressed by the stark realism of Tuthmosis' art. The incident had culminated in Amio commissioning several busts of himself, Neferu and the children.

In the execution of these works it was necessary to have many sittings and, especially at the later stages of the work, Amio and Neferu would go to Tuthmosis studio for the work. In the beginning Tuthmosis worked mainly from the drawings he had made, and in the case of the children, he worked wholly from his drawings. Neferu found it very tedious having to sit still for long periods and she would always strike up a conversation. She told him about her own humble origins and about the customs and history of the Keftiu. He seemed genuinely interested and would make the occasional pertinent comments. Tuthmosis was married to a rather quiet and shy lady, appropriately called Meresger, which means 'Lover of Silence'. They had no children and seemed to be happy enough, though Tuthmosis was reputed to be a frequent visitor to the House of Joy, which existed on the other side of the Nile at Hermopolis. Akhetaten did not have a brothel of its own as this was deemed unseemly for the new religion. Neferu wondered whether Meresger knew of the gossip about her husband. Perhaps this was the reason for her silences.

One day Neferu was presumptuous enough to ask Tuthmosis whether it grieved him not to have children. She was surprised when he told her that it did not particularly bother him. He told her that he liked children, and his sisters and brothers had many. He shrugged nonchalantly and remarked that if they came, they came, and if not, well that was the way of things. Neferu was totally taken aback. 'But there will be no one to carry on your name,' she said in amazement.

'My name is not important. I am important for my own sake, not for the generations I do or do not produce,' he replied equably.

'Yes,' she admitted uncertainly. 'But who will remember you in one-hundred years? Aren't you afraid that you will be forgotten?'

'If you are correct, Your Majesty,' he replied with cynicism in his voice, 'the living god will remember me and no one else is important. If I am remembered, it will be for my work and my skill. Someone will look at this bust I am making of you and say, "This is Grand Queen Nefertiti. It is the work of the grand queen's sculptor, Tuthmosis." So, you see, my name will come down to posterity whether I have children or not.' He grinned at her, and she was forced to admit that he was right. A man was important for himself alone, not for the number of sons he would or would not produce. Later that day, she reported the conversation she had had with the sculptor to her husband. In their situation it seemed to be particularly relevant, and they drew comfort from the views of Tuthmosis.

Another time, Neferu tried to persuade Tuthmosis to change his name to one incorporating the name of Aten, but he flatly refused. He was a stubborn man and said that he had been named Tuthmosis and that was what he would stay. If Neferu was slightly annoyed, it was to no avail. He told her that names were not important to the Aten and that probably other foreign peoples called him by a different name in their own language. A beloved child has many names, he said. He also said that the Aten would look upon those people with as much favour as he did upon the Egyptians, and that he looked upon the quality of spirit of men, not upon which name they called him by.

Neferu was interested in these views, which developed an aspect of her faith which she had never considered before. He made her think. His logical mind and straightforward manner of speaking impressed itself upon Neferu and she had to concede that he was correct. Again, she reported the conversation to Amio. Later on, Tuthmosis and Meresger became frequent visitors to the palace and Amio and Tuthmosis would have long philosophic conversations on all aspects of life. Sometimes, when they did not agree, the arguments would become quite heated, but Tuthmosis would always stick to his point of view and not allow the pharaonic status of Amio intimidate him. Sometimes Amio would become quite irritated, but in truth, it was the very reason that he liked Tuthmosis so much. Pararameses, Ay and Tuthmosis were the only men whom Amio could discuss anything with and who were capable of defeating his arguments by intellect alone, and who possessed will and strength of character equal with him. In other respects, each man was entirely different in personality. Ay could be extremely dangerous because of his deviousness. He would strike at his enemies in such a way that they were never able to point a finger of accusation at him. Pararameses was cool and placid and not easily roused to passion; a man of outstanding common sense and decency who planned his moves with precision and was reasoned and methodical in everything he did. Tuthmosis was direct in his anger and aggressive in his manner sometimes, but possessed warmth and passion that was evident in everything he said and did.

Meresger was like a timid butterfly, and it was a long time before she felt at home with Neferu and her husband, in spite of all Neferu's efforts to facilitate this. She became most clearly herself with the children and it was obvious to Neferu that her childlessness was a source of great pain to her. Meresger and Maatnofret developed a warm friendship and in time Meresger would visit Neferu's friend and interact with the younger children even when Neferu was not around. Neferu knew of this through Maatnofret and was happy that the quiet soul had found a source of solace in her children. Maatnofret was pleased to have found a reliable help with the children when she was busy with other things. These were the sort of people Akhetaten had taken unto itself and were an example of the kind of decent and worthy people Neferu would otherwise never have known if she had remained in Thebes.

CHAPTER 24

Not long after Neferu's return to Akhetaten, a message was received from Thebes that Pararameses would be coming to visit, in accordance with the invitation issued to him. Amio was in high spirits, really looking forward to this visit of his old friend, and he went to a lot of trouble to organise some hunting expeditions and some archery competitions to entertain him.

The old friends were obviously very pleased to see each other and that first evening was spent reminiscing about times past and childhood days. Neferu sensed, however, that there was a purpose to Pararameses visit other than its mere social aspect, though the courteous Theban was always careful to say nothing that would upset her.

After they returned from a hunting trip the next day, Neferu noticed that her husband was preoccupied and troubled. In the privacy of their bedroom that evening, she taxed him with questions, and he told her that Pararameses had indeed come to Akhetaten with another motive. It seemed that unrest in Thebes amongst the priests of Amun was still seething and they were actively seeking support from units within the army itself. Mutnedjmet's husband, Horemheb, had used his position as the son-in-law of Ay to further his control over important offices within the administration and he had, with or without the knowledge of Ay (Pararameses did not know) formed powerful friendships within the hierarchy of the most important high priests. Horemheb had become relatively openly critical of Akhenaten and seemed to be surreptitiously stirring up talk of what would happen when, as seemed certain, Akhenaten died without a male heir. It appeared that the subject was common gossip about the court. There was also a lot of subversive discussion about Akhenaten's favour towards foreigners and strange gods and strange ways. Pararameses was eager for Amio to go to Thebes on a prolonged visit to see for himself and to put an end to speculation and gossip.

Amio was very worried about the situation and Neferu said that perhaps he ought to consider going. Amio said that he could not go. He was bound by his vow. If he were to break it, he would be shamed before all of his people. Together they sat up half the night, discussing the possible options. The only other course open to them that offered itself as a practical solution was the hurried development of the north of the country as the chief administrative domain. Amio could place Pararameses as assistant chief vizier of Lower Egypt, with charge of all the delta regions, Memphis and On. Pararameses was to encourage the natural sway of the priests of Re to counterbalance the power of the priests of Amun in Upper Egypt. They decided to send for Tiya to inform her of what was going on, if she did not already know, and to see what her advice was on this situation. Having arrived at these conclusions, they settled down for the night.

The next day, Amio informed Pararameses of his decision and told him that his appointment was to become effective immediately. He himself could choose where he wished to make his headquarters, but Amio recommended Memphis or On because the large Keftiu population there would give him their support as a personal friend of Nefertiti. A messenger was despatched to Demi in Memphis immediately.

Pararameses was taken aback. It was obviously not a move he had anticipated, but he was quick to see the advantages it offered to him. Lower Egypt was a much more fertile and lush area, and as Amio's trusted friend, he would have a pleasant life with his family, away from the intrigues of the Theban court, which were not to his tastes. He could see the political sense in strengthening the hands of the northern priests in what was, after all, a longstanding rivalry between the two factions of Amun and Re. As a non-religious man himself, he found the concept of Aten attractive and it did undoubtedly resemble the Re religion of Lower Egypt, though personally he did not care for priests of any religion. He thought them purveyors of magic. He did not go so far as to profess himself atheist, but he found it difficult to believe in anything he could not perceive with his five senses. Some people might have considered Pararameses lacking in imagination, but he considered himself as having his feet firmly on the ground.

Pararameses stayed one more day at Akhetaten before departing to Thebes with his message for Tiya and his instructions to set in motion his rapid departure to Lower Egypt. In order to avoid alerting the priests of Amun to the real reason for his departure, they had concocted a 'Pageant of Empire' festival which would be held at Akhetaten to celebrate a state visit by Tiya, the grand queen. What could be more natural?

Within a decan, Tiya's letter of acceptance was officially received and the tentative arrangements for the festival gained rapid momentum. Amio also received an official letter from Pararameses stating the grateful thanks of himself and his family for the elevation of position accorded to him. He would be setting out for Memphis without further delay and his family would be following as soon as it was feasibly possible to organise the move. There was no mention of Ay or his reactions in his letter and Amio was compelled to swallow his questions and his curiosity until the arrival of his mother. Neferu had suggested that she could travel to Thebes for him, but he had refused her offer, saying that those with evil tongues would say that she was the pharaoh and not he. He told her that he did not want to put her at risk of unpopularity. It was already against her that she was of Keftiu origin and an ardent supporter of Atenism, not to mention her upbringing as a follower of Re. He was afraid that the priests would try to harm her. They had a long-held reputation for poisoning those they wanted out of their way. Amio therefore forbade her to go. In the circumstances, there was nothing they could do until Tiya arrived.

By the time that Tiya did arrive, three decans later, they had learned to live with the uncertainty and were beginning to wonder if they had over-reacted. There was no indication of trouble at Akhetaten, and Thebes was four-hundred kilometres upriver. Amio sent out spies to gain information from the river boat captains but did not glean anything useful. At length, he discussed the subject in a rather neutral way with Tutu, his foreign minister. Neferu was uneasy about this because she had always had an instinctive mistrust of the man. She was never able to explain why she should feel like this and Amio told her that she was becoming over-sensitive about the matter. He dismissed her fears concerning Tutu as groundless. She held her tongue and decided to let time tell which way the wind would blow.

Tiya finally arrived, along with her daughter Baketaten and Tutankhaten, who was now three years old. They went into deep discussion over the situation. Tiya was, as always, quite pragmatic. She pointed out that Neferu had not had a pregnancy for almost three years now and the physician had informed her that the severe inflammation she had suffered after the birth of Satenpare had probably rendered her sterile. Neferu nodded, knowing this already. Tiya continued that under other circumstances she would have been able to pass Tutankhaten off as the rightful heir because only the court knew that he was not Nefertiti's son, but unfortunately, Pararameses was correct in his surmise about Horemheb's treachery, though Ay could do nothing without proof of his son-in-law's intriguing. Tiya said that Ay was reluctant to accuse Horemheb in public as it would cause a lot of family trouble and he felt that he could effectively control the general without jeopardising the marriage of his daughter unnecessarily. Ay had told Tiya that if

Horemheb did entertain covetous ambitions regarding the throne, there was no way he could legally back them up. He himself was a commoner and Mutnedjmet had produced only a daughter, and even if Amio should die, Smenkhare and Tutankhaten were both in direct succession, and should anything happen to them then he, Ay, would be next in line to the throne.

Put in this way, it seemed that there was nothing to really worry about. Amio trusted his uncle completely. Neferu was less convinced, but she could not openly state her doubts about the character of the charming, intelligent but devious grand vizier in the presence of his sister. In any case, she felt there was a lot of his father in the old Hebrew and that in his heart of hearts, he was an Atenist. For all his moves to placate the Amunists, she knew it was only for political reasons.

What truly did upset Neferu was Tiya's re-introduction of an old topic. She wished Amio to take a new wife to put an end to the speculation regarding the succession, once and for all. It surfaced that Tiya was worried about her own health. After the birth of Tut, she had gone directly into the menopause and had had no show of blood for more than a year. Now, however, she had begun to have frequent haemorrhages and her physician was worried about her. None of his treatments had been effective and just lately she had lost weight and felt continually tired. Now and again, she suffered vague pains in her abdomen, but nothing of a severe nature. She was worried but not unduly so. Being a political pragmatist, as ever, she had drawn up her will, making Nefertiti the adoptive mother of Tut should she die.

Amio was alarmed but could not seriously entertain for long fears that his mother was in danger of imminent death. Even Neferu thought that Tiya seemed as indestructible as ever. Neferu attempted to observe her mother-in-law in a more objective light and saw clearly that the queen had aged considerably in a short time and that there were dark shadows beneath her eyes. An unnamed fear washed over her. Whatever Tiya's faults, she had always been completely behind her son, and as long as Tiya lived there could be no possible danger to Amio. Knowing this, Neferu decided she would do all she could to prolong the life of the grand queen.

Neferu was more than happy to adopt Tut as her official son, though it was not the solution she had envisaged. Her agreement pleased Tiya and relieved her fears concerning her small son's future. He was the same age as Neferu-tashery, and they got along very well except for minor squabbles over toys. Not only that, Tut was such an amiable little boy that Neferu had instinctively loved. She felt that he could very well have been her true son. Gratifyingly, he seemed to be equally fond of her too.

When Tiya realised that Neferu was totally opposed to Amio taking another wife, and would remain adamant about it, she dropped the subject and substituted another one. She suggested that Meretaten, now eleven years old, should marry Smenkhenre, who was now twenty-two, and that Amio should make Smenkhenre co-regent with him.

Although such an early marriage was alien to Neferu's plans for her daughter's future, both she and Amio favoured the plan. It took no account of love, and somehow she felt that the quiet, studious Smenkhare and her boisterous, extrovert daughter would not make a particularly good match. In the difficult circumstances, though, it seemed an expedient match and Amio was particularly positive about it. He told his mother that he had no inclination to take another wife to bed. Since his marriage to Neferu, he had not lain with any other woman and they both felt that the Aten intended them for each other. Neferu told Tiya that she truly felt that if Amio laid with another woman, she would not be able to forgive him. It would spoil their perfect understanding.

Tiya argued that such thoughts were just romantic nonsense, but it was to no avail. She knew that Neferu was a very determined character, and she did not wish to spoil her son's marriage. Privately, she thought that Neferu was being selfish. Tiya reminded Neferu that her own husband had had many other wives beside herself.

'I did not make a fuss about it,' she said equably.

'But Amenophis was not the love of your life,' her daughter-in-law reminded her. 'I think you would feel differently about it if Archduke Tuthmosis decided to take another wife now,' Neferu remarked sagely.

Tiya gave Neferu a sharp glance. 'Mmm,' was her only comment.

Thus it was that during Tiya's state visit some fateful decisions were made, and actions taken to bring them to fruition. During this prolonged visit of three months, Tiya's condition did not appear to deteriorate in any way, but she remained convinced that when she returned to Thebes, Tutankhaten was to remain at Akhetaten and only Baketaten would accompany her back as her consolation.

In order to celebrate Tiya's state visit, great festivals had been arranged and the citizens of the new city turned out in force to celebrate the presence of the grand queen. In commemoration of the event, Amio bestowed some new honours on several worthy citizens, including the artists Tuthmosis and Luwty, who were made noblemen, elevated to the aristocracy for their services to the arts, luwty for his work in mosaics and Tuthmosis for his sculpting.

During her visit, Tiya ordered busts of both Baketaten and of Tutankhaten to be made by the great sculptor and she was delighted with the results, so much so that she also asked for, and received, the preliminary drawings that the artist had made of the two children.

During some of the state functions, Amio allowed his two elder daughters to participate. He had decided that as Meretaten was to marry Smenkhare, she must quickly become used to public functions and the part she would play. To facilitate their awareness of their positions, the girls were allowed to help by handing medallions to their father for him to ceremonially place them over the heads of the worthy recipients. The girls both behaved splendidly and even their grandmother told them that she was very proud of them.

Sometime later, Neferu was upset to discover that Tiya had discussed with her eldest granddaughter the probability of her marrying her uncle and becoming queen. Neferu was very surprised to discover that Meretaten, at least, was amenable to the idea. She was fond of her grown-up uncle but had never considered him as a possible husband. In spite of this, it seemed that she was wholly prepared to marry him. Neferu was horrified that Tiya had broached the matter without her consent. She had wished to discuss all the pros and cons with Meretaten herself. She suspected that her daughter was in love with the idea of becoming queen and did not fully understand the implications of marriage. Much as she was fond of Smenkhare, she had wanted a love match for her daughter. Everything was now out in the open at any rate, whether she liked it or not. She felt very cross with Tiya, who seemed to be taking the reins into her hands once more. She could feel only relief that her mother-in-law appeared to have backed down over the question of Amio taking another wife. She supposed she should feel grateful.

Over the few days following the disclosure to Meretaten of the news of her planned marriage to Smenkhare, Tiya continued her logical discussions with Amio and Neferu. It was finally decided that Meretaten would travel to Thebes with Tiya on her return and her marriage would take place in Thebes soon afterwards, when the two young people involved had been given a little time to get to know each other. Neferu was somewhat shocked by the speed of it all. What had been suggested as a far-out theory was fast becoming an actual event. She felt that she had no influence in the matter anymore.

Neferu soon ascertained that her daughter had a natural taste for power and was very much of the same ilk as her grandmother. The two of them got along extremely well and once Neferu surprised them huddled together discussing the details of the event.

The seed, once sown, had germinated quickly, Neferu thought.

Neferu was jealous. She recognised it herself and felt humiliated by it. Recognising it, moreover, did not help her to come to grips with it. She felt she should have been able to rise above it, but she seemed incapable of doing so. The whole 'Pageant of the Empire' was fast becoming a nightmare to her. She felt she was becoming an outsider in her own home and that Tiya had succeeded in driving a wedge between herself and her eldest daughter. Once she was even disgusted to find herself trying to curry favour with her daughter. She realised then that the inherent competitiveness between herself and Tiya was seriously destructive. It was as if in giving up her small son voluntarily to her, Tiya had to have something or someone in exchange. The two women were unable to discuss the things between them as they were so emotionally charged, and all their old conflicts were suddenly made obvious and remained unresolved.

To add insult to injury, Tiya suddenly suggested that Amio should later marry Meketaten if Meretaten and Smenkhare did not produce a son. Neferu was startled. More than startled, she was shocked beyond belief. The very thought of incest was completely repugnant to her. It was not practised generally in Egypt, though she knew that it was quite usual in past royal dynasties. Amenophis III, Amio's father, had married Sitamun, Tiya's eldest daughter, so there was a close precedent. The idea was abhorrent to Neferu, and she assumed that it would be so to Amio too. In the beginning he did indeed object, but not half as strongly as she would have hoped, and Neferu could see that some part of him was not averse to the idea.

Neferu felt sick and dispirited. Her whole life seemed to be falling to pieces. That evening she was totally miserable and Amio felt guilty for something he had not yet done but was considering. For the first time in their marriage, she refused to yield to him that night. It was not a good omen. They quarrelled and Amio sulkily turned his back on her. In the dark, Neferu cried silently.

The next morning her eyes were swollen. She was due to go to the studio of Tuthmosis for a sitting for a bust he was making of her. She was unusually silent that day, but the artist did not comment upon it. He too was quiet, most unlike his usual talkative self.

Neferu was at a low ebb. She felt that the Aten had let her down. He had cheated her, she his most fervent follower. Why could she not have been given a son? At home, jealousy was her most constant companion. Now she felt not only an outsider in her own home but also that she was on trial and soon to be replaced.

In her jealousy, Neferu made demands upon her husband's sexuality that she would not normally have made. At the same time, she felt angry with herself for doing so and angry with him for making her feel so insecure. Neferu felt from this time onwards that a poison had been introduced into her marriage and spoiled its quality forever. On the surface they seemed to go on as before and Neferu was careful not to let Tiya see the extent of her turmoil and inner torment. Any warmth that had previously developed between them was now irrevocably lost and there was only an icy coldness in Neferu towards Tiya beneath the polite surface put on to smooth the wheels of family life.

In order to come to terms with the feelings raging inside her, Neferu took to attending the temple daily to pray to the Aten alone. Penhasi, the chief servitor, noticed, and was worried. He asked her what was wrong, but she shook her head. She could not discuss this with anyone, even him. He was a dear old man but not a suitable recipient for such confidences as these.

Day after day, Tuthmosis noticed her anxiety and low spirits. One day just prior to the departure of Tiya, he asked her if there was something seriously wrong. He asked her if he could help in any way. His tone was so sympathetic and friendly that Neferu just burst into tears. Once they started, she just could not stop them coming. Tuthmosis came over to her and held her tightly. He did not say anything, just patted her on the back. When she had calmed down a little, she told him everything. She felt he was the only friend she had. The people she loved and had most trusted were suddenly enemies whom she could no longer look to for her happiness. Neferu told Tuthmosis that she must contact her father, who was always a tower of strength. She tried to smile through the blotchy tears as her obvious distress was very upsetting to him.

Tuthmosis told her that he would always be her friend and that she could always confide in him. He would never reveal what she told him to anyone. Then he told her that he had been in love with her from almost the first time they had met. He knew that she loved her husband and that there was nothing that she could give to him, but he wanted her to know it anyway. Neferu was shocked into silence. She had never dreamed of this but, somewhere deep down inside her she felt a still small voice of calm which said to her, 'You see! You are not alone. There is someone who really loves you and will be your true friend.' When Neferu had collected her thoughts, she told Tuthmosis shyly, 'I am very fond of you, Tuthmosis, but I have only ever considered you as a friend. In spite of our divisions, I do love my husband very much and I hope that our marriage can be healed. I dearly value your friendship and hope that you will continue to be my dear friend.' Tuthmosis nodded but made no verbal reply, turning away so that she could not see his face. After a moment Neferu defused the delicate atmosphere by expressing a desire to wash her face before leaving. The master sculptor indicated to her where she could go to repair the ravages of the emotional outburst she had experienced.

As she left the studio, Tuthmosis bowed deeply and took both of her hands in his. 'Remember,' he said simply, 'if you need a friend, I am here.' Neferu extricated her hands, feeling that she was somehow caught in an act of betrayal towards her husband. Once in the chariot, she shrugged her shoulders. It was he, after all, who was guilty of betrayal, she thought, not her.

On arrival back at the palace, Amio was busy with Tutu, the foreign secretary. Neferu had never really liked him. She did not know why; there seemed to be no outward reason for her distrust. Amio had once told her that she was too swayed by her emotions and should keep them under control. Particularly in the case of Tutu he had dismissed her comments, saying that there was no more able politician in Egypt than Tutu, excepting his uncle, of course. Neferu had remained unconvinced but had never since discussed the matter with Amio. For such an intelligent man, he could be remarkable unperceptive.

On this day, she avoided interrupting the pair of them and went to play with the children instead. The children were playing by the lotus pool. Little Tut had become accustomed so quickly to the life at Akhetaten that her ran to greet her just as naturally as the others. Maatnofret, who was sitting with Tiya on the lawn, looked up. Neferu knew that Maatnofret was in her element with the children. She considered them as the children sent in place of the ones she would have loved to have had but had never been blessed with. It was good to see her so happy.

Strolling over towards the two women, Neferu looked around the beautifully landscaped gardens. As she sat down on the grass beside them, she remarked, 'Isn't it wonderful. To think that just a few years ago these beautiful gardens were just a barren stretch of semi-desert.' Tiya and Maatnofret looked around them. They agreed that it was indeed a miracle what the Aten and hard work could accomplish.

'How did your sitting go?' Tiya asked.

'All right,' Neferu answered neutrally. 'I think Tuthmosis is reasonably satisfied with it. I find it hard to sit still for so long while he is making the drawings though.' It was a safe reply, she thought.

Maatnofret laughed. 'If I had to sculpt a head, I would be there for years, and you still would not be able to recognise it. I'd be pleased even if people realised it was meant to portray a human being.'

The others laughed in response.

'I think that goes for all of us sitting here,' Neferu replied in an amused tone. Her eyes wandered over to where the children were playing tag, chasing each other around the shrubs and flower beds.

'I shall miss Tut very much when I leave the day after tomorrow,' Tiya said wistfully. Neferu followed the queen's gaze over to where Tut was chasing Neferu-tashery around a prickly shrub to squeals of excitement. She felt herself soften a little towards the older woman.

'Don't worry about him,' she said reassuringly. 'I will love him as if he were my own child.'

Tiya turned to look at her. 'I know that, Neferu, or I would never have brought him. Between you and Maatnofret, he could not be in safer hands,' she assured her. Neferu bowed her head at the compliment. The thought crossed her mind that in other circumstances she and Tiya could have been the closest of friends. In another time, another place and circumstances, they could have been as close as sisters. There were many qualities she admired in the older woman as a person, she thought. It was a shame that she was Amio's mother and the grand queen of Amenophis III. Would it be the same with herself later on, she wondered. There seemed a considerable danger of it being so, she suddenly realised. Where had Neferu Stassopoulos disappeared to? Was she still there beneath Nefertiti Nefer-Neferu-Aten, chief (and only, if she had her way) wife of Akhenaten, Neferkheprure, Amenophis IV, pharaoh of all Egypt? Neferu felt a shiver of presentiment. She did not wish to lose sight of Neferu Stassopoulos. She was real. Nefer-Neferu-Aten, queen of all Egypt, was just a layer she had put over herself like the layers of an onion. She must not let the alter ego take over.

'What is the matter?' Tiya asked, noting her troubled look.

'Oh, nothing.' Neferu smiled. 'I was just thinking and hoping that Meretaten and Smenkhare will be happy together,' she said glibly.

'They like each other, and they have a mutual interest in the future of our country,' Tiya admonished her. 'If, later on, they fall in love with someone else, well, these things can be arranged with finesse.' The queen added after a short pause.

'I suppose so,' Neferu replied. Privately she believed that the Aten did not approve of such goings on, though he certainly seemed to sanction them time and again, she thought resentfully.

The housemaid came to tell them that lunch was served. The children were rounded up and taken to eat. Over lunch, Amio seemed to be in a good mood.

'How did your sitting go?' he asked her cheerfully. Neferu looked at Tiya. There was no possibility of saying anything privately and, in any case, what could she have said?

'Fine,' she replied quietly. 'I think Tuthmosis is satisfied with the work so far.'

'Oh, good!' Amio said. 'Did he say how long it will be before it is ready?'

Neferu shook her head. 'I don't think he really knows yet,' she answered. At least that was true, she reflected, feeling a little guilty.

In bed that night, Neferu considered the events at the studio that morning. Amio was being particularly loving and trying his best to lift her recent moodiness with his charm. Neferu knew that what had been said between herself and Tuthmosis had been important, in some way she could not define it had been fundamentally important, and she had never kept any secrets from Amio. Yet now, when a golden opportunity presented itself to discuss it, she passed it over. For the first time in her marriage, she kept something from her husband.

Neferu felt very relieved when Tiya finally left to go back to Thebes. Their goodbyes were friendly enough on the surface, but the invisible gap between them remained unfilled. Meretaten was both sad and excited to go. She did not want to leave her family and yet Neferu sensed that she was more excited than sad. She was young, and the future was the unknown just opening up before her, filled with promise, happiness and grandeur. It was Neferu who had the tears in her eyes for the departure of the small eleven-year-old, who still seemed such a child to her.

Tiya, too, had tears in her eyes as she clung to her young son. Tut cried a little and Neferu hugged him as she knelt beside him, telling him to wave to his mother as the ship pulled away. They stood on the riverbank until *The Aten Gleams* was far upriver and Tiya just a tiny speck on its deck. Neferu looked at Tut. She had lost a daughter but gained a son. She remembered an old saying of her grandmother's that a fair exchange could not be considered robbery. But she had not wanted an exchange, that was her trouble. She wanted everything. Was she greedy? Perhaps the Aten was telling her that she could not have everything. She sighed and took Tut and Neffie by the hand. Maatnofret carried Satenpare and Amio walked ahead, hand in hand with Meketaten and Ankhsenpaaten. Was their closeness symbolic of things to come? She tried to push the thought away and concentrate on the present. It seemed the only sensible course of action. She looked down at the little boy. 'We love you very, very much, Tut. I hope you will be happy with us. Your mother loves you very much too, but she thinks that it will be much better for you here while she is not very well. Here you will have lots of friends to play with.'

The small, innocent face looked up at her. Its dark brown eyes were limpid and showed an expression of serene trust. He squeezed her hand.

'I love you and Amio too, Neferu,' he replied placidly. 'When Mummy is better, she can come and live here too, can't she?'

'Yes, she can, if she wants to,' Neferu answered neutrally. 'I think Akhetaten is much prettier than Thebes, don't you?' she asked, trying to change the subject.

'I like them both,' the little boy stated diplomatically. Neferu felt a smile tug at the corners of her mouth at his reply, but she said nothing, and their conversation broke off as they settled themselves into the various chariots. Soon Neffie and Tut were involved in a game of 'I Spy' which lasted until their arrival back home.

Within a few days of Tiya's departure, a messenger arrived from On announcing the death of her grandfather. Neferu was inconsolable, the whole foundations of her life seemed threatened. When she was able to think rationally, she could not decide what to do. It was unthinkable that she should not go to her bereaved family, but should she take her children with her, or should she go alone? On was so far and Tut had only just settled in – she did not wish to disturb his security by suddenly disappearing, albeit for a short time only. She knew she had to go and see her father, who had always been a cornerstone of her well-being, and she knew that Grandma still missed her sorely. Amio was quite equable either way. He was prevented from leaving by the now obviously ill-advised vow which seemed to be imposing impossible restrictions on their options for action at every turn.

There was not much time, but Neferu vacillated still. She desperately wanted to leave, but she did not want to leave Amio alone with Meketaten, although her conscious mind told her she was being unreasonable. The girl naturally loved her father. Strangely, she of all of them had always been his favourite, and perhaps this was why Neferu was behaving so unreasonably now. Part of her intuited that had Tiya suggested that Amio marry Meretaten instead of this daughter, she would not have taken it quite so badly. Neferu tried to analyse her feelings objectively but was unable to define that intrinsic difference which set Meketaten apart from her older sister. She only knew that she felt tormented and that any remark by Amio could unexpectedly trigger off the tumult, or even if he failed to make an expected reply.

Previously, Amio had always been tremendously jealous of Yussef, and he had always pre-empted any talk of an invitation to Akhetaten to try to patch up the quarrel between them. Now when Neferu broached the subject, Amio scarcely looked up, agreeing that it was high time that she see him again and issue an invitation to him to come to Akhetaten. To Neferu, this sudden capitulation seemed to be a further indication of his cooling ardour towards her. Instead of the pleasure she would have felt earlier, she now felt brushed aside. She tried to remind herself that they had now been married for twelve years and that it was quite normal to reach a plateau of feeling after all this time. They had experienced such a close relationship and such passion together that she had begun to take their happiness for granted, and now she was faced with a sudden threat which made her realise that happiness was not an eternally solid emotion that could be relied upon to look after itself. Neferu told herself dismally that perhaps Tiya's intervention in her marriage was forcing her into a healthy period of reappraisal. In the end, he was responsible for his own life and actions. She wanted his love freely or not at all.

It was in this sudden realisation of the core of the problem and her own insight into her nature that she decided to leave for On. She decided to take Tut and Neffie with her and leave the others with their father. The older children were agreeable to this and Maatnofret said she would accompany her and look after Satenpare too. In the end, therefore, the three younger children were to go and Meketaten and Ankhsenpaaten would stay with their father. Amio argued that he did not want all the children to go in case they met with an accident on the boat; with no surviving heir the situation would become even worse. When Amio said this, Neferu found herself looking at him with a sudden, if temporary, intense dislike. The feeling was so intense that it frightened her. This was her husband. It was not right for a wife to dislike her husband.

Afterwards, Neferu thought how much Amio had changed. Gone was his boyish optimism and also his faith in the Aten, and in its place had grown this obsession for a son. It had come to rule his thoughts and all his plans for the future. She wondered what her place in that future would be, now that she could no longer bear children, male or female. It seemed a sterile prospect emotionally as well as physically. Perhaps she would be better off elsewhere for a while to consider what options were open to her.

During the past few decans, Neferu had been unable to prevent herself retreating from Amio in every way, step by step. She was conscious that she was doing this and knew that it was her way of anticipating the hurt that lay ahead and seeking to minimise its emotional impact upon her. She knew that Amio was angry and hurt but she knew of no other way of dealing with the situation without her breaking down. If she could not have his love wholly, she would not have it at all. She felt with all the force within her that what Tiya had suggested would come to pass. She wanted to be prepared for that day in advance.

Once her mind was made up, the travel arrangements were settled quickly. Neferu was not sure whether Grandpa was to be embalmed or not. The normal Keftiu tradition was that the dead were to be buried before sundown on the day of death. She assumed that this would be the case with her grandfather, who had always expressed a strong distaste for the concept of embalming so beloved of many wealthy Egyptians. He had always said that in the new life, he wanted a new, young body, not the old worn-out one. Neferu had always sympathised with him; in fact, she had always felt exactly the same thing.

Neferu had not been home to On in any real sense for more than twelve years and it was like going back in time. Her visit was a private one and she did not want to be recognised. She was in no mood for the role of gracious queen in her present circumstances and apart from an official visit to see Pararameses on Amio's behalf, she was under no obligation to perform any functions of an official nature.

At On, she and the children were met by her father and Demi and quickly ushered to waiting chariots, which took them the remaining journey home. After all this time, the rooms of Grandma's house looked tiny to her. Grandma herself looked remarkably unchanged, although she too seemed to be much smaller. To Neferu's surprise, she was taking the fact of her husband's death very well.

'It is good that he has gone first,' Grandma told Neferu with satisfaction. 'If I had gone first, he would not have known how to cope with looking after himself. Now I can go peacefully when my time comes.' Neferu hugged her grandmother, even now, she was more concerned with others than with herself. She had spent her whole life in looking after others and had found her happiness in doing so. Her selfless devotion made Neferu feel small and selfish.

Grandpa had already been buried, as Neferu had guessed he would be, and all the rest of the family were settling down to the return to the normal routines of living. Grandma was happy to have Neferu and her great-grandchildren with her and busied herself making space available to them in her small home. Neferu marvelled that her battered old heart even had space for affection for these unknown children who were her kith and kin. Neferu herself felt that the house was empty without the presence of her grandpa, but Grandma admonished her that she at least felt his presence everywhere and wondered at her granddaughter. Neferu felt tears prick at her eyelids and was reassured by Grandma's enormous faith.

It was unbelievably easy for Neferu now to fall back into the world of her girlhood. Although Grandma was now seventy, she was in full possession of her faculties. At first, Satenpare had refused to go to her. She was not used to old people and her great-grandmother was dressed all in black, which was also alien to her. Gradually as she watched Tut and Neffie warm to the old lady, she too gradually allowed the old lady to pick her up and sit her on her knee.

Tut and Neffie were fascinated by the stories that Grandma told them about when she was a little girl and about Neferu herself when she had been small. They wanted more and more, especially at bedtime. 'You are spoiling them, Grandma,' Neferu told her gently.

'Nonsense,' her grandmother retorted. 'You can never spoil children with love.'

Here in On, Neferu felt the ragged, jagged edges of her emotions calm and she began to find herself, Nefertiti Stassopoulos, once again. A decan went by, and she felt a strange reluctance to return to Akhetaten. She started to go outdoors, dressed in the long dark habit of a Keftiu widow, face partially covered. She visited the market with Aunt Lea to buy fruit and she even walked the distance to her father's house without arousing any comment or even interest.

At the end of her first decan in On, Neferu sent word to Pararameses that she was ready to meet with him privately. Her visit was arranged under the auspices of Demi, who was now married and resident in Memphis itself. Demi was married to an Egyptian lady called Sentnofret. They already had a two-year old son and Neferu knew that Demi's wife was expecting their second child. The two women had never met before but when they did so, Neferu understood at once that her brother was supremely happy. He had, at last, finally met the love of his life, he told her. Neferu was very happy for him and tried to stem her own misery, which was bitterly underlined.

Neferu asked her brother about Yussef and told him that she had an invitation from Amio for Yussef to visit Akhetaten. Demi looked at her gravely and shook his head.

'I don't think it would be wise, Neferu,' he said gently. 'Yussef has changed. He is not at all the same person we used to know.' Demi paused and Neferu waited curiously for her brother to go on. She raised a querying eyebrow and Demi shrugged. 'Yussef has become hard, bitter and ruthless. As a general he has a reputation for using people without mercy to further his own ends,' he said firmly.

'It doesn't sound like Yussef,' Neferu said uncertainly, remembering suddenly his cold steeliness towards her in Thebes.

'I'm sorry, Neferu,' her brother said. 'The Yussef we both knew is dead. He cut off Grandma and Grandpa years ago and even Father and I only see him in the course of business. He has refused all family invitations for years.' Demi's voice was flat and uncompromising. Neferu remained silent for a while. She stood up and went over to the window of Demi's study to look out upon the garden. There was a large, bright blue butterfly on one of the flowers under the window. She watched it and was reminded of Smenkhare's collection, beautiful but dead.

'They tell me that Yussef married Anula Charalambides,' she said finally.

'Yes, that's right,' Demi answered. 'They have two children, a boy and a girl, I believe.'

So, Yussef had a son. Neferu felt suddenly tired. 'Who do the children look like?' she asked, not knowing even why it should matter.

Demi shrugged. 'It is some time since I saw them,' he admitted. 'The boy struck me as resembling Yussef, as far as I can remember. The girl was so young that it was hard to say. She was more of a mixture of them both, I think.' Demi looked at his sister. 'Why do you ask? Does it matter?' he asked.

'No,' Neferu replied with a shrug. 'I don't know why I asked. Just wondered, I suppose.'

Demi looked at her reflectively. 'It's no good trying to resurrect the past, Neferu. It's dead and gone. This is not like you. What's the matter?' Neferu felt cold, in spite of the heat outside. She sat down again suddenly and there was an expectant silence in the room. The chirruping of the crickets outside seemed all the louder.

'You are right, Demi,' she said quietly. 'The past is gone and there is no going back to it, no matter how much I would like to.'

'Why do you want to go back to the past, Neferu?' Demi asked her gently. His sympathetic tone was too much, and she felt the tears pricking her eyes again. 'What is it, Neffie?' he asked gently, using her childhood name. His kind face was worried.

'I can't produce a son, Demi. You must have heard,' she said in a controlled tone.

Demi nodded. 'Yes, I know, Neffie. What is Amio going to do? Marry another wife?' There was a sudden comprehension in his voice.

'He probably will,' Neferu replied, not moving at all, the tears streaming down her face, falling in noiseless plops upon her dress. Demi watched silently as the tell-tale wet marks spread into little circular shapes on the dark cotton material.

'Who is he planning to marry?' he managed eventually.

'Probably my own daughter, Meketaten,' Neferu answered with an anguished cry and began to sob.

Demi crossed over to her and knelt down, putting his arm around her shoulders. 'I don't know what to say,' he said gruffly. 'This is awful!'

Neferu made a determined effort to control herself. 'There is nothing I can do about it in any case,' she said, taking the handkerchief he proffered and blowing her nose loudly. With Demi she could not pretend. He knew her so well that it was impossible to deceive him.

'Will you go into seclusion if he marries Meketaten?' Demi asked.

'Seclusion?' she almost spat the word out. 'I most certainly will not. I shall ask him to divorce me and make a new life for myself here in On. It has been done before,' she said defiantly.

'I don't think Amio would allow it; he would lose face,' Demi responded.

'Ah, yes. That would be a problem,' Neferu commented cynically. 'Amio could not bear to lose face.'

'Perhaps you are over-reacting, Neferu,' her brother said hopefully.

'Perhaps, but I don't think so. I still love him though, and I have no intention of letting him go so easily.' Even to her own ears, her words had the emptiness of bravado.

Demi stood up silently and looked down upon her. 'That it should come to this,' he said, half to himself. 'You will always have a place here with us, Neferu,' he said heavily.

Neferu shook her head vehemently. 'No! My place is with the children and in spite of everything, I feel that my destiny is with Amio.' She paused before continuing with a sigh, 'Nothing has worked out as we planned, even though we tried so hard.'

'I always imagined that you were both so happy. It seemed to be the perfect marriage, despite its unusual beginnings,' Demi spoke despondently, seemingly just as disillusioned as she felt herself to be.

Neferu now felt a little sorry that she had confided in him. 'We have been supremely happy together until now,' she admitted to her brother. 'I shall pray to the Aten that an acceptable way out of this predicament can be found for us.' Her tone sounded more cheerful, Demi was relieved to note.

'Let's go and have some refreshments!' he suggested. 'You can wash your face in Sentnofret's chamber,' he said, pointing to a curtain at the other end of the room.

'Is it a mess?' Neferu asked anxiously.

'Your eyes are all black where the kohl has smeared,' he said, peering at her. Neferu laughed. Demi was as practical as ever, she thought.

Over refreshments, Demi confided that he and Sentnofret had become very close family friends with Pararameses and his family.

'He is a good fellow!' Demi declared.

'Pararameses?' Neferu asked, somewhat unnecessarily. 'Yes, he is. I have always liked him. He is very loyal, and he has his feet firmly on the ground.'

'We have invited them to Rashid with us later in the year,' Sentnofret informed her. Rashid! Neferu sat electrified for a moment. The very name of the place conjured up a deep nostalgia to return there. She knew that she would never see it again. Amio would never agree to leave Akhetaten, and she could never imagine going there without him by her side. A lump came to her throat as the memories of those happy times past now rushed upon her. She pushed them away resolutely and turned the conversation to less painful subjects.

Demi informed Neferu that Pararameses and his wife were very popular here in the north. The governor-general was noted for his sense of fair play and his efficiency. He combined justice with his authority and seemed to get on very well with all groups, the Keftiu in On and Memphis, the Israelites in Goshen as well as the great bulk of Egyptian nobles themselves. Amio's choice had borne fruit and Pararameses had a great following now in all the delta regions. This at least was very good news and Neferu looked forwards to reporting it to Amio back in Akhetaten.

The following day, after a very congenial reception with the governor-general himself and his family, Neferu received a messenger from Amio. He sent word that he was missing her and the children and wanted them to return as soon as possible. Neferu smiled, cheered up by this indication that she had not yet been replaced in his affections completely. She made plans to return in two days and sent a message to that effect.

Pararameses called upon her with his latest reports to take back to Akhetaten with her. Once all his business had been concluded, they turned to private matters.

'I would hate to have to return to Thebes now,' he told her. 'We are so very happy here.'

This confirmed what Demi had told her and what Orelia also had said. Neferu had found this especially pleasing, as she knew that Orelia had never left Thebes prior to their move to Memphis.

'Amio will be very pleased about this,' Neferu said cheerfully. 'You know that you are the only person outside the family whom he really trusts.'

The governor-general smiled. 'I am flattered at your compliment. Amio and I grew up together. We know each other's best and worst points. No surprises that way.'

'It's true!' Neferu replied, laughing.

With a graver tone, Neferu asked Pararameses about Yussef. He told her that with his marriage, Yussef had become a frequent visitor to Thebes, where his wife's family still lived. The Keftiu general had apparently become great friends with Horemheb over the past year or so. Neferu confided to him what her brother had said about her former childhood friend, but Pararameses could tell her little more. He shrugged. 'He is always very amiable with me,' he assured her. 'It is rumoured that his marriage to Anula is not a, what shall we call it?' Here he paused before finding the expression he sought. 'Not a perfect match,' he said succinctly. 'He has caused quite a few broken hearts, I believe. He is certainly very popular with the ladies.' Neferu was interested to hear this, but she really wanted a more exact picture of Yussef's real opinions, which Pararameses was unable to give her. Yussef had always been so secretive by nature that she guessed few would be able to determine his true state of mind. She had hoped that Pararameses would be one of them.

'Yussef has always been very clever at hiding his real feelings, Rameses,' she said, using his familiar name. 'What do you think his real opinions are towards Amio and myself, now that all this time has gone by?'

Pararameses shrugged again. 'I doubt that he will ever disclose his true opinions to me, Neferu. I have, however, noticed that he has a tendency to adopt a very frigid tone when referring to "the pharaoh". He never discusses Amio by name and he has never mentioned you to me as far as I can recall. If I have mentioned you, then he has certainly not prolonged the subject.' Pararameses looked at Neferu closely. 'Is that what you expected to hear, Neferu?'

This time it was Neferu's turn to shrug. 'I don't know. It does tell me, however, that he has not forgiven us, and in that case, I feel it would be quite useless to issue him with an invitation to Akhetaten,' she replied in a resigned tone.

Pararameses lifted his eyebrows in surprise. 'Had you planned to?' he asked, somewhat superfluously.

'I have considered it frequently. I always wanted Amio and Yussef to be on good terms. It has taken until now for Amio to agree and it seems that Yussef never will.' Her tone was sad. 'I do not like to be on bad terms with people, especially the people I love,' she added.

'Neferu. If I may speak plainly,' Pararameses declared softly, 'I think it would be very unwise to issue such an invitation. Yussef is no longer to be trusted. He is a close friend of Horemheb, and both men are not averse to seeing misfortune befall Amio, and that would mean yourself too. Don't lower your defences to your enemies. There are too many of them already.'

Neferu looked up at him sharply. 'Is Amio in danger?' she asked worriedly.

'Not while Ay lives and I am strong,' Rameses assured her. 'The army will remain loyal to me here in the north and Horemheb is safely under the control of Amio's wily old uncle there in Thebes.' He softened his words with a smile. 'Still, Neferu. Egypt is changing and I believe it was most unwise of Amio to have made that vow never to leave the new city. It is good for the pharaoh to be seen out and about now and again in public and in the most important cities in the Two Lands. What has been done has been done and we cannot do anything about it now. The damage is done. I will do my best to minimise it,' he said to her reassuringly. After a pause he continued. 'I hope I have not offended you by speaking so directly.'

'No. I prefer straight talking to all that diplomatic hogwash so many officials love to plunge themselves into,' Neferu spoke feelingly.

Pararameses grinned. 'I don't believe Egypt has ever had such a straightforward queen, or such a political one,' he said.

'What do you mean, political?' Neferu was genuinely amazed. 'I am not interested in state affairs at all,' she protested.

'I have heard it said of you that you are a witch who has great powers over men, especially the pharaoh,' he answered her.

'But you know that that is rubbish!' Neferu answered indignantly.

'Yes, I know,' Rameses answered calmly. 'But it is the kind of thing that the priests of Amun have put about to discredit you. They say that you have no son as a punishment for desecrating the temples of Amun.'

Neferu was furious. 'How dare they?' she cried hotly.

'Don't worry about it too much, Neferu,' Pararameses said placatingly. 'But try to get Amio to agree to some kind of conciliatory steps towards re-establishing peace with the priesthood. It would help to stop that kind of malicious gossip. You, at least, can still travel.'

'I will report what you have told me, Rameses,' she said, still stung by the ridiculous accusations of the priesthood. 'I cannot promise you anything. I truly have never tried to interfere in the affairs of state, and I am certainly no witch. I can assure you that if I were, I would have managed my affairs quite differently.'

Pararameses laughed. 'You don't have to convince me, or anyone else with any intelligence, Neferu. Don't worry about it anymore,' he spoke reassuringly. They switched subjects to more mundane matters over refreshments and soon afterwards he gave her an affectionate hug and departed.

In spite of Pararameses' calming words, Neferu remained shocked and upset by his revelations. A witch indeed! What a lot of rubbish. She began to feel a strong sense of looking forward to going back to Akhetaten again. It seemed that Yussef was now her permanent enemy and the priesthood of Amun were slandering her to the people. Once again, Akhetaten began to appear as her refuge. Unconsciously, her thoughts reiterated Demi's words. So, it had come to this.

That evening Neferu had a long chat with Grandma after the children had been put to bed. She had not wanted to burden the old lady with her problems, but Grandma was very astute and though she professed to be very poor sighted nowadays it seemed to Neferu that the old eyes missed nothing. 'What's the matter with you, my girl?' Grandma had said after their informal evening meal, eaten with trays perched on their knees. The sorry tale had slowly unfolded and Neferu realised that she should have told Grandma earlier. The old lady's down to earth approach cheered her up more than anything else thus far. 'Never forget, Neferu, that the lives of us all are in the hands of the Father Almighty. Mine, yours and Amio's too! You don't believe that he has any helpers maybe, but it makes no difference in the end. Remember that and keep your heart still. If he has not given you a son then there is a reason for that and you should wait for that reason to be made plain, as I'm sure it will, before it is your time to leave this life.'

Grandma reminded her that generations of peoples came and went before them, and everything was no doubt as it should be in the vastness of the heavens. It was Amun now but who knew whose turn it would be in the future. Although Neferu did not strictly believe this, she loved her Grandma too much to even question her thinking and valued much more the love behind this attempt to relieve her worries. Neferu relaxed and she and Grandma spent a very enjoyable evening reminiscing and laughing. Neferu told her grandmother how much she loved her and had missed her and Aunt Lea. When they said goodnight, she pressed her cheek against the wrinkled old one of Grandma and the only moderately less wrinkled one of her aunt, and hugged them both.

'Thank you, Grandma, and you too, Aunt Lea, for all the love, care and happiness you have always given me.'

Grandma glowed. 'I have had such a good life, Neferu. A good husband and children, and then such happiness from my grandchildren. I am ready to go when the god calls me. When I go, don't grieve for me. I will wait for you. I am only sad that Yussef is estranged from us. I will continue to pray for him. You do it too, will you?'

Neferu felt herself close to tears again. 'I will, Grandma. Tomorrow is my last day here. Perhaps we could pay him a surprise visit. Would you like that?' she asked.

'I would like that, Neferu. I had no chance to talk to him at Grandpa's funeral. He came but left as soon as the coffin was interred. He cared enough to come, you see,' she said softly.

Neferu nodded and pulled her grandmother close. 'It's still there somewhere in his heart, Grandma. He has lost his way, but the Aten will find him when the time is ripe, I expect.'

'Yes,' replied Grandma. 'Maybe tomorrow.'

Neferu woke early the next morning. Satenpare was an early riser and Maatnofret was in Memphis, visiting relatives. The little girl was climbing into her mother's bed.

'Stay here, Satenpare,' her mother whispered to her. 'I will bring you a drink.'

The little girl snuggled down in her mother's bed and Neferu went with bare feet through to the kitchen. There was only old Irene now to help with the chores and she was still asleep. The house was completely quiet. It suddenly struck Neferu that Grandma was usually up and about by this time. She popped her head into Grandma's room, but she was still asleep. She looked so peaceful that Neferu decided not to disturb her and withdrew gently. It was only when she heard old Irene rising that something fluttered inside her. Satenpare used the pot and then Neferu tucked her in firmly, telling her that it was far too early for her to get up yet. When her daughter had settled down again, Neferu returned to Grandma's room. She still lay in the same position and this time Neferu approached her quietly.

'Grandma?' she said hesitantly.

The old lady did not move and when Neferu touched her hand on the coverlet, it was cold.

'Bye, Grandma,' she whispered out loud. She bent and kissed the old lady's face for the last time, but was all the while conscious that she was kissing only a shell. Grandma had already left on her infinity journey. Perhaps Grandpa had waited to accompany her?

Neferu went through to the kitchen where Irene was making a morning drink.

'You are up early today, Neferu! Not like Elena.'

'Grandma has left us, Irene,' Neferu said in a tremulous voice.

'She went very quietly,' the old Keftiu woman said impassively. 'She went exactly as she always said she wanted to. Well, I expect it will be my turn next,' she continued matter-of-factly. 'We'll have to inform your father first thing.' Neferu nodded. She was feeling deeply the loss of her grandmother, but she remembered her words the previous evening and she felt relief that she had had this chance to let her grandmother know how much she loved her and appreciated her.

Later in the morning her father and Demi arrived, and plans were rapidly made for Grandma's burial in the traditional Keftiu manner. She was to be buried by sundown in the grave next to Grandpa's, at the family plot in the necropolis.

'It is very fitting that Grandma did not have to be separated long from grandpa,' Vassiliou said comfortingly to Neferu.

'We had planned to go and visit Yussef today,' she told her father sadly.

'I have sent word to Yussef, but I don't know whether he will come,' her father told her.

'We will see,' Neferu replied, not believing that even the iciest Yussef could fail to turn up for Grandma's funeral.

As they started on their journey to inter Grandma, Yussef still had not appeared and Neferu felt how icy could be the hand of hatred upon her. She felt it like a cold ring of metal squeezing her heart. It was only as they stood by Grandma's graveside late in the afternoon, listening to the prayers of the priest of Re that Neferu looked up and saw through her blur of tears the figure of Yussef. He came to stand beside her father on the opposite side to herself and Demi, pushing his way through the many friends and relatives mourning the old lady. His jaw looked set and determined but Neferu's spirit lifted that he had not rejected Grandma finally. She would never have recovered from it if he had not come.

After the chanting had ceased and the wailing of the mourners quietened a little, everyone prepared to go for a family meal at her father's house. Neferu went over to Yussef.

'It is good to see you, Yussef,' she said quietly. He nodded coldly but said nothing. 'It is strange, but just last night Grandma and I were planning to visit you. We planned to come and surprise you today.'

Yussef looked at her sceptically. 'What would have been the purpose of such a visit?' he asked coldly, but with a certain amount of curiosity.

'It was her wish that you become reconciled again,' Neferu said quietly.

'Grandma and I have never had any quarrel,' he said in a resolute tone.

'I know that,' Neferu said quickly. 'She wanted us to be friends again. I want it too,' she added.

Yussef sighed impatiently. 'We can never be friends, Neferu. You know that!' He spoke as if explaining to a small child.

'I have never stopped being your friend, Yussef,' Neferu said, feeling the tears flowing freely down her cheeks yet again. 'I don't want you to hate me.'

'I don't hate you, Neferu,' Yussef replied, less harshly. 'There can never be any social contact between us, though. Our paths have gone different ways and they can never cross again.' There was silence for a while and Neferu pulled the black headdress more closely about her face. 'I don't hate you, Neferu, if it means anything to you.' He repeated for a second time, before bowing low and taking his leave.

Neferu stood breathlessly for a moment. There had been a crushing finality in his words, and she knew now that there would never even be a semblance of any kind of relationship between Yussef, Amio and herself. Only death was big enough to erase that bitterness, she thought. She took comfort from his words that he did not hate her and from the fact that he knew that she wanted to be his friend. She looked down at her Grandma's grave. I did try, Grandma. I really did. She mouthed the words silently, wondering if the spirit of her grandmother had heard.

Heavily, Neferu walked to her father's chariot. She stayed only a token time at the meal to honour her grandmother's memory and then she left to go back to the old house where Maatnofret was now arrived and looking after the children.

'It's time to go back home,' she told her friend. 'I'm just so glad that I came. Now, with Grandma gone too, it has been a very special time. I miss Amio and the girls,' she said with a wan smile.

Maatnofret admitted that she was more than ready to leave too. 'I am missing Paranefer too,' she answered. 'Let's go home.'

Delayed by one day for Grandma's funeral, they left the quayside early the following day. Pararameses and her father and Demi were there to see them off. It was how she wanted it. No fuss. She watched them until they disappeared from view.

'I have such a strange feeling, Maatnofret,' she spoke almost involuntarily.

'What kind of feeling, Neferu?' her friend asked curiously.

'I know that I will never see On again,' Neferu said slowly.

'Nonsense! It's just the end of a chapter in your life,' the other woman said sharply. 'You are feeling low after such a draining time.'

'No,' stated Neferu. 'I feel calmer now than I have for months. I just know that I will never come here again.'

Maatnofret shrugged. 'It is in the hands of the Aten,' she said.

Neferu smiled. 'You are right, Maatnofret. Everything is in the hands of the Aten.'

CHAPTER 25

At an hour before sundown on the second day after leaving On, the royal ship docked at Akhenaten. Long before then Neferu's heart had flown to meet her husband in spirit and as the boat came in, she recognised his silhouette on the quay waiting for her. Without even the briefest of hesitations, she walked into his open arms, not caring for the modesty demanded by protocol. They had been apart just two decans and it seemed like a lifetime. Neferu greeted Meketaten and Ankhsenpaaten and hugged them closely to her before the children were led away to the large chariot by Maatnofret. Amio and Neferu travelled back to the palace together in the small chariot.

Later, in their chamber, their reunion was all she could have wished. Their separation had been a salutary lesson to them both that happiness is very fragile, and love should be nurtured. Their separation proved the truth of the saying that distance is like the wind, it extinguishes the small flames but only fans the big ones. Their lovemaking lacked none of its former passion and hunger as they told each other how much they had missed the other. They both cried tears, but they were cleansing tears, washing away their hurt and bitterness.

Gradually their marriage recovered from the blow it had suffered. If neither of them forgot their temporary estrangement, then they never mentioned it and outwardly everything was as it had always been. A report arriving from Ay in Thebes indicated that the situation there was calm and that there was nothing to worry about. The priesthood was completely under control. Amio relaxed and began to plan with Paranefer the architectural outlines of a new military barracks, which would vastly increase the defence capacity of Akhetaten. Neferu looked upon this as a kind of war game, not to be taken seriously.

In truth, Neferu had learned an important lesson. She had come to understand herself better than ever before and she knew that it would not hurt her substantially if the throne were to pass out of her hands after Amio's death. She had no interest whatsoever in building a dynasty. It seemed to her to be a vain goal. She did want to maintain Atenism and see it grow throughout the Two Lands, but she was not prepared to take steps to accomplish it on a great scale, only at a personal level. The Aten must make his own insurance for the future, and would do so, she believed.

As a woman she perceived, as many women before her and since, that she had invested all her life and emotional resources into one man and his children and that that had left her extremely vulnerable to his whims. She now had first-hand experience of his capacity to hurt her, and she was afraid. She knew that she could be destroyed if he betrayed her and so she decided to form a broader base for her personal happiness in the future. This had to be achieved in such a way that Amio would not be offended, or that nothing significant would be detracted from their relationship.

She looked around for something interesting to fill her days. Her possibilities were limited to what society considered fit functions for the wife of the pharaoh. She did not want to arouse any more negative comment in Thebes than she had done already. In the end, Penhasi, the chief servitor, came to her aid when he happened to mention that he wished he could start classes for the smaller children, to teach them about the religion of Aten. Penhasi assured her that the secret of building a strong faith in the Aten was to start with the children. When they grew up, they, in turn, would teach their children. Neferu saw the logic of that and agreed to use her influence to get more mothers to form small classes for the little children.

Several other mothers came forward and Neferu became part of a roster of teachers who took classes on a daily basis, helping the children to learn to read and write also. Through this, Neferu also became involved in another project started by Penhasi. The servitor had become concerned about the increasing numbers of poor and homeless who had begun to arrive in Akhetaten, drawn by the stories of a new social order being built up there. Many of these poor were disabled and handicapped in some way. There was now a sizeable population of children with no visible means of obtaining a living other than by begging.

Penhasi came to see Amio about the problem and Amio ordered funds to be released for the building of an infirmary for the old and sick, and a school for the children. The school was a total disaster in the beginning as the people refused to send their children, preferring them to work at home or to beg for alms. Amio, Penhasi and Neferu were at a loss until Amio thought of a system of payment in kind. Those families who sent their children to school regularly were issued with food and household requirements for as long as the children attended. In this way, they envisaged a future population of young adults who would be loyal to the system and ready to defend it if necessary. Such adults with the ability to read and write would not be so impressionable to the superstitious sway of the priests of Amun.

Neferu threw herself into the project with great enthusiasm. She felt it made for her. In Akhetaten, at least, she knew that she was very popular, and her face was known everywhere. She found it easier than they had ever imagined persuading the more influential citizens of Akhetaten to contribute to the project, both in provision of actual goods and in their time. Many other of the noblewomen became actively involved and Neferu gained tremendous satisfaction from doing what she considered to be the Aten's work. Amio, at first very dubious about the extent of her involvement, later came to support her completely. A strange, new and exciting world began to open up to her. The crisis she had been through seemed to have released an inexhaustible stream of energy within her, which she needed to channel into something positive.

In addition to her part in Penhasi's project for the poor, Neferu persuaded Tuthmosis the sculptor to teach her how to make pottery and how to paint and glaze it. She often took the two older girls along with her and they all had a good laugh with their first attempts. The girls were very proud of their somewhat lopsided pots and such objects began to adorn the palace at the oddest nooks and crannies, much to Amio's amusement.

Grandmother Tiya became the proud owner of a whole collection of such artefacts. Even the three younger children became involved and Tut and Neffie also became busy, if unskilled potters. Although their painting was frequently smudged and it required a great deal of imagination sometimes to make out what it actually represented, the happy little artisans were proud of their handiwork and the adoring recipients were not over critical of the donor's skills.

Tuthmosis was a willing teacher and if he sometimes regretted his generosity in offering his services, he did not make it apparent. He and young Tut got on especially well, which came in handy when the boy had to sit for drawings. He was quite at ease and Tuthmosis was able to capture a series of very charming and natural expressions. Even Amio eventually became involved in the family pottery-making efforts, and with practice their skill increased until they managed to produce some quite presentable specimens. Tut became quite ambitious and insisted upon making a clay head. Neferu had to pretend to pose for it and it was difficult not to laugh as the determined five-year-old boy concentrated on his masterpiece with a set look on his face and his tongue clamped between his teeth. It was not long, however, before the young fellow realised that great works of art are more than the products of enthusiasm and determination and he fast became frustrated with his masterpiece, eventually abandoning it in a corner of the atelier's yard, where it became baked brick-hard by the sun and remained as a memento to posterity for as long as Akhetaten stood.

All of these activities were originally born of an instinctive survival mechanism in Neferu, in order to reduce her overwhelming emotional dependence upon her husband. They were not threatening to him, and they brought her much happiness. She felt she was needed by a wider circle than her family.

True to her word, Neferu had reported to Amio everything which Pararameses had told her. Amio had vaguely conceded the need to bring hostilities between himself and the Amunists to an end if it could be achieved without any loss of face on his part. Neferu never again questioned her husband on this subject. She was no longer interested in what went on outside Akhetaten. If Amio specifically requested her opinion on anything political, she would give it as far as she understood the question, but she deliberately refrained from initiating conversation on anything other than the goings on in Akhetaten. She never intruded upon his sessions with Tutu each morning, when the latest emissaries were received, and messages sent. In this way, she preserved her peace of mind intact and lived each day at a time, feeling a sense of accomplishment as her city grew and prospered.

Neferu continued her sittings for her statue and neither she nor Tuthmosis ever again discussed the fateful day of her breakdown. She was grateful to him for the adroit way he handled the aftermath of it, not ignoring what had happened but rather preferring to let it lie. She never felt ill at ease with him, on the contrary, there grew a silent bond between them of a friendship cemented by trouble, not broken by it. When the head was finally finished Neferu was very pleased with it. She felt that Tuthmosis had captured not only her outward looks but also something of her inner strength. Amio was thrilled with it and wanted to remove it to the palace right away, but Tuthmosis persuaded him to let it remain at the studio for a while longer. He wanted to make another copy to serve as a model for the smaller ones he would make for sale in his shop. Amio agreed, flattered that there was such a large market for the likenesses of both himself and his wife. It was indeed a sign of their popularity in Akhetaten that Tuthmosis had such a thriving business in these small statues. Tuthmosis took on two assistants to train as sculptors. They were two poor local boys who had shown an aptitude for drawing. He did the finishing work while they did the basic outlines of the busts. Gradually they too would learn the techniques of the great artist.

The summer was long and hot and many times Neferu dreamed of going to Rashid to spend a couple of decans at the seaside with her children. It would not be the same, however, without Amio, and he was bound by his vow to remain in Akhetaten. Amio now openly admitted his deep regret at having ever made such a vow, but there seemed no way out of it except by death. He too felt that it would have done them all good to go to the coast for a short holiday and there was really no reason why they could not have done so. Life was quiet and serene in Akhetaten and the situation in Thebes was under control, according to the reports of Ay. Still, Amio felt he could not renounce his vow without losing face.

Halfway through the cool period, Tiya informed them that she intended to make a short visit to see them privately, especially her son, Tutankhaten, whom she was greatly missing. As soon as Neferu heard of it she began to dread it. She was afraid that Tiya would start again with the suggestions which she found so intolerable to her soul. Amio perceived her anxiety immediately and lost no time in reassuring her that he would not allow his mother to upset her. Partly reassured by this, she said no more and made an effort to plan for the visit with as much composure as she could manage.

When Tiya arrived, Amio was true to his word and must have forbidden his mother to mention the subject of the accession, because she never once brought the subject up. Tiya did, nevertheless, spend several times in prolonged conversation with her son out in the gardens and Neferu, who quietly observed them from the veranda, guessed that they were not discussing the varieties of plants that were now blooming. She had an impending sense of trouble but made colossal efforts to quash it. Tutankhaten had missed his mother greatly when he had first come to Akhetaten but that was now a year ago and he had now settled down with the girls. Amio and Neferu had come to love him as their own child, and he seemed to be completely happy with them. When his mother arrived, he was, conversely, shy and even slightly in awe of her. Perhaps he had felt abandoned and in his childish five-year-old way was showing his anger for this. Whatever the reason, Tiya obviously felt rejected by him. He clung to Neferu as if she were his mother, and at first he refused to go to Tiya at all. After, Neferu wondered how much this little drama contributed to what was to follow.

Tiya was now forty-six and she was beginning to look old. She did not have the energy she had had formerly for matters of state, and she had relinquished almost all her power to her brother. She told Neferu that she was still bothered by her woman's problem and was losing a lot of excess blood. Her physician was not able to do anything about it. Her relationship with Archduke Tuthmosis was as close as ever and he wanted to make her his wife officially. So far, she had resisted, in order to maintain for Tutankhaten a clear and legal right to the throne through herself as the widow of Amenophis III. She was afraid that marriage to her lover with its consequent loss of official status would in some way, inconceivable to Neferu, compromise Tutankhaten's rights. Neferu felt that Tiya was mistaken but did not voice her opinion, as she felt that she did not want to become involved any further in the affairs of Amio's family than she already was.

The visit of her mother-in-law to Akhetaten passed without any contretemps but also without any expressions of warmth. Tiya made several overtures of a friendly nature to Neferu, but Neferu could not bring herself to respond. She behaved with great politeness but could not find it in her heart to forgive Tiya the rift she had caused between Amio and herself.

It is said that danger always comes from where you least expect it. Over the years of her marriage, Neferu's initial wariness of Tiya had dissolved in the afterglow of her love for Amio. A certain tenuous friendship had slowly grown between them but now when Neferu was in the presence of Tiya she felt that she was in the presence of a subtle enemy. It was anathema to Neferu's basic nature the manipulative way that Tiya always sought to secure alliances in every possible direction, and she thought it dangerous too because it sought to override people's natural inclinations. Indeterminate honours and half-bribes would not buy the soul of someone. Neferu felt in her bones that one could sway one's opponents by power, but in order to bring about true and permanent change it was necessary to change the heart of someone and that could never be bought. Tiya sought to neutralise dangers before they were even on the horizon, whereas Neferu preferred not to look for them. It seemed to Neferu that Tiya's strategy could only ensure that trouble would come because in courting allies she brought to the very attention of them their value as a bargaining factor and thus increased their greediness to hold her hostage in her weakness. The saddest thing about their relationship was that she perceived that Tiya was just as unhappy as she was with the situation.

When Tiya left, Neferu felt some of the tenseness leave her. Amio made no reference to the succession and Neferu did not question him. In some vague way she could not escape the feeling that once again their relationship had been tarnished, but she could not decide what it was that made her feel like this. Things settled down again and she took up active work with Penhasi once more.

Neferu felt that Tiya was very disappointed with her. She herself supposed that she did not live up to the traditions of past pharaoh's wives, but she felt she was only queen by accident. She remembered her early days at the Theban court and reflected that Asenaath would have made a much better queen than she had. Certainly, Asenaath and Tiya had much more in common with each other than she had ever had with Tiya. Probably Tiya bitterly regretted having asked her to stay, she thought wryly.

Months went by quietly for Neferu and then Ay sent word that he would be coming to visit early in the new year. Amio was pleased. He enjoyed conversing with his witty and lively uncle and more and more he began to feel frustrated by the restrictions on his movements by the vow which he had imposed upon himself.

The cooler period was almost over when Ay arrived with his wife, Teya, the great royal nurse. There was a party atmosphere around the royal apartments and Amio seemed rejuvenated in the wit and good humour that animated the grand vizier and his wife. Teya made much of the children and they, in turn, adored her. The news from Thebes that Ay brought with him served to allay Amio's fears. He told Amio that Horemheb had to appear to be in sympathy with the priests in order to gain their trust, whereas he was actually keeping an eye upon them and reported back to Ay, either directly or through Mutnedjmet, everything of importance. Neferu found something very distasteful in this and it only served to underline the wiliness which was an integral part of the grand vizier's nature.

Life was very quiet at Akhetaten after the departure of the grand vizier, and Amio became rather introspective. He seemed to be wrapped up in some problem of his own and would answer absentmindedly if Neferu spoke to him at such times. Their marriage seemed to be on a plateau yet again. They were happy but they had lost the excitement of exploring each other's minds to discover new and engaging characteristics. Now they no longer looked, assuming that they knew all there was to know about each other. Neferu knew that she was just as guilty as Amio in this, too used to being happy and taking one another for granted. Whatever was amiss in their psychological relationship did not spoil their physical attraction for each other, so this helped to tide them over an otherwise unsatisfactory phase in their relationship.

With the beginning of the truly hot weather, news came from Thebes that turned their lives upside down. Tiya was dead. At first, they simply could not believe it, it was so unexpected, and she had always seemed to be indestructible. It was impossible to believe that this formidable woman was no more. Their incredulous request for more information was answered with a confirmation, giving more details of her final illness.

Amio's indomitable mother, to whom all illness was a weakness to be hidden at all costs, had succumbed to a major haemorrhage. Her 'woman's problem' had turned out to be far more serious than any of them had realised. In the decans leading up to her death she had apparently suffered severe abdominal pain that only opium had been able to relieve, though her last moments had been peaceful, according to Ay. Even this last illness had been kept secret until the very last days as Ay's precaution against a perceived weakness in the throne being utilised by their enemies. Neferu was both amazed and shocked by this subterfuge on the grand vizier's part. Surely, he could not be so totally blind to the glaring loophole within the bosom of his own family?

Neferu was stunned and Amio was thrown into a frenzy of grief, the like of which Neferu had never seen before. For the first time she was witness to the extent of the bond between Tiya and her son. Now as never before he raged at the stupidity of the vow he had made. Neferu begged him to break it and go to his mother's funeral. She got Penhasi to come and absolve Amio from the vow with the Aten's blessing, but this only made Amio even angrier. Neferu felt cold shivers pass over her.

Once the initial acute reaction of his grief was spent, Amio began to make resentful remarks to Neferu, concerning her attitude to his mother during her last visit to Akhetaten. Neferu did feel guilty that she had not been more friendly the preceding year and she was sorry for his mother's death, but she withdrew coldly from his remarks. Once again, they retreated behind the barriers of silence they had erected to protect themselves from each other.

In spite of his grief over her death, Amio refused to travel to Thebes for Tiya's funeral and sent word that her body, once embalmed, was to be brought to Akhetaten for burial in the tomb which he had had made for her in the cliffs in the wadi. In Thebes there was consternation and uproar over this and, for the first time, Ay and Amio openly quarrelled. Ay contended that his sister should be buried at Luxor in the Valley of the Queens, as befitted the wife of Amenophis III. Amio remained insistent that his mother's body be brought to Akhetaten, where a team of artists were working flat out to complete the work necessary to decorate the tomb as rapidly as possible.

Amio's fury was increased by what he perceived as lack of support from Neferu in this quarrel. He considered her neutrality as hostile and demanded an explanation. Neferu replied to his angry interrogation thus: 'I believe that Tiya should be buried wherever she herself expressed a desire to be buried. As she never mentioned the matter to me, I do not consider myself well-placed to argue the point.' Neferu tried to put her point of view diplomatically but to no avail. Amio ranted and raved, destabilised by his extreme grief. Neferu felt sorry for him but, in her heart of hearts, she felt that Ay was right. Tiya should be buried with her husband. She understood that Amio's insistence on bringing the body to Akhetaten was a subconscious desire on the part of Amio to bring her close to him again, but in his present state of mind there was no way she could explain this to him without further enraging him. She tried as best she could without upsetting him, she hoped. 'Amio, I don't believe that our earthly remains are of any real importance. Where your mother exists now, she has no need of that body; it is just an empty shell. Her spirit is free and with the Aten and will always be close to you. The whereabouts of her body has no relationship to the whereabouts of her spirit.'

Amio listened haughtily and an icy atmosphere existed between them for days, so that even in death Tiya became a cause of strife between them. Finally, Amio issued a decree that Tiya's body was to be brought to Akhetaten for burial. Ay was furious and sent a message that the whole of Thebes was scandalised.

From this time onwards, the relationship between Amio and Neferu began to deteriorate. At first, she tried to comfort him, but he was cold and accusatory towards her, and she grew more resentful. Their marriage began to fragment in tiny ways that seemed of no consequence in themselves but which she knew were important. She did not know how to get through to him. To have picked up on one particular incident would have seemed carping and trivial. She just knew that something destructive was pervading the air around them.

In public they continued to maintain a facade of their former loving closeness but, in private, Amio had become cold and bitter towards her and she, in turn, withdrew from him more and more. Nowadays they only made love when his physical frustration could be put off no longer and there was no tenderness in it anymore. Although she needed him as much as he needed her, she always felt abused afterwards. She herself no longer initiated any lovemaking, and she stopped using terms of endearment to him, preferring to use his name, Amio, instead. At first, she would forget and call him 'darling' or 'my love' as had been so natural in the past. As time wore on, however, she used the terms less and less. Inside she felt that her heart was breaking. Sometimes she felt that she loved him as much as she ever had done but at others she felt as though she hated him. She could not believe the speed at which their marriage was disintegrating.

Notwithstanding these unhappy circumstances, it still came as a shock to her when Amio suddenly and coldly brought up the subject of the accession one day. It was true that Meretaten had not yet conceived, but she was still only thirteen years old, and she and Smenkhenre had only been married for one year. They had a whole lifetime ahead of them. She reminded him of this.

'Meretaten is fourteen next month,' he answered coldly. 'If she does not conceive during the coming year, I shall have to consider marrying Meketaten to secure a son for the throne.'

Neferu was bitter. Amio shrugged. 'You have known for a long time that it might be necessary,' he answered, refusing to discuss the matter further. Yes, she had known, she thought to herself. She felt cold, alone and rejected. She knew beyond doubt that it was the beginning of the end. She was thirty years old, and she felt there was nothing left for her.

More and more, Amio took to having Meketaten accompany him on state functions. Occasionally, Amio would come to her and request that Neferu accompany him instead of Meketaten, but he was always careful to point out that this was only to maintain the public image of a happy and successful marriage. It made Neferu feel cheap, but she played the part required of her as best she could.

Hardest of all for Neferu was the difficulty of maintaining a semblance of unity in front of dinner guests and at the frequent social functions that they were required to attend. It took all of her acting ability and Amio's too, no doubt, and she suspected that some of their closest friends saw through the sham. One person who certainly did was Tuthmosis. During a party one evening, when he happened to be alone with her for a moment, he commented, 'You are falling apart before my very eyes, Neferu. Can I do something to help?' Neferu almost lost control there and then in public. Tears came into her eyes, and she had to turn to face him fully in order to avoid anyone else seeing. He looked acutely concerned but continued to make inconsequential small talk, as if she were answering him, until she managed to regain control over herself. To an onlooker, it must have looked as if they were discussing a subject of a problematic nature.

'Come and see me at my studio,' he told her in a low voice. Neferu shook her head firmly.

'I can't Tuthmosis. It is out of the question.' He made no reply to this, but ever afterwards, whenever he was present, she would catch him looking at her.

Just after Meretaten's fourteenth birthday, she and Smenkhenre arrived back at Akhetaten for the ceremony to make Smenkhenre co-regent with Amio. Amio's brother was a quiet, kindly young man and Neferu knew that he would always treat her daughter with great delicacy. They were very different in personality, and she suspected that it would be the headstrong, outgoing Meretaten who might go astray if a problem should occur between them. After the celebrations, the young pair returned to Thebes, where the priests of Amun were to perform further rituals, in accordance with tradition. This was an attempt by Amio to be conciliatory towards the Amunists. Shortly afterwards the young couple were to move to Memphis to take up residence there. It was a further attempt to increase the status of the ancient capital and weaken the importance of Thebes as the centre of politics and administration.

Just after the departure of the junior pharaoh, Neferu began to feel that there might be a chance of finding Amio again. It started the day after the departure of their guests. The family dined alone that evening, and afterwards Meketaten left to attend the birthday party of one of her friends. Ten-year-old Ankhsenpaaten was playing in the nursery with Tut and Neffie. Amio and Neferu were sitting on the veranda enjoying a goblet of wine. There was a silence between them. The housemaid brought Satenpare to kiss her parent's goodnight. The child had been very fractious that day and had not slept during her afternoon rest period, so she was going to have an early night. Neferu kissed her daughter and Amio took her upon his knee for a cuddle before the maid took her away. The sun was slowly sinking in the sky and Neferu knew that in half an hour it would be night. She watched the sun sinking as if mesmerised. The stirring sight never failed to impress her. 'It is beautiful, isn't it?' Amio said in a companiable voice, turning to look at her. She turned to look at him, surprised by the gentleness in his voice. It was a long time since he had used such a tone to her. She wondered if she had imagined it, but he was smiling at her slightly.

'Yes, it is very beautiful, and very stirring,' she agreed. There was an awkward silence for a moment, neither of them daring to say anything for fear of breaking the truce, then Amio said, hesitatingly, as if trying carefully to choose the right words and the right tone, 'I hope that what has been accomplished here will remove from us the onus of responsibility, Neferu.' His tone was conciliatory, and she knew that he was trying to reach her. She wanted to meet him halfway.

'What do you mean, Amio?' Although she knew to what he was obliquely referring, she was genuinely puzzled at his wider implications. She was afraid to read too much into his words and wanted him to make it quite clear as she had no intention of ever letting him make such abuse of her again.

'I mean that if Meretaten and Smenkhenre have a son, then we are free to be ourselves again. They are young and have many chances.' There was a slight note of appeal in his voice. She loved him so much, in spite of everything, and she hoped so desperately that he was right that she could not even bear to think of the alternative.

'I will pray that they have a son and soon,' she replied with intense sincerity.

His next question was totally unexpected.

'Do you still love me, Neferu?' she looked away, not wanting to concede any ground. He had hurt her too many times. On the other hand, the question was such an important one that if she skirted around it, she might lose the only chance they had of reconciliation. She would have preferred to know whether he still loved her before answering, but she decided to dump her pride and answer honestly and directly.

'Yes. I still love you, Amio.' She did not look at him. Across the table he reached out and took her hand. She looked at him now and saw that he was looking at her with a gentle and tender expression.

'And I still love you, Neferu. I always have,' he said quietly. Tears came to her eyes and began to fall down her cheeks. She felt too weak to hold them back this time. How could he have been so cold and cutting towards her if he had loved her? Amio got up and came round to her. He knelt on the ground and pulled her face down to his.

'Don't cry, my darling. Don't cry.' He kissed her. It was useless to say 'don't cry' to her when she was either on the point of doing so or already was. It just made the tears come all the faster. In spite of her efforts to stop them, they quickly became a torrent.

Neferu hated her weakness for crying. She always felt that it took control of the situation right out of her hands, as well as making her nose red and shiny and making her eyes swollen. It was hard to be dignified when you felt such a fright. Amio did not seem to mind. He wiped her face gently with his cloak and just at that moment the sun slipped over the horizon and darkness came suddenly.

'Come, my love. Let's go inside,' he said, gently pulling her up. She rose and he pulled her to him, stroking her hair. It was the first act of spontaneous tenderness between them for months and she did not want to move for fear of spoiling the moment. Sometimes there were times when she felt that she hated him, but always underneath she knew that she would love him as long as she lived. He was her destiny. In the cool evening air, she shivered slightly, and he felt her arms. 'You are cold, darling. Come now.' They walked towards the sitting room where the servants had lighted the oil lamps. Amio picked up a rug and put it round her shoulders.

'I want you, Neferu. You are my wife and I love you. Do you want me too?'

'How could you doubt it?' she kissed him gently on the lips. 'Yes, I want you, Amio,' she replied.

Their lovemaking that night was again as it used to be in the old days before things had soured between them, and they miraculously found each other again, in spite of all the bitterness and cold words. They made a promise to each other that night, that they would never let such an estrangement separate them again.

For a brief period of several months, Amio and Neferu lived out a second honeymoon period. If it lacked the youthful excitement of the first, it made up for it in the sweetness of lovers who had trodden the edge of despair and permanent separation and stepped back just in time. They both made a tremendous effort to avoid stepping on the sensibilities of the other. It was a time of renewal of their love and a time when there was still hope for the future. As the months passed, however, each developed a silent concern with the lack of positive news from that distant city which seemed to haunt their nightmares, Thebes. There was still no sign of a pregnancy for Meretaten and, reading between the lines of the messages that came, there was something else, unstated. Neferu asked if she should travel to Thebes, where the pair were presently staying on a prolonged visit from Memphis. She wanted to investigate but he was unwilling to let her go. He told her that he could not bear her to be away from him and that he could put up with anything just as long as she stayed close. She could not consider going after that. Although Amio was unwilling to adopt an attitude of laissez-faire, he was once again bound by the vow he had made so rashly so many years before. He sent for Ay to come to Akhetaten eventually.

The news was not good. It appeared that Meretaten showed no sign of pregnancy and Ay was having to make more concessions to the army to keep the priests of Amun under control. Lower Egypt, effectively under the control of Pararameses, remained completely loyal to the pharaoh, so there was no problem there, but Ay admitted that he was beginning to find Horemheb very difficult to manage. It appeared that Horemheb had the backing of the priests of Amun and the overall control of the army of Upper Egypt. Ay suspected that his son-in-law had ambitions for the throne, though there was no way he could legalise such pretensions even if both Amio and Smenkhenre were to die without male issue. There was always Tutankhaten, who was a direct link with his grandfather Tuthmosis IV, even if he was actually the son of the archduke. Officially he was the son of Amenophis III and had now been formally adopted by Amenophis IV, Akhenaten.

Neferu was angry with Ay. She could not understand how he had come so quickly to lose control of the situation, even if Horemheb was his daughter's husband. Ay admitted that he was getting old and tired and had come to depend more and more upon his son-in-law. Neferu was not convinced that this was the essence of the matter but consoled herself that Mutnedjmet had produced only a daughter, no son. When she looked at the grand vizier, she felt troubled by something vaguely familiar which fluttered inside of her. She could not put her finger on what it was, however.

One thing which was certain was that Horemheb had no legal claim to the throne whatsoever and Mutnedjmet had no direct link by blood to the royal family. It did not look likely that she would produce any more children after all this time, a factor of considerable relief to Neferu in the present situation.

'It is very likely that Meretaten will soon conceive,' she reminded the grand vizier.

He gave Neferu an enigmatic look. 'It might not solve the problem, Neferu,' he answered cynically.

She lifted her eyebrows in perplexed surprise. 'Why on earth not?' she asked uncomprehendingly, exchanging a sharp glance with Amio.

'Because Meretaten has been … How shall we say it? … A little generous in her affections.' The grand vizier looked apologetically at them both.

Neferu felt her blood run cold. 'She has been unfaithful to Smenkhenre?' she asked in a shocked voice, and yet there underneath a still, small voice asked 'Why are you shocked? Isn't this what you feared?'

Ay shrugged. 'Your eldest daughter is a very beautiful girl, Neferu, and she loves flattery and admiration. There are many at court willing to give it to her. Smenkhenre is quiet, and if we are honest, he is not a handsome man. They are not the same kind of people, Neferu.' He spoke without condemnation.

'I foresaw this!' Neferu said furiously. 'Why did no one listen to me?'

'Everything was under control as long as Tiya lived,' Ay answered. 'She kept a firm hand over the girl, but with the death of her grandmother, there was no one to whom she would listen.' Ay paused. 'Her indiscretions are widely known and there are few at court who would be willing to guarantee with certainty the paternity of any child she might produce.'

Neferu felt nauseated and sat down suddenly. Amio looked just as shocked as she felt. 'You will have to go to Thebes, Amio. I don't see any other way of your establishing your authority once and for all if you do not go.' Her voice sounded tired and defeated, even to herself.

'You know that I cannot go, Neferu,' her husband stated obstinately.

'Penhasi has said that he will publicly absolve you from your vow in the temple of Aten,' she cried in anguish.

'Penhasi is not the Aten, and the word of the pharaoh is law,' Amio answered in a dispirited voice. 'I cannot break my own vow.'

Neferu looked to Ay for support, expecting that the grand vizier would give her unequivocal support in this, but strangely, he did not do so and agreed wholeheartedly with Amio. The wind was taken out of Neferu's sails and instinctively she knew what was going to come next. She even composed her face in resolute readiness for it and was not surprised when Ay suggested it.

'Amio must formally marry Meketaten and secure an heir to the throne as soon as possible.'

She looked dully at the grand vizier. Did he know what he was doing to her? She looked at him and suddenly she knew what it was that was so familiar about him, it was the small, pinpoint pupils. She had seen them before on Amenophis III. Was Ay also addicted to the seeds of the poppy? If he were, it would be so easy for Horemheb to manipulate him. For the first time she began to wonder if this whole visit were not some political strategy to drive a wedge between herself and Amio. The priests of Amun would surely have gained a victory if they could accomplish that. Was it possible? Had Ay concluded some kind of deal? It seemed hardly likely and yet. And yet.

Effectively, Neferu knew that she was cornered. If she said the wrong thing now, it was possible that Ay would go straight back to Thebes and report that she and Amio were estranged and that he was left without support, stranded in his own city. The priests would say that the Aten did not look after his own so he must be a powerless god. It would be the denial of everything she believed in.

'You win, Ay,' she said quietly, shrugging her shoulders.

A look of surprise crossed his face, as if he had expected resistance. Amio, too, looked amazed, but said nothing.

'Well!' said Ay, still gazing at Neferu. 'I take it we are all agreed?' Neferu shrugged by way of reply. In her heart of hearts, she had known for years that it would come to this.

In the privacy of their chamber later on, Amio made strenuous attempts to reassure Neferu that the marriage was only for the sole purpose of securing a son and he would discontinue the relationship directly this goal had been attained. He told her that no one could replace her in his affections. In spite of herself, Neferu kissed him. Dear Amio. He really was so naïve in some ways. She felt the wisdom of an old, old woman, already foreseeing what would happen.

Neferu wondered why the Aten had chosen Meketaten for this role. Did he not know that she was the child she loved most out of all her children? She feared that now this love would turn to hate, and she prayed to the Aten to control her jealousy in such a way that she would not cause her daughter any harm. She was afraid of the depths to which that weakness in her might drive her actions.

Next day, in the presence of Amio, Neferu tackled the unpleasant task of telling her daughter that a marriage was to be arranged between her father and herself, in order to secure an heir to the throne. According to the plans she had arranged with Amio the previous evening, his and Meketaten's belongings were transferred to a suite at the other end of the palace, and she informed Maatnofret of what had been decided so that Maatnofret could organise the spread of information amongst the rest of the staff. She knew that she would not be able to bear doing it herself. Maatnofret understood her anguish and was, as always, a tower of strength. She supervised the apartments which had been chosen, knowing that they had been chosen for their inaccessibility. Neferu did not wish to be an accidental witness to the embraces between her daughter and her husband. So began the most difficult and painful period in Neferu's life.

Neferu began to consider Yussef. Was this how he had felt about her, she wondered. If so, she could understand it for the first time and she could forgive him. She felt an immense regret for the Keftiu boy she had once known and put so easily aside. Thoroughly shaken, Neferu sat up on her bed. She was filled with a desire to destroy. She wanted to hurt Amio, and in such a way that he would never recover, but she did not know how. Neferu called for Maatnofret and asked her to prepare her bath. While she bathed, she considered what to do. In the bath she carefully appraised her figure. She was thirty-one now and had borne five children. As dispassionately as she could in the circumstances, she assessed herself. She was still slim, but her bottom was now bigger and had lost the firmness it once had had. Her thighs were no longer as slim and as firm either, she had to admit, and her breasts were no longer firm. Her ankles and her arms were still good, and her face was still beautiful. Her face had been praised so many times that she had come to think of it as some kind of public work. It was on her but not really her.

Neferu observed her face in the silver mirror objectively. Her skin was still good, and she had no wrinkles. Yes, without doubt, her face and her hair were her best features. She had let herself go, she realised. She never wore makeup or did her hair in a fashionable way. She wondered if she should change, smarten herself up a little. On the other hand, if she began to wear cosmetics, Amio might think she was making a pathetic effort to win him back. He might despise her and then she would feel really sick. Right now, she hated him, and this feeling empowered her. She felt she had wasted nearly sixteen years of her life on a total rat. She looked at herself sombrely in the mirror. She would waste no more. She began to make her plans.

The next day at lunch, Neferu told Amio that it was high time that he got Tuthmosis to model heads of the younger children. Neffie and Tut were now seven years old and quite capable of sitting still for reasonably lengthy periods. In any case she could go with them and make the day enjoyable by playing games with them. It might even be possible for Tuthmosis to do the five-year-old Satenpare too. The unsuspecting Amio was delighted to arrange this and happy to see that she had something to interest her. He had something to tell her, and he had been wondering how to do it without hurting her. He was now given a golden opportunity.

'Neferu, Meketaten is pregnant,' he said to her gently.

Neferu felt her heart thud and then stop for a moment. She decided to give him one last chance. She knew in advance, though, that he would fail the test. Looking up innocently, she answered carefully.

'I am pleased to hear it. Does that mean that you will be moving back in with me again?'

He realised immediately that he had fallen into a trap. He could not look her in the eyes. He turned away and began to bluster. 'Well, I can't desert poor Meketaten just like that. She needs me now more than ever until the baby is born.'

'And what afterwards, Amio?' she asked in a carefully measured tone. He did not answer, just shrugged his shoulders. Neferu looked at his back as he stood there, and she suddenly realised that she did not even like him. He was a total sham. All his life he had relied on other people to organise his life and solve his problems or clean up the mess he made. He was a man without the courage of his convictions. Her judgement was merciless. 'Do not worry, Amio. I am not going to object,' she said calmly.

He turned around in surprise and relief. He had obviously been expecting a scene. 'Do you mean that?' he asked, as if needing further reassurance.

'Oh, yes,' she replied. 'In fact, I'm going to ask you never to approach me again.'

His eyes narrowed. 'What do you mean?' he asked ominously.

'It is very simple,' she said with an immense feeling of calm. 'You have destroyed my life and happiness, and now I want you to grant me the same rights that you have granted yourself. I want your permission to take a lover if I fall in love, without fear of your retribution.' Amio was fundamentally shocked. She saw it in his face. He appeared to have thought of that possibility, however.

'You are thinking of going to Yussef after all this time?' he asked, amazed. She was not, she knew that that road was well and truly spoiled, but she perceived that it might be useful to have him think that. She merely shrugged by way of reply. Amio considered the request. He did not want her going off to Thebes, he would be the laughing stock of the city. On the other hand, if he granted her request, he could continue to live with Meketaten without feeling guilty about Neferu. He loved her still as a person and did not want her to be unhappy. 'Very well! You may take a lover, but it must be someone from Akhetaten. I will not allow you to leave the city. Secondly, you must be discreet so that I do not lose face publicly.'

To his surprise, she nodded her head in agreement immediately. 'I agree to your terms, Amio. One more thing. Do you promise me that you will not attempt to harm my lover in any way whatsoever?'

She wanted there to be no cause for accusations later. Amio lifted his eyebrows in surprise.

'Are you already in love with someone?' he asked, showing an inexplicable annoyance on his face.

'No,' she said neutrally. 'But I want the rules to be clearly laid out in advance.'

He seemed relieved 'Oh, I see,' he said expansively. 'Well, I don't see how I could refuse you that. I hope I am not a mean-spirited man.' She smiled slightly at his words and at his obvious lack of understanding. She had always thought of him as an intelligent man, but he was obviously capable of great stupidity too. In that moment she despised him.

'Thank you, Amio. I want nothing more from you,' she said, giving him a deep curtsy before turning and walking out. Amio watched her go. That curtsy, done in private, brought home to him, more than anything she had said, that they were now separated. It had happened so painlessly that he could not believe his luck. The Aten was on his side, after all. In spite of his vast relief, a part of him felt sad as he thought of all the happy times they had had. Still, one could not live in the past and he had a new love now.

Neferu was very careful not to rush things. She knew that Tuthmosis was in love with her, but she did not want to use him as a sop to her ego. She found him physically attractive, and she liked him a lot, but she had never allowed herself to think beyond that. Now she could allow herself that freedom.

Amio was as good as his word and arranged for her to visit the studio the next day. If the sculptor was surprised to see her, he did not show it. It was the first time Neferu had been out for several decans. In her misery, she had been living in virtual seclusion. Today, though, she had made a special effort. Her hair was neatly coiffured as usual, but she had put a lotus in her hair and outlined her eyes with kohl. She had gone back to her Keftiu roots and chosen a soft, white linen dress in the classical Keftiu style, falling in folds down to her ankles. She had only changed after breakfast, which they all still shared as a family. She had not wanted Amio to guess anything. After all, was it not he who had wanted her to be discreet?

Tuthmosis was, in spite of his earlier words, very fond of children. He gave the younger children clay to play with, in the room in which his assistants were working and he set about making copious drawings of Tut. In an odd way, the little boy had become the focus of Neferu's attentions of late, almost as if having removed her regard from Amio she had transferred it to Tut. The boy did have a very sweet nature and was highly intelligent, which Neferu found gratifying. He quickly grasped concepts that most seven-year-olds would not even consider. For instance, one day after telling Tut about the living god and discussing the fact that people had a spirit as well as a body, and that it was the spirit which survived when the body died, he suddenly interrupted her to ask whereabouts in the body the spirit lived. When she explained to him that it pervaded the whole body, he had asked what happened to those people whose bodies were damaged or who only had one leg. Was the spirit damaged too? Neferu was taken aback, and after considering the matter further she told him that she supposed that the spirit was somehow closely connected with the mind and therefore its centre must be in the head. It did not make any difference if the body was damaged, the spirit was intact. Tut had had no difficulty in understanding this. Neferu loved him very much and though she did not dare to say it aloud, she loved him more than any of her own children, even more than Meketaten, whom she had been remarkably close to prior to the present. Neferu knew instinctively that this child was her kindred spirit. Sometimes he seemed to know what she was thinking, he tuned into her moods and emotions so correctly. Once, after a quarrel with Amio, which he had inadvertently overheard, he had stepped forward and said very gravely, 'Never mind, Neferu. I still love you. I will always love you.' She had crushed his little body to her and kissed his head. There are times when one can derive a lot of comfort from a small child, as she had then from little Tut.

Tuthmosis began to chat to Tut. He told Neferu that it was important to get to know a child to bring out the personality a bit more. Unlike an adult face with its wrinkles and expression lines, a small child's face was an empty frame in which only the basic features were mapped out. She understood that when he pointed it out to her, and she realised that his work led him to a very good understanding of the personalities of his various subjects. Tut and Tuthmosis seemed to get on very well. Although the boy was quiet, he was not shy, merely reserved. Tuthmosis was outgoing and he spoke to Tut as an equal. He did not talk to him in a patronising way as many adults do to children, or treat him as some kind of mentally deficient adult, which again many adults do to children.

At the end of the first day's sittings, Tuthmosis had many drawings of all the children, and it was decided that she would bring Tut back the following day. Before they left, Tuthmosis said he would like to do a full-length statue of Neferu for his own pleasure. He asked her if she would sit for it. Neferu sighed. 'Perhaps it should have been done ten or fifteen years ago, Tuthmosis. I am far past my best now.'

Tuthmosis laughed incredulously and said, 'You have never been more beautiful, Nefertiti.' It was bold, and she noted that he had never called her by her full name before. It was very flattering, and it gave her ego a much-needed boost at this difficult time.

She smiled and asked, 'Why do you call me Nefertiti? It seems strange to me now after not hearing it for so long.'

'Because Nefertiti is your name, and it somehow epitomizes the essence of you so well. I will always call you Nefertiti. It is a beautiful name for a beautiful woman,' Neferu found herself blushing like a young girl, something she had not done for years. She lowered her eyes so that he would not see her pleasure at his words. Tuthmosis looked at her for a long moment and then he invited her to visit his home. The invitation was issued to her alone and did not include Amio, she noticed.

'My husband is engaged on other matters at the moment,' she said. 'His wife is expecting a baby.' She spoke in a detached fashion and Tuthmosis observed her clearly.

'I invited you, Nefertiti,' he said clearly and firmly.

'I don't think Meresger would be happy to have an unaccompanied female dine with her husband,' she said it feelingly, having suffered this herself.

'Meresger and I have not been man and wife for many years, Nefertiti.' Neferu was shocked. She wanted to ask him why but could not find the words, so she looked at him questioningly. He shrugged his shoulders. 'She finds lovemaking painful and distasteful, so I have always found my consolation elsewhere.' She had to admit that he was disarmingly frank. So that was why he was such a frequent visitor to the House of Joy. She became aware that they were now on dangerous ground. All pretence of maintaining any barriers of rank between them was now permanently shelved. This frank conversation had taken them beyond those borders. That being so, she decided to satisfy her curiosity on one more score.

'Why have you never divorced her?' she asked wonderingly.

Tuthmosis shrugged again. 'She has no family of her own. She was an orphan. There would be nowhere for her to go to, and anyway,' he continued frankly, without any sign of embarrassment, 'I like her. I am very fond of her. Once, I loved her. The memory of it is surely worth something and on top of everything else, she runs my home smoothly and competently. If I were on my own, I would get into a terrible mess,' he said, with an engaging grin. So, he was kind as well, she thought. Not many men would have been so understanding. She smiled at him.

'I would love to come, but for the purposes of discretion,' she emphasised the word slightly, 'I think I must bring the children with me.'

He smiled, obviously pleased at her acceptance of his bold invitation. 'I understand. I think Meresger will enjoy their company.'

Neferu nodded her head. 'We will discuss it tomorrow,' she said, making to take her leave.

'Peace be with you, Nefertiti.' Tuthmosis smiled and bowed slightly.

'Peace be with you also, Tuthmosis,' she replied and took her leave. As her chariot drew away, she looked at the door of the atelier and he was standing there. He lifted his hand in salute and bowed his head slightly. She lifted her hand in reply and then was gone.

Back at the palace she was still slightly flushed with the pleasure of the day and the open attraction which Tuthmosis has shown so frankly but so delicately. Amio was the last person she wanted to run into. As is invariably the case on such occasions, he was the first. He and Meketaten were coming down the open corridor of the courtyard.

'Neferu,' he said in surprise, obviously having forgotten where she had been.

Neferu had just handed over the children to their nurse so she could not use them as an excuse to get away quickly. She felt a slight sense of surprise. Only a few days ago, the sight of him hand in hand with her daughter would have been like a knife in her entrails, now she was pleased to notice that it had no effect upon her. She merely replied, 'Yes?'

Amio looked at her closely. She was suddenly conscious of the lotus in her hair and the kohl around her eyes, not to mention the ochre on her lips nor her sudden taste change in fashion. His long eyes narrowed slightly.

'Ah, yes. You took the children for a sitting, didn't you?'

'Yes, Amio. Is there anything wrong?' she asked demurely.

'No!' he said and she turned to pass him on her way to her room. As she got properly past him, she turned as if she had just remembered something.

'Oh, by the way, Amio, Tuthmosis and Meresger have invited us to dinner. I told him that you were very concerned on behalf of your new wife and therefore wouldn't be able to go, but I have accepted on behalf of myself and the youngest children. That was all right, wasn't it? Of course, if you want to come, I will be able to tell him at tomorrow's sitting.' Her whole tone was purposely very casual, and he answered in the only way that he could have.

'No, No. You did quite rightly.' She turned away and continued to walk on. 'Neferu!' She stopped at the sound of his voice and turned round again. He seemed puzzled. 'Have you been somewhere else today?'

'Well, yes,' she answered. 'I called on Penhasi to take a new prayer I have written to the Aten. His new assistant was there. He seems a very charming man and it was such a pleasure to speak Keftiu again, for he is Keftiu, of course, as you already knew.' That should deaden the trail, she thought. Actually, the new assistant to Penhasi was a very charming and handsome man, what was more, he had recently been widowed and, as she was well aware, Amio had not met him, having stopped visiting the temple. It had been a source of great worry to Penhasi.

'Oh. I haven't met him yet!' Amio said. 'But you like him, then?' he added speculatively.

'Very much so,' said Neferu, smiling innocently. She was very much tempted to tell him that the new curate was also very handsome, but she did not want to go into overkill. Better not go too far, it could backfire on the young man. She felt very pleased with herself, sure that any possible suspicions which Amio might harbour were now located other than at the studio door. Not that she really expected Amio to be jealous, but she did not want to arouse his instinctive curiosity or possessive instincts.

This incident was a useful lesson to Neferu. From then on, she decided that she would continue to dress carefully and to apply cosmetics daily, even if she were staying at home. In this way, Amio would not notice either from her dress or her makeup her comings and goings. She no longer cared if he thought she was trying to recapture his attentions. In fact, that would have been conducive to her plans, as it would be bound to make her look pathetic and achieve the opposite effect. Fooling him was going to be much easier than she had thought, and she was beginning to enjoy it. She secretly nursed the thought that the best revenge was when the victim did not even realise that vengeance had been wreaked.

At dinner one evening a few days later, Amio complimented her on her appearance. He seemed vaguely irritated for some reason, but she thanked him sweetly. She looked at Amio and she said that she thought it best if, from now on, they dined separately. They could dine together, and she would dine with the rest of the children. Neferu said simply, 'I don't think that we need to further disturb an already inflamed situation. We must be civilised about this, don't you think?' Amio seemed doubtful, but after hesitating, agreed.

Neferu sighed. Did the dunderhead expect to have his cake and eat it too? She reflected that Amio was remarkably naïve, considering he had been brought up in the bed of intrigue that the Theban court was. She had thought that he would have absorbed the ability to handle this kind of situation with his mother's milk. Something had gone wrong. Perhaps he had had a wet nurse, she thought, with sudden amusement. That woman must have been the only honest one in the whole palace complex.

That night she went to bed early and, for the first time in weeks, she slept soundly. She woke the next morning refreshed and looking forward to the coming day. She was no longer at the mercy of other people's actions and was once again in control of her own feelings. It felt wonderful. She had her own excitement now at the marvellous sexuality of her feeling for Tuthmosis.

The day following the corridor incident with Amio, she had arrived early for the sittings. The children were boisterous and chatty and provided just the right background for the unspoken conspiratorial understanding she now had with Tuthmosis. Just like little Tut, she did not need words with this man. He knew that she was attracted to him, she sensed that he was aware of it, and it acted as a catalyst on them, increasing the attraction merely on the strength of that knowledge.

Neferu watched the sculptor as he worked. He wore a simple loin cloth and sandals. He was taller than Amio, and of a much sturdier build. He was not fat at all, but he was not thin, rather, well-covered and muscular. He had a beautiful body, she thought, and there was a strong air of sexuality about him. She felt aroused by the thought. He was not an overtly handsome man, but he had a very open, masculine face which appealed to her.

When Tut became tired, Tuthmosis sent the little boy to play while he poured out drinks for them all. He told them that he would expect them in the evening, two days hence. For the next two days he would not need a sitting because the first rough work did not require it, but if she wished to visit, she would be very welcome, and he would do the drawings of her which he had previously planned. She replied that she would come alone on the following day to inspect the work. He smiled at this. He was standing very close to her, and she could almost touch the attraction in the air between them.

Neferu was now free to do as she liked. She was always careful to visit the temple daily as she always did, to pay her respects to Penhasi and she made a deliberate effort to be charming to Xerlon, his new Keftiu assistant. It was not difficult as the man was very likeable for his own sake, and Neferu reflected that if Tuthmosis had not already engaged her affections, she could quite easily have found solace in Xerlon. Neferu had obviously been a little too friendly with Xerlon because Penhasi made haste to tell her not to encourage the young man too much. She was a very beautiful woman, and one could not tell! Neferu wanted to laugh but she was so genuinely fond of the old servitor that she could not. Penhasi had witnessed her terrible distress earlier and he was very happy to see that she had recovered her equilibrium. Indeed, she seemed blooming of late. He sympathised with her greatly because he too thoroughly disapproved of Amio's behaviour. He had several times told his wife that he would not be surprised if the Aten punished him severely. He had even said as much to Neferu earlier and been very taken aback when Neferu had replied that she wished he would.

Consequently, Penhasi was puzzled by Neferu's present good humour, and he was quite at a loss as to how to explain it. When Penhasi commented again to Neferu that he was very disappointed at her husband's non-attendance at prayers, he was amazed to hear her reply. 'Well, Penhasi, you must be patient. He has waited so long for a son that he wants to make sure this time!'

Privately, Penhasi thought that her words did not make sense. What had that to do with his non-attendance at the temple? However, there was no mistaking her placating tone of voice. He told her sincerely, 'I do admire your wonderful generosity of spirit, my dear! After all you have been through!' Neferu looked down demurely, not quite up to facing his honest gaze. If he only knew, she thought to herself. Later, as she left the temple, she overheard Penhasi telling Xerlon, 'Wonderful woman! Absolutely devoted to her husband, you know!' She was overcome by a fit of laughter and had difficulty swallowing the sound. She hoped they would not notice her back shaking. Devoted? Not anymore.

The dinner party with Tuthmosis and Meresger went off beautifully. From the start, she noticed that Meresger appeared to be in on the conspiracy and appeared not to mind, even to actively promote it. Later Tuthmosis confessed that he had told her because he needed her help to avoid public suspicion. She had agreed immediately, feeling that the queen would not at least take away the security of her position by marrying her husband. She had openly said so. Neferu found it a very curious arrangement, but Tuthmosis was used to it.

Meresger came strangely to life with the children, and it was odd to watch her come out of her shell with them. She adored them and they sensed it and abused it outrageously. Satenpare especially used all her charm, putting her arms around Meresger's neck and scrambling onto her knee. Neferu told Tuthmosis that children are sometimes a decided asset.

After dinner, the children stayed with Meresger while Tuthmosis showed Neferu around the villa. She had been there before, of course, with Amio and other guests, but not into the private rooms. Now, he showed her the whole villa, which was full of his paintings and statues. She gasped at the beauty of it. He had arranged everything so tastefully. There were beautifully carved female nudes in alabaster and frescoes on the walls of scenes from natural life. He paused in front of one room before taking her in. She wondered why, but soon all was revealed. It was his bedroom. Here the paintings were all erotic, scenes of tender love and passion, as if to compensate for the lack of it in his marriage. There was nothing coarse or pornographic about it, she noticed. She realised that behind the cynical image which he presented to the world, he was a born romantic.

'Do you like it?' he asked, almost diffidently.

'It is beautiful,' she said, genuinely impressed.

She thought that if she had known about this earlier, she would have commissioned such paintings for her own and Amio's room, but she did not say that. Neferu knew that Tuthmosis had brought her into this room for one reason only and that he was waiting for a sign from her. She turned to look at him. He lifted her chin with his fingers and said, 'Nefertiti.' Bending down, he kissed her on her lips. When his lips touched hers, she found herself responding immediately. He put his arms around her and pulled her to him. She could feel his frustration. After a while he released her and looked at her warily. She said nothing and began to remove her dress. He helped her to do so. She laid it carefully over a table and removed the rest of her clothes. He examined her body carefully, as if memorising it for a drawing. The eternal artist. Then he removed his loin cloth and came towards her. Suddenly he put his arms around her and lifted her bodily, carrying her over to the bed. He lay her gently on it and then climbed on it himself. He kissed her breasts and skilfully moved his hands over her body before finally entering her. When his passion was spent, he lay back and laughed quietly. She knew that he was surprised by her passionate response to him.

'You and I are made for each other, Nefertiti, we are two of a kind,' he said, looking at her with amusement in his eyes.

'What kind are we?' she said, smiling.

'The kind who need love to survive,' he replied. She did not deny it, nor did she feel guilty at what had happened between them. It had all seemed so natural, as if it was meant to be. 'Look!' Tuthmosis rolled over and pointed to two small doors about forty centimetres wide on the wall.

'What are they?' she asked, because she saw that they were fitted directly into the wall itself. He got up and opened them and she drew in her breath in a gasp as she found herself faced by a portrait of herself. Neferu got up to take a closer look at it. 'When did you do that?' she asked him finally.

'About twelve years ago,' he answered, smiling. She was stunned. Had he been in love with her all those years? As if he knew what she was thinking, he lifted her face to his and said to her, 'I told you before. I have always loved you.' Neferu felt suddenly small in the face of such devotion. She wondered how she had never noticed. 'I have waited a long time for this,' Tuthmosis said quietly.

'Was it worth it?' she asked, wonderingly.

'Yes. It was worth it,' he replied.

She reached up to him and embraced him. 'We could be killed for this, you know,' she said to him.

'Yes, I know. It will not stop me,' he said determinedly.

She smiled at him. 'You are a reckless hothead, Tuthmosis.'

'No. I am only a man driven by love for a woman he met too late.'

Tears came to her eyes, as they always did when she was moved. 'I think we had better go back,' she said.

'When will I see you again?' he asked.

'I will come to the studio the day after tomorrow,' she replied. 'Should I bring Tut with me?'

'Yes,' he answered. 'It is time to do some more detailed work.'

She smiled up at him. 'I am happy that sculpting takes such a long time.'

'Are you?' he asked her gently.

'Yes. I am,' was her answer. Quickly she washed herself down in his bathroom and then dressed. He tidied her hair with his deft fingers before they rejoined the others.

Meresger was telling the children a story and they stopped to listen to her as they entered. The children were spellbound. Once again Neferu found herself wondering about this very tolerant woman. Meresger looked at her husband. He regarded her steadily. She smiled slightly and gave him the slightest of nods, as if she was pleased for him. Neferu intercepted the look. To make a world, it took all kinds of people, she thought.

When the story was over, Meresger sent for the servant to bring the chariot. It was not far to the palace, but it was dark. Neferu thanked Tuthmosis and Meresger and then they left. In the chariot she asked them if they had enjoyed themselves and they answered in the affirmative. Tutankhaten asked her where she and Tuthmosis had gone. 'To see some of his beautiful statues and paintings,' she answered easily. The boy asked nothing more.

When they reached the palace, Neferu helped Maatnofret and the nursery nurse to put the children to bed. When they were tucked in, she went to say prayers with them. She wondered what the Aten was thinking about her right now. She hoped he would forgive her, but she could not help the feeling that it was partly his fault. If he had prevented the whole thing happening in the first place, by giving her a son, it would not have happened, she thought resentfully.

The next day, Neferu was writing a poem, sitting on the veranda, when Amio approached. She carefully turned the papers upside down and looked at him inquiringly.

'How are you, Neferu?' he said by way of greeting.

'I'm fine, Amio, thank you. And you?' she answered.

He smiled and sat down opposite her, looking at her thoughtfully. She wondered what it was he wished to say. 'Did you enjoy your dinner last night?' he asked.

'Yes. It was fun. Tuthmosis showed me all his work. He really is exceedingly talented. I hadn't realised that the villa is so beautiful.' She spoke naturally and truthfully but instantly felt very wary inside.

'Yes, the children said that they enjoyed themselves. I suppose Meresger enjoys having children around her, having none of her own. It is very understandable,' he spoke pleasantly.

Neferu heaved a sigh of inner relief. 'Yes. I really think she would have made a superb mother,' she said smoothly. 'How is Meketaten?' she asked by way of a rapid change of subject.

'She is suffering from nausea in the mornings but apart from that she seems very well.' He seemed slightly surprised by her question. 'You are really taking all this very well, much better than I had thought,' he said to her warmly. Neferu shrugged her shoulders slightly. 'You are really an exceedingly wise woman, Neferu. No man could have a better wife,' he said sincerely. Neferu smiled with cynicism. And yet he had been able to discard her so easily, she thought. He looked at her papyrus. 'What are you writing?' he asked.

'Just a poem,' she replied. She did not offer to show it to him as she once would have.

There was a slight pause and he merely said, 'I am glad that you have started to write again. It is a long time since you wrote your last poems.' It was three years, in fact, she reflected. He obviously assumed that the poem was for Penhasi, because he added, 'Penhasi must be pleased with it.'

She smiled and nodded. 'Penhasi was wondering when you are going to visit the temple again for prayers,' she said tentatively.

Amio scowled, as he always did when his will was crossed. 'That is my business. I will go when it pleases me.' Neferu nodded and did not pursue the subject further. It had obtained the result she desired. Amio rose, his mood now slightly irritated.

'I will go and see the children,' he stated. She nodded and he took his leave. She sat back in her chair and when she was sure that there was no danger of him returning, she lifted the papyrus up and, after meditating for a while, she continued to write. It was a love poem for Tuthmosis.

CHAPTER 26

The following day, Neferu and the children set out for Tuthmosis' studio. She had been pondering over the problem of how she and Tuthmosis could meet more frequently without arousing suspicion and she thought that she had the answer.

Tuthmosis greeted her as he always did, but drew her away to the seclusion of the empty courtyard where he gave her a long and passionate kiss. Afterwards, she strolled around the courtyard, out of view of his assistants and, in a low voice, discussed their future meetings. Tuthmosis told her that he would obtain one of the long, all-covering gowns of the fellahin women so that she would be able to walk around unrecognised. It was a very good idea and would afford her much more freedom. They arranged to meet the following night after sundown when the children were asleep.

Neferu realised that she would not be able to manage this alone and she would have to take an ally into her confidence. That ally could only be Maatnofret, as there was no one else she could trust with such an intimate confidence. She did not relish the prospect of asking her friend to collude in something this dangerous, but she did not know who else to ask.

That evening after sundown when the children were already put to bed, Neferu drew Maatnofret into her room and hesitantly told her plans. The older woman was so terribly upset that she cried and Neferu felt really bad about it. Still, she could not resign herself to going back to her old life, wondering if Amio would ever spare her any of his time or affection. She would no longer know how to handle it if he did. Her disillusion with him was far too profound for her to go back to being the faithful little victim of whatever whim of state happened to take him by storm. Neferu hugged her friend and tried to comfort her. Maatnofret confessed that she had known something was going on, but she had not known what. Neferu told Maatnofret everything of her feelings and the behaviour and cruel words of both Amio and Meketaten. She spared Amio nothing in the telling. Maatnofret understood Neferu, even if she did not approve of her actions. Neferu was like a daughter to her, and she herself bitterly blamed Amio for the distress he had caused Neferu. Finally, in spite of her qualms, she said she would help. All that Neferu wanted her friend to do was to keep a room for her near to the palace exit, where she could leave the clothes which Tuthmosis would obtain for her and to make sure that the room was not used by any other personage. In this room Neferu would be able to change and leave the palace unrecognised. Maatnofret was to cover for her if necessary and should Neferu be needed quickly, then she could send a coded message by one of the very junior servants, who would not be suspicious as they were very often sent on all kinds of messages, often after dark also. This was just a precaution, as Neferu did not really think this would be necessary. She would always take care not to be away too long and never the whole night. For their coded message they devised 'Please call tomorrow morning as soon as possible for plans for a painting.' The message was signed by herself, and she and Maatnofret hid it under an alabaster statuette on a high window ledge in Neferu's private sitting room. She had to stand on a chair to place it so she was satisfied that no one would find it. Amio had not been into her room for months. Only Maatnofret entered and the maid who cleaned the room, but Maatnofret was always there to supervise that.

The system worked wonderfully well and Neferu found herself free to come and go at will. She rarely saw Amio during the day and she took care never to venture to that part of the palace where he and Meketaten had set up home. Life became fresh and exciting again for Neferu. There was something exhilarating about her forbidden trysts. Tuthmosis was a completely different kind of lover to Amio. He was capable of selfishness and was fiery at times, but he was also sensitive and passionate. His body was strong and muscular, and he could lift her as if she were as light as a feather. Often after they had made love, he would draw her.

Early on in their relationship he asked her not to wear cosmetics. 'Why not?' she asked, mystified.

'It is like painting a rose gold,' he told her.

He made her feel like a young woman again, and he was good for her. She became as slim again as she had been before having had her children and she felt her body firm up. Some of it was no doubt due to the extra exercise she was getting, walking and running backwards and forwards under cover of darkness, some was probably due to the excitement of wondering whether or not she would be found out, and some was due to the beauty-giving factors of being in love again. Whatever it was, a lot of people began to comment on her radiance.

One day when she visited the temple. Penhasi and Xerlon offered her refreshments. She had no makeup on except a little red ochre on her lips and she could not help noticing the admiration in Xerlon's eyes. He was very attentive and Neferu was purposely just the tiniest bit flirtatious with him. Penhasi looked on disapprovingly but said nothing.

Neferu was careful not to visit the temple for several days afterwards. She had not done that to spite Amio – that motive had long disappeared from her mind. She had done it to protect her new love, who was growing increasingly important to her at a deep psychological and emotional level. She did not expect Amio to suspect anything, but she wanted to throw up a smoke screen in case he did suspect anything later. This particular smoke screen could be fully investigated and found to be innocent. Neferu became aware for the first time that her long association with the Theban royal family had made her just as devious and conniving as they were. Neferu had tried to persuade Tuthmosis to come to the palace at night as there was ample space there for him to go unnoticed and she felt that ultimately it would be safer for them both. Tuthmosis was, however, a very proud man and told her that he would never make love to her in her husband's home.

Soon after this, Amio began to be much more visible in their former quarters too. At first Neferu thought he was checking up on her, but after a while, Neferu realised that this was not the case. She then wondered if he was trying to stage some form of reconciliation. She was prepared for that and continued to be coolly friendly with him, but did not encourage further intimacy. She felt irritated that her old life appeared to be encroaching upon her new one.

Work on the statue of Tut was now finished and she brought it home with her. Work on the bust of Neffie had already started so she had irreproachable reasons for her frequent visits to the studio. When she brought home the statue of Tut, she showed it to Maatnofret, who was admiring it when Amio came in. Seeing the object of their conversation, he was momentarily diverted and generous in his praise of it. Neferu placed it on a shelf in the main sitting room for everyone to admire. When Maatnofret left, Amio cleared his throat and said he wanted to speak to Neferu.

'What is it, Amio?' she said neutrally.

'I have been to the temple this morning,' he said, looking annoyed.

'Oh,' she said, wondering what was coming next.

'Penhasi tells me that he does not think it wise that you show undue favour to Xerlon,' he said in a tight voice.

'Ah,' replied Neferu. 'I think Penhasi is worrying unnecessarily.'

'I do not!' said Amio coldly. 'Don't think that your new lifestyle has gone unnoticed by me, Neferu. If you have been encouraging Xerlon, then I forbid you to show your favour publicly!' Neferu looked at him sharply. This was unexpected. She even thought she detected a note of jealousy in his voice. She would have to placate him; she did not want him to be watching her.

'I assure you that you are mistaken, Amio. I am very discreet in my behaviour.'

He was not satisfied. 'Is Xerlon your lover?' he snapped.

'No. Xerlon is not my lover, Amio,' she replied truthfully. 'Though that is really none of your business, if you recall our pact,' she continued carefully.

'I do not believe you,' Amio said nastily.

'I am not a liar,' Neferu said coldly. 'Are you jealous, Amio?' she continued to speak in the same even tone.

'I do not care who your lover is!' he said angrily. 'But I will not have you bringing shame on my name.'

Neferu looked at him icily. 'Have I brought shame on you, Amio?' she asked quietly.

His manner calmed and he spoke in a controlled tone. 'No. You have never brought shame on me, Neferu. I just want you to be discreet.'

'I promise you I will be discreet,' she answered quietly. He seemed at a loss as to what to say for a moment, then he bowed and turned and left.

Neferu told Tuthmosis what had happened. He sighed. If Amio had been anyone else in the whole of the Two Lands, they could have left together and made a new life for themselves. It was what she wanted, and it was what he wanted too, but they both knew that no one could walk out on the pharaoh and remain alive for more than a few days.

As the decans passed, Neferu began to notice that the balance in the palace had changed. She was no longer the outsider, in fact everything now seemed to revolve around her. Amio and Meketaten had isolated themselves in the beginning, but now it was almost as if they had been forgotten. The children turned to her and Maatnofret for all their little wants and pleasures. They were much less demonstrative with Amio than before and he was obviously beginning to feel himself out on a limb. He made several enigmatic remarks to this effect. He seemed glum and her radiance and happiness seemed to be a thorn in his flesh. The one worry that Neferu had entertained seriously had never materialised. She had worried in case she had become pregnant. She did not, though, and she was completely certain now that she was barren. She would never again have children. The inflammation following Satenpare's birth must have been responsible for it. She was pleased not to have to worry about it anymore. She did not wish to have any children anymore.

One day, Amio and Meketaten informed Neferu that from now on they would be taking most of their meals with her and the children again. Amio also told Neferu that he had requested Ay to visit them. Neferu guessed, therefore, that the sharing of meals was a subterfuge in order to present a united family image in front of the grand vizier. Neferu was severely rattled by his decision as it would curtail her freedom of movement considerably. Still, as long as he did not decide to move back to her end of the palace at night, there was no real danger. Mealtimes became a strain for her once again, though the reasons were totally different now. On the surface everything was friendly, and she was careful to maintain a casual manner. She made no attempt to seek any closeness with either of them, but she was careful to observe all the necessary protocol. It soon became obvious to her that Amio was not happy. She did not know why. He had got what he wanted but he was not happy. It was nothing to do with her, however, so she did not dwell on it.

Out in the garden one afternoon with the children, she sat on the grass enjoying their boisterous playing. It was a happy occasion, and they were playing hide and seek with lots of squeals and lots of laughter. Nefer-Neferu-Aten-tashery was trying to do a somersault and Tut was helping by holding up her legs. Neffie junior collapsed in a sudden heap, and they all fell around laughing when plump little Satenpare tried to have a go too. Her little roly-poly arms could not take the plump little body and she was most annoyed with her efforts. Neferu went to help her and noticed Amio watching them. Casually she walked towards him. 'Is there anything wrong, Amio?' she asked.

'Does there have to be anything wrong when I come to see my family?' he replied in an offended tone.

'No,' she said and shrugged. 'I just wondered, that is all.' She curtsied and turned to go.

'Neferu, don't go. I am sorry. I didn't mean to snap,' he said apologetically.

'That's all right, Amio. I was just going anyway. You stay and enjoy the children,' she said.

'Neferu, can't we be friends?' he asked.

'But we are friends, Amio,' she said surprised. 'I wasn't aware that we had quarrelled?'

'I love you, Neferu. I don't like this division between us,' he said.

'I love you too, Amio. You are a good man. We have known each other for a long time. You are still my friend.'

'But you are not in love with me any longer,' he said questioningly.

She looked at him directly and frankly. 'No, Amio. I am not in love with you any longer.'

'Do you love someone else?' he asked in a flat voice. Now he had put her in a difficult position. She was not willing to deny the man she loved but she did not want to place Amio's anger upon him. She tried to skirt around the issue.

'What do you think?' she asked neutrally.

'I think you are evading my question,' he said, looking her in the eyes firmly. 'Do you love another man?' he asked again. Neferu was quiet for a moment as she let her gaze drift over to where the children were playing.

'Yes. I'm in love with another man,' she finally admitted.

His face went white suddenly as if he were actually shocked by her answer. 'May I know whom?' he asked eventually, after what seemed to Neferu to be an eternal pause.

'Please do not ask me, Amio,' she begged him. 'I have been very discreet. Remember your promise. You said you would never harm him.'

There was a long silence that was filled with her dread as she saw him battling with himself. At the end of it he said, 'I promised that I would not harm your lover. I take it you have been lovers?' she did not reply, and he saw the answer from her face. 'Who is it, Nefertiti?' he said, using her full name. 'I will not harm him in any way. You have my vow as the pharaoh, but I want to know whom it is that you love.'

'I love Tuthmosis, the artist,' she said simply. She had never expected him to react in this way. He was furious and looked jealous even, though there was no reason for this as he was in love with Meketaten. He surely had not expected her to live a life of solitude, waiting for him to consider bestowing his favours upon her now and again. Amio pulled her roughly by the arm, into the sitting room out of sight of the children.

'And has he taken you here in my home?' he raged.

'No. I always go to him,' Neferu tried to speak coolly.

He seemed flabbergasted. 'Then the whole city knows,' he gasped.

'No. I go at night, dressed in peasant clothes with my face covered.' She could not keep a tiny note of pride out of her voice at the cleverness of her disguise.

'Who else knows?' he asked bitterly.

'Why do you want to know, Amio? Surely you aren't going to break your vow?' she said worriedly.

'No,' he said. 'I have no intention of breaking my vow. I tell you for the second time! I just want to know how many other people know.'

'Just Maatnofret and Meresger,' Neferu replied.

'His wife knows and approves?' he asked in a surprised voice, momentarily diverted from his anger.

'Why not? You expected me to!' she answered, unable to contain a note of bitterness. He was silent and she continued, 'You made your choice, Amio. I cannot change my feelings on and off again to suit yours. I am sorry.'

Amio was very proud. She knew that he could order both herself and Tuthmosis to be put to death at any moment, but she knew that having given his promise, he would not do it. She realised too late that he hadn't promised not to punish her. She did not think he would do it, though, because she was the mother of his new wife, and the grandmother of his new child. His dynastical needs were being met and therefore he could afford to be generous. Amio remained looking at her for a long time with an unfathomable look on his face before turning with an icy bidding of his leave and marching back to his own part of the palace. Neferu was left standing and wondering what the next few days would bring. She held firm to the hope that the memories of their past love would assuage his anger and shock. She tried to keep out of his way as much as possible and sent word to Tuthmosis via Maatnofret that for the moment it would be unwise for them to meet. Maatnofret returned tight-lipped and said only that she had explained the situation to Tuthmosis. She said that he had sent word back that he was ready to die for her if necessary but not until they had seen each other one last time. Neferu had to smile. She did not think it would come to that.

Neferu now became a virtual prisoner of the palace once again, though she was not too distressed at first as she considered it as a time of diplomacy, and it was only right to give Amio a chance to adjust to the situation, which had obviously come as a great shock to him. She was sure that from now on he would have one of his spies follow her everywhere she went, and she did not want that. Although she missed Tuthmosis enormously, it was her considered evaluation of the situation that once Meketaten had given birth Amio would relinquish all emotional nostalgia for her and concentrate on his new heir. She prayed desperately that the baby would be the son he craved so that her part in their lives would be at an end. He would let her live in freedom so long as it was discreetly, she felt.

Meketaten was growing very big now, and Neferu was able to be more honest in running her own life now that things were out in the open and Amio knew of her feelings. She felt a little more nicely inclined towards her daughter, with no jealousy there to intrude on her relationship with Meketaten. She felt only a sisterly affection for Amio. Neferu found it easy to forgive now. She had a new love, a talented and brilliant man who was ardent and passionate for her alone. She loved him and he loved her. She could afford to be friendly with Amio.

Everything was steadily improving between them all when, a few decans later, Meketaten went into premature labour. Neferu was out that evening with Tuthmosis and they had just made love when she received her own coded message. She knew that something serious had happened and dressed as quickly as possible, leaving her lover to worry as she rushed back to the palace. In her secret room, she changed into her ordinary clothes and went to find Maatnofret. On the way, she met the nurse, who informed her of what had happened. As fast as she could without running, she made her way to Meketaten's suite. The physician was present. Neferu went over to the bed where her daughter was lying.

'How are you, Meketaten?' she asked quietly.

'Mother, I'm so glad you're here.' Her daughter's face looked very pale and wan and Amio looked afraid. He was holding her hand. As the night unfolded and the situation became increasingly serious, Amio held Meketaten's hand and told her again and again that he loved her. Meketaten lay, wracked by contraction after contraction, and then would sink exhausted into the pillows as the pains ebbed away.

At first, Neferu was not worried. Labour is, after all, like that, but after twelve hours there was still no sign of the baby. Morning came and still nothing. The physician gave her something for the pain and for a few hours after that, her daughter slept. When she woke up, the contractions started again and afternoon past into night once more. The physician was looking desperate himself by now and they had given up questioning him as to when things were likely to progress. Yet again, Neferu and Maatnofret took him aside and despairingly wondered if there was anything they could do. They did not want him to put in his hand and force the baby out, as he now suggested in desperation. They could only wait.

It was almost midnight when the baby was born dead. It was a girl. Meketaten was bleeding badly but she was conscious. She asked about her baby. Neferu told her that it was a beautiful little girl and Meketaten asked to see her. Amio began to cry and told her that the baby was dead. Neferu wrapped the baby in a pretty shawl as if it were alive and handed it to her daughter. She could hardly see Meketaten for the tears in her eyes. She had just noticed the amount of blood gushing from her daughter and knew that she was dying too. Suddenly all her guards were down, and their quarrels forgotten. As she placed the baby into her daughter's arms, she told her how much she loved her and how sorry she was that they had quarrelled. Meketaten took her mother's hand and kissed it.

'Don't cry, Mother,' she said. 'I love you so much. Don't cry!' Neferu tried to control herself so as not to upset her daughter further. Meketaten looked at her daughter proudly.

'She is beautiful, isn't she?' she asked Neferu.

'She is, my darling,' her mother replied.

Meketaten said that she felt very cold. She looked at Neferu again. 'I am dying, aren't I?' she asked her.

Neferu looked at Amio. He looked terrified. She looked down at her daughter again. 'Yes, you are, my darling. But don't be afraid. Amio and I are here with you, and you are going to the country of eternal life. Will you wait for us when you get there?'

Meketaten nodded. She looked from one to the other. 'I love you both so much,' she said quietly.

Neferu took her hand. It felt very cold. She bent down to kiss her daughter. 'We love you too, with all our hearts,' she said simply.

Amio took the baby from Meketaten and laid it by her side. He sat down beside her again and took hold of her other hand. He kissed her tenderly and stroked her hair. When he asked her if she had any pain, she whispered, 'No.' After a slight pause she asked them to kiss all the other children for her. Soon after that she complained of the cold again and then said that it was getting dark. Her final words before slipping into unconsciousness were, 'I love you both. Always remember that.'

Within a few minutes she was dead. She was fourteen years old.

Neferu howled like a wild animal and burst into hysterical sobs. She cried out to the god she had put so much faith in. 'Why did you let this happen, Aten? Why? Why? Why?' The physician tried to take her away, but she refused. She said she would prepare her own daughter with Maatnofret. Amio refused to leave also. The physician was shocked and Amio asked him to leave. He bowed low and opened his mouth as if to speak, thought better of it and left.

Together, Amio, Neferu and Maatnofret lifted the little body of Meketaten off the bed, away from the lifeblood which had seeped away from her, onto a fresh couch. Maatnofret prepared the bed with clean linen and she and Neferu carefully washed Meketaten's body.

Neferu closed her daughter's eyes and she and Meketaten put her favourite dress on her. They combed and arranged her hair and lay her in a natural position on her bed again. When they had finished, her young daughter looked beautiful again. Neferu went into the garden and returned with a long-stemmed red rose. She wrapped the stem in a small linen cloth and lay the flower on Meketaten's breast. Afterwards she lay the child within the crook of Meketaten's arm. Amio sat mesmerised as they worked, seeming unaware of anything going on in the room. Neferu and Meketaten brought water and together they cleaned the floor and furniture of all blood. Maatnofret tried to insist that it was a job for the servants, but Neferu would have none of that. 'She is my daughter, of my body, and I am a servant too. I am the Aten's servant. He has seen fit to take my daughter away from me and I wish to do these last services for her myself.'

Amio sat by Meketaten's body neither speaking nor moving. He seemed to be frozen in time and space, with a dull empty look in his eyes. Neferu busied herself with the cleaning until the room was spotless and there was nothing else to block out the pain which was pushing itself mercilessly over the threshold of her mind. When everything was done, she went to sit by her daughter's body and cried heartbrokenly until there were no more tears left inside her. She prayed, begging her daughter's forgiveness for her hardness and asking that her spirit stay close by her until it was time for her to leave also. Neferu remained with her daughter until dawn, when she bent over and gave the cold cheek a final kiss before leaving her alone in the room with Amio. They had exchanged no words all through the night, each locked separately into their own private nightmare. Something died in Neferu that night. It was called 'hope for the future'.

Neferu informed Tutu, the chief minister, and he promised to send word to Ay forthwith. She went to her own room and lay down on her bed. During that long night, she had cried so much that she now felt completely drained of emotion. There was such an emptiness inside that she wondered if she were dying too. For the first time since her awakening to faith, she began to doubt the existence of the Aten. After a while she brushed the thought away. Yes, he was there all right. Was he good, though? It was his benevolence she began to doubt. In spite of her doubt she prayed, asking him to give her the strength to go on, and then she closed her eyes in exhaustion and finally slept.

When Neferu woke up the house was completely silent. She could hear nothing, and this was most strange. She got up quickly and washed and dressed before going to look for the children. She found them quietly huddled together in the nursery. Death was something they had never experienced so closely before, and they were finding it frightening and difficult to come to terms with the finality of it. Maatnofret's face was ravaged by the tears she had shed and suddenly Neferu saw that she looked like an old lady. Neferu hugged her, both of them afraid to speak for fear of losing control in front of the children and frightening them more than they were already. From their closed faces, Neferu knew that Maatnofret must have already told them. Later Maatnofret told Neferu how they had taken it.

'Meketaten has gone to the Aten with Grandma Tiya,' she had told them simply.

'Will we see her again?' Satenpare had asked doubtfully. Satenpare now came to her mother and asked her for confirmation if Meketaten was coming back. 'We will see her again when we go in our turn, and that probably won't be for a long, long time,' Neferu told her youngest daughter.

'Has the Aten got a nice palace?' Satenpare asked.

'A beautiful palace in the sky,' Neferu tried to smile.

Tut looked at her swollen eyes. 'Why have you been crying then, if it is so nice?' he asked suspiciously.

Neferu was forced to smile at the logic of his words. 'I have been crying for myself, Tut,' she answered. 'I am sad because she has gone, and I won't see her again for a very long time. I am sad because I remember those times when I was angry with her or mean to her, because now I know how stupid it is to waste time hurting those people you love the most. I know that she has forgiven me, but I cannot forgive myself. I loved her very much and yet I made her sad. That was not nice of me.' Her eyes filled with tears as she spoke.

Tut came over and put his arms around her. 'No one can hurt her now,' he said astutely.

Neferu hugged him. 'That's right, Tut. No one can hurt her now,' she replied, wondering at his ability to understand.

'She's not alone, is she?' he asked. Neferu knew that for a small child, nothing is more frightening than being left alone.

'No, Tut. She is not alone. Grandpa and Grandma, your mother and Meretamun are all with her. You always go back to those you love,' Neferu answered reassuringly.

'It will be all right then, Neferu,' the child said, pressing his warm, round cheek against hers. 'And you've still got us,' he added earnestly.

'Yes. I've still got all of you,' she replied, grateful for that, at least. Neferu thought of Amio and wondered if he was still locked in his grief in that forlorn little room. She had better get up and go and check on him, she thought to herself, and said out loud, 'It will be very hard for your father now. You must all show him how much you love him.'

It was the darkest period in Amio's life. His peace of mind was completely shattered and Neferu began to feel sorry for him for the first time since she had known him. She had lost her daughter many months before, in a bitter and hurtful way, and yet in death they had found each other again. There was no bitterness in Nefertiti any longer. The period of mourning brought her and the other children closer than ever before. On top of this, she had Tuthmosis to love and support her and provide a much-needed respite from the heavy and oppressively grief-laden atmosphere of the palace.

In the immediate days following the death of Meketaten, Amio appeared to be completely cut off from reality, existing in his own dark world of grief. Intuitively, she sensed that he was experiencing a double loss, that of herself as well as the loss of Meketaten. He was lost in the situation. There had never been a time in his life when he could not have what he wanted. For the pharaoh everything was possible, and now he was having to face his limitations as a man without his mother, his wife or his future heir. Neither power nor status nor wealth were of any help. There was no one to ruthlessly intrigue on his behalf as Tiya had always done. Death was above them all, touching the high and the low with an implacable equality and sternness. Amio felt himself deserted and alone.

Neferu did not know how to approach Amio in his grief. She felt that she had failed him. She felt that he needed her and was trying to reach out to her, but she felt afraid to come too close for fear he would demand more of her than she could give. She analysed an ambivalence within herself. In part she still loved him as a person and as the man at the centre of her existence for so many years, but she knew that underneath she had not forgiven him for betraying her love and, perhaps in her very heart of hearts, she blamed him for the death of Meketaten. Deep down inside of her there was still that cold, hard area which even her grief could not dissolve.

When Neferu had satisfied herself that the children understood and accepted the situation on that first day of Meketaten's death, she went, with much misgiving, to the end of the palace area where Amio's quarters were. She did not know what to say to him or how to say it and she went as one does to visit a familiar neighbour, well-liked but with the wariness of not knowing what kind of reception to expect. She reflected as she walked that she and Amio had become strangers to one another, but armed strangers, capable of hurting each other. She certainly was not prepared for the extent of his grief.

At the entrance to his room, she hesitated before asking permission to enter. He seemed not to hear her at first, sitting staring at the wall in front of him. She had the impression he had been immobile for several hours. 'Amio. May I come in?' she asked, wondering if it had been wise to come at all. Slowly he turned his head towards her, and she saw the dullness of his gaze. He nodded. She went in and drew up a chair opposite him. Once, she would have seated herself beside him.

'Amio. Have you had anything to eat?' She asked it already knowing that he had not, since Maatnofret had told her that he had refused everything put in front of him.

He shook his head. 'I am not hungry,' he replied, dully. Neferu sighed. He would have to be coaxed like a child, she thought, and why her? Why should she be the one to always have to clean up the mess and chaos he caused? It was an uncharitable thought and she pushed it away with self-disgust. This was not the moment for feelings of martyrdom.

'Amio. Come and eat with us. You cannot sit here all the time. Life has to go on. I am sorry but it is true. You have other children, and they need you. You cannot ignore them. You must make an effort to live out your daily routine. You are the pharaoh.' She tried appealing to his sense of duty, which Tiya had sometimes seemed to inculcate in him to the exclusion of all else.

'Pharaoh!' he said bitterly. 'Yes, I am pharaoh, but a pharaoh with nothing! No wife to love or be loved by, no son and no happiness!'

She said nothing for a moment, but then, 'You have Egypt. Egypt is above all those things. That is why you must try, on the outside at least, to carry on. The pharaoh is above all personal happiness. Egypt and its people must come first.'

He smiled at her cynically. 'You begin to sound like my mother, Neferu. She could not have put it better herself. And it is easy for you, of course. You have a new love.' Her compassion died a sudden death at the hostility of his attack. In his hurt, he was trying to hit out and she was the only one available. She decided to retreat.

'I'm sorry, Amio. I was only trying to help.'

She got up to leave but just as suddenly his tone changed, and he said pleadingly, 'Please don't go, Neferu.' Reluctantly Neferu sat down again and nodded. She felt trapped and uncomfortable, not knowing what to say. He had become unpredictable to her. She no longer knew him. Amio lifted his shoulders helplessly. 'I loved her so much, Neferu,' he said. Neferu nodded again. She was really the last person he should have been telling this to, she reflected. It still hurt her to think about it. Did he not understand? As he spoke the tears filled his eyes and he cried like a child. 'Hold me, Neferu,' he said, holding out his arms. Neferu was shocked. After a slight hesitation, she stood up and went over to him. He put his head on her breast and his arms around her waist and she held him to her as if he were a child. It was an incongruous situation, she meditated. She now felt more like his mother than the woman he had taken to wife.

When he had sobbed his fill and his heaving chest had quietened a little, she said gently to him, 'Go and wash your face, Amio, and then come and have refreshments with us. We will wait for you.' He nodded in agreement, and she loosened herself from him gently. He took her arm and kissed it as she did so.

'You are a good woman, Neferu,' he said, trying to smile at her.

'Don't be too long.' Was her answer, and then she turned and was gone. When she was outside in the corridor, she comprehended that over and above the spoken words between them, something else had been exchanged. Had it been a goodbye?

Two days later, the grand vizier had arrived with sombre mien. His look of cold appraisal was not lost on Neferu. She realised that he was probably surprised to see her so calm and detached. He smiled with a hint of approval on his wily face. 'You have handled the situation well, Neferu.' Neferu inclined her head. This was unexpected praise indeed from the old politician. His sharp eyes took in Amio's ravaged appearance in comparison, and he shook his head slightly before offering his nephew his condolences. Amio felt no need to disguise his feelings in front of his uncle and he broke down and cried. Neferu excused herself so that they could speak alone. The astute Ay looked momentarily surprised and took in the obvious lack of warmth between them, they who had formerly been so close.

Neferu went for a walk in the garden. She was glad that Ay was here. She reasoned that he would be an immense support to Amio, who was very fond of his uncle. She felt tired and drained. The atmosphere of the palace hung over her. Her daughter was gone, and nothing would bring her back. There would always be a place for her in Neferu's heart, but Neferu was tired. Tired of heartbreak, tired of pain and death, tired of emotional conflict. She wanted to run away and never come back. To start all over again with Tuthmosis in a place where no one knew them. She truly loved this man, who had so unexpectedly come into her heart just when she thought she could never love again. She half-entertained a wild dream of them going to Caphtor or one of the other Greek islands that her father and grandfather had told her about. Almost as quickly as it had come, she discarded it. She knew it was an impossibility. There was no escape from her situation. She could never leave the children. They depended upon her for their happiness and security. There was no way of knowing how long Amio would remain in his barren state of devastation but, until he pulled himself together, the children would obtain no emotional security from him.

With that thought came another unbidden, one she really did not wish to contemplate. What then, when Amio recovered enough to plan for the future? He still had no son. He must marry again. This time she would have no objection to him taking another wife. There were many beautiful women in the harem which Amio had inherited from his father, and if not from there, there were many beautiful daughters of the Theban nobles at court, or his many relatives. If he could not go there to choose, then Ay could arrange for some of them to come to Akhetaten for appraisal. She would openly encourage it. Their relationship was irredeemably broken, but she did not begrudge him a new chance of happiness. She considered and decided that it would be wise to prime Ay on this as soon as possible so that he could encourage Amio to look outside of himself and to the future. Penhasi had a beautiful daughter too. There was no harm in encouraging her to visit the palace and even try to promote a relationship between them.

Neferu turned her thoughts to Tuthmosis. She must get a message to him soon. She felt in need of his common sense and, above all, of his physical presence. She toyed with the idea of asking Maatnofret to visit him with a message but rejected it. Maatnofret was far to grief-stricken and would disapprove severely. Neferu did not want to run the risk of general outrage in the present tragic circumstances. She was trapped.

Restricted as she was to the confines of the palace now, Neferu began to feel imprisoned. For the moment there was no possibility of her leaving surreptitiously. Her absence would be quickly discovered if one of the children were to ask for her, or even if Amio or Ay were to request her presence at some meeting or other. If only there was some way that Tuthmosis could come to her. She needed his strength now more than ever. She knew that by now he must be aware of all the facts, and she knew that he must be waiting for her to make further contact. She knew that he would never come to the palace under any circumstances. She was also aware that meeting him now would put them both in mortal danger. There was nothing for it but to wait until the grand vizier returned to Thebes.

Neferu meditated on what Amio would tell Ay. She felt certain that he would discuss her affair with Tuthmosis with his uncle. Discontentedly she kicked at the edge of the small fish pool on whose low wall she was sitting. Not for the first time, she wondered how her life had ever come to be in such a mess. She was assailed by the sudden thought that maybe the Aten did not like her. Come to that, she was not at all sure that she liked him either.

Nothing was said by Ay, at first, to indicate that he was aware of Neferu's situation. They both parried their conversation around inconsequential topics, studiously avoiding any reference to anything which might lead to a quarrel. Neferu noticed that Ay's visit seemed to be bringing Amio back to life again and she welcomed this at first as a good omen. The new Amio though very quickly began to prove himself a very different man from his previous personality. This man was stern and lacking in all joie de vivre. She found him so distant to her that she could hardly believe that she had ever loved him, or that he was the father of her children. Any regrets she had harboured for him now disappeared. They did not fight. Their relationship crystallised into a coolly polite and formal one. Neferu still wondered if Amio had requested his uncle to intervene concerning her relationship with Tuthmosis.

It came after lunch one day. Ay was voluble and affectionate with the children and there was a semblance of old times in the noisiness and chatter. Amio had been making an effort to win back the closeness of the children and had taken them down to the pool. Neferu sensed right away that it was a ploy to leave her alone with the grand vizier. She was not reluctant, however, to bring things out into the open. Her thoughts had been hovering unspoken just beneath the surface for so long.

'You and Amio are no longer close,' the grand vizier stated matter-of-factly.

Neferu shook her head before replying. 'No,' she admitted. 'We have lost that bond we once had, Ay.'

'Do you still love Amio?' he asked directly.

Neferu considered a moment. 'I love him Amio as a person, but I am not in love with him,' she said coolly.

'You are in love with someone else?' Ay raised his eyebrows in question but Neferu knew that his question was largely rhetorical.

'Yes,' she replied. 'I am sure you have been informed of it.' Her tone was dry.

Ay nodded. There was no censure in his voice when he asked, 'Is there any chance that you and Amio will ever be reconciled?'

'I don't feel that is a possibility,' she answered frankly, looking at Ay directly.

He sighed. 'Then there is no chance of you ever having a son then,' he said in a resigned voice.

'There is no possibility of my ever having another child anyway, I think. I believe that I am barren now,' she answered with a shrug of her shoulders. It was not painful to her. After a slight pause she continued. 'I have no objection to Amio taking a new wife. Our marriage is only a nominal one now. I think it might be a good idea for you to seek a suitable one for him from Thebes. I have no desire to deny him the chance of an heir or happiness with someone else.'

Ay looked at her speculatively. 'There is really an enormous change in your attitude, Neferu,' he said finally.

Neferu gave a bitter laugh. 'I was pushed too far!' she replied. 'I did try to warn you that my feelings are not like the resin of the gum tree. Something broke in me, Ay. I cannot help it. I think I lost the ability to respect Amio. That was important to me.' She looked at him directly to see if he understood but he merely nodded.

He sighed again. 'It cannot be helped. Feelings are strange things. This was not a situation which could have been predicted at the start.' He spoke almost as if reassuring himself that it was not due to his bad planning. 'Do you plan to continue your relationship with the sculptor?' he asked.

Neferu was instantly wary. She knew she was putting herself in a very dangerous position to be so frank. Ay was dangerous. She knew that it was his nature to use anything she told him to his own advantage. In spite of that she could not deny publicly the man she loved. It would be like denying her faith in the Aten would be to her.

'Yes. I plan to continue my relationship with Tuthmosis. I love him,' she answered.

'Strange,' he mused. 'How that name has figured so prominently in the lives of the women of my family.' Neferu knew he was thinking of his sister, Tiya, and her love for the archduke.

She shrugged. 'It is a common name in Egypt,' she remarked.

He nodded in agreement. 'I hope you will continue to be as discreet as you have been so far, Neferu.'

'You need have no fear, uncle,' she spoke emphatically. 'I will allow no shame to come on Amio or the crown. You have my promise.'

The grand vizier nodded again and when he spoke his tone was serious. 'I knew I could count upon you, Neferu,' he answered smoothly. The interview was over. It had not been any more difficult than that. She breathed a sigh of relief. 'Tomorrow I shall be returning to Thebes,' said Ay. 'It is extremely regrettable that Amio persists in his refusal to leave Akhetaten even for a short visit to Thebes, but I will do as you suggest and discuss with Amio this evening the possibility of him taking a new wife from Thebes. To tell you the truth, I had considered the matter myself on my way here and I also had reached the conclusion that it would be the wisest course to take. I was wholly unprepared for your acquiescence in the matter. It will be much easier now.'

Neferu nodded. 'You have my full support,' she replied.

Ay stood up. 'Let's join the children and try to lighten the mood of their day. I fear that they have been very much unsettled by all this.' Neferu stood up and they walked across the room. Ay took Neferu's hand in a gesture of affection. Neferu looked at him. She sometimes considered him shallow in his affections, but he did possess a happy knack of smoothing over the rough edges. There was no doubt of that.

The three adults covered their feelings as they played with the children, and on the surface, a good time was had by all. After half an hour or so, Neferu shooed the children to their afternoon rest and took her leave of Ay and Amio to partake of her own rest. As she walked across the lawn, she felt the eyes of both of them upon her back. They had a lot to discuss, she knew. She was now aware that Ay would report to Amio her full backing for him to take a new wife. The crown of Egypt would soon be safe, even if Meretaten and Smenkhare did not produce the long-awaited son. She expected an imminent improvement in Amio's mood and vision of the future.

Once in her room, Neferu closed the shutters and undressed in the gloom. She brushed her hair listlessly before lying down on her bed. Once it had been their bed. She began to remember some of the moments of happiness and passion she had spent with Amio here. It all seemed so long ago now and so far away emotionally that it was almost as though it had happened to someone else, not her. She sighed, shutting off the memories, and closed her eyes.

Neferu was awoken from her rest abruptly by an agitated Maatnofret. The older woman's face was drawn with distress.

'Neferu! Your Majesty! You must wake up!'

Neferu woke instantly. Maatnofret never called her 'Your Majesty' in private. Something awful must have happened. 'What is it, Maatnofret?' she cried, alert to the anxiety in her friend's face.

'It is Amio, Neferu! He is furious and his shouting can be heard all over the palace.' Maatnofret was wringing her hands – not a good sign, Neferu knew. Neferu jumped up quickly and, pausing only to quickly brush her hair, she left her room with Maatnofret at her heels. Her dressing gown swung about her hips as she almost ran towards the furious tones of Amio. She felt worried that he might have lost control altogether and gone mad. Her long dark hair was swinging down her back and she was aware that she was most inappropriately dressed for walking the palace corridors. Finally, she reached the entrance to his study and went in anxiously. He caught sight of her and stopped in his tracks. Ay rose and bowed low.

'You catch us at a bad moment, my dear,' Ay commented superfluously. His eyes passed over her admiringly and she pulled her gown more closely to her. She now regretted her impetuosity in rushing here half clad. She looked at Amio and was pleased to see that although he was obviously enraged, he was in full control of his faculties.

'Ah! My beautiful and ever-loving wife!' He sneered sarcastically, after his initial stare. 'To what do we owe this honour?' he demanded.

'The servants were frightened and intimidated by the shouting. They wondered if there was something seriously wrong,' Neferu observed. As soon as she had said the words, she realised that it was not the most diplomatic way she could have put it, but it was already out, and she could not take the words back. She bit her lip.

'Wrong! What could possibly be wrong?' Amio said icily. 'I have lost my daughter and my child, and my chief wife and great queen wants nothing more to do with me. What could possibly be wrong? This same wife, who just two years ago refused to entertain the very idea of me taking a new wife to secure an heir, is now conniving with my uncle to that very end.' Gradually his voice lost the icy tone and heated up to what she knew would end in a storm. He glared at her accusingly. 'If your jealousy had been less then we might not be in this mess now. You make your about-face too late, my dear.' His words came out staccato-like and cutting.

Neferu was stung into replying. 'Perhaps the Aten does not wish you to father a son, Amio. Tutankhaten is a fitting heir to the throne. There is no danger of the throne passing out of the family while he is alive.' Ay looked surprised and for once was silent. There was even an air of curiosity about him, and he did not try to interfere between them.

Amio almost spat the words out at her. 'I want a son of my OWN!' he said, hitting his chest with his fist to emphasise the word 'own'. 'I loved you and you have betrayed me with another man. I will not marry any other woman, but I will take Ankhsenpaaten to wife! She will bear me a son!'

His eyes glittered with rage and hate. Neferu was terrified. 'No, Amio! Please do not do this. It is against the will of god. The Aten will punish you severely if you do this terrible thing. If you do this then you are no better than the followers of Amun,' she cried hotly. Amio stepped forward and raised his hand to hit her. Neferu clenched her teeth to take the blow, but his hand stopped in mid-air.

'No. I will not strike you, Neferu,' he said coldly. 'But from now onwards you are no longer the grand queen. I will order your name to be struck from all buildings, and statues of you will be replaced by statues of Meretaten. You are disgraced for denying your husband his conjugal rights.' Neferu inclined her head. She then looked at him, his face set hard in anger, and she curtsied low first to him.

'Your word is law, Your Majesty.' She curtsied to Ay and then in a tone of marked formality, as if she had just met the pharaoh as one of his unknown subjects, she asked, 'Do I have your leave to retire, Your Majesty?'

She looked up at him and for a moment his eyes softened ever so slightly before the hard look came back into them and he merely shrugged and said coldly, 'You have my leave.'

Outside in the corridor, Maatnofret sobbed and sobbed. Neferu took her arm tiredly and led her friend back to her sitting room. Maatnofret was inconsolable and blamed herself for interfering. Neferu assured her that it was not her fault and that it must be the will of the Aten. She was shocked at Amio's behaviour, but she knew that he could never have really loved her to treat her in this way. What she has perceived as love had just been a combination of lust and possession. Amio had never been a good loser. There was one tiny consolation in it all which did not fail to avail itself to her consciousness. Tuthmosis had always railed against the difference in their public rank. Now that she was disgraced, he was far superior to her. It would be a test of their love if he could stand by her now that she was lower than he was.

When Neferu had managed to calm Maatnofret a little and sent her to make sure that the children were not upset, she sat down on her bed. Her legs felt like wool. Her heart was thundering, and she found she was shaking all over. Her lips felt stiff when she tried to say the words out loud.

'I am disgraced,' she managed to say eventually. She tried to collect her thoughts together and decide what she must do. The practicalities of it began to sink in and her anxiety galvanised her into action. I must move to the northern palace, she thought to herself. That is my very own property, unless he should demand the gift back. She did not think he would do that; it was not in his nature. But she had been wrong about his nature before, she reminded herself.

Deep inside her she felt a growing fear and insecurity. She knew that she had very few real friends. Certainly, none who would dare to stand up for her against the pharaoh. She began to doubt Tuthmosis. It was so long already since she had seen him. More than a decan. Had he abandoned her? She tried not to let the feeling of panic loose and tried to tell herself that it was a test by the Aten to see if she could go through all these things and still retain her belief. Part of her did not believe it but she made herself get down on her knees and pray for his strength to go through whatever she had to with dignity and not let her family be ashamed of her.

Later in the evening, Ay came to her suite to talk to her. He tried to persuade her to formally renounce Tuthmosis and beg Amio to forgive her. Neferu's weak resolve was only strengthened by her anger at this. How dare he? That she should beg his forgiveness! Neferu was outraged and said so. 'I wish that I had never ever met Amio. He has been a curse on my life and made it worthless.' Ay was very sympathetic and held her to him. He told her that he would always be her friend and that from now on he would come often to Akhetaten and visit her. The grand vizier also told her that Amio intended to remain in the palace here at Maruaten and that she was to retire to the northern palace with Tut, Neffie and Satenpare. There a large wall would be built around the palace to guard it from the public gaze.

Neferu was from now on allowed no place in public life and was to live as a recluse within the palace. She was not allowed to leave Akhetaten but would be allowed to receive guests as she wished at her new home, or, more appropriately, those who were not ashamed to be friends of the former queen. On top of everything else, she was to be deprived of her official royal name, Nefer-Neferu-Aten, and was henceforth to be known by her family name of Nefertiti. These were harsh punishments, she felt, for all the years of love and kindness she had given this man, but she felt that they would not crush her. The humiliation of public censure would be the hardest to bear, she thought. She was glad that Ay did not intend to reject her. She was grateful to him for that. She was also relieved that Amio had let her retire to the northern palace. It saved her having to grovel for it. When she thought the matter over, she was surprised that he still intended to entrust the care of the children to her. She was afraid he might change his mind on this, and she brought up the subject with Ay. She felt inordinately pleased when the grand vizier informed her that Amio had told him that Neferu was a good mother and that the younger children still needed her. Neferu was grateful to him for that, at least.

The very next morning, Neferu transferred to the northern palace with the children. It transpired that the servants had been up well before dawn, taking furniture and personal belongings over to her new residence. The hardest moment was saying goodbye to Ankhsenpaaten, and she could not stop the tears from falling then. Almost as difficult was saying goodbye to Maatnofret, who was to stay and look after the young princess. Neferu knew that with Maatnofret her daughter would have the very best care. Her friend could not, in any case, be separated from her husband, Paranefer, who was Amio's valet. Maatnofret hugged her and told her that she would come to see her regularly and bring Ankhsenpaaten if she was allowed to.

Neferu felt deeply sad to leave the home she had been used to for more than a decade. She felt that she was virtually a common prisoner. She would have preferred to have been banished to Rashid, away from everyone who knew her, but Amio would not hear of that, Ay said, because of the children. Ay embraced her and told her that she must not become depressed. He would keep in regular contact and act as a go-between herself and Amio, should she wish to discuss anything important to her. Neferu nodded, grateful that she would have some contact with the outside world. She begged him to contact her brother and informed of the situation, but not to inform her father, unless he were likely to find out by some other route. Ay promised to see to the matter. She felt desolate when he left.

The northern palace faced the austere eastern mountains and was close to the police security buildings. The very day that she moved in, the workmen came to start the building of the enclosing wall. The palace had been cosily furnished from the beginning, but it had not been used, except sometimes to house guests not invited to reside in the home palace, for whatever reason. Its walls were bare for the most part and Neferu wondered if Tuthmosis would desert her now. She imagined the walls covered in his art. She needed his friendship more than ever now that Amio had made her his enemy. She took a chance and passed a message to him via one of the servants, who appeared to be sympathetic to her plight. She recalled the man from their time in Thebes when she had bestowed an appointment on him in the palace valet service, for whatever she could not now remember. She waited nervously for a reply. Had her message been intercepted? She almost cried with relief when the servant returned with an instant reply from Tuthmosis. The message said that he would come to see her that evening. She still had one friend left, it appeared.

Tuthmosis was as good as his word and soon after darkness he arrived. The children's nanny brought him in and if she was surprised, she said nothing to comment on his presence. As soon as they were alone, he took her in his arms. It was not a passionate embrace, but rather that of a friend, someone she could rely upon. Tuthmosis asked her to tell him what had happened, and she did so. When she had finished, he told her that Amio had visited his villa two days previously. Meresger had been stunned by the knowledge of his visit, when later Amio had requested a visit to the villa to inspect the art of the house, unknown to Tuthmosis. Meresger had tried to avoid showing him Tuthmosis' private chamber, but Amio had insisted. He had apparently greatly admired the murals and then had opened the little doors covering the painting of Neferu. Meresger had been severely frightened when the portrait was exposed, but Amio had not commented upon it, merely gazed at it for a long time. Before leaving the villa Amio had thanked Meresger politely for showing him round and then taken his leave.

Neferu was stunned to learn these things. She wondered if the visit had been the catalyst for the outburst that day. Even if he did not love her himself, he felt she was his property and his property had been stolen. Tuthmosis acknowledged that he had been taken completely off guard by the visit, but as Amio had not contacted him, he was reasonably sure that the pharaoh did not intend to take the matter further. Knowing Amio so well, Neferu felt that this was probably true. He could not break the vow he had given her, and he did not wish to publicise the matter any more than was necessary. As the northern palace was so close to the headquarters of the security guard, Neferu felt that Amio would receive daily reports on the comings and goings of visitors to the palace. Tuthmosis made it clear that he had no intention of abandoning Neferu and made it plain that he would come to visit her daily, if possible. That night he stayed at her side and the world became less dark and frightening for that.

A new, very private life opened up to Neferu from this time onwards. She met very few people other than Tuthmosis and her immediate family. Her beloved artist spent many evenings and most of his nights with her, but other guests were very few and far between. Neferu did not visit the temple any longer, but Penhasi came regularly to see her and to pray with her and for her. He was a good man and she felt he was fond of her. His wife also came, with small titbits for the children and little presents. Although they discussed little of importance, she knew it was their way of showing their support of her. Penhasi would often shake his head and sigh deeply as he left. Sometimes Neferu felt that both she and Amio had let the people down. She sometimes tried to say to herself, 'But I am only a woman, I was not born to be queen.'

CHAPTER 27

Three decans after Neferu moved from Maruaten, she received word from Demi that both her father and Shosen were dead from cholera. Her father had died first, followed by Shosen two days later. Although she was devastated by her father's death especially, she was consoled by the fact that they had gone together. She was also relieved that they had known nothing of her disgrace and that their lives and happiness had not been disturbed by it. Neferu felt that death was becoming her close companion and she wondered how long she could retain her instinct to survive without Tuthmosis and the children. The Aten seemed to have abandoned her.

Maatnofret was as good as her word and visited the northern palace every day. It seemed that Amio's fury continued unabated, and he had sent for Meretaten and Smenkhare for the official change of status. Maatnofret informed Neferu that Ankhsenpaaten was well, though she missed her mother and the other children a lot.

It appeared that Maatnofret had not yet dared to raise the subject of bringing Ankhsenpaaten to visit her mother. Maatnofret also informed Neferu that Amio had ordered all references to her to be hammered from all public places and this had now been accomplished. She no longer existed, to all intents and purposes. Neferu was terribly shocked by his actions and not a little afraid that her outlaw status would be used to deny her even her most basic human rights by her enemies. It was at this time that she began to entertain thoughts of her own death. She would have rather resorted to suicide than to suffer the abuse of his ignoble hangers-on, who were certainly cowardly enough to use such a situation to their advantage. The only thought that comforted her a little was that she knew Amio would never lift his head honourably afterwards if she were to be physically abused or mistreated. She wondered whether Meretaten and Smenkhare would be allowed to visit her when they came to Akhetaten.

Her only real news from the outside world now came via Tuthmosis, who stoutly stuck by her. He told her that the great tide of public opinion was with her, and Amio was fast losing all favour with the citizens of their city. They were shocked by his public outrage against her. They spoke openly about how she had publicly humiliated herself in front of them all and of the Aten when he had been mortally sick, ten years previously. It seemed that there was real public anger against the pharaoh for his treatment of her. Neferu was surprised and pleased that the people were so strongly for her, but she felt sad that their marriage had come to this. She knew how unhappy Amio must be to be goaded into taking such steps.

The visit of Meretaten and Smenkhare came and went and Neferu saw nothing of them. Tuthmosis told her that the pomp and splendour of the visit was great, and the people hoped that the young couple would soon have the desired son. Ay came to see her and greeted her as he had always greeted her. He told her that news of her disgrace was not generally known in Thebes or elsewhere. Not even all the members of the royal family itself knew. Teya hugged Neferu and told her that Mutnedjmet and Horemheb sent their very best wishes to her. Ay had obviously spoken very sympathetically of her in Thebes and rather than being made a social outcast, there seemed to have been an effort to portray her as some kind of martyr. Neferu felt a bit uncomfortable about this as she did not wish to appear as a weak victim. She was afraid of the tendency of bullies to be drawn by the weakness of their victims. She began to see that Amio was being portrayed as a sadistic monster, which he obviously was not. Neferu tried to explain her feelings to Ay and Teya. It was all very difficult and made more so by Amio's edict forbidding her to leave Akhetaten.

As time went by, life in the northern palace settled down into some kind of normality. Tuthmosis was a joy to her. He came and spent many hours painting frescoes on the walls and making sculptures for the rooms and gardens for her. When he was not there, Neferu spent all her time with the children. The children were taken daily to Maruaten by their nanny to see their father and they sometimes chatted about what daddy had said or done. In general, though, they were very reticent about him, and she did not encourage their confidences in this respect in case Amio thought she was trying to cause trouble. She learned to cut all reference to him out of her speech, although not out of her mind. In spite of herself, she worried about him, more so than about Ankhsenpaaten, who knew that her father loved her.

When Neferu heard that Ankhsenpaaten was pregnant, her old fears revived, remembering Meketaten. She prayed to the Aten with everything in her that this daughter would not die too. By now she was resigned to the fact that this baby would also be a girl.

She did not even consider that the Aten would possibly allow Amio to have a son after disavowing everything he stood for. As she entertained no hopes herself on his destiny to father a son, she discouraged Maatnofret's speculations on the matter. With time, she was becoming more and more strong again, with the constant love and companionship of Tuthmosis. He was an infinitely practical man and very intuitive. Once, he told her how strange it felt when he sculpted the small busts of the pharaoh for sale. They were popular articles and sold as well to traders from the north and south as in Akhetaten itself. He said that he often reflected upon the vagaries of a fate that had decreed that he should continually sculpt the head of his rival.

'Rival? Amio is not your rival,' Neferu replied in surprise.

'Yes, he is,' Tuthmosis replied with an enigmatic expression.

'Why do you say that?' Neferu asked, mystified. 'It is you that I love.'

'Yes,' he agreed. 'But underneath you still love him too.' He looked at her levelly.

'That is not true, at least in the sense in which you mean it,' Neferu answered honestly. 'I love Amio as a person, but I am not in love with him at all.'

'You still love him as a man, even though you do not know it yourself. One day he will come for you and you will go. I will be without my love once more.' His tone was one of resignation. Neferu denied the words hotly, but he would not be convinced.

In order to maintain contact with her brother, Demi, in Heliopolis, it was necessary for her to pass her messages via Maatnofret. Demi was now an important official in the judicial system. Maatnofret had to pass the message to Amio to censure prior to his sending it on further. It was in this way that Neferu heard that Demi was coming to Akhetaten to see her. Neferu was overjoyed. By now, she had achieved a certain peace of mind and was not unhappy. Meresger was a frequent visitor to the palace, and this was very useful as it prevented gossip. Meresger was also a genuinely nice person, and over the months she and Neferu became friends. It was an odd situation, but it worked very well. Meresger spent a lot of time with the children and seemed honestly comfortable with the situation.

Nefer-Neferu-Aten-tashery was now eight years old and was a very pretty child. Tutankhaten was slightly younger than she was by a few decans only and the two of them were as close as twins. Even Satenpare was now at an age where Neferu could have quite deep conversations with her. Occasionally they discussed the meaning of life and ethics and other profound subjects at a depth she felt they could understand. She tried, as always, to bring her religious feelings into their everyday life in such a way that whatever the future might bring, they would never have to feel themselves alone or that they would feel it right to turn to cold stone statues for comfort and solace.

Maatnofret brought word that Amio was very worried by the increasing power of the priests of Amun at Thebes. He had become stern and morose, according to Maatnofret, and he was becoming increasingly introspective. Apparently, his only frequent social visitor was Penhasi, with whom he would discuss theology until late in the evening. Maatnofret told her that Amio had resumed his daily visits to the temple of Aten. It was several months now since Neferu had seen Amio at all.

One day, Amio allowed Maatnofret to bring Ankhsenpaaten to see her. Neferu was ecstatic to see her daughter again. Already, Ankhsenpaaten's abdomen was beginning to swell with her pregnancy. Neferu was sad that her daughter's childhood had been so short. Neferu found her daughter happy, in spite of everything.

After this first visit, Ankhsenpaaten was allowed to come and visit frequently, and Neferu was able to teach her daughter about the coming delivery of her child and how to look after it. Neferu was glad that Ankhsenpaaten was much more sturdily built than her older sister had been. Her robust little frame seemed vibrant with health but, as Neferu well knew, even this was no guarantee of a safe delivery, and she was worried about her daughter. She tried to make Ankhsenpaaten's pregnancy a point of learning for the other children and they were all interested in feeling the baby's movements. Tut was just as fascinated as the girls and Ankhsenpaaten loved being the centre of attention. Ankhsenpaaten asked her if she would be present for the birth and Neferu did not know how to reply. She replied that she would desperately love to be there with her if her father would allow it. Ankhsenpaaten promised to ask and when Ankhsenpaaten arrived for her next visit she found that the answer was in the affirmative. Both Neferu and her beloved daughter were pleased and Neferu was much relieved. If things should not go well, at least she would be there with her daughter to help as best she could.

It was almost a year to the date of Meketaten's death when Maatnofret arrived one night to wake to inform her that Ankhsenpaaten was in labour. Neferu rose anxiously and begged Maatnofret to return immediately to her daughter's side. She jumped up and dressed quickly, trying not to disturb Tut, who was sleeping in the bed with her, following a nightmare earlier on. Tut woke up, however, and Neferu told him what was happening and settled him down again. Her lover Tuthmosis was on her other side, and she kissed him and told him she might be away many hours. Tuthmosis grinned and said with amusement that he might get a better night's sleep now that he was not so squashed.

She laughed and blessed his good humour always in the face of the most uncomfortable moments. She made to leave but felt compelled to turn again and go back to her lover. She knelt beside the bed on the floor and planted a loving kiss firmly on his sleepy lips before jumping up again and rushing off along the cold corridor.

Outside in the courtyard, the air was chill and there was a wind blowing. She shivered and pulled her cloak more closely about her. She was going alone on foot, in order not to alert attention. Officially she was disgraced and therefore not allowed within the grounds of the palace of Maruaten even. Neferu walked briskly, unafraid. This was still her city, she felt. She entered Maruaten by the gate entrance reserved for the royal family and quickly crossed the once familiar courtyard into the main corridor. Maatnofret was waiting there for her and escorted Neferu to her old quarters. Somehow, Neferu did not mind at all that Ankhsenpaaten should be using her old room. She noticed that there was only a narrow bed there and she wondered where Amio was now living.

Soon after her arrival Amio entered the room and Neferu was truly shocked by his appearance. His face was thinner than ever, and he looked haggard. In her reaction to him she had forgotten the protocol, suddenly realising this, she quickly knelt in a deep curtsy and said, 'Your Majesty.'

Amio looked at her. His expression was hard to determine, but he seemed pleased to see her. 'There is no need for formality between us, Neferu,' he said. She noted that he had used her familiar name. Curiously, she realised that she was pleased to see him again.

'I hope you are well, Amio,' she said, uncertainly. He certainly did not look it, she thought privately. He nodded but made no further comment as he advanced towards his daughter's bed.

Neferu turned to the physician, who bowed to her and then began to relate to her the events of the delivery so far. The doctor said he was pleased and that everything was proceeding normally. Ankhsenpaaten was strong, albeit young still, and he did not expect any problems this time. There really was nothing for Neferu to do apart from sit with her daughter and help her to while away the time until the birth of the infant proper. Neferu kissed her daughter and then she prayed out loud a short prayer to the Aten for a healthy child and a safe delivery for her daughter.

Amio sat opposite to Neferu on the other side of the bed. He looked at his former wife many times but hardly spoke, except to smooth Ankhsenpaaten's forehead occasionally and tell her that he loved her. Neferu took a good look at him. He seemed a shadow of his former self and she knew instinctively that he was deeply unhappy. Inside of her she felt that hard core of unforgiveness beginning to melt. She had not anticipated that events would have torn him so far apart.

Soon events left them no time for speculation. Notwithstanding Ankhsenpaaten's youth, her labour was short and within a few hours she had given birth to a healthy daughter who gave a lusty cry. Neferu picked up the baby and wrapped her up in a soft cotton blanket. She held it to her and crooned at the baby's red and angry face. She gave the baby to her daughter, who held her for a few minutes before handing her back and lying back tiredly. Looking up, Neferu saw Amio watching her, and she took the baby over to him to show him.

'Look, Amio! She is beautiful, isn't she?' she said, relieved at the happy outcome.

Amio looked at the baby and at her. 'Yes. She is beautiful,' he said slowly.

Neferu suddenly thought of his disappointment at the birth of another girl, and she remarked sympathetically, 'I am sorry she is a girl, Amio.'

Amio smiled at her wanly. 'I have come to believe as you do, Neferu, that I am not destined to have a son.'

Neferu put her right hand on his arm. 'I am truly sorry, Amio.'

He looked at her steadily and then said, 'I am truly sorry too, Neferu.'

She had a distinct feeling that he was not talking about a son. 'Amio …' she began, and then stopped. She did not know what to say. She wanted to make her peace with him, but so many wounding words and actions had passed between them that she could not find the right words.

Amio looked at her expectantly but shrugged as her silence continued. 'You may come and visit Ankhsenpaaten and the baby every day,' he said eventually. 'But in view of our circumstances it must be secretly.' Neferu nodded. She understood that his pride was all he had left now. She could forgive him that. Amio went over to his daughter and took her hand and kissed her gently. 'Well done, Ankhsenpaaten! I am proud of you! Thank you for giving me such a beautiful daughter.'

Neferu felt the tears smart her eyes. She loved him for that generosity in the midst of his anguish and disappointment. She watched his back as he left the room. In his defeat he was regal. She felt proud of him then. He was a true pharaoh.

It was dawn when Neferu left the palace. She knew that soon word would be on its way to Thebes that once again the long-awaited child was a girl. Time was running out for Amio. He had refused to take another wife from outside and Neffie was still too young, if Ankhsenpaaten could not provide him with a son.

Neferu took to visiting her daughter every evening. Sometimes she would run into Amio, and they would exchange a few words. There was still obvious goodwill between them and yet their conversations were like sparring matches, as if both of them expected the other to make some decisive concession. Gradually Neferu began to feel her pride ebb away as she realised that Amio was not only unhappy, but he was also ill.

From Maatnofret she ascertained that Amio had been celibate from the onset of Ankhsenpaaten's pregnancy. He had not taken a concubine as she had thought. Her friend also informed her that for decans now he had been suffering fevers and swollen joints. His knees especially seemed to be affected and caused him great pain. His physician gave him something for the pain, but it did not cure the condition. Sometimes he was a little better and sometimes much worse. Neferu felt sick at heart. With the information had come the thought that he might die and with that thought came the blinding realisation that she still loved him. If he died, she would be desolate. The stupid quarrels and bitterness, even her pride, were as nothing when faced with that. They had torn each other apart and, in doing so, they had torn themselves apart.

Neferu was wracked with pain, guilt, indecision and love for two very different men. What should she do? She cried bitter tears in front of Maatnofret and told her what was in her heart. Maatnofret begged her to go to Amio. She told Neferu that she was convinced that Amio still loved her and that it was only pride that was keeping him from her and his hurt that she loved Tuthmosis. Neferu needed to know that Amio really loved her and did not just need her because he had no one else left.

For several days she thought of nothing else. Tuthmosis sensed her inner turmoil, and it was he who took the bull by the horns and brought the subject out into the open. His tremendous intuition almost made words redundant.

'You will have to choose between us, Neferu,' he said quietly in a controlled tone.

'I love you both so much,' she cried bitterly.

He held her tight. 'I understand, Neferu. I have always known that you still love him. You must be certain, though, that it is love that you feel and not pity.' Neferu nodded, very distressed. He stroked her hair and spoke soothingly. 'I will always love you, Neferu, and I will always wait for you. You are the only woman I have ever really loved. If ever you need me, I will come, just as long as there is strength in me. I will leave now, and I will not return until you ask me to come,' Tuthmosis said his words with tremendous dignity and Neferu clung to him in her grief. He was such a tower of strength. She had no right to put him through this. Gently, she disengaged her arms and wiped her eyes.

FOR THE LOVE OF ATEN

'Come now, Neferu, my love. You must be strong.' He kissed her swollen eyelids and gently sat her in the chair close by. 'Whatever is to be, will be,' he whispered to her with a wry philosophy. 'If Amio died and you had not gone to him, could you be happy with me? If you go to him and he dies, will you come to me? I don't know, Neferu, but I am willing to take my chance. I have enough love for both of us.' He kissed her one more time before rising to his feet. 'I am going now, my love. Remember that I will always love you.'

Tuthmosis left and Neferu sat there in the chair for a long time, blinded by her tears. She prayed to the Aten to make the right decision. She asked him for a sign so that she could know what to do. Suddenly a memory came back into her mind from all those years ago, almost seventeen years, when Amio had risked his life and reputation and prestige to save her from a whipping and how when he had asked her to marry him, he had asked as if she were going to refuse him. She smiled slightly through her tears. He was still that blend of infuriating arrogance and charming, undemanding modesty. He was still, underneath, the man she had fallen in love with. Circumstances had tried them sorely and they had both failed the tests, not just him. It was the fault of both of them. She loved him still and she always would. Even death would not be able to part them. Somehow, she knew that throughout eternity they would be linked together in some form or another. She could not fail him now. It would be a betrayal of everything tender and precious that they had ever experienced together.

CHAPTER 28

That evening Neferu dressed carefully for the man she was going to woo. She had made her choice and she knew that there could have been no other. She had to finish gracefully the life that the Aten had shown to her. She went to kiss the children goodnight and told them that she would see them in the morning. She put her cloak on and pulled the hood low over her face, and, in the company of her lady-in-waiting, she walked to Maruaten. When she reached the courtyard, she bade the lady-in-waiting to return with one of the chariots if she was afraid to walk alone in the dark.

Neferu went swiftly to her old room to see her daughter. Ankhsenpaaten was resting in bed. She looked very well. There had been no problems with her recovery from the birth and she was beginning to be a little bored. Her father was continually busy with affairs of state, and she was missing the attention she had received when she was pregnant. Neferu took her cloak off and told Ankhsenpaaten that she was going to talk to her father.

Amio was in his study when she found him. He looked up in surprise as she curtsied low to him. He rose to greet her. 'Neferu! What can I do for you? Is there something wrong?' he asked courteously.

Neferu was silent. Now that she was here, her courage failed her somewhat. 'Yes. Something is wrong, Amio,' she said quietly.

'What is it, Neferu?' he said anxiously, stepping forward.

It was a very difficult moment for Neferu. She had to swallow her pride and that was something which nearly choked her. 'Amio. I still love you with all my heart and I want us to be together again.' She managed to get it out quickly before her pride stopped it altogether. Amio stood stock still, so still that she thought he had not heard her half-eaten words.

Suddenly, he opened his arms to her and said in a moved voice, 'Neferu. I love you too and I want you back again.' Without knowing who moved first, she was in his arms, and they were both crying. They clung together for a long time, neither of them wanting to disturb this moment of peace and surrender. The war was over and both of them knew it. Destruction was all around them but through it all they had found one another again. The wounding words were not forgotten but in this moment of great sweetness, they had lost their sting. Finally, Amio whispered, 'Come back to Maruaten, Neferu. I need you with me.' He began to kiss her face and continued incessantly. Through the mingled tears they smiled at each other.

'Yes, I'll come, Amio,' she said.

'What about Tuthmosis?' he said, his face darkening.

'Tuthmosis knows that I had to come back. He is a good man, Amio, and I love him very much and I always will, but I love you more. Let's not discuss the past or the future. Let's live just for now.'

He nodded and pressed his face next to her own. 'We can't ignore the past, Neferu, but it is time to forgive. I have always loved you and there has not been a day I have not thought about you and prayed that you would come back to me.'

'I wanted to hurt you, Amio. Just as you hurt me.' She looked at him directly to see if he understood.

He nodded again. 'I understand, Neferu. It is gone now. We have both suffered. Let there be no more suffering.' *Let there be no more suffering*. It was a futile hope. There was to be much more suffering, but never again of the kind which could tear Neferu's heart in two with bitterness. The two of them went into the bedroom next to the study, which Amio had made his own. They undressed slowly, without their old passionate haste, and Neferu saw how wasted Amio had become. In her shock she commented on his thinness, and he smiled ruefully and admitted that he had not been well. He now confessed to the pains and problems he had been having and showed her his right knee, which was red, hot and very painful to the touch. Neferu was really worried, but he brushed it aside. He said that his lack of appetite had been due to jealousy more than anything else and that now she was back, he would be sure to eat more. He drew her towards him and told her that jealousy had almost driven him crazy and the pains in his limbs were as nothing compared to that. He told her, as if he was particularly concerned that she should know it, that he had not been with any other woman and not with Ankhsenpaaten since the day she had conceived. He told her that if he could not have her then he wanted no one else.

Time melted away for Neferu as she became again the lover she had once been to her man. She felt his need of her, and she fondled him gently. For a moment he lay feverishly and then, with a cry, he took her quickly and afterwards he lay in her arms, still inside of her and he groaned.

'You make me crazy, Neferu. I can't live without you.'

She smiled in the dark and kissed him gently. 'I am glad,' she said. Afterwards they went to wash and played out their old ritual of him washing her intimately, and her washing him in turn. When they went back to bed, she asked him if she should massage his knee for him. He was silent for a second and then he answered with surprise in his voice. 'It is not hurting.' They fell asleep in each other's arms.

When Neferu awoke in the morning, Amio was lying awake beside her looking at her. They smiled at each other. Amio sighed. 'I would like to take you, Neferu, but I am so stiff in the mornings that I have to move carefully.' He winced as he tried to turn towards her to kiss her.

She kissed him gently and said, smiling, 'In that case, my darling, I will just have to take you, won't I?' There was desire in his eyes, and she felt him hard against her. She thought for a moment and then got up quickly and brought some cushions from a couch. She placed two of them around his inflamed leg, just below the knee and then placed more cushions over them and gently lifted his left leg over onto more cushions so that his legs were separated, and the left leg slightly bent. He winced slightly as she bent the knee a little and she was careful to handle it gently. When she was finished, she asked him if he was comfortable, and he replied that he was. She moved her hand down into his groin and began to massage him. The sight of his arousal also excited her, and she felt his pleasure as she kissed him and then took him in her mouth. Her lips glided up and down his most vulnerable parts gently and he came quickly. Afterwards he lay quietly. She moved back up to face him and lifted his hands against the warmth of her breasts and she put her arms around him.

She asked him how he felt, and he replied simply, 'Wonderful.' He did not try to move, and they lay still for half an hour before it was time to rise. Paranefer came in and stopped in surprise when he saw Neferu. Amio smiled. 'My wife has come home again, Paranefer,' he said.

Maatnofret's husband looked embarrassed and Neferu said cheerfully, 'Just give me a minute, Paranefer, and then you can help Amio up.' The old man nodded and withdrew. Neferu kissed Amio and laughed. 'Do you need me to help?' she asked him.

'It is very strange, this!' he said wonderingly.

'What is?' Neferu asked.

'The pain and stiffness have gone,' he said, tentatively flexing his fingers.

Neferu laughed again. 'Making love is good for you, you see,' she teased.

'Yes. It really is!' Amio said seriously. Slowly he sat up and gingerly moved his legs over the side of the bed. 'I have hardly been able to get out of bed by myself in the mornings for decans,' he said as he drew himself to his feet. 'You are good for me, Neferu,' he said, turning to her.

'Well. If that is so, then you won't be suffering any more stiffness in the mornings anymore,' she promised. When Paranefer returned, he was pleased to see the pharaoh up and making his way to the bathroom without help.

That first day of their total reconciliation Neferu spent with Amio and the children. Amio was full of remorse concerning the changes he had had made to all the public buildings and was anxious to organise the restoration of her name to them. Neferu no longer cared about such things and was too anxious herself about his physical condition to do more than tell him to forget it for the time being. He could see to these things when he was stronger. Nothing seemed to matter to her anymore except the world within the family. She thought often of Tuthmosis, and her heart ached to think of how much pain she had caused him in doing this thing. She prayed that he would forgive her.

Neferu was sad to see how easily exhausted Amio became. He complained that his vision had also deteriorated and that he was no longer able to read the documents properly. She was thoroughly alarmed and felt very bad about not having perceived the true state of Amio's health sooner. They had seen so little of each other, and it was her fault. Now she regretted the time she had spent away from him. Amio wanted to organise a state ride through Akhetaten so that the people could see that they were reconciled, but she knew that he was just not up to it physically. She told him that that too could be postponed until he was stronger. He himself seemed to have no real perception of his extreme state of emaciation, though he did recognise that he was seriously ill. In spite of the chronic pain he was in, his mind was as alert as it had always been, and he continued to make wry and witty jokes about his situation.

Neferu became so concerned about him that she asked Maatnofret to arrange for all the children to be brought over from the northern palace. She told Amio that she intended to spend some time alone with him and was arranging for Ankhsenpaaten to be transferred to the other end of the palace with the baby, Maatnofret and the other children. This way, he could spend his mornings with them and then rest in the afternoons.

Neferu sent for the chief physician and, in front of Amio, she asked him to tell her the truth about Amio's condition. Amio shrugged. 'Tell her,' he said. The physician bowed to her and said in a grave voice that he could do nothing for Amio except to reduce his pain and that he did not expect the pharaoh to live more than one year. Although she had known in her heart that she could not keep him long, she had hoped against hope that it could change. Hearing the physician say it out loud was very shocking for her. She thanked him for telling her the truth and gave him leave to go.

When the physician had gone, Amio made a joking grimace and then matter-of-factly he began to discuss what would be the best way to plan for what was to come. Neferu felt cold and shivered violently. He held her close, and they clung together for a while. She saw that he was becoming agitated for her and made a supreme effort to calm herself for him. When she regained control of her mind properly, she told him that he must give up all affairs of state and relinquish them to Ay, Tutu and to Smenkhenre. She told him that when he died, Egypt would have to go on without him anyway and therefore it could do so now. She told him that she and the children wanted him full-time for the period left to them. Amio agreed to send for Ay to discuss the matter and said he would speak to Tutu, the state secretary, and delegate as much as he could to him. He confessed to her that he had, in any case, lost all interest in the affairs of state and that these things had become very exhausting to him. They discussed how best to plan for the inevitable separation, how to put it off as long as they could and how to obtain maximum pleasure out of the time left to them.

Tutu was summoned and Neferu implored him to handle as much as he could without disturbing her husband. Tutu understood the situation very well and was pleased that it had been brought out into the open. He promised to send a messenger to Ay right away and seemed pleased to see Neferu in her former position. Neferu guessed that he was more pleased to have the power to administer as he thought fit. She knew that he was aware that she did not have a warm regard for him and that he was a dangerous intriguer, possibly in league with Horemheb and the priesthood, but she did not care anymore. The Aten must take care of Egypt and its people. They were his responsibility. Hers was to prolong the life of her man as long as she humanly could, for her sake more than for his own probably. The thought of going on without him was intolerable to her.

In the afternoon they all sat in the garden and Neferu watched Amio as he sat chatting to the children while they played. They were all keen to play with the new baby and Ankhsenpaaten proudly held her baby out for them all to give it a cuddle, before the nurse took it away to feed it. As she observed the happy little scene, Neferu decided that she must make a strict regime and that they must stick to it scrupulously. As Amio's mobility was worse in the mornings, then it would be best for him to have a massage and then a warm bath first in the mornings and then breakfast. The children would be brought to him afterwards and then after lunch she would spend the rest of the day with him alone, plus the nights, of course.

Because she did not want the children to feel rejected, Neferu told them that their father was very ill. Now that they were all quite physically independent, she could leave them largely in the care of the nursery staff, all of whom had been with them for a very long time and were completely reliable and kind. Maatnofret would have overall charge as they were almost as much her children as they were her own. Neferu spoke separately to Ankhsenpaaten and told her she was in charge, and she felt herself quite grown up. The children were excellent about all these things and Neferu realised that she had an enormous benefit from their adaptability in this. They understood their mother's situation and seemed not to take offence at being relegated to a secondary role. Neferu set about re-organising the furniture and the household in general to suit Amio's physical limitations better. If Amio resented her pushiness now, he did not show it.

One thing that preyed heavily upon Amio was the legality of Neferu's position. He insisted upon Penhasi coming to arrange a renewal of their marriage vows, according to the law of the temple of Aten. He would not rest until the servitor had visited and performed a simple ceremony there in the palace for them. Amio relaxed after this. Everything else could wait, he said, but he did not want to take the risk of dying with his marriage vows broken.

Amio's illness caused him most pain at night when he had gone to bed. The aching was worst then, or perhaps it just seemed so, more noticeable because the light of day was gone, and the palace was so silent in the dark. He could not sleep and refused to take the extract of poppy, which the physician had given him, because it gave him bad dreams and sometimes made him confused. He liked Neferu to stay awake with him and talk to him. When the pain was bad, she suffered it too, with him, and felt useless and frustrated at her inability to cure him. Now, their great sexual affinity came to their help. She would massage him gently all over and then continue sexually until his desire was greater than his pain and he climaxed. She discovered that afterwards he would inevitably say that his pain was less and that he could fall asleep. Once asleep, he was often able to sleep for several hours. In the morning she would stimulate him again and this really did seem to settle his condition. He no longer required the poppy extract until just before his death eight months later.

In those first weeks back together, Amio seemed to improve considerably. Most of the time, he was able to make love to her by taking her and his mobility was reasonable. The health regime she had arranged for him was largely successful and his frequent rests fitted in with the children's school schedule and their rest periods too. Apart from the constant worry over his condition, Neferu was tremendously happy and fulfilled. All the children were well, and the family grew together more closely than ever before. This time, Neferu knew how to appreciate her happiness. She lived for the day and tried not to think of the future at all. Only now was important and she no longer left the palace at all, even to go to the temple. Every morning Penhasi came to visit them and take a small service of prayers. Amio could no longer kneel but lay on the couch while Neferu knelt on the floor beside him.

Ay was visibly shocked by the deterioration in Amio's condition when he arrived and Neferu begged him to take over all aspects of the pharaoh's position, in order to relieve her husband of all personal pressure. Amio and Ay were very close, and Ay was the only other one apart from Pararameses whom Amio trusted. Smenkhenre was too introverted and inexperienced to rule on his own. Ay told them that he would carry out all the affairs of state with the integrity he had always shown. Amio wrote out a decree, expressing his will that at his death, Tutankhaten should be made co-regent with Smenkhenre. As the son of Tiya and Amio's half-brother and adopted son, he was Amio's heir. Ay swore in the name of Aten that he would uphold Amio's wishes in this matter and would always support Tutankhaten until he was able to rule independently.

There remained one area of contention between Ay and Amio. It was the question of burial place. Amio insisted with all the force of his will that he should be buried in the tomb he had had hewn out of the rock in the eastern mountains just outside the borders of Akhetaten. Ay was very disgruntled with this and tried to insist that Amio's body be brought back to the Valley of the Kings. Amio would not hear of it and Ay was unable to move him. In the end, the old vizier promised to do as his nephew wanted in this matter. Next and finally, Amio made Ay promise that Neferu's position would be restored to her formally, if he should die before he could do it himself. Ay promised this too and Amio lay back satisfied that he had done all he could to ensure the safety and well-being of the people he loved and cherished and the country and the people he loved. Neferu felt a great sense of relief. From that time on, Amio was pharaoh in name only and they were able to spend his last months as a private family.

Strangely, in spite of the adversity of sickness and its resultant restrictions, this was one of the happiest times in their marriage for both of them. Time was so precious now that there was no time even for the banality of impatience. They were both seized by a sense of urgency and the quality of their relationship was different now from the early days of their marriage, characterised by its wild, passionate abandon and the excitement of exploring each other in every sense, the heartbreak of their petty quarrels and the ecstasy of making up. Now their love was tried and tested to almost breaking point and found to be real and true. It was a quiet passion now, with the certainty and security of knowing each other's quirks, weaknesses, strengths and needs. Now, they were almost an extension of each other. There was no longer any urge to test each other; it would have been a waste of time when it was running out for them. They had already squandered enough and misunderstood too often what was important.

Once, after a moment of great physical tenderness between them, Neferu asked Amio the question that she had so often asked him in her mind. If she had not come to him that fateful day, would he have sent for her or would he have gone on without her until he died? Amio smiled.

'I wanted to send for you so many times, my darling, but my pride would not let me. Just before you came, I was so desolate that I was on the point of surrendering my pride to the four winds and asking you to come back to me.'

She kissed him gently. 'It was the answer I wanted to hear. I would have been inconsolable if you had died without me by your side.' They could speak of death without fear now.

Another time, Amio came out into the grounds without her hearing him and caught her crying bitterly. He was jolted by the sight and held her closely to him, asking what was wrong. She told him the truth letting the tears come freely. 'Amio, I am frightened.'

'Why are you frightened, Neferu?' he asked anxiously.

'Because I am only thirty-three and very strong. I might live for many years after you go. We must pray to the Aten that he will take me too, soon after you go.'

Amio was very upset. 'I will stay with you always, Neferu, when I have gone to eternal life. Don't be afraid, my spirit will be with you always, I promise. You must live until the children are able to manage by themselves. The Aten will take you when he is ready. You must fulfil your responsibilities to him before he will take you.' He held her and crooned soothingly to her until she calmed down again, and they were able to enter the house without raising the children's anxieties.

When Penhasi came to give them benediction the following morning, Neferu shocked him by praying for a short life so that she could rejoin her husband quickly after death. He insisted upon adding the words 'If that is the will of the Aten' before adding his amen to the prayer.

Amio and Neferu spent the rest of their decans and months together in isolation from the rest of the world, seeing only the most trusted advisors and the servants whom they had known for many years. The world outside Maruaten did not exist anymore for them and they had lost all desire to concern themselves with it. Neferu once broached diffidently the question of not having fathered a son and asked Amio if he still felt bitter about it. He shook his head in reply and answered that he now understood that it was never meant to be. The Aten had destined Tutankhaten to be his successor and he could now accept the Aten's will with serenity. Neferu was overjoyed to hear that and felt a real warmth pervade her at his words.

Five months after her return to Maruaten, Amio's physical condition began to deteriorate quickly, and it became necessary for him to remain in his bed almost all the time. To have the servants lift him out into the chair became more than he could bear sometimes. Neferu now began to give him the poppy extract ordered by the physician to reduce the pain. To prevent his isolation from the rest of palace life, she had their bed moved into the sitting room so that occasionally he could be moved out to sit in the garden, on a good day. The sitting room was large enough for them to sleep there, for the family to congregate there and for them all to eat there.

In this way, Amio never had to be left alone by Neferu. When he was awake and the children were playing outside or if they were with their tutor, she would either sit or lie with him. She took over all his personal care herself now it was too painful for him to be lifted into the bath by the servants and she bathed him carefully and then get Maatnofret to help her to change the bed linen. She attended to all his toilet needs and did not allow the servants to help in this because she knew how humiliating it was for him to ask them to help with these things. She knew that he would have done the same for her without experiencing any embarrassment and for her, his body was just an extension of her own.

The poppy seed extract relieved the worst of Amio's pain, but it made him confused sometimes and gave him nightmares. He hated this and always refused the drug unless his pain was unbearable. Their sexual life was wholly dependent upon her now that his movements were so limited, and he hated that. He retained his desires to the full, however, and she enjoyed this power; she had to beat the pain and enable him to still experience some pleasure from his body. It was one of the few physical pleasures left to him now and she exploited it to the full. She learned every possible way she could to bring him pleasure with her hands and her mouth and to make him feel that life was still worth the living.

Once, he told her that she was like a gifted musician: she had learned how to play his body like a musical instrument so that there were no discordant sounds, only beautiful music. She laughed at his witty analogy. It was strange but, in spite of everything, they laughed a lot together. Amio had always been very quick-witted with a tendency to sarcasm, and he was a gifted raconteur. Even now, he was able to detect humour in the everyday routine going on around him.

Earlier in their marriage, he had written her many poems and stimulated her interest in poetry too. During the past few years, though, he had not written any poetry at all. In these, their last months together, he wrote her the most beautiful love poems of their marriage. When his hands became so painful that he could not utilise the stylus himself, he composed them mentally and would ask her to write them for him. It felt odd to her to be writing down some ardent comment about herself. She wondered that he could still envisage her in terms of such physical perfection after all these years, when she knew herself that both her face and especially her body were showing marked ravages of time. Sometimes she would stop writing and stare at him and find that the passionate words were accompanied with an equal passion in his eyes. This always succeeded in arousing an answering passion in her too, which required a physical response, even if only a tender kiss.

Neferu could not bear to spend a moment away from her beloved husband now. Her thoughts of every waking moment were with him. True to his word, Tutu had taken over completely the work of state and only came to visit them when the royal seal was not sufficient authority for some decree or other. Then Amio would sit with the stylus in his hand and painfully and laboriously write his name. His daily struggles caused her great heartache, but she took care to hide it from him as well as she could to maintain an atmosphere of serenity in their home.

It was only sometimes, when she lay awake in the dark while he slept, that she would silently cry and pray in despair to the Aten that he would not take her husband from her yet. In the last few decans of his life, Amio became a total prisoner of his body. This was his own description, and it was a truthful one. Neferu reflected that this fate was far worse for Amio to have to endure than it would have been for many men because his nature was to be impulsive, energetic, aggressive and independent. The Aten had given him a body that was none of these things. It was a tribute to the strength of his personality that he had been able to accomplish so much.

Neferu expected her husband to rant and rave in his frustration against the disease that was ravaging his body so relentlessly, but he took it with surprisingly good will. He did not complain much of the pain, which she knew must have been considerable at times and which made her feel so helpless. Sometimes he became depressed, but she would sit on the bed and take his hand or kiss him and smooth his forehead and remind him of some of the many happy memories of their past life, until he cheered up. Fortunately for them both, at this most difficult time of his life physically, his faith was at its strongest. He would outline to her all the things he most truly believed in and which he wanted her to inculcate in young Tut.

It had been Amio's aim to simplify a theology which was largely inaccessible to the masses of ordinary Egyptians and to show that the one great god, who was the creator of all things and all peoples, was impartial. He truly hated the sway of the priests over the people and wanted to proclaim that all men were born equal in the sight of god. Most of all, he wanted to suppress the practice of magic, which the priests used to manipulate the people and hold them enslaved.

Many years earlier Amio had adopted the policy of using the spoken vernacular for all official documents. This had been previously prohibited by the religious and civil authorities and an archaic form of Egyptian had been used for many generations since the ancient times. This ancient form of the language had long since ceased to be comprehensible to the ordinary people and its use served to limit the spread of knowledge to those of an elite power-based few. Amio had felt that this contributed to the mystification of the people in general, which the priests of Amun used to their benefit in amassing power. He was proud of his success in this desire to liberate the people from the bonds of tradition that had outlived its usefulness. He wanted to broaden the vision of the people and force them to look beyond the rigid formulae which had governed their thinking for centuries.

In his enthusiasm, Amio could be very irritated with those who did not understand or share his ideals. Although Neferu adored him and agreed with those visions a hundred and one percent, she did sometimes tease him that the way he taught his theories of peace and goodwill could sometimes be very aggressive. Often he had been able to take such criticism from her, but he had often been ferocious with outsiders who had voiced opposing views, especially when such views came from the priesthood of Amun.

Now that it was almost over for him, Amio could see clearly where he had made mistakes and been too hasty in passing judgements. Neferu eased his mind by reminding him that the Aten was in charge of all things and even his mistakes would not have been allowed to happen without the will of the Aten. It must have been in some mysterious way that even the mistakes somehow served the ultimate purpose of their god. Perhaps the Aten had not allowed him to complete his plan because it was part of an even greater plan which would remain undiscovered for many generations. Perhaps they would complete the plan in another time and space. Perhaps they would return in a future time to this space to complete their task. Amio was much comforted by the thought. 'If I am to be born again, Neferu, I want you to be born again at the same time. I will pray to the Aten that we can always be together.'

Neferu lay down beside him and kissed him. 'I think that as long as we wish to be together then the Aten will allow it, if we follow his will. I believe that those who love each other, in whatever kind of relationship, will always be together as long as love exists between them. Perhaps he wished to test our love sometimes, to see whether it is strong enough to survive in the face of adversity. If it does survive, then it can only grow stronger, I feel.'

'Our love has survived, even though we almost let it slip away,' he said softly.

'But we did not let it slip away. We could have, but we chose not to let it happen,' she reminded him.

Once, he told her touchingly. 'The Aten is taking me first because he knows that I could not bear to live without you.' His voice firm and certain.

'But what about me? Will I be able to live without you?' she asked desolately.

'Yes! You will have the children and you will have Tuthmosis. I will allow you to obtain some happiness by letting Tuthmosis borrow you for the rest of your life,' he said magnanimously. 'But only on condition that you do not marry him. You will remain my wife until you die.' Neferu was amazed that he should have been thinking such things, and a little amused that his plans were so detailed.

She gave a small laugh. 'Amio. You are impossible,' she said at last. 'I am not an object to be borrowed.'

'No, you are not an object,' he agreed. 'But the Aten meant you for me.'

Neferu had to laugh that the old arrogance was still there. The shell was destroyed but the spirit within remained intact, temporarily imprisoned, peeping out of the windows of the shell as fiery as ever.

'I hope the Aten is not a man!' she said humorously.

'I hope so too!' came the irrepressible reply. 'I don't want to share you there either!' He moved his head towards her to kiss her and she moved up closer to him, slowly, so that she would not jar his limbs. 'If I could, I would take you now,' he said mischievously. 'So, why don't you take me instead?'

She smiled and moved her hand downwards to his groin. Neferu became so used to Amio's body that as the limbs atrophied and became contorted, she did not fully comprehend the extremeness of it. What a stranger would have seen as grotesque abnormality, was to her merely her husband's body. It was part of him and therefore to be cherished. She did not find his deformities ugly, only painful because of how she knew he suffered. Even on the night before his death, when his pain was severe and he moved his head about on the pillow restlessly, she was able to soothe him by massaging him gently and fondling him until the opium took effect.

Neferu had been expecting the end for so long and yet, when it did finally come, it caught her unawares, leaving her shocked and bereft. She realised that in her supposed anticipation, she had been fooling herself. The moment came, as her brain had known it would, but her heart would not accept it. Amio had had a very bad night, with pains in his abdomen as well as his joints this time. Neferu had given him the opium, but it had not really helped much, and she had given him more, perhaps too much, until he had finally fallen into a deep sleep which lasted for many hours. When he awoke, he felt a little better, but he still had some pain, and she gave him more of the poppy extract so that the pain would not grow. He had a profound pallor and his abdomen seemed very bloated, but the extract settled him. She noticed that he was a little breathless and she took her pillow and pushed it under his own to lift him up a little bit. He said he was more comfortable. Neferu suddenly experienced a feeling of acute anxiety approaching panic, and to overcome it she leaned forward and kissed him, saying, 'Amio, my dearest darling Amio. I love you so much.'

He looked at her with such a look of love that she felt her eyes fill with tears. 'I have always loved you, Neferu, from the very first time I saw you, and I always will. We will come again, and I will search the earth over until I find you. Will you wait for me to find you?'

'Yes, my darling. I will always wait for you.'

Amio smiled. 'Peace be with you until we meet again, my love.' The last words came out in a gasp and then there was nothing more. The eyes that looked at her were empty. Amio had gone.

She cried out aloud in terror. 'No, Amio! Not yet, not yet!' She knew that her words were useless.

She flung herself on his body, kissing him and holding her to him. It was in that position that Maatnofret found her when she entered, some time later.

When Neferu did not answer her greeting, Maatnofret came closer and saw that Amio's eyes were open and staring. She bent over and closed them gently and pulled Neferu away. Like a zombie, Neferu allowed herself to be pulled off the bed.

'Neferu! Neferu!' She could hear Maatnofret's words, but she could not respond. There was a crack, and she felt a sharp pain on her left cheek.

Slowly her eyes filled, and she said 'Amio has gone, Maatnofret.'

'I know, darling. I know.' Maatnofret put her arms around her and hugged her and then Neferu cried and cried. Maatnofret held her for a long time and then she said, 'Look, Neferu. I want to show you something.' Neferu turned to look where Maatnofret had gone. Maatnofret was standing by the bed and was pointing down to Amio. She did not understand what the other woman was trying to say to her. Maatnofret pulled back the covers to reveal Amio's distorted body. 'Look, Neferu! He stayed as long as he could for you. You would not have wanted him to suffer any more of that, would you?'

Neferu shook her head. 'No,' she answered softly at last. 'I am being selfish. There is no more suffering for him now.'

Neferu lay on her bed, staring unseeing at the ceiling with a dreadful feeling of emptiness inside her. There were no more tears for Amio's death. It had gone far deeper than tears. She felt that if she could cry now, she would feel better, or alive anyway. She had the oddest feeling that she too was dead, and she felt so cut off from her own actions that she even experienced a slight sense of shock when later she noticed that the hands mechanically arranging her hair in the mirror were her own.

Maatnofret came with some extract of poppy seed, sent by the physician, but Neferu brushed it aside. That was for pain, and she had no pain. She had nothing left in the way of emotion at all. She felt completely calm and slightly irritated by the look of worry on the face of her old friend and confidant. Even the thought of the children could not break through the sense of unreality she felt. She knew that word would be already on its way to Thebes and that presently the grand vizier and his wife would be here to take charge of things. She could not arouse herself to pay attention to the routines going on around her and she felt a profound inertia that prevented her from event trying.

CHAPTER 29

Neferu continued in her half-dreamlike state even after the arrival of Ay and Teya to Akhetaten. Part of her noticed that the palace administration and care of the children carried on under the loyal auspices of Maatnofret and that part of her was grateful for this respite from the routines of living. The other part of her was living in a strange, anaesthetised world where nothing really touched her. She did not want to leave it, knowing that there was no partial shield, and if she surrendered to the mundane, the pain would also come flooding back.

Maatnofret came to tell her that Ay wished to talk to her about the future. It was a strange word. She could not envisage time ahead anymore. When she tried, she could only see a long dark stretch of empty days with no meaning. The future was for others, not for her. What point was there in living when you had lost all possibilities for happiness? She remembered her promise to Amio, and she would honour it as best she could, but beyond that, she could see nothing. Dully, she rose from her bed and straightened her gown around her.

When she entered the sitting room, Ay rose to greet her. He came forward and took her hands. She smiled at him mechanically and he looked at her anxiously. He led her to the couch and gently pushed her down, drawing up a chair and sitting just opposite her.

'Forgive me, my dear,' he said, clearing his throat. 'I know that this is the worst possible time to discuss these matters.'

He stopped and sighed, and she said, dully, 'It's all right, Ay. I am perfectly composed.'

He looked at her sharply, as if her appearance belied her words. 'Neferu,' he continued. 'I would not bring these matters up now unless it were anything but the most extreme importance.' She nodded and said nothing but patted his hand in an absurdly maternal gesture.

'Continue,' she said softly.

Ay cleared his throat once again before beginning. 'Neferu. As you so earnestly requested me eight months ago, I have administered the affairs of state almost without reference to Amio.'

Neferu nodded. 'I am very grateful to you for that, Ay,' she said quietly.

The grand vizier looked at her with softness in his face. 'Yes, I know, Neferu. There are some things, however, which I must bring to your attention now, though. These past years have not been easy for me since the death of my sister. Nowadays, I need eyes in the back of my head to watch what is going on around me at court and in the temples. Our present situation in Upper Egypt is critical, most especially in Thebes itself. From the point of view of foreign policy, we are threatened with attacks on our allies in the east by Hittite hordes from the north and Asiatic peoples from the east. We cannot rule out the possibility that one day they will attack Egypt itself.' Neferu shrugged. She could not see the point in worrying about potential disasters in years to come. The Aten was in control of that, surely?

'I do not see that as a primary cause of concern right now,' she replied quietly.

'No. That is true, Neferu, nevertheless, it must be taken into account because of the politically weak situation we find ourselves in right now,' he answered sharply. The sense of urgency in his voice managed to pierce the cocoon of indifference she had surrounded herself with.

'Do you mean the priests of Amun?' she said.

'I do indeed,' Ay replied. 'You know as well as I do, Neferu, that my family have been resented for a very long time and for many reasons.' Neferu nodded again and he continued. 'Our Semitic origins, our favoured position with the old pharaoh, Tiya's marriage to Amio's father. This alone has been enough to cause us many enemies amongst the nobility. Above all, the Egyptians have always found our religion strange and unacceptable, in Upper Egypt anyway. Even the fact that you are Keftiu in origin irritates some people, not to mention your very public conversion to Atenism, which we ourselves have always been very reticent to proclaim. Amio was, perhaps, too uncompromising in his attitude towards other gods and in that he was very much influenced by you, Neferu.' He softened his tone as he said the last words, as if to detract from their harshness. Neferu nodded in admission that it was true. She had made enemies in Thebes, she knew that. She still remembered clearly her encounters with Asenaath and Sinefrew in her early days at court.

'Where is the main trouble coming from?' she questioned Ay with a sense of resignation.

Ay replied slowly as if describing it for his own clarity as much as for her understanding. 'I am pretty sure that Sinefrew and his relatives have been the prime instigators of unrest. He never forgave Amio for crossing him in public, in the whipping incident. They have always envied us and always harboured great bitterness towards us since Tuthmosis was born. Sinefrew's mother was Amenophis' second wife and Sinefrew was born three months before Amio, but Amenophis made Tiya his chief wife and therefore Sinefrew was denied the right of accession. When Tuthmosis, Amio's elder brother died, Amio became crown prince, even though Sinefrew was older. It made him doubly bitter. I am afraid that your encounter with him so many years ago was a catalyst that he had only been waiting for. It served to ferment a hatred that had been there a long time, Neferu. If only you had been able to settle down and be happy in Thebes, perhaps all this could have been averted, but then, maybe it would not have made any difference. When you and Amio did not provide a son for the throne, they began to see their possibilities improving dramatically. That is why I and Tiya were so anxious for Amio to take a second wife, you see.'

Neferu was surprised that Amio had never mentioned that Sinefrew was his half-brother, but then, his father had several wives, and he was so used to the situation of having dozens of close relatives that he did not think it a strange thing. She suddenly realised that he probably had many more half-brothers and sisters, who were themselves intermarried. He probably only thought of them as some kind of cousins. It was all very complicated and slightly unpleasant to her, even if it did not affect her directly. 'I understand your worries over the accession, Ay, but I disagree with you regarding the result. Even if I had given birth to a son, his character or his physique may not have made him suitable to be pharaoh, whereas Tut is a fine boy, strong and handsome, as well as intelligent and in direct line to Tuthmosis IV, his grandfather.'

Ay nodded. 'That is true, Neferu. No one can doubt Tutankhaten's right to the succession and Smenkhenre must make him co-regent immediately in order to strengthen our hand. Tut has been brought up here in Akhetaten, however, and I fear that unless we make some further moves to placate the priests of Amun, then there is a danger of revolution, with a coup d'état a distinct possibility.' Neferu was profoundly disturbed by this news. She knew she was forced to do something to strengthen the position of this true son of her heart.

'What do you want me to do?' she asked.

'Move to Thebes immediately, with the children,' he stated abruptly. Neferu was jolted out of her lethargy of indifference with one blow. She swallowed hard, all her instincts telling her to refuse. She loved Akhetaten, it was her home, and she did not want to leave it ever. She had planned to grow old here with her husband and it was here that she wanted to die. She hesitated. 'I am afraid that it is necessary, Neferu.' Ay's voice was stern. 'You must bring the children to Thebes. Tut would be miserable there without you and the others and yet, if he stays here, I might not be able to control the situation much longer. Horemheb has control! As my son-in-law, I know I have his loyalty, but even you must be made aware that he is a firm anti-Atenist.'

'Horemheb against us too?' Neferu was stunned. 'Why?'

Ay sighed. 'Not against you personally, Neferu. I think that he felt very slighted all those years ago, when you and Amio refused the invitation to his wedding to Mutnedjmet. He felt that it showed no gratitude for all the work and planning he put into the design and construction of Akhetaten. I am sorry, Neferu. I would not have told you, except that it seems relevant to our present situation.' He sighed again, not used to speaking so openly.

'But I never knew he felt like that,' Neferu said slowly. 'Of course, both Amio and I were grateful for his excellent work. It was just that we were so eager to start our life here. I was so unhappy in Thebes, and I just wanted to get away as soon as possible.'

'I know, Neferu, I know. Don't worry about it now. I have explained all that to him and he has forgiven you, I'm sure.'

Neferu bit her lip. 'This is all my fault, Ay. I should never have married Amio. I have never had the right sort of personality to be queen and I have always resented his duties. Perhaps I was too possessive. I wanted him for myself alone. I was jealous of Tiya and her influence over him and I shut my eyes to the things I did not want to see. I should never have become queen. Fate played a strange trick upon me and then refused to give me the son who would have allowed me to relinquish my role. If only I had had a son! He would be married by now and the throne would be safe. Instead, Tut is only nine years old and we must provide him with a secure background until he reaches puberty.'

There was a long silence at the end of her speech before Ay replied. 'The situation is not yet lost, Neferu. There is always the possibility that Smenkhenre and Meretaten will have a son, though the situation there is not hopeful so far. Do you agree to come to Thebes?' he asked.

'I suppose that I have no choice,' she said simply, already resigned to the upheaval.

'I thought you would understand,' he said with satisfaction, laying his hand over hers in a gesture of warm approval. 'This is our ace card,' he continued. 'And we must play him soon.'

Neferu felt tired. 'Will it be enough?' she asked.

'No,' he answered. 'There is one other thing.' He paused.

'What is it?' she asked with cold trepidation.

'We must arrange for the marriage of Tut and Ankhsenpaaten to take place as soon as possible,' he declared firmly. Neferu was shocked to her core. She felt sick. So, all the intriguing was going to start all over again.

'Is that absolutely necessary?' she asked in horror. 'They are so young and Amio has only been gone a decan.'

Ay nodded. 'I know, but Ankhsenpaaten was officially Amio's chief wife at the end of his life and if she marries Tutankhaten as Amio's widow, then his right to the accession becomes totally incontestable.'

At these words a terrible stab of pain went through Neferu, although she realised that the grand vizier had not meant to wound her. He was just being his usual politically pragmatic self. She sighed loudly and he misinterpreted its cause. 'It will not prevent them from forming liaisons in later life, should they wish to do so, once a son has been born,' he stated cynically. Neferu looked down. Probably he and Tiya had once spoken like this about herself and Amio, she thought. Feelings were of no consequence where the acquisition and retention of power was concerned, to the likes of Ay.

'Could we not wait a little, regarding this matter?' Neferu pleaded, needing time to think. 'It is only ten days since Amio's death and it does not seem proper to be discussing a marriage, when his funeral ceremony has not even taken place.'

This time it was Ay who sighed, contemplating her with a certain amount of undisguised impatience.

'It will be another sixty days before the necropolis workers will be ready to deliver Amio's body for the ceremony,' he reminded her. 'Anything could happen during that time if we remain here at Akhetaten.'

Neferu knew that she was beaten. 'All right, Ay. Do what you think fit, so long as your arrangements do not preclude myself and all of the children being brought back to Akhetaten for Amio's funeral,' she said sternly.

Ay looked offended. 'Amio will be given all the honours of his position, Neferu. How could you doubt it?'

Neferu nodded. 'I'm sorry. I did not mean to offend you,' she answered placatingly.

Ay inclined his head to show his acceptance of her conciliatory words. 'I have kept some news until now, Neferu, because it did not seem apt to reveal it before, in the light of your grief,' Ay spoke hesitantly and Neferu looked at him directly, wondering what new blow was to come. 'Meretaten is pregnant, but it seems that the father is Sencherib, the son of Sinefrew.' He shrugged his shoulders.

Neferu drew her breath in. So, her foolish, vain daughter had been inveigled into the enemy camp.

'Poor Smenkhenre,' she voiced finally.

Ay shrugged again. 'It is very much to be regretted but their marriage was a mismatch of personalities. It was to be expected, though not, I had hoped, so soon.'

Neferu meditated silently. No wonder Ay was so impatient to strengthen Tut's position. This turn of events had enormously increased Sinefrew's ambitions. If Smenkhenre died, Sencherib would be in a very good position to claim the throne. Inside of her she felt a little tremor of fear for Amio's brother. Death could be made to occur much earlier than fate had planned in environments like that of the Theban court, she knew full well.

Neferu felt she was having a rude awakening into a world she had managed to shut out for so many years. She wondered what else was still to come. Whatever happened, they could never hurt her Amio now. He was safe and there was some comfort in knowing that.

'All right, Ay. You win.' She gave him a rueful smile. 'I will talk to Ankhsenpaaten and Tutankhaten today. If they agree and have no distaste for one another, then you have my leave to arrange everything. I myself have no desire to take any further part in political life and would like to be considered a private person from now on.'

Ay looked at her curiously and Neferu knew that he found her an enigma. 'You really loved him,' he said wonderingly.

She knew that he meant Amio. 'Did you ever doubt it?' she asked and stood up, not expecting an answer to what was more an exclamation than a question.

'I never truly knew for sure,' he said openly.

'He was my destiny,' she said. 'I was meant to love him and he me. The right man, the right time, perhaps the wrong place. I only know that we will meet again. For Amio and me, it is not over yet.'

Metaphysics irritated Ay. He felt himself on a more practical plane. He coughed discreetly and smiled at her. 'You may very well be right, Neferu, but at this moment I am more concerned with the here and now, where all our problems are unfolding.' His tone was gentle, notwithstanding his words. He was silent for a moment, as if lost in thought, then he lifted his head up to look at her again. 'On a practical level,' he said apologetically. 'When will you be ready to leave?'

Neferu reflected. 'It will take two or three days to organise and transfer everything to the ship,' she estimated, half to herself. She looked at him again. 'Three days from now,' she stated.

'Good,' Ay answered with satisfaction.

At the doorway, Neferu hesitated. 'I will come with you to Thebes and stay until the children have settled in, then I must return here. I have some affairs to settle and some goodbyes to make.'

Ay nodded his acquiescence. 'You are a formidable woman, Neferu,' he remarked in a tone of involuntary admiration. She inclined her head in acknowledgement of his compliment, turned and was gone.

Thus was Neferu so brusquely shaken out of her anaesthetic cocoon into the real world again. For the next few days, however, there was no time for private grief with so much preparation to be made. Three days later, as promised, they were standing on the quayside ready to board *The Aten Gleams*. She knew that with her leaving, there would eventually be an exodus from her beloved city of many of the senior officials, who would make their ways back to the centre of political life in Thebes. She felt a sharp pang pierce her grey mood at seeing her beloved home receding into the distance. She thought of Tuthmosis. Did he know that she was leaving? She had deliberately not sent him a message. She knew that in returning to Amio, she had hurt him deeply. Did he hate her too now, like Yussef did? Did she have any real friends left?

During the journey, Neferu concerned herself only with the children. Tutankhaten was aware that he was soon to be made co-regent and that Ay would teach him how to administer the affairs of state. He had been very sad to leave Akhetaten, although he had shown interest in the plans made for him. He had shown surprise at the plan to marry him to Ankhsenpaaten and confessed touchingly that he thought he would marry Neffie. Still, he loved Ankhsenpaaten, and it was made clear to him that this was a marriage of convenience which would not later preclude him loving someone else. Neferu felt no qualms about returning to Thebes on what she felt sure would be a temporary basis. She truly felt that she could soon withdraw from public life altogether. Once Tut was crowned, no one would concern themselves with her any longer. She had outlived her political usefulness. Once Tut had settled into the court and happily adapted to his new position, perhaps she could return to Akhetaten immediately and permanently.

It was not to be. On reaching Thebes, they were presented with the disastrous news that both Smenkhenre and Meretaten were dead. The cause of death was thought to have been poisoning and they had been found three days previously. Their bodies had been taken for embalming. In the heat, they would have started to decompose quickly so Horemheb had had to deal with the matter immediately. Both Ay and Neferu were profoundly shocked and Neferu saw Ay age visibly before her eyes. She knew from that, at least, that he had had no hand in the matter. Her initial suspicions rested with Horemheb, but he too seemed devastated by the crime. Neferu found it hard to believe that the handsome face she saw in front of her could be responsible for such a foul deed and yet someone had done it. Someone in very close proximity to the young couple, but who?

Neferu found that she and the children had been placed in Tiya's old suite, just across the alley from Ay and Teya. Amio's old suite had been occupied by Smenkhenre and Meretaten and now lay empty. The other upper suite, formerly that of Mereta, was now occupied by Horemheb, Mutnedjmet and their daughter. In Smenkhenre's boyhood suite now lived the old Archduke Tuthmosis, whom Neferu found to have aged tremendously.

Maatnofret was tired and Neferu settled her old friend and Paranefer into her suite. She wanted to have her friends close by her. They also intended to return to Akhetaten with her when the time came, to spend their retirement there. They were both sixty now and such shocks were too much for them. Maatnofret sobbed and sobbed for the young queen she had brought up as her own child. Maatnofret had always been such a tower of strength and she now gave way. In looking after her and the children, there was no time for Neferu to reflect on her own feelings. It seemed that death had been her constant companion for so many years now, that she wondered when it would visit her. She felt a curious comfort in the thought. She tempered this with the thought that although she did not fear death itself, she had no desire to be poisoned.

The more thought that Neferu gave to the matter – who had the most to gain from the death of Smenkhenre and Meretaten – the more she came to suspect Horemheb. Sinefrew most certainly had nothing to gain from the death of his unborn grandchild, it was sure. Ay was old now and although he loved power and was eminently capable of intrigue, he could and did have that power without the aid of the crown. The death of his nephew and great niece diminished his claim to power. If Tutankhaten should die, then the throne would now pass to Sitamun's son. She was the daughter and wife of Amenophis III, therefore neither the family of Sinefrew nor Ay had anything to gain from the deaths in question. It was also interesting that the murderer had chosen to act while Ay was away in Akhetaten, perhaps because the grand vizier's proximity would have been close enough to prevent such an act if he were in Thebes. At least she now knew that Ay would move heaven and earth to protect Tut from the same fate.

Neferu's thoughts chased themselves around her head. In the privacy of her bedroom, she sent out a silent call for help to Amio. 'Wherever you are now, my darling, please stay close to me. I need your help to make the right decisions.' Over and over again she tried to make sense of the puzzle. Neferu had never really cared for Mutnedjmet. She was a clever woman, in the same fashion as her father, also she was extremely ambitious and something of a snob. She was not a warm person, but Mutnedjmet was definitely no murderess, Neferu was certain of that. What about Horemheb, then? She had always sensed that he was utterly ruthless, and she was sure that he was capable of doing it, but how could it serve his purpose? That was what she could not understand. Horemheb had no connection with any of the royal blood lines whatsoever. It was Amio who had raised him from the role of minor scribe to court architect and thence to a position in the army. His marriage to Mutnedjmet had seemed to be a love match and had certainly been the cause of him entering the court proper. That could not bring him respectability as a serious contender for the throne, however, as there were too many other relatives with acknowledged blood ties to the royal family who would have much stronger legal claims than he could ever have. Neferu was suddenly stopped in her tracks. She had been missing the real point all along. As field marshal of the whole army of Upper Egypt, he controlled virtually all the possible routes to power. It was not legality he was considering, it was might. If Ay was dependent upon opium, as she suspected, he would be easy to manipulate. The ageing grand vizier wanted a quiet life, after all, and what was more natural than to rely upon his son-in-law? If Horemheb really did have the support of the priests of Amun, as she suspected, then it was only Pararameses who would be between him and the throne in any practical situation. It was only too possible then that Tut's life too was in danger. But what was it then that was stopping Horemheb from toppling them now? He had all the power to do it. The more she thought about it, the more she realised that it was because Horemheb needed the alliance of Pararameses to secure power, and for some reason he still did not have it. As long as Pararameses had control of Lower Egypt, she knew they were safe.

Neferu pondered her options to no avail. With the death of the young pharaoh and his queen, Ay moved quickly to organise the marriage of Tutankhaten and his bride to be, Ankhsenpaaten. By now, Neferu bitterly regretted bringing the children to Thebes at all. If they had all stayed in Thebes, it was possible that Tut would have lost the throne, but his life might have been spared. Here in Thebes, he was the next possible victim of the murderer.

Neferu watched the wedding ceremony of her daughter to Tutankhaten. The children looked so sweet, but she could have cried for the way their young lives were being manipulated to save a dynasty from collapse. In her heart she knew it was not right, and she wondered once again why their god was not watching over them.

After the wedding, Neferu found Ay jealously guarding them ever more closely. She began to feel herself excluded from their company and to be more and more irritated by the open efforts to nullify her teaching. He insisted that Tut's name be changed to Tutankhamun, at the obvious instigation of the priests of Amun. She was outraged beyond measure and for the first time since leaving Akhetaten, she cried. Tut was very upset by this and hugged her tightly. 'They are trying to turn you against me and against Amio and everything we have taught you,' she told him.

'They can never turn me away from you and Amio, Neferu. I love you both more than anyone in the whole world.'

She kissed him and wiped her eyes. 'There is only one real god, Tut,' she told him. 'I have never lied to you about it.'

'I know, Neferu. I will always believe you rather than anyone else, whatever happens,' he whispered to her.

'Tut. I am afraid for you. Your brother was murdered. You had better do as Ay tells you until you are old enough and strong enough to do the things you believe in yourself. If you do as he tells you, you will be safe,' she told him seriously. 'In the meantime, keep the truth in your heart and pray only to our god, the Aten, when you are alone.' The boy nodded, and she hugged him to her again. 'I am so proud of you. You are such a good boy,' she said.

'And I am proud of you too, Neferu,' he replied.

At Thebes, Neferu spent most of her time with Teya and Maatnofret, choosing not to join in the social life of the court, except to give support to Tutankhamun, as he was now called. This went largely unnoticed because she was still officially in mourning. As soon as it was possible, she made her plans to leave, Teya taking charge of all the children while she returned to Akhetaten to complete her funerary arrangements and settle the things that needed still to be done. Maatnofret and Paranefer left with her. Once on the boat, she turned to look at the city as the ship pulled away. It had got much worse now, she reflected, glad to be leaving. Even with Amio beside her, she had found Thebes oppressive and unfriendly, now, without him, she found it terrifying. What would it do to her children?

Neferu stood on deck, two days later, the boat having made very good time, waiting for the city to come into her line of vision on the horizon. It had always been a pleasurable sight to her before and it did not fail to delight her now. The pleasure was dimmed now by a premonition that this would be the last time she might see it. As they sailed into view of it, she lovingly searched the skyline, knowing every familiar shape of it as if etched upon her heart. This city had arisen from the barren desert, the product of Amio's imagination and their joint dream. She experienced a sense of poignancy at returning and knowing that he would not be there to greet her this time.

It was mid-morning when they docked, and the heat of the sun beat down on them. The river was busy and the noise of the fellahin on both sides sounded round the busy docking area. Once on dry land, she went forward to meet the greeting party. Most of these officials would soon be on their way to Thebes themselves. They were only waiting for the final funeral arrangements to be completed. Only a skeleton staff of noblemen would remain to administer the city and she knew that their dream was fast fading. Only the most committed Atenists would remain to live out their beliefs here. She found the thought very sad, but also found comforting the concept that the ones who did stay would be her kind of people and she would always be welcome here because of that, no matter who else abandoned her.

One of those who had elected to stay in Akhetaten was the portly old chief of police, Mahu. He had been a loyal servant to Amio and herself, even in her disgrace. She remembered his embarrassment and how he had continually apologised to her, as if it had been his fault that he had been ordered to remove her name from all the public buildings. He had gone into voluntary retirement on Amio's death, and he did not wish to uproot himself and his good wife to return to Thebes.

Neferu was greeted by Nakhtmin, the ageing general who was a cousin of Tiya from her mother's side. The old Nubian was still lean and fit, although old now. The old general was well-liked and respected in the military. For this reason, he had been chosen to be Tut's tutor and advisor in the Kap and would presently continue that work in Thebes. Maya, Amio's chief finance officer and chief scribe, would also be leaving later. These two men were above reproach and Neferu had complete faith in them. It was for this reason that she had insisted that they were to take over the special care of Tut. Ay had not demurred, though he had pointed out that it would be an unpopular decision with the priesthood of Amun. She had pointed out to him that the preservation of Tut's life was her paramount anxiety, and she knew that he would be safe with them. Ay had fully supported her in this, and he knew that his cousin Nakhtmin would be better placed than most to put down any talk of rebellion in the army.

Back at Maruaten, Neferu gave orders that all her personal belongings and those of the children that remained should be transferred to the northern palace of Hataten. Hataten was Neferu's own private property, a gift to her from Amio, who had registered the gift to her family for posterity. Apart from a loving gesture, it had also been part of a more general plan to ensure that his daughters would inherit substantial property on his death and hers. Later on, when she was disgraced, it had become her home temporarily and, thanks to the work of Tuthmosis, it now rivalled in beauty the much larger palace of Maruaten. Because it was so much smaller, it seemed much cosier to her now; there was not the hustle and bustle of family life to fill it. When the transfer of furniture and belongings has been accomplished, Maatnofret and Paranefer were settled in there. It was to be their home now for the rest of their days. Paranefer was ten years older than his wife and now, at sixty-two, he was totally overwhelmed by the tragic events that had overtaken them. He had not only been a father substitute to Amio, but he had also been a very close friend and it was heart-breaking to Neferu to see how the old man seemed to have lost his bearings. He needed Maatnofret now, more than the children needed her, Neferu felt. Much as she would have loved to keep Maatnofret with her in Thebes, Neferu knew it would have been unjustifiably selfish. They belonged here in Akhetaten now. They deserved a comfortable retirement and, as long as they lived, she and the children would always have a loving place of refuge from the frenetic life of Thebes, should they need one.

Neferu concentrated on settling the living arrangements of her old friends and those of her staff who wanted to remain in Akhetaten. They were all loyal people, and she was fond of them. They had served her and Amio well and it was her duty to ensure that they were comfortably placed in their old age. They assured her that they would keep the gardens and grounds in immaculate condition and would report any problems to Paranefer and Maatnofret. Maatnofret told Neferu that she would send frequent messages with the riverboat messengers and all that remained was for Neferu to settle the rooms for her own personal use at Hataten, her own castle to the Aten. She chose the three rooms she had shared with Tuthmosis when she had lived there previously. They were very comfortably furnished from that time and required almost no extra furniture. The walls were beautifully painted with frescoes, which brought that time to her memory once again in all its depth and emotion.

At Maruaten, a skeleton staff of six men and women, who were not Theban in origin, were left to maintain it. These people were all young with children who had been born here in Akhetaten. Neferu arranged for some of the furniture to be shipped to Thebes for Tut to use as the new pharaoh. When she felt strong enough, she went to Amio's study. There was an air of expectancy about it, as if it expected its master to enter at any moment. Papyrus was strewn on the great desk. She felt a great lump come into her throat and in the end, she left it untouched, exactly as he had last used it.

Feeling desolate, she entered the room where Meketaten had died. It was bare now and the furniture neatly stacked. The couch bed was stripped and already there was thick dust over everything. There was nothing here to indicate the passions and the tragedy that had been played out here, such a short time ago. With a heavy heart she left and began to walk down the long corridor. Her footsteps echoed and that made her feel worse. When she got as far as the open corridor, she stopped to admire the view of the beautiful pool and the gardens. As she stepped out onto the grass, she could almost hear again the sound of the children's laughter at play. Neferu remembered the day when Meretaten had fallen into the pool soon after they had arrived, and how Amio had jumped in to save her because she could not swim. It had given Meretaten a terrible fright but had had a salutary effect on her and on the other two. Amio had been very annoyed with her, and she had howled loudly. Neferu smiled at the innumerable memories of cosy domesticity they had enjoyed here.

After a while, she sighed and went back in to continue her solitary tour of the palace. As she left each room, she said a quiet goodbye out loud and finally she stood in their bedroom. The silence overwhelmed her, and she sat down, looking around. Closing her eyes, she began to remember their loving, their laughter, their quarrels, their hopes and fears, their reconciliations. The hard lump inside her chest grew to granite-like proportions. It was so large that it would not go up nor down. She opened her eyes again and looked around. Was this all there was left of all that? Was it all gone without a trace? She searched for a way to make time go back so that she could recapture those moments of love and live them all again. Why had she not understood then and appreciated each precious second with the perception she had now? She had taken for granted all those blissful days so that they all ran into one another, and she had not paid attention to them. They had all flown away and it was only now, when she had lost it all, that she understood how truly blessed she had been. She envied Amio that he had gone first. How desolate it was to be left behind. Slowly, the tears began to trickle down her cheeks as the full extent and misery of her loss hit her. She cried and cried for Amio, for herself and for all of them. She began to sob, and her sobs rose to a crescendo, wracking her body. Where was her god now? Why had he allowed this to happen to her, who had always believed in him? Why? No answers came to Neferu as she sat there all alone. She felt only the bitterness of betrayal by the god she had believed in. When her sobbing finally ceased, she felt her eyes hot and swollen. She rose and went to the bathroom to wash her face, but the water pitcher was empty, and she had to make do by wiping her face on the hem of her gown. Coming back into the bedroom, she felt a little better. At the doorway, Neferu turned to look again at the room behind her.

'Goodbye, Amio, my love,' she said softly before finally leaving.

In the sitting room, Neferu took the bust of Tut that Tuthmosis had made, and one of Amio, and she wrapped them up in a linen sheet before putting them in a basket to take with her to Hataten. She took her leave of all the remaining servants and thanked them for their trustworthiness and care. She gave them presents and leave to use the wine cellars to a moderate extent for themselves and then she dismissed them to their duties. Before she left, she looked around the sitting room once more. It would be so easy to live here with all the ghosts of my memories, she thought, and yet I would not be happy. Happiness had disappeared for her with that last breath of Amio's body. Perhaps she was meant to go to Thebes? Perhaps the Aten still had work for her to do, though just what she could not imagine.

Neferu knew that over in the necropolis, the workers were hard at work embalming Amio's body, but she knew that that was of no importance. Wherever Amio's spirit was, it was not there. She knew it was soaring free, somewhere out in the universe. Perhaps it was even here with her now and she, in her blindness, could not see or feel him. She closed her eyes and said a quick prayer and then spoke out a plea, softly, 'Remember your promise, Amio! You said you would always stay with me. Stay with me!' Suddenly, she had such a strange feeling that there was someone with her in the room and she opened her eyes quickly. There was no one. 'Is it you, Amio? Are you here?' she whispered out loud. There was no answer or movement to signify that he had heard, but she felt his presence so strongly that she held her breath. 'I'm leaving now, Amio,' she whispered. 'Come with me, my love.'

From that time onwards, a sense of peace began to grow in Neferu and gradually, the grey gloom of anaesthesia began to lift. She did not expect any further happiness for herself in this life, but she perceived that she had a job to do which was important. Tut and Neffie were still only eleven years old and Satenpare only eight years old. She must make sure that the faith in which they had been born and brought up was not twisted and warped by the nefarious plans of Ay and Horemheb.

Much as she liked Ay, Neferu realised that his sense of right and wrong was different from that of most people. What he wanted was right and what he did not want was wrong, and moreover she sensed that in Horemheb Ay had received a son-in-law of the same ilk as himself. Both of them were capable of acts of great evil if they felt it to be expedient and both were capable of rationalisation of such actions. It was precisely because they were so charmingly amoral that she found them so difficult to deal with. A downright evil person would not have posed a problem at all, but these two were not evil, they merely had no sense of right and wrong when it concerned their ambitions and desires. They both lacked a sense of ethics and sensitivity to the sufferings of others. What was she to do? One person she felt might be on her side was the old Archduke Tuthmosis, Tiya's beloved and the true father of Tut. Neferu had found him very much in tune with her feelings when she had spoken with him in Thebes, and he had treated her almost as a daughter this time. There was something very paternal about him and she felt able to confide in him. He was very old now, it was true, and he held no sway over the doings of the court, but he was held in tremendous respect as the only surviving brother of Amenophis III, and second son of the great Tuthmosis IV. Neferu wondered if he was the ally the Aten had sent to her aid, though he was by birth and by religion an Amunist, or more properly, likely an agnostic.

That first evening at Hataten, Neferu discussed freely with Maatnofret the position as she saw it. Maatnofret was deeply troubled. Neferu was like a daughter to her, and they had been together since Neferu's first visit to court. Now Neferu was a widow of thirty-two and it seemed her life was over to all intents and purposes.

'You have one other friend you could turn to,' Maatnofret reminded her.

'Who?' Neferu queried.

'The other Tuthmosis who loves you,' she said earnestly.

'Oh, Maatnofret, I don't think there is any emotion left in me now to give to any man,' sighed Neferu.

'I expect Tuthmosis would understand that,' replied Maatnofret. 'But you owe it to him to contact and talk to him.' Neferu sighed again. She had been thinking the same, but she was afraid to put a stick in a hornet's nest. Tuthmosis was a true friend and she truly loved him, but he was like Amio in many ways, impulsive and unpredictable and she could not manage either of them. On top of that she had hurt him very badly and she had not the right to stir it up again. Would he, could he ever forgive her that? In her heart of hearts, though, he knew that she would have to go and say goodbye to him, if nothing else. She told Maatnofret that she would go the following day.

Early the next morning, Neferu rose and breakfasted with Maatnofret and Paranefer. She noticed that Paranefer ate very little, and she urged him to partake of more. He smiled at her wanly and made an effort to please her by taking some pitta. It distressed Neferu almost as much as it did Maatnofret to see him like this. After breakfast she gave them both a hug and set out.

Her first call was to the temple of Aten to see Penhasi. Together with the old priest, she knelt to say special prayers for the spirit of Amio and the rest of her departed loved ones. Afterwards, she asked the servitor to say a special prayer for herself and the children, requesting strength and guidance for them all. A final prayer was directed to the Aten on behalf of Tut and his coronation. Especially earnestly, they prayed that the priests of Amun would not be able to shake the faith of Tut's belief in the Aten. After their prayer session was over, Neferu took an emotional farewell of Penhasi and his family and asked her chariot driver to take her to the atelier of Tuthmosis. To her surprise and consternation, she found it closed and shuttered, with no sign of either Tuthmosis or his assistants. She wondered at it but guessed that he was taking a holiday. After a moment's hesitation, she asked the driver to take her to the sculptor's villa.

It was Meresger who received Neferu and cordially invited her in. Notwithstanding the emotional triangle which existed between them, there was liking and friendship of a kind between the two women. Meresger told Neferu that Tuthmosis was in Memphis, and he had been there for almost half a year, apart from three short visits home.

'What is he doing in Memphis?' Neferu was both disappointed and curious.

'Don't you know?' asked Meresger, in surprise.

'No, I don't,' Neferu assured her.

'Oh!' the other woman replied. 'Somehow I assumed that you would.'She looked at

Neferu and saw that she was perplexed. 'It was just after you went back to Maruaten,' she explained. 'Tuthmosis received an important commission from Pararameses to do some work on the temple of Aten which is being built there.' Meresger paused before adding, 'We assumed that the pharaoh wanted my husband out of the way for a while, at least.' Neferu lifted her shoulders to express her ignorance of the facts. She reflected that it very probably was Amio who had arranged the commission. It was very much his style of doing things, she thought, but he certainly had not mentioned it to her.

'If Amio arranged it, he said nothing to me about it,' she told Meresger.

Meresger nodded, seeing that Neferu was telling the truth. 'When will he be coming back permanently?' Neferu asked, as casually as she could.

'I don't know yet,' came the prompt reply. Neferu changed the subject and told Meresger about the deaths of her daughter and Amio's brother. Meresger was visibly shaken and put her hand to her throat in an involuntary gesture of fear. Neferu told her that Tut was possibly also in danger and that was why she was tying up her affairs in Akhetaten so quickly. All the children were in Thebes now and she must go back quickly. Tut was soon to be crowned pharaoh and she was afraid for him and Ankhsenpaaten. Neferu saw that Meresger was examining her. She knew that she looked tired and haggard, far from the woman in the portrait in Tuthmosis' room.

'You look ill, Neferu,' Meresger said.

'No. I'm not ill, Meresger. I am exhausted emotionally, that is all. How are you?'

'It has been lonely since Tuthmosis left.' Meresger paused before continuing quietly. 'He took it very hard when you went back to your husband.'

Neferu swallowed. 'There was nothing else I could do, Meresger. I loved them both, but Tuthmosis did not need me and Amio did. I had to go to him. Do you understand?' Neferu asked.

'Yes, I understand, and so did Tuthmosis. It did not make it any easier for him, though.'

'Does he hate me?' Neferu asked slowly.

'I don't think he hates you. He is just bitter at the way things have gone for him. He still has me,' Meresger said softly.

Neferu smiled slightly. 'You have always stood by him, Meresger. You must love him very much.'

'Yes. I do love him very much,' she said.

'Do you hate me?' Neferu asked.

Meresger smiled. 'No, I don't hate you, Neferu. In a strange way you have made my life easier.'

Neferu was both startled and mystified. 'Easier? How can that be, Meresger?' she wondered.

A closed expression came over Meresger's face and, at first, Neferu thought the other woman was not going to reply. Eventually, Meresger said painfully, 'I could never be a proper wife to Tuthmosis or any man.'

Neferu felt embarrassed to ask and shy to know, but could not control her curiosity. 'Why not, Meresger?'

'Because I come from Upper Egypt where the girls are circumcised. I don't know what went wrong for me but making love is impossible – no man could penetrate me.'

Neferu was horrified. 'Could the physician do nothing for you?' she asked sympathetically.

'Before, when we were first married, we were too poor. Now it is too late, you see.' Meresger shrugged miserably.

'But how have I made your situation easier?' asked Neferu, still mystified.

'Because Tuthmosis fell in love with you many years ago and from then on he was mainly faithful to me. Oh, I know that he visited the House of Joy, but I knew that he would never leave me for anyone else. Even when you favoured him, I knew that you could not marry him. As long as he is in love with you, he will never leave me.' Neferu was silent, beginning to get a glimpse of the misery this woman must have lived through for so many years. Tuthmosis had never discussed Meresger with her, apart from the very first time they had sensed the special feeling between themselves. She knew that he was very fond of his wife and respected her very much.

'I am so sorry, Meresger. I don't know how you can be so nice. I'm sure I would be a hateful hag in that position. I would hate everybody.' Neferu leaned forward and gave the other woman a hug. 'You make me feel ashamed for complaining of my lot,' she added.

Meresger smiled. 'I know that you have suffered too, Neferu. Perhaps we have more in common than we think.' Meresger hesitated and then asked if she could give Tuthmosis a message on his return.

Neferu was silent as she thought what to say. What the other woman had just told her had altered any conception that she could continue her relationship with her former lover. To take him away from Akhetaten would destroy Meresger.

'Just tell him that I came to say goodbye. I did not want to leave without seeing him. Will you do it?'

Meresger nodded. 'Is that all?' she asked, with a questioning look.

'Yes. That's all,' said Neferu. 'If we never meet again, Meresger, I wish you well and the blessing of the Aten. Peace be with you.'

'Peace be with you too, Neferu,' was Meresger's reply as Neferu left.

As the chariot returned to Hataten, Neferu thought to herself, 'I did try, Tuthmosis, but fate was against us.'

Back at the palace, Neferu related to Maatnofret what had happened and asked Maatnofret to visit the studio when Tuthmosis returned from Memphis and tell him that if he wanted to contact her, he should send a message via Maatnofret herself. That afternoon, she wrote a letter to Demi telling him about her return to Thebes and the forthcoming coronation of Tut. The next day she was due to leave. That evening Maatnofret reported some gossip she had picked up from the servants. It appeared that some cases of leprosy had been diagnosed amongst some poor latecomers to Akhetaten and they had been quarantined to some hastily erected dwellings on the outskirts of the city. The unpleasant news was glossed over as it did not seem to touch their lives and was just one more depressing incident in lives that were becoming increasingly bleak. It appeared that since the initial quarantining there had been no new cases reported.

'How awful to be exiled from one's family,' Neferu had uttered.

Maatnofret had agreed. 'What could be worse than to have a disease like leprosy, where you were shunned by everyone?' The older woman shuddered.

The next day, Neferu and Maatnofret said an emotional goodbye and Neferu boarded the ship to go back to Thebes. With her she took those senior officials who would be needed at court in Thebes to support the new pharaoh. They had all served Amio loyally and they were all Atenists. It seemed to Neferu that from now on she would only have a maternal role to play and that thankfully, her political life was over at last.

CHAPTER 30

Arriving back in Thebes, Neferu noticed that Ay had accomplished much during the decan that she had been away. During that time, he had transferred Tut and Ankhsenpaaten to Amio's former suite, between his own and that of Horemheb and Mutnedjmet. Installed with them were Maya and his family and Nakhtmin and his family. Although Neferu was upset that the move had been initiated without her permission, she knew that the children would be safe in the hands of the devoted Maya and the old general.

The two younger girls, Nefer-Neferu-Aten junior and Satenpare, had had a good time in the care of Aunt Teya, who spoiled them thoroughly. Neferu felt that they preferred to be with Teya rather than herself in this anxious and preoccupied frame of mind that she was in. Satenpare complained to her, 'You are no fun nowadays, Mummy!'

Neferu made an effort to give more of herself to the girls, but it was difficult to behave cheerfully and appear serene in such circumstances. She brooded over the possibility of buying a villa outside the palace complex itself and leaving court altogether. Once the seed had been sown, the idea became increasingly attractive to her. There were many beautiful villas in the city and the children could come and visit her regularly. She really did not see why the two younger girls could not stay with her for a lot of the time.

Neferu bided her time and waited for a suitable moment to broach the subject to Ay. She was certain that he would not approve, and she needed to formulate her plans if his grounds for objection were to be made minimal. Gradually it dawned on Neferu that the handsome and charming Horemheb was going out of his way to win her approbation. He was always kind and attentive to her and made an effort at conversation to seek out her opinion. She was flattered but, more than that, she was curious to know why. Although Mutnedjmet seemed to be the tiniest bit jealous, Neferu felt there was no reason for her to be so. Horemheb wanted something but she was not sure what. She found him agreeable to talk to, but she definitely did not trust him. It was an instinctive gut reaction.

Neferu understood Mutnedjmet better. The couple had produced only daughters, but no sons, and she knew that Mutnedjmet was feeling the same sense of inadequacy and guilt that she herself had done earlier. She wondered if Horemheb was planning to take another wife and thought that must be why Mutnedjmet had become so shrewish and watchful. For all these reasons, Neferu was constrained to give a cool reaction to Horemheb's discreetly flirtatious manner. She perceived that he was offended by this, but she saw no alternative in the circumstances. He wondered if she had another enemy at Thebes now.

It rapidly became apparent that Ay and Horemheb were working in close co-operation towards an official reinstatement of the supremacy of Amun amongst the official gods, though, no doubt, with differing degrees of willingness. She began to feel sick at heart when the archduke told her that architects, intendents and workmen were all working frantically to replace the name of Amun, which Amio had had obliterated during his early reign. Neferu decided to tax Ay on the matter. Ay reacted angrily to Neferu's chidings, more angrily than she had ever known him. He told her that the threat of an insurrection led by the priests was not only possible but probable if attempts were not made to placate them decisively and soon. He told her that he did not want to do it but that it was vital. Tutankhamun's coronation was to be the occasion of the official reinstatement. At this meeting, for the first time, Ay cast some doubts upon Horemheb's trustworthiness and feared that without Horemheb's approval and support, he would not be able to rule. It appeared that Horemheb was without a belief in any god but that he valued the importance of the support of the priests of Amun. Neferu was chilled to the bone. Everything she and Amio had worked for was being overturned in the space of a few decans. Poor Tut was to be an innocent tool in their hands. Neferu raged to no avail.

For the first time, Neferu brought up her desire to move out of the palace. She informed Ay that her life at court was over, and she wished to be considered as a wholly private person. She would have preferred to move back to Akhetaten, On or Rashid, rather than live here in Thebes, but she wanted to be near to the children, even if she could not have them with her. Initially, Ay cajoled and pleaded with her. He told Neferu that she could still play an important role in strengthening the crown for Tutankhamun. Neferu asked how this was possible and Ay told her that his hand would be greatly strengthened if she would agree to marry him. Neferu was so completely astounded that she merely gaped, wondering if she had heard right. Ay obviously mistook her silence for interest in his suggestion (she could hardly call it a proposal). She reminded it would do him no good if he was considering an heir as she was barren and, in any case, she would never marry again, the very idea was distasteful to her. Amio would be the only husband she would ever have; she wanted no other.

Ay was furious beyond belief at her refusal to consider the matter. He told her that if she had married him, he would automatically have become co-regent and thus secured both Tut's future and her own at court where, he reminded her, she was intensely disliked in some quarters as a reminder of Amio's unpopular views. Neferu was flushed with anger and answered that it was for that very reason that she wished to move. She intended to remain a firm Atenist and would never deign to enter a temple of Amun or be thought of as associated with such heresy.

'Heresy?!' he shouted at her. 'We are considered the heretics here, and Amio has jeopardised all our futures with his intransigence. If you wish to leave the court then I will arrange a suitable place for you, where you can practise your ideas of freedom and equality. I promise you that you will be back begging me to reinstate you within six decans!' His tone was sneering, and she was mortally offended. How dare he talk to her like that? He would never have dared to do so while Amio was alive. For the first time she had quarrelled openly with Ay, and she began to experience a side to him that he had always previously kept hidden. Neferu lifted her head proudly and said icily, 'I never thought to hear you speak to me in such a way, Ay. I will pack my belongings and move out as soon as I have arranged a suitable place to live.'

'Leave it to me, Nefertiti,' he said, using her full name as a sign of his formality. 'The whole court knows that you disgraced Amio's trust. You must be placed in an area where the neighbours are unaware of your identity in order that no more shame be attracted to the throne.' His voice was cold and hard, and she felt the menace of his implied threat. She felt afraid but she tried not to show it.

'So be it, Ay. I trust the Aten will stand by me.' Without more ado, she turned and left the room.

Going straight to her apartment, Neferu wrote a message to Maatnofret and hurriedly sent one of the servants to take it to the barracks as an urgent message from the queen. She knew that she had to move fast before Ay restricted all her rights and privileges. Fortunately, she was in time, and she heard from the servant that the messenger had left immediately. When she received word that the message was already on its way, she quickly departed for the suite of Tut and Ankhsenpaaten and sought out the redoubtable Maya. To him she confided her position and asked him to contact Pararameses for her and also Tuthmosis, if he was still in Memphis. She asked Maya to ensure that both of them would be informed as to where she would be situated. Amio's trusty advisor was distraught but promised to keep in touch with her and to ensure that the children were kept safe and well cared for at all times. Neferu correctly surmised that Ay would ensure that she had no possibility of leaving with the children and she did not want them to share in her punishment anyway. Punishment was what she knew it was meant to be.

Maya went to interrupt Tut's preparations for the coronation, which was to take place in a few days' time. He returned with Tut and then left them alone to talk privately.

'Tut, my darling, I am going away,' she said, hugging her to him.

'Where are you going, Neferu?' he asked her anxiously. She sat down so that their faces were adjacent and told him as briefly as possible that times had changed now and that she no longer had any power or influence at court. She told him that she could never renounce the Aten and that therefore she was disgraced in the eyes of the court as she had been once in Akhetaten, though for a different reason. She told him that he would be used as a pawn in a chess game, in which the real struggle was for the power of ruling Egypt. Tut listened intently as she continued, 'You will not be able to do anything about it, Tut, until you are a grown man, so do not defy them openly. If you do so, you run the risk of them killing you just as they did Smenkhenre and Meretaten. I don't want to frighten you, I just want you to understand that you are safe only as long as you do as you are told. You are not strong enough to make a stand yet. Wait until you are a man and then do what you feel to be right.' Neferu felt the tears prick her eyes as she held her adopted son, as much hers as if she had born him herself. 'I love you with all my heart, Tut. Do you know that?'

He pressed his face to hers. 'I do know it, Neferu,' he said, with tears in his voice.

'I will think about you every day, Tut, and I will pray to the Aten for you specially. Remember me in your heart. I hope that we will meet again soon but I don't know if they will allow you to see me. I will try to send you messages, but they may try and prevent that too. I will never, never forget you or stop loving you. Will you remember me too?'

Tutankhaten nodded, his eyes bright with tears. 'When I am grown up and strong, Neferu, I will bring you back. You will live here, and everyone will kneel before you,' he said fiercely. Neferu smiled in spite of herself.

'That is not important, my darling. It is only important that you grow into a good man. I have always been so proud of you, and I know that I always will be. Amio and I could never have had a better son than you even if we had had a dozen sons. You would always have been my favourite.' For a moment they clung together and kissed until Maya returned to take him back to the priest to continue his practising for his coronation.

Neferu felt the return of that deep lump inside her chest. Was she going to lose her children as well as her husband? Was there going to be nothing left to her? She got up just as Tut's major domo entered. She asked him to bring Ankhsenpaaten to her. He bowed slightly and returned a few minutes later with the princess, soon to be queen. Neferu took her daughter by the hand. She was a tall girl for thirteen and very grown up. Not surprising perhaps, in view of all the things which had happened to her already. Neferu hugged her daughter and told her that she was leaving. Ankhsenpaaten was upset, but not as upset as Tut had been. Ankhsenpaaten was sweet and already sophisticated, but Neferu knew it would be difficult for her head not to be turned by the trappings of power and the privileges of her position. She was already developing the guile of a woman of court. Neferu told her that she loved her very much and would think about her every day and pray for her and for her baby, little Ankhsenpaaten tashery, who was now a plump and adorable one year old. She would miss her, but she knew that Ankhsenpaaten was not made in her mould and soon she would not want to be associated with the mother who was disgraced. It was not her fault, she knew, it was just that Ankhsenpaaten was not strong by nature. Ay would find it much easier to bend her to his will than he would find with Tut.

Within a few hours, Neferu found that she was virtually a prisoner inside her suite. She was allowed to move about freely in the palace gardens and to visit the apartments of her friend the archduke. She was allowed periodic access to the children but never alone. In the case of her two youngest daughters, they were allowed to visit her apartment but only in the company of Teya. Poor Teya was heartbroken, but she did not dare to defy her husband's orders. Neferu told her that she bore her no malice for the sequence of events and indeed she did not. She knew that Teya was an unwilling participant in all this, and she needed to keep her as an ally, albeit a passive one. Teya would vouch her life for the safety of the children and Neferu knew that. She also foresaw that she might need Teya's assistance in the future, if she was to live away from the palace complex. Furthermore, without Teya, she would not be able to get messages to her children.

Teya preferred to ignore her husband's part in the deterioration of the situation, and she heaped condemnation upon her son-in-law, Horemheb, instead. She was apparently aware that he was philandering elsewhere and was confidante to Mutnedjmet's misery. She appeared to believe that it was Horemheb who wished to marry Neferu, and this made Neferu wonder what the wily grand vizier had told his wife. Rather than upset the old lady by giving her the true version of events, Neferu merely reminded her that as she was barren; there would be no point in Horemheb marrying her. She could not provide him with an heir to give a semblance of legality to any possible claim to the throne by him. This was an aspect that Teya seemed glad to latch onto. Perhaps she sought it to cheer her daughter up with.

The following day Ay visited Neferu in her apartment to tell her that he had obtained a villa suitable to her purposes. He warned her that it was very close to the edge of the western desert, right on the edge of the city close to the poorest area and not far from the exile of the lepers. She saw that his aim was to frighten her into submission, and when she did not reply, he continued by telling her that if she wished to return to the palace at any time, she could send a message via the physician in that quarter, who had been told to make sure she had what she needed. Of course, he gave her the ultimatum that if she returned, it would only be on his conditions.

Nefertiti felt afraid and lonely. This was not at all what she had envisaged. She began to wonder what it was about her that caused so much destruction and unhappiness. She did not believe that she was evil but without doubt, evil things happened around her and she felt that she was always being punished for crimes she had not committed. In effect, she was being sent into exile. Her pride refused to allow her to show her feelings and she merely asked when it was that her belongings would be transferred. She was told it would be the following morning. She made to turn away, to show her dismissal of this hostile stranger, but stopped to look at him again as he told her that he was sending Asenaath, Sinefrew's sister, to be her lady-in-waiting. This was his final insult and in doing so Ay lost all contact with Neferu. Anger replaced her fear and she snapped at him. 'I refuse to have your spies in my home, Ay. You may keep Asenaath. I do not need a lady-in-waiting. I am quite capable of looking after myself. You seem to forget that I am a commoner by birth.'

'Don't be stupid, Neferu!' he hissed. 'You are only making it harder for yourself.'

Neferu looked at him coolly. 'No. Ay. It is you who is making it hard for me, but know this – Amio's spirit is watching you. The dead do not rest easy when their loved ones are wronged. Remember that when the time comes. This will bring you no good.'

'Are you threatening me?' he said, suddenly losing his temper.

'I threaten no one,' she said icily. 'I have no power to hurt you or anyone else. It is you who will be your own undoing. The Aten sees all.'

'The Aten! Bah!' he sneered. 'And what did the Aten do for you or for Amio? If the Aten has any strength, why are you in this position now? Tell me!'

'I don't know,' she replied honestly. 'I only know that there is a purpose in everything and that if the Aten wishes that I should suffer these trials, then it is not to break me but to use me for his own purpose. I will not turn against him now.'

'You may keep your Aten, then, and suffer the consequences. I have tried my best for you. It is your own fault.'

'No, Ay! You have done your best for yourself. Power is what you love. You are not capable of loving any other human being in more than a purely physical way. Lust you understand but love is beyond your comprehension. You are not evil, you are merely amoral. You have no sense of what is right and what is wrong, only what Ay wants and what Ay does not want. You know how to hate, Ay, but you do not know and have never known how to love. I think it is too late for you. I want nothing from you for myself, my life ended when Amio died, but this I do ask of you, that you will protect my children, especially Tut, from all harm. If anything should happen to them whilst they are separated from me, then let the curse of Aten be upon you from that moment until your death and then beyond that into any other life which may come. What you do to me and to them, let that be done to you.'

Ay listened intently to her words. He seemed to have lost his anger. At her last words, he looked up at her and only said, 'So be it!'

Having said her piece, Neferu bowed her head slightly and left the room, leaving him staring pensively at her back. This was the last time that Ay and Neferu ever met before Amio's funeral. That night in her prayers, she prayed that whatever the future would bring to her, she would never need to ask either Ay or Horemheb for help. Not in that life or in any other life to come. 'Please grant me this, Aten,' was her last thought before she fell asleep. She was in Tiya's room, in Tiya's bed, but she knew that she totally lacked the queen mother's political acumen.

Waking early in the morning, Neferu jumped out of bed, wanting to be ready before they came to collect her. She did not wait for her lady-in-waiting, realising that from now on she must learn to be completely self-sufficient. She had supervised the packing of her clothes already the evening before and had chosen only those which would be suitable for a widow in exile.

Sighing again, she looked at the many beautiful gowns in her wardrobe, remembering the occasions when she had worn them last. Neferu was a great hoarder of clothes and could never bear to part with those clothes she associated with the happy times of her life. She kept them for years on end and now as she looked at them again, she chose the white dress made by her grandmother all those years ago and the dress which she had worn on the day that she and Amio had made love for the very first time. On impulse she stuffed them in one of her linen bags strewn on the floor, already full of her things. She considered putting in a lovely deep lilac silk dress as well but rejected it from the purely practical point of view that it would require very careful handling and cleaning. If no servants were to be available to her, she would not be able to manage it herself and it might spoil. She felt as though she was being sent to prison.

In order to cheer herself up, Neferu went to take a bath. The water was cold though, and she decided she could not face that, but would rather wait until it had heated. When the maid came to light the fire in the oven below the heating surface for the cauldron, Neferu watched her carefully, in order to learn how to do it herself. In reality, she was not too worried about having to do these things for herself. She was basically an independent soul and she had never relied upon the servants to do things for her personally. She knew that she would be able to clean and make food for herself if she had to. What worried her more was the conspiracy of silent hostility around her. She could be killed, and they would cover up her tracks as if she had never existed.

Apart from her brother and Pararameses, maybe, no one would even think to inquire where she was. Their fabrications were so skilful, only the closest people at court knew the truth and they dared not say anything. She could be dead for all the world knew. Knowing Ay, she guessed that her true whereabouts would remain a secret known to him and Horemheb only. In effect she would cease to exist for almost everyone else. If Pararameses did not receive her message and find out where she was, anything could happen to her. She felt nervous at the prospect.

It was just twenty-four hours to Tutankhaten's coronation, when he would receive his accession name of Nebkheprure, meaning 'The Master of Transformations in Re'. With his name now officially changed to Tutankhamun, the title was apt in the extreme, she thought, cynically. Amio had also been known as Neferkheprure in the early days of his co-regency with his father, 'Master of Beauty in Re'. It was as if everything that had been had never really existed.

While the water for the bath was heating, Neferu put on a pretty morning coat and stepped out into the garden. She looked across at the lotus pool and smiled as she remembered the shocked face of Tiya that time eighteen years ago when she had decided to have a secret swim. Not very secret, as it turned out. Amio had been watching her too, though she had not seen him at the time. She had laughed so much later, when he told her how his eyes nearly fell out of his head in surprise as he glimpsed the girl he secretly loved jump naked into the pool. Well, she would not be swimming today. She did not want to provide a titillating show for Horemheb or her other gaoler.

At a signal from the maid, Neferu interrupted her daydreams and returned inside to prepare herself. She decided that if she were going to be disgraced, then she was going out in style. After her bath, she towelled her hair and made up her face, outlining her eyes in kohl and carefully applying red ochre to her lips. When her hair was more or less dry, she brushed it through carefully and piled it high upon her head into a fulsome chignon. From the jewellery that Amio had given to her, she chose a silver necklace inlaid with lapis lazuli and matching earrings, which dangled almost to the level of her chin. To complete this statement of her defiance, she chose as her gown a becoming shift of pale blue cotton damask, cut in the traditional Keftiu style. It seemed to say 'I am different. I am not one of you'. When she was ready, she checked herself in the mirror and felt pleased with the results of her efforts.

When Ay's messenger came to collect her, she was ready. She supervised the removal of her luggage and then went to say goodbye to the old archduke, Tuthmosis. Tiya's lover was so moved that there were tears in his old eyes. He gripped her hand tightly and apologised that he no longer had the power to undo this crime or even to mitigate it. He promised he would find out where they were taking her and visit her regularly as long as he lived or until Tutankhamun brought her back, whichever came first. She told him that the thought of his visits would give her strength and that one's friends in adversity are one's true friends, and the only real ones worth having, even if they could not alter the situation. She worried about how he would manage to discover where she had gone, but he told her not to. Ay would not dare to refuse him, son of Tuthmosis IV, knowledge of her whereabouts. She kissed him goodbye, and he told her that he would see her within two days. It was a promise.

Much relieved, Neferu went next to see her son and Ankhsenpaaten and the baby. Tutankhaten was visibly upset, but she told him that she had a friend in Tuthmosis and that he could confide in the archduke if he wanted to get a message to her urgently. She warned him, however, that it would not be wise to overuse this channel of communication otherwise Horemheb's spies might discover it and cut off their chances of passing on information. Neferu wished her son and daughter well for their coronation, told him that she would pray for him and that he would be a great pharaoh, perhaps the most famous of them all. He smiled at her words, not really believing them but not wanting to make leaving the more difficult for her. She hugged him so tight that it almost hurt, but he did not complain. When she eventually released him, there were tears in her eyes, but she was smiling. She kissed him once more and then stood up quickly and with a last wave she left.

Maya, her husband's most trusted advisor, took her hand in his and squeezed it tightly. She saw that he was so upset that he could not get any words out at all, and she nodded at him to show that she understood. Finally, he managed to ask her if she had everything she needed. She nodded and kissed his cheek. Nakhtmin was put in a similar situation and kept clearing his throat over and over again. It warmed her heart to know that she still had good friends who loved her.

Finally, Neferu went to say goodbye to her two youngest daughters in the home of Teya. Teya cried openly and that almost undid her. She had great difficulty in maintaining her mask of calm in front of Neffie and Satenpare. The little girls asked her when Mummy was coming back and Neferu had to swallow hard before she could reply. 'I don't know, my darlings. I hope that you will be coming to see me soon. I shall miss you both so much. Remember how much I love you. I will pray for you every day. Be good girls for Aunt Teya, won't you?' Satenpare nodded gravely and then clasped her arms around her mother's neck.

'I love you, Mummy,' she said and Neferu's heart almost broke.

If Ay had returned then, she knew that she could not have gone through with it, but for better or for worse, she did not know which, he did not come. It was heartrending to have to leave her children behind her and she knew that she would never forgive Ay as long as she lived. She looked at them in the doorway for the last time. Satenpare touched her heart, she had such a look of Amio about her. She examined the little face of Neffie, too. Her namesake and the one who was most like her in looks out of them all. She blew kisses to them and then turned to go.

In the courtyard her chariot was waiting, and she climbed in. The driver was a senior officer from the Theban military headquarters, and she had often seen him with Horemheb. He looked at her curiously but bowed deferentially and said nothing. They drove for about twenty minutes, using the lesser thoroughfares. Neferu had never been along these routes before and she began to be aware of another side to the city of Thebes, which she had never known about before. Eventually, the dwellings began to thin out and they arrived in a part of town that had seen better days. There were several large villas, but they showed signs of decay, overgrown gardens and flaking whitewashed walls. The shops here were smaller and dirtier than in the area around the Malkata complex and the people in the streets looked much less affluent.

The chariot drew to a stop in front of a small white villa with closed shutters. For some reason, she was reminded of their old holiday home in Rashid, and she felt her heart lift a little. It seemed to her to be an omen. She stepped down, helped by the soldier, and while he was trying the locked door with a big, old, copper key, she looked around the garden. It was surrounded on all sides except the front, by high, whitewashed walls of brick. The villa had obviously been empty for some time, and the garden was overgrown. She realised that she would have to do some work on it and regretted that she had not absorbed more knowledge on that score from the many gardeners they had had at Maruaten.

The officer managed to open the rusty lock and pushed the door open for her. She entered into the dark interior of the house and immediately went to open the shutters. As the sunlight flooded in she looked around her with relief. She noticed that the room was scrupulously clean. Ay had done that for her, at least. The furniture was rather sparse, but she would direct the officer to bring more, and she had brought some of her favourite pieces from Akhetaten, including the chair that Amio had found most comfortable. They would fit in well here. She noted the officer scrutinising her every reaction and made a mental note to keep an expression of indifference. She did not want the two conspirators to be made aware of her feelings any more than was necessary.

Neferu wandered round the house examining the rooms and the officer went to wait in the hallway for further instructions. There was a large kitchen where she could eat also, and a reasonably sized bathing room with a huge old cauldron and three large pitchers for water. Altogether there were seven rooms in all, including these utility rooms. It was far smaller than the palace, of course, but more than big enough for her needs. All the rooms were clean, and she noted that the little pantry was well-stocked with bread, fruit, wine and juice. Altogether, her spirits rose considerably. It was much, much better than the images of her frightened mind had produced.

Neferu returned to the hallway and asked the soldier if he knew who was responsible for providing the provisions, but he did not appear to know very much about anything, and she perceived that his replies were genuine. After ascertaining the name of the street her new home was located in and its number, she gave him some detailed instructions as to some specific pieces of furniture that she wanted brought to the villa and then she dismissed him.

Once the soldier had left, Neferu was struck by a nesting instinct and she went from room to room again, planning how she would furnish them and which room she would use for what purpose. There was a discreet cough behind her, and she turned to see one of the palace servants standing there, carrying some of her bags. She realised that the baggage chariot had arrived, and she asked him to bring the things in and set them all down in the first room off the hallway. He deposited the bags and left, to return a minute or so later with more, followed by a second servant. While the two men deposited her luggage where she had shown them, she let herself out into the garden at the back of the house. It looked very forlorn and was dry and arid with bare patches of red sandy soil showing. She decided to think about that later and went back inside.

When all the articles had been left in the side room, the servants came to her to request dismissal and she thanked them. Once they had gone, the thought came to her that she was now quite alone in the world. There would be no one here to care what she thought, said or did. She suddenly felt a bit engulfed with it all and shook herself inwardly. 'Nonsense! You can cope. The Aten will give you strength and there are still some people who love you, even if they are not with you.'

For the rest of the day Neferu worked, unpacking her things and putting them away in the old rosewood cupboards. For lunch she ate some fruit and then she investigated the bathroom and toilet facilities further. The fire grate had been packed with the usual mixture of reeds and dried cow dung ready for use and there was naphtha and flint available. She had so expected to be alone for evermore that when the sound of approaching footsteps alerted her to the presence of another person in the house, she was quite startled. In the hallway, looking at her shyly, stood a young girl of about fifteen or so. Neferu smiled at her.

'Hello. Who are you?'

'I am Serapina, Your Ladyship,' the girl answered quietly.

'Who has sent you, Serapina?' Neferu asked, mystified by the sudden intrusion.

'The gentleman sent me, Your Ladyship. The gentleman who ordered the provisions. He said I was to come back today to see if you wanted to take me on as your maid. It was me who cleaned the house, Your Ladyship.' The girl spoke Egyptian with an accent which Neferu had not heard before, but she could understand it without difficulty. Neferu raised her eyebrow as the girl handed her a piece of papyrus. The message was from Maya.

'There is no possibility of discussing anything here at the palace. I know the address. The young girl who will deliver this note has been hired by me to make the villa comfortable. Her brother will contact me daily. He is a minor servant in the palace laundry and trustworthy, I think. The girl seems pleasant, and you might need her help. I will organise payment etc. I hope you will find her suitable.' The message was signed 'Your most devoted servant, Maya'.

Neferu smiled at the girl and said, 'I am Neferu, Serapina, and I would like you to work for me. I would be grateful for your help.'

'Oh, I would like to work for Your Ladyship,' the girl said quickly. After a pause she continued hesitantly. 'Do you want me to live in or out, Your Ladyship?'

'Which do you prefer to do?' Neferu asked her.

'Well, there's a lot of us at home, ma'am. Twelve of us and not much space and my mum's got a lot on with the baby being ill and all,' the girl said frankly.

'Well, of course, it's clear you must live in then. It's just that I have only just arrived myself, so I don't know yet where everything is myself. You come around with me and we'll work everything out together, shall we?' Neferu spoke as kindly as she could as the girl seemed a little ill at ease with her.

'Yes, Your Ladyship,' came the diffident reply.

Together they moved around the villa assessing the suitability of the rooms. Neferu decided that the large room off the hallway would be the sitting room. It had a long low window, which made it bright and cheerful. The next room, which also faced the front, they left free for the moment. Opposite that room was a large room, which she decided should be a guest room, assuming that she might need such a room on the odd occasion at least. The third room facing the front, Neferu chose as her bedroom. Opposite that was the bathroom with its sloping stone floor and its high, narrow window. Off from this was the toilet closet, which drained into a septic tank in the back garden somewhere. She guessed it must be located at the left side wall of the back garden as here the topsoil showed the lush fertility such areas always produce. Going back towards the hallway again on the same side as the bathroom were two rooms which adjoined each other, and one had a separate exit. Neferu decided that these would be suitable for Serapina and possibly another maid later, depending upon her circumstances. Neferu offered the girl the small rooms. 'This one could be your bedroom and this one your sitting room,' she said, pointing out to the area in question. Serapina seemed to be delighted with the arrangement and together, she and Neferu lifted a bed from the end front bedroom into the girl's new quarters. Neferu promised her some more furniture when the rest of her things arrived. Serapina was thrilled and informed Neferu that she had never slept in a real bed before. At home they always slept on mats, which were rolled up the following morning. Neferu realised that there were some aspects of life in her country about which she knew nothing as yet.

Neferu soon saw that Serapina knew all about hard work. She had evidently had to do a lot of it in her short life. From now on the girl took over all aspects of the cleaning and bathroom and kitchen preparations, without Neferu even having to explain anything. In the beginning, Serapina was very shy and in awe of Neferu, however, she gradually began to unwind, and they began to get to know each other at a human level. Neferu was shocked to discover that the girl could not read, and she set herself the task of teaching her. Naturally, she also taught her about her religion. She sensed that the young girl thought she was somewhat quaint, but she always listened quietly, and in turn, she told Neferu all about the various members of her family who, it seemed, all lived close by in one of the many small workmen's cottages on the edge of town.

Serapina seemed to be unusually incurious about Neferu's background and she never asked personal questions. Neferu wondered if she had been warned against doing so. Once, Neferu looked up and caught Serapina staring at her. 'What is it, Serapina?' she asked.

The girl blushed. 'I was just thinking, ma'am. You're very beautiful!' the girl replied in her local vernacular. Neferu laughed. It was a long time since she had received such a sincere compliment.

'Thank you, Serapina. I am glad you think so.'

Serapina wanted to bring her family to see her new quarters and obviously felt she had gone up in the world. Neferu allowed her to do so, partly because she was curious to meet these individuals about whom she had heard so much, and partly because she was so touched at Serapina's pride in her new circumstances. When the little army crowded in, she stayed in her room while Serapina showed them around and she could hear the choruses of 'Ahs' and 'Ohs' as they admired her things. She liked their natural curiosity and their lack of guile in expressing it. She was amused to hear Serapina telling one of them in a stern voice, 'Don't touch anything!' When Neferu came out to observe them and to make her greeting, they were struck dumb as of a man. Some of them stared at her open-mouthed and others stared down at their feet as if just having discovered them for the first time. Neferu felt they were sweet in a slightly uncouth but very human way.

Neferu asked Serapina to introduce her family to her and the girl did so, starting with her father, who bent low and looked down. The man mumbled something in a most humble way, causing all his family to follow suit. Neferu felt angry inside that a grown man should be humbled in front of his family in this way. The Aten did not assess some people as high and others as low, she felt sure. She knew it was only an accident of birth which had led to the difference in the present positions of this man and that of herself. She herself had always felt the equal of anyone at the Theban court when she had first gone there.

To make her guests feel at ease, Neferu invited them to be seated in the sitting room, and she noticed that the small room was suddenly full with small children and young men and women. The parents seated themselves precariously on the edge of the couch that she pointed out to them, but the others sat on the floor cross-legged. Neferu offered them juice and wine for the older ones and tried to speak to them naturally. She told them that she was a widow and had several children of her own. she told them that she came from a city in the north of Egypt and now wanted to spend a quiet life. They did not really appear to comprehend what she told them, or more probably, they did not believe it, but they nodded vigorously, trying to please her. The small children were quite dirty but rather charming and very talkative. They, at least, chatted to her freely and one little girl of about six offered to come and be her maid when she grew up. Neferu smiled and thanked her for her generous offer. When they had departed, escorted by Serapina into the street, Neferu sat back and smiled at her unusual entrance into the local society. She had a feeling that Amio was laughing in amusement somewhere, and the thought made her smile again. Neferu entertained the thought that if life was going to be harder from now on, it did seem likely to be interesting anyway. She wondered what the Aten had in store.

True to his word, Archduke Tuthmosis became her first guest on the evening of her second day at Malarma, as the district was known. Neferu was overjoyed to see the old man. It was a victory of sorts that he had been able to find her, she knew. Now they had an opportunity to speak frankly without being overheard. Tuthmosis told her that finding her had been easy. He had merely stationed one of his servants in the courtyard with orders to request the address from the returning driver who had brought the furniture and other belongings.

What was more sinister, however, was that Ay had given out the story that she had returned to Akhetaten to live in her palace at Hataten with her servants. Neferu was furious at this blatant lie, but she understood, as indeed Tuthmosis was not slow to point out, that Ay was aware that his deeds had been reprehensible and that if she publicly disclaimed what he had said and why he had said it, Ay would be disgraced. Angry though she was, Neferu declined to do this because to undermine Ay would also be to undermine Tut's possibilities, as the crafty old grand vizier well knew. In effect, Ay was hiding behind a young boy. Her contempt for him was enormous and she knew that nothing he could ever do would ever make her afraid again. She told Tuthmosis, 'In any case, it is only a choice between Ay and Horemheb.' She did not want Horemheb in power.

The archduke told her that he was pleased to see that she was tackling her new situation with a certain amount of aplomb. He had been afraid of finding her stricken with depression. He informed her that all the children were well, and that Tut's coronation had gone off well. He had been very proud of his son. Although he had been brought up an Amunist, he had become a confirmed Atenist in his older years but, like Tiya, he had always made an effort to placate the believers in other gods and had attended their ceremonies if it was deemed expedient. He also told Neferu that it pained him to have always had to hide the true paternity of Tut and that he was sorely tempted to divulge the truth to Tut and intended to do so when a suitable occasion arose. Neferu nodded. She too felt that her adopted son should know who his true father was.

Tuthmosis described for Neferu the events of that day, all the pageantry culminating in the actual coronation. He described his pride as he watched the khepresh, or blue crown, being placed upon the head of Tutankhamun. He told her that Tut had held his head high and firm and walked with all the straightness of a much older pharaoh. Neferu remembered the many times her husband had worn the khepresh and tears came to her eyes. Now it had passed to a new generation.

Perhaps the most important news of all that the archduke had to impart to Neferu was that Ay had decided to recall Pararameses back to Thebes from Memphis to lead the army of Upper Egypt. Horemheb was soon to depart to Memphis to take direct control of the whole of northern Egypt. In effect, it meant that Horemheb had superseded Pararameses as chief of the general staff and second power to the pharaoh.

In that moment Neferu knew that she and Amio had lost everything they had ever worked for. Pararameses was not tainted with Atenism in the eyes of the priesthood of Amun, but he was known to be completely loyal to his childhood friend, Amio, and also to Neferu. It had been his undoing, she realised. In the event of a rupture between him and Horemheb, with a consequent split in the army, she knew that the priesthood would go with Horemheb. This event seriously weakened Ay's position, she thought.

His intriguing was all coming to nought. The pair of them still needed each other for the time being, however, as Ay needed the support of Horemheb to continue with at least partial power and Horemheb needed his marriage to Mutnedjmet to give even a semblance of legality to his ultimate aim to usurp the throne. Neferu wondered how Pararameses would react to the news. It must be very galling to be so publically demoted. She felt angry on his behalf. He had always been a loyal, intelligent and fair-minded man. Perhaps he lacked charisma, but he was infinitely preferable to the scheming, over-ambitious Horemheb, with his penchant for intrigue and cruelty.

Neferu asked the old prince to inform Pararameses of where she was staying upon his return and Tuthmosis promised to do so. When she asked him if he had found it easy to slip away from the celebrations to come and see her, he had smiled and said that everyone understood that old men of his age had to retire early. She hugged him, grateful for this good friend that the Aten had bestowed upon her so unexpectedly. She regretted that she had not taken the opportunity to get to know him better in the early years of her residence at the Theban court. Neferu felt very lonely as she watched his chariot start up in the darkness. He had told her that he would return again in a few days, or earlier if anything very important were to happen.

After a few days, Neferu began to realise how lonely she would have been without the company of Serapina. She discussed visiting the souk with her and making a short tour of the quarter in which she now lived. She decided to leave the matter for a few more days, however, as some inner instinct told her that events at Malkata might change quickly now that the coronation was over. Ay would begin to feel himself more secure now, especially with Horemheb about to depart for Lower Egypt any day. She reflected that he must have been aware that Horemheb would eventually set his sights on Lower Egypt and that his position there would be very secure, being a native of the area himself.

It was not long now before Amio's funeral would take place and Neferu wondered how Ay would suddenly produce her again for that event. In the meantime, she set about rebuilding her life. She began to explore the new quarter with Serapina by her side. She walked the streets in a long cloak with a hood to largely cover her face, although she felt it unlikely that she would be recognised here. She soon noticed that even the style and quality of her clothing attracted attention. Her hooded cloak was typical of the dress of many Keftiu women of Lower Egypt but there were very few Keftiu here and the style singled her out. In spite of her attempts to live incognito, she realised from Serapina's talk that she had already aroused curiosity and speculation in the locality. She regretted it but knew that a certain amount of talk was inevitable. Even if she were to be recognised, it was doubtful that news of her would go any further than hereabouts. The very fact that one of her daughters bore the same name as she did would help to obscure the fact that she was not present at court.

On her visits to the market, Neferu would look about her with interest. Her villa was built on the very edge of the 'respectable district' and it backed onto the poor district proper. Living in the poor district were many beggars, the vast majority of whom were physically handicapped in some way. There were the blind, the deaf-mutes and the deformed. Neferu had never seen such human misery before and in such large numbers. Almost overnight, her view of herself and her station in life changed.

Gradually, Neferu came to feel that the Aten had sent her to Malarma for a purpose. She began to feel a sense of responsibility for these people and that she had to try to do something to alleviate their condition in some way. But how? The more she thought about it, the more she sensed how little equipped she was to accomplish anything that could help these forgotten ones of the Aten. At the same time, she recognised a need for a goal in life if she were not to go mad from missing the children. Most of all she missed Tut, even though he was not of her flesh. The closeness between them was so uncanny that if she closed her eyes and concentrated, she could almost see what he was doing and what he was thinking. It was because of her implicit faith in her ability to contact him in this way that she did not unduly worry about his safety. She felt that she would 'know' immediately if he were in danger.

Serapina knew the streets of Malarma like the back of her hand and each day she and Neferu would take a different route, until Neferu had become acquainted with the layout of the district. The very humblest hovels were right on the edge of the desert, and it was strange to see the abrupt line of demarcation of the fertile ground and the desert scrub. Neferu wondered at the importance of the artery that was the Nile, without which the whole of Upper Egypt would be arid desert.

Malarma was on the south-western edge of Thebes and was composed of several moderately large villas like hers, all of which were old and had seen much better days. The rest of the area was made up of workmen's houses of white, sundried mudbrick. They were built in narrow streets and alleyways with sharp bends to make as much use as possible of the fertile land that was already much poorer here. Within these little alleyways were small shops and hundreds of people. It was like a small city within a city. A few hundred metres to the south-east of the city proper was an isolated area with white buildings, whose occupants never left the area. This was the leper colony, and the local people were very afraid of it. Food and water were delivered to a halfway area of no man's land at sunrise and again at sundown by the locals, who were responsible for supplying the colony with its needs. These people would then step back some twenty paces or so and wait for the lepers to collect the goods. Messages were shouted across to each other, but no physical contact was attempted or permitted. Many people had loved ones in the colony, and this was the only way they could communicate.

Serapina had an aunt in the leper colony and Neferu went with her once to observe the ritual for herself. It distressed her very much and she came away feeling very humble after comprehending just how lonely and isolated the existence of these people was. That night she prayed to the Aten to show her how she could help to relieve the deprivation of the people of Malarma. She told him, 'You have taken away from me the people the I love, please give me someone or something to make my life worthwhile.'

Two days after observing the heartrending ritual of the lepers and their loved ones, Neferu was pleased to receive a visit from Pararameses. Unlike the archduke, he arrived in his chariot before sundown, while it was still full light. From this, she surmised that he was visiting on the orders of Ay, or at least with his tacit permission, and this proved to be so. He looked a lot older than when she had last seen him and there were deep furrows around his mouth. He was a little stockier too, but he seemed fit and well. Pararameses bowed low to greet her with a grave air. He appeared to be examining her when he straightened himself. She supposed she looked older too and felt sorry that she had not paid much attention to herself of late.

'You look very well, Your Majesty,' he said finally.

'Please don't be formal, Rameses,' she said with a smile. 'I am a private person now. I prefer you to call me Neferu as in the old days.' He smiled and acknowledged this with a slight inclination of his head. Neferu dismissed the nervous Serapina, who had undoubtedly heard him call her 'Your Majesty'. She would have to swear the girl to secrecy when Pararameses had gone.

Pararameses took the glass of wine which she proffered and seated himself on the couch as requested. He seemed unusually ill at ease, as if he did not know how to take this new change in her circumstances. 'I passed on your message to the royal sculptor Tuthmosis as soon as I could, Neferu,' he said.

Neferu nodded, pleased at this. 'Where is Tuthmosis now?' she asked.

'When he received your message, he decided to go back to Akhetaten. The work was finished anyway on his statue for the temple of Aten, and he had not yet started on the private commissions, so he was able to refuse them.' Neferu was disappointed at his reply. She had half-hoped that Tuthmosis would have sent her a message of moral support at least.

'Did he send no message?' she insisted.

'Only that he hoped you are well, and that the Aten is with you.'

Neferu was stunned at this apparent lack of regard for her well-being. So Tuthmosis had not forgiven her. Perhaps he was now her enemy, as Yussef had become? She felt bitterness well up in her. No one was interested in her now that she was no longer associated with power and wealth. Well, if that was the way it was to be then let it be. She would banish them from her mind just as effectively as they had banished her. She composed her face so that Pararameses would not see that she was upset. 'Oh!' he said. 'I have something for you.' He fished into a pocket of his mantle and brought out a small piece of papyrus on which was written 'I love you, Neferu. Tut.' It was exactly what she needed at exactly the right time. She felt overwhelmed with love for her young son.

'Tell Tut that I love him very much too,' she said with a quiver in her voice. 'In fact, I will write him a message too,' she said. With her stylus and some black ink, she wrote. 'I love you, too, Tut. Neferu.' She gave the papyrus to Pararameses. He took it carefully and put it in his pocket.

'I will give it to him this evening,' he said.

She nodded and thanked him. 'How long are you going to stay here, Neferu?' Pararameses asked worriedly.

'For the rest of my life, I assume,' she said with a shrug. 'I would prefer to live in On or Rashid or Akhetaten, but I cannot leave the children while they are still so young. I am easily available from here if they need me.'

'But what will you do here alone?' he asked uncomprehendingly.

'I haven't thought it out properly yet,' she said uncertainly. 'But I want to do something to help the people. You should see the suffering and deprivation here, Rameses. It's awful! I never knew there were so many people living out such desolate existences. I would like to help somehow. It cannot be right in the eyes of the Aten that some of us have so much and some so little. There must be some way I can help our people.'

Pararameses nodded. He had always been basically egalitarian at heart. 'I understand your feelings, Neferu, but what can you do to help?' He had placed emphasis on the word 'can'.

Neferu lifted her shoulders in defiance. 'I don't know, but the Aten will show me. I know, for instance, how to look after the sick. I have had a lot of experience since I was very young in doing that. Even the physician at Akhetaten said that no one could have looked after Amio as well as I did. I don't believe he was just flattering me.'

Pararameses considered the matter. He knew that Neferu could be very obstinate, but he doubted that she understood the enormity of what she was considering undertaking. As a general and a soldier, he had been acquainted all his life with suffering and he had frequently seen men die from disease and injury. It was not a pleasant sight. 'I believe you, Neferu,' he said finally. 'But I don't think you understand how hard such a life would be or how gross the sights and the stench of disease can be.'

'Yes. I know that you are right and that it will be hard, but I feel I must try. I am not a young woman anymore, Rameses, and I have no wish to be involved in the intrigues and dirty tricks of the court. I intended to move away anyway. To retire to a nice villa on the riverbank to the north of town, but Ay has seen fit to deposit me here. He has done it because I refused to marry him. He wishes to be co-regent with Tut, you see.' Her tone rose angrily, and she saw that Pararameses was genuinely surprised at her words. It was obviously new information to him. Neferu continued her tale. 'He is debasing everything I have believed in for the sake of furthering his own personal power, and I will not make the public obeisance to gods I do not believe in to suit him. On the other hand, I fear Horemheb. He does not like me, and I suspect that it was he who was responsible for the deaths of Smenkhenre and Meretaten, whoever may have done the actual deed,' she said bitterly. 'Horemheb is a man of great ambitions and very few scruples about removing people who stand in his way. As long as Ay is alive and holding onto power, I know that he will support Tut and look after him, because without Tut he has no claim to the throne or to power and under Horemheb, he knows he would be immediately replaced. It is the only reason I am prepared to accept this humiliation quietly until Tut is old enough and strong enough to take power himself. I want to ask you an honest question, Rameses, and I hope you will give me an honest answer.'

Pararameses lifted his eyebrows. 'Ask away, Neferu,' he said with a slight smile.

'Who would you support in a showdown between Ay and Horemheb? It is important because I know that you would have the backing of the whole of Lower Egypt, and probably much of the army here in Thebes. Your father is still alive and has spent his whole lifetime in the army. He carries much prestige.'

Pararameses sighed and was silent for a while before replying. 'I will be as truthful with you as you wish, Neferu. As you know, I am not a religious man and I feel that, sincere as you and Amio have always been, this quarrel with the priests of Amun has torn the country into two and seriously weakened it. I believe as you do that if there is a god, and I am not at all sure that there is when I look around me and see all of this misery, then there is only one and he is intangible. He is not to be found in stone or in magic. I believe that people should not have their minds manipulated by priests of any religion who are often only out to increase their own material prosperity and political power.' Here he stopped for a while to look at Neferu, and then stood up and walked up and down the room as if collecting his thoughts. 'The problem is, Neferu, that I have no love for Ay. My father and I have watched him manipulate people all our lives. He is devious and selfish and only interested in his own ends, as you have so eloquently pointed out. He is the son of a foreigner to boot. For forty years he has spent his time cheating both Egyptians and his own family in order to get what he really wants, and that is the crown. Amio was my best friend and as long as you and Tut are alive I will continue to give Ay my support for your sakes. If, however, he harms you or the boy in any way, then I will transfer my allegiance to Horemheb. Believe me, I too have my profound doubts about him as a person, but he is an able administrator, and he does have the backing of the priests of Amun. To oppose him then would mean putting Egypt into civil war, and I am not prepared to do that.'

Neferu had been listening to him intently and she too now stood up. 'Thank you, Rameses. I agree with you completely. It is what I wanted to hear from you. I know that you do not believe in the Aten, but I will pray to him that he will give you his protection. It was Amio's wish that if anything did happen to Tut and there not be a male heir then you were to have the crown of Egypt. It is my wish too. Egypt will continue to be blessed under you as pharaoh, Rameses. I can rest more easily now I know that Tut has you for support.'

Paramesses looked at her sternly. 'Make no mistake, Neferu. If it comes to a showdown between myself and Horemheb, then I have no claim to the throne. I am a commoner with no royal blood and Horemheb is married to Mutnedjmet, who is the niece of Amenophis III. Although his claim to the throne is exceedingly tenuous, it still would be far greater than mine, and therefore it would be he who would take the throne. I have no intention of stealing a crown to which I have no legal right,' he said, uprightly.

Neferu laughed and replied serenely. 'Rameses! If the Aten wishes you to be pharaoh, then you will be pharaoh, and no one will be able to prevent it. Now, let's change the subject. How is your family?'

Pararameses smiled at Neferu's rather blunt diplomatic tactics. 'Amio must have had his hands full with you, Neferu.' He laughed.

'Well, he did used to say that I was impossible at times,' she admitted with a mock demure smile.

'I can well believe it,' was Pararameses' reply.

From then on, they turned the conversation to more general topics and the evening passed quickly. It appeared that his family had been loath to return to Thebes. They much preferred the bustling life of northern Egypt and its cooler climate to the extreme aridity of southern Egypt and its isolation from the populous north. Two of Pararameses sons had elected to stay in the north – Seti, his eldest son, who was now an army officer himself, and Pararameses Junior, who was also in the army now. Pararameses told Neferu that they found Thebans to have very rigid outlooks on life and its isolation from the international atmosphere of the delta area made life here rather dull and restricted after the social mixtures and tolerant attitudes of the northern lands. Neferu agreed with him entirely. Pararameses told her that they had kept their private villa on in Memphis and intended to retire there when the time came round. Neferu laughed. 'I think it will be a long time before you retire, Rameses,' she said with some amusement.

Before he left, Pararameses told Neferu that he would only come and see Neferu if she sent word that she needed to see him. He did not wish to arouse comment and perhaps cause more trouble for her. He told her that the local physician was to be her contact and would be coming to see her soon. He asked her to contact him at least three times a decan so that he would know that she was all right, and he would pass her messages on to the children. He promised to liaise with Archduke Tuthmosis, who had insisted upon coming to see her twice a decan in person, much to Ay's chagrin. Neferu asked Pararameses to have a word with the physician about letting her help him and her friend agreed to do so. He promised not to discuss the matter with Ay.

When Pararameses had gone, Neferu sat down to reconsider the events of the evening. She was well pleased with the outcome of their frank discussion and perceived that Amio's boyhood friend was a man of his word and did not shrink from taking the bull by the horns. She knew that he liked her. Now she knew he liked her as a human being, not because she was the queen. It would have been so easy for him to ignore her, and he had not done so. Remembering the incident at the beginning of the evening, she called Serapina to her and cautioned her to say nothing to anyone. She made Serapina swear never to divulge her identity to anyone and Serapina did as she was asked. Neferu felt that she was too much in awe of her ever to break her promise.

Finally, Neferu considered the most painful note of the evening, Tuthmosis' reaction to her news. It hurt but she knew that she had hurt him, and she could not really blame him. She had expected too much, more than she had had a right to. With that, she sighed, got up and went to bed.

CHAPTER 31

When the physician of Malarma came to visit Neferu, he turned out to be an older man of forty-five or so, very tall for an Egyptian and with a dry, leathery skin, lined with deep furrows. He had the face of a man inured to suffering. Where once had probably been empathy there was now only resignation, coupled with anxiety to receive his payment. Neferu was disappointed in him somehow. She did not know what it was she had expected but it was not this rather seedy man, who looked as if he had long since abandoned any ideals and now had as his goal the desire to make it comfortably from one day to the next. Accompanying the physician was his assistant, who was a more pleasing prospect. He was a youngish man in his late twenties, rather thin and with a sympathetic mien and a gentle smile. In contrast with the good quality garments of his patron, the assistant wore somewhat shabby clothes. Neferu thought he looked kind and a far more preferable prospect than the senior physician. From his deferential manner, she guessed that the older man knew who she was.

Neferu explained that she wished to help out with the care of the doctor's patients. The senior physician could not disguise his incredulity, although he did say that the honourable general had informed him of this. He obviously thought she was quite mad, or at the very least slightly unhinged and he had difficulty in concealing this. He did not, however, go so far as to refuse her offer of help should a suitable occasion arise. Neferu wondered what he meant by a 'suitable occasion', but she did not argue her point. She wanted him to accept her as someone to be reckoned with rather than a half-crazy noblewoman with do-good intentions, and she needed his help to even get started on the path she had chosen.

The following evening when the archduke came to see her again, she related to him the conversation she had had with Pararameses and with the quarter physician. He laughed as she comically mimicked the physician's expression of incredulity. More to her surprise, Tuthmosis thought her idea praiseworthy. He too had often pondered on this question of the equality of man and the apparent injustices of the social realities. Neferu found that she could talk to the old prince just as easily as she had been able to talk to her own father. He told her that Ay was a sorry shadow of his father. He had the same kind of looks and the same sharp intelligence, but he had always lacked the strong morality which had so characterised Yuya. Yuya had been a lion of a man, whereas Ay was a fox of a man, he told her. The comparison was not flattering to Ay, but Neferu felt that it must be true, coming as it did from this good-natured man who had nothing to lose or to gain by stating the truth. When Tuthmosis bade her farewell, she watched him go with regret. She looked forward to his visits, when she could talk and say whatever was in her heart and know that she would receive an honest and balanced reply.

Two days later, Imsetre, doctor Siptamun's young assistant, came to her villa in the heat of the afternoon rest period to ask her assistance at a case. Neferu had been lying awake fantasising with nostalgia for the times past. Her mood, bordering on melancholy, was quickly dispelled by the unexpected arrival of the visitor and a sleepy Serapina came to announce the doctor's arrival.

Rising rapidly, Neferu went to the sitting room, where the young man was looking round curiously. He drew himself upright and bowed deeply at her entrance. 'Your Ladyship, Siptamun would be grateful if you could attend one of our patients in her confinement. It is a particularly difficult case, and he has another patient he must tend to urgently, while I must visit a man with severe burns of the hand. I will return to relieve you as soon as I have dealt with my patient. Would you consider coming to help?'

Neferu was pleased to have something useful to do at last. Having been delivered of five children herself, she considered that she knew something of the process. She felt that she might be useful and could handle the situation. 'Yes. I am happy to come. I will bring my maid, Serapina, with me in case I need help while you are away.' Imsetre nodded and, pausing only to collect her shawl to put over her head, and make sure that Serapina did too, the three of them left quickly in a westerly direction along the dusty street and through the narrow alleyways to the very western edge of the town.

There, in a small, dark room in one of the workmen's overcrowded dwellings, Imsetre led her to a young woman lying on a mat on the floor. The first thing Imsetre did was to shoo out the majority of the small crowd of women who had collected there. They had been apparently offering a diversity of advice to the young woman lying there, whose face was presently contorted with the cramp of a strong contraction. During their journey, Imsetre had told her that the labour had already lasted for thirty-two hours and there was a danger of the woman dying of exhaustion if the delivery did not progress to completion soon.

The women seemed annoyed at being pushed out and Neferu overheard a comment of,

'We don't need any fine ladies here, thank you. We can manage on our own.' Neferu knew that she was on trial. Imsetre palpated the woman's abdomen and told her that the lie of the baby was abnormal in that it was a breech birth, but if Amun was on their side it would proceed normally.

'If the Aten is on our side,' she gently corrected him. He looked at her sharply but did not reply. Before he left, he gave her some crushed poppy seeds but told her not to give them unless the pain became extreme because it would slow down the procedure and only prolong the labour even more. Neferu gathered that he did not expect her to do more than sit with the patient until he came back, when he intended to try to force the labour by opening the neck of the womb further, if he could. It was a very delicate procedure to turn the baby around and he was not sure that it could be managed. Neferu felt very nervous on behalf of the woman. She seemed very frightened.

When Imsetre had gone, Neferu thought to utilise the presence of the women hanging around the doorway by asking them to bring water from the well. At first they seemed truculent, but she told them that they would be doing it for the young mother, not for her. After a few minutes of arguing they went off to bring the water, still grumbling. In the meantime, Neferu went over to her patient and made herself acquainted. The poor girl looked dreadfully uncomfortable and there was a film of perspiration over her top lip. Her thick, long black hair was greasy and matted and to Neferu she had the look of a hunted animal that has been cornered. Neferu took her hand and spoke soothingly to her. She smiled up at the girl's mother, who was sitting on the opposite side of her on another mat. She asked her when the waters had broken. The older woman was glad to talk. She might have been the same age as Neferu, but her face was withered and lined with the toil of a life of care and burden. As she spoke, she wiped her daughter's forehead periodically with a dirty old rag.

When the village women returned with the water, Neferu sent Serapina home to bring two linen towels and one of her old cotton shifts. Left alone with the slightly hostile women, she poured some of the water into a cooking pot and washed the girl's face. Afterwards, she helped the girl into a semi-sitting position with the help of the mother and one of the village women helped to put some rugs behind the girl's back to support her. It was all very primitive compared to the care she herself had received, but the facilities were almost non-existent. Another of the village women put the water on to heat as requested and a third began to clean an area on the other side of the room so that they could transfer the mother there after her delivery. There was nothing to do then but to wait. Serapina returned with the linen and put it in a small basket weave chair, one of the few pieces of furniture in the room.

Now that the village women realised that they were not going to be evicted, they lost some of their truculence and began to chat. Even the young mother to be seemed to become more aware of her surroundings and Neferu managed to get her to drink some water. The women spoke with the same accent as Serapina. Neferu knew that they were watching her curiously and had marked her out as a stranger. In answer to their questions, she told them that she was Keftiu, from On. The way that they looked at her she might as well have been from some distant exotic land. They observed her all the time.

Neferu monitored the warming water and when it was the required heat, one of the village women removed it from the fire. The room was stiflingly hot and rank with the smell of human bodies. Just as Neferu had decided to bathe the woman, she gave a loud scream and slid down the rug to a lying position. Her abdomen was contracting rhythmically, and her fists were clenched, her head twisting from side to side. Suddenly the baby was born, bottom first and the umbilicus around its neck. It was an alarming blue colour. Neferu was taken by surprise at the speed of its entrance into the world and almost let the baby fall. Just in time she caught it and quickly twisted its slippery little body round to release the neck from the asphyxiating grip of the umbilical cord.

For a moment Neferu lay the baby between the mother's legs, while she went to get the knife that Imsetre had left. She carefully washed the knife in the hot water as the physician had instructed and then she tore a piece of rag from the old shift that Serapina had brought. First, she tied off the umbilicus close to the baby and then close to the mother, then with the knife she cut the cord and released the baby from the placenta, which was expelled a few minutes later. Neferu held the blue baby up by its feet and it gave a splutter as some mucus was expelled from its mouth. There was a weak cry and she cradled it to her. She suddenly became aware that the room had been totally silent, but now, with the child's cry, there was an explosion of noise as everyone started to talk and smile at the happy outcome. Neferu was enormously relieved. In the end she had not had to do anything, Mother nature had just completed her job. The drama was over.

Neferu handed the baby to the grandmother, who smiled down at the tiny, wizened face, still red and angry looking from its recent efforts. Neferu tore off some more of the old cotton shift and wet it in the warm water and gave it to the grandmother, who immediately began to clean the baby up. She turned her attention to the mother and began to wash her all over. This appeared to cause the village women much consternation and Neferu wondered if she had broken some local taboo. When the mother was clean, including her hair, Neferu put on her the now ragged hemmed shift as a nightdress. With the help of three of the women, she transferred the new mother to the clean area they had previously prepared. She then left the exhausted mother entirely in the care of the women and went to peer closely at the little boy who had made such an unceremonious entrance. Satisfied that all was well, she smiled at the grandmother, who had wrapped the baby up and wanted to give it to the mother. Soon all the women were crowded around the mother and baby, and she was left to consider the events. Evidently the women were pleased with her as several came to touch her arm with hesitant touches and say 'Well done.'

Neferu had not actually done anything, but she felt happy and proud anyway. She was tired and sweaty and smelly, but she felt Amio would have been proud of her and that wherever he was, he was watching and approving. She washed her hands in the rest of the water and then was unsure what to do next. There seemed to be no further need of her here, but she did not want to to be deemed to have deserted her post by leaving before Imsetre returned. Neferu hovered about anxiously, wondering how long he would be. Fortunately, she did not have to wait long. As he entered the little dwelling, she greeted him with a happy smile, secure in the confidence of the happy outcome and a patient who was sitting up happily suckling her infant. Imsetre looked around the room with surprise and satisfaction. 'You have done well,' he said quietly.

Neferu's heart almost burst with pride. She felt enormously important. She had helped another human being into the world and helped its mother through a crisis. She was sharply aware of the loss of Meketaten in childbirth and this event in this little home somehow helped to take away some of the pain of that loss. She knew that this child would have none of the advantages her own children had had, but she prayed that it would survive and thrive into adulthood. Here in this little cottage on the edge of the desert Neferu perceived for the first time in a realistic way the enormous gap between the wealthy and the poor and deprived. She looked again at the tiny little boy and compared it with the greedy, power-hungry men at the court. Was it less important than they were? She did not think so, and yet it was almost certainly condemned to a life of dirt and poverty because of an accident of birth. It seemed scandalously unjust. Neferu felt a desire to take the child and protect it from all the harm and danger she could see it would have to contend with. She knew it would be no use, however, as she could do nothing about all the other babies being born into similar conditions all over Egypt. She felt helpless in front of the enormity of it. What she could do was just a drop in the sea. There must be a better way of living, but she could not see how it could come about. She sighed and turned away. Imsetre thanked Neferu and asked if he could call upon her help in the future if necessary. Neferu dragged her eyes away from the little bundle and looked at the physician. 'Yes, indeed!' she assured him.

It was past sundown when Neferu and Serapina walked home. Imsetre had accompanied them to the front of the villa and then took his leave. Neferu noticed that she already thought of the villa as home. When they arrived, they discovered that the house was cold as they had forgotten to close the shutters on leaving. Serapina set about making the fire as Neferu went round and closed all the shutters and lit the oil lamps.

The following morning, Neferu rose early and ate a light breakfast with Serapina before they left to go to the market to buy their fruit and vegetables. Neferu loved the souk; it brought back memories of her childhood with Grandma and Aunt Lea. All the noise and bustle still held a fascination for her. Afterwards, they walked back leisurely and once home, Neferu continued with her reading lessons with Serapina. The girl was making good progress and took a pride in her ability, which was very pleasing to Neferu. As the morning sun rose still higher, Serapina went to prepare their lunch, which was usually a very simple meal of pitta, olives and tomatoes with goat's cheese. Neferu realised that she was very lucky that they had their very own well in the garden. It would have been very tiring to have to hump the containers of water from the village communal well. To Serapina, this was a luxury beyond measure, and Neferu wondered once again how she had lived so long without an appreciation of the difficulties that such a large part of the population seemed to be enduring throughout a whole lifetime.

Standing out in the back yard, Neferu assessed the so-called garden. It was beginning to look greener now. She and Serapina had made a determined effort to keep it watered. Every evening after sundown they had drawn up bucket after bucket of water and the garden was now beginning to show the results of their efforts. She stood back to admire their handiwork and remembered with a sense of pleasure that the archduke was coming to visit her that evening. The old man had a very sweet tooth and she had remembered to buy his favourite nougat in the market.

'Hello, Neferu!' Neferu jumped at the sound of a familiar voice so close, and she whirled round in amazement.

'Tuthmosis! I never thought to see you again!'

The sculptor said nothing but just looked at her. 'Did you think I could ever forget you?' he said finally.

Neferu shrugged her shoulders, not sure what to say. 'I thought you might hate me after what I did to you. I would understand,' she managed to say.

'Yes. I did hate you, loved you, hated you, loved you. Many times in the same day. Now I have come back. I don't hate you anymore and now that I have seen you, I know that I still love you, in spite of everything. You sent for me. Why?'

Once again Neferu shrugged her shoulders. 'I needed you, why else?' she answered simply.

'Do you love me?' he asked.

'I have always loved you. I loved Amio too. He needed me more. He understood my feelings for you because he had loved Meketaten too. Because you love one person does not mean that you cannot love another at the same time. It is strange but it is so. Do you believe it?'

Tuthmosis nodded. 'I believe you, Neferu. You said you needed me. In what way can I be of assistance to you?' he asked coolly.

'By being here with me,' she answered frankly.

'Nothing else?' he asked with raised eyebrows.

'No. Nothing else. I am asking you to stay and live with me here, Tuthmosis. Of course, I understand that you must bring Meresger, and she is very welcome.'

Tuthmosis smiled at her.

'I have already come to stay, Neferu. I have brought my things. Meresger refused to leave Akhetaten. She is happy there at the villa. All she asks is that I go back to see her every ten decans or so to make sure that she is all right. She is in constant contact with Maatnofret, who sends you all her love. Her husband is very ill. She would have come to see you, but she fears for his life, and she cannot leave him now.'

'Oh!' Neferu exclaimed, distressed at the thought of Amio's trusted friend dying. Was there to be no end of these bereavements so close to her?

'Are you not going to kiss me, Neferu?' said Tuthmosis teasingly. She smiled for a moment and then stepped up to him and kissed him on the lips with her eyes open. He too, kept his eyes open as he responded. It was a kiss of assessment. They stepped apart, both seemingly satisfied at their evaluation.

'Come inside, Tuthmosis! You must have some lunch with us.'

Taking Tuthmosis by the arm, Neferu led him back inside the house and to the kitchen where all three of them sat down to the lunch that Serapina had prepared. She introduced him to Serapina as a very dear friend who was coming to live with them. His presence at lunch stultified the girl's normally voluble outbursts and she sat quietly and shyly, although Tuthmosis tried to draw her out. After lunch Tuthmosis carried his bags through to the room next to Neferu's, which had an inner doorway adjoining her room. 'This can be my work room and my sitting room, but we sleep together in your room,' he said firmly.

Neferu had no desire to argue. It was what she had wanted. She was not the kind of woman who could enjoy living without a man, but it had to be the right man. Tuthmosis was her kind of man. Like Amio, he could be difficult and quarrelsome, not to mention self-opinionated and arrogant, but he was also warm, kind, affectionate and had a generosity of spirit that more than made up for his shortcomings. If men such as Amio or Tuthmosis were ever to kill, it would be in a passion of fury, not a cold, devious, premeditated poisoning such as Ay, Horemheb or Tutu were capable of. Neferu found that she could accept the heat of fury far better than the coldness of cunning and malice. That was not her style at all. The former she could forgive, the latter made her feel cold inside.

After Tuthmosis had settled his things, he came to join her in bed. She had expected him to take her in a hurried passion, born of their long separation, but he did not. She looked at him expectantly. 'Are you not going to take me?' she asked in surprise.

'Not yet,' he replied.

'Why not?' she asked intrigued.

'Because, Neferu, you are not just the receptacle of my physical frustration, you are the woman I love. I want us to get used to each other again first,' he said slowly, looking at her closely as he leaned on his right elbow and kissed her right hand. She marvelled at his sensitivity, or was it his cleverness? The very fact that he was willing to wait for her increased her responsiveness to him immediately. She leaned forward and kissed him. He smiled but did not follow this up. She traced the outline of his lips with her finger.

'Do not play hard to get with me, Tuthmosis. I know you too well.' She noticed that there was a slight note of petulance in her voice. Tuthmosis threw back his head laughing before swooping down on her and gathering her into his arms. After their lovemaking, Neferu lay back at peace. It felt good to be loved again. She felt that Amio would not mind now. It was almost six decans since his death and soon it would be time for his funeral ceremony. She would say goodbye to his body then and ask his spirit to bless her relationship with Tuthmosis. He would understand that this love did not represent any lessening of her love for him. He and Meketaten were together now, and she needed someone to share her existence here as well.

Tuthmosis asked her what she was thinking, and she told him carefully. She looked at him closely to see whether he was annoyed with her, but he only nodded his head and smiled at her. He told her that they would go back to Akhetaten together for the funeral and he would arrange his affairs before they finally returned to Thebes. Neferu was pleased. She wanted to see Amio's body safely to its last resting place but was glad not to have to go there alone. So far, Ay had resisted all her requests to be allowed to see her children and she hoped the occasion of the funeral would be a meeting point for them.

That evening, the old archduke came to pay his visit and came face to face for the first time with his younger namesake. Tuthmosis, her lover, told the archduke that they had once met, in fact, but it was such a transitory experience and he had been so unimportant that he did not expect the older man to remember. It was quite natural in the circumstances. As the younger brother of Amenophis III, the archduke had had a strictly regulated order of social acquaintances and a young artisan from the poorer classes would not normally be amongst them. They had apparently met briefly during Amio's great plans to build Akhetaten, his new city. Amio had wanted to attract the young, poor but talented, who were more likely to be motivated by ambition and who still had an open mind for change and to better their lot in life with a young pharaoh in a new city. The older, established professionals had not wanted, in the main, to uproot their lives and take their chances elsewhere.

The two men seemed to get on well together and Neferu was pleased. In spite of the disparity in their backgrounds, they chatted freely and without constraint, appearing to enjoy each other's company. The archduke said he felt much better now that Neferu had someone close whom she could rely on. Although there was no evidence to substantiate his fears, he was worried that he might not live much longer. Neferu hushed him to talk no more like that. The archduke told Neferu that Ay had sent orders that she was to travel to Akhetaten for the funeral with his entourage. The elder Tuthmosis also told her that he suspected that Ay had already come to regret his spitefulness and needed to show his detractors at court that Neferu was alive and well. It seemed that he wanted it to appear that there was no rupture between them. So! Ay needed to shore up his political reputation, did he? It must be at a very low ebb indeed, she commented to the archduke.

The royal barges were not due to depart for Akhetaten for six days hence and this gave Neferu time to consider her position. The elder Tuthmosis looked at his younger namesake seated next to him and commented, 'Ay will be furious when he finds out that you have a lover.'

Neferu shrugged her shoulders. 'Amio told me explicitly that when he died, he would not object to my resuming my relationship with Tuthmosis, so long as we did not marry. I promised him that I would abide by that wish so that Tut's position would not be jeopardised in any way,' she explained.

The old prince looked at her. 'Amio said that?' he sounded surprised.

'Amio changed a lot in that final year. I think he knew that he did not have long to live, and he did not want me to be alone,' Neferu said softly. The archduke nodded and Tuthmosis the younger remained silent but listened with interest.

'You must be very careful, my dear, in spite of that. You do not wish to give the priests of Amun any ammunition to use against you. Your public reputation is important. Still!' he added with a crafty smile, ' I might be able to help there.'

Neferu looked at him with a puzzled expression. 'What do you mean, Uncle Tut?' she asked, biting her lip.

The archduke chuckled. 'I think that your Aten has devised a very good plan to protect your reputation,' he said enigmatically. Neferu exchanged glances with her lover and Tuthmosis shook his head slightly to denote his incomprehension of what the old man meant. Noting that they were both in the dark, the archduke continued, 'Well! Don't you think it a happy coincidence that young Tuthmosis here and myself both have the same name?' he asked her. She frowned, unable to see what he was driving at. 'No?' he chuckled again. 'It seems the Aten is very clever, Neferu. When I continue to come here regularly, as I shall, the court will say, "Ah. Old Tuthmosis visits Nefertiti regularly" and it will be true. If the priests of Amun try to smear your reputation by saying that Nefertiti has a lover and his name is Tuthmosis, the court will laugh at them. They will say that the old prince is like a father to Nefertiti and that again will be true. Only Ay, Pararameses and the family will know the truth. Pararameses is your sworn friend and would never divulge it and Ay would not dare to do so in case he himself is found out. No, Neferu! You are not at risk as far as your reputation is concerned.' The archduke seemed to derive great enjoyment at the thought of bamboozling everyone with this subterfuge. Neferu looked at him and thought that he must have had many years of such ploys himself and thus was very well versed in this kind of drama.

'In any case, Uncle Tut, my reputation is in the hands of the Aten, not in their hands. They cannot destroy me without destroying themselves.'

The younger Tuthmosis laughed. 'You have so much faith, Neferu!' he said.

'You are wrong, Tuthmosis. My faith rises and falls like your own,' she replied. 'But I know that there is a purpose in all things, and I feel that I was meant to come here and see for myself the deprivation and hardship under which so many of our people live. I could never go back to court and forget them now. I must try to do something to improve their lot and I would never be allowed to do that at court. Since Amio died, there is no one at court who cares for these people except, perhaps, Tut, but he is too young to do anything.' Tuthmosis smiled in resignation. He knew better than to interrupt when she was on her high horse, he told the archduke. The two men smiled at each other conspiratorially and Neferu sighed, knowing that they did not take her seriously.

The archduke left, promising to return soon. He kissed Neferu affectionately and slapped Tuthmosis on the back in a friendly gesture. 'Don't plan anything too ambitious,' he warned them with a smile.

When he had gone, Tuthmosis turned to Neferu again. 'What is it exactly that you mean to do, Neferu?' he asked with a frown.

'I don't know yet,' she admitted. 'I don't know enough about the problems – that is why I want to go with the physician and find out how these people really live and then devise a practical plan to help on a large scale.'

Tuthmosis shook his head. 'But why here? Why not at Akhetaten? We have our poor there,' he spoke doubtfully.

Neferu sighed at his lack of understanding of her position. 'Because I must stay in Thebes until the children are older. If they should need me, I can be with them quickly from here. In any case, in Akhetaten we have our projects for looking after our citizens to some extent. I do want to go back there, believe me.'

Tuthmosis was not convinced. 'I don't see what one woman can achieve. Or even one man and one woman, come to that.' Neferu put her arms around his neck and kissed him by way of reply. He drew her to him. 'What would I have done in my life if I had not met you, Neferu?' he murmured.

'You would have been a very successful artist and led a very boring life planning your tomb and ensuring that you were always in favour at court. You would have become very very wealthy and decadent, wasted your wealth in the House of Joy, and all the time you would have had a secret feeling inside yourself that you were selling yourself short and living your life on someone else's terms.' She spoke lightly but with a hint of seriousness in her voice.

'Whereas now?' he asked, moving her away from him slightly so as to look at her.

'Well. You may or may not be killed by a scheming old man who never looked beyond his own desires in his life. You may or may not become a famous artist, depending upon how much time you give to your work, and you will feel love and tenderness because I promise to give it to you until either you or I die, or you find someone else. You won't become wealthy. You won't have children. Life will be hard and dangerous, and you probably won't live to be an old man.'

Tuthmosis guffawed with laughter, throwing back his head in genuine amusement. When he stopped, he said, 'I really don't know why I am laughing because I feel it is more than likely to be correct! I must be mad, but I am going to choose the second alternative. I can't think of any other woman I have ever met in my life who could possibly make it sound even halfway an attractive proposition, but you!'

Neferu smiled. 'I forgot to tell you one thing.'

'What was that?' he asked, smiling.

'You will be under the protection of the Aten, and you will never need to feel that you are alone. You will guarantee your future in the afterlife, and we can always be together.'

'How could I refuse, when you put it like that?' he said tenderly, drawing her to him again. 'Are the Aten's women always so beautiful?'

'Always,' she said firmly.

'Oh, well then, I'm definitely on his side.' He was laughing again.

Neferu looked up at him and said in all seriousness. 'I will never bind you, Tuthmosis. If you ever want to leave me, I will try not to hold you back.'

'I have bound myself to you, Neferu. It was meant to be,' he replied, equally seriously.

CHAPTER 32

A chariot arrived a few days later after sundown to convey Neferu and Tuthmosis to Malkata. Neferu told Serapina to look after the villa and its contents until she returned in one decan. The girl was puzzled by their departure. Neferu had not discussed the true purpose of her journey, merely told her that she was going away for a while. She deemed it possible that Serapina may have overheard snippets of conversations, but she was a very loyal girl and never made reference to a subject unless it had been specifically mentioned to her. In any case, Neferu felt that Serapina appreciated her job and would not willingly endanger her position.

Ay was furious at the inclusion of Tuthmosis to the party but Neferu had had enough of what Ay did or did not want and she made it clear to him that she would brook no interference in her private life. She would call his bluff sharply and publicly if he went too far. Just for good measure, she tackled him in front of Horemheb, who looked startled to be witness to their quarrel. It was Neferu's way of showing Ay that enough was enough. She knew that he was absolutely dependent upon Tutankhamun's survival for power. After the quarrel, in which she felt that she got the upper hand for once, she noticed that Horemheb was going out of his way to be pleasant to her. She responded with sweetness and light, to Ay's obvious chagrin.

Tuthmosis had not been to the Theban court since his early days as a young artist when he had come as a guest of Amio, during the planning phase of Akhetaten. The whole atmosphere had changed since then, and he felt it heavy and oppressive. He watched Neferu play out her little strategy between Ay and Horemheb and commented to her, 'It seems that you too have learned how to use political strategies to your own use, Neferu.'

She looked at him and smiled. 'They used me without mercy to their own advantage and I learned quickly and well, Tuthmosis. I am only playing them at their own game, and you see how they do not like to be on the receiving end. Basically, they are only bullies. They like to mete out their will, but they have no stomach for taking their own medicine.'

'Harsh words, Neferu!' replied Tuthmosis.

'But you know that they are true ones,' was her only comment.

During the trip to Akhetaten, Ay accorded Neferu all the outward politeness she could have wished. She knew that underneath he was now her arch enemy but then, he had few friends left now anyway. For the sake of her adopted son, however, she also made a show of outer friendliness. Her act was obviously successful because Teya was overjoyed about this 'reconciliation'. Poor Teya. She wanted so desperately for things to be as they used to be, but then, she had never really known how they had truly been. Perhaps, deep down, she had never wanted to know.

On this journey, Neferu took the opportunity to try to get close to her children again, She saw that they felt strange and ill at ease with her. Were they angry with her for leaving them? She felt very sad about it. Only Tut and Ankhsenpaaten seemed glad to see her and they were affectionate with her, hugging her and chatting away merrily. Neferu sensed that Ay was unhappy at having to leave Horemheb alone in charge, even for such a short space of time as a single decan. There was no way he could have avoided attending the pharaoh's funeral, however.

Neferu was jealous when she saw how Neffie and Satenpare clung to Teya. She wanted to snatch them back and tell her.

'They are my children!' she told Tuthmosis.

'You cannot bring them to live in that district, Neferu,' he said. 'If you do, you will ruin their material future. They would blame you for it later. If you want them back, then you must go back to court to live. Ay cannot do anything to you now. His own position is too insecure. If you do go back to court, then you will be unhappy because you do not fit in there. If I came with you, it would make your position worse. Two known Atenists. There would be criticism of your influence over the pharaoh. In short, Neferu, you are between the devil and the deep blue sea,' was his down to earth opinion.

Neferu was galled but she knew he was speaking the truth.

'We could stay at Akhetaten with the girls,' she said hopefully.

'Would they want to stay there with you, now they have got used to Teya?' he asked.

'I will ask them later,' Neferu replied defiantly.

Once at Akhetaten, Neferu stayed at Maruaten with the others and Tuthmosis went home to Meresger. The officials, who had earlier stayed to oversee the funerary preparations for the entourage, had performed their tasks well and everything was in a state of readiness. Without the presence of Tuthmosis to sustain her, Neferu knew that she could not have returned to her beloved home without breaking down. It was all changed now, and these people seemed out of place in the quietness of Maruaten. They did not belong there.

Out in the garden, she walked with Tut, remembering this and remembering that. She found herself looking for signs of Amio in his half-brother's face, but although she caught a glimpse of him now and then, Tut had a look all his own and his personality was completely different. Tut had an inner serenity which Amio had never possessed. There had always been a kind of restlessness about Amio, as indeed about Tuthmosis. This was missing from Tut. Amio had been impulsive, Tut considered everything carefully before acting or making a judgement. Both were warm and affectionate, and both were very intelligent. They had that in common, she thought.

The following day, Neferu led the procession as widow and chief mourner. The chariots proceeded slowly in the direction of the lonely wadi in the eastern mountains where Amio had had their tombs hollowed out. To Neferu it felt like a charade. She would have preferred to have followed her husband's sarcophagus with just the children and his friends, the people who had really loved him. The tomb looked lonely and forbidding, notwithstanding the beautiful paintings. Inside, she patted the sides of the sarcophagus containing the mortal remains of the man she had loved and whom she still loved, believing that somewhere in the great expanse of the sky he still existed and still waited for her. She would never accept that he was here in this cold stone coffin. Never! Wherever his spirit was, it was not here. Neferu left the tomb with a sense of having done her duty and felt a sudden impatience to be gone from this lonely place. Gradually, after everyone had paid their last respects, the cortege moved in the direction of Akhetaten once more, at a much faster pace this time than on the outward journey. They left the workmen to seal up the tomb under the eagle eyes of Maya, head of the necropolis work.

Later that day, when the memorial honours were over, Neferu asked her two younger daughters what they would like to do. She explained that her little villa could in no way compare with the opulence of the court apartments, but that she could buy a much nicer place if they wished, and they could move in with her. The other alternative was that they could all stay here in Akhetaten with her. She explained why she could not stay at the court in Thebes. Her views on religion were very different from the people around her and she had many enemies because of it. She wanted to be a private person now that their father was dead. She told them that she had no taste for politics. The last possibility was that they remain with Teya in Thebes, close to Tut and Ankhsenpaaten and she would try to see them as often as she could. The girls chose the latter alternative. They wanted to be near to their elder brother and sister, and Uncle Ay and Aunt Teya were very nice to them, they assured her. Neferu felt totally rejected and wondered how long it had taken Ay to mould their minds and loyalties in this way. Would Amio think she was a terrible mother? Would he understand and forgive her? She felt that in the handling of the children she had let him down. She wondered what, if anything, she had ever accomplished in her life. She had failed at everything.

The following day was spent by most of the entourage as a kind of tourist day prior to returning to Thebes. They left by chariot to see the new town and its shops and sights. The servants packed up again and Neferu went to pay a final visit to Penhasi and his family before going to see Meresger and Tuthmosis. Penhasi was worried; he feared a mass exodus of people from Akhetaten now that the new pharaoh was installed at Thebes. He was very emotional about it, saying that Akhetaten would bleed to death.

Neferu was struck by his words and felt a shiver pass over her. She felt like a traitor herself, feeling that if she stayed, then at least some of the importance and prestige would carry some sway. She feared more, though, for the lives of Tut and Ankhsenpaaten in Thebes. She must stay close to her beloved children. Neferu tried to comfort the old man who was so dear to her. She told him that she intended to return to Akhetaten once Tut was strong enough to rule on his own. Neferu was moved to tell Penhasi about her quarrel with Ay and her move from the palace. She left details with him as to where she could be located in an emergency. She knew that the Israelite was from Goshen and had never set foot in Thebes, but she thought he could pass the information on to someone who might need to know, such as any old friend from On or Memphis. The old man was shocked by her revelations, but she reassured him, telling him about her new job in the district of Malarma and how she felt that she was serving the Aten in this way. Neferu asked Penhasi to pray for her every day and to remember her to the people. The chief servitor informed her that he always had and would continue to do so until he died. She was very moved by his admission and gave him a hug and a kiss, much to his surprise. When she left, she felt that she had cheered him up and herself also.

On the way to the villa of Tuthmosis and Meresger, she felt a little nervous as to the kind of reception she would receive. Meresger must have been devastated by Tuthmosis' decision to go to Thebes. Neferu alighted from the chariot with trepidation and felt a mixture of guilt and sadness as the servant showed her into the vestibule. On entering the reception room, she was greeted by a most unexpected sight, a fat baby sitting on a rug and biting a wooden toy animal. Meresger saw Neferu's incredulous gaze and laughed out loud. 'It's my new daughter!' she said proudly.

'How did you acquire her?' Neferu asked, pleased to see the woman's cheerfulness and her amiable manner.

'The mother died of a fever and the father already has three other small ones so this one is now mine and I help out with the other three. Life is so busy now that I scarcely have time to think,' she said with a mock grimace. Neferu looked at her curiously. So Meresger had also found her own salvation, she thought. She considered that there was no point in delaying the subject uppermost in their minds, so she pitched straight in.

'Are you angry with me that I have asked Tuthmosis to stay with me in Thebes?'

Meresger was suddenly serious. 'Not angry, heartbroken at first,' she admitted candidly. 'But now, I have someone of my very own.' She stooped to scoop up her daughter into her arms as she spoke. She looked around her and gestured with her free hand. 'I have the villa and I have rented out the workshop. I weave on my loom and the things I make sell quickly. I have everything I need and Tuthmosis has promised to visit me regularly ...' She stopped suddenly.

'You are very welcome to come and live with us, Meresger,' Neferu said frankly.

The other woman shook her head. 'I could not settle in Thebes anymore. I have not even visited the place in twelve years and there was never anything there for me anyway. I love my home and my friends here and I have a comfortable life. I don't want to go back to the old gods or the old ways. Here I am accepted for what I am, and my origins are unimportant. Here we are all the same.' Meresger was adamant in her refusal to leave and Neferu could not change her mind. She had not really wanted to, but she had felt she must make the effort for the sake of her own conscience. Meresger had given her the answer she had wished for.

'I want to come back to Akhetaten someday,' she said wistfully.

Meresger nodded. 'I think it would be better for you, Neferu,' was her reply.

When their ship left Akhetaten the next day, Neferu stood and watched her city disappear into the distance without once taking her eyes off it. Tuthmosis came to stand beside her. 'What is it, Neferu?' he asked quietly.

'I'll never see Akhetaten again,' she replied. When she turned to look at him, he saw that there were tears in her eyes.

'Nonsense!' he said emphatically. 'We will retire here when Tut grows up.'

'No,' she said, calmer now. 'You will go back, but it is finished for me.' Abruptly, she changed the subject. 'I have told Maatnofret that when Paranefer is gone, she must come to us if she is lonely.'

'Of course!' he answered. 'Maatnofret is always welcome, she knows that.'

Neferu nodded. 'I wish that Demi could have been at the funeral. It would have been so good to have seen him again. I have the strangest feeling that there is no home for me in the whole of Egypt, that I am in the wrong time and the wrong place, that I really don't belong here at all.' Her tone was dismal.

'You have such quaint notions at times, Neferu! You must stop being so fanciful. You know that you can have anything you want if you really want it and you can live where you want, no one can stop you going if you wish to go,' he said in a tone of slight impatience, feeling left out as he did sometimes when she had her musings, as he called them.

'Maybe that's the problem,' she commented. 'Do I know what it is that I really want? Yes, I do, but I have never been free to choose. Even now there are constraints on me. Unseen ties upon my soul which tell me I must stay near the children, even though I would prefer to live elsewhere. It is as if there is something inside me which pushes me to do the things I do, though I would infinitely prefer to have an easy life and not concern myself with the doings of others. Sometimes I do things against my own better judgement.'

Tuthmosis shook his head. 'You are a very complicated woman, Neferu. On the one hand it can be very exhausting but, on the other, it's what makes you so interesting.' He smiled to soften his words.

She supposed she was complicated. How could he expect to understand her when she did not even understand herself?

She hoped that he was not sorry that he had forsaken his former life for her. 'Are you sorry that you ever met me?'

He shook his head, and she noticed the way his eyes crinkled at the corners when he smiled. 'No! You are different from most people, but so am I. We are both outsiders and we complement each other. We never have to play roles with each other, and I can relax with you and be my true self. It has been rare in my life, and it is worth all the complications. Also!' he said, leaning forwards as he lowered his voice. 'You are a very good lover and that is important in a woman.'

She smiled as he rolled his eyes round comically. 'Well, that is something I suppose!' she laughed.

The remainder of the two days it took to take them back to Thebes passed quickly and without incident. Neferu was aware that she and Tuthmosis had caused a lot of comment and Teya informed her that some of the more censorious gossips had commented on his lack of nobility. Neferu was incensed and told Teya that Tuthmosis was born a true nobleman by nature and did not need the approval of the hypocrites who made the disparaging remarks. Teya soothed her feelings and Neferu did not mention the matter to Tuthmosis, as it would have hurt him unnecessarily. Once back on dry land she made haste to ensure that their brief sojourn at the palace did not prolong itself beyond a sad goodbye to her children.

In the end, Neferu and Tuthmosis decided to stay in the Malarma district and in the same villa. The back garden became Tuthmosis' work area and one corner of it was made over to his work completely. The rest of the garden was gradually rearranged about the work area, and it was separated from the rest by some rose bushes. There were shards of pottery everywhere and Neferu had to constantly warn Serapina not to go there on her bare feet.

Neferu continued to help Siptamun and Imsetre out occasionally and slowly she became accepted in the community as someone who would help out in a crisis if she could. Sometimes people would come to the door and ask for help and she would slip on her cloak and go. More often than not, her patients were women in labour who could not afford the fees of the doctor, though she found out as she got to know them better that they rarely got paid. It perhaps accounted for some of Siptamun's sourness. He told her that he charged his more affluent clients more to make up for the fees he did not get from the poor ones. Neferu began to see a nicer side to him than she had imagined he had possessed, and thought that when he was young he had probably been as idealistic as his young assistant still was. She and Imsetre got on particularly well together and he would teach her what he knew of a particular condition as they walked back after attending a patient.

The plight of the lepers bothered Nefer a lot and she wondered who looked after them. No one, it seemed. Imsetre told her that the dying lepers were looked after by the relatively fit ones and that when they died, their bodies would be taken out into the desert just before sundown and burnt with naphtha. At first, she felt horrified, but Imsetre said that it was the best thing. The fire consumed the infection, and in his opinion the body was only the house of the soul. Neferu perceived that in Imsetre she had found a kindred spirit, although he was always quick to change the subject if she broached the concept of Atenism. Either he was not interested, or he was afraid of the priests. Either way she did not really care. What was most important was what people were, not what they called themselves.

Once every decan, Neferu would travel to Malkata to see the children. She realised after a few months that they were growing further and further apart. She was now becoming that faraway aunt figure that Teya had once been to them. It was galling to her, but Tuthmosis always managed to cheer her up afterwards. It was only Tut who always seemed overjoyed to see her, the one who was not the child of her flesh. It was strange to her that it should be this way. As the months went by, her visits became less frequent, and she realised that she was subconsciously cutting herself off from then. Their life was no longer hers. When she did go, she was never left alone with them, Teya was always present, and this restricted Neferu's ability to be herself with them.

Over that first year in Thebes, she watched Tut grow taller and more self-confident. He was very popular at court and with his fellow officer cadets in the Kap. These were the sons of the highest nobles in the land, many of them Nubian and many of them were distant relatives to him. She was happy to see how self-assured he had become with these people. His closest friend was a boy called Huy and he often spoke of his friend to Neferu when she visited. He tried to include her in his life in this way and showed his love and affection far more demonstratively than any of her daughters.

Teya told Neferu that her visits to the court never went uncommented upon by the priests of Amun. She had noticed that the robed priests were much more prominent around the court now than she had ever seen them before in the past. Teya's comment worried her. She knew that the priests hated her, referring to her as that 'witch wife of the heretic'. She began to fear for Tut in case her visits undermined his position. She knew that he was under the close influence of the priesthood continually. She guessed that he was trying to reconcile the opposing points of view to himself as a balance between herself and the priesthood. It was too big an emotional burden for an eleven-year-old, she decided and, from then on, she took care to go to Malkata secretly at times which had been prearranged with Nakhtmin and Maya.

Pararameses continued to visit her now and again, bringing small presents from his wife. He did not seem surprised at meeting Tuthmosis there when he came for the first time after the arrival of the sculptor. Tuthmosis enjoyed his visits and they got on extremely well together. They seemed to have a lot in common. Now and again Maya, the treasury officer, would come to visit her, and he was never quite sure how to react to the presence of Tuthmosis. He seemed vaguely shocked but was too diplomatic to say so. Neferu discovered that he was having a very hard time at court, trying to balance the various factions. He was not a popular man with the priests of Amun as he had remained an Atenist and he was part Hebrew, as the suffix 'ya' in his name denoted. He managed to stay his ground because he was a mathematical and financial wizard, and no one could afford to ignore the portly forty-five-year-old.

From Pararameses and the archduke, Neferu learned that Horemheb was now firmly established in the old pharaonic palace at Memphis and that the whole of northern Egypt from Akhetaten downriver to the seacoast was under his direct jurisdiction. Neferu felt a tremor at hearing this but there was nothing she could do about it. She consoled herself by once again reminding herself that she was merely one woman with extremely limited influence, and that it was the Aten who controlled all.

On one occasion, Neferu asked Pararameses what he knew about Yussef. The field marshal had lifted his shoulders and told her that he had developed an unfortunate habit of drinking too much. Horemheb found him useful because of his influence with the wealthy Keftiu business community and therefore Yussef retained his position, in spite of his ever more frequent drinking bouts. Neferu was so saddened to hear about Yussef's mores that she never asked about her childhood companion again.

Six months after Amio's funeral, Paranefer died also and Maatnofret moved back to Thebes to come and live with them. Until Maatnofret's arrival, Neferu had heard almost nothing of Akhetaten. Tuthmosis no longer visited as often as before, Meresger was happy and doing well and had lost her emotional dependence upon him in her new role of mother to the children of the widower. Neferu was absolutely overjoyed to have her friend back with her and Maatnofret professed herself happier at Malarma than living alone in the loneliness of the beautiful but empty Castle of the Aten. The three of them and Serapina became a little family again.

For almost two years they continued a quiet life in the deeper shadows behind the struggle for power for the throne. They were happy in their memories and the knowledge of the love and friendship between them, and they learned to enjoy a quieter kind of life, such as none of them had earlier been accustomed to. Towards the end of their second year, Tuthmosis, the old archduke, died and with his passing was the end of an era. He was the last remaining child of Pharaoh Tuthmosis IV, who was, in the eyes of the priests of Amun, the last of the rightful pharaohs.

They were very upset at Malarma at this passing of their old friend and protector at court, but he was a very old man and had lived an honourable life – it was to be expected. Soon after this, however, came news of the spread of leprosy in Akhetaten and Pararameses reported that Horemheb had declared the whole city out of bounds to all visitors. This seemed to be a very draconian measure and they were all worried that there must be something serious behind it, unconnected with the outbreak. Neferu and Tuthmosis were worried about Meresger, and Tuthmosis decided to go back to find out what the position was. Pararameses told him that it would be quite useless as Horemheb had put all the entrances to the city under armed guard. Tuthmosis became very agitated but calmed down when Pararameses promised to investigate and find out how Meresger was. It was a worrying time having to wait and several times Tuthmosis was ready to leave on impulse, wracked with guilt for having left her there. Eventually, Pararameses received word from Horemheb himself that Meresger was safe. Tuthmosis settled better after that and sent a message to her via the auspices of Pararameses.

Now Neferu began to receive messages from Ay that she should come to visit the court more frequently and he started to hint that she should come back to live permanently at the court. He was showing his age now and she sensed at how isolated he had become, although outwardly he still retained his grip on power as before. Neferu even began to consider the matter herself. She knew that they would accept Tuthmosis as her lover now and Ay had even hinted that she would no longer be expected to make public obeisance to the gods of Amun. Was it time to let bygones be bygones? Could she ever again accept the restrictions placed on her by being constantly under the scrutiny of the court with its now heavy preponderance of ecclesiastics. She promised Teya that she would consider the matter and discuss it with Tuthmosis. In the end the matter was taken out of her hands.

Neferu had noticed for some time that Imsetre was becoming increasingly depressed. At first, she had not paid much attention to it and had even teased him about it. She liked the young man. He was kind and friendly in a shy sort of way and she thought they had become good friends, but gradually she became aware that he was shunning her. He no longer called on her to help with his patients and if she saw him when she went to market with Serapina, he would openly avoid her. She wondered what she had done and felt very hurt. Eventually, she contacted Siptamun to try to find out. The older physician did not know why Imsetre was avoiding her, but he too had noticed a marked change in the young man's attitude to life recently. As Imsetre was not married and lived alone, there were no clues to be gained from his family.

Puzzled, Neferu discussed the matter with Tuthmosis, and Tuthmosis was nothing if not direct. He suggested that they call on the physician unannounced. Accordingly, when the pair of them left for their promenade in the late afternoon, they called at the home of Imsetre. The young servant who answered their call said that his master did not wish to see anyone.

'Is there anything wrong?' Neferu asked worriedly. The young man bit his lip but then denied that anything was amiss. He seemed a little frightened to her eyes, but she could not force him to tell her anything. 'Tell Imsetre that if anything is wrong and he needs help I will come. Will you remember that?' The young man nodded but his eyes were evasive. When they left, Neferu said to Tuthmosis.

'He lied to us. Did you notice that he was frightened?' Tuthmosis agreed with her but said that if they did not want help then she should do nothing further.

A few days later, Siptamun came for her help with a patient who had scalded herself severely. He needed her help to dress the wounds because Imsetre was not at home, according to his servant, and he had not appeared at work for several days. Neferu was puzzled and told Siptamun about her visit to the house with Tuthmosis. The physician's rather cynical comment was only, 'We shall find out eventually. Things always come out in the end.' Neferu looked at him sideways, wondering if that applied to her too.

Things did indeed come out in the end for two days later, the servant of Imsetre came to the villa and a nervous looking Serapina ushered the distraught young man inside. 'Come quickly, your Ladyship! I think my master is dead.' He sounded terrified. Neferu and Tuthmosis exchanged glances and, grabbing their cloaks from the hook in the hallway, they ran out, telling the young man to go immediately for Siptamun. When they reached the physician's house, they found the door left ajar by the servant in his hurry and they entered within. The young physician lay on his bed as if sleeping but the pallor of death was on his face.

When Tuthmosis lifted Imsetre's hand, it was cold and there was no beat at the wrist. As Tuthmosis lifted the arm, the wide cotton sleeve fell back to reveal a white discolouration on the forearm. It was leprosy. They looked at each other aghast. No wonder the young man had been depressed. Tuthmosis put the hand back onto the bed carefully and told Neferu to back away from him. They went into the kitchen and Tuthmosis washed his hands thoroughly. He looked grim. 'He was shunning you to spare you, Neferu. Not because you had offended him.' Just at that moment they heard footsteps running and soon after they were joined by Siptamun and Imsetre's servant. Tuthmosis gave a grim shrug and said to Siptamun. 'It is too late, he is dead. It seems he has leprosy.' The older doctor took a sharp intake of breath and went into the chamber where the body lay. While they waited for him to return, Tuthmosis said to the young man, 'You knew, didn't you?'

The young man nodded miserably and began to cry softly.

Siptamun returned and poured water from the pitcher into the washing bowl. He proceeded to wash his hands carefully. 'Leprosy all right,' he said at length. 'Must have had the symptoms a good few weeks, I'd say. The only symptoms are on the forearms. The cause of death was poisoning. He killed himself rather than go to the leper colony. Can't say I blame him,' he said, more to himself than to them. Siptamun turned to the young man. 'Have you got any symptoms?' he asked grimly.

'No.' The young man shook his head in terror. 'Will I get it?'

Siptamun shrugged. 'Who knows? Maybe, maybe not. I've been diagnosing patients with it for thirty years and I never got it. Been in contact with it hundreds of times.' The young man did not look very comforted by these words. 'Everything will have to be burnt,' Siptamun continued.

'Everything?' the young man asked.

'Well, everything which he touched,' Siptamun modified his words. 'His clothes. The furniture must be washed down with strong natron solution and the house must be cleaned and left empty for one decan.'

'Where will I go?' asked the unhappy young man.

'I suppose you could stay here if you wash yourself and all your clothes and then bring the priest of Amun to say prayers over the house.'

Ritualistic magic rubbish, thought Neferu to herself when she heard his words. What could Amun do?

Neferu and Tuthmosis left the unhappy man to set about his tasks and the physician to organise the removal of the body and its burning. 'Poor Imsetre must have been very frightened. I don't think he was so much afraid of the disease as of being ostracised,' Neferu said thoughtfully.

'Mmmm,' said Tuthmosis. 'What would you do if I got leprosy?'

'I suppose I would hide you in the house so that no one would find out. I would not let them take you away from me. Just like Imsetre, I suppose.'

He put his arm round her. 'I guess you would too!' he replied.

Gradually, the shock of Imsetre's death passed. Maatnofret wanted Neferu to stop helping to nurse the poor, but Neferu found it impossible to turn anyone away when they arrived asking for help for some loved one or other, so she carried on the work, though the thought of contracting leprosy now frightened her. Just to be sure, she did not go near the children for several decans, and she examined her skin frequently. There was nothing.

Since the arrival of Maatnofret, the villa had felt comfortably full and had a much cosier atmosphere to it. Serapina had been rather jealous of Maatnofret at first and she had resented her taking over the household. Little by little, the friction between them eased and Maatnofret taught Serapina how to be a lady-in-waiting at court. She made Neferu sit still while she showed Serapina how to do her hair and Neferu had to submit to having her hair done for several days until Serapina got the hang of it. Maatnofret took it upon herself to teach the girl court manners and motivated her by telling her stories about life at court. Serapina was fascinated and began to entertain ambitions of becoming a maid at court. She begged Neferu to help her and Neferu promised to do what she could. On her next visit to the palace, she brought the matter up with Teya, who promised to consider the girl when a vacancy next arose. It could not be as a lady-in-waiting, of course, as these positions were largely chosen from within the court circle, but there were other jobs of a similar, if less exalted nature. It was another six months before such a position arose and Serapina was despatched to the palace to be a proud assistant nursery nurse to the three-year-old Ankhsenpaaten tashery.

After Serapina's departure the house was quiet, but Maatnofret now came into her own.

'I liked her,' she told Neferu. 'But I can't get used to young people at my age!' Neferu smiled, she knew that Maatnofret liked things done her way. Now there were just the three of them, it was like old times. Life settled down to a mundane serenity. Siptamun's new assistant never came to call on her and she rarely saw the older physician unless she needed to pass on a message to the palace via Pararameses. Maatnofret would make the evening meal and she and Neferu would wash the dishes together. In the evening Tuthmosis would light the fire to heat the water and then they would sit in the sitting room playing backgammon or sewing. Sometimes Tuthmosis would work on a small painting and Maatnofret would take her little hook and make lace by the light of the oil lamp. She complained that her eyes were not what they used to be, but she still managed to produce the most intricate patterns. Most often, if they were not just sitting comfortably chatting, Tuthmosis would sit and draw them as they sat in the light of the lamps, asking them occasionally to move their faces or shoulders into a position more pleasing to his aesthetic eye. He enjoyed the effects of the shadows thrown by the flame. He made hundreds of sketches of them.

The life-sized bust of Amio sat on a round rosewood table in front of the window and in the evening light it looked particularly realistic. Neferu liked it there. It was almost as if Amio were watching over them. She could think of him now without pain of loss, now she remembered only the good times that they had spent together and the great love that had existed between them. It was not a love that hurt her anymore and she knew that one day they would meet once again. Once, Tuthmosis had followed her gaze as she looked at the statue and he told her that he had once hated Amio for taking her away from him. He had gone to his studio and smashed every single statue of him and afterwards he had closed the studio and had never worked there again. Neferu had been very distressed at hearing this and, hastily, he assured her that his animosity had long since evaporated and that he did not mind the bust of Amio on the table. He said that it was his own work, and he was proud of it. She laughed at that.

As the hot spring developed into the unbearable heat of summer, they discussed going to On to visit Demi. It was a long time since Neferu had seen her brother, though he wrote to her fairly frequently. Generally, his news was at least a decan old before she received it. Demi had informed her that Horemheb had made Yussef his deputy administrator, thus making him one of the most powerful men in Egypt. Demi also told her that Yussef now shunned all contact with him and, reading through the lines, Neferu sensed his hurt and sadness at this. On the few occasions that they had had cause to meet, Yussef had apparently made several derogatory remarks about her, referring to her as a witch. For this reason, Demi warned her to be very careful and begged her to make no contact with their half-cousin. Yussef had become dangerously malicious, he said. Neferu was anxious for her brother; he must be suffering under the new regime because of his sister's perceived crimes. Could Yussef not forgive, even after all this time? He was not the person they had once known.

Neferu discussed the matter with Tuthmosis and decided to take his advice and not write to Demi any more in case the letters were being intercepted. Her letters to him could be extremely detrimental to him and his family. She wrote a short note to him, sending them all her love and saying only that they were all well and that she would only write again if something serious were to happen. She was upset for many days afterwards and Tuthmosis was furious, threatening to give Yussef's carcass to the vultures. She made a determined effort to cheer up as she did not like to see him so angry. She told him that she was just very tired and perhaps they should just go to Akhetaten instead.

For several days Neferu had had a tingling sensation in her cheek. It did not go away, and she asked Tuthmosis to have a look at it. He could see nothing, however, and she decided to ignore it. After a while the tingling disappeared, and she forgot about it. Later on, she noticed that she had lost sensation in that area. She looked in the mirror, not really worried, but there was nothing to see. She shrugged and said nothing to the others as it seemed to be such an unimportant little problem and she was otherwise quite well.

During the mornings, Maatnofret and Neferu spent time in the garden. They had learned quite a lot now about plants and the garden was looking very neat. They were proud of it and spent time religiously every afternoon making sure that the plants were well watered. They were companiable days, Tuthmosis working on some piece of sculpture or other in his little corner, Maatnofret and Neferu washing and drying the clothes on their little bushes and the walls and all the time chatting and laughing.

A few decans passed and one day, as all three of them sat on the back doorstep, Neferu put her hand to her cheek again. It had become a habit with her since the first tingling had started. Now she noticed that the area of insensitivity seemed to have grown. Tuthmosis was looking at her.

'What's the matter?' he asked.

She shook her head. 'I don't know,' she replied. 'The tingling has gone now, but now I can't feel this area at all.' She pointed to the place in question and Tuthmosis peered at it. She detected an almost imperceptible look in his eyes which quickly disappeared. 'What is it?' she said slowly.

'Oh, nothing serious, I don't think,' he said smiling and leaned forwards and planted a kiss on the area.

'Lovely skin you have always had, Neferu,' said Maatnofret. 'And you don't look a day older now than twenty years ago when I first met you.' Neferu started to laugh, forgetting her cheek. She told Maatnofret that now she really did believe that her eyes were seriously deteriorating! On this light-hearted note, they went in to have lunch.

That evening, Tuthmosis told Neferu that if they intended to go to Akhetaten, then they should leave quickly. Neferu asked him why he was in such a hurry. Was he worried about Meresger? It was more than a year since he had visited Akhetaten, and she did feel a bit guilty about it. All the messages that they had received from Meresger had indicated that she was happy and in good health though, so she supposed that she had let the matter slide, in her selfishness. A strange expression came into Tuthmosis' eyes, and he said he thought it best that they travel before the real heat of summer came. During the next few days, Tuthmosis became insistent that they should start to make their preparations to travel as soon as possible and Maatnofret also appeared to have now developed a nostalgia to return to Akhetaten to see how it was going on. Neferu agreed to contact Pararameses and in the evening she wrote a letter for Siptamun to deliver. The next morning Tuthmosis took it himself to the physician's house to deliver it. When he had gone, Neferu joked to Maatnofret about his eagerness to return home.

'I think Tuthmosis must be very homesick,' she laughed.

'Well,' said Maatnofret slowly, 'it is the place that I love the best. The court is not the same since Tiya died and anyway, there is no place there for an old woman like me. I want to die in Akhetaten and have my bones placed next to my husband's.'

'Die?' Neferu asked in sudden alarm. 'Are you feeling unwell, Maatnofret?'

'No. No. Be calm, Neferu! I am quite well, but you can never be sure when the Aten will call for you!'

'That's true,' said Neferu, still feeling that something was not quite right. Both these people that she loved so much were behaving slightly out of their usual style. Well, she was tired too and a holiday would do them all good, no doubt. Everything at court seemed to be going smoothly and the children were all well.

'If we go to Akhetaten, we probably won't want to return here afterwards,' she commented.

'No. Perhaps not. Let's wait and see. For the moment it would just be nice to see home again, don't you think?'

Neferu nodded in agreement. She stood up and touched her cheek and noticed that there seemed to be a small rough patch on it. 'Do you know where my mirror is, Maatnofret? I couldn't find it this morning, or yesterday.'

Maatnofret frowned in apparent puzzlement. 'No. I haven't seen it, Neferu.'

'I'll go and have another look for it,' said Neferu, somewhat mystified. She stood up to go.

'Neferu!'

Neferu turned round at something in Maatnofret's voice. 'What is it, Maatnofret?'

'I love you, Neferu.'

Neferu looked at her intently. 'I love you too, Maatnofret. Something is wrong, isn't there? Tell me what it is, Maatnofret!'

Maatnofret's eyes filled with tears, but she shook her head stubbornly. 'I'm just an idiotic old woman,' she cried. Neferu was really upset now. Maatnofret never cried. Her homesickness must be really bad.

'Don't worry, Maatnofret. We'll all go home as soon as possible.' Maatnofret nodded and Neferu went to look for her mirror.

Neferu searched everywhere in her room, but she could not find the mirror. It was very strange. She decided to go and look in Tuthmosis' art room, in case he had needed it for something. She found it there under his work apron. She wondered what he had been doing with it. She lifted it up the glossy, polished silver surface to her face and looked closely at the small white, scaly lesion on her cheek. Like a thunderbolt she suddenly knew the reason for their strange behaviour and their desire to leave for Akhetaten so precipitously. For a moment blind panic seized her and she felt as terrified as she had done as a small child when she was afraid of the bogeyman. 'Why me?' she asked of the Aten, mutely. 'Why my face, where everyone will see?' Quickly, Neferu stripped off and examined her body. There were no tell-tale signs anywhere else. What was she going to do? As she stood there naked, Tuthmosis entered the room quietly. He looked at the mirror in her hand and accurately assessed the situation.

'So you know?' he said levelly.

She burst into tears and the tears came like a storm. 'Tuthmosis, I'm so frightened!'

He crossed the room to her in an instant and took her in his arms. 'Don't be afraid, my darling. We'll go home. Don't be afraid, I will never leave you.'

'You must leave me now, Tuthmosis, or you will get it too.' Her voice was shaky with the crying.

'I will never leave you and we are not even going to discuss it anymore!' he said, pulling her even closer to him. 'Without you there would be nothing left for me. We stay together until death parts us.'

'It's easy to say it now,' she wept. 'But later on, when my face becomes completely disfigured, then you'll wish you had left me earlier. I don't want to be ugly, Tuthmosis,' she cried like a child, and it drew Maatnofret to the door.

'Stop that, Neferu!' she said sharply.

Neferu stopped, momentarily shocked by the sharpness in Maatnofret's voice. 'And would you not weep, in my position?' she cried bitterly.

'No doubt,' Maatnofret replied. 'But giving in to it is not going to help so you had better shut up and forget it. We are going home where we belong.'

Neferu felt a bit hard done by. She had expected more sympathy from Maatnofret at least. 'Well, at least you can pray with me that the Aten will take me before my face becomes completely destroyed and I become a source of horror to everyone.' She felt full of self-pity, and so undeserving of this disaster. Tuthmosis and Maatnofret exchanged glances.

'Neferu,' Tuthmosis said, with such a grave tone of voice that Neferu was compelled to concentrate. 'I have obtained a very deadly poison from the doctor. He has assured me that it is quite painless. When the time comes that you want to go, you can have it. I will keep it on me, and you must ask me for it. I don't want you ever to take it when I am not with you. Do you understand?' Neferu looked at him and, for the first time in their relationship, she fully understood the depth of his love for her. He was giving her a choice in her own destiny. She was not condemned to suffer the agony of mutilation. She could choose to die with dignity. With that knowledge she no longer felt afraid. She wiped her eyes and smiled tremulously at him.

'I'm not afraid any more now that I know that,' she said.

'Good!' he said, relieved. 'And remember! Nothing has happened since yesterday, nothing has changed, except that now you know and yesterday you didn't. Yesterday you were happy; cling on to that today and tomorrow. The mind is powerful, and it can see beauty when it is attuned to it, even where others can see only ugliness, and the mind can also see ugliness where others see only beauty. You are beautiful, Neferu, and you will always be beautiful because you care for others, and you show it.'

His words touched her heart. For the rest of her life she remembered them, and his reaction to her illness. She wondered if Amio would have taken it so well, she was not sure that he would have. She would never know that. Neferu only knew that Tuthmosis was not only her lover but that he was her twin soul and that she would go through eternity and search for him to be with her in the final, unknowable future, when she believed the Aten would ultimately possess them all. That night when she prayed, she thanked him for sending this giant of a man to share her last days with her.

In fact, Neferu's prayer was a little premature because the lesion on her cheek grew only slowly and it was not until just before she died that other lesions began to appear on her forearms. They never did go back to Akhetaten. Pararameses came to visit them and Neferu had to warn him not to come in because she had leprosy. He ignored her and came in anyway. He looked at her cheek closely and then said that he was sad about it. He took her hand and squeezed it sympathetically. It was his quiet way of showing her that he did not reject her, and she was very moved by it. His news, however, was not good. He was able to inform them of something that hitherto he had kept from them in order not to upset them. Six months previously. Akhetaten had been sacked by the troops of Horemheb. They were all profoundly shocked at this news and wanted to know the reason for the atrocity. Pararameses looked ruefully at Neferu. "There was a widespread outbreak of leprosy and the priests of Amun said that the place was cursed because of the Atenist's heresy and so must be destroyed.'

It appeared that many of its people had left already, drifted away as the work had gone when the bulk of the administration had returned to Thebes. The city had already begun to die and more left when the extent of the outbreak of leprosy became clearer. The troops had killed all the lepers, some had fled across the desert towards the direction of the Red Sea. It was not known what their ultimate fate was except that groups of them were heard to have migrated eastwards and the Hittites called them 'Gypsies', as this was their form of 'Egyptians'.

Since the sacking, no one from Thebes had been allowed to go to Akhetaten to see who was left. The buildings had been left largely undamaged by the events and it was rumoured that some of the populace still resided there, mainly the old or infirm. To all extents and purposes, it was now a ghost city.

'So you see, Neferu, you must stay here.'

Neferu nodded, stricken at the news. 'I will remember Akhetaten as it was. Please, Rameses, try to find out if Penhasi and Meresger are still alive and well, will you?'

Pararameses nodded. 'I will do my best, Neferu. In the meantime, you must obviously not leave the confines of the villa. If the local people realise what you have, they will drive you to the leper colony or even kill you. So long as you stay here, you are safe.'

Neferu nodded. 'I promise I will not leave, Rameses. In return, will you promise me that you won't divulge to the children that I am sick. I don't want them to be afraid for themselves or for me. Tell them that I love them very much but that I can't come to see them anymore because I have hurt my back, but that it is not dangerous.' Pararameses agreed that it was not a good idea to tell anyone. They agreed to continue the same system of messages and after he had partaken of a goblet of wine, he returned to Malkata. Tuthmosis said that he had never realised before what a good fellow Pararameses was.

'Yes,' Neferu agreed. 'Pararameses is not a man of flowery words or poetic gestures, but he is brave and solid. The kind you can rely upon in a crisis.'

CHAPTER 33

Neferu now came face to face with the understanding that for her, death was no more some vague, nebulous concept to be accepted at some far date in the future, but that it was a slowly progressing inevitability. She could not think in terms of decades anymore but in terms of a few years or even only one or two. She had always known that death would come, of course, and there had been times when she might have welcomed it, but now she was forced to come to terms with the things she would not have the time or opportunity to achieve or experience.

The worst feeling was knowing that she must never again hold or kiss her children, or perhaps even see them again. She would never know Tut as a strong pharaoh, bringing the truth of Aten to a people being manipulated by priests representing a panoply of animalistic images and using magical hocus-pocus to control their minds. She had so hoped to see her people free and strong and dignified in the knowledge of their true worth and real potential. Would Tut be able to do it on his own? It was asking a lot. She knew that as long as Ay lived, he would manipulate the boy in any way he deemed necessary in order to secure his own grip on power. Without Tut and his innate sense of justice, Egypt had no real future. It would be a choice between an amoral and undisciplined old man and an ambitious and ruthless dictator. She sent a special prayer to the Aten that all their work would not disappear forever. 'Aten, god of all creation, please deliver Egypt out of the hands of the evil one and into your truth. Please don't let all that Amio and I dreamed of be lost forever. Make the people know that you are the only god and that you have created all men free.' This was her prayer for Egypt.

The lesion on Neferu's cheek grew slowly, and gradually her skin in that area lost its olive colour and became white and scaly. That part of her face was completely anaesthetised and so she felt no physical pain. She tired very easily but otherwise she felt quite well and her life at the villa with Tuthmosis and Maatnofret continued as before. The Aten had spared her the horror of having people shrink away from her in disgust. Neither Tuthmosis nor Maatnofret ever showed any fear of catching the disease and, in reality, they all seemed to be drawn more closely together than they had ever been before. There were no more silly irritations, and every day became precious as it had during the final months that she had spent with Amio. All the beauty of everyday life took on new meaning and she saw things with a fresh eye, no longer taking them for granted; the velvety softness of a rose petal and the subtle variations in its colour for instance. These became things to wonder about. It seemed such a miracle how the bud opened and the flower blossomed, giving out its heady fragrance for a short while before it began to wilt and die. She saw the analogy with their own lives and gained a lot of comfort from it.

These things had come and gone every year without her stopping to give it more time than to enjoy the beauty of their colours and the perfume which they imparted to the garden. Now she began to perceive a wonderful symbolic order in it all, just as she watched the mosaics created by Tuthmosis take shape, made piece by piece from tiny fragments of dozens of different colours. Out of an apparent jumble, he would create the forms which she could see only with difficulty after hundreds of the pieces had already been placed. What to her was a vague, partially formed picture was already to him a completely formed image in his mind just waiting to come out. When she watched him working delicately and with tremendous concentration, she wondered if that was how the Aten worked with the lives of people.

One day, Neferu had cleaned Tuthmosis' workroom, she remembered, and she had thrown away some ugly useless bits. That afternoon after their rest, he had started to work and the pieces that he required were the very ones she had thrown away. She had had to go outside with him, looking in the rubbish until they had found them. What to her had been rubbish was useful to him and he had chosen them for the very qualities that she had rejected as worthless, their indiscriminate brown colour and the granular, rough surface. Was it like that with people, she wondered? She rather suspected that it was. The god of creation could surely use anyone and anything which he himself had created.

Neferu continued to work on the garden and to meditate on the profundities of life, using the botanical changes constantly occurring as analogies of the situations which had occurred in her life. Sometimes she would look up and find that Tuthmosis was looking at her. He would always smile at her then and there was always love in his eyes. Sometimes it was the other way around and he would catch her staring at him. They knew each other so well and yet now that she knew she must leave him, she realised that there were vast areas of his mind about which she knew nothing and which she would have liked to explore.

On one subject Neferu was very firm. After her death she did not wish to be embalmed and she did not want her body to be placed into a sarcophagus in the Valley of the Queens. She wanted her body to be burnt in the desert. Like Amio, she wanted to have a new body in her new life. She certainly did not want to have this diseased one back.

This state of quiet serenity continued for many months. Maatnofret was sixty now and her hair had become completely white. It was thinner and wispier now and she wore it in a knot at the back of her neck. She was thin and wiry, but her eyes were dimmer now and she had had to give up her lace making. She sorely missed having something to do with her hands in the evenings. In spite of this, she remained healthy and active and complained of little except the creaking of her bones now and again.

Pararameses came to visit and was obviously relieved to find that the little family were coping well and were comfortably placed. 'Do you find me much changed, Rameses?' Neferu asked.

He shook his head. 'You still look the same to me, Neferu, except that now you have got a mark on your cheek that was not there before,' he said laconically. She smiled. Pararameses could never be accused of having a wild imagination, so she guessed it was true. Not that she was afraid now. She had control of her own life and could choose her death whenever she wanted, life therefore had no horror for her. She could afford to enjoy what was left to her. She never asked Tuthmosis for the small phial.

Just after the fourth anniversary of Amio's death, Neferu was doing the gardening one day and she pricked her finger on a rose thorn. She winced and withdrew her finger rapidly. At the end of her finger was a small puncture mark and the tiniest suspicion of blood. Tuthmosis looked up.

'What is it?'

'Oh, nothing,' she answered. 'I just pricked my finger on a thorn.' She stuck her finger in her mouth and rubbed her tongue over the wound. After a moment it stopped hurting and she went back to her gardening. After lunch everyone had a nap, and later they played backgammon. Tuthmosis was pleased because he beat her several times and she had always thought herself the better player. That evening he made several sketches of her, as he often did. In his sketches he never drew in the lesion on her cheek. She had sometimes told him that he should do it to portray her as she really looked, but he always refused.

'It isn't part of you,' he would say. She was flattered by his refusal to show her face as damaged, of course, as most women would be, but she would not really have minded Tuthmosis showing her damaged cheek. She did not need to hide from Tuthmosis in any way. Later on, when they went to bed, Tuthmosis was particularly romantic, and he wooed her in a tenderly passionate way. Perhaps he sensed something she did not. Afterwards, while she still did have full awareness, she wondered if it was a premonition and a tender farewell.

The next day, Neferu awoke with a heavy head, and she felt flushed. Her finger was throbbing slightly and looked red and swollen. On her arm she noticed that one of the veins seemed more prominent than usual and it travelled up her arm in a red route to the elbow. She showed the offending digit to Tuthmosis, and he was worried that she might have blood poisoning from the rose prick. Maatnofret said that the best thing to do in such circumstances was to put the hand into hot water and soak it. If that did not work, then the finger was to be pricked with a needle to let the poison out and then soak it again. This is what Neferu did, but it did not appear to help much. The swelling of the finger did go down but by the evening she felt worse with a bad headache and was very feverish.

That night Neferu lay quite still and could not sleep. Tuthmosis was beside himself and wanted to go and fetch the physician right there and then. He kept touching her forehead to feel how hot it was and brought rags soaked in cold water to take the heat out. Neferu would not let him go for the physician and told him that she would be all right in the morning.

Towards dawn she did fall asleep and when she woke up, she felt a little better. Her head still throbbed when she lifted it from the pillow, but she was able to drink and to chat to Tuthmosis and Maatnofret. She persuaded them to wait a while before sending for the physician. In the afternoon she and Tuthmosis fell asleep together, but when she woke up again, Neferu felt much worse, and she began to experience rigours. First came a terrible feeling of coldness and then the sudden feeling of hotness followed by intense perspiration. Tuthmosis was almost out of his mind with worry now and insisted on getting Siptamun immediately. Maatnofret sat by her bed while he was away. Neferu tried to drink some of the water that Maatnofret offered to her, but she could not take much. She felt more tired than she had ever felt in her life.

Siptamun came and brought several lotions and potions to treat her. None of them seemed to be effective and the pattern of rigours repeated itself over several days. The fever took all her energy and left her listless and apathetic. Sometimes she would dream that she was in the garden at Akhetaten and that the children were playing. At other times she dreamed that she was back in On or Rashid and the three of them, herself, Demi and Yussef, were having a swimming race to the rock. Sometimes she saw Amio looking down at her and saying, 'You must drink, Neferu.' Sometimes it was Tuthmosis saying it to her. Sometimes Amio and Tuthmosis would blend into the same figure, and she was not sure who it was. 'Is it you, Amio, or is it you, Tuthmosis?'

Sometimes she was not sure whether she was awake or whether she was dreaming, but when she was awake and she knew it for sure, she always knew her beloved Tuthmosis and Maatnofret. She would put out her hand to hold theirs, and when they were tending to her, she tried to help as much as she could, though she felt so powerless. Through it all she felt no pain, only a deep tiredness and weakness.

The physician had told Tuthmosis that Neferu would undergo a crisis and either get better slowly or die quickly. He said that the crisis would occur about one decan after the onset of the first symptoms, but the crisis did not occur. After five days or so, Neferu seemed to improve, and she was more awake and could sit up in a chair while Maatnofret and Tuthmosis arranged her bed. Nine days came and went and though she had improved, she did not get better. The fever still raged, though not as high, and she was now lucid all the time, but she had no appetite and was becoming increasingly thinner.

Neferu knew that she must eat if she were to get better and Maatnofret would try to tempt her with appetising morsels. Neferu would try to please her friend but as soon as she took a mouthful, she just did not feel hungry and after swallowing the first bite, she could not take more. This was not like her at all – she had always enjoyed food. Strangely, she did not feel worried about herself or about the children anymore.

Neferu knew that she was dying. She had dreamed it so clearly one afternoon. They had all been there, shouting and waving at her, standing at the end of an enormous lotus pool. There had been Father, Grandpa and Grandma and Meketaten, all standing together holding hands and, coming to meet her with his arms outstretched was Amio. She started to walk towards him but when she was almost there she woke up and the vision disappeared. She knew that it was a sign that it was now time to write her goodbye letters to the children. When Neferu told Tuthmosis about the dream and that she was going to die soon, he cried. She had never seen him cry before and it tore at her heart. She could not bear to see him cry and she began to cry too.

'Please don't cry, Tuthmosis. I can't bear you to be unhappy.'

'How could I be otherwise when you are going to leave me?' he said in a choked voice.

'Tuthmosis, I am not leaving you. I will be with you wherever you go, I promise you that. If it is possible, I will give you a sign. I will never leave you. I will wait for you to join me in the afterlife.'

Tuthmosis lay his head against hers on the pillow. 'I always knew that it would happen like this,' he said, quieter now. 'Somehow, deep down inside of me, I always knew it. This is not something I can fight. I am so helpless,' he cried.

'No, Tuthmosis. You are so strong and so good. You have had such a hard life in many ways and yet I have never known you bitter or cruel to others. I feel so proud of you. You are a great man.' She paused and smiled at him. 'I would not normally tell you this, of course,' she said, trying to lighten his mood, 'but in the circumstances, I feel I must tell the truth.' A hint of a smile came to his eyes at this evidence that there was a flash of fight still left in her. Their relationship in the past had sometimes been a stormy one.

When, later on that day, Tuthmosis had written the letters to the children that she had dictated to him, she lay back satisfied. Neferu gave Maatnofret much of her jewellery that day. She wanted to be sure that her old friend would have everything she needed for the rest of her life. The special pieces that she had loved the most, she gave to Tuthmosis to remember her by. Neferu then made Tuthmosis send for Pararameses and the physician to be witnesses to her will. Until that time she had not informed anyone at the palace that she was ill, and she knew that Pararameses was a man of his word and that he would have kept her secret. Now, when Pararameses arrived, he told her that he must inform Ay. She agreed to that but told him he must not inform the children until she was dead. Once she was gone, there would be a finality about it that they could deal with better than the thought of her being ill and they not being able to visit her. In the presence of Pararameses and Siptamun, Neferu bequeathed the castle Hataten in Akhetaten and everything in it to Tuthmosis and Maatnofret for as long as they should live, and after their deaths it should revert to her two youngest daughters. Everything that she and Amio had jointly owned was to go to Tut and Ankhsenpaaten. To Tut, she also bequeathed her bust of Amio and of himself as a small boy. Both of these statues had been sculpted by Tuthmosis and she felt it was a fitting way of interconnecting all the people she loved.

When Neferu had finished with her will, she made Pararameses and Siptamun witness it and then Tuthmosis helped her to sit up well enough to sign it at the bottom. Finally, she gave the physician a small gold brooch for his wife and to Pararameses she gave a heavy gold necklace for his wife, for him to remember her by. The tall field marshal smiled at her and said that he could never ever forget her as long as he lived and that it had been a pleasure to have known her. To complete her responsibilities, she handed him a gold and lapis lazuli necklace to give to Yussef. Yussef had made it for Tiya twenty years earlier and she had received them on Tiya's death. Now they would go back to their home in Lower Egypt.

Another two days after the making of her will and Neferu's condition began to deteriorate once more. It was as if her body was giving up the fight now that her affairs had been put into order. Tuthmosis told himself that he would have to grieve for two soon, as Pararameses had told him privately that the scout whom he had sent out to reconnoitre Akhetaten had returned to inform him that Akhetaten appeared to be deserted apart from a few lepers. He had not dared to enter the city proper and one of the lepers had told him that there was no such person in Akhetaten as Meresger, wife of the sculptor Tuthmosis. He was depressed but resigned to the inevitable and decided that after Neferu's death he would go back to Akhetaten. He was not afraid of leprosy anymore. His love for Neferu had helped him to overcome that. In any case, he meditated, one had to die of something, Neferu had once said.

Neferu heard the quiet voice from a long distance, 'Neferu. You must drink!' With an effort she opened her eyes and saw the deep brown eyes of Tuthmosis looking at her. She smiled up at him. 'You must drink, my love,' he repeated gently. She sighed. Why could her darling not accept that it was of no use? He gently, very gently, slipped his right arm under her shoulders and raised her up from the pillows. With his left hand he lifted the goblet to her lips, and she felt the cool scented water touch her parched lips. She swallowed two or three times and he whispered encouragingly, 'More!' When she would drink no more, he lowered her gently onto the pillow and, almost against her will, her eyes closed. She felt so tired, so hot and tired. She felt something wet touch her face and she opened her eyes again. There were tears running down the face of Tuthmosis and falling upon her.

'Dearest Tuthmosis,' she whispered. 'No one could have had a more loyal friend or lover.' A great sorrow welled up inside her to see him so distressed. He was only forty-one and yet he had lived through more heartbreak than many old men. She thought of all they had gone through together. He had always defended her and come to her aid. How many men would have done what he had done, faced her leprosy and lived with it day by day? Her face was slowly being ravaged by it and yet he had always made her feel beautiful. She looked at the deep furrows on his face. He looked much older than his years now. Tuthmosis lifted his fingers to her face and with the index finger, he traced the outline of her eyebrows and then, very gently, touched her right cheek. 'Not beautiful anymore,' she whispered ruefully. She tried to laugh but her parched throat only allowed a croak. He shook his head as if to stay her words.

'You will always be beautiful, my darling Neferu.' The words ended on a choked finish. After a moment, he said fiercely, 'Always!' Again, he paused and then asked softly, 'Do you have any pain?'

'No,' she replied, shaking her head slightly.

'I'm afraid, Neferu. Afraid of living without you. Even Meresger is gone. There is no one in this world whom I love now. It will be so hard to live in a world without love.' His voice was bleak. She started. It was the first time he had acknowledged that she was dying. He had fought hard against it but she was glad that he had finally acknowledged it. She tried to find the words to bring him comfort. She knew it was always easier for the one who was leaving than the one who was left behind. She knew. She had been through it herself.

'Don't be afraid, my love. Even though you won't be able to see me, I will be right there with you, waiting for you. You will never be alone, I promise you.' She had said the words before, but she felt that she must repeat them over and over again until he really believed them. Tuthmosis' faith had been a rather hit and miss thing in the past, but she had worked on him and now she trusted that when she had gone, his faith would be strong enough to see him through and bring him comfort. At her words the tears fell faster down his cheeks. He took her left hand from the coverlet and lifted it to his lips.

After a minute he said in a calmer tone, 'I will miss you so much, Neferu, when you have gone. If you definitely promise with all your heart to wait for me, I won't be afraid.'

'Yes. I do promise you with all my heart, my soul and my mind, that I will wait for you, my dearest Tuthmosis.' He bent down to kiss her, and as she felt his light kiss upon her lips, she felt herself drifting off again into that twilight zone between wakefulness and sleep. His voice sounded close to her ear. 'Sleep for a while, my queen.'

Later, Neferu woke to find herself on the couch under the window. Tuthmosis and Maatnofret were putting fresh linen on her bed. Maatnofret noticed that she was awake, and they both came over to her. 'I will wash you, Neferu, and then you will feel better.'

Neferu nodded and thanked her. 'I'm sorry to be such a burden. You know how I hate to be ill.'

Maatnofret shook her head angrily and her old eyes moistened. 'Don't talk like that, Neferu. You know how much we love you. It is no burden to us.' Neferu nodded, sorry to have upset her.

Tuthmosis took her hand. He seemed to hesitate for a while and then he said carefully, 'Neferu, I have sent for Tutankhaten. I think he should know, and it is not right for you to do this to him.'

At this Neferu became very agitated. 'If Ay and Horemheb find out, they will kill him. In any case, he must not risk becoming contaminated. There is too much at stake,' she cried.

'I have asked Pararameses to arrange everything with Maya so that they will bring him late, when the court has retired. If you are very afraid, we will not let him actually enter into the room, but he can speak with you from the doorway.' Neferu was still very disturbed. She had not seen her darling Tut for nearly a year, and he must feel that she had rejected him. Perhaps he had forgotten her now. He had only just been eleven when they first came to Thebes, and now he was fifteen. If the priests of Amun had managed to make him their man, he would not want to be associated with her any longer anyway. She could do nothing now but wait and see. The situation had been taken out of her hands. Even if he did come, would he be disgusted and repulsed by this dreadful disease which marked her out from the rest of mankind?

'When did you send for Pararameses?' Neferu asked Tuthmosis.

'Just a short while ago,' Tuthmosis answered. 'It may be many hours yet before Pararameses has an unobtrusive opportunity to speak to Tut,' he continued. 'There is no point in you upsetting yourself by thinking about it.'

She nodded her head and smiled. 'You are sometimes so unpredictable, my love,' she said.

Tuthmosis shrugged. 'I only thought how I would have felt if I were him and the woman I loved as my mother were dying. I would want to be with her.'

'Even if it was leprosy and you felt that she had rejected you?' she asked, doubtfully.

'Tut will know in his heart that you have not rejected him and, yes, even if it were leprosy,' he replied firmly.

'Tuthmosis. How long have I been lying here in fever now?' Neferu asked.

'Almost two decans,' he answered calmly. She lapsed into silence, shocked to hear how long she had been sick. Maatnofret came and began to wash her. She looked down at herself and saw how thin she had become. Her body was very wasted, and she knew that the end must come soon. Today, though, she felt her mind very clear and alert. When Maatnofret had washed her and put on her a pretty cotton gown, Tuthmosis came and lifted her into his arms and carried her back to the bed. She put her arms around his neck as he walked and pressed her healthy left cheek close to his right one.

When he had lowered her carefully onto the bed, he sat down beside her and held her hand. Maatnofret busied herself cleaning the room. 'Will you promise me one more thing, Tuthmosis?' she asked him in a serious tone.

'If I can, Neferu. What is it?' he said, lifting his eyebrow quizzically.

'Promise me that you will take my body and burn it in the desert so that there is nothing left of me. I don't want to be entombed in the Valley of the Queens. Please don't let Ay do it to me. I want to be free and part of the earth. I want to have a new body in my new life. This one is worn with disease, and I don't want it anymore. The Aten will give me a new face that I will not be afraid to show. Will you promise me, Tuthmosis?' she begged him.

'I promise you, Neferu, if that is what you really wish.'

'It is what I really wish,' she replied emphatically. 'Be with me, my love, when my time comes. I will be calm and unafraid if you are with me,' she said softly.

'I will be there with you, my love,' he replied quietly. Neferu smiled and relaxed back onto the pillow.

Tuthmosis began gently to brush her hair. He spread it out artistically on her pillow, noticing how much more silver there was in it now. For a final effect he covered her right cheek with a large soft wave of hair and then he leaned back to look at her. She smiled up at him, amused by the eternal artist in him, who could not look at any sight without some inner eye seeing it as a painting. Struck by a sudden thought, he jumped up and Neferu watched silently as he began to look searchingly around the room. Finally, he saw what it was he wanted, and he brought it to her.

'Look!' he said triumphantly. 'You are still the most beautiful woman in Egypt.'

Neferu looked curiously into the mirror and sucked in her breath in surprise. The ugly lesion on her cheek was almost hidden. Her face looked much thinner than she had ever seen it before, but she was still beautiful. She smiled at her man again. 'And you are still the best artist in the whole of Egypt,' she replied. Some of his former fire came back to his eyes and he seated himself beside her again, taking her hand.

'Our dreams won't die, Neferu. They will live on in the minds of those who got away. They will carry them with them wherever they go and because they were born of free will, they will transmit them to their own children. One day in another time and place, it will begin again. The Aten is with us, I know it. There will come a time when men will rise up against the chains of ignorance and slavery that shackle their minds, and I cannot believe that the Aten will allow the evil ones to prosper. The time will come when man will see the light of truth. Perhaps we will come again to witness it.'

Neferu felt herself swept along in the fervour of this passionate outburst of emotion from Tuthmosis and she nodded enthusiastically. At that moment, they heard an outcry from Maatnofret and Neferu exchanged an anxious look with her lover. Tuthmosis jumped up frowning to go and see what the matter was, but before he even reached the doorway he suddenly stopped in his tracks and looked very taken aback. A very agitated Tut was standing there.

'Neferu!' Tut cried, looking past Tuthmosis to the figure lying on the bed.

'Tut!' answered Neferu weakly, shocked at his sudden entrance. 'How did you get here?'

Tutankhaten came forward into the room, but Tuthmosis pushed him back. 'No, Tut! You must not come any closer,' he said firmly.

The handsome youth angrily drew himself to his full height and said imperiously. 'I am the pharaoh and I command you to stand aside.' A glint of amusement came into Tuthmosis eyes as he bowed deeply and stood aside as he had been ordered to.

'No, Tut! You mustn't come any closer. You might become infected, my darling!' Neferu cried in alarm but to no avail. Tutankhaten ignored her and came right up to the bed. He knelt down on one knee and asked in a strangled voice why she had not let him know that she was ill, he would have come sooner. 'I knew that, Tut, and that is why I could not tell you. I was so afraid that you would become sick too. I could not take the chance.' She wanted to stroke the bent head, but she did not dare to touch him. As if he had read her thoughts, he rose and leaned over the bed to kiss her on her lips. His eyes were full of tears and her own also. She managed to force them back. 'It has been so long since I have seen you,' she said. 'You are a man now, so handsome and tall. I have missed you so much. You must give my love to the girls when you go back. How are they?'

Tutankhaten told Neferu that all her children were well and that Ankhsenpaaten was pregnant with their first child. The whole court was praying that it would be a boy. His voice broke as he told her of his plans to bring her back to the court to live with them.

'Please don't be upset, Tut. It was not meant to be. The Aten controls our destinies and the plans we make are as nothing if they do not have his backing. Have you forgotten the Aten, Tut?' she asked sadly.

'No. Neferu! I have waited as you told me to. Ay says that the time is not yet right for a return to the Aten. First, I must become strong and learn all the secrets of the Kap. When I have control over the army, then I can make the priests do as I wish.' He said it with a boyish swagger which made her both amused at his youthful confidence and afraid for his inexperience of the evil of some men's minds.

'The Aten does not need armies, Tut. It is not his way. His way is the way of peace,' she said, and then to change the subject, she asked, 'But tell me more about the girls.'

Tut smiled as he told her. 'Uncle Ay and Aunt Teya say that Neffie looks just like you when you first came to the court. There are dozens of the boys in the Kap who are madly in love with her and want to marry her. Uncle Ay says she is still too young. My best friend Huy is very serious about her and says that as soon as we pass out of the Kap next year, then he is going to ask her to marry him. I know that Neffie likes him a lot and I think she will say yes. I know that she is in love with him because they always ask me to carry messages between them so that Uncle Ay won't find out.'

Neferu was amused to hear this. 'I hope Huy is a nice boy,' she said.

'Oh, yes!' answered Tut. 'His grandfather was Amenhotep Hapu, my grandfather's grand vizier before grandfather Yuya.' Neferu wondered if Tut knew now that it was the Archduke Tuthmosis who was his real father, not Amenophis III. If he did, it had not upset him at all, it seemed, as he had not bothered even to mention it. 'Satenpare is quite tall now, just as tall as Neffie. The two of them are always squabbling and Aunt Teya says that they are turning her hair white with their petty quarrels,' Tut continued, smiling. Neferu was pleased to hear how cosy and domesticated it all sounded. Teya was a good woman and had looked after them well, it seemed. She was grateful for that. A thought suddenly crossed her mind.

'How did you get here, Tut? It is still daylight,' she asked haltingly.

'I came by horseback. 'He grinned. 'I took the horse out of the stables myself and came bareback.' His face became serious. 'I came as soon as I could, Neferu.'

Neferu looked at Tuthmosis in alarm. 'You were very reckless, Tut,' she said as severely as she could. 'If Ay or the priests find out, you will be severely criticised. You must be careful, for my sake. I love you very much and I don't want to be the cause of any trouble.'

'I had to come, Neferu!' he cried hotly, stung by her reaction.

'I know, I know, my love,' she said soothingly. 'And I am so happy to see you and to have had this last opportunity to speak with you and see how you have grown. It's just that I worry so much about you all. I have always loved you so much and I always will. My hopes rest in you now and I know that you will be a great pharaoh. Much as I would like to keep you here with me, my darling, you must go back now before your absence is discovered. Have you no cloak to cover your head?' Tut shook his head. Maatnofret looked at her and mentioned the old white cloak of Amio's, which Neferu used to wear.

'Has it been washed clean since I last used it?' Neferu asked her anxiously.

'Yes. It's completely clean,' Maatnofret reassured her.

'Take that then, Tut,' Neferu begged him. He agreed to use the cloak to conceal his identity. He seemed reluctant to leave her. 'You must go, darling! Don't be sad for me. I am going home to the Aten and to all our loved ones. There is your mother, Amio, Meketaten, Meretaten and Smenkhenre and all my family too. I won't be lonely, and I will wait to greet you when your time comes as I will wait to greet Tuthmosis and Maatnofret. Always remember that I love you very much. You were my very special child! Give my love to the girls too.'

'Peace be with you, Neferu, until we meet again,' Tut said. He leaned forwards and put out his hand onto her forehead and smoothed back her hair to reveal her cheek. He looked at it for a moment and then said, 'You are still beautiful, Neferu. Just as I remembered you.' He bent down and carefully kissed both her cheeks.

Neferu was terrified. 'You should not have done that, Tut,' she cried in her alarm. 'You must go and wash yourself immediately.'

He shook his head. 'Nothing about you can ever hurt me, Neferu! I am not afraid. Don't be afraid for me. I will always love you.' Quickly he donned the cloak and went to the door. In the doorway he turned to thank Tuthmosis and Maatnofret and told them to come to the palace as soon as it was all over. With a last look at Neferu, he blew her a kiss and then turned and was gone.

There was a long silence in the room and Neferu felt that something important had been finished. Her final goodbye had been said. 'I am worried about him, Tuthmosis,' Neferu said finally. 'It was very reckless of him to come in broad daylight on horseback.'

Tuthmosis smiled. 'He is a youth after my own heart,' he replied. 'Don't worry! Remember that the Aten is in charge of everything. You said it yourself.'

'It's true but ...' Her words trailed off. He smiled. 'He has grown so tall and handsome,' she said. 'Did you not think so, Maatnofret?'

'I certainly did,' the old lady replied.

'He has character too!' interjected Tuthmosis and laughed. A companiable silence descended on the room. Maatnofret brought in a jug of sweet wine and even Neferu was able to drink it. Tuthmosis got out his papyrus and, coming to sit by Neferu, he began to draw. First, he drew Tut as he had just seen him, and he showed the drawing to Neferu. She was enchanted by it. The likeness was excellent, and she took it into her hand and kept it, not wanting to put it down. Next, he began to do a profile sketch of her. She was tired now, but she felt content. After all, Tuthmosis was right. These were not her problems; they were the Aten's.

Neferu relaxed back on her pillows with a light sigh. Tuthmosis looked up. She smiled at him with love and trust. 'I'm so tired, Tuthmosis. Do you mind if I sleep for a while?' Tuthmosis looked at her for a long moment, then he leaned forward and kissed her gently on her lips.

'Sleep, my love. Dream of me and remember that I have always loved you.'

'I have loved you truly, Tuthmosis.'

Neferu closed her eyes and she slept. Tuthmosis continued to draw. Somehow, he did not feel tired at all. Sundown came and still he sat there with his stylus. He lit the oil lamps and Maatnofret brought food and drink. She went to take a drink to Neferu, but Tuthmosis told her not to disturb her. Maatnofret went over to the bed and was disturbed by the shallowness of Neferu's breathing. The pair of them exchanged glances and there was a question in the old lady's eyes. Tuthmosis shrugged his shoulders in reply and then told her to go to bed as there was nothing she could do. He promised to wake her immediately if something untoward happened. Neither of them used the word death.

Evening passed into night and midnight came. Tuthmosis continued to draw, sketch by sketch, from memory, of Neferu in different poses and attitudes, sitting, walking, smiling, serious. Occasionally he stopped to feel her pulse and observe her breathing. Sometime after midnight, he put down his sketches and carefully replenished the wick in the oil lamps. When he had done that, he came to sit by the bed again and took her left hand into his own. She stirred slightly and he felt her forehead. It felt cool now. The fevered flush was gone and there was a pallor about her cheeks. He leaned forward and said quietly, right up close to her ear, 'Can you hear me, Neferu? I want you to know that I really love you.' She stirred slightly but did not wake up. He felt a heavy stone in his chest that did not move. It was so heavy that it was almost preventing him from breathing. He suddenly felt that he must keep hold of her hand at all costs. Her hand felt small and cold now inside his own, but she was still breathing. In the light of the flickering oil lamps, he watched her constantly. His eyes began to feel tired, and every now and then he would close them and nod off for a moment or two, only to be awakened with a jump by heaven only knew what prompt.

Just about three in the morning, still well before dawn, Neferu's breathing began to fail. She would stop breathing for a minute or two and then several deep, sighing breaths would come in rapid succession. Gradually, the intervals between the breaths became longer. 'Neferu,' he whispered, trying gently to rouse her. There was no response. A wave of grief washed over him and jumping up quickly he called loudly, to wake Maatnofret, telling her to come right away. He turned his attention back to Neferu immediately. Maatnofret appeared beside him in an instant and together they sat and watched over the figure in the bed. Finally, in the darkest hour just before the dawn, a long sigh came, and it was all that heralded the cessation of that beating heart. Maatnofret leaned over and kissed Neferu. 'Goodbye, until we meet again, Neferu,' she said simply.

Tuthmosis bent over her and kissed her gently, all over her face. 'Remember, Neferu! You promised to stay close by me.' He continued to sit there holding her hand and remembering her words and promises. Maatnofret put her arm around his shoulders. Tuthmosis seemed not to be aware of her.

'Are you still here in this room, Neferu?' he whispered, but there was no answer. A feeling of panic came over him and desolation engulfed him. Silently he begged. 'Please send me a sign that I can recognise, Neferu.'

All of a sudden, a voice inside his head said to him, 'Go to the door now!'

Gently he lay Neferu's hand down on the coverlet and went to the door. Down the corridor he turned to the hallway and opened the main door. He looked east towards the sky and at first all he could see was the bright pink of the beginning of dawn, but as he looked an enormous red ball rose up over the horizon, growing ever larger. The sun was his sign, and he felt the panic inside him subside. He returned to the room where Neferu lay and noticed that the dawning light of day was making the flickering light of the oil lamps superfluous, and so blew them out. He went over to the bed and looked down at the figure of Neferu. 'Thank you, my love,' he said quietly.

Maatnofret asked him what they should do next and Tuthmosis exclaimed that he had something he must do quickly before they took Neferu's body away. Maatnofret covered her head and left for the home of the physician Siptamun to send a message to Pararameses and to obtain enough naphtha for their purposes. While Maatnofret was gone, Tuthmosis quickly began to mix the paste and when he had obtained the necessary consistency, he spread it carefully over Neferu's face and left it to dry. Maatnofret returned while it was still drying, and she had with her the necessary articles and the news that Siptamun would contact Pararameses as soon as possible. A chariot would be arranged within an hour or two at most. Tuthmosis nodded; it left him little time. In the meantime, Maatnofret cleansed and prepared Neferu's body and covered it with a shroud, leaving only the masked face free. As soon as the mask was dry enough, Tuthmosis removed it carefully and cleansed the remaining bits lovingly from Neferu's face. With a last kiss from both of them, he covered her face.

They had barely accomplished this when the chariot arrived. The driver was impatient, anxious not to be seen hanging around this district. Tuthmosis and Maatnofret carefully lifted the body of Neferu and carried it out to the chariot. Maatnofret then went to bring the naphtha and warned Tuthmosis to be careful, as the flames had the habit of leaping out towards the source of the ignition. Tuthmosis promised her that he would be very careful, and he got in the chariot.

The chariot driver was so unnerved by the extraordinary freight he was carrying that he was very quiet and cooperative and drove as fast as he safely could, until they reached the edge of the desert. Tuthmosis was as anxious to get as far from the city edge as it was possible, and the chariot continued until the ground beneath them became far too soft for the wheels to roll easily. Tuthmosis looked back and decided that it was far enough. He told the driver to stop.

The sun was blazing overhead now already, and he was covered in perspiration. He climbed down from the chariot and chose a spot about three metres further into the desert. In his haste, he had forgotten to bring a spade to dig out the sand. Now he had to hollow out a suitable grave in the sand with his hands. When it was long enough and deep enough to make a shallow grave, he lifted out Neferu's body from the chariot and carried it over to the makeshift grave.

The driver of the chariot was very jumpy and made no attempt to help. Tuthmosis lay the body carefully into the grave and then went back to the chariot for the little bottle containing the naphtha. With precise, even movements, he poured the naphtha over the body as uniformly as he could and then he began to rub the flints. The first sparks did not ignite the naphtha and he had to continue laboriously for about ten minutes before the material suddenly ignited. The blue flames stretched out towards him, singeing his hair, and he jumped back quickly to avoid being burnt.

In the still desert air, the body quickly became an inferno, and he watched the hot waves of air as they rose and danced above the body before he turned away, not able to watch the final destruction any further. The driver took his turning away to mean that he was ready to leave, and he shook the reins slightly. Tuthmosis shook his head sharply and said, 'Not yet,' in a peremptory tone.

He wanted to stay until he was sure that the body was completely destroyed. The man seemed mutinous, but Tuthmosis was adamant. Tuthmosis guessed that the whole process would not take long because Neferu had been so thin by the time of her death. Periodically he turned to look and see if the flames were still high. The most horrible thing about it, and what really sickened him, was the smell of the charred flesh as it carried towards him in the air, and he had to move further away.

Once the flames had died away, he forced himself to approach the remains. What was left of the body was charred beyond recognition and though he felt horribly sick, he began to push sand over the smouldering heap with his hands. When the body was fully covered by the sand, he stood back and said a silent prayer to the Aten. He asked the god to bless this final resting place of the body of Nefertiti. Finally, he threw down the goatskin bottle which had contained the naphtha over the grave, perhaps as some kind of impromptu memorial. He stood for a moment and looked around the desert and then up at the sky before making his way with a heavy sigh to the chariot.

The chariot driver needed no further sign and made top speed to be away from what he obviously felt to be an accursed place. Once back in Malarma proper, Tuthmosis made the driver drop him off some way from the villa and he continued his journey on foot. Maatnofret met him at the doorway of the villa and, in response to her unspoken question, he answered, 'It's done.' His face and hands were blackened by the smoke and Maatnofret directed him to the bathroom where she had already supplied several pitchers of water. She herself had already bathed and changed into clean clothes, he noticed. When he had bathed and changed, Maatnofret made him have something to eat. He noticed that she had cleaned the sickroom so completely already that it was already devoid of any signs of personality. There was no longer any ambience of Neferu in the room at all. The realisation caused a wave of pain to flow over him anew. At the table, Maatnofret was all common sense.

'We should leave for Akhetaten without delay,' she said.

'We must wait for Pararameses to contact us before we do anything,' he replied. Maatnofret nodded. After quickly finishing his meal, Tuthmosis returned to the sickroom, which had become his makeshift studio. He still had one important job left to do. Taking the death mask of Neferu, he found it sufficiently dry to start to make a mould, and he began to work on it.

The arrival of the physician caused Tuthmosis to lay down his work. He wondered what the message was. Siptamun entered and told him that Ay had sent a message that he was to examine them both, and if there were no signs of leprosy, they were to be taken to Malkata to see the grand vizier. Tuthmosis told the physician that the body of Neferu had been disposed of according to her wishes. The physician's distaste registered momentarily upon his face before it assumed its usual professional, non-committal look. 'It is, of course, none of my business,' he said, not unkindly.

The physician examined Tuthmosis first but could not find any signs of the disease, neither on Maatnofret. Soon after he had left, they began to sort out their possessions for what might be a prolonged stay at Malkata. Tuthmosis wondered how much Pararameses had told Ay. Did he know about the disposal of Neferu's body, for instance? They could only wait and see.

Tuthmosis recommenced working on the death mask. He indicated to his many sketches of Neferu and said to Maatnofret, 'Maatnofret, Choose which of my sketches of Neferu you most prefer.' Maatnofret looked through the pile of sketches and chose the ones she wanted. Tuthmosis filled the mask he had made with his plaster and then put out in the sun to dry. He felt very tired all of a sudden and realised that he had not slept at all for more than twenty-four hours. He knew that there was no point in lying down now as the court chariot could arrive for them at any moment. Maatnofret seemed to have completed all their packing and the linen bags were closed and fastened, waiting out in the hallway to be picked up. Neferu's clothes were left hanging in her wardrobe except for a few which Maatnofret knew to be clean and not used for a long time. Now, on an impulse, Tuthmosis went through her wardrobe and stuffed her beloved white dress, which her grandmother had made for her, into the bag of his personal belongings. 'To remember her by. Something that she wore,' he said to Maatnofret by way of explanation. She nodded and did not reply. They were both very tired now and lapsed each into their own memories of happier times when the clothes had been worn in totally different circumstances. Maatnofret looked up at the walls and ceilings, where Tuthmosis had painted frescoes that were identical with the ones in Amio's study at Akhetaten.

Tuthmosis' eyes followed her gaze. 'She wanted it,' he said simply. Maatnofret nodded again wordlessly, looking sad. They both felt burdened by the weight of bereavement and of circumstances for which they were not responsible and in which they had both tried to do their best, seemingly to no avail. Tuthmosis reflected that even Maatnofret, with all her great faith in her god, seemed crushed by the impact of Neferu's death, coming as it did at the end of a decade of one tragedy after another. Like Tuthmosis, she too felt that there could be no further purpose in her life and that she had lived too long. Sensing her deep desolation, Tuthmosis flung his arm around her shoulders, and they stood united in their mutual grief.

Tuthmosis took a last survey of his work. The only thing to denote his long stay here in Malarma would be these carefully executed frescoes on the walls. Now that the person he had painted them for was gone, he felt no sense of pain in leaving them. They had no meaning without the love which had inspired them. 'Will this time of evil never end?' Maatnofret asked him, with a note of hopelessness in her voice

'Yes. It will end,' Tuthmosis replied grimly. 'It will end with the deaths of Ay and Horemheb, but you and I will be long gone by then.' It was said quietly and without any drama, but they were both seized by a sense of despair. What the future held for them they did not know, but they knew for sure that they would never be returning to this place again.

When the chariot came to collect them, Tuthmosis carried out the bags, while the servant who had arrived made a quick inventory of what was left behind. Maatnofret took with her the bust of Amio and the one of Tut. She could not bear to leave them behind, they had both been so dear to Neferu. Tuthmosis went to get the mould of his death mask, which was now dry, and then he locked the back door and went to make a final tour of the place. At the doorway of the sickroom, his eyes focused on the empty bed, and he looked down at again at the delicate mould in his hand. He had wanted it to be as closely representative of her as possible, but now, half-finished, it seemed like some tawdry toy. He decided that he would start again and make another mould and would give it a more true to life look which he would not paint. It would remain as a stark statement of her final expression. With that goal uppermost in his mind, he departed from the house and locked the front door. In the carriage, he saw that Maatnofret was crying, and he drew her to him. They travelled the journey to Malkata in silence.

In the courtyard at Malkata, Pararameses' adjutant received them and after stepping down from the chariot, they were conducted to the field marshal's home. Here,

Pararameses received them himself in a large reception room facing the courtyard. Tuthmosis had never been inside the house before and he looked around curiously. He and Pararameses looked at each other squarely. They both seemed at a loss as to what to say after the initial greetings.

'What are your plans?' Pararameses asked.

Tuthmosis shrugged. 'We plan to return to Akhetaten, but first I must go to On and Memphis to take these articles which Neferu gave me. She wished to bequeath them to her brother, Demi and to her half-cousin, Yussef.'

Pararameses looked surprised. 'Yussef? I wouldn't have thought that Neferu would have wished to maintain any form of contact with someone who has worked so steadily against her and Amio for so long. I was surprised that she wished to send him some of her jewellery.'

'He was the one who made it, many years ago, for Tiya. Neferu never wore it,' Tuthmosis explained.

Pararameses lifted his eyebrows but said nothing. After a short pause, he said, 'I could have one of my messengers take it for you if you wish.'

Tuthmosis shook his head. 'I feel that I would like to see Demi myself and explain her death to him,' he replied.

'How did the end come?' Pararameses asked. At that moment a servant entered, and a silence descended on the room. Maatnofret seemed to be immersed in her own thoughts and did not attempt to make conversation.

It was Tuthmosis who broke the silence. He sighed heavily and said, 'She died peacefully in her sleep early this morning, just before dawn.' Pararameses nodded, waiting for him to go on. 'She didn't want any pomp or ceremony, or a tomb covered with the symbols of false gods. She believed that in the afterlife she would have a new body and she did not want the old one to be a possible source of contamination for others. She wanted her body to be burnt in the desert and her remains to go unmarked. I have done as she wished and she, at least, will never have to undergo the desecration of her tomb by grave robbers, as so many before her have done. Tonight, the desert will cover all traces of her burial ground to all eyes except the Aten's and her own.'

Tuthmosis fell silent after this report and cleared his throat. Maatnofret nodded, as if in vindication, but she said nothing.

'You have carried out her wishes, Tuthmosis, therefore you have done the correct thing,' Pararameses remarked. 'But I fear that Ay will be furious when he finds out. I suspect that he will feel that you have usurped his rights in this matter and caused him to lose face in what he considers is a family matter.'

'Rights!' Tuthmosis shouted, incensed. 'What rights did he have? It was his intriguing and deviousness, along with his accursed son-in-law, Horemheb, that brought down everything Neferu stood for! He has no rights as far as Neferu is concerned.'

Pararameses did not deny it and merely sighed again. He rose from the couch and went over to look out of the window to the courtyard below. Finally, he turned round and admitted, 'He will think otherwise, I warn you, and he is very unpredictable these days. He spends much of his time nowadays under the influence of the poppy seeds, like the old pharaoh. He is liable to fly into the most profound rages over the most trivial reasons, or conversely, he may accept news of a most dire catastrophe with the utmost placidity. One can never say in advance.' Pararameses meditated a while and then said speculatively, 'I think you would be very wise not to inform him of your intention of returning to Akhetaten. He has recently issued an edict that no one must go there on pain of death. It is now called "The Forbidden City".'

Tuthmosis nodded. 'Thank you for that advice, Pararameses. I thank you also on behalf of Neferu, for remaining loyal to her when the others discarded her.'

The field marshal bowed his head slightly. 'It was my duty as a servant of the pharaoh and my pleasure as her friend.'

'Nevertheless, it must have cost you much popularity,' Tuthmosis said shrewdly.

'There are some things in life worth more than popularity. Honour and integrity, for example,' Pararameses answered gravely.

'Why has Ay never discovered that!' Tuthmosis replied bitingly.

'I think it is time we go to meet him. Are you afraid?' Pararameses asked.

Tuthmosis shook his head. 'My life doesn't hold much importance to me now. There is no reason for me to fear dying,' he replied. 'Will I have an opportunity to speak with Tutankhaten?' he asked.

Pararameses started at the name. 'You must be very careful to call him Tutankhamun now,' he said quickly.

Tuthmosis nodded. 'I will not say or do anything which might put the pharaoh at risk,' he said seriously.

'I'm afraid that the pharaoh may already be at risk. His visit to Neferu was rather foolhardy and many people recognised him. The news got back to the priests of Amun, and he was severely censured. They feel that he is still too much tainted with the so-called heresies of Amio,' he replied tonelessly. 'I will do my best to contain the damage.' Tuthmosis felt his blood run cold, and he clenched his fists. It was his fault. He was the one who had informed the boy of Neferu's condition, via Siptamun's messenger service.

'I trust that you will be able to succeed,' he said with emphasis. 'I'm ready to go now.'

Moving quickly, Tuthmosis helped Maatnofret to rise and then picked up the linen bag containing his sketches and the death mask. Pararameses indicated that he could leave his remaining belongings there and that he was invited to stay with them if he wished. Tuthmosis thanked him but stated that he wanted to set off for Lower Egypt as soon as possible. Pararameses escorted Tuthmosis and Maatnofret to the grand vizier's office on the second storey above the great reception hall. The grand vizier was seated at his desk, and he rose as the three of them entered the room. Pararameses and Tuthmosis bowed deeply, in accordance with the demands of protocol, and Ay inclined his head.

The grand vizier turned his attention to Maatnofret, whom he seemed genuinely overjoyed to see. He greeted her warmly and told her that he hoped she would decide to stay and live here with them from now on. Maatnofret seemed surprised but pleased by his response to her. Pararameses and Tuthmosis exchanged glances. Tuthmosis remembered that Maatnofret had known Ay almost all her life, though she rarely spoke about it. He guessed that she was torn between this invitation and her plan to return to Akhetaten. He could understand that. She was sixty years old, and she had lost almost all of the people she had loved. She looked at Tuthmosis with a question in her eyes. Tuthmosis knew that she was wondering if he would consider her disloyal if she stayed. 'Stay here, Maatnofret. You belong here. You spent many years here at court, you know the people and they know you. You will have the pleasure of watching Neferu's daughters grow up and I will be happy knowing that you are safe. Neferu would have wanted it.' His voice was very soft and gentle with her.

Tears filled Maatnofret's eyes.

Ay looked at her with concern and patted her arm. 'He is right, Maatnofret. Teya will be so happy to have her old friend back. There are so few people left now from our youth. Will you stay?'

Maatnofret nodded and put out her arm to Tuthmosis. 'Tuthmosis, I will miss you. We have been through so much together. Thank you for being so understanding. You will always be in my thoughts.'

For reply, Tuthmosis lifted the gnarled old hand to his lips and kissed it. 'It has been a great honour to have known you, Maatnofret. Wherever I go, you will always have a place in my heart. Pray for me and may the peace of Aten be with you.'

'May the Aten be always with you too, Tuthmosis,' Maatnofret said and reached up to kiss him.

Ay asked Pararameses to escort the lady-in-waiting down to his wife, who was eagerly awaiting her arrival. Tuthmosis watched her depart. He was happy that she had found a comfortable home for her last years. There was credit for Ay in that at least.

CHAPTER 34

After the other two had departed, Ay requested Tuthmosis to sit down. Tuthmosis looked at him curiously. The grand vizier was a withered old man now, but the eyes were still bright and alert. Tuthmosis had expected a more overtly aggressive reaction to him and was thrown off-balance. He remembered that Maatnofret had told her that Ay was sixty-two now. He sat in his chair calmly while watching Ay appraise him. When he did speak it was a full-frontal attack. Most unusual coming from the old fox, he thought.

'Why did you take it upon yourself to dispose of Neferu's body, and in such a way?' Ay asked haughtily.

'Because it was what Neferu wished for herself, and I was honourbound to carry out her wishes,' Tuthmosis answered calmly and without any trace of irritation.

'You did not consider the protocol requirements of the situation?' the grand vizier interrogated him coldly.

'I considered them, and I rejected them in favour of the queen's personal wishes,' he said quietly.

Ay gave a sudden throaty laugh which turned into the wheezy cough of an asthmatic. When the paroxysm passed, he said sarcastically, 'Ah! You rejected them.'

Tuthmosis felt that the remark required no answer, and he allowed his eyes to stray round the room. It was an elegant room, though a little overfurnished to his taste. All the furniture was beautifully carved and decorated and he noticed that the table next to him had a copper top with fluted edging and it was intricately worked in designs of flowers and a large peacock with a fanned tail. He thought that it did not look like the work of an Egyptian artist, and he wondered vaguely where it had come from.

Ay's cough brought him back to the present and he studied the grand vizier across the table. He remembered Neferu saying that Ay was a strange personality for whom she had felt an ambivalent mixture of fondness, respect and deep mistrust. She had said that he was unlike any other man she had ever met. He did not assess situations as being right or wrong in the same way that other men did, rather what he wanted he considered right, and what he did not want he considered wrong. He was not basically evil, but he was totally amoral, responding only to the stimulus of what he desired or needed and to nothing else. To have ultimate control over this situation, he needed to have ultimate power, and this was the driving force behind him, nothing else. Neferu had considered him highly dangerous because his amorality was combined with a very highly developed intelligence which allowed him to manipulate people in the most part without them even being aware that they were being manipulated.

Neferu had acknowledged Ay to be the most intelligent man she had ever met, and she had also told Tuthmosis that Ay was also the most devious person she had ever met. Tuthmosis was very tired, not having slept for more than twenty-four hours. He realised that he was not at his most alert and that he must retain control of his situation. Bearing all this in mind, he was very wary and determined not to let this wily old man deceive him. Ay noticed his expression and his intuition immediately detected the latent hostility emanating from Tuthmosis. He smiled at him ever so slightly and Tuthmosis gave a perfunctory smile in return.

Imperceptibly, Ay's mood seemed to change, and in an almost affable tone he inquired what it was that Tuthmosis was carrying with him. Tuthmosis looked down at his bag and observed the rolled papyrus.

'They are only sketches of Neferu which I have made,' he said. 'I don't think you will find them interesting.'

Ay lifted his eyebrow in slight derision. 'On the contrary, I would be most interested to see them,' he remarked. Tuthmosis took the sketches from his bag with care and handed them to Ay. The old man opened them out and examined each one carefully with an almost expressionless face. When he had seen them all, he looked up. 'I congratulate you, sir, you seem to have captured the very essence of Neferu.' Tuthmosis bowed his head slightly to acknowledge the compliment. 'You have a prodigious talent!' Ay commented. Tuthmosis was silent, not wanting to be put off his guard by any possible verbal manoeuvres by the grand vizier. He knew himself to be articulate but guessed himself to be no match for the old fox. He planned to answer as far as possible in non-committal monosyllables. 'I loved her, you know,' said Ay, with a smile.

Tuthmosis felt momentarily astounded and then a well of fury rose up inside of him. 'You never loved her for a moment,' he said bitterly, realising immediately that he had blown his intentions of parrying all possible inflammatory remarks.

Ay looked at him coolly and then said almost with compassion, 'It had to be done, you know, and it need not have ended like this. Nefertiti's fate was in her own hands.' Tuthmosis was silent, afraid that he might not be able to master the anger that was so close to erupting. Ay continued, 'With the death of Tiya and Amio and no male heir, the throne was left in a very weak position. The priests of Amun are very powerful. It was necessary to placate them in order to secure the throne for Tutankhamun. I had to move quickly to prevent a coup by the high priests.' Tuthmosis was silent but continued to listen with interest. After a pause to see the effect of his words, Ay continued, 'I did offer to marry Neferu in order to strengthen her position, but she refused.' He shrugged as if in recollection.

'So you decided to humiliate her publicly and send her into exile because she refused you.' Tuthmosis could not bite off his bitter comment.

Ay answered icily. 'I decided to teach her a lesson. I did not intend it to go on and on. I thought a little discomfort and rough living would bring her to her senses. I underestimated her tenacity, that is all.'

'That's all? That's all?' reiterated Tuthmosis furiously. 'Neferu had to be condemned to be treated as a common criminal outlaw because she refused you?' There was a cutting contempt in Tuthmosis' voice which was not lost on Ay. The grand vizier did not immediately respond to it, however.

When he did speak again, his voice was measured and even. 'All that was required of her was a public obeisance to the gods Amun-Re. She could have privately continued to worship the Aten. It would have cost her very little,' Ay said with a shrug.

'It would have cost her integrity,' Tuthmosis said savagely. 'And she could not live a lie.'

Ay shrugged again. 'And did the Aten rescue her in the end?' he inquired sarcastically. Tuthmosis was silent, not knowing how to answer that. He too had pondered that question and it truly did seem that the Aten had rejected them all. Had it all been a beautiful fantasy, and was it all wasted? He wanted to believe that it wasn't, but he did not really know and was finding it hard to convince himself that it was worth the pain. He wished that he could see some meaning in it all. He looked up at Ay, keenly observing him and asked, 'And what about you, sire? Are you satisfied with the consequences of your strategies?'

Ay suddenly looked defeated and turned his face away. The reaction was momentary only and was quickly replaced by a somewhat sardonic smile, but Tuthmosis had seen it. Nothing could take that instant away. His artist's eye had registered that moment of vulnerability and defeat and his heart rejoiced in it. He needed no overt answer to his question. Tuthmosis was beginning to feel more in command of himself in this strange interview. He knew that Ay could have him killed at any time, but he felt that the other man would not do this unless he deemed it absolutely necessary. He was not a brutal killer, he merely wanted to be in control.

Tuthmosis began to understand what Neferu had meant. This man's character was fascinating, without a doubt. He was undoubtedly decadent and enjoyed his powerful, wealthy lifestyle, but he was not a snob. He showed an interest in people which bordered on the scientific; he was an alchemist of the human psyche. Tuthmosis remembered in the past when he had been a frequent visitor to the home of Amio and Neferu. He had always been treated as an equal in the privacy of their home, although he had always been careful not to take advantage of his position. He was considered to be the best artist in the whole of the Two Lands, and he knew this to be true. He was not a man of false modesty. He remembered that Ay, who was very interested in art and had an appreciation of beauty, had never stood on ceremony. If he had felt uncomfortable at all, it was in the presence of Tiya, who had seemed to be a very reserved and undemonstrative woman. A very correct woman, always aware of her position, not unkind but certainly lacking in warmth. Ay, on the other hand, possessed the ability to put another person at his ease, even when the other person was an adversary. It was in strange contrast with his basic ruthlessness. In the long silence following his question, Tuthmosis and the other man looked at each other, each pursuing his own thoughts.

Beyond the strict public adherence to his position, Ay was inclined to cross the barriers of status in his social life because of his innate curiosity about the emotional workings of the men and women around him. Tuthmosis knew all this and that to Ay – he was just an artisan, a very skilled one, but an artisan, nevertheless. That being so, he knew that he was dispensable. The silence between them was becoming unusually long and Ay did not appear to be intent on breaking it. Tuthmosis wondered if it was a ploy to make him lose his nerve. If so, it had not worked. He continued to observe the grand vizier with interest. The old man seemed to have some difficulty with his breathing and his large barrel chest was out of proportion with the still slender limbs of the small, previously agile figure. In his old age, Ay's face clearly portrayed his foreign origins, with its markedly aquiline nose and the small goatee beard that was typical of the nomadic Semites but alien to the Egyptians, who were almost uniformly clean-shaven.

It almost appeared that Ay could read his thoughts for he suddenly began to discuss his origins. 'My father was a remarkable man,' he said pensively. 'He was sold as a bondsman to a minor river administrator by his own brothers. Some family, eh?' Ay gave a short rasping laugh which ended on a wheezy cough once more. When it had passed, he continued, 'He was just a youth, betrayed by his own brothers. He belonged to one of the nomadic clans of Semites who roam the countries east of our border. The tribe call themselves Israelites after my grandfather, whom I only met once or twice as a boy. My father's name was Joseph and when he arrived in Egypt, he could neither speak the language nor knew the customs. He was clever though. Yes, he was clever!'

Here Ay paused and tapped his forehead to emphasise his father's intellectual capabilities. 'He did his work well and ensured that his master's fortune grew but, like many men before him, he fell foul of the devious tricks of the master's wife. She tried to seduce him, but when he refused, she had him thrown into the prison at Zoan, near Goshen, on the border. She turned her husband against him in case he told her husband what she was like, you see.' Here, Tuthmosis perceived an analogy between the fate of Joseph and that of Nefertiti, but Ay did not appear to have noticed this irony.

'He was in prison for seven long years, for a crime which he had not committed. But, as I said, he was clever, and he made himself a model prisoner. The warders found him indispensable, and in the end, they gave him the run of the prison. They almost came to think of him as one of them. He probably would have been there for the rest of his life, except that fate intervened in a strange way. The Israelites come from a long line of religious people, originating in the area between the Tigris and Euphrates river called Chaldea. The city my family originated from was Ur. Chaldea at that time was a melting pot of cultures from the east, north and from the west. There were many religions and just as many gods. My ancestor Abraham belonged to a clan who only believed in one god. It was a religion that had come down to him from the ancient times before the great flood of the legends. His ancestor, Noah, was one of the few survivors of the great flood when many of the other peoples perished, and the clan has always continued to give thanks to their old god who saved them, wherever they have roamed or settled. They worshipped the old god from the ancient days, and they are great believers in him contacting them through dreams. They are a very intuitive people. They have to be! Their existence depends upon finding water and grazing for their sheep. They constantly have to read the sky to determine the weather. Unlike the Egyptians, they have few material possessions apart from their animals. They put their faith in their god, Yahweh, for their survival and well-being. Their god has no particular form, they have no possibilities of carrying around large statues of him, after all, but for them, he is ever present in the winds which pervade the universe.'

Tuthmosis gave a start. It seemed to him that the Aten and this Yahweh were very similar. Ay noticed the slight reaction of Tuthmosis to his words and interpreted correctly the cause of it. 'I see you are beginning to understand,' he said softly. After a moment, he continued, 'Father prayed constantly to his god while in prison. It was a very difficult situation for a nomad to be in. Until he had been brought to Egypt, he had never stayed in any one place for more than a few days, perhaps a decan at the most. Always moving around to fresh grazing. He felt like a bird with its wings clipped but eventually he learned to adjust to the situation. Finally, his opportunity came. Two servants of the pharaoh, Tuthmosis IV, were imprisoned for fraud. While they were there, they both had strange, symbolic dreams that my father was able to interpret for them correctly. One of them was executed but the other one was later released and went back to the palace to work. He had promised to speak to the pharaoh of my father, but with typical human ingratitude, he promptly forgot his promise until more than two years later, when the pharaoh himself was troubled by a recurrent dream that caused him deep anxiety but which no one could interpret. When he heard the pharaoh talking about his dream, the wine taster remembered my father, Joseph, and told the pharaoh about him. Tuthmosis sent for my father and asked him to interpret the dream, which my father did to the best of his ability. The dream denoted that there would be seven years of good harvests followed by seven years of bad harvests with consequent famine widespread throughout the Two Lands. He advised the pharaoh to make all provision to save all the extra grain during the good years in specially built silos, which would keep out the vermin. This would be available for bread then in the bad years. A very practical man, my father,' Ay mused. 'Just plain common sense really. Still, the pharaoh was so impressed that he did just that, when many other of the private landowners did nothing. When the famine came, they were made destitute by their barren land and my father advised the pharaoh to buy their land at the current reduced market value and rent it out to them later. Many of them had to sell just to get grain for bread and fodder for their animals. It made Tuthmosis enormously rich and powerful and he, in turn, raised my father to the nobility, and made him grand vizier, the second most important man in Egypt. Not unnaturally, there are still many members of the old nobility who lost land and status in this way who still resent us for it.'

Tuthmosis interjected here with a sudden insight into the story. 'I have heard about this, Ay. My own grandfather became destitute. We lost all our land. I still remember his bitterness and the hardship under which my father grew up because of that famine.'

Ay looked at him reflectively and nodded. 'It was not only the ordinary people,' he remarked. 'Even the priestly class became impoverished and was seriously weakened to the pharaoh's advantage. It is hardly surprising that they don't like us, is it?' The question was a rhetorical one and Tuthmosis did not answer. He was fascinated by this opening up of Ay and wondered what the grand vizier sought to achieve by telling him all this. Ay spoke pensively, 'During the famine, my father brought all his clan in Egypt and settled them in the Goshen area. They have prospered because father made special dispensation for them not to have to pay taxes, but they are not wholly secure there. The Egyptians associate us with the Hyksos, you see. Actually, they are nothing to do with us, though they were Semites of another clan. My father hoped there would be a gradual integration, but it has not happened.' The grand vizier leaned forward slightly and said softly, 'They still hate us.'

'But Nefertiti was not descended from the Hyksos,' said Tuthmosis. 'She was Keftiu and there have been Keftiu in Egypt for centuries, since the great flood.'

'She was different, and to be different is to be distrusted,' said Ay cynically.

'No,' said Tuthmosis. 'That depends upon the person. I cannot agree with you.' After a pause, he asked. 'Do you believe in this god of your forefathers?'

Ay looked startled and then laughed cynically. 'I believe in no god. I believe in wealth and power. I will be my own god!'

Tuthmosis was shaken by this blatant admission of ambition. 'You want to be pharaoh,' he said. 'And Neferu was your chance. She denied it to you. You still want to be pharaoh.' Tuthmosis half expected Ay to deny it, although he would not have believed such a denial.

Ay leaned forward and said with quiet menace, 'Yes. I wanted to be pharaoh and, in a way, I am. As Tutankhamun's advisor, it is I who controls the administration of this great country.'

'Tutankhamun is a man now, soon he will be a father. He will not allow you to dominate him for very much longer, Ay. He has his own ideas, and you are an old man now,' Tuthmosis said slowly.

'A dying lion can still bite,' Ay answered cryptically to this. Then Ay yawned and said, 'I think we have come to the end of our conversation. Can I ask you your plans? You know that you are very welcome to come back. The palace can always use a good artist.'

'I have not made any long-term plans as yet. There has not been time,' Tuthmosis lied.

'Well, think about it,' said Ay. 'Come, let's go to lunch with Tutankhamun and Ankhsenpaamun. They're expecting us.'

Ay led Tuthmosis out of the office across the block and down the steps close by the house of Pararameses. They walked along the covered corridor alongside the inner courtyard and through to the pharaoh's suite. Tuthmosis had not expected to be received into the pharaoh's private apartment but guessed that the grand vizier wanted his presence to go unnoticed, as far as possible, by the larger court circle.

In the main hallway, they were met by Tutankhamun's main mentor, Maya. Tuthmosis bowed to the official, who was well known to him from his occasional visits to Neferu at Malarma and from their earlier acquaintanceship at Akhetaten. The administrator smiled at him affably. Tuthmosis was not aware of whether Maya knew of Neferu's death as yet and he decided not to mention it in his greeting.

Maya led them to the royal apartment and went in to announce their arrival. Tut stood up as they entered and came informally to greet him. First of all, Tuthmosis made a deep bow of obeisance to the young pharaoh and then to his queen. Ankhsenpaamun was seated on a couch and appeared to be in the later stages of her pregnancy. Tut turned to Ay and said somewhat coldly, 'You may go, sire. I will send for you if I require your presence.' Tuthmosis felt inner surprise at this statement of the young pharaoh's increasing command of his own life and awareness of his station. Tutankhamun was indeed well on the way to assuming his royal authority.

For a moment, a flicker of opposition showed on Ay's face, but he suppressed it quickly and merely answered, 'As you wish, sire.'

When the grand vizier had left, Tut listened intently as the sound of his uncle's footsteps disappeared down the corridor and then he dropped his formality and advanced towards Tuthmosis and put his arms around him in an affectionate hug. Tuthmosis, still holding his bag, tried to do likewise. He was moved by the spontaneity and affection of Tut. The young queen stood up and also came forward, her back ramrod straight as she walked with the stance of the woman who is heavily pregnant. Tuthmosis watched her, noticing what an equal blend she was of both her father and her mother. He embraced her in turn.

Recalling Nefertiti, Tuthmosis was reminded of her possessions, which he carried in his bag, and he relinquished the bag into the hands of Tut. 'The sketches are a present from me, and the rest of the things are to you both from Neferu. Tut lifted out the bundle of papyrus and the bust of Amio, which was very heavy. He set it carefully on the table and looked at it gravely. The jewel box he handed to his wife and while she was examining its contents, he unrolled the sheaves of papyrus and with an expression of pleasure, he began to study the sketches of his adoptive mother. From his pocket, Tuthmosis took the smaller death mask of Neferu and showed it to Tut. The boy looked at him.

'May I have it?' he asked.

Tuthmosis nodded. 'I would like to make a copy of it first, if I may,' he replied.

'Of course,' the young pharaoh replied.

Tutankhamun touched the uneven right cheek. 'It could just be a mistake in the pottery,' he murmured. 'No one need ever know that it was leprosy,' he said wistfully. Looking up at Tuthmosis, he said, 'No one need ever know if we do not tell them.'

Tuthmosis agreed. The young queen had shrunk back involuntarily when the word leprosy was mentioned. Tuthmosis noticed it and said to her gently, 'Your mother was a very beautiful woman and she died before the disease had time to disfigure her. Do not pity her; she died deeply loved and the immediate cause of her death was a high and continued fever whose cause the physician was unable to ascertain.' The young queen appeared reassured and nodded.

Tutankhamun picked up one of the sketches. 'It seems almost alive,' he said of the drawing. 'You have a very special talent, Tuthmosis.'

Tuthmosis smiled. 'I loved her,' he said simply.

'I know,' answered Tut, smiling at him.

Tuthmosis hesitated and then deciding that frankness was the best policy, said. 'I fear I may have put you at risk by informing you of her condition. I had no desire to imperil you. I merely thought you would want to see her before she died.'

'Don't regret it,' answered Tut sharply. 'Nothing could have kept me away. I only wish that you had informed me earlier.'

'She forbade it,' Tuthmosis informed him. 'And when the fever first began, I had hopes that she would overcome it,' he continued flatly.

'Where is she now?' asked Tut in a measured tone.

Once more, Tuthmosis explained what he had done and why he had done it. He saw that the young man was shocked and upset, but he nodded understandingly.

'If that was what Neferu wanted then it was right to do as she wished,' was his comment. He looked at Tuthmosis and seemed to become aware of the other man's visible exhaustion. 'Forgive me,' he said suddenly. 'Shall we lunch now? We can discuss further tomorrow. Has Rameses arranged your room?' Tuthmosis nodded gratefully. He was both hungry and tired and, although he had developed his own strategy of action, it did not require to be carried out immediately. Tut took his arm by the elbow and guided him to the dining room, which Tuthmosis could see from his present position. Ay and Maya joined them for lunch and the conversation proceeded upon more formal and general lines.

CHAPTER 35

Over lunch, Tutankhamun asked Tuthmosis to stay and work for him. He told him that he would be very comfortably housed in a home of his own. Tuthmosis thanked him for his kindness and said that his first duty was to proceed to On, where he would meet with Neferu's brother and give Demi the details of Neferu's final moments and give him the articles she had bequeathed to him. He told Tut that after that he would return. He did not wish to divulge his real plans. The young pharaoh commissioned two busts, one of himself and one of his queen, Ankhsenpaamun. That same afternoon, after a brief rest, Tuthmosis made moulds of the faces of both his subjects.

Tuthmosis observed the face of Tut carefully. Four years previously it had still been a child's face, now it was the face of a handsome youth. In many ways Tut resembled his mother, Tiya. He had her full lips and cheeks and the same unusually shaped skull as Amio and Ay. He was definitely Tiya's son all right, he thought. Tuthmosis mused about the way things had turned out. It was obvious that the boy had strength of character, that was plain. His visit to the poor district to see Neferu had proved that. He sighed as he looked at the young man now; already in his short life he had experienced the death of several of the people most close to him. He thought it must inevitably leave its mark upon the youth. Tut and Ankhsenpaamun appeared to have a close and loving relationship, they must have been each other's support during the hard times. The girl seemed to be more lacking in spirit than the young pharaoh. She seemed reserved and timid. Poor soul, she must have been afraid when the end came at Akhetaten. Tuthmosis wondered where the other children were. Neffie was the same age as Tut, fifteen, and even Satenpare must be thirteen now.

Tuthmosis asked about the two younger girls of Neferu, and Tutankhamun smiled. 'I will send for them,' he said and rang a bell. The manservant who entered was requested to bring the two princesses. When he returned with them, ten minutes later, Tuthmosis jumped to his feet and stood immobile. Neffie, the taller of the two girls, was the image of Neferu. Looking at her, Tuthmosis knew what Neferu must have looked like at that age. The likeness was uncanny, and he felt mesmerised. The same face and the same name. The younger girl, Satenpare, was a blend of both her father and mother. She had the same rather exotic looks that the two oldest girls had had. The younger girl could not remember Tuthmosis very well and seemed very shy of him. Nefer-Neferu-Aten junior, however, came forward confidently.

'It has been a long time, Tuthmosis,' she said with a smile. 'I remember you well.'

Tuthmosis suddenly found himself wishing that this girl would have an easier life than her mother had had. 'You look so much like your mother, Neffie,' he said quietly.

The girl's face lost its smile. 'I am not allowed to discuss my mother or to use the name "Aten" anymore,' she said uncomfortably. 'Now, they call me Nefer-Neferu-Amun.'

Tuthmosis smiled. 'They can change a name, but not the soul of a person. To me, you will always be the daughter of a great and beautiful queen.'

'I have seen the drawings you have made of mother and Tut has promised that I can have one for my own,' she replied.

Tuthmosis bowed. 'It is my pleasure,' he answered.

Tuthmosis was pleased to have this opportunity to speak with Neferu's little family. He spared them the sadder parts of Neferu's illness and told them instead of how the poor people had brought gifts of fruit and flowers to the house by way of thanks when their mother had been to help in some crisis or other. He wanted them to be proud of her.

At the evening meal, Ay proved to be a genial host and, in spite of their differences, he seemed drawn to Tuthmosis. The artist sensed that for all his machinations and love of power, the grand vizier was lonely. For him, all the best years were gone and the struggle to maintain his grip on power was becoming increasingly difficult. From the acute remarks that Pararameses had allowed to escape, it seemed that it was really Horemheb who now controlled everything, and Ay was more and more the puppet while the puppeteer waited his turn in the background. Remembering the suspicious deaths of Meretaten and Smenkhenre, Tuthmosis could not help feeling a frisson of fear for Tut and his young queen. The fact that Ankhsenpaamun was pregnant must be a bit problem for the ruthless Horemheb. Tuthmosis wondered how Horemheb would fix the legal position so that his accession was linked at least tenuously to the laws of succession. He guessed that it might involve marrying Neffie or Satenpare. If that was so, then Neffie's little love affair with Tut's best friend, Huy, was going to have to be sacrificed. In view of the fact that the great majority of the population had never seen Nefertiti in person, it was quite possible for Horemheb to pass her off as Neferu. Perhaps that was the reason that Ay had informed Tut that his second cousin was too young to marry. The more he thought about it the more probable it all seemed to be. After all, no one knew that Neferu was dead, except this little circle here.

Tuthmosis' meditations upset him so much that he told them to Pararameses, who was outraged. 'That would be a diabolical plan,' he said with horror. 'However, if you are capable of conceiving it, how much more so Ay and Horemheb,' he continued cynically.

Tuthmosis added, 'No one could dispute his right to the throne if her real identity was blended into that of her mother. With the approval of the high priests, who else would dare to protest? Certainly no one at court.'

'Horemheb has come to dislike the Atenists and would willingly use their presence to inflame the situation with the priests of Amun, but I don't believe he would go so far as to murder Tutankhamun, and the boy seems to be in excellent health, so he is not otherwise liable to die,' Pararameses remarked shrewdly.

'I wonder!' said Tuthmosis. 'It's what Neferu feared most.'

Pararameses shook his head. 'Even the priests would not sanction such a blatantly criminal act … unless …' His voice trailed off.

'Unless Tut made a play to revive Atenism,' Tuthmosis finished for him.

'It is possible,' admitted Pararameses, 'but not probable. This is just malicious speculation, Tuthmosis. Horemheb is ambitious and would love to be pharaoh, but I don't think he would go to the lengths which you are suggesting. He is not a bad fellow,' he said with a slight smile.

'I wonder,' Tuthmosis said. They chatted for a while longer before rising to retire. It had been a very long day for Tuthmosis, and he was very satisfied that it had resulted in Maatnofret being so comfortably settled. He was free to continue his journey northwards now without having to worry about the old lady.

That night in bed, Tuthmosis came to grips with the half-formulated ideas that his mind had been mulling over for several days. The more he wrestled with his doubts and fears, the more certain he became that Neferu had been right, and Tutankhamun was in grave danger. For the moment perhaps, Ay had the situation more or less under control, but it was clear that he was losing his grip and he was an old man himself. There was no saying that he would not die suddenly and then the young pharaoh would be entirely at the mercy of Horemheb and the priests of Amun.

Tuthmosis did not share Pararameses complacency towards the issue of Horemheb and the extent to which he was capable of going in order to gain supreme power. Out of the vague and nebulous notions that crossed his mind, that of vengeance, for past and possible future crimes, fitfully invaded his consciousness. What if Horemheb were to be removed from power? How could he successfully accomplish such a strategy? If he killed Horemheb, the threat to Tut would be effectively removed. The priests of Amun would not dare to usurp the throne and if they tried, he was certain that Pararameses and the army would oppose the coup. Just before he slept, he thought of Neferu and knew that in spite of her bitterness towards the plotters, she would not sanction such a course of action.

When Tuthmosis woke up the following morning, it took him several seconds to realise where he was. He turned his head from left to right, not recognising the room at first. Gradually awareness sank in, and he began to ponder over the events of the previous forty-eight hours. He felt refreshed after the long dreamless sleep and was without that deep sense of melancholia that had haunted him the previous day. He reflected on his life. He was forty-one and his life seemed to have been a constant journey between summit and trough and back again. For years he had had the sense of being carried along on the tide of circumstance, unable to initiate any important moves himself. Now, since the death of Neferu, he had lost that sense of his own impotence in the face of events and an awareness of a sense of drama was beginning to develop in him. He smiled slightly at himself, quite enjoying it. The drama which would soon unfold would be his, in that he would be responsible for some of the action, even if it were to lead to his own death. Although a distinct premonition told him that such a course of action as he envisaged would cost him his life, he had not the slightest fear or dread of it. A man who has nothing left to lose can afford to be reckless, he thought.

As he rose, Tuthmosis noticed from the angle of shadow on the floor that the sun was already high in the sky. He was struck by surprise that he had been left to sleep for so long. Meditating on the coming day, he made his way to the bathroom. As he washed himself, he had a definite feeling that time was standing still, or that he had suddenly slipped out of his own time. It was most odd but not an unpleasant feeling. He dressed leisurely and when the servant appeared, he asked the man to ensure that his dirty clothes would be laundered ready for him to leave the following morning, soon after sunrise. The servant dutifully took the dirty clothes away and returned a little later to say that the grand vizier requested the pleasure of his company for breakfast. Tuthmosis felt his time warp come to a sudden end. 'So the drama begins,' he thought.

Over breakfast, Tuthmosis informed Ay that he wished to depart for On the following morning, to carry out the commission entrusted to him by Neferu. Ay was very affable and even asked him if he would deliver some messages for him to Horemheb at Memphis. They were not very important, he revealed, and it would save sending a messenger. Tuthmosis' heart jumped. It was the very opportunity he had been seeking and it had happened in such a casual fashion that he could hardly believe his luck. He acquiesced immediately and Ay said he would arrange a suitable berth for his departure on an early morning boat to Memphis. Tuthmosis thanked him with a slight bow of his head.

After breakfast, Tuthmosis decided he had better set about his work on the death mask of Neferu. He made his way to the studios of the court sculptors and stood watching for a while the master sculptor of the court as he taught his assistants the finer techniques of dimension and perception. It was all so familiar to him. He had learned his craft in these very studios so many years before. Tuthmosis acquainted himself with the master and spent a while in professional chat before setting to work making a copy of the mask. While the copy was in the kiln, he and the master discussed variation in style and form over a simple lunch. It was an enjoyable interlude, bringing back memories of his own apprenticeship.

In the afternoon Tuthmosis rested and then took refreshments with the young pharaoh, presenting him with the original death mask of Neferu. It was a moving moment and somehow fitting that they should say goodbye on that note. Tut expected to see the artist again within the decan, but Tuthmosis knew that once he had carried out his plans, he would never be able to return to Thebes again. He comforted himself by reminding himself that what he was to do would ensure a long and safe life for this youth whom Neferu had loved so much. On leaving Tut, Tuthmosis went to visit Maatnofret. Teya invited him in and escorted him to see the old lady-in-waiting herself. He had to acknowledge to himself that Ay's wife was a remarkably nice old lady. He took into account that Teya and Maatnofret had known each other since girlhood.

Maatnofret received him with pleasure in her comfortable sitting room. She told him that she was being treated very kindly and was now pleased not to be returning to Akhetaten. Here she would be able to see the girls and Tut regularly once more. She was most taken by Neffie's resemblance to her mother, and it seemed to have helped to assuage her grief. Already she had lost that look of hopeless despair that had so unnerved him. Maatnofret was anxious to know if Tuthmosis resented her staying, and was delighted when he confirmed that, from the bottom of his heart, he was happy that the Aten had seen fit to make her last days comfortable and happy with her loved ones. Maatnofret hugged him like her own son before he left and told him that he would always be in her thoughts. They each requested the Aten's blessing for the other one and said an emotional goodbye.

That evening, after sundown, by the light of the oil lamps in his room, Tuthmosis sorted out his luggage. He rolled up his remaining sketches of Neferu, some of which he would give to Demi, and then checked the earrings and necklace that was meant for Yussef, now deputy to Horemheb. Scoundrel, thought Tuthmosis, how could he have behaved so badly towards Neferu? Wrapped up in a linen garment, he placed the death mask copy on the top. He intended to keep that for himself. Dinner with the entourage that evening passed off in an informal manner and, pleading excessive fatigue, he begged leave early to retire. Tut granted his request with charm and informality and Tuthmosis left the court to itself for the last time.

In the morning, he breakfasted with Pararameses, who led him to Ay and the young pharaoh for a brief farewell. Their goodbyes over, Tuthmosis left them, reflecting that perhaps it was a good thing that Horemheb were not here in Thebes. He might have felt impassioned enough to kill him here and now. He intended to do that, but he would leave that until last. There was something else he had to do before that.

Pararameses came to bid him farewell. Although he was a hard soldier, lacking in warmth on the surface at least, Tuthmosis thought, there was a kindness in him. He was a down to earth, prosaic man, firm and strict, but not a cruel man. He was no schemer or intriguer like Ay or Horemheb, in spite of his ambition. He had been Amio's boyhood friend, and he had known and liked Neferu and always treated her well in her disgrace, to the detriment of his own personal popularity with the power groups. He had remained their loyal friend as best he could, while endeavouring to protect his own interests too in a situation where his advice had been ignored and he had thought their plans folly. In such a situation, his loyalty was all the more admirable, Tuthmosis thought. Now, once again, this seemingly indifferent man showed his better nature. He gave Tuthmosis a safe pass in his name to move about Memphis freely. Tuthmosis thanked him. He would have like to have forewarned Pararameses of his plans, but he dared not. He and Horemheb were, after all, working together.

The journey downriver would have been very pleasant on any other occasion. It was the first time that he had sailed past Akhetaten for four years and a lump came to his throat as the eastern mountains came into view. Even when they had sailed out of view of that once splendid city, which just a few short years ago had contained all his dreams, he found that he still had tears in his eyes. For Neferu and for himself, the dreams had ended there. The love which had been born again between them was the only thing that had given them both the strength to live on. Now that she was gone, he felt that there would be no more happiness or emotional security left for him in the world.

It was another two days before Memphis came into sight. When the boat docked at the riverside, Tuthmosis watched as the vast majority of the passengers disembarked. From his vantage point on the deck, he looked around at the city in his range of vision and re-acquainted himself with the layout of it. He would need to move quickly when he returned. Once the boat set sail again, this time for On, he felt a rising impatience in himself and had difficulty in suppressing the sense of excitement. He was swept along by the strangest feeling that it was all meant to be and that his reason for existence was about to uncover itself in the drama which he meant to cause to unfold.

Tuthmosis alighted with pleasure when the boat docked at On and as soon as he put foot to dry land, he set off to look for a tavern to stay for the night. There were several such establishments in the dockside area, and he chose the most respectable looking one. Inside he paid his lodging in advance and went to inspect his room. Having satisfied himself that the room fulfilled his wants, he left to obtain the information he needed. An obliging fruit and vegetable seller pointed him in the direction of the centre of the city and he looked around himself with interest as he walked. It seemed a busy and pleasant town and he walked until he found the souk. From one of the wealthier looking shops, he received directions to the Stassopoulos villa. The name was evidently well known, and he found the home of Neferu's brother without any difficulty. The servant who answered the call was very suspicious but said that his master was home that day and asked him to wait.

The servant soon returned and escorted Tuthmosis into Demi's study. The two men faced each other across the room. They had not met for more than five years. Demi spoke first. 'Welcome to On, Tuthmosis.'

Tuthmosis inclined his head. 'I do not bring good news, Demi.'

Demi sighed and moved forwards to greet Tuthmosis. 'Neferu is dead?' he asked.

'Yes. Six days ago,' he answered, watching the other man's face.

Demi sat down heavily and motioned Tuthmosis to sit down too. 'In a way it is a relief,' he said. 'I have worried about her day and night for so long. Now at least, she is safe from all harm.'

Tuthmosis nodded. He too had had similar sentiments. 'I brought you these,' he said, handing the bag to Demi. Demi opened it and, one by one, took out the small personal objects that had belonged to his sister. His mouth began to work but he managed to control his expression. Finally, he took out the roll of papyrus comprising Tuthmosis' sketches of Neferu. Separating the sheets, he examined them individually, occasionally smiling at some secret personal recollection of times past.

'You have caught Neferu's spirit in these drawings, Tuthmosis. I can see my sister as if she were here in front of me.' Demi looked up at the artist sitting by him. 'Tell me,' he said simply. 'How has it been?' Tuthmosis told Demi everything he wanted to know. When he had finished Demi said, 'I suppose that, in spite of everything, I ought to tell Yussef.' His voice was immensely sad.

'Do you want me to tell him?' Tuthmosis asked. 'Neferu commissioned me to give him some jewellery which she has bequeathed to him.'

'I think perhaps I will do it myself, Tuthmosis,' Demi replied.

'Nevertheless, I would like to accompany you, if I may,' Tuthmosis answered.

Demi shrugged. 'I don't see that it will do any harm if you wish to come with me.' Demi was somewhat mystified at Tuthmosis insistence. 'I will inform my wife of our errand and we can go immediately after you have eaten and rested,' Demi continued.

'I would prefer that, as I have promised the pharaoh that I will return to Thebes within the decan,' Tuthmosis replied.

Demi nodded. 'Of course. I understand. You will stay the night though.'

'Thank you. It may be a good idea.' Tuthmosis smiled his thanks. Demi sent a messenger requesting an audience with the deputy governor in advance for the evening of the following day.

The next morning, Demi and Tuthmosis set sail by one of the small express boats for Memphis. They completed the last part of their journey by fast chariot late the following evening. It was a more than slightly drunken Yussef who received them.

'To what do I owe the honour of this rare visit, my dear cousin?' he asked Demi cynically.

Demi bowed his head stiffly. 'I have come with Tuthmosis to inform you that Neferu is dead, that is my only motive,' he replied. Tuthmosis watched the face of the Keftiu general and noted the very sobering effect Demi's words had upon him. He became quite pale.

'Neferu dead? When?' he asked.

'Six days ago. Tuthmosis arrived yesterday. He was with Neferu when she died peacefully in her sleep.' The blurred eyes swivelled round to look Tuthmosis squarely in the face.

Tuthmosis stepped forward. 'I have something from her to give to you.'

Yussef's eyes focused on him silently for a while as if still shocked by the news, then he seemed to relapse into his former mood. 'Well, Neferu was a stubborn woman. What do I care if she has gone? She never cared about me.'

Demi pulled himself angrily upright. 'I have not come here to listen to insults about my sister. Goodbye, Yussef. I do not feel we will ever have cause to meet again. I wish you peace.' Yussef stepped forward and began to remonstrate but Demi turned haughtily and left, as quickly as his limping leg would allow. As he passed Tuthmosis, he gave the other man an inquiring look as if to say 'Are you coming too?' but Tuthmosis shook his head ever so slightly. Yussef looked at him curiously and when Demi had gone, he sat down and indicated that Tuthmosis should also sit.

'Tell me about her,' he said coldly.

'I thought you weren't interested,' replied Tuthmosis just as icily.

'Oh, I always found Neferu interesting, didn't you?' Yussef had resumed his sarcastic tone. Tuthmosis put down the small curved, wooden box containing the gold and lapis lazuli jewellery onto Yussef's desk.

'What is this?' The Keftiu asked curiously, picking it up and opening it. He stared at the contents for a long time without saying anything. Finally, he snapped the box shut and put it back on the desk.

'What did Neferu die of?' he asked in a toneless voice.

'Leprosy and a fever,' Tuthmosis answered in a voice as expressionless as he could assume.

'Leprosy?' There was horror in Yussef's voice. After a pause. 'So she lost her beauty in the end then?' There was a note of satisfaction almost, in his voice. Tuthmosis noted it and took pleasure in taking his papyrus sketches out of his bag. He lay them on the desk.

'No. Neferu did not lose her beauty. She died before the disease could destroy it. I drew that one a few hours before her death,' he said sharply, indicating one of the sketches on the table. Yussef looked up at him for a moment before picking up the papyrus and opening it out. He stared down at the smiling face of Neferu as she had looked at Tuthmosis with love in her eyes, that last evening they had had together. She was thinner but otherwise exactly as Yussef remembered her. Tuthmosis saw his face soften, but then his lips tightened, and he threw the picture down onto the desk again.

'I feel nothing for her. She betrayed me and I don't want to see her or her picture ever again.' He stood up and came to stand in front of Tuthmosis. 'She got her punishment in the end. She could have rejected that deformed fanatic she married, she could have saved herself after his death by turning to Amun, she could have married Ay and been living in luxury at Malkata. Her own intransigence was her downfall.'

The impulse of fury that suffused Tuthmosis was such that his carefully thought-out plans were overturned, and he was seized by the impulse of the moment. He drew out his small artist's knife and plunged it directly into the heart of the man in front of him. Yussef's face took on an incongruous expression of amazement as his arm went up to his chest. Tuthmosis watched him with a cool objectivity as he began to gasp for breath. 'You have outlived your usefulness,' he said softly to the dying man. Yussef slumped forwards onto the floor and lay there in an unnatural position. After a minute or so, the body stopped its heaving, and a large red stain began to spread over the rug. Tuthmosis picked up his sketches of Neferu methodically and, with no precautions for his own safety, he walked unhurriedly from the room, out of the house and onto the street.

Once in the street, he began to walk briskly in the direction of the river. All the time, he expected to hear a hue and cry of pursuit to follow him but there was nothing. Down at the dock, he was fortunate to obtain a passage on a boat that was due to leave upriver immediately, and he paid his passage and went on board. He knew it could not be long before the militia were after him, but he felt surprisingly calm. He had the feeling that it was all predestined and therefore there was nothing he could do but to wait for whatever destiny had decided. For the first time in his life, he understood the total and implicit faith that had motivated Neferu. He felt no fear as he stood on the deck and watched serenely the onset of twilight when it came. The setting of the huge red disc of the sun over the horizon appeared as an omen that it would soon be the end of his story too.

The evening air was cold, and he shivered slightly. He moved towards the canopied part of the deck and joined the other passengers, who were huddled together for warmth. Tuthmosis sat next to an old man, who, it appeared, was travelling to Hermopolis. He had been visiting his son's family in On. The old man asked Tuthmosis where he came from and Tuthmosis told him that he had been born in Thebes and had also been visiting On to see friends. He felt it was not a complete lie, as he considered Demi as a kind of friend by proxy as Neferu's brother.

Throughout the evening, the garrulous old man chatted, glad to have an attentive listener. Eventually his chatter ceased, and he pulled his rug around him more closely. He noticed that Tuthmosis had no rug and kindly, if slightly reluctantly, offered to share it with him. Tuthmosis accepted with gratitude. After a while there was the sound of soft snoring and Tuthmosis smiled a little in the dark. He leaned back against the cedarwood benches and let his thoughts drift back to Neferu and the relationship they had shared. It had been a strange, stormy relationship, with periods of ecstatic happiness and periods of intense misery for him. Tonight though, he felt that he would have done the same all over again, even if he had known how it would end. He had loved and lost and found and loved again but it had been worth all the pain. He felt tired and closed his eyes.

When Tuthmosis woke up, he felt very cold and stiff. It was the damp, gloomy grey light of the birth of morning before the dawn proper. Slowly he began to collect his thoughts together and remembered the events of the previous day. He became aware that he was hungry but knew that the boat would not dock in Dahla for another hour or so. The old man woke up and complained bitterly of the cold. He took out of his bag some pitta and some olives and began to munch. After a couple of bites, he offered Tuthmosis some and they ate companiably, watching the sun rise over the horizon bringing with it warmth and light.

As the boat docked at Dahla, Tuthmosis looked around for a search party but there seemed to be nothing unusual, just a few people waiting for the boat to dock. Tuthmosis disembarked for a while to buy some provisions and a warm blanket for the following evening. He returned to the ship with his purchases. Tuthmosis sought out the old man who had been his companion of the previous evening and went to sit beside him. They began to chat. Tuthmosis was curious to ask the old man about Akhetaten as he lived so close to the ghost city, but he dared not. Times had changed and he did not want to bring suspicion upon himself. He still had something to do. He knew that Tutankhamun was safe as long as Ay was alive. The grand vizier was ruthless and power hungry, but he was attached to his nephew and Tut was also his only claim to power. Horemheb, on the other hand, would have no such scruples. Tuthmosis wished that he had not lost his temper the day before. It would have been better to deal with Horemheb first. What he had done would only make his real aim so much harder to achieve. It would be difficult now to remain undetected long enough to plan his revenge. He realised that he must formulate his plans better if he were to survive long enough.

The old man began to chat again and Tuthmosis listened willingly. He asked

Tuthmosis if he had ever visited Hermopolis and seemed pleased when Tuthmosis replied that he had been there many times.

'Ah!' the old man said. 'Was it in the old days of Akhenaten and Nefertiti?'

He looked round as he spoke. 'Yes,' answered Tuthmosis in a non-committal voice.

The old man looked at him craftily. 'Were you an Atenist?' he asked it softly, so as not to be overheard. Tuthmosis hesitated before replying, but he knew he could not deny his principles. He could have made some kind of evasive reply, but he chose to answer openly.

'I still am!' he said, proudly but quietly.

The old man chuckled and leaned forward, saying in an undertone, 'So am I.' Tuthmosis smiled. The old man was also a survivor. The old man looked at him afresh and more searchingly than before. 'I know you,' he said at last. 'You're the sculptor Tuthmosis! I bought several small statues from your studio.'

Tuthmosis nodded, pleased in spite of himself, to be recognised. 'How did you get away when the soldiers came?' he asked the old man.

'Easy,' the old man replied with a grin. 'My eldest daughter lives in Hermopolis with her husband, who owns a goldsmithy. When my wife died, I moved to Hermopolis to live with them. It was just a decan before the pharaoh died. I had sold my house and already moved my belongings out. The Aten was on my side, you see!' Tuthmosis wondered at the mysterious workings of life. How strange that the old man should have been so fortuitously spared the harrowing experience of the sacking of Akhetaten. He nodded at the old man, who said confidentially. 'They say that Nefertiti now lives in Thebes and has forsaken the Aten.'

Tuthmosis shook his head vigorously to rebuff the accusation. 'It isn't true! Nefertiti's daughter lives at the palace but the queen would not deny the Aten and was banished from the court. She is now dead,' he said savagely.

The old man was taken aback. 'Dead? When did she die?' he said, shaking his head with regret.

'She died six days ago in exile. I know because I was with her when she died.' Tuthmosis put his hand inside his pocket and withdrew the papyrus sketch that he had lost. Silently he smoothed it open and handed it to the old man, who took it with an inquiring look.

The old man looked at it carefully. 'It's the queen all right,' he said slowly. 'She looks older, and her face is thinner, but it is Nefertiti. I know because I have seen her many times in the temple.' He carefully rolled the papyrus up and made as if to hand it back to Tuthmosis.

Tuthmosis asked him. 'Did you like Nefertiti?'

The old man sighed before speaking. 'I remember a long time ago, soon after the old pharaoh died, and his son moved to the new city. The pharaoh became ill, dangerously ill. Everyone thought he would die.'

Tuthmosis nodded. 'I remember that,' he said.

The old man looked at him keenly. 'Well, I went to the temple to pray that day when the queen asked all citizens to pray for the life of the pharaoh. Do you remember that?'

'Yes. I remember it well,' said Tuthmosis. 'It was very moving.'

'Yes,' replied the old man. 'But most of all, I remember the way she spoke to that old man who wanted to offer his life up to the Aten, in exchange for the life of the pharaoh. She didn't accept his offer, although she was so afraid of losing the husband she loved. I thought then that underneath all the pomp and circumstance, she must be a nice person.'

Tuthmosis nodded again and let go of the papyrus. 'Keep this in memory of her,' he told the old man.

'Don't you want it?' The old man asked, surprised.

Tuthmosis smiled. 'I don't need it. I have made so many drawings and sculptures of the queen that I could make another one from memory,' he answered. The old man smiled and thanked him for the gift, promising to keep it safe. He told Tuthmosis that he was honoured to have an original work from the famous artist and such a talented one.

During the afternoon, most of the passengers slept. It was very hot and Tuthmosis was glad when the boat docked at one of the small villages along the riverbank. He disembarked to walk up and down for a while and to get himself a drink of the barley beer that a dockside vendor was selling. One other person disembarked and went on his way, having reached his destination and a couple of well-to-do looking men boarded the boat. After a while, Tuthmosis boarded once again.

The old man had woken from his afternoon siesta, and he greeted Tuthmosis like a long-time acquaintance when the younger man returned to his seat. The two new passengers were seated close by. They obviously knew each other well and from their speech it became clear that they were local officials on their way to Thebes. Tuthmosis' ear suddenly pricked up when he heard one of them mention Yussef. 'Bad business that! I wonder if they'll ever get him now? Well over the border by now, if you ask me.' One of them said and the other replied.

'Stabbed in his own home, and him the deputy of Horemheb. Whatever next!'

'Maybe he didn't leave Egypt. He could be in Thebes, gone on one of the river boats.'

The first one said. The other one sounded disbelieving. 'Why would he do that? It seems to me that there is no way he could escape detection in Thebes.'

'He's apparently well known at court,' The second one replied.

'Must be mad if you ask me!' the first one continued. 'Why did he do it, I wonder?'

The other one shrugged. 'Who knows! I expect that there is a lot going on at court that we never hear about. Best to keep out of it.'

The two men lapsed into silence and after a while they nodded off. Tuthmosis was now wide awake, and his brain was clicking over in a very alert fashion as he pondered his possibilities. If these two minor officials had already heard about the death of Yussef, then it was possible that one of the larger and faster riverboats was well on its way to Thebes by now. He would be arrested for sure if he should be foolish enough to return there. He felt angry with himself for allowing Yussef's malice to goad him into spoiling his strategy. What was he going to do? Tuthmosis became aware that the old man was talking to him again and shifted his attention onto his words.

'I went back there once, you know,' he said conspiratorially.

'Where?' asked Tuthmosis, not registering the meaning of the old man's speech.

The old man leaned over and whispered, 'Akhetaten, of course!'

'Really?' remarked Tuthmosis. 'Is there anything left?'

The old man shrugged. 'It was last year in the cool season. I went with my son-in-law just out of interest. There are most of the buildings still standing, but empty, of course. It was almost deserted. Just a few lepers there. We didn't go too near,' he said.

'Who were the lepers and where did they come from?' Tuthmosis asked curiously.

The old man shrugged again. 'I don't know. I expect that they were some of those who fled into the desert when the army came to destroy the temple and kill the priests. Weren't you there then?' he asked.

Tuthmosis shook his head. 'No. A few days after the death of the pharaoh, Ay, the grand vizier, and his entourage came. They pressured Nefertiti and the children into going back to Thebes. She didn't want to go but she felt she had to do as they wished. When they left, I was working in Memphis.'

'It was probably just as well,' the old man answered. 'After the queen left so did most of the officials. Some stayed on but just a few months afterwards there was an outbreak of the leprosy and many other people left then too. They said it was the curse of Amun on the city. Didn't believe it myself!' he said cynically. 'After all, every city has its lepers, doesn't it?' Tuthmosis had to agree. The old man shook his head and then continued, 'Anyway, about two years ago, a company of soldiers came on the orders of general Horemheb, they say. They forced everyone left to renounce the Aten or be banished. Some were killed, most fled and some renounced the Aten. I was already in Hermopolis, so I was saved. Still, the body of my good wife is still buried there and sometimes I go there to put flowers on her grave. I always feel sad when I come back so I don't go very often.'

Tuthmosis nodded. He could understand that. A thought crossed his mind. 'How many people remain in Akhetaten?' he asked.

The old man thought for a moment. 'Oh, I don't know,' he said musingly. 'Maybe a couple of hundred, maybe more, maybe less. Some returned after fleeing from the soldiers. They couldn't cope with the trek across the desert, or they were old and didn't want to settle elsewhere. Then there are the lepers. It's a ghost city really. Why do you ask?' he asked curiously.

'Well, I was thinking that perhaps I would disembark with you tomorrow and go and take a look myself,' Tuthmosis said slowly, giving the man the impression that it was more or less a spur of the moment decision.

'I think you'd find it a waste of time,' the old man commented. 'And morbid somehow. They say that even the grave robbers are afraid to go there. The pharaoh chose himself a lonely tomb, up there in the wadi. I wonder what his spirit thought of all the goings on there have been? His splendid city a ghost town of lepers and exiles. Perhaps one day he will take his revenge?' he continued fancifully. 'Life is strange. I've seen some changes in my lifetime, I can tell you!'

They were both quiet for a while and then the old man began to tell Tuthmosis about his grandson and the wild goings on of the youth of nowadays. Drinking too much and visiting the houses of pleasure too frequently. Tuthmosis smiled, reassured to hear that the vast stream of mankind was continuing to survive out there in the great backdrop of Egypt.

The following morning, the boat docked at Hermopolis and Tuthmosis and the old man, along with a few other passengers, alighted at the busy port. The old man apologised for not being able to invite Tuthmosis to stay with them. He seemed reluctant to say goodbye. The pair of them went to find a donkey for Tuthmosis to buy at a suitable price and the old man gave him much advice as to the characteristics to look for in the animal. When they eventually found a suitable beast in the animal market, Tuthmosis paid for it in gold. The price was more than he had anticipated, even after stiff bargaining, but he was left with enough to buy his provisions and the other requisites he needed, such as his precious papyrus, which might no longer be available in Akhetaten if it were almost deserted and derelict.

The two travelling companions parted amicably and said warm goodbyes. The old man told Tuthmosis that he would be sure to treasure the drawing of Nefertiti that he had been given and he imparted his address to Tuthmosis in the case of the sculptor needing assistance. Tuthmosis thanked him and they left in different directions. Tuthmosis brought sufficient provisions to last him for several days and then set off with the donkey back down to the riverbank to find a ferryman. The ferryman whom he approached seemed surprised that he wished to be ferried across to Akhetaten. He knew the few Atenists who came over for provisions and he did not recognise this one. He was not a curious type, however, and took the proffered payment. There was a difficult moment in trying to get the donkey on board the boat but eventually they managed to accomplish it and they moved away from the back.

Once on the other side, Tuthmosis adjusted the provisions more equally onto the donkey and then set off, walking beside it. It was already hot, but the journey was not far. He could see the white- washed walls in the distance and it still gave him the feeling that he was going home. It was a journey he had first made nineteen years previously and it now seemed a lifetime back. He wondered what to expect when he arrived, but he was struck by the air of desolation about the place as he got nearer. It was not until he reached the outskirts of the town that he realised that his advance had been observed.

A bowman stepped out of the shadows of a building with his arrow placed and aimed at Tuthmosis. There was a distance of about thirty metres between them and Tuthmosis stopped in his tracks. 'Who are you and what do you want?' The archer asked.

'I am Tuthmosis the sculptor to Akhenaten and I have come home,' Tuthmosis said squarely.

The bowman did not reply but two other people stepped out and Tuthmosis recognised the figure of Penhasi's son. 'It's true, it is Tuthmosis,' he said to the archer. He turned to face Tuthmosis and shouted to him. 'You can't come back here, Tuthmosis. We are a community stricken with leprosy.'

'I'm not afraid of leprosy, Mahmoud. I have lived with it for more than a year,' Tuthmosis replied.

'Are you a leper?' Mahmoud cried in surprise.

'No, but I have looked after the queen, Nefertiti, who was. She died just one decan ago.'

'The queen had leprosy?!' Mahmoud's voice was incredulous.

'Yes,' answered Tuthmosis. 'It did not have time to seriously advance before she died. She died from a high fever which she contracted four decans ago. The physician did not know the cause of it.'

Mahmoud was silent for a while. 'All right, you may enter Akhetaten,' he said eventually. The bowman lowered his bow and Tuthmosis advanced towards the little group. When he drew close, he noticed a small tell-tale patch of discoloured skin on Mahmoud's forehead. He went forward to offer his hand in greeting but the other drew back.

'Don't touch me, Tuthmosis. I'm a leper.'

Tuthmosis gave a grim laugh. 'Believe me, I'm not afraid of either leprosy or of death, Mahmoud. If it's my destiny to develop leprosy, then it will come. Give me your hand!' Mahmoud hesitated still, then he stepped forwards and thrust his hand into the extended hand of Tuthmosis.

'It's good to see you again, Tuthmosis.' He grinned at the sculptor. 'How are you and what brings you to Akhetaten? We have few visitors these days.' Tuthmosis said that there would be time to talk all about that later when they were more privately placed. Quietly, he asked if Penhasi was still living. Mahmoud's face took on a grim expression and he answered. 'No. They killed my father because he would not renounce the Aten. He and my mother were too old to flee and too proud.' Tuthmosis sighed before expressing his deepest regret. 'What about the queen? Did she renounce the faith?' Mahmoud asked.

'No. Never,' Tuthmosis answered vehemently. 'For that, they exiled her to the outskirts of the poor district of Thebes and she was not allowed to live with her children again. In her adversity, she put her faith in the Aten.'

'She was a good woman. May the Aten bless her soul and give her eternal life in the heavenly sphere,' Mahmoud said devoutly. They were silent for a while as they thought about the past and then Mahmoud said with a smile, 'What can we do for you now, Tuthmosis?'

Tuthmosis recounted to Mahmoud the death of Yussef at his hands and how he would like to stay for a few days until he went back to Memphis. He told Mahmoud about his plan to kill Horemheb. Mahmoud listened silently before saying. 'Killing is not the Aten's way, Tuthmosis. You knew that. Why don't you stay with us permanently? We have a simple life here nowadays, but no one bothers us anymore.' Tuthmosis thanked the other man but replied that he was afraid that if he stayed longer, he would be traced back to Akhetaten and put them all in danger. Mahmoud shrugged. 'Here we face death all the time. Almost all of us are tainted with the disease, or we stay because we cannot bear to leave the people we love who are tainted. We have learned that there are some things that are much worse than death. I stayed because my wife was sick, and now I stay because I cannot leave. Larya died last spring. We sent the children to Lower Egypt to be cared for by my father's family in Goshen, three years ago. We never saw them after that, but I know they are well and sometimes it is possible to get a message through. We both missed them sorely, but it is better for them like this. I gave instructions that they were only to be brought back to Akhetaten in the event of them becoming sick with the leprosy. As they have remained well thus far, it is not likely now that they will develop the sickness and so I am left here alone to arrange my own fate.' There was no hint of self-pity in his voice and Tuthmosis wondered at his serenity.

'If the others share your lack of fear of the danger I represent, then I would dearly like to stay for a short while,' Tuthmosis answered.

'Be our guest. Choose your home or come and stay with us, whichever you prefer,' Mahmoud offered.

'I would like to go down to my old studio and do some work if I may,' Tuthmosis replied.

'That's good. Create something beautiful for us, Tuthmosis. We are tired of death, disease and destruction here. Make something in stone or pottery which will last so that we can look at it and remind ourselves that there is still something beautiful and indestructible in what we made here.' Mahmoud spoke with feeling and Tuthmosis was touched by the poignancy of his words.

Taking his arm, Mahmoud took Tuthmosis to meet some of his former friends and associates. Tuthmosis was grieved to see the extent to which the disease had already ravaged some of his former fellow citizens. He genuinely did not fear the disease though, and was able to move about among them with no thought of shrinking back, as perhaps he might have done a few short years earlier. The people he met greeted him with friendship and familiarity and he told them truthfully why he had come. Some of them were openly grieved at news of the death of Nefertiti and none of them had any love for the traitor they considered Horemheb to be. Tuthmosis told them that his coming might put them all seriously at risk and that he understood and would respect their wishes if they preferred him to leave the following day.

The band of citizens that Mahmoud appeared to be leading left to discuss the matter together and a quiet woman came to give him a goblet of water to drink. He sat down gratefully on a small wicker chair outside the nearest house and waited. After about fifteen minutes, Mahmoud and the others returned and Mahmoud told him that it was the decision of them all that all life is in the hands of the Aten ultimately and, if they were attacked, they would rather all die together and quickly than by the slow ravaging and lingering death of leprosy to which they were condemned. Tuthmosis felt that he had truly come home to his brothers in faith. His faith had never been stronger than in that moment and he had never felt more in his life that he belonged, he who had always felt himself to be an outsider.

Over a convivial meeting of kindred spirits, Tuthmosis learned that the bulk of the remaining population of Akhetaten were domiciled round a small group of villas in the part of the city between Maruaten and the temple. This area included Tuthmosis' former villa and it was thus that he soon found himself once again in the home that he had previously shared with Meresger. Meresger, who had refused to follow him to Thebes and who had opted to stay in Akhetaten with Penhasi and his wife. Tuthmosis felt guilty. He had not even asked Mahmoud about Meresger. It was almost as if she had never existed. He had left her behind, thinking her safe in her beautiful villa and familiar surroundings, while he had gone to face danger in Thebes, and all the while it had been the other way around.

Tuthmosis entered the main reception area of the villa and looked round in surprise at seeing several old people sitting there. In a bemused fashion he greeted them. Their faces were strange to him, but then Akhetaten had always been a populous city. The old folks looked at Tuthmosis rather fearfully, but he reassured them and asked if they knew of the fate of a woman called Meresger. There was an exclamation from behind him and Tuthmosis whirled round to see Meresger herself standing there. She looked older and there were lines of suffering etched on her face. Her arms were discoloured with the patchy loss of pigmentation caused by leprosy.

For a moment they stared at each other and then Tuthmosis went forward to greet his wife. Meresger shrank back. 'Don't come near, Tuthmosis.'

Tuthmosis advanced. 'Don't be afraid, Meresger,' he said reassuringly. He went up the two steps towards her and stood in front of her. 'It's good to see you, Meresger,' he said with a smile. He took her hand in his and kissed it. She began to cry, and he took her in his arms. 'Don't cry, Meresger. Everything is all right now.' He patted her back comfortingly. 'Do you forgive me for leaving you behind?' he asked finally.

'I forgive you, Tuthmosis, but I don't forgive those who came to destroy us,' she said bitterly. After a pause, she asked him if Neferu was dead now. Tuthmosis answered in the affirmative.

'Leprosy and a fever,' he added by way of explanation.

'Aren't you afraid, Tuthmosis?' Meresger asked, drawing back from him.

'No, I'm not afraid and, if you will have me, I would like to stay here with you for a while,' was his reply to her question.

Meresger listened while he told her his plans and he listened while she told him how she and many others had fled out into the desert when they heard that the troops were coming. The horses and chariots had not been able to follow them over the hot sands and they had stayed far out in the heat of the scorching sun until nightfall. The soldiers had finally left after three days but by that time many of them had died from lack of water and dehydration. When they had finally plucked up the courage to return, Akhetaten had been almost deserted. Some had gone to Hermopolis if they had been given a free pass by the soldiers for recanting their faith. All the lepers and those who had refused to recant had been killed. The troops had said they were acting on the instructions of Horemheb himself. Meresger said that there had been rumours before the event that the lepers were going to be targeted and some of them, with the healthy ones who loved them, had already left in a caravan across the desert to the countries of the eastern border. She did not know what had happened to them. Tuthmosis told her that Pararameses had told him that some of them had reached Hatti, as his scouts had informed him of them. The Hittites had given them free passage to who knows where in their fear of the leprosy. Tuthmosis wondered how much Ay had known of the massacre.

Meresger told Tuthmosis that he was very welcome to stay with her at the villa. She had always kept his old room free for him in case he had come back to her. He was touched at that.

'If I stay, the soldiers may come again,' he warned her.

'Then we will die together this time. Death holds no fears for me now,' she replied.

'Yes. We will die together,' he said, embracing her.

Meresger took Tuthmosis to his old room and tears came to his eyes as he looked about him. Even the portrait of Neferu behind the two small doors was intact.

'I loved her so much, Meresger,' he said.

'I know, Tuthmosis,' she answered quietly.

'How can you not hate me, Meresger?' he asked wonderingly.

'You are the only real family I have ever known, Tuthmosis, and you have always been so kind to me. How could I hate you? I love you like the brother I never had. Once there was a time when we had love and passion and later it grew to the love born of friendship. I was not able to be a proper wife to you and you never castigated me for it. I am happy that you have come home,' Meresger said with dignity.

In spite of everything, Tuthmosis felt a sense of peace. 'I want to go to my studio and work as if everything was as it used to be,' he said.

Meresger nodded. 'I understand. But not today, Tuthmosis. Go in the morning and I will bring your lunch to you so that you can work throughout the day if you wish to.' Meresger was quiet for a moment before continuing, 'I haven't been there for a while but there was a lot of rubble there and all the work you left was smashed,' she told him.

'No,' Tuthmosis replied. 'I did that myself when Neferu went back to the pharaoh. I smashed all the busts and statues of him that I made and all the ones of Neferu too. I was very destructive in my fury.' He smiled ruefully. 'After that I made only animals and birds for sale and drew portraits to ensure our living.'

Meresger smiled slightly and nodded. She pointed to the portrait of Neferu on the wall. 'But you never destroyed that,' she said softly.

His eyes turned to the portrait once more. It was as fresh now as it had been then. 'No. I could never destroy that,' he replied. His eyes moved round the walls of the room. 'I have always loved this room,' he said.

Meresger moved in a businesslike fashion. 'I will make up the bed for you and then you must come and eat,' she said, in her most down to earth manner. Tuthmosis smiled at her tone. She was a tower of strength and calmness, this woman. He was lucky to have found her again.

It was no burden to Tuthmosis to share a communal life with those of the survivors of Akhetaten with whom Meresger was sharing her home. He was a gregarious man, and for some reason he felt in need of company now. That night he went to bed early and enjoyed the luxury of sleeping in his own bed again. He realised that he was exhausted from the mental and physical strain of many consecutive days of stress. He was safe here and he could afford to relax now.

The next morning, Tuthmosis rose and after eating breakfast with Meresger he walked to his studio. Except for the deserted streets, and the air of desolation that had descended over Akhetaten, he might have gone back in time five years. His feeling of ease was so pronounced that he surprised himself by whistling as he walked. He knew what he was going to do, and it was to be his best work ever.

At the studio, Tuthmosis ignored the piles of rubbish and set about his work. There was love in his heart as he worked, and it seemed to him that his fingers had never been so strong or so supple. Some hours later, Meresger brought him some bread and fruit and a pot of barley beer. He worked on through the afternoon and reluctantly put down his work only when the light began to fade.

Leaving the studio, he retraced his steps of the morning and made his way to his old home. When he arrived, Meresger greeted him, and the room was cosy with the light of the oil lamps. That evening he played backgammon with Meresger, and they smiled and talked of old times, remembering old friends now gone. They prayed together for the people they loved, both dead and living, and in a somewhat solemn mood they went to bed. They shared the bed without passion but wrapped around each other for comfort.

Tuthmosis was consumed by an instinct to finish his work quickly the following morning and he worked long and hard and methodically. From time to time he stopped and stepped backwards to assess his work. One more day and it would be finished. He left the studio earlier that day and walked along the main street to the northern palace where he had spent so many happy hours and also one of the most heart-breaking moments of his life too. He remembered the time again when he had lost Neferu to Amio again. It seemed to have lost its sting now, he realised.

The palace had been locked up, but someone had forced one of the gates. He entered by this gate and looked around. The gardens were overgrown with weeds and in some places the plants had withered and died of lack of water. There was no one to care for them and he knew that in time it would all revert back to desert. The desert would claim its own and no one would know that they had ever existed. All that love and passion would be as if it had never happened. He wondered idly how long it would take. He sighed and went inside. His footsteps echoed eerily along the long empty corridors. He looked around at the walls and ceilings he had so lovingly painted but the very emptiness of the place struck a melancholic chord inside him, and he felt he wanted to get away from there. It had been wrong to come back. There were only ghosts here now. He wanted the warmth of life and human voices. Here were only whispers of the past in the pale anaemic tones that were an insult to the vibrant colours of the emotions that had lived here. His heart was heavy as he passed through the doors. It was not a good idea, he thought, to try to recapture the yesterdays, far better to let them live on in memory and keep them alive to feed on in the privacy of the soul.

That evening, Tuthmosis felt in need of more stimulating company than that of the old folks whom Meresger had befriended and cared for. After dinner, he set out in search of Mahmoud. He guessed that the eldest son of Penhasi would be residing at his father's former home and his surmise proved correct. The chief servitor's former home appeared to have become the small seat of government for the diminished city and there was a small congregation of people there.

Mahmoud greeted Tuthmosis and asked him to join them in a prayer service to the Aten. Mahmoud conducted the service and for once Tuthmosis felt in tune with the mood and occasion. He was not normally an introspective man by inclination but this evening he found beauty and peace in the words of the last prayer of Akhenaten before his death.

'I breathe thy sweet breath every day,
Thy beauty I behold.
Oh, Let me hear thy voice always.
In winds of heat and cold.
Touch thou my hands, that still in me,
Thy spirit should prevail.
Through life and death I call to thee,
Whose name shall never fail.'

The words brought tranquillity to Tuthmosis and after the short service, he chatted to the other people present. He told Mahmoud that he had spent the last two days working feverishly to complete a bust of Nefertiti. Mahmoud asked if he could come to the studio to see it and Tuthmosis agreed, although it was not quite finished, and he intended to start work on it soon after dawn the following day. When most of the group had dispersed, Mahmoud and Tuthmosis walked the empty streets back to the villa where Meresger was waiting. The three of them sat chatting late into the night. Both Meresger and Mahmoud tried to dissuade Tuthmosis from his plan to kill Horemheb and Meresger reminded him that all life is in the hands of the Aten and only he had the right to wreak vengeance. Tuthmosis had lost heart for the plan if the truth were to be told, however, he remained adamant that it must be done and that after the next day, when he had completed his statue of Neferu to commemorate her life, he would make his way back to Memphis to bide his time. It was very late when Meresger made up a bed for Mahmoud, and they all retired. The house settled down to silence as they all slept.

Tuthmosis rose early and ate a light breakfast, which Meresger prepared for him. The rest of the house still slept. Tuthmosis told Meresger that he would return to the villa for lunch that day and not to bring it out to him. At his atelier, he settled down to work on the sculpture of Neferu. He was meticulous in his attention to detail and a perfectionist in his art. This work was to be his homage to the woman he had loved and the queen he had served so faithfully. At lunchtime he placed the bust on a shelf to dry. He had completed the right eye and when it was dry after lunch, he would start work on the left. Tuthmosis stood back to admire the work he had executed so lovingly. It was a masterpiece and he felt pleasure at the thought of Neferu's reaction to it if she had been alive. He closed his eyes and concentrated on his thoughts. 'Wherever you are, Neferu, come and see this work, which I dedicate to you.' After a while he opened his eyes. He started at a slight sound behind him and turned quickly, but it was only Mahmoud. Mahmoud stared in silence at the bust, obviously deeply impressed by it, and he said so openly. Tuthmosis flushed with pleasure at this sincere praise and, clapping his arm around Mahmoud's shoulders, they set off for lunch.

Lunch was a strangely happy meal. Just like old times, Mahmoud said as they sipped the wine taken from the deserted palace wine cellars. 'I'm sure Akhenaten wouldn't mind!' Mahmoud added with a laugh. There was a moment's silence, as if they almost expected the dead pharaoh to give his permission. Lunch over, Tuthmosis and Mahmoud left together. At the junction of the street, they parted company and Mahmoud turned right and Tuthmosis left. There was only a distance of about twenty metres between them when they became aware of horse's hooves in the distance. Both men turned to look at each other and the same thought struck both of them simultaneously. 'Troops!' called Mahmoud, and he ran up to the steps alongside the nearest villa to gain height and see how far from them the threat was. Tuthmosis ran up beside him and looked into the distance where about forty or fifty archers on horseback were approaching.

'It's me they want,' said Tuthmosis in consternation. 'I'll go out to them now and then they will do you no harm.' His tone was agitated, denoting his fears for his companions.

Mahmoud put his hand on his friend's arm. 'No. Tuthmosis! This is our last stand! This time we stay. If they take you, they take us all.'

There was a sudden and unexpected throng of people in the streets, all alerted by the first hearers of the horsemen's advance. The crowd came silently and Tuthmosis was startled when he looked down and saw how quietly the grey ghosts had appeared.

'My friends! It's me they're looking for and you must hide. Go back to your homes I tell you. I will go out alone.' There was a silence after his words, and no one moved. Then the bowman who had halted Tuthmosis' advance when he had arrived at Akhetaten shouted to his compatriots.

'We run no more. This is our last stand. If we die, then we die faithful to the Aten. Come and band together.'

Mahmoud said to the anxious Tuthmosis. 'The old man must have betrayed you.'

'No,' answered Tuthmosis. 'It must have been Ay. He was astute enough to guess that I would come home.'

Tuthmosis ran down the steps and called to the people as he ran that they were to stay where they were. He moved as fast as he could to meet the approaching riders, who were now only about two-hundred metres from the edge of the town. On seeing him, the leading horseman called out to the others, and they reined to a halt. The leader advanced a little towards Tuthmosis and called out. 'Who are you?'

'I am Tuthmosis, the sculptor in chief to Akhenaten and Nefertiti, Nefer-Neferu-Aten. I believe you are looking for me.' There were murmurs amongst the horsemen, which were audible to Tuthmosis only as indistinct sounds, but he saw from their faces and gestures that it was him they were seeking.

The leader unrolled a papyrus and read out an order demanding the arrest of Tuthmosis to stand trial for the murder of Yussef Leandrakis, general in chief of the Egyptian army and deputy to Horemheb, the general commander in chief of Lower Egypt. The warrant had been issued in the name of Ay. Tuthmosis bowed and stepped forward, but the sound of protesting voices caused the horsemen to redirect their gazes to a position behind him. Tuthmosis turned to see the population of Akhetaten standing behind him in, it seemed, its entirety. Meresger ran towards him crying and Tuthmosis held her. He heard a cry of 'Lepers, kill them!' The horrified voice came from one of the horsemen.

Tuthmosis turned round again quickly. 'Let them go, they have done nothing. I will come with you.'

A general cry now swept through the horsemen. 'Kill them. Lepers! Lepers!'

The leader lifted up his hand to still them and shouted. 'It is the orders of Ay that there is to be no bloodshed,' He Commanded.

'Ay is an old man. Horemheb knows these heretics. They are trouble causers! This Tuthmosis has already killed one of our leaders. How do we know if he isn't a leper too?' one of the officers shouted. 'I say, kill him!'

'I am not a leper, and I am willing to come with you. Leave my friends alone,' Tuthmosis shouted angrily.

Mahmoud shouted. 'We are not afraid to die. We are at peace with the Aten. You murderers are right to fear. You will pay for your misdeeds in the afterlife.'

These were the last words that Tuthmosis heard him say as an arrow sank deep into his chest and he staggered backwards. With this act of violence, the atmosphere changed and Tuthmosis ran to help Mahmoud. The people of Akhetaten thronged around Mahmoud as he lay on the ground. Meresger began to take charge of the wounded man and Tuthmosis turned his attention again to the hostile horsemen. He began to walk towards them, wanting to avoid further bloodshed. As he walked in face of the troops, whose bows were all now at the ready, he could hear the people behind him calling him to come back.

Suddenly an arrow whizzed past him in the air and struck one of the front riders in the thigh. He turned to see the lone Atenist standing defiantly on one of the buildings and suddenly a whole volley of arrows descended upon the vulnerable people of Akhetaten. He saw Meresger fall to the ground and lie unmoving. He ran towards her. That single arrow had been the catalyst for the undercurrent of hatred to burst to the surface and he looked on in horror at the ensuing massacre until he felt a sudden and acutely sharp pain in his back. He felt that he could not get his breath and turned to look at his assailants for a moment before two more arrows hit him and he fell to the ground. The pain was agonising for a few moments and then everything began to go dark. 'Is this death?' he thought. 'If it is, why am I not afraid?' There was pitch blackness all around him now but no pain. He felt as though he was in a long dark tunnel travelling forwards at a very fast rate. As he looked ahead, he began to see a dazzling white light and he tried to shade his eyes but without success. The light was all around him now and he turned around. Slowly he began to perceive a figure in front of him. She was smiling and her arm was outstretched.

'Is it you, Neferu?' he asked soundlessly.

'I told you I would wait for you, Tuthmosis. Welcome home,' she said simply.

EPILOGUE

Monotheism came to an end in Egypt officially with the death of Akhenaten, Amenophis IV, the beloved husband of Nefertiti, Nefer-Neferu-Aten. It survived underground during the reign of the young pharaoh Tutankhamun, who had been named Tutankhaten by his mother, grand queen Tiya, at his birth. Unfortunately, the young pharaoh died in mysterious circumstances during his nineteenth year of life. The cause of his death was unknown, but is believed to have been poisoning. His mummy also shows a small hole in his skull behind and slightly below one of his ears.

Tutankhamun's wife, the young queen Ankhsenpaamun, third daughter of Nefertiti and Akhenaten, was compelled to marry again quickly in order to secure the throne from the control of the most senior military commander of the Egyptian armed forces, Horemheb. It is known that someone offered his hand in marriage to the young Ankhsenpaamun but that she rejected the applicant. It is known from Egyptian archives that she sent to the king of the neighbouring country of Mitanni for one of his sons as a spouse, because she did not want to marry 'One of my servants who is repugnant to me'. The letter to the king of Mitanni is preserved in Akkadian, though it is not known whether she was referring to Ay or to Horemheb. It seems probable that it was the former, her great-uncle. The prince of Mitanni, who was sent by his father, was ambushed and killed on his way to Egypt to take up the offer and it was Ay who became pharaoh. For all his intrigue and scheming, Ay was already an old man and he died after only four years on the throne.

After the death of Ay, the throne was seized by Horemheb, who used his position as the son-in-law of Ay as his legal link to the claim to the throne. With this accession, all blood ties to the last pharaohs of the eighteenth dynasty were lost and a new dynasty began, although not officially until the accession of the aged army commander Pararameses, who took the name Rameses. Rameses lived for two years before his son took over from him.

Horemheb and Mutnedjmet had no son. It seems that Horemheb married Neferu junior in order to cement his ties to the throne, although the Egyptian archives are not wholly clear on this as not all of them have survived. Nefer-Neferu-Amun (formerly Aten) tashery was approximately twenty-four at the time of Horemheb's succession to the throne. He was in his early forties and went on to reign for thirty-four years.

Under Horemheb, Memphis became the official capital of Egypt once again, for the first time since the great flood and the consequent occupation of northern Egypt by the Hyksos, several hundred years previously. Ay, or Horemheb, it is not clear which one of them, seems to have married off Satenpare to the king of Ugarit, a country situated within modern-day Syria. Thereafter, there is nothing known of her. During the reign of Horemheb, all traces of the Atenist pharaoh and his queen were systematically obliterated from all the buildings and the archives. Much of the evidence of their existence and the roles they played out was discovered in the remains of Akhetaten, which is now known as Tell El Amarna. Even today, the desert there is strewn with the ruins of the city, which has been mummified by the sands of time.

If we accept that grand vizier Yuya was indeed 'Yussef whose god is Yahweh', i.e. the Joseph of the coat of many colours, whom the Biblical book of Genesis tells us of, then Amenophis IV, Nefertiti's beloved Amio, was his grandson and therefore was surrounded from his earliest youth with a vision of one god. All the circumstantial evidence identifying Yuya as Joseph is very strong.

The Bible tells us that Joseph was 'second unto pharaoh' and that he travelled in the 'second chariot after pharaoh'. Without doubt, this places Joseph in the eighteenth dynasty, because there were neither horses nor chariots in Egypt before this period. Other factors denoting Yuya's real identity are also hinted at. The Bible says that Joseph married the daughter of the high priest of On (the present-day suburb of Heliopolis in Cairo). Yuya married Asenaath, the daughter of the high priest of On. The tomb of Thuya, wife of Yuya, contains murals and hieroglyphics which state that she was the high priestess of On. The Bible calls her Asenaath, a fairly common Egyptian name, but the name Thuya shows definite signs of the Ancient Aramaic suffix 'ya' which denotes an abstract concept of 'spirit' or 'breath' and which in Hebrew at least was associated with the divine creator god. Thuya may have been a form of this that was acceptable to both Yuya himself and the Egyptians around him.

We know by simple mathematical deduction that Joseph had a daughter, although the Bible does not tell us so directly. In Genesis it is written that sixty-six Israelite 'souls' entered Egypt and that this made a total of seventy Israelite 'souls' in Egypt altogether. This means there were four Israelite souls in the country before the rest of the tribe came to live there. Joseph must have been one, his two sons, Manasseh and Ephraim were another two, but who made up the fourth soul? It was not Thuya because she was totally Egyptian in origin and the Bible has a habit of leaving out the names of people it does not consider important, most likely because they were female. Sixty-six and three make up sixty-nine and it is my view that the seventieth soul, who was not important enough to have been named, must have been female, i.e. Joseph had a daughter.

Genesis says that Joseph became 'father unto pharaoh', but Joseph could not have become father unto pharaoh unless his daughter married the pharaoh. Who could this daughter be if not Tiya? In addition, we know from the extant Egyptian texts that Tiya was the daughter of a former slave, and here again we have the typical Semitic 'ya' suffix. Genesis tells us that Joseph was the slave of a potiphar prior to his imprisonment on trumped-up charges. A potiphar was an important, middle-ranking Nile security administrator. This word is also important in showing that Ancient Egyptian showed important root analogies with Ancient Greek in that the words for river come from the same source.

The mummy of Yuya shows that his ears were not pierced, and this was exceedingly rare amongst upper class Egyptians, for whom it was a sign of their social position and their class. Perhaps the most telling indication that Yuya was not Egyptian in origin is that he was buried with his hands across his chest, whereas Egyptians were always shown mummified with their arms straight down by their sides.

The father of Akhenaten, Amenophis III, seems to have been a young boy of thirteen when he became pharaoh. Nowhere in the archives does it say that he was co-regent with his father, to my knowledge, therefore we can assume that he succeeded to the throne on the death of his father, the Pharaoh Tuthmosis IV. There is no doubt that Yuya was very much a father figure to him as his chief advisor, but this position alone would not be sufficiently powerful for him to be called the father unto pharaoh unless there was a real and official reason for it to be deemed so, i.e. he was literally the father-in-law of the pharaoh. Although Amenophis III was an Amunist by birth, he too would have been exposed to the effects of monotheism via his advisor and father-in-law, had this been Joseph. It is true that Amenophis III began early on to introduce a previously unknown god into the Egyptian pantheism. The name of the god was Aten. Amenophis had a boat made for Tiya, his grand queen, which was called *The Aten Gleams*.

Linguistically, the word 'Aten' had both a concrete and an abstract meaning for the Egyptians. According to the hieroglyphical evidence, it means the disc of the sun with its corolla and had an abstract meaning of 'breath' or 'spirit' corresponding to the Ancient Hebrew word 'ruach', meaning 'breath' or 'spirit'. Semantically it would not be a big psychological jump to equate the Hebrew word 'Yahweh', which was originally a verbal noun meaning 'The great I am' or 'Here am I', with the word Aten in Egyptian to mean 'the breath of life'. Under such already well-developed language connotations, the god could easily come to be symbolised by a painting of the sun's disc and its rays, just as today the cross symbolises Christ to most Christians, or the Star of David symbolises Judaism to most Jews. It is a simple fact of humanity that most people need symbols to jog their memory, and symbols such as stars and crosses are ancient symbols that have served to keep concepts alive down through the generations, especially in times of poverty or great troubles, when the lives of people are more directed to the task of surviving and there is not much opportunity to dwell on ideal or the hereafter. For the unwary, these symbols can come to be a trap and have a meaning for the follower in itself, so that the true religion becomes tarnished with the statues and symbols which were only meant to represent it. This was what Moses was only too aware of when he meted out the commandment 'Thou shalt not make graven images'. The tribes of Israel made the golden calf when they felt their god had abandoned them, as do modern-day Catholics who pray before the statue of the Madonna. This response is deeply rooted in man. It was not something unique to the ancients. Akhenaten and Nefertiti lost sight of the fundamental spirituality of their religion at times, as so many of us do. Perhaps they too were beguiled into believing in the picture of the sun's disc, which they represented symbolically with its rays sent forth and ending in two benevolent hands. Sometimes it is hard to know when true faith blends and becomes blurred with the symbols that represent it. Because of the Ancient Greek belief in sun worship, which probably reinforced Nefertiti's belief, at least, it is even possible that they perceived the sun as the dwelling place of their god the Aten. With all his later troubles, it does seem that Akhenaten did at least temporarily lose his faith around the time that he and Nefertiti were separated, and she was banished to the northern palace called Hataten, or Castle of the Aten.

With the accession of Horemheb, persecution of the Atenist began in earnest and it may have partially been the reason for the later persecution of the Israelites of Goshen under the reign of Seti, and perhaps Rameses the second. Akhenaten was referred to as the heretic, if he was referred to at all, and there were attempts to obliterate all traces of Tutankhamun also. There was a decree passed that Amio's name was never to be mentioned and if referred to at all officially, it was as 'that scoundrel'. Apart from the question of religion and the threat it represented to the powerful Amun priesthood, it was also a question of Akhenaten's part-Hebrew origins. Hebrews were associated, unfairly in this case, with an earlier Semitic tribe called the Hyksos who had invaded Egypt on horseback when it was seriously weakened in the aftermath of the great flood. They had ruled the whole of northern Egypt, the Lower Land, for one-hundred and fifty years before being finally pushed out by the first pharaoh of the eighteenth dynasty, Akhenaten's ancestor, ironically. Although there had been a certain amount of intermarriage in the north, we know that even in Joseph's day, Egyptians and Semites never ate at the same table. Genesis chapter nine tells us this.

There is no doubt that the Egyptians perceived the Israelites to be a threat to them. There are numerous references in Genesis and Exodus to their wealth and prosperity and, in Exodus, the pharaoh (which one?) himself is said to have incited the Egyptians to subjugate them. It is probable that the material success of the Israelites, which Joseph instituted by allowing them exemption from the payment of tax and the allocation of land to them, may actually have been more important in their downfall than the question of their monotheism. Horemheb's public dominance, which began with his military role as controller of the delta area and continued with his pharaohship, lasted a long time and in spite of his efforts to secure the throne with a son, he too died without male issue and with him the eighteenth dynastic period ended officially. The short, two-year reign of Rameses the First heralded the warrior pharaohs who, for a short time, renewed Egypt's former power and glory.

Tuthmosis was a common name in Egypt, incorporating the name Moses with the god Toth. It is interesting though, that the Hebrew prophet was given this name, minus the reference to the pagan god, of course. The Bible tells us that he was given this name by the Hebrew nurse who was designated by the pharaoh's daughter to look after him until he was weaned. Why did the pharaoh's daughter take such a risk in adopting a Hebrew baby? At this stage of his life, he was indistinguishable from an Egyptian in that he probably was not circumcised. His poor mother must have had to abandon him to save his life at a time when the Israelites were under very hard-pressed circumstances. This was probably the factor that enabled the princess to hide his origins from her father. It would seem from the fact that the princess had a Hebrew nurse him that Hebrews were at least within the palace confines in some numbers.

According to Exodus chapter four, there were four generations between Levi, the half-brother of Joseph, and the life of Moses. Levi had a son, Kohath, who had a son, Amram, who had two sons, Moses and Aaron. If Yuya was Joseph, then Akhenaten and Moses were distant cousins, and the children and grandchildren of Akhenaten and Nefertiti would be contemporaneous with Moses. Since we have the story of Moses being found in the bulrushes, and we know that the Israelites lived in the Goshen area of Northeast Egypt, then the pharaoh must have been living in the delta area when Moses was born. If we reckon that the generation gap was roughly the same for both the Levites and those descendants of Joseph, then we must assume that Moses was born during the reign of Horemheb and at least thirteen years after the death of Akhenaten (Tutankhamun was pharaoh for nine years, and Ay for four years). This being accepted, then if the pharaoh's daughter was the daughter of his wife Mutnedjmet, she was partly Hebrew in origin as her great-grandfather was Yuya. It might explain the princesses' compassion for the little Hebrew baby.

The history of the whole of this period is covered in obscurity and will probably never be deciphered with certainty. The players themselves made determined efforts to cover their own tracks at the time and, later on, Horemheb completed their efforts by his obliteration of the remaining monuments, some of which is still visible on the statues and pillars at Luxor, where the workmen were in a hurry and only partially completed their task. Through the mists of time, however, we glimpse a people involved in scandals and passions, people of high ideals and mortal failings, no different than our own. These were real people just like you and me, capable of great strength and great weakness. It might be true to say of them that they were the very first personalities of the ancient world who can still reach out to us and touch us today with the depths of their emotions as flesh and blood characters.

Atenism was an ambitious project and it failed in Egypt, but perhaps it was only a short phase in a long line of monotheism which has flourished on and off since humans first developed. Noah already contained in his name the element of 'ah, ha, ya', which, from the extent of their use in names of Ancient Aramaic origin, must have been semantically significant. The very story of his survival suggests that he was saved simply because he believed in one god. This implies that there were others who believed in several gods and his little clan did not approve of that, and that is why they thought that the others perished. It is known that in the Middle East there was a widespread monotheistic religion that existed well before the dawn of Christianity and that was apparently very close to Christianity in its beliefs and modes of ethical behaviour, and which existed separately from the Hebrew monotheistic faith. No one knows what it was called, but in about six hundred BCE, one of its followers took the faith to Persia where it became widespread and lived until the Muslim invasion of about one-thousand CE. The last known prophet of this religion in the East was Zoroaster (Zarathustra in Pharsee). The Zoroastrians were eventually pushed out of Persia and mainly exist today in India. Some Persians secretly kept up the old religion, but their numbers are not known, and many were forced to convert to Islam. There is in the story of the birth of Jesus a hint of their presence, where it is written that three magi came from the east, following a star. The word 'magi' is a Persian word and denoted the title of 'priest'. Jesus himself is thought to have belonged to a Hebrew sect called Essenes. This sect existed alongside the Sadducees, Pharisees and Zealots. It was known to have espoused pacifism and to have followed a code of behaviour very similar to modern Christianity and to Zoroastrianism.

What is certain about the Atenists is that some of them did survive and remained true to their faith. When the Israelites left Egypt, they took with them something which much, much later became known as Psalm 104 of the psalms of David. Psalm 104 contains almost word for word sections of Akhenaten's 'Hymn to the Aten'.

'How manifold are thy works,

They are hidden from the face of men, O Sole God!

Like unto whom there is no other.

Thou madest the earth at thy will when thou wast alone.

Men, cattle, all animals, everything on earth that goes on its feet,

Everything that is on high that flies with its wings …'

From Hymn to the Aten, translated by HW Fairmen.

(See 'The Lost Pharaohs' by Leonard Cottrell, published 1961 by Cox and Wyman Ltd – London, Fakenham and Reading.)

From the rest of Akhenaten's poem, it seems that he believed that he was sent by the Aten with a special mission to promote his cause, and because of this he expected to be the recipient of the Aten's favours. He was undoubtedly quite egocentric and perhaps this was his downfall. In spite of this, it is most heartening that, for the first time in known history, a powerful dominant male publically declared his love for a woman. He acknowledged the role of his wife and treated her, for most of the time, as an equal. The

'Hymn to the Aten' ends with the words by which Akhenaten asks for the protection of the Aten for himself and for Nefertiti.

> 'The king of Upper and Lower Egypt, who lives on truth:
> Lord of diadems, Akhenaten, whose life is long:
> And for the great royal wife, his beloved,
> The mistress of the Two Lands,
> Nefer-Neferu-Aten, Nefertiti,
> May she live and grow young forever and ever.'

APPENDIX I

The Dynastic Line

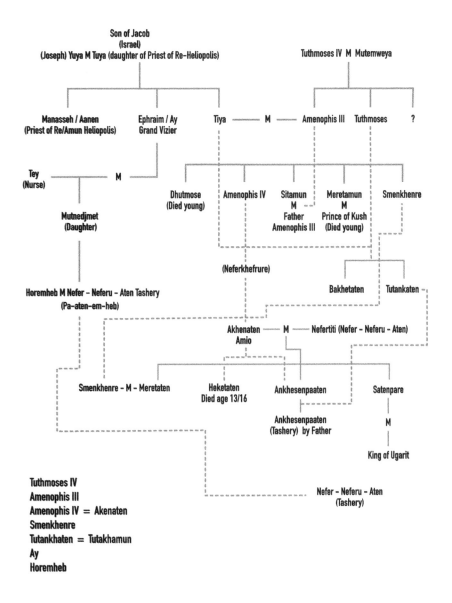

APPENDIX II

The Great Hymn to the Aten is the principal source for the radical reformulation of Ancient Egyptian belief in the reign of Akhenaten. It is inscribed in thirteen columns of hieroglyphs on the west wall of the courtier Ay at Amarna. The original hieroglyphic inscriptions have suffered from vandalism since discovery.

There are numerous translations of the Great Hymn, and the following is only one rendering of this, one of the most influential of surviving Ancient Egyptian writings.

Akhenaten's Great Hymn to the Aten
You rise beautiful from the horizon on heaven,
living disc, origin of life.
You are arisen from the horizon,
you have filled every land with your beauty.
You are fine, great, radiant, lofty over and above every land.
Your rays bind the lands to the limit of all you have made,
you are the sun, you have reached their limits.
You bind them (for) your beloved son.
You are distant, but your rays are on earth,
You are in their sight, but your movements are hidden.
You rest in the western horizon, and the land is in darkness in the manner of death,
sleepers in chambers, heads covered,
no eye can see its other.
Anything of theirs can be taken from under their heads, they would not know.
Every lion goes out from its den,
every snake bites.
Darkness envelops, the land is in silence, their creator is resting in his horizon.
At daybreak, arisen from the horizon, shining as the disc in day,

you remove the darkness, you grant your rays,

and the Two Lands are in festival,

awakened and standing on their feet.

You have raised them up, their bodies cleansed, clothing on,

their arms are in adoration at your sunrise.

The entire land carries out its tasks,

every herd rests in its pastures,

trees and plants are sprouting,

birds flying up from their nests,

their wings in adoration for your spirit.

Every flock frolics afoot,

all that fly up and alight,

they live when you have shone for them.

Boats sail north and south too,

every road is opened at your sunrise,

and the fish on the river leap at the sight of you

Your rays penetrate the Great Green.

You who cause the sperm to grow in women,

who turns seed into people,

who causes the son to live in the womb of his mother,

who silences him in stopping him crying.

Nurse in the womb, who gives breath to cause all he has made to live,

when he goes down from the womb to breathe on the day of his birth,

you open his mouth in form,

you make his needs.

When the chick in the egg speaks in the shell,

you give it breath within to cause it to live,

you have made him, he is complete, to break out from the egg,

and he emerges from the egg to speak to his completion,

and walks on his legs, going out from it.

How numerous are your works, though hidden from sight.

Unique god, there is none beside him.

You mould the earth to your wish, you and you alone.

All people, herds and flocks,

All on earth that walk on legs,

All on high that fly with their wings.

And on the foreign lands of Khar and Kush, the land of Egypt

You place every man in his place,

you make what they need,

so that everyone has his food,

his lifespan counted.

Tongues are separated in speech, and forms too -

Their skins are made different,

for you make foreign lands different.

You make a Flood in the underworld, and bring it at your desire

to cause the populace to live, as you made them for you,

lord of all they labour over,

the lord of every land.

Shine for them, O disc of day, great of dignity.

All distant lands, you make them live,

you place a Flood in the sky, to descend for them,

to make waves over the mountains like the Great Green,

to water their fields with their settlements.

How effective they are, your plans, O lord of eternity!

A Flood in the sky for foreigners, for the flocks of every land that go on foot,

and a Flood to come from the underworld for Egypt,

your rays nursing every meadow,

you shine and they live and grow for you.

You make the seasons to nurture all you mae,

winter to cool them,

heat so they may taste you.

You have made the far sky to shine in it,

to see what you make, while you are far, and shining in your form as living disc.

risen, shining, distant, near,

you make millions of forms from yourself, lone one,

cities, towns, fields, the road of rivers,

every eye sees you in their entry,

you are the disc of day, master of your move,

of the existence of every form,

you create ... alone, what you have made.

You are in my heart, there is none other who knows you

beside your son Neferkheperura-sole-one-of-Ra.

You instruct him in your plans, in your strength.

The land comes into being by your action, as you make them,

and when you have shone, they live,

when you rest, they die.

You are lifetime, in your body,

people live by you.

Eyes are on your beauty until you set.

All work is stopped when you set on the west;

shine, and strengthen (all for) the king.

Motion is in every leg, since you founded the earth,

you raise them for your son who come from your body,

the king who lives on Right, lord of the Two Lands,

Neferkheperura-sole-one-of-Ra,

son of Ra who lives on Right, lord of Risings,

Akhenaten, great in his lifespan,

and the great king's wife whom he loves, lady of the Two Lands,

Neferneferuaten Nefertiti, eternally alive.

APPENDIX III

Biblical References

Genesis 39:20
Joseph's master took him and put him in prison, the place where the king's prisoners were confined.

Genesis 41:40
'You shall be in charge of my palace, and all my people are to submit to your orders. Only with respect to the throne will I be greater than you.'

Genesis 41:43
He had him ride in a chariot as his second-in-command, and people shouted before him, 'Make way!' Thus he put him in charge of the whole land of Egypt.

Genesis 41:45
Pharaoh gave Joseph the name Zaphenath-Paneah and gave him Asenath daughter of Potiphera, priest of On, to be his wife. And Joseph went throughout the land of Egypt.

Genesis 43:32
They served him by himself, the brothers by themselves, and the Egyptians who ate with him by themselves, because Egyptians could not eat with Hebrews, for that is detestable to Egyptians.

Genesis 45:8
'So then, it was not you who sent me here, but God. He made me father to pharaoh, lord of his entire household and ruler of all Egypt.

Genesis 46: 26 & 27

All those who went to Egypt with Jacob—those who were his direct descendants, not counting his sons' wives—numbered sixty-six persons. With the two sons who had been born to Joseph in Egypt, the members of Jacob's family, which went to Egypt, were seventy in all.

Exodus 1: 8, 9 & 10

Then a new king, to whom Joseph meant nothing, came to power in Egypt. 'Look,' he said to his people, 'the Israelites have become far too numerous for us. Come, we must deal shrewdly with them or they will become even more numerous and, if war breaks out, will join our enemies, fight against us and leave the country.'

Exodus 2:10

When the child grew older, she took him to pharaoh's daughter, and he became her son. She named him Moses, saying, 'I drew him out of the water.'

Exodus 2:23

During that long period, the king of Egypt died. The Israelites groaned in their slavery and cried out, and their cry for help because of their slavery went up to God.

Exodus 3: 13 & 14

Moses said to God, 'Suppose I go to the Israelites and say to them, 'The God of your fathers has sent me to you,' and they ask me, 'What is his name?' Then what shall I tell them?'
God said to Moses, 'I Am Who I Am. This is what you are to say to the Israelites: 'I Am has sent me to you.'